Sisterhood of Suns
Pallas Athena

by

Martin Schiller

Edited by Quiana Kirkland and Heather Reasby

PANTARI
PRESS™

Pantari Press, Seattle Washington, USA

Roza Shanina--a young fighter, and Carlos--an old fighter

CHAPTER 1

Kaly n'Deena swore for the tenth time at the broken hydro-pump. It
was bad enough that she was missing the Founder's Day celebrations, but
to make matters worse, the *kekking* replacement unit wasn't fitting in its
fekking slot. It was supposed to, but of course on this day, of all days, it
wasn't cooperating.

"Ooo! You *bitch!*" Kaly cursed, "Get in there!" She had been a Repair
Tech for the colony's automated farm complex since turning 13, and after
three years on the job, she *knew* that she had the right part for the unit. The
problem was, the hydro-pump either didn't agree with her assessment, or its
innards had distorted with the passage of time. Whether she liked it or not,
the new component was not going to work.

"*Deas dam va!*" she snarled. She sat back and brushed away some of
the sweat from her brow with the cleanest part of her hand. *All right, fine*,
she thought, grabbing up her *elzlate* pad, *I'll double, triple check.*

Unfortunately, the part listed for the hydro-unit, and the part she had
been attempting to install, were one in the same. The entire unit would have
to be replaced.

"Of course!" she said aloud, "Of *kekking* Mother *fekking* course!" As
near as she could tell, the entire universe was conspiring against her. A full
replacement would take a good hour, not to mention the time involved in
driving her crawler back to the nearest maintenance shed just to get the new
unit.

By the time she had it in and online, the dance would be over, and
with it, any chance that she would have had to get closer to Ayleen. And
she had worked *so* hard on her dress for the Founder's Day Dance!

"Maarta did this to me on purpose!" she shouted, kicking a dirt clod
into the air. "Ooo! I'll get her for this."

Maarta had been her rival for the beautiful Ayleen's affections for the
last year. She was also in charge of scheduling who was on emergency call-
out for repairs.

She must have known that this would happen, Kaly decided angrily.

Howling with frustration, she tromped back to her crawler. Whether
she liked it or not, she was stuck with the situation. The colony's huge
farms were vital to its existence, and keeping their automatic units on line

had a higher priority than one girl's desire to attend a dance. Even so, she vowed that Maarta would pay dearly for her treachery.

A loud hollow noise, high overhead, interrupted her plans for revenge, and she looked up through the crawler's canopy, trying to spot the source. It took her a moment to find it, and another to put together what it was.

A spaceship, she thought. The contrail that it left as it cut through the upper atmosphere was unmistakable. It also made no sense; the Colony was isolated, at the very fringes of the Sisterhood, and the monthly supply ship had come and gone a week earlier.

Who could it be?

Just then, something small and dark dropped away from the ship, and arrowed towards the ground. From the direction it was taking, it seemed to her as if it was going to land squarely on the Colony's communications complex, several kilometers to the east.

The object never reached the earth however. Instead, 300 meters from impact, it lit up from the inside, becoming a bright point of light.

Suddenly, it became the sun itself, and Kaly turned away, unable to bear its brilliance. Then the shock wave from the detonation hit her crawler, sending it tumbling end over end like a dry leaf in the wind.

***

It was full dark by the time she came-to. The crawler was lying on its side and her head felt like someone had been beating on it with a hammer. When she reached up and felt along her scalp, she winced as her fingers made contact with something warm and wet. Switching on the canopy light, she saw that her hand was covered in blood.

A painful, sideways glance at the gory streak on the canopy told her the rest of the story. Somewhere in the explosion of the whatever-it-was that had gone off over the communications complex, she'd been thrown against it and knocked unconscious.

Her reflection in the plexiglass also revealed a nasty looking gash and she gingerly re-explored her skull. She wasn't any kind of medic, but it didn't seem to her as if it had been broken.

Reaching for the first aid kit, she discovered that it was just out of reach and she fumbled with her seat harness trying to get it to loosen up. For a moment, it refused to comply, and she pounded on the locking mechanism with her fist. After a few blows, it came open with a metallic "click", spilling her roughly onto the canopy and sending a black wave of pain rolling down from the top of her head.

Several minutes went by before her agony had subsided enough for her to pull the kit from its rack and begin treating herself. Once she had sprayed it on however, it only took a few seconds for the Medispray to do its job. Right away, the analgesic solution deadened the pain, and the nanites suspended within it went to work repairing the damage. A sterile dressing, impregnated with a skin sealant did the rest, and Kaly was finally able to take stock of her situation.

I've got to get out of this thing, she thought, *and go warn the Colony Mothers.*

When she punched the emergency release however, the canopy only opened a quarter of the way before it became jammed in the soft earth. The space that this offered was a narrow one, but she was small for her age and after a few contortions that would have made her gymnastics instructor proud, she was able to wriggle her way out.

"Now what?" she asked the night around her. A few kzizka bugs chirped out a meaningless response, but beyond that, there was only silence.

It was going to be a long, lonely walk back to the Living Center, she realized, and she wasn't afraid to admit that she was frightened.

***

A half-kilometer from the center, she spotted a vehicle coming towards her from the opposite direction. Just from the configuration of the headlights alone, she knew it wasn't anything that the Colony used.

Abruptly, a brilliant spear of light stabbed out into the darkness, and swung around towards her. Instinct made her dive into the nearest irrigation ditch—and just in time to avoid being cut down by a burst from an energy weapon. As she hugged the muddy bottom, she heard the vehicle stop, then the sound of the doors opening and heavy footsteps.

Her heart pounding in her chest, Kaly kept low and prayed to the Lady, begging for Her to keep whoever was up there from finding her. Then the footsteps stopped, and a conversation began.

The voices were deeper than a woman's, and oddly nasal. They were also speaking in a harsh, guttural language that wasn't Standard, or anything else that she could recognize.

But she could still tell that the speakers were arguing about something. Then someone else barked out what was clearly an order. The discussion ceased and everyone returned to their vehicle.

Kaly waited until the noise of the vehicles engine had grown faint before she risked climbing up the bank to take a look. By that point, the machine had reached the end of a neighboring field.

Its searchlight came on again, and she thought that she saw someone running across the open field, but then the energy guns opened up, blinding her. When they finally stopped, the field was dark again and she couldn't tell if her eyes had been playing tricks on her or not.

Not that she was going to go over and find out. She had to make it back to the Living Center.

Keeping to the shadows, Kaly reached the outskirts of the settlement an hour later. The first outbuildings seemed untouched, and her spirits momentarily lifted, but as she walked along, she realized that the entire Center was dark. Hugging herself for reassurance as much as warmth, she pressed on, trying to spot any signs of life.

Her hopes fell when she saw the places where the fires had scorched the buildings. What had been once been one of the dwelling units was squashed flat like a kzizka bug under a giant's heel. Another seemed intact at first glance, but a regular pattern of blast marks scarred the entrance, and its automatic doors hung off an odd angle. The signs of violence were everywhere.

And when the Gathering Square finally came into view, she saw that the young trees that her primary class had planted there just a few years earlier were now nothing but charred skeletons. There were also piles of what looked like discarded clothing, arranged in odd little clumps all around them.

Drawing closer, Kaly realized that they weren't someone's laundry after all. They were bodies.

"Oh, goddess," she whimpered, unwilling to go any further. But her legs had a will of their own and she found herself moving towards the square, unable to stop herself. With nightmarish slowness, the details became clearer with each leaden step.

A girl roughly her own age was face down on the grass, her arm missing from the elbow down. The orphaned limb lay nearby, looking like a discarded part from a child's doll.

That was when Kaly recognized the dress that the girl was wearing. It was Maarta's—she'd seen her working on it just a few days earlier in preparation for the Dance. The pattern was unmistakable.

Ayleen was near her, lying on her back and staring up at the stars with an expression of surprise. And where her stomach should have been there was nothing but a blackened hole.

Stupefied, Kaly stared down at the wound, unable to fully accept what her eyes were telling her. Then the smell of burnt flesh reached her nostrils, and she dropped to her knees and vomited until nothing would come up.

In the midst of catching her breath, she heard someone calling out to her. This time it was in Standard.

"Kaly! Get over here! They're coming back!"

She looked up and spotted the ragged features of Anna n'Gwyn peeking out from behind a broken section of wall. "Come on!" the girl cried, "They'll kill us if they find us!"

Kaly rose, and ran to her, keeping low and nearly tripping over another corpse in the process. "What happened?" she asked her.

"Raiders," Anna whispered, her eyes wide with terror and tinged with madness. "They attacked us during the dance. They k-killed everyone. Kaly—I'm afraid. What do we do?"

"We hide," Kaly answered, amazed at the strength in her voice. "We find anyone that's still alive--and we hide."

With that, she pulled Anna to her feet. Back behind them, the harsh staccato of an energy weapon firing ripped through the darkness.

Someone screamed.

***

Just below the crest of the hill, Kaly got down on her belly and crawled the last few meters. One of the other girls was at the summit, lying prone with a pair of binoculars and peering out through the long grass at the valley below. Like Kaly, she was also a Star Scout.

"Anything?" Kaly whispered.

Susyyn n'Tina shook her head and answered in a hushed voice. "Nothing so far. One of their tanks went by just before you got here, but it didn't stop. I think they're going to keep on moving by us."

Kaly nodded and took the binoculars to survey the activity for herself.

The invaders had not wasted any time consolidating their victory, she reflected bitterly. A group of automated earthmoving machines was at work down in the valley, carving out a kilometer-wide swath in the earth as they sucked up every ounce of valuable minerals from the soil. The land that they left in their wake was bare, and utterly devoid of life. That was what the invasion had been all about, she realized, the robbery of vital resources from a people that had no real means to resist.

Not that there were many who could resist. Most of the colonists had been killed in the first hour of the assault, and to the best of her knowledge, only their small group remained, hiding out in a small pumping station. How long they could remain there before the enemy sent a patrol to investigate the building was anyone's guess.

They needed a survival plan, and they needed it fast. But with all of the adults either dead, or injured beyond being able to help, there was no one for her to turn to for advice. She was the oldest of her little group, and as the highest-ranking member of the colony's Star Scout troop, she was now also the de-facto colony leader, and its military strategist.

The problem was, she didn't have the foggiest idea what to do, or how to go about doing it. The Star Scouts had trained her in the rudimentary aspects of leadership and survival, but nothing had prepared any of them for a full-on alien invasion.

Kaly only knew one thing with any certainty; surrender was not an option. The invaders had systematically killed anyone that they had encountered, regardless of age, or ability to fight. And armed resistance was just as futile. The raiders had landed in force, and with heavier weapons than anything the colony had ever possessed.

While the alien machines continued to move by, Kaly felt a cold thrill of fear and despair fill her to the core, and when she glanced over at her companion, seeing the same thing her eyes. It nothing new though. It had become a familiar sensation for all of them in the last few days.

She took a deep breath and whispered the Star Scout motto to herself. As a new Scout, the ritual had seemed silly and idealistic, but since the invasion, it had taken on a much deeper meaning, lending her the strength and the focus that she needed.

"I am a Star Scout," she said, "I am loyal, I am helpful. I am an asset to my sisters and my community. I am the shining star of hope when everything and everyone around me has been plunged into darkness. I am strong. I will persevere until I cannot draw another breath. I am a Star Scout."

Susyyn heard her and began recite the litany herself. Gradually, their common fear retreated into the background—for a while at least.

Once agian in control of herself, Kaly took brought the field glasses back up to her eyes and considered their options.

But she she already knew what they were. The only solution that they had was to hide long enough for rescue to come.

If it came, she thought grimly. Their survival hinged on the one, faint signal that they had managed to send off before the transmission had been jammed. And the odds that someone would actually hear it, was poor at best. They needed a miracle, and they needed it soon.

Her sense of dread began to rear its ugly head again, but Kaly wrestled it down. "I'll send someone up in an hour to take over for you," she said.

Returning the glasses to her companion, she backed herself down the slope and made her way to the pumping station. Her *psiever* told her it was 00:07:26, and as she re-slung her rifle, she made a mental note to send someone up to relieve Susyyn at 00:49:93.

9

It took a second for her eyes to adjust to the dimly lit interior as she entered the small building. The little ones were finally asleep, huddled together in the corner of the tiny room on makeshift beds made from jackets and other garments, and Kaly moved past them as quietly as possible. She was glad that they were asleep. When they were awake, they were frightened and hungry, and there was nothing that anyone could do to alleviate this.

For the hundredth time, she took stock of their resources. It was something that the Scouts had taught her to do; to know what was available and decide the best way to use it.

They didn't have much. What food there was, had been scavenged from emergency kits hidden at the edges of the settlement, and the few weapons that they possessed had come from those same caches. These were chemical weapons, and hardly a match for what the invaders carried. Ammunition was also running short, and medical supplies were almost non-existant.

Water though, was not an issue. The pumping station helped to irrigate the colony's fields and it offered this substance in abundance. But Kaly knew from her Scout training that once the food finally disappeared, water alone would only give them a metric week of life at the outside. Then starvation would begin to take its toll, and it would be the little ones that would go first.

Somehow, they had to get more food. It would mean taking dangerous risks though. Risks that up until then, she had avoided in favor of the safety of concealment.

I'll go, she decided at last. *I'll be the one to go out and get what we need.* If she succeeded, then she would save some lives. If not, then at the very least, there would be one less mouth to feed. It was a reasonable proposition, and exactly what a Star Scout was expected to do.

She had never expected to live forever anyway.

Propping her rifle against a wall, Kaly made her way over to Anna n'Gwyn. The girl was seated in a corner with a small remote diagnostic terminal on her lap. Before the raid, Anna had been the class valedictorian with an affinity for electronics. She had hoped to attend one of the great universities off-planet. But now, like Kaly, she was just another survivor, her life in ruins and the future looking more and more doubtful with each passing second.

Kaly sat down next to her, but before she could say anything, Anna answered her unspoken question. "No," the girl said tiredly. "I haven't heard anything. Just space-noise."

Kaly looked at the small display screen but failed to decipher its readout. The hiss coming out over the RDT speakers told the whole story however, even to her untrained ears. There was nothing out there.

"They heard us, Anna," Kaly said. "I'm sure of it. They'll come."

"Sure," Anna spat. "And maybe if the little ones pray to the Goddess hard enough, cookies will rain down from the sky for all of us to eat!"

One of the little ones started to wake up and Kaly resisted the urge to slap Anna. Instead, she clenched her fists, and contained her anger.

"Go back to sleep, Lissa," she whispered to the child. "Anna didn't mean what she said." The child regarded her with an expression filled with fear and doubt, but obediently lowered her head back to the jacket she had been using as a pillow. And as was the way of small children, she was fast asleep in seconds.

Kaly was starting to whisper a stern reproach to Anna when a deep, rasping cough interrupted her. Her head snapped around towards the evil sound.

It was Jenna, the last adult in their group, and one of their most severely wounded. Krissi, the closest thing that they had to a medic, was already bending over the critically injured woman and examining her. The 13-year-old's expression was strained.

Jenna's injuries were well beyond her capabilities and everyone in the shelter knew it. Krissi's medical training consisted of what she had received in the Scouts, combined with one season spent volunteering in the colonies' small medical clinic. Doing data entry.

Watching Jenna over Krissi's shoulder, Kaly didn't like the pallor of the woman's skin. She was looking worse, and Kaly knew instinctively that her death was near. As this grim realization took hold, Jenna's body went into convulsions.

"Kaly," Krissi cried, "Something's wrong with her. Help me!"

11

By the time Kaly was at her side, Jenna had stopped moving. She had also stopped breathing.

"Kaly, what do we do?" Krissi squeaked.

Kaly put her ear to the womin's mouth and nose. She heard nothing. She felt for a pulse. Again nothing.

"Breathe for her," she ordered, quickly seeking the right spot on the sternum to place her hands. "I'll start the compressions."

Krissi was frozen in place. "I can't do this!"

"Anna," Kaly yelled, "Get over here!"

Anna dropped her diagnostic set and rushed over. Giving Krissi a look of pure disgust, she got on her knees and gave Jenna two deep breaths through her mouth. Then Kaly started chest compressions.

They worked on the woman for ten minutes before they finally realized that she was past saving.

"It's not going to work," Anna finally declared in a flat, emotionless voice. "She's dead." Without further ado, she got up from the body and walked back to the diagnostic terminal to resume her vigil.

No one said anything, not even Kaly. The only sound in the room was the hiss of space-noise coming from the RDT, and one of the little ones, crying softly.

USSNS *Pallas Athena*, Battle Group Golden, Miranda System, Pantari Elant, United Sisterhood of Suns, 1042.10|30|02:50:26

Commander Lilith ben Jeni sat cross-legged on the floor of her cabin, breathing in the delicate fragrance of the Kalian incense scenting the air around her. Her eyes were closed, and her mind was empty of everything but peace and silence.

A chime sounded, softly, but insistently, and she reluctantly focused her attention on it and opened her eyes. The bridge wanted something.

"Yes?" she asked, trying not to lend any impatience to her tone. One of the great pleasures that she allowed herself during a *freeday* was spending the first part of her morning in quiet meditation. The demands of duty generally prevented her from doing this during a normal working week.

A hologram of her second in command, Lt. Commander Katrinn Bertasdaater, materialized. "I'm sorry to bother you, Lily, but you said to let you know if anything interesting happened."

Banishing the last traces of her annoyance, Lilith addressed the image. "What do we have?"

"We received some fresh intel on the *Spacewitch*, ma'am," Katrinn answered. "She's in a convoy out of Ananti 4, headed our way. But before she joined up with the other ships, Customs Police in Ananti notified the DNI about her. An informant told them that her captain loaded up with a large quantity of *glass*. According to DNI, she's carrying it in a pair of false holds."

In addition to protecting the Sisterhood from external threats, it was the Navy's job to help enforce martime laws—especially when it came to drug smuggling. And Szalian crystal was one of the biggest probelems that they faced.

Glass was a highly addictive drug. Addicts known as 'cutters' slashed themselves with glass shards, releasing an enzyme into their blood stream. The infernal substance tricked the nerves into believing that what was pain, was actually pleasure.

But what brought the cutters ecstasy the first few times, failed the next. More and more injury had to be inflicted in an ever-expanding, never-ending cycle of self-abuse. Only death from infection or trauma ever freed the glass addict from this slavery.

In Lilith's opinion, anyone who trafficked in glass deserved to be jettisoned into space, without trial, or the bother of a spacesuit.

"Yes, that *is* some interesting news," she agreed.

"I took the liberty of arranging a little surprise for her," Katrinn continued. There was a gleam of mischief in the Zommerlaandar's violet irises. "I've ordered the *Artemis* and the *Demeter* into positions in and around the main shipping lane, and I have us on standby to help coordinate the stop."

A holo of the Miranda system appeared alongside her Second, showing the two *Macha*-Class cruisers in their group, parked inside the concealment of an asteroid belt. A smaller pair of symbols marked out the locations of two F-90A Valkyrie aerospace fighters. Her own ship, the

Pallas Athena, was standing off at a good interval from the others, and moving on a heading to take up station behind a small planetoid.

All in all, it was a good ambush, Lilith reflected. But after three years of serving with her Second Officer, she was not surprised. Katrinn was an able commander in her own right and Lilith had never been disappointed with her Second's tactics.

"Everything looks good Kat. And I completely concur," she said.

"Port Authority registered her leaving space-dock just behind the convoy," Katrinn added. "So when we see them, we'll see her."

"Excellent," Lilith beamed, "How long before we can expect her?"

"If our information is correct, and the convoy didn't run into any trouble in Null, we should see them in about twelve minutes standard."

"Good," Lilith replied, "I'll be up in three."

"Thank you, ma'am. I'll have your breakfast waiting." Katrinn's image winked out and the room went dark again.

Lights, Lilith thought. A psiever, a tiny bioelectronic receiver implanted deep inside her brain at birth, interpreted the thought impulses, and translated them into a signal. Receivers in the room around her responded to that signal, and the lights came on.

Her *kaatze*, Skipper, who had been using Lilith's meditation exercise to occupy the entirety of her empty bed, looked up in irritation, and the same everyday miracle that had turned on the lights, broadcast his thoughts from his own psiever directly to her mind. Not that she really needed to hear his tart commentary.

I was quite comfortable before all that commotion, the kaatze protested. *And we don't need any lights on.*

"I'm sure that you were," Lilith retorted, "but unlike you, *I* have *work* to do. You should try it sometime. It might be a nice change from lying around and sleeping all day."

The kaatze answered this with a profanity that only felines fully understood, but Lilith ignored it. Instead, she made her way into the tiny private bathroom that adjoined her sleeping quarters. After a few minutes, she reemerged relieved, showered, and feeling reasonably human.

At a thought, her closet opened and revealed her uniforms. Freeday or no, she was required to report for duty properly attired and she quickly selected one of her day uniforms. It was a simple 'star-service black' tunic with minimal decoration, matching trousers and knee length boots.

She put this on, and then stopped for a moment in front of the closets full-length mirror to smooth out the uniforms creases and straighten its collar. Then she ran a brush through her short, military-length hair.

It was almost completely jet-black, except for splashes of grey here and there, and despite the occasional urging of her friends and co-workers, Lilith had steadfastly refused to have it colored over. Instead, she had kept exactly it as it was, telling anyone who commented on it that she had earned every grey hair in her years of service. To her, they were a badge of honor--not a sign of age. Patting a few of the more rebellious strands into place, she headed out of her cabin, pausing only long enough to make the Lady's Sign in the direction of her personal shrine.

As always, there was a sailor on duty in the common passage that ran through Officers Country. The woman saluted her, and Lilith returned the gesture reflexively as she strode by her and out into the main hallway to the Lifts. At this time of the ships 'day', the residence deck was comparatively empty, and she found herself alone in the central lift.

Bridge, she thought. The elevator responded obediently, and rose smoothly until it reached the Command Level, and then opened up onto the bridge itself.

Like any other *Isis*-class warship, the *Athena's* primary bridge was a large cylindrical chamber. It located deep in the heart of the great vessel, and protected by the surrounding decks and thick layers of blast resistant armor.

In the very center of this space, Lilith's command chair floated in its own grav field, above a raised dais. Directly below it, and facing towards the ship's bow, were two conventional workstations that were reserved for her senior officers when she was on the bridge. Beyond them, orderly rows of control stations radiated outwards in every direction, separated by departments.

With a nod to Katrinn, who was speaking with an officer over in Fire Control, Lilith took a moment to allow her eyes to adjust to the dim light. Except for the illumination from the holojectors and control surfaces all around her, the bridge was as dark as a mining shaft on her motherworld of

15

Ara. The only notable exceptions were the three gigantic situation screens that encircled the bridge.

At the moment, the forward-most *sitscreen* was displaying a detailed diagram of the Miranda system and all local space traffic. It also showed the current positions of the battle group's three ships and the fighters. Each one, Lilith saw, had gotten themselves into position and had gone over from standard running to full stealth mode.

Seeing this, she smiled in anticipation. For the last standard month, Battle Group Golden's tour of the Pantari Elant had been uneventful, and she was as eager as the rest of her command for anything that would break up the monotony. The *Spacewitch* was about to provide them with that very diversion.

As she walked over to her chair, and took her place, her smile widened as the light breakfast that her Second had promised popped up from the chair arm. Toasting her Second with her tea, she took a deep appreciative sip and waited as Katrinn finished her conversation and came over to assume her own place at one of the Senior Officer's workstations.

"Any update on the convoy's arrival?" Lilith asked.

"The convoy escort signaled that they would be coming out of Null on schedule," the Zommerlaandar replied. "If they hold true to that, we should see them in another two minutes."

Lilith nodded. "That should give me just enough time to enjoy my breakfast then. I'd hate to meet the good Captain without being properly nourished."

Katrinn laughed, and left her to it.

Lilith managed get in a few bites of her sandwich before the Senior Ship's Advocate, Lt. Commander Ellyn n'Dira appeared and took her place her place at the Third Officer's station. The seat's official owner, Lt. Commander Mearinn d'Rann, was off duty at the moment, and the two women shared the workspace together. It wasn't a formal arrangement, but something that the pair had come to mutually agree upon over the years.

"Have I missed anything?" N'Dira asked.

"Not at all, Ellyn" Lilith replied, inclining her head towards the sitscreen "The fun is just about to begin. Relax. Enjoy the show."

16

"Good," the other woman said exhaustedly. "I needed a break from those briefs anyway. *Some* of us might actually *have* free time on a freeday, but I don't think any of them are Advocates."

"Or Commanders, it seems," Lilith remarked dryly. N'Dira was in charge of the ship's legal affairs and she knew that the woman was working on a dozen or more cases at the moment. But with a crew of 10,365 women including officers and techs, a workload like that was simply to be expected.

Unfortunately, the Star Service also required that N'Dira drop everything that she was doing and run to the bridge to advise the Commander every time they were about to get involved in anything that might have legal repercussions. At least this time she hadn't brought her work topside with her, Lilith reflected, returning her attention to the sitscreens.

At exactly the two minute mark, the number two sitscreen display showed the unmistakable signs of ships coming out of Null. An area on the screen had been marked out with a graphic, while a real-time image appeared in a window alongside it, showing an empty stretch of space beginning to ripple and distort. Within seconds, the disturbance increased in magnitude. Then, there was a soft burst of light at its center, followed by a line of freighters coming out of the area like beads on a string.

As each ship came back into normal space, the *Athena's* sensors read their transponder code and identified them on the sitscreen. And then, just as the Nullgate was about to collapse, a final ship popped out, straggling well behind the rest of the pack. She read off as the CSS *Harmony*, out of Cerridwen, but Lilith and the *Athena's* computers knew from her engine signature that she was really the *Spacewitch*.

"That's the first count, eh, Councilor?" she said to the Advocate. Falsifying transponder codes wasn't a Class-A offense, especially since the captain could always claim a malfunction, but every little bit counted in the end. N'Dira nodded absently in agreement as she called up a holo at her own station and began entering the data into a fresh case file.

"Commander? The Valkyries are asking for permission to make the stop," Katrinn advised.

"So be it," Lilith replied. "Also inform Captain taur Minna to have the *Artemis* come into play."

Katrinn relayed the order, and the *Artemis* came out of stealth as the Valkyries closed the distance with the *Spacewitch*. Their transmissions played out on the bridge as they hailed the freighter.

"Freighter *Harmony*, this is the Sisterhood Navy. You are ordered to power down and heave-to for inspection," the flight leader said. "Have your manifests and licenses ready for download."

The *Spacewitch* did not obey the order. Instead, the little freighter turned around and started heading away from the Miranda system towards open space, at top speed. On the surface, this seemed to be an utterly futile maneuver. Like most merchanters, she lacked the ability to transit into Null, and even if she had possessed that capability, the *Indwellers*, the amorphous life forms that inhabited Nullspace, would have made short work of her without a heavily armed escort ship tagging along to defend her.

Lilith was an old hand at dealing with smugglers though, and knew exactly what the Captain of the ship was really about. The *Spacewitch* was making for the border of the system in the hopes of crossing its legal boundary, and jettisoning her cargo in open space. If the *Spacewitch* managed to do this, then the charges against her might be reduced. Especially if her Captain were able to convince a Judge Advocate that she'd taken the drugs aboard without being aware of them, and had tried to dispose of them like a good citizen. But all things being equal, this was highly unlikely.

"I repeat—power down your engines and heave-to," the Valkyrie flight leader demanded. But the *Spacewitch* kept right on going.

"That's our second count--and a felony I believe," Lilith observed. Failure to power-down and submit to a lawful inspection was a serious offense.

Katrinn looked up to Lilith. "The Valkyries are asking for permission to fire a warning shot. May I grant it, ma'am?"

Lilith looked over at N'Dira.

"Yes," the Advocate nodded, "but only that. I was specifically advised by the Advocate General's office that we need to keep the *Spacewitch* as

18

intact as possible. We don't want any damage to the ship if it can be avoided."

Her response puzzled Lilith. Normally the AG's office didn't get involved in the process of enforcing the law—they generally left the tactical end of things to Commanders in the field. Unless something very important was involved.

"Very well," Lilith finally said. "Kat—please inform the flight leader that she may fire a warning shot."

Katrinn nodded and passed the order along.

"Freighter *Harmony*, this is your last warning," the Valkyrie pilot said, "Heave-to or be fired upon!"

The merchanter ignored this order, and one of the fighters launched an *Elf* anti-ship missile. It detonated near enough to the vessel to show its Captain that they were serious, but without causing any damage.

Realizing that they would not reach the border of the system in time, the *Spacewitch's* Captain made the only move left to her. The *Athena's* sensors registered the merchanter's cargo bay opening up, and then the discharge of a number of small objects.

A sensor scan came back with the results of the analysis a moment later. They were cargo containers. Just as Lilith had predicted, the *Spacewitch* had dumped her glass. Not that this had done the merchanter any good: once they were recovered, their contents would be inspected and confirmed.

"And that would be our third count," Lilith remarked with a pleased expression, "blatant possession of contraband cargo."

In the meantime, the *Spacewitch* was still moving at top speed towards open space. Lilith was betting that they still had other contraband aboard

"It also doesn't look as if we'll be able to avoid damaging her if we want her to stop," she added.

"If we must," the Advocate agreed reluctantly. "The AG won't like it, but I think that we can justify it if it doesn't cause any perminant property damage."

Lilith nodded in agreement. "Kat, instruct the pilot to limit her damage to their sensor electronics. They can get those fixed whenever they get out of jail."

Martin Schiller

Her Second smiled and relayed this out to the fighters.

"Understood, *Athena*. Target acquired," the Valkyrie pilot said. "Firing." Another missile arrowed towards the freighter and the screen registered an explosion almost directly on top of the vessel. It was at this point that the *Spacewitch* finally decided to answer their hails.

"*Deas dam va!* This is the *Harmony*!" a voice crackled," Stop firing! You *bitas* just fried all my sensors! We're running blind!"

"Then power down your engines, and slow down to boarding speed," the pilot responded. "Now."

The civilian Captain replied with an expletive, but the ship's in-system drive went offline. Braking thrusters engaged next, and the vessel's speed reduced to no more than a slow crawl.

Immediately, a *Nixie* SR-113 rescue ship carrying a squad of Marines and rescue-paramedics left the hangar of the *Artemis*. As it began to work its way towards the crippled ship, Lilith rose from her chair. "I'll be in my Office, Kat. Please bring the *Athena* into range and see to it that the captain of the *Spacewitch* is brought to see me at at once."

The Commander's Office was immediately adjacent to the bridge. Lilith entered it and came around her desk. The holofile for the *Spacewitch* and her captain was already on display and she quickly read through the material in an attempt to glean anything from it that she didn't already know. There was nothing surprising contained in the file, however. The ship had a long and checquered past, and so did Captain d'Orsi.

A career criminal, she thought with disgust. The Sisterhood was nowhere near as wild and anarchistic as the Gaian Star Federation had been, but there were still those who chose to break the law. It would be a pleasure to send Captain d'Orsi off to a correctional colony.

She paged over to the case history section and added in her own summary of the day's actions. On a small side screen, information was already pouring in from the search team aboard the *Spacewitch*. From what they'd found so far, it was going to be an open-and shut affair.

Katrinn called as she completed her entry. "Commander? You have a message from Dessica." Dessica was the largest city on Aridia, and the local capitol of the Miranda system.

20

"Fine, Kat," Lilith replied. "Put it through." As part of their standard operational protocol, the *Athena* had immediately sent out an after-action report to the nearest Star Service Headquarters, and something about the event had triggered a flag of some sort. She was fairly certain that it had everything to do with the orders that N'Dira had received from the AG's office.

The transmission that came to her was in real-time, sent from the planet, through Nullspace via relay satellites, and then out again to the *Athena* in normal space in encrypted form. A holo of two women, one dressed in a Star Service uniform, and the other in a civilian comerci, manifested before her desk. By her insignia, Lilith knew immediately that the Navy woman was part of the DNI, the *Divis da Naval Intelle*, the Naval Intelligence Division, and the small black rose on the other woman's business suit meant that she was affiliated with the OAE, the *Orgón par Avaní Extér* or the Agency for External Affairs.

To most women of the Sisterhood, the OAE was a little non-descript sub-department of the Supreme Circle, a humble diplomatic corps that acted as a liaison with other sentient races. Which was exactly what the OAE wanted everyone to think.

In reality, it was a gigantic spy agency, with tentacles reaching out everywhere. And the OAE and the DNI were old bedmates.

She addressed the pair. "Ladies? What can I do for you today?"

"Commander, I am Captain Hari n'Kyla" the DNI officer began, "and this is my associate Willa bel Jeanna. She is a representative of the OAE. We'd like to talk to you about Captain d'Orsi and her ship."

Lilith had other business that she wanted to address first though. "Before we go into that, let's talk about my daughter," she said. "Have you any news?"

"No," Bel Jeanna replied. "I was advised that you might ask after her, but we have nothing to tell you aside from the fact that she is still unaccounted for. Believe me, if we knew anything more—"

"Then you might or might not tell me," Lilith retorted. "Depending upon how the information fit in with your objectives."

"Commander, —"

"Let's get on with your business," she said with a curt wave. "What do you want with the *Spacewitch*?"

The two intelligence officers proceeded to explain their mission. Despite her dislike of the pair and what they represented, Lilith listened carefully, and when they had finished, she sent a message for Ellyn n'Dira to join them. The Advocate's presence, and her powers of persuasion, would be useful when the Captain of the *Spacewitch* was brought to her office.

Several minutes passed, and then the door hissed open revealing the smuggler captain herself, accompanied by two large Marines.

"This whole thing is outrageous!" Captain d'Orsi bellowed. "I demand to see an Advocate! I'll press charges against all of you for the damage that you did to my ship! I want to file a complaint immediately!" The woman pushed her guard's arms away and stepped towards Lilith's desk, chin held high.

"I am the Senior Ship's Advocate," N'Dira, said, rising from her seat. "And you can file your complaint with my department *after* the Commander speaks with you. For now, I strongly advise you to keep silent."

"No! I want you to hear my complaint first," D'Orsi insisted. "I have rights!"

"The only right you have is to shut your mouth and sit down," Lilith snapped. There was a deadly, no-nonsense tone to her words and D'Orsi's face registered a mixture of surprise and outrage. She began to mouth an objection, but one glance at the Zommerlaandar troopers standing to either side of her made her reconsider. Instead, D'Orsi took her seat.

"Now, Captain," Lilith said calmly, "Let's talk about your situation, shall we? From what my search teams have reported, your ship was carrying some *very* interesting cargo."

D'Orsi started to protest again, but Lilith gestured her to silence. "First, there is the matter of all that glass you had on board," she began. "I'm sure that you're well aware that this substance is illegal in the Sisterhood."

"I can explain that—"

"I'm sure you can, but I'd rather not hear your lies. Instead, I would prefer to continue with what *I* have to say."

Lilith took a platinum case from her desk and withdrew a Zommerlaandar *czigavar*. The smokeless cigarette contained a low intensity hybrid of Old Gaian cannabis.

As she touched it to her lips, it ignited, and she took a long, deep drag off it. She didn't smoke often, but in her opinion, this was one event where the indulgence definitely heightened the pleasure of the moment.

"A second item worth mentioning are the 12 cases of military grade long-arms," Lilith went on, referring to her data screen, "and battery packs for the same. We also found some pirated *realie* orbs tucked in along with everything else."

D'Orsi shifted nervously in her chair, and Lilith arched an eyebrow at her guest. "I gather that the realies were for personal use and the weapons for self defense?"

The smuggler suddenly looked as if she had just eaten something disagreeable, and Lilith grinned, enjoying every nanosecond of her discomfiture.

"And, if all *this* weren't enough," she added, "there's the business of using a false transponder code, *and* your failure to follow a lawful order for inspection."

N'Dira chimed in. "Commander, I believe that we are looking at something in the neighborhood of 20 to 35 years of incarceration if the Captain is convicted on all counts. With time off for good behavior after 15 of those years, of course."

"I have to defer to your expertise on sentencing, Advocate," Lilith returned. "One thing that I *do* know is that the Captain here is facing some serious legal issues that will earn her substantial prison time *when*, and not *if*, she is convicted."

D'Orsi slumped in her chair. "What do you want from me?" she asked quietly. She knew the game.

Lilith leaned forwards abruptly, her ice-blue eyes flashing with anger. "What do *I* want?! *I* want to see you sent away to a correctional colony to break rocks for the rest of your goddess-cursed days. *I* want to see that ship of yours blown into atoms, right along with your filthy cargo."

Then she frowned, and leaned back in her chair, her cold gaze steady on the pirate captain. "It seems that we can't always get what we want," Lilith said. "However, the Lady *does* tend to make sure that we get what we truly deserve."

The holo of the two intelligence officers, who had been monitoring the entire conversation, winked into view at this point. The OAE woman rewarded D'Orsi with a hungry, wolfish grin.

"They have an offer that I think you should accept, given your present legal situation," N'Dira suggested.

Lilith extinguished her *czigavar*, and gestured to the two guards behind D'Orsi to leave, and wait outside the office. "I won't wish you any luck in your new career, Captain d'Orsi," she said.

***

Lilith and N'Dira came out of Lilith's office, followed by a thoroughly dejected Captain d'Orsi. As the Marines marched the smuggler off the bridge, Katrinn joined the two officers. "Well, what happened?"

"It seems that the OAE decided to take advantage of Captain d'Orsi's predicament," Lilith informed her. "So, instead of having the pleasure of transporting her to a correctional colony, it looks like we're going to have to cut her loose in the name of national security."

"That's a damned shame," Katrinn replied with genuine regret. "We had her pegged in our gun-sights on some solid violations."

"Oh we still do," Lilith assured her. "She's 'volunteered' to spy on the Hriss for the OAE—that, or go to prison. It seems that the government has a new program to recruit smuggler trash like her to help them gather intel. D'Orsi and her ship have just joined their brave ranks."

"A correctional colony would have been kinder," Katrinn smirked. The Hriss, a warlike race that neighbored the Sisterhood, was sometimes known to kill traders after a deal was done. In their warped way of thinking, this was considered a normal part of doing business: if a trader was smart enough, and resourceful enough, to escape with their profit, they earned respect, and the chance for more lucrative deals. If they weren't, then the Hriss didn't believe that they deserved to keep their profits, or their lives.

It was an odd way of ensuring that only the most cunning of merchants dominated the illicit trade between their two races. For this very reason, few smugglers attempted to deal with the Hriss, but those that did became very wealthy for their troubles. In Lilith's private estimation, D'Orsi wouldn't see much in the way of a profit, or enjoy a lasting business relationship.

"Let's hope the Hriss test her business acumen to its limits," Lilith remarked irreverently. "In the meantime, please make sure that Security dumps all of her cargo out of the nearest airlock and vaporizes it. Since she's going to be working on the right side of the law now, she won't need all that nasty contraband aboard her ship, now will she?"

"Certainly not," Katrinn chuckled, "It will be my pleasure, ma'am."

Lilith mirrored her smile, and then accessed her psiever. The time of day, down to the nanosecond, appeared in the corner of her vision. She saw that she still had plenty of her freeday left.

"Well, Kat," she said, "If there's nothing else, I think I'll go and enjoy the rest of my freeday."

Her Second sketched a salute. "Have fun Lily, and don't forget we have a lunch date."

Promising to keep their appointment, Lilith left her and took the Lifts down from the bridge to deck 6, going straight to the Ship's Library. There, she took her place in the small cubicle that had been set aside for her exclusive use, and activated the holoviewer.

For the last two years, she had been pursuing a Doctorate in Military History, and her thesis, *"Lilya Litvak and Her Influence on the Military Campaigns of the Eastern Front,"* sat on the virtual desktop.

She had completed it three weeks earlier, and a copy was being reviewed by her Third, Mearinn d'Rann. In addition to her duties as an officer, Mearinn was also her Doctoral Supervisor, and the Program Coordinator for the University of Thermadon's Military Extension Courses aboard the *Athena*.

Until the Tethyian was done with it, Lilith had some time on her hands, and it was her policy to spend this rare commodity as wisely as possible. Today, she intended to accomplish this by catching up on her reading and broadening her general understanding of history.

25

A file folder next to the thesis contained several virtual books, and she considered each one carefully. Two of them were about the Soviet Military in the second of Old Gaia's five world wars.

Originally, these had been intended as reference material for her thesis, but she had managed to complete the project without having to consult them. And although they represented her favorite period in pre-Sisterhood history, *"Lilya Litvak"* had oversaturated her on the subject. She wanted something else.

Another title in the file was a recent edition of Lena Calydraith's *"Where the Blue Flowers Grow"*. Historians considered *"Blue Flowers"* to be one of the most definitive accounts of the Plague from the standpoint of an average woman, and over the years, Lilith had read many versions of it. This particular edition promised a more in-depth examination of the pre-Sisterhood era and Calydraith's personal life, but it failed to entice her.

This left her with only one choice; *"The MARS Plague and Its Origins"* by Dr. Maria ben Rilla. The book had been recommended to her by Mearinn herself, and according to her Third, it was quickly gaining popularity in the academic community, and would undoubtedly become a classic.

I suppose this is it then, she decided, opening the book with a thought, and ordering herself a cup of tea with another.

The introduction appeared before her. Most readers would have paged past this to get the meat of the text, but Lilith felt that it was essential to read everything that an author wrote—including and especially the introduction. It was the only way to gain a true grasp of the writer's intent and the overall spirit of the book itself.

As she began, an optical tracking program embedded in the book automatically spawned a hologram. This was a common feature of many virtual books, and although she could have easily deactivated it with another thought, Lilith allowed it. Like the introduction, the images that an author chose to accompany their work were often just as revealing as their words. They tended to add another layer of meaning to the message that the writer was trying to convey.

This particular image was of the MARS virus itself, in all of its terrible glory, and a reflexive shudder went up her spine as she read the caption.

Magnified image of the MARS virus. Courtesy of the University of Thermadon, Department of Epidemiology.

As soon as the book sensed that she was done with it, the holo disappeared, and the introduction began.

"MARS was the perfect killer," Ben Rilla stated, *"and a virologist's worst nightmare. It was airborne, dormant for up to twelve years, constantly mutating, and 100 percent fatal at the onset of symptoms. It was also extremely unique in the annals of pandemics. Male Acute Respiratory Syndrome was gender-specific. Women were completely immune to its ravages.'*

"Because of this, early researchers quickly realized that MARS was not a naturally occurring pathogen, but the deliberate creation of some unknown laboratory. The issue that remained, and continues to spark heated debate to this very day, is who was responsible for it, and why it was ever created in the first place.'

"What no one can argue with were its effects. In less than a decade, every human male in existence had perished, no matter his age, or station in in life.'

At the end of this sentence, another hologram manifested. This time, it displayed a huge pile of male bodies being burned, and the caption underneath indicated that it had been taken on Essylt, the very world that Lena Calydraith had called her home. Calydraith herself was in the image, standing off to one side with several other women, and watching as the flames took hold.

Lilith paused, and took a moment to zoom in on the woman and her companions. Each of them wore a mask to filter out the stench of the burning flesh, and they carried portable flamers. It was one of the images that had found a place for itself as an essential part of the Sisterhood's Secondary school curriculum. And, as always, she was struck by the profound weariness in Calydraith's eyes. Eyes that had cried themselves dry, and were gazing towards an uncertain future.

An old nursery rhyme that Lilith had learned as a child came back to her. It went, *'See-Saw, mother and dau! Burned their da to obey the law!'* On many worlds, including Esyllt, the authorities had mandated the immediate immolation of plague victims. But this tactic, like so many others, had failed to halt the disease's advance.

After a moment more, she closed the holo and resumed her reading.

"Human society very nearly collapsed," Ben Rilla continued, *"and to compound the situation, an alien invasion followed right on the heels of the disaster. The Hriss, believing us to be weak, chose this point in history to wage a war of conquest and indiscriminate slaughter. What they didn't count on was the reliance of women, or their determination to survive."*

Being a naval officer, Lilith was well-acquainted with the desperate battles that had been fought to repel that invasion. They had become the stuff of military legend and the inspiration for generations of cadets at the Naval Academy on Calaphis; from the first bloody engagement at Tennos-9, all the way to the defeat of the Hriss battle fleets at Fomalhaut.

And also, the terrible tragedy of Solara, where the Hriss had perpetrated one final atrocity. In revenge for their disgrace at Fomalhaut, the invaders had rallied their remaining forces and attacked the birthplace of Humanity.

A new holo came up, and Lilith found it even harder to look at than its predecessors. Not simply because of its subject matter, but also the nearness of it to her own professional experience. It was another classic image, and although it was over a thousand years old, it still hadn't lost any of its visual impact.

The shot had been taken on the bridge of the USSNS *Deborah Gannett*, and showed a Navcom tech, looking back over her shoulder at her captain. She had been captured at the very instant that she was announcing the terrible news to her superior about Old Gaia's fate.

Alerted by the inhabitants of the planet, the fledgling Sisterhood fleet had rushed to intercept the Hriss battle group, but had come out of Null only to discover that their motherworld was gone forever, pulverized into dust by planet-buster missiles. It had been the last, and greatest loss of what would become known as the First Widow's War.

Lilith's throat tightened involuntarily as she imagined what it must have been like for the *Gannett's* crew, and their captain, as they realized that they had failed. She also whispered up a small, secret prayer of thanks to the Goddess that she had been born when she had, and had not been the one sitting in that command chair.

28

She continued reading.

"Our enemies also didn't realize our capacity to learn from the lessons of history," Ben Rilla stated. *"MARS was not the first great disease to ravage our species, even if it was the most devastating. Centuries before interstellar space travel was even a concept, another plague cut a swathe through our ranks. This was the Black Death of the Middle Ages, and there are many parallels between it and MARS that bear serious examination.'*

"One of these was the pivotal role that travel and commerce played in both catastrophes. The ability to move over long distances and transport goods has always been the key to great wealth and power. However, it was this very freedom that proved to be our undoing.'

"In the Middle Ages, trade between Europe and the Far East provided the mechanism for the Black Death to be introduced into European society. In the great city state of Florence, this occurred in 1348 BSE, when a merchant ship laden with exotic goods—and infected fleas--made port. By the time that the disease had finally burned itself out in 1356 BSE, an estimated 200 million people had perished.'

"Centuries later, interstellar trade was the agent of disaster. Although a civil war between the Gaian Star Federation and the Kasiegian Confederation had been raging for several years, trade had continued unabated.'

"In the process of transporting legal and illegal goods from one star system to the next, infected merchanter crews unwittingly transmitted the MARS plague throughout all of the human worlds until no place had been left untouched. This time, the casualties were in the trillions.'

Another hologram appeared with this. It was an example of the ubiquitous Widow's Stone. Every world in the Sisterhood had at least one of these monolithic black stones on display, etched with the names of the Plague's victims, and those who had fallen in the three wars that the Sisterhood had fought with the Hriss.

Lilith took a moment to make the sign of the Lady in respect for the dead, before closing it, and moving on.

"Another common point was the sweeping social change that the two epidemics ushered in. Like the Black Death, the MARS Plague transformed human society completely. Established governments fell, religious beliefs

29

were questioned and discarded, and the very fabric of civilization
underwent a radical transformation.'

"For the ancient Europeans, the result was the Renaissance and some
of the finest art and inventions that our species has ever created. For the
women of the 23rd century BSE, it was the enlightenment of Motherthought
and the greatest society ever conceived of, the United Sisterhood of Suns.
As terrible as it is to admit, the illumination that Motherthought has
brought to our lives, and the freedom and prosperity that we now enjoy,
would not have been possible without the MARS Plague. It freed us from
the domination of men, and gave us the chance to flourish on a scale that
our ancestresses could never have imagined for their daughters.'

"Today, more than a thousand years after this catastrophic event, we
tend to assume that MARS no longer touches our daily lives. And yet, its
effects are still being felt. One example of this is religion.'

"Prior to the Plague, it was a given that the universe had been created
by a male God, and that 'he' was represented by the patriarchal religions
of the time, including Christianity. With the advent of MARS, this viewpoint
fell into disrepute, and was eventually replaced by the worship of the
Goddess.'

"Even so, a remnant of this archaic male-centered belief system has
managed to survive to this very day, but not without experiencing a
wholesale alteration to its fundamental beliefs. Instead of a male serving as
its spiritual leader, a female was elected to become Pope in 03.24 ASE, and
in order to bring about what it believed would be the 'Second Coming' of
its redeemer figure, its followers were compelled to engage in a genetics
program to resurrect the male human. Today, we call them the neomen.'

Lilith paused the book, and took a long sip from her tea, pondering this
statement. The New Catholic Church of the Revelation of Mari was a tiny
minority in the Sisterhood, and generally despised and distrusted by most
women. Personally, she didn't feel any particular hostility towards them,
and she didn't share the general view that the Marionites were any kind of
credible threat to society.

Nor did she harbor any antipathy towards the neomen themselves. In
her opinion, these 'new males' were too small in number, and too
marginalized to ever wield the kind of sociopolitical influence that their

forbearers had once enjoyed. As she saw it, they were really nothing more than a genetic curiosity, however much the Marionites and their sympathizers wanted it to be otherwise.

Even so, she would have preferred that the neomen had never been created in the first place, and that Christianity had died with the Plague. Like Islam, Judaism and the other patriarchal religions that had once existed, the historical record amply demonstrated how this belief system had managed to stunt the spirtual and technological growth of humanity for millenia.

And the fact that there was still a minority of otherwise enlightened women who chose to believe that a 'god' governed their lives, rather than the Goddess, both astounded and disappointed her. For all of its advances and progress, the Sisterhood still had its fair share of ignorance and superstition, she decided.

Setting down her cup again, she resumed reading.

"Another dramatic effect that MARS continues to exert on us is the very process of reproduction itself. We simply take it for granted that we can have a child completely free of any male influence. We have only to apply for the permit, pass the parenting classes, and let a doctor handle the rest."

She was tempted to close the book right there. At the outset, she had expected some of Ben Rilla's material to bother her, but this was a particular sore spot. Every time birthing was mentioned in any context, she was always forced to recall her marriage, and the daughter that she and her wife had given birth to.

That, and the pain of losing them both.

She was too dedicated a student of history, and too well trained as an officer to allow her regrets to overwhelm her however. Even now, at this time of year. Mastering herself, she pressed on. Her ghosts would have to wait until she was ready to deal with them.

"But before the MARS Plague, and for literally millions of years, this was not the case." Ben Rilla went on, 'Having a child in the pre-Sisterhood era required that a woman submit herself to a messy, animalistic union with a male in order to receive the 'contribution' of his XY chromosomes.'

"This primitive, and often savage means of reproduction was at best, a desperate gamble. Sometimes, when the Y chromosome subjugated the

31

female's egg, it produced an inferior male offspring, and at other times, when the X chromosome triumphed, the mother was blessed with a female.'

"The degradation did not end there by any means; once impregnated, women quickly found themselves enslaved by the 'fathers' of their children, and were forced into a life of utter servitude.'

The holo that supplemented this depicted a pregnant woman standing before a stove in a primitive 20th century kitchen. She was barefoot, and screaming children were tugging at her skirt. Off in the corner, a male dozed in a chair, with an empty bottle of alcohol lying on the table in front of him.

The woman was the very epitome of weariness, and she sported several bruises and a black eye that had clearly been visited upon her by her husband. While Lilith understood that the image had been deliberately overplayed in order to underscore the wisdom of Motherthought for young girls, she had read enough accounts from the pre-Sisterhood era to accept its basic message. Before MARS and the Sisterhood, women had been nothing better than chattel, especially in what historians had called the 'third world' nations.

There was also another, optional holo embedded in the text, which promised her a graphic example of the ancient sex act itself, but Lilith pointedly ignored it. She had viewed 'vid clips just like it in Tertiary school, and wasn't interested in seeing another.

Most modern women considered heterosexual sex to be on par with bestiality, and just as socially unacceptable. But although she shared this attitude, she didn't consider it to be a crime like so many of her countrywomen did. Instead, it was like the neomen; something that nature had discarded in favor of something better.

MARS had certainly been a terrible thing, she reflected, but Motherthought was correct. The Plague had elevated womankind to a state of evolutionary perfection. Unlike the beasts of the field, her species no longer required a weaker counterpart to reproduce, which was a claim that few races could make. Now, sex was just for pleasure and not a tool of domination.

She sent a thought and turned to the next page.

32

"We have a woman to thank for our liberation from this genetic tyranny" Ben Rilla continued. *"She was the great scientist, Dr. Rachel Landa, and although every schoolgirl knows her name, her story deserves retelling, not only to award her memory the honor that it merits, but also to bring to light certain details of her work that the average reader might be wholly unfamiliar with.'*

"Our reproductive revolution actually began well before the MARS Plague, in 2004 BSE. Researchers in a Japanese laboratory were able to create a 'fatherless' mouse from two female parents. The technique involved the modification of an immature egg and combining it with a normal, mature egg. The result was a genetically diverse female mouse that could also reproduce in the same manner."

Lilith took another long, speculative sip of her tea. She hadn't been aware this particular fact.

So, we owe it all to a pair of mice? she wondered. The universe could be a surprising place at times. Mice it was then.

She also made a mental note not to mention this particular detail to Skipper. The kaatze would be utterly appalled.

"At the time, the Human race, unenlightened as it was by the tenets of Motherthought, viewed this experiment as nothing more than an anomaly, and some (especially among the male population) were even frightened by its implications. Dr. Landa however, saw past these narrow attitudes, and envisioned a shining future for womankind.'

"She immediately relocated to Japan, joined the project, and soon secured support from several progressive corporations, which allowed her to take the experiment to the next level. Working in secret, she eventually overcame the technical hurdles, and enabled two female volunteers to produce a daughter without any male involvement whatsoever.'

"The first human woman, born of women, had arrived on history's stage and she was named Nozomi (which meant 'hope' in the ancient Japanese language). Nozomi soon became one of the most studied children in pre-Sisterhood history."

This was another surprise. Lilith hadn't been aware of the child's name, or the fact that she had been Japanese, and she felt a surge of ethnic pride course through her. Her motherworld, Ara, had been colonized by the

33

ancient Nippon, the Chin, and Eurasians like herself. It was also the birthplace of Motherthought, and now, Ben Rilla had linked it with this momentous event.

The women of Asia have contributed a great deal to the Sisterhood, she mused. *However quietly.* Eager to learn more, she paged forwards.

"The announcement of Nozomi's birth created a firestorm of controversy. Landa was immediately vilified by the scientific community, and the male-dominated media as a 'mad scientist' and a 'monster'. And although her fellow lesbians embraced her discovery, Landa ended her days in disgrace and obscurity. But thanks to her selfless dedication and sacrifice, the doorway to a fully functional, all-female society had been opened, and would never be closed.'

"But when MARS arrived, Landa's work ceased to be a curiosity, or a marginal 'alternative' birthing process. Instead, it proved be the very key to our survival as a species. The women of the Sisterhood owe Dr. Landa a debt that can never be fully repaid, and this book has been humbly dedicated to her memory and to the memory of all those women who fought and died to preserve our nation, and our species.'

"--Dr, Maria ben Rilla, Thermadon Val, 1041.05"

Thoroughly impressed, Lilith started in on the first chapter. It highlighted the early efforts by the ancients to create biological weapons at various points in history, and then the circumstances that gave rise to the civil war between the Gaian Star Federation and the Kaseigian Confederacy. Although she found the material to be detailed, and well-reasoned, she couldn't agree with the author's conclusions.

The Kasiegian's certainly deserved the suspicion that historians viewed them with, but the MARS virus had affected them just as deeply as it had the GSF. Ben Rilla's contention that the Plague was their creation, and had somehow gotten out of control, simply didn't wash.

Lilith's personal theory was that it had had its genus elsewhere, either among the many cults and political splinter groups of the time, or came from one of womankind's many alien enemies. In her estimation, the Zeta Reticulans were the most likely culprets.

The 'Greys' as they were often nicknamed, had secretly enslaved humanity for thousands of years, and farmed it for genetic materials. After humanity had rebelled and overturned the puppet leaders that the Greys had put in place, they had earned their eternal enmity.

But the Greys were not fighters in the conventional sense. They worked in the shadows, and their weapons were subterfuge and treachery. Instead of engaging in an open war with the Sisterhood, many including herself, believed that they had goaded their client race, the Hriss, into doing all the fighting and dying for them.

Unfortunately, there was no firm proof of this, but what intelligence the Sisterhood did possess pointed strongly in that direction. And only their status as a member race in the Collective, and its mutual protection pact, was what had kept Womankind from seeking a direct conflict with them. Seeding a deadly plague was well within their means, and just the kind of loathsome thing that the Zeta Reticulans would stoop to.

As certain as she was of their complicity, Lilith still allowed Ben Rilla to present her case, and kept an open mind. An hour later though, and despite learning additional information, her opinion remained unaltered.

It was also time for her lunch date with Katrinn. Rubbing the fatigue from her eyes, she set a bookmark, and closed the file.

***

If there was one thing that the Star Service prided itself on, it was its food; brunch, as always, was good and filling. By necessity, the meals *had* to be good: long tours of space-duty ate at a crew's spirits. Appetizing food, decent entertainment and continuing education through a half dozen universities ensured that morale aboard a ship on active patrol stayed as high as possible. To Lilith's mind, of all the ships in their battle group, or in the Topaz Fleet for that matter, the *Pallas Athena* boasted the best of all these things. For this reason, it came as no surprise to her that the Captain of the *Artemis* was also dining aboard that day.

Lilith took her plate and sat down at Captain taur Minna's table. "Erin? Getting tired of your cook?"

"Hmm, perhaps," the Nemesian replied. "She still has no idea how to properly prepare *sq'ueeka*. She still insists on *cooking* them!" Erin shook her head in dismay, and looked down at the bowl in front of her. Two of the

35

tiny amphibians were swimming around in it, completely unaware that they were about to become her mid-day meal.

"Care for one?" she offered, knowing full well that Lilith would refuse. Like most women, Lilith did not agree with the Nemesian view that all food was at its best when it was still alive, and wriggling.

"No, Erin. Thank you, though," she replied politely.

Erin shrugged and fished one of the *Sq'ueeka* out of its bowl with a special fork, neatly biting off its head with her sharp canines. True to its name, the hapless creature gave a short squeak of protest before expiring. But this did not shock Lilith in the least. She'd seen the spectacle many times before and sat opposite the jungle-dweller without making any comment.

"I heard about the *Spacewitch* being let go," Erin said between bites. "You really think it was worth it, this 'big plan' that the spooks have in mind for her?" Her tone was casual, but her light green skin darkened and her prehensile tail flicked in the air behind her, betraying her actual mood.

"Yes," Lilith replied. "I had my doubts when they explained their plans to me, but all things considered, I have to agree that she's more useful to us as a spy-ship. Besides, it will make certain that Captain d'Orsi is too busy keeping her skin intact to have any spare time left to smuggle."

"I guess," Erin sighed, "Just the same, she's someone I'd like to see staked-out in the 'Green, but even the Neversaw would probably spit her out once it got a good taste of her."

"More than likely," Lilith agreed with a small laugh. She'd never seen the predator that Erin was referring to, but she imagined that any self-respecting monster from the endless forests of Nemesis would probably avoid dining on such tainted fare.

"Oh well," Erin sighed, her tail movements slowing a bit. "Maybe we'll run across her again some time." Then an evil grin spread across her elfin features. "And who knows? Maybe she'll be enough on the wrong end of things to give us cause to blow her out of space. People like that always trip themselves up in the end."

Lilith made the Sign of the Lady. *"The Goddess wills the way,"* she said. "One can always hope that she'll see to that."

As pleasant as their conversation was however, she did have some important business to discuss with the Mistress of the *Artemis* and changed the subject. "We should be pulling out of Miranda tomorrow for the next leg of our patrol. Is that problem with your engines getting itself worked out?"

Erin ran a hand through her fire-red hair and cursed. *"Teeshka'rek!"* she spat. "Hardly! My Chief told me this morning that the secondary impulse engines were still vibrating a few too many points towards the yellow-line. She wants at least two more days to set things a'right. That woman is an endless fiddler!"

"Tell her she can have one day, no more," Lilith told her. "We have to be in the Telesalla Elant in two days."

"Done and done better," Erin acknowledged. "I gave her five hours to finish with her tinkering. I also told her that anything else could be tightened up once we reached port."

Lilith nodded in satisfaction. She and Erin generally saw eye-to-eye on how a ship and its crew needed to be run—even if they would never agree on their choice of meals.

At that point, the Senior Ships Activities Officer Saara sa'Vika walked up to join them. "Ladies? Is everything to your liking?"

Both women smiled up at the Kalian. Of all the officers aboard the *Athena*, or on any Sisterhood ship for that matter, the Ships Activities Officer was always the most popular member of the crew. The SAO or 'AO' as she was sometimes nicknamed, was directly responsible for the crew's morale. Today, Lilith knew that she was making the rounds of the mess, checking to see that the food that it served was up to her exacting standards. From what she had heard, a ruthless leader lurked behind Sa'Vika's easygoing manner, and she let nothing escape her notice.

"I had hoped I'd catch you here, Commander," Sa'Vika said, with a bright smile that lit up her dark brown skin. "I have just gotten my hands on the latest *Celina* realie, and I wanted to make *sure* that you got a copy."

She held out a gold and black plastic cube. On one face was a holopic of the famous singer, and on another the cryptic title "*A Concert for Eversea*".

"Why thank you, Saara." Lilith took the cube from her with genuine gratitude. "However did you manage it?" she asked. "We're a long ways from port."

"Ah now, Commander," Sa'Vika scolded, wagging a finger at her, "how many times have I told you? Don't ask me *how* I do it. I have my ways."

Lilith strongly suspected that one of those 'ways' had involved a brief meeting with Captain d'Orsi about her pirated realies, but the gift was too fine to really press the matter. "Of course, Saara. Tell me, how is your department fixed for things? Is there anything that you're running short of?"

"It's gracious of you to ask, Commander, but we seem to be well stocked for the present. I could use a slight accommodation in the second shift's scheduling however. The workshop on light-weaving is going to run slightly overtime, and some of the crew will be forced to miss it."

"I'll do what I can to smooth things out, Saara," Lilith replied. It was always give-and-take with the SAO. Nothing was ever truly free.

Saara's pleasant expression never betrayed even the tiniest fraction of the triumph that Lilith knew she was feeling. Forcing an entire ship to change its duty rosters was no small feat.

"Thank you, Commander. I'm sure you'll do whatever you can for us. Oh, and I'd almost forgotten this," Saara reached into one of her pockets and produced a tiny can. "Tethyian pinfish in oil. For Skipper."

"Of course," Lilith replied. "We mustn't forget a gift for the *real* Commander of the *Athena*." Both women laughed as she took it.

Then the Kalian caught sight of someone else that she needed to curry favor with, and with a polite gesture of farewell, departed for the next table.

"She greased you up good," Erin said tartly, stabbing her fork in the direction of the *Celina* realie.

"You're just jealous," Lilith rejoined. They both knew that the same tactics worked on the Nemesian just as effectively, even if the bribe took a different form.

"Well, if she isn't jealous, *I* am," a voice said. Lilith turned around to see Katrinn bringing up her tray of lunch.

Katrinn threw herself down into an empty seat with an exaggerated sigh of relief. "I know it's probably not the best subject to bring up just now," the Zommerlaandar said, "but the *Demeter* has the *Spacewitch* in tow. Captain bel Sarra estimates that it will take them about three hours to reach Aridia and drop them off."

"Hmm," Erin said. "If it were me, I'd cut the tow beam about halfway there--in an asteroid field. I think it'd be fun to watch them try and crawl their way out with all their sensors down."

"That's an idea," Katrinn conceded. "But actually, Bel Sarra told me that she plans to talk with the Portmistress and see if she can at least delay the daylights out of any repairs. Apparently, she knows her family and intends to call in a favor or two."

"Isn't it strange how red-tape can just *pop-up* all of a sudden?" Lilith observed.

Kat smiled and looked away. "Oh well..." She let her words die away, and then turned around suddenly. "So? When are *we* going to get to play that realie?"

"Soon enough," Lilith laughed. "First things first. *I* get to play it before '*we*' do. Privileges of rank, don't you know?"

"Yes, ma'am!" Kat said with a mock salute. "Just don't take too long before you get around to sharing it with us lower life forms, Lily. I have a freeday coming up too!"

"Oh, I'll keep that in mind," Lilith replied, fondling the realie in her hand. Then her tone became serious. "In the meantime, how are things going for our scheduled transit into Null?"

"Well, on our end, all systems check in," Katrinn answered. "Engineering says that the drive is operating at 99.995 percent and our power reserves are at 90. Fire Control told me that all defensive systems are on line and ready. They also asked me to let you know that they fixed the traverse problem with gun 2430." Katrinn leaned back in her chair and folded her hands behind her head. "So, barring any mischievous *Aalfen* making trouble for us, we should be ready to transit on time."

"Good," Lilith said with satisfaction. Her meal had arrived and she took the time to enjoy it, and the company of of her friends. When she had finished, she excused herself.

"Well, I believe I may still have some of my freeday left to enjoy. Ladies?"

Katrinn eyed the realie with undisguised avarice. "I'll drop by your quarters when my shift is over."

Lilith flashed her a knowing smile and then departed. It was time for her to keep her promise with herself, and visit the Ship's Temple.

Whenever she had a freeday, she always made a point of visiting it, even if only briefly. But today, she sorely needed the comfort that it offered. Although her lunch with her officers had been pleasant enough, it had done nothing to dispel the emotions that Ben Rilla's words had dredged up, or allowed her to forget what day it was.

The Temple was on the same deck as the recreation facilities, and to a newcomer, it looked like any other compartment there, except for two distinct features. The first was a triple faced lamp that hung on a long chain over its doorway, and the second was its open hatchway. Except in times of ship-wide emergency, the entrance was always open as a sign of welcome and sanctuary.

Just inside this there was a small basin filled with cucumber scented water and Lilith stopped for a moment to wash her hands and face, ritually cleansing herself. Then she stepped inside the temple proper.

In keeping with the beliefs of most of the major sects that worshiped the Lady, the room was circular. Rows of low padded benches ringed the walls, facing towards the center where the cylindrical altar stood. She entered the space, and the ship's computer registered her presence, and religious preference.

A signal from it to her psiever created the image in her visual cortex of a full moon, the Selenite representation for the Goddess, hovering above the altar. Lilith kneeled and recited the words of the traditional Naval Prayer.

> *"Oh Eternal Goddess of Heaven,'* she began,
> *Who alone laid out the heavens, and*
> *Who rules over the raging fires of the stars;*
> *You who have encompassed the void with*
> *Your bindings until day and night come to an end.*

40

Receive into Thy gracious protection the persons of us,
Thy servants, and the ship in which we serve Thee.'

"*Preserve us from the dangers of space, and from the violence of the*
enemy; That we may be a safeguard for our sisters, and
Provide security for those who pass among the stars. Grant that we
may serve Thee in peace, great Lady;'

"*And ordain that we might return in safety from our voyage*
To enjoy the blessings of our motherworlds,
Our labors completed, and in thankful remembrance
Of Thy mercies. So may it be."

Then she closed her eyes and meditated, drinking in the peaceful silence of the place and letting it soothe her.

***

From a corner of the room, the Most Reverend Ophida n'Marsi watched Lilith as she prayed. She had expected her, and as the Ship's High Priestess, she always made herself available when the *Athena's* commander visited her Temple.

Ophida waited until Lilith had finished with her devotions and then went over to the woman's side. "Blessings of the Lady be upon you, Commander," she said.

Lilith stood. "And Blessings be upon You, Mother."

"It is always good to see you here, Daughter," Ophida said. "Is there anything that we can do for you in the Lady's House?" But Ophida already knew full well what Lilith wanted, and why she had come.

"Yes, Mother, there is," Lilith replied. "Could we retire to the Sanctuary and speak together?"

"Of course, child." The old woman led her to a curtained alcove in a corner of the room. They entered the small chamber, and the Priestess drew the curtain shut behind them. Then they sat and faced one other.

41

Ophida recited the ritual words of the Sanctuary. "How can I serve you, Daughter?"

"Mother," Lilith said, giving her the traditional reply, "I would have you hear me."

"Speak what is in your heart, Daughter."

Lilith's shoulders sagged. "Oh, It's the same old thing," she sighed.

"Perhaps it is, but I will still listen," Ophida answered gently. "Go ahead, Daughter. Share with me."

Lilith took a deep breath. "It's that time of year again. It's my daughter's birthday. And today, two women from Naval Intelligence and the OAE contacted me. They didn't have any news, but their visit made me think of her. Then I read a book in the library. It was a history piece, and it talked about the birthing process."

Ophida nodded patiently.

"I can still remember the day that Jan and I went to the doctor and saw the holo of how she would look when she grew up," Lilith said wistfully. "She was so beautiful..." Her voice trailed off, and Ophida gave her her moment.

She had heard all of this many times, and knew the story well. Years before Lilith had taken command of the *Athena*, she had married, and the union had produced a daughter. The girl had been a bright child, and she had quickly shown an aptitude for psychic abilities. Then at 18, she had joined the Navy, and had gone on to serve aboard the USSNS *Habondia* as a psi working in Navigation/Communications.

Finally after several years of space-duty, the young woman had transferred to Naval Intelligence. There, she demonstrated a knack for making accurate assessments from raw intelligence data, often seeing connections that her co-workers had overlooked. This, and a keen interest in field work, had led to her being assigned to train as an agent, and once she had graduated, she had proven herself to be both adaptable and resourceful in undercover assignments.

When she had helped the DNI to uncover a network of corrupt servicewomen selling off military supplies to the Xee, and then a conspiracy to use naval vessels to smuggle glass into the Sisterhood, a promotion had come her way. More successes had followed, and more promotions. And the OAE, always on the lookout for promising assets, had approached her with an offer to leave the Navy and come work for them.

Contrary to Lilith's wishes, she had accepted the invitation. A few more years passed, and then, without any warning, she had vanished without a trace. The official account was that she had been on a joint mission for the OAE and the DNI, and was 'missing, presumed dead'.

But Lilith had steadfastly refused to accept this, and continued to insist that her daughter was still alive, somewhere.

"You know me," Lilith said at last, her eyes misting. "I can't help it. I worry about her. I wonder where she is, and if she's safe. And I keep asking myself if there was anything that I could have done. Anything that I could have changed to keep things from turning out the way they did."

"And bearing a galaxy full of guilt in the process," Ophida observed. "You and I have talked about this before, Daughter, every year on this date since you came aboard the *Athena*. You already know the answer: you can't hold yourself responsible for her disappearance. Nothing you could have done would have changed her fate, whatever it was."

"I know," Lilith admitted. "But a part of me will always be missing until I find her again."

"Yes," Ophida agreed. "And the Goddess may see fit to reunite you with your daughter. But even if that miracle happens, there will still be a void in your heart. It has been there since Jan died."

Lilith looked away, her eyes now dark with pain, and Ophida continued. "You know what I'm speaking about. You may or may not have the power to bring your child back to you, but you *do* have the power to find joy for yourself, and fill that void."

"I don't know," Lilith replied doubtfully. "I still haven't healed. I'm not certain that I ever will."

"That is something for the Goddess to decide," Ophida told her. "But if an opportunity for happiness comes your way, accept it with open arms and an open heart, lest you spit on the gift that the Lady has given you. The *Cauldron of Wisdom* puts this plainly: '*Our road is laid out by the Lady, and She sets us on it in accordance with Her great design. We have no choice but to travel its length until our journey is at an end. The Goddess Wills the Way.*'"

43

"Yes, Mother," Lilith agreed, remembering the scriptural passage, "She does, and I will try. Thank you for your wisdom."

"Is there anything else that you would share with me, Daughter?" Ophida asked.

"No, Mother. I have shared all that was within my heart."

Ophida rose and placed her hands upon Lilith's head. "May the Lady always guide you, Daughter. May She sooth your troubled brow and be a comfort to you as you perform your duties. Blessings of the Goddess be upon you as you go forth from this place."

Lilith stood and clasped the Priestesses hands in her own. "And Blessings be upon you, Mother. Thank you for listening to me."

"My pleasure, Daughter," Ophida replied. They stepped outside together and walked towards the exit. "I do hope that we will have the pleasure of your company at the next holy festival."

Lilith's expression brightened. "Of course, Mother. I wouldn't miss it. In the meantime, let me know if there is anything that you need before then."

"I shall," Ophida assured her.

As Lilith departed, Ophida considered how their session had gone and wondered if the day would ever come when the woman would be allowed to learn what had truly happened to her daughter--and why it had been necessary. Only time would tell.

The priestess turned and went into her private office. There, she secured the door for privacy and sat down at her comscreen. An encrypted message from Dessica was waiting for her.

Met with subject via holo, it read, *Requested assistance with Project Merchant Princess. Subject was reluctant to cooperate, but complied. Subject also made the usual inquiry regarding 'Galenthis.' Your orders; Monitor subject's loyalty closely and continue to divert interest from Galenthis--Bel Jeanna*

Ophida typed in her response. *Subject's loyalty remains intact. Will update on progress as needed --N'Marsi.*

Then she sent the message.

The OAE had women like Ophida embedded aboard every major starship, and the Agency considered their jobs to be absolutely vital to the stability of the Sisterhood's naval forces. The success of the Navy's mission utterly depended on the healthy state of its officers' minds, and on their unwavering loyalty. There were simply too many enemies poised to destroy Womankind to accept anything less.

Ophida understood this better than most field agents did. Before she had shaved her head and donned the robes of a Priestess, she had been a naval officer herself, and had commanded a ship of her own. And like Lilith, she had had her own handlers, watching her and guiding her from the shadows.

She still had no idea who they had been, but she was grateful to them for their clandestine service. Anyone who was responsible for the lives of thousands of crewwomen, and controlled a ship capable of destroying entire planetary systems, deserved close observation, and extra attention. Ophida had, and so did Lilith.

***

Lilith's freeday deteriorated rapidly after leaving the Ships Temple. As soon as word had gotten around that the Commander had suspended her off-time to tend to the *Spacewitch*, everyone with ship-related business found an excuse to seek her out. They were all very apologetic of course, but each one of them had felt that they had had matters that all required her personal attention.

The first person to waylay her had been Dr. elle'Kaari, the *Athena's* Chief Medical Officer, who had presented her with a list of badly needed requisitions for the medbay. The doctor had been followed in-train by the Chief Engineer with a pressing issue concerning fuel consumption by the ships engines. Then the Stores Officer had pounced on her, and after her, others had descended, each with equally important business. By the time it was all over, so was the freeday.

CHAPTER 2

Marpesia District, Thermadon City, Thermadon, Myrene System, Thalestris
Elant, United Sisterhood of Suns 1042.11|01|00:64:79

It was raining on Thermadon; a miserable cold drizzle that managed to
seep into every centimeter of Maya n'Kaaryn's plastic coat no matter how
tightly she'd sealed it. It was like a living thing, determined to get past her
jackets feeble defenses and steal away her body heat. Several blocks earlier,
she had finally given up trying to fend it off and trudged down the street,
doing her best to ignore her discomfort.

It had been two days since she'd hitched a ride to the capital of the
Sisterhood on the CSS *Carol Curtiss*, a merchanter out of Corrissa, but
only a few hours since she'd stepped foot on the planet itself. The assault of
the incessant rain made it seem like that journey had taken even longer.

To make matters worse, her *inocular*, which was embedded in her left
forearm, hurt like the blazes. Born from the ravages of the MARS plague,
the Sisterhood had learned from the fatal mistakes of its predecessors. Like
the psiever, and the *biochip*, the inocular was implanted at birth, and served
as a permanent site for the injection of vaccines, which everyone was
required to receive.

This was especially true for space travelers. Exit from a spaceport was
not granted until the inocular had been scanned for its record of previous
vaccinations and new ones had been administered for the latest local bug
that was going around.

And whatever it was that was causing the sniffles for the women of
the capital city apparently required a cure that felt like it was worse than the
disease. She only hoped that her reaction to the vaccine would limit itself to
simple discomfort. Like any seasoned *nulltrekker*, she'd gotten good and
sick a few times from the shots that the locals had mandated, and she didn't
relish this happening to her again.

Frowning at the possibility, she fished around in her jacket until she
had reassured herself that her chit was still there. She'd obtained it at the
spaceport and it guaranteed her temporary lodging at a worker's hostel. As
far as anyone would know, she was just another migrant spacer, with
nothing on her record.

The truth was a great deal different, however. Before making the trip
to the capital, Maya had had the identity in her biochip changed out, and
her inocular history altered to match. Modifying these devices was highly

46

illegal and also extremely expensive. But Delgen had been getting too hot for her, and Thermadon had promised a fresh new start, justifying the expense.

Unfortunately, the directions that she'd gotten from the chit dispenser to the hostel had been poor, and she had been wandering the streets for the last hour looking for the goddess-cursed place. A hovercab would have been the ideal solution, but Maya hadn't seen any around, and she didn't have enough credits left in her stolen account to afford one even if she had.

Like the rain, she told herself that this was a temporary inconvenience. Thermadon was not only the capital; it was also the largest city in the Sisterhood, and fat with possibilities. Anyone with special abilities like the ones that she possessed could make money fast. For the moment though, she would have to satisfy herself with the few credits that she had, and walk to her destination.

Leave it to the Sisterhood to just assume that everyone somehow knows their way around T-Don, she thought unhappily. As she wiped a strand of wet hair from her face, she suddenly felt the all-too-familiar sensation of someone watching her. Her talents told her right away that it wasn't a criminal like herself--it was a *kaaper*.

A police hovercar came out of the shadows of a nearby alley and pulled up to the curb. But Maya resisted the urge to lower her head, or to run, and kept on walking like any normal, law abiding citizen. She was also careful to project the feeling that everything was normal and that she was really nothing worth bothering with.

It didn't work, but this didn't surprise her either. Although street kaapers didn't tend to be psis, some of them did possess the innate capacity to sense when something, or someone, just wasn't 'right'. This kaaper was obviously one of those women.

Although Maya could have tried pushing a little harder, she hestitated. There was a chance that this would backfire, and actually heighten the kaaper's suspicions. Moderate sensitives sometimes reacted that way, especially when they were on their guard.

The passenger window of the cruiser rolled down and she turned to face the driver.

"Heyas, girl," the policewoman said with a thick North Zommerlaandar accent. "Vat you doing out here zo late?"

Walking, as if it were any of your business, the girl thought. But instead of saying this, she answered the kaaper*'s* question in the politest tone that she could muster, "I'm trying to find the Transient Worker's Hostel, Officer."

"Vat's your name?"

After years of living under assumed identities, her response was smooth and seemed unrehearsed. "Mindi bel Tala" she replied.

"Show me za chit."

She produced it, and a bright ribbon of blue light from the car's roof array played over her body, and Maya held her breath. The vehicle was scanning her identification from her biochip implant and the inocular. A casual reading from a spaceport chit dispenser was one thing, but a scan by the Police 'Plexi was quite another. If the alteration to her identity had *any* flaws, the remainder of her visit to the capital would be spent in a holding cell, followed by a one-way a trip back to Delgen for trial.

But when the policewoman glanced at the information in her data-monocle and frowned, Maya relaxed. The scan hadn't discovered a wanted criminal, at least as far as the TMPD Police Network was concerned.

Still not entirely convinced, the kaaper regarded her suspiciously for a long moment, and Maya responded with her best *I'm-innocent-and-going-about-my-lawful-business-but-I-am-ever-so-happy-to-help-a-member-of-law-enforcement* smile. This was met with a dark scowl, but Maya wasn't concerned. After all, she told herself, wasn't under arrest, and the policewoman didn't even look like she was going to get out of her car.

"You're two streets too far to za north," the kaaper finally said, inclining her jaw in the opposite direction. "Turn left at za corner and go down to N'Rina Boulevard, n' zen right. You'll zee it about halfvay oop on za left."

Maya thanked her and started to walk away, but the policewoman wasn't finished with her. "Mind you, girl, I don't vant to see you hanging around at zis hour again. I know vat you look like now and I don't need any trouble on my shift. *Zat klaar?*"

"Yes, ma'am," Maya replied deferentially. The window rolled back up and the cruiser drove off into the shadows in search of other wrongdoers, or more likely, a place to hide so that its driver could get some sleep.

Welcome to Thermadon, she thought sourly. She only hoped that whoever she eventually found in the capital to make the next change in her biochip would be just as good as her last connection, and not quite as expensive.

The hostel turned out to be exactly where the policewoman had said it was. A young woman was seated in one of the few beat-up chairs in the lobby, paging through a holomag. Even though Maya had been in many ports of call, and seen her fair share of strange looking people, this one *was* remarkable.

She was dressed in an outfit that was a combination of leather and projected light-fields. Her skin was as pale as a Nyxian and she sported what was either a tattoo or a body painting of some kind of beast on one side of her face. But it was her irises that really stood out; they were a shocking shade of bright yellow that glowed so brilliantly that Maya was half certain that they were either artificial lenses, or had been augmented in some way.

As she passed, the woman looked up at her with a feral grin, exposing fangs that immediately identified at least part of her genetic heritage as Nemesian. Maya tried not to reward her with any expression of shock or surprise, and ignored the amused chuckle that followed her as she walked up to the front desk. Thankfully, the clerk appeared to be fairly normal, if somewhat disinterested. Undaunted, Maya presented her chit for scanning.

"That gives you one free night and a meal," the woman said. "After that, you pay like any other guest worker. Your bed is in dorm 3, upstairs, cot number 14. The house rules are simple: no drugs, no overnight guests, and no weapons. Got that, girlie?"

Maya only nodded, and took the grav-lift upstairs. She hadn't expected a warm welcome, just a bed.

The dorm she had been assigned to was crowded with small cots and sleeping bodies. Her own little bed sat next to a single, grimy window that looked out onto N'Rina Boulevard.

Right away, she opened the storage locker next to the cot and threw her *trekker's* kit bag inside. Then she undressed and tossed her clothes in after it. The locker read her bioplasmic signature and keyed itself to her as she closed it shut. Short of someone blasting the thing open, theft was unlikely, and she'd learned to sleep lightly.

Letting herself into the the bed, and drawing the thin sheets over herself, she began making her plans for the morning. Bel Sharra Memorial Spaceport wasn't far from the hostel, and it was one of the busiest in the Sisterhood. She didn't imagine that she'd have much trouble finding a legitimate job there, or illicit opportunities to make some *real* credits. Spaceports were the perfect workplace for a thief, and she considered herself to be a good one. It wouldn't be long until she would be on her feet, she assured herself. Despite her bad start, T-Don looked like the perfect place to set up shop.

As visions of all the credits that she would make danced enticingly in her head, Maya started to drift off. She was nearly unconscious when she felt *something* that shocked her back into wakefulness. Her eyes flicked open, and she tried to identify the source of the disturbance.

But she detected nothing out of the ordinary. Except for her, everyone else was fast asleep. She listened for any sounds out in the hall, but it was equally still.

Finally, she rose and looked out the dirty window down to the street below. A single hooded figure in a long, dark cloak was moving along the wet sidewalk, barely visible in the poor lighting.

Abruptly, the woman stopped and looked back up in her direction, and Maya immediately backed away from the window into the shadows. Although she knew that it was impossible, she could still feel the woman's eyes finding her in the darkness.

Then, inexplicably, the woman was *gone*. She hadn't just walked away; she was simply not there any longer. Maya shook her head, uncertain of what she had just seen, and waited. But when the mysterious stranger failed to reappear, she went back to bed.

That night, the image of the cloaked woman haunted her dreams.

***

Sarah n'Jan watched as Maya retreated from the window, and then waited to see if anything else happened. The streets around her remained silent though, and, with the exception of a stray kaatze, passing from one alley to the next, they were also completely deserted.

Finally, satisfied that the young woman had been nothing more than a rogue psi—a rarity to be sure, but nothing threatening, she touched a gem set in the center of the ornate silver clasp on her cape. With this action, special fibers woven into the garment deactivated, and she seemed to materialize magically out of thin air.

In reality, it was hard science, and nothing supernatural had been involved. When they were active, submicroscopic cameras embedded in the fibers captured the colors and shades of the world around them. The data was transmitted to equally diminutive displays, which rendered them perfectly, and made the wearer optically invisible.

This was not a standard feature by any means, either in the Capitol City, or anywhere else in the Sisterhood. Outside of the military, or professions like her own, this kind of technology was highly classified. So was the mission that she was on.

Sarah blew a kiss up to the empty window. "Sleep well, my little *esper*. Perhaps we'll meet again," she whispered. Then she walked on, staying alert.

Her relationship with her contacts had changed over the last few days, and it made her uneasy. It hadn't been anything overt. Rather, it had been a collection of subtle discrepancies that might have been missed by a less experienced agent. And in her expereince, it was the small things that could prove deadly.

Even now, her instincts were warning her to leave the area immediately, but she pushed them to the back of her mind. The transaction that she needed to make was too important to cancel, and she knew that her superiors would demand more than just intuition to justify such a drastic decision. She had to see the meeting through to its end and take things as they came.

The street ahead of her ended at the fringes of N'Dayr Memorial Park, one of the largest outdoor recreational sites in the Sisterhood. It was a wild space, even larger than some of the towns that bordered the Capitol. And at that time of night, it was empty, making it the perfect location for a clandestine meeting. Or an ambush.

Reaching the border of the park, she stopped once again and checked the weapons that she had concealed in the folds of her cape; a tiny needlegun with poisoned rounds, and a black market smart-grenade. With luck, they wouldn't be needed, but having 'back-up' was only prudent, and a matter of habit. Satisfied that they were ready, Sarah surveyed the streets one last time, and left the sidewalk for a paved walking trail.

The shadows grew thick around her, and she briefly considered embracing her *symbiote*. But she discarded the idea immediately. If things went badly, she knew that she would need all of her reserves for the fight, and the classified implant always exacted a heavy toll on its users.

So instead, she reactivated the cape, and let it wrap her in the darkness. Her form became less than a shadow, and more than a ghost.

After going only a short distance, she spotted the wan light of the park's lamps shining through the shrubbery, and then her contact. The woman was where she was supposed to be, seated on a bench with her back to her.

Sarah watched her quietly for a few minutes, and then, extending a gloved hand, felt out into the night. But aside from the woman herself, and a few small animals, nothing else registered against the background energies of the area. She wasn't entirely reassured by this, but in the absence of any discernible threat, she left the cover of the foliage and walked up to the bench, deactivating her cloak.

Her contact jumped at her sudden appearance. Then anger replaced suprise. "Damn you!" the woman snapped, "You didn't have to do that! You scared me half to death!"

"Let's talk," Sarah said, ignoring the woman's protests and taking a seat. "When can I get my shipment? I need it by the end of this week."

"This week? Are you *fekking klaxxy*?" the other woman replied, her breath misting in the chill night air.

"The kaapers have been cracking down at the port. Getting in a shipment like that is going to be difficult. We can't just walk it off the ship and out to the street! Someone's got to be paid off!"

Translated into Standard, this meant that the woman wanted more credits. "How much will that take?" Sarah asked.

Her companion was just about to answer when Sarah suddenly *felt* an esper somewhere close by. Whoever the psi was, she was good—very good, she thought. She had managed to mask her presence completely, and that wasn't an easy trick.

She looked around her trying to get a fix on the intruder, and failed. Then a second presence registered in her consciousness. It was another psi.

One glance over at her contact told her, even without using her talents, that the woman was completely unaware of the new arrivals or the ambush that they intended to spring. Despite herself, Sarah had to smile in admiration.

Someone had tipped the smugglers off that she was a psi, or they had simply puzzled it out for themselves. Whatever the case, they had obviously realized that a non-esper would have been unable to conceal the knowledge of their betrayal. So they had opted to sacrifice an unknowing pawn, just to get close to her.

Capture the queen and checkmate. *If* it worked.

Sarah had no intention of letting this happen however. Nor did she grant any reprieve to the woman seated next to her. She was still a potential threat, even if she had been nothing but a lure.

"What's wrong?" the woman asked. Comprehension was just beginning to dawn on her features, and she started to reach into her jacket pocket.

Moving with bioaugmented speed, Sarah reached out and expertly snapped the woman's neck. As the corpse slumped over, a compact needlegun fell out of the dead woman's grasp and clattered off the bench onto the wet grass.

Then Sarah ran.

Behind her, she could hear her pursuers as they cursed and pelted after her. A needlegun round buzzed past her ear, and despite the threat it posed, she found another reason to smile. Whoever they were, they either didn't have symbiotes of their own, or they were reserving them just like she was.

And their employers were also cheap; the round that had been fired at her was the 'dumb' variety, and not one of the more expensive, self-guided 'smart' models. Had it been otherwise, she wouldn't have been alive and able to gloat. Or to pause, and return fire with a three-round burst from her own weapon.

Her rounds *were* smart, and they found their targets. The women behind her screamed and dropped. There were more psi's coming though, and they didn't even bother to conceal their presence. She counted at least four who were in the process of closing the distance, and several others that were in the vicinity.

The time to embrace her symbiote had definitely arrived. With a thought, she accessed the alien device embedded in her skull, and the world transformed. Everything became grainy, colors paled and drained away, and the shouts of her hunters became distant, muffled whispers.

In reality, the universe hadn't changed. Only the space around her had. The implant had surrounded her with an invisible bubble of time that ran faster than her surroundings. And she used it to its fullest advantage, running through the frozen trees, past leaves suspended in mid-fall, and out onto N'Rina Boulevard.

There, she released the bond, staggering for a moment as a heavy wave of nausea washed over her. Sarah was a veteran of such after-effects though, and drew in a deep, steadying breath as she made for a line of parked hovercars. More needlegun rounds sought her out, ricocheting off the 'cars, and she fired back at her attackers as she sent a thought to her aircar.

Aria! Start your engine and come to me! She was well aware that there was a good chance the enemy psi's would overhear the psiever conversation, but there was no helping it. Speed was more important than stealth at the moment.

The AI responded immediately. *On my way, mistress! Hold on! Estimated arrival five seconds.*

In the meantime, another pair of psi's had exited the park and were moving down the line of vehicles in an attempt to flank her. Sarah shot at them, but this time, her smart rounds failed her. Instead of taking out their targets, they went wild, and she realized that her enemies were using some kind of portable countermeasure. *Not so cheap after all*, she thought grimly.

She needed to buy herself some time. Reaching into her cloak, she bought out the grenade and flipped the arming switch, setting it for dumb-fire. Then she flung the tiny metal sphere in the general direction of her attackers. It detonated with a bright flash that lit up the nearby buildings and shattered the windows of the 'cars nearest the blast. There were more shouts, but her attackers stopped advancing on her position.

Sarah wasn't deceived. Her opponents were only waiting for reinforcements to arrive. Then they would assault her in earnest.

Aria, hurry up, she thought.

Then a shadow passed between her and the streetlights overhead, and she looked up at the razor sharp outline of her *Falcaan 490* as it descended and opened its gullwing doors.

I'm here mistress!

Sarah sprinted for the vehicle, emptying her needlegun in a burst of suppressive fire, and threw herself inside.

"Drive!" she shouted. "High speed, evasive."

The vehicle was equipped with powerful engines that could easily outrun most police cruisers, and it took off like an anti-ship rocket down the rain-soaked street, pressing her into her seat.

"Destination?" the AI asked cheerfully.

"None specific. Leave this area by the most expedient route," Sarah replied.

"Mistress, we are being followed," Aria informed her.

Sarah immediately called up an image from the rear-view traffic camera. A hovercar was behind them, trying to catch up. It was an *Aerhawk* 3350 she saw. It wasn't quite on the same performance level as her *Falcaan*, but it was still more than adequate for the pursuit.

A second later, the enemy driver engaged her afterburners in anttempt to close the distance, and narrowly avoided a collision with a row of parked vehicles in the process. Whoever she was, she was an amateur, Sarah thought, or her AI simply wasn't as good as Aria when it came to computer-assisted steering.

"Shall I engage weapons, Mistress?" Aria asked.

She was just about to grant the AI permission to do so, when a Thermadonian Metro Police car came down and joined the chase.

A message appeared simultaneously on her windshield HUD: "YOU ARE IN VIOLATION OF SECTION 44523.4, 44525.5: EXCESSIVE SPEED AND RECKLESS DRIVING. LAND YOUR VEHICLES AND STOP NOW!"

"*Deas dam va!*" Sarah growled. "There weren't supposed to be any police in this area." The very last thing she needed right then was this complication.

"Should I actually *obey* that order?" her hovercar inquired.

"Don't be ridiculous," Sarah responded. "Disregard and continue evasive action."

"Thank you, Mistress. I do *so* love a good chase!"

Sarah ignored the AI's remarks, and kept her eye on the vehicles behind her instead.

Another message appeared on the HUD: "YOU HAVE TEN SECONDS BEFORE YOUR ENGINE WILL BE DEACTIVATED! STOP NOW!" A set of numbers accompanied this dire proclaimation, displaying the countdown.

Sarah was not concerned in the least. Aria had much more under her skin than just a fast pair of engines. "Initiate countermeasures," she instructed.

"Countermeasures employed," the car responded, laughing. "Engine override signal blocked successfully, and quite easily I might add."

The fact that the *Aerhawk* also hadn't been affected indicated that they had the same countermeasures at their command, and Sarah frowed.

No, she thought with distaste. *Definitely not so cheap after all.* Clearly, the gang's leadership was willing to expend some signifigant resources to make an example of her. Not that she intended to let that happen.

Then the *Aerhawk* revealed another nasty little secret. Ports opened up on its nose, and bright blue flames spat out as it fired a pair of railguns at the *Falcaan*. Aria spotted this nanoseconds before her mistress, and ascended without instruction, banking sharply to the right at the same time.

Sarah was thrown violently into her safety straps as her 'car neatly evaded the depleted uranium rounds.

Now it was their turn to play a trick or two. "Drop proximity mines! Key to the *Aerhawk*," Sarah commanded.

There was a dull 'thump' behind and beneath her seat as two mines were released from their tail. To their credit, their pursuers responded to the threat immediately, letting loose with a matching pair of ECM pods and dropping low. But with only a little room to work with, the Aerhawk's undercarriage hit the pavement and sent a shower of sparks into the night sky.

At the same time, the first mine that Aria had launched fell for the deception and chased after the decoy, exploding harmlessly overhead. The second mine was also fooled and stupidly chased its pod straight into the police cruiser's hood.

Only the fact that it still hadn't caught up with what it believed to be its target, and had remained inert, was what saved the policewomen. Instead of exploding, the mine smashed into pieces and although its shrapnel cracked the windshield, the cruiser remained aloft, and part of the pursuit.

As they passed an intersection, another police cruiser joined the chase, coming down and pulling in behind the pack. It wasn't an ordinary patrol hovercar however; it carried a rack of air-to-air missiles under its stubby winglets.

The message that it broadcast was clear, and imperative. "THIS IS AN ARMED POLICE RESPONSE UNIT. STOP YOUR ENGINES AND LAND OR YOU WILL BE FIRED UPON!" An alarm came to life on the *Falcaan's* dash. Simultaneously, the APRU unit acquired a lock on their engines.

"Aria! Discharge flares on launch!" Sarah barked. The police cruiser fired as she said this, but again, Aria had anticipated this and let its flares go along with a pair of ECM pods. The *Aerhawk*, which had also been targeted, did the same same thing and then followed through with another railgun attack.

As Aria jinked and twisted away, the APRU's missiles exploded harmlessly in mid-air, and Sarah realized that the group of aircars was now approaching a busy intersection.

The traffic signals controlling the junction were standard models, and shielded from normal psionic interference, but Sarah wasn't a normal woman, with a normal psiever. Throttling Aria's engines to maximum, she concentrated on the lights and pushed with her talents.

Unable to withstand her projected will, they obediently changed from red to green. Robot trucks, which were the only traffic passing through at that hour, stopped abruptly and the *Falcaan* blasted by them.

Then Sarah *pushed* a second time. The lights reset to green and the trucks began to move again. There was no time for the *Aerhawk* to avoid the collision. It plowed full speed into the forward section of a large truck, shearing in half and exploding into a fireball.

The two police vehicles that were behind it swerved wildly to avoid the blast. The armed unit managed this, but rammed into a traffic pylon instead. The impact sent it spinning into the side of a nearby building. Its companion was even less fortunate. The cruiser plowed straight into the burning remains of the *Aerhawk*, and became wreckage itself.

Flaming debris spewed over the intersection, and Sarah bit back an oath as she ordered Aria to climb and join the flightlanes high overhead.

"That was an exciting chase!" the AI chirped, blissfully immune to the carnage below them. "I especially enjoyed the opportunity that it gave me to run my engines at maximum throttle."

"I'm glad that *you* had so much fun" Sarah replied, acerbically. It had been bad enough that things had gone awry with her contacts, she thought. Now there was this, on top of it all. Although the casualties had been unavoidable, there would still be some serious fallout to deal with.

Aria interrupted her dark ruminations. "Mistress, I have a bulletin concerning us on Police Channel 1493," it informed her. "Would you like to see it?"

"Yes, Aria."

The message flashed in a corner of the windshield. It contained no surprises and Sarah had read many like it before:

HOT SHOT: CRIME IN PROGRESS--WANTED BY THERMADONIAN METROPOLITAN POLICE:

Reckless Endangerment, Flight to Avoid Arrest, Assault on Police Officers, Murder.

Name: Unknown (No Record Found). Height: Unknown, Weight: Unknown, Hair: Unknown, Eyes: Unknown, Motherworld: Unknown. DOB: Unknown. Known Alias': Unknown.

Hazard Level: HIGH. NOTE: If you observe the suspect, DO NOT attempt apprehension. Suspect may be a military-grade psi and should be considered armed and dangerous. Contact APRU for further instructions.

Subject was last seen traveling 01:16:36 hours westbound Marpesia District, Sector 7 in a black Falcaan 490, Registration number 115386G773. Advise if spotted.

"*That* simply won't do," Sarah responded. "Change transponder codes and modify your skin."

"Do you have a skin preference?" the AI asked her.

"Nothing in particular. I'll leave the choice up to you," she replied.

The car obeyed her command. Outside, the molecules of the dynamic skin that coated its metallic body reorganized themselves, changing the car's pigmentation from jet black to a rich, dark crimson.

"Skin and transponder code changed, Mistress," Aria reported. "And if I may say so, I do so like the shade of red that I chose. It's really quite stylish and I think that it compliments my body quite nicely."

Sarah laughed dryly. "Good. I'm glad for you. Now, get us to *Jackie's*. I think it's time to lay low for a bit."

Aria pondered her request for moment before responding, "Mistress, I've located *Jackie's*. It is currently in the Agamede District, Sector 20, sub-sector 121-B. I'm taking us there right now."

Jackie's was one of Sarah's unofficial offices and hideaways when she was in Thermadon. Floating on permanent suspensor fields, the bar changed its location constantly, but this feature was not what made it so special. Many businesses on Thermadon were portable and relocated themselves according to customer demand, and shifts in purchasing patterns from sector to sector.

What was different about *Jackie's* was that it did not officially exist. Instead, the floating structure plugged in to the empty slot of a host building like any other transient business, but registered with the structures' virtual landlords with a new identity every time. One day it would list itself as a private club, another a restaurant, and another as something else, each with different names, and different fictitious owners.

Only its carefully screened customers knew what it really was, or where it was at any time. And as long as the rent was paid, the AI's of the host buildings seldom asked any questions. When they did, *Jackie's* either moved itself, or paid off the investigating parties with enough credits to quell their curiosity. Tonight, *Jackie's* was docked on the 751st floor of the 1500-story Bel Shanris building.

While Aria brought them around for a landing, Sarah noted the holographic sign wrapping around the bar's exterior, which advertised the business as the *Antiope Club*. It was a private joke that only the bar's owner, Jackie, knew the meaning of, and Sarah had never pressed her terribly hard for the truth; everyone was entitled to their secrets—as long as they weren't dangerous ones.

The car entered the hangar at last and slid into the parking space that had been reserved for her. As Aria powered herself down, Sarah exited and walked to the entrance. There was only one woman on duty there.

She wasn't the only security by any means; the bar had plenty of automated systems that it could call upon to deal with unwelcome visitors, but Jackie had always preferred the "human touch". The figure at the door was probably the furthest expression of what could be considered human, however. She was an Aviaa, from Tetra in the Chandi Elant.

After Humanity left Old Gaia and began to settle alien worlds, concerns arose over the environmental effects of terraforming on previously pristine worlds. And a new movement was born. It had called itself Biosyncronism, and its principle belief had been that instead of changing an alien planet to suit humans, that humans needed to adapt themselves to their new environment. The Bios had linked forces with geneticists and sympathetic lawmakers, and as their philosophy had taken hold, strict environmental laws were passed, and *Homo Sapiens* underwent a wide range of physical transformations. Some, had been minor, while others were radical.

On Nemesis, which had been one of the first true Bio Worlds, the settlers opted for their offspring to be born with prehensile tails, retractable claws and color-changing skin—along with a digestive system that allowed them to survive on a predator's diet. On Tethys, which was dominated by gigantic oceans, humans became amphibians with gills and webbed digits. And on Tetra, bioengineering had created a race of blue skinned, winged people, who were adapted to live in an environment where almost everything had the capability of flight.

None of these alterations had saved human males from the MARS plague, however. But the legacy of Biosyncronism remained, and because of it, Womankind was far more diverse than anything the ancient pre-spaceflight Gaian's could have ever imagined.

The Aviaan standing before Sarah was a typical example of her genotype. She was much taller than women from other worlds and her fine boned frame and translucent wing membranes made her seem far too frail for the post that she manned.

Sarah knew differently. In reality, Aviaan women were formidable opponents with supernaturally quick reflexes. They also compensated for their lighter bodies with a wicked set of claws, flexible hollow bones that bent instead of breaking, and employed a deadly martial art they called *Sass'kaalat* which was perfectly tailored to their physique.

Given the choice, Sarah always preferred a heavier opponent with normal physical abilities to an Aviaan. As she passed over the threshold, she exchanged nods with the woman, partially out of mutual recognition, but also because of the respect that each had for the other as fighters.

It was dark inside the bar, except up near the stage where a band was playing Neo-Kryxian music. The latest rage on Thermadon, it was slightly less grating and more harmonious than the original form that was its inspiration. Genuine Kryxia music from the world of Noween was a cacophony of eerie wails and atonal sounds that only the native women could tolerate. Although the 'updated' version had a much wider appeal and even possessed something resembling a formal melody, Sarah was forced

61

to recall the old adage that anyone who was not from Noween and claimed to like its music, was actually stone deaf.

Sarah did her best to endure the racket as she lowered her hood and made her way past the polished *baaka* wood bar. In the process, she caught the eye of the bar's owner and Jackie saluted her with an empty glass.

"Nice to see you," the woman said. "Your table's ready, and it looks like your secret admirer has sent you a flower and a little note."

Sarah returned her conspiratorial wink with a smile, and walked past the other patrons to her private booth. The booth was expensive, but worth every credit. It was in the back, shrouded in enough shadows to make her invisible to anyone who entered the bar, and right next to an exit to the garage. It was also surrounded with its own silent-zone, which not only saved her ears from the din, but also helped to ensure her privacy when she had guests.

Just as she had been promised, a single black rose sat on the table. Next to it was a small plasti card. Despite what Jackie believed, they were not from the same person however.

Taking her seat, Sarah pointedly ignored the card. She knew who had sent it, and decided that it could wait--if she even bothered with it.

Instead, she ordered herself a glass of Zommerlaandar white wine and regarded the rose pensively. News of the night's operation had traveled fast, she reflected. She only hoped that the repercussions would not be as great as she feared.

Finally, when she felt ready, she picked up the flower and inhaled. To the casual observer, this action seemed innocent enough. In reality, the rose's scent bore a carefully engineered protein, keyed to her specific DNA. Once its molecules were absorbed into her bloodstream, the message that the protein contained was passed on to her brain as a false-memory. It was from her employers.

As if played itself out, a woman that she had never actually met sat with her at the table minutes before she had really arrived, and spoke to her in a voice that her ears had never heard. And as always, the counterfeit memory did not include the woman's features, and her words were deliberately unaccented, making any identification of her motherworld impossible. What the phantom had to say was quite clear however.

"We understand that your contacts attempted to sanction you this evening. This is unfortunate, and given the evidence that we have subsequently uncovered, we believe that an individual in an organization we are partnered with compromised you. We have long suspected this person to be a mole, and are investigating the issue.'

"There is a high likelihood that this will be confirmed. If this occurs, we would consider awarding you the task of handling its resolution, should you desire it. If not, then another operative can be assigned.'

"As for the attempted intervention by the Metropolitan Police in tonight's activity, we feel that any collateral damage that they incurred, while regrettable, was unavoidable. Our liaison within that agency was specifically advised to make certain that no police units were on patrol in the area. This is a matter that we will address with their Chief shortly.'

"Since the situation with your contacts has proven untenable, we are removing you as the primary in this operation. We are giving that task over to another agent, who will explore different avenues of approaching the problem. Once they are in place, given your experience, you will be their controller and direct their activities.'

"In the meantime, you have been assigned another mission to undertake for us immediately. Due to recent events in the High Court, and your prior relationship with the Marionites in other matters, we require that you make a delivery to them at your earliest opportunity. This delivery will augment other measures that we already have in place, and assist us in our long term efforts."

The details followed, and Sarah let them un-spool in her mind without worrying herself about any of it. They were already stored in her long-term memory and would be accessible when they were needed.

Instead, she took another sip of her wine and inhaled the rose's scent again. With its message delivered to its intended recipient, the special proteins had already decomposed, and the flower's perfume was exactly what it seemed to be. Although it always presaged serious business, Sarah had to concede that her employers had chosen an elegant way to communicate with their agents. And roses had always been one of her favorite flowers.

Finished with it, she laid the flower down and looked at the folded piece of plasti, regarding it with a mixture of desire and revulsion.

I won't read it, she vowed, but her hand reached out almost of its own volition, and shaking slightly, she opened the card.

"See me. Tonight. T," was all it said, printed in a dark, elegant font that she knew all too well. The only thing that remained to make her self-betrayal complete was to follow the sender's instructions, and go to her.

I won't do it, she told herself. This was a lie though, and what little was left of her will abandoned her completely. She *needed* to see her, especially after the debacle in the park, and she hated herself for being so weak. But she hated the sender even more for using her weakness against her.

"Fek it!" she said under her breath. *Just this once, and never again. Just for tonight, to take the edge off.*

Before she could argue with herself any further, she rose and made her way back out to her hovercar.

Bel Sharra Memorial Spaceport, Cyrene District, Thermadon City, Thermadon, Myrene System, Thalestris Elant, United Sisterhood of Suns, 1042.11|01|03:94:90

Bel Sharra Memorial Spaceport lay on the west end of the gargantuan city, a sprawling complex of runways, landing pads and docking cradles. It was one of the largest spaceports in the Sisterhood, rivaled only by Zommerlaand's Waanderstaad, or the naval spaceport at Rixa. Merchandise from all corners of the Sisterhood flowed in and out of Bel Sharra by way of a constant stream of spacecraft that filled the sky with their comings and goings.

The seemingly impossible task of maintaining order over such chaos was accomplished by the watchful eyes of Bel Sharra's control tower. Nicknamed "the Needle", the shining silver structure was almost as tall as the golden pyramid of the Great Assembly itself, and nearly as famous.

Maya pressed her nose against the plastiglass as the magnorail turned south and descended down the long track-way to the Terminus Station. In a few more seconds, it was gliding into the passenger platform, and opening its doors with a soft hiss of compressed air laced with jasmine and the sounds of water from a nearby public fountain. Taking in the scene, Maya got out, a little unsure of where to go next.

Fortunately, a bright yellow omni information terminal stood nearby, sited there for the benefit of newcomers like herself. She went over to it, and provided her false name and phony planet of origin. The station thought this over, and promptly unlocked its access pad.

She requested the 'Plexi's local module. "Employment opportunities, Thermadon, Bel Sharra Spaceport only."

"Nexus Corporation is hiring for an administrative assistant," it answered. "Two years experience required. References a must. From this station, walk to the multi-course terminal and take concourse 71-b."

"Next listing please," she requested.

The omni dutifully ticked off all of the current job openings at the port, and as Maya listened, she became more and more disheartened. Most of the positions weren't things that she was qualified to do, and didn't offer the chance to get close enough to anything worth stealing. But just when she was about to give up hope, a listing for the Customs Warehouse came up, and her expression brightened. It was perfect.

"Dock workers needed to work in the Customs Warehouse. No experience necessary. Apply in person at dock 201-Z. Clean background history required. From this station, walk to the multi-course and take concourse 51-R. Board the tram at station H and ride it to dock area 'Z'."

"Show me the way," Maya said. The omni obediently transmitted the data to her psiever, and then immediately disengaged the connection. This was mandated by law. Although psievers and the omniplex could be linked, abuses by government agencies and commercial interests in the centuries before the Sisterhood, had mandated their separation from one another. Except for brief exchanges like this one.

As her psiever broadcast an image of a red ball moving away from her at a walking pace towards the multi-course building, Maya followed it. If she got the job, she vowed, the first thing that she was going to do was treat herself to a decent breakfast.

But when she arrived, the yard boss was not impressed with her at all. "You seem a bit small, girlie. This job calls for a lot of heavy lifting. You think you can handle hard work like that?"

"Yeah," Maya replied. "I can handle hard work."

"You know anything about running a hovercarry?" the yard boss asked.

"Sure," Maya said. "I ran them all the time back on my motherworld." This was true enough, but what she didn't mention were all the other places she had run the devices, or what she had carried away with them.

"We'll see," the yard boss said skeptically. "The job pays 10 credits per hour for a 10 hour day, less taxes. You show up at 01:67 sharp. Got that?"

"Yeah."

"Go over to the office and tell them to give you a jumpsuit. I'll see you here tomorrow. *Klaar*?"

Bel Sharra Memorial Spaceport, Cyrene District, Thermadon City,
Thermadon, Myrene System, Thalestris Elant, United Sisterhood of Suns,
1042.11|03|05.58:27

Maya came in from the spacedock and entered the main cargo holding area. Once she was inside the huge chamber, she pulled her hovercarry in between a row of storage racks.

She needed a break. This was the fifth trip she'd made from the CSS *Andromeda* and the heavy crates of electronics were starting to take their toll.

A few rows up, she spotted the Yard Boss. Fortunately, the woman hadn't seen her yet and Maya allowed herself the luxury of a few more moments of inactivity, although she knew that she couldn't stay like that for very long. The Yard Boss' eye caught everything happening on the docks and if she spotted Maya slacking off, it was a guaranteed fine of two credits.

"Evil bitch," Maya cursed under her breath. Reluctantly, she turned the hovercarry back on and started off on the long trip to 'E' section where the rest of the *Andromeda's* cargo was being stored for Customs inspection.

The Yard Boss watched her critically, but when she saw that Maya was working, and that her 'carry was full, she went back to talking with another supervisor.

That's right, fat buns, Maya thought bitterly. *Go back to your gossiping and let the rest of us work. Don't want you to change your routine.* Even so, she kept her head down and her expression bland. The Yard Boss could fire at will and Maya was still certain that the Customs Warehouse had the potential for profitable thefts.

Reaching 'E' section, she wound her way back through the towering rows of cargo-boxes to the zone assigned for the *Andromeda*. As she pulled in, she noticed two other 'dock rats' standing over one of the boxes that she'd brought in earlier. One of them, a Tethyian, was her immediate supervisor.

"Just drop the cargo here," the woman said, waving a webbed hand, "We'll put it in place".

This was strictly against regulations. Each box had to be placed into a pre-designated slot in the storage racks by the worker who had brought it in. This was intended to ensure that a clear chain of custody was maintained until Customs checked it against the ship's manifests. The Tethyian was definitely up to something.

"Sure thing," Maya replied suspiciously. She powered the hovercarry down and started to offload it.

"Heyas," the Tethyian asked with a sly grin, "you want to make a few extra credits for yourself?" Her gills opened and closed slowly, suggesting that she was *very* interested in what her response would be.

"Yeah, who doesn't?" Maya replied carefully.

"I thought so," the supervisor said, "I can usually spot the right kind of girls working this dock. From now on, you just keep an eye on the shipping labels. If you spot something like these realie-players, just make sure that a box or two of them gets dropped off here. You do that, and I'll make sure there's a little something extra waiting for you at the end of the shift."

"What about the manifests?" Maya asked her boldly. "Won't missing boxes get noticed?"

The Tethyian turned to her companion. "Like I said, the new girl's no dummy." Then she turned back to address Maya again.

67

"Boxes get lost in shipping all the time. Sometimes we find out where they've gone and someone goes to a correctional colony. And sometimes it was just an error made by a clerk." She spread her webbed fingers wide in a gesture of false-helplessness.

"Errors are better," Maya agreed.

Her fellow conspirators proved good on their word. That night, when she went back to the hostel, she was 80 credits richer. Things were definitely starting to look up at last.

CHAPTER 3

The *Athena* had finally settled into its patrol of the Cenadel system, and Lilith saw the chance to make up for the time that she'd lost on her freeday. She had the option to use up an occasional elective day for mental health and she had taken it with Katrinn's help, and blessings. Her Second had assumed most of her duties, with Ellyn n'Dira and Mearinn d'Rann handling the remainder. They had done this before for her, and they knew without having to ask, that she could and would, reciprocate.

Skipper was less cheerful about the sudden change in their routine, however. Lilith had risen earlier than normal, breakfasted, and had gone straight to the library. When she returned to her quarters, well before her usual time, the animal was beside himself with impatience and dismay at this manifest break in "the way things were supposed to be".

Where did you go? Why are you back so early? the kaatze demanded. Y*ou've been gone so long! Did you bring me anything?*

"The answer is that it is none of your business, and no, I didn't," Lilith retorted.

You didn't bring me anything?

Skipper's slitted eyes widened in shock and his tail flicked with annoyance. He couldn't believe that his mistress hadn't brought him something tasty. In his estimation, it was only right and fitting that he should be given some kind of gift as an apology for her serious breach of protocol. The fact that she hadn't, and that she wouldn't even tell him *where* she had gone was utterly beyond his comprehension.

Lilith let him believe this for a moment longer before she smiled and revealed the tiny can of pinfish that she had been hiding behind her back. She'd kept it in her office after the SAO had given it to her, just so that he wouldn't bother her about it. Realizing what it was, Skipper pawed at it greedily.

"In a moment, you glutton," she said breezing past him. "But first things first. I have a new realie I want to play and I don't want you bothering me. I'll give you the fish *only* if you promise to behave and let me be."

Yes! Skipper agreed. *Anything.Just give me the fish! Now!* His tail quivered with excitement.

69

"Fine," Lilith said, walking into the bathroom. Skipper trailed after her, or rather the can she was holding, and circled impatiently while she opened the seal and dished the spicy fish out onto a small plate.

"Remember, let me be," she warned him, wagging her finger, "or this is the last treat that you'll get for a while."

Skipper ardently promised to behave himself and the moment that the plate touched down, he pounced on the food and began gorging himself as if he had been starving for months. Lilith shook her head in disgust at his theatrics and walked over to the closet. She quickly undressed, stowed her uniform, and slipped into her favorite nightgown.

Filled with anticipation, she went over to the realie-player. The device sat on a small table by itself, its playing-arms spread wide. A slim wireless headset lay next to it, and Lilith put it on, fitting it snuggly over her temples.

Then she opened the plastic cube that contained the realie, and gently withdrew the shiny metallic orb. The moment that she placed the sphere into the player's arms, they closed over it and a tiny blue-white beam of light shot up from the player. A muted beep accompanied this, signaling that the device was ready to start transmitting.

Glancing over at Skipper one last time to make certain that he would stay where he was, Lilith laid back onto her bed.

Play realie, she thought, closing her eyes. For a fraction of a second, all she saw was the inside of her eyelids, but then the player began sending its signal to her psiever.

The darkness around her faded, and a scene coalesced while the notes of the first song began to play. It was a gentle, romantic theme, and as it increased in intensity and volume, she found herself standing naked on a windswept beach, looking out over an ocean that reflected a huge moon hanging in a wine-red sky.

She could feel the wind as it played gently over her skin, and the grains of sand under her bare feet. Then Celina lent her magnificent voice to the song, appearing like an apparition over the face of the moon. As always, Lilith was overtaken by her masterful performance and she let herself sway to the music.

70

After a few more notes, Celina's face disappeared from the moon, and she reappeared on the sand next to Lilith, beckoning her to follow her into the sea.

Lilith trailed after her willingly, a part of her marveling at the sensation of the warm water as it lapped around her legs. Celina's realies were always like this; incredibly detailed and realistic, making it easy for her to lose herself inside of them.

The waters closed around them, dancing with the rays from the moon above and sparkling here and there with eldritch fires in the depths. Celina swam ahead of her, drawing Lilith ever downwards towards whatever mysteries awaited them.

Somewhere in the song and halfway to the bottom, Lilith watched the singer's lithe nude form shift and change into a marine animal. A distant part of her mind recognized the creature as one of the Gaian life forms that had accompanied humanity to colonize other worlds. It was a dolphin, she recalled, and its species had found a new home for itself on Tethys and several other planets.

Then, to her amazement, she realized that she had transformed into one herself. An incredible sense of freedom and happiness overcame her as she reveled in her new form, and chased playfully after Celina. The water around her caressed her new skin and the song itself took on glorious proportions that her human ears would never have been able to fully appreciate. She literally felt the notes as tangible things, as part of a world of sound that she had never dreamed existed before this experience.

In the meantime, Celina had changed direction, moving upwards towards the pale lights at the surface, and Lilith willed her powerful body to follow. Before she quite realized it, they had broken the surface together. For what seemed like an eternity, they hung there, their transformed bodies glittering in the moonlight before plunging back into the welcoming sea just as the music reached its climax.

They descended into the depths again. Far below, something glimmered in the darkness. It was beginning to take on a halfway recognizable form when the realie cut off abruptly. A message flashed in front of her eyes: "Command Override. Player Disengaging."

71

Lilith sat up, blinking in disorientation for a moment. "Yes?" she asked.

A holo of Katrinn appeared. "Lily, I'm sorry to bother you, but we have an emergency. We'll need you in the conference room."

"I'll be topside straightaway," Lilith answered, already moving towards her closet. *Well*, she thought, *at least I got to enjoy a little more of a day off*. It was better than nothing at all, and the price that one paid for being the Commander.

Katrinn and the rest of the *Athena's* command staff were waiting for Lilith when she arrived. A holo of Erin taur Minna of the *Artemis* and Commander bel Sarra of the *Demeter* hovered behind the assembly like a pair of ghosts. Everyone's expression was grim and businesslike, which meant that something big had come up.

The only exception was Erin, who flashed Lilith a wide grin that exposed her canines. With the exception of those who had become acclimatized to the customs of the greater Sisterhood, Nemesian women generally only 'smiled' as a response to a threat, or in anticipation of combat. Whatever this was about, it was not only serious, but a bloody fight was probably going to be a component.

Lilith took her seat. "What do we have?"

"Sagana Territory, Demeter System," Katrinn ordered. A holo of the star system appeared in mid-air over the dark *baaka*-wood table. "Center on Persephone."

The holo changed to a close-up of the tiny Class G planet. Lilith saw that it was sparsely settled, boasting only one central town called Newhearth, and a few outlying settlements that dotted its otherwise untamed surface.

"Star Service Field Headquarters in Almaran picked up a distress call from some colonists," Katrinn stated, "and they requested that we respond and investigate. In the message they sent, the colonists said that Hriss raiders had attacked them, but they didn't know how large a force was involved.'

"The message is a week old, and we were lucky to get it. The colony's emergency distress beacon was either never launched, or it got lost in Null. According to Field, the message was sent out as a burst transmission from a weather satellite that the raiders missed. One of our ships just happened to be scanning that sector and picked it up."

"That's luck all right," Lilith agreed. But whether the colonists' good fortune had held after that was the question. Ever since the War of the Prophet had ended ten standard years earlier, the defeated Hriss Imperium had unofficially encouraged their semi-independent Clans to roam into Sisterhood space at will, attacking merchant convoys, or raiding outlying systems like Persephone.

Although there were exceptions to the rule, such raiders didn't tend to loiter. They got what they came for and they left. With seven days already gone, the odds were high that the battle group wouldn't find anything but wreckage, dead bodies, and a planet stripped down to bare earth.

"Let's see the message."

The star system disappeared and a badly modulated transmission replaced it. The woman in the holo looked tired, and a bloody bandage covered her forehead.

"This is Dr. Sharra n'Terri of the Newhearth Colony on the planet Persephone in the Demeter system," the woman said. "Please, if anyone is out there listening to this, we need help! We've managed to gather a few survivors together and hide, but I don't know how long we have. The Hriss have invaded us—they destroyed our main communications complex and the Living Center.'

"Please, come and help us. They've been shooting anyone they've found. I can't tell you where we are; they might be listening to this, but we'll hold on as long as we can and watch for you. Once we know we're safe, we'll send another signal. Please, send help now." The message ended there.

"Demeter system," Lilith requested. "Wide view." The system reappeared over the table and enlarged itself.

She studied it for a long moment and then turned to Col. Marya Lislsdaater. Lislsdaater was commander of the 115th Marine Combat Regiment. She would be in charge of any ground operations, and her troopers would be tasked with rendering aid to the survivors. And if the battle group got lucky and the raiders had overstayed their visit, they would also deal with any hostile ground units. "What is your state of readiness?" Lilith asked her.

"We're all set, Commander," Lisldaater reported, "We will be able to field the entire regiment, along with some armor support. I also have a Marauder team that I'd like to send out ahead of my force to recon the area and secure any survivors."

"We'll certainly do what we can to accommodate them, Colonel," Lilith promised. She knew, without having to ask, that the Marauder team would also be dropping off a few spybots on its way in. This would give the battle group some valuable advance intel to work with.

She addressed the Ships Senior Medical Officer next. "How is your department doing?"

"My staff is standing by," Dr. elle' Kaari responded. The Nyxian's expression was unreadable beneath her black, full body *Qada*-robe, but her tone was somber.

"We can set up an extra ward in the enlisted mess hall, and we have enough supplies on-hand to treat the entire territory if we have to. I also have some of my staff assigned to follow the Marines when they go downside."

Lilith nodded in approval. "We're going to treat this as an active incursion until we learn otherwise."

The captains of the *Artemis* and the *Demeter* indicated their understanding. Standard procedure for an active incursion called for the battle group to go into stealth mode just before it re-entered normal space. Its exit-point from Null would also be well outside the orbit of the last planet.

This would make its signature minimal, if not impossible for any enemy sensors to detect--if there were still any enemies to be concerned with. Although the low probability of an engagement might have enticed a less experienced Commander to choose speed over stealth, Lilith knew better. She had spent too many years patrolling the Sisterhood's frontier zones to rush in blindly. In the face of an unknown, prudence was always her preference.

She leaned back in her chair and steepled her fingers. "All right, we sound as if we're as prepared as we could be under the circumstances. How soon can we be under weigh?"

"Within the hour, Commander," Mearinn d'Rann answered.

"Good. Let's prepare for transit."

***

As soon as the ComTechs had reported that all ships were ready, Lilith signaled her Helmsmistress, Caleda bel Tridis and her two assistants. "You have the ship, Helmsmistress."

Caleda adjusted the oversized psiever headset that she was wearing and went to work, starting the sequence for the transit to Null. "Routing power from the main generators to the Pavilitas," she announced, her transmission sounding over the entire bridge. "Pavilita generators coming on line and powering-up."

Next to her, one of her assistants, and also a trained psi, was calling up a computer-generated image of the stars as they would appear several AU's out from the limits of the Demeter system.

"Astrographic visualization complete. Pavilita generators at one-hundred-percent," Caleda stated as the holo appeared in front of her station. The Helmsmistress looked up at the display and taking a breath, sent herself into a deep trance. With trained precision, she quickly memorized the star-patterns until the entire array of heavenly bodies was firmly in her mind as a whole, unbroken concept.

Holding this image in her consciousness, she reached out with her thoughts through her psiever, down through the ship into the Pavilita generators. Psionic receivers within the devices responded immediately, translating her mental impulses into coherent signals. The energies that had gathered in the psionic generators began to change as Caleda wove them into the configuration that she desired.

Her assistants had been waiting for this moment, watching their mistress and sensing her progress through their own psievers.

"Secondary wings online," one of the assistant helmswomen said and then when Caleda was ready, "Discharging Pavlitas to the collector wings."

75

A deep hum resonated through the *Athena's* massive frame as the power transferred over. Sensors outside the ship showed the stern wings crackling with lightning as they were flooded with power from the Pavlitas. Caleda was unaffected by all this; her mind stayed with the energy, continuing to command its form as it played out over the huge wing surfaces.

"Boosting the signal," her assistant continued. The drone deepened and just as the vibrations became uncomfortable, Caleda spoke in a distant voice.

"I am ready." With this, the collector wings discharged, their energies flashing along the sides of the warship to another pair at the bow. The power gathered there for a microsecond, and then it coalesced into two brilliant spears of sapphire light that stabbed out from the wingtips into the void.

Several kilometers away, the beams met, and the fabric of space began to buckle and distort under their onslaught. Then a misty rift opened up, widening until it was large enough to accommodate the *Athena* and her companions.

The hole that had been created opened up onto an entirely different universe; a non-place that women called Null. And on its opposite side, would be the normal universe, and their destination.

Caleda came out of her trance at this point. "Returning power to standard engines. All ahead, half," she said.

Then she turned around and addressed Lilith, "Commander, the *Artemis* and the *Demeter* have fallen in-line and are following us in. I calculate a two hour transit."

"Well done, Helmswoman," Lilith answered. She rotated her chair to face Fire Control directly. "I want all defensive batteries online as we make the cross-over. Sound general quarters."

The senior fire controller nodded, and an alert tone began to wail throughout every corner of the ship. Simultaneously, overhead illumination winked off, replaced by red battle-lights.

As Battle Group Golden entered the gate and left the normal universe behind, the temperature aboard the *Athena* plummeted immediately. No one knew exactly why this effect occurred, although there were many theories. One thing was certain however. Hell was not hot, but freezing cold.

"Adjust environmental levels to compensate," Lilith requested, reorienting her chair. The techs over at the EviroCom station were already doing this, but it was standard protocol for the Commander to issue the order. In a few moments, temperatures rose again.

Satisfied, Lilith focused her attention on one of the sitscreens. Unlike normal space, Nullspace was not empty. Instead, the *Athena's* main displays were filled with a seemingly endless panorama of roiling cloud forms painted every color of the spectrum. Mysterious flashes of energy permeated their depths, revealing hidden layers of unknown gases with actinic bursts of light. Occasionally, discharges of what would have been ball lightning in the normal universe, danced across the cloud banks in an almost lifelike ballet of light. To the uninitiated, it seemed to be an idyllic panorama of fantastic beauty, but neither Lilith, nor her crew, were fooled in the slightest.

Their wariness was justified. The battle group had just crested a magenta and gold bank of gases, when a feeling of total malice washed over everyone on the bridge. It was a pure undiluted loathing that they all felt on a visceral level – something utterly foreign to the world of matter, and more alien than the strangest of races that lived in the galaxy that they called home.

It also carried a taint that was ancient beyond reckoning, a corruption that had been born before matter had ever been created. And although she had felt this unholy presence many times, a shiver still went down Lilith's spine. Something dark, on both a material and spiritual level, was moving through the clouds. It was an Indweller.

The *Athena's* sensors spotted the thing and relayed information about the target. "*Indie* located at 280.30.10 mark 70, paralleling our course," a NavTech announced. Lilith glanced over at Fire Control again, and the senior controller answered her unspoken question.

"We have a solution, Commander. Monitoring the Indie." As the woman announced this, a soul-piercing screech of rage sounded across the murky gulf, penetrating the hull. Then a mass of black plasma flew out of the mists, coming straight for them.

"Fire!" Lilith barked. Fire Control responded with the *Athena's* forward facing guns and the plasma-ball exploded halfway to the ship, but the Indweller was not finished with its assault. With another hellish shriek, it burst out of the clouds, revealing itself, a huge formless blob of dark not-matter.

Spreading its lightless form wide, it flattened out into an immense black curtain that was larger than the entire battle group combined. For those aboard with any psi talents, it radiated a palpable and absolute hatred of them and wanted nothing less than their utter destruction.

As the thing closed the distance, the corners of its body curled over and oozed outwards, stretching into angry tendrils that reached out for the ships. When they made contact with the *Athena*, energy levels across the boards began to drain dramatically.

"Route power to grav field!" Lilith ordered. The temperature had dropped again, and her breath misted the air. "Fire Control, all forward guns to bear--fire!"

The *Athena's* defensive batteries let loose with everything they had, focusing their destructive power onto one point on the *Indies'* irregular shape. The being collapsed in on itself with a demonic howl of pain and immediately retreated back into the clouds.

"Good work, ladies," Lilith said, signaling to EnviroCon to bring the heat back up again. "That looked like an old one. Let's hope it doesn't have any relatives lurking about. Stay sharp."

But the Indweller had been alone, and it made no reappearance. It had had enough, and had decided to go off and sulk. For the next hour and a half, the battle group's transit was as peaceful as Null could be and Lilith allowed herself to relax a bit.

She even managed to enjoy the vista. Absent the monstrous creatures that inhabited it, she had always found Nullspace itself to be rather beautiful. In its own nightmarish way.

Then Navcom interrupted her. "Commander, we have a vessel ahead, bearing 340.029.70 mark 34. She appears to be dead in space, and not answering our hails."

The sitscreens displayed a close-up of the ship. Its transponder was out, but in a few moments, the *Athena's* computers had matched the pitted hull with a ship that it had on record. The *Sabrina* was her name, out of Calaphis in the Solara Elant, and according to the computer, the merchanter had been missing for the last two standard years.

This was no surprise. Although merchanters travelled with armed escort vessels through Null, there was always the careless Captain who strayed too far from the protection of the convoys' guns and fell prey to the Indwellers.

"Any signs of life, Navcom?" Lilith asked.

"No, ma'am, nothing reads on our sensors," the tech replied.

Lilith suppressed a shudder. "Very well. Amend the ships file to read *'found derelict in Null. All hands presumed lost.'*"

If a ship was unfortunate enough to become engulfed by the Indwellers, it lost most of its energy and quickly became helpless. And once the *Indies* got inside its hull, anything alive inside of it died.

Scientists who had studied the phenomenon claimed that such deaths were instantaneous, caused by the complete cessation of bioelectrical activity. But in all her years as a Commander, she'd heard too many crewwomen screaming in agony to believe such patent nonsense. Whatever the *Indies* did once they got to the crew was neither instant, nor painless.

"Let's move on, helm." she said grimly. "We have a colony to rescue."

The battle group accelerated and moved away from the *Sabrina*, leaving her and her crew of ghosts alone in their mist-shrouded grave.

***

With one minute remaining to the transit through Null, the helm signaled Lilith. "Commander, approaching our exit into normal space." Ahead of them, the mists were thinning, and she could see stars beginning to appear on the sitscreens.

Lilith patched herself through to the *Artemis* and the *Demeter*, "All ships, this is the *Athena*. Switch to stealth mode. Silent running until contact."

At that, all three ships went invisible. From there on out, the battle group would be running silent, listening with passive sensors for the first signs of their enemy.

The Helmswoman had done her job well, Lilith reflected. The battle group exited Null 29.5 AU's out from their destination, or nearly 4,413,200,000 kilometers. At such a distance, it was highly unlikely that the invaders had noticed their re-entry into normal space.

Even so, she knew that they had a lengthy trip ahead of them; at their maximum speed, one-sixth light, it would be over eight hours before they reached Persephone. That was a long time to be sneaking through open space, and there was always the chance that the raiders had seeded passive mines or sensors throughout the system.

If they ran into one, and if it detected them, the odds were that they would survive the encounter, but their quarry would have enough warning to make an escape. Whispering a prayer to the Lady, Lilith fervently hoped that this would not occur. She had been in too many situations where they had arrived just in time to find their opponents gone, with nothing but their murderous handiwork left behind. Calling up a cup of tea from her command chair, she settled in to wait.

Six hours passed without incident and Katrinn was just coming on duty to relieve her, when Navcom alerted them that they had something.

"Commander, we have a track on a target in orbit over Persephone."

"Give me what you have," Lilith requested.

"It's not much at this range, ma'am, but it's definitely one ship," the Mariner informed her. "From the data, my best guess would be a *Hilla*-Class light cruiser. I don't see anything else parked over the planet, or in near space. My *Hriss'ka* isn't the greatest, but they seem to be talking to shuttles making trips to the surface. Nothing that sounds like they know about us."

"Well, Lily, it looks like you were right about them being Hriss," Katrinn remarked. "One light cruiser, eh? She probably just has a few fighters running picket-duty. That's a small raid by anyone's standards."

"Yes," Lilith agreed, and they both smiled. A lone light cruiser was no match for the battle groups' firepower, fighters or no.

"Now, you need to talk to those *Aalfen* of yours and make sure our friends don't get our scent," she added. They both knew that unless the enemy captain was insane, he'd run the moment that he knew they were there.

"I'll do my best," Katrinn promised. "Maybe I'll even set out a little bowl of ginger milk, just to buy their help."

"Whatever it takes," Lilith replied, not entirely certain whether her second was being serious or not.

USSNS *Pallas Athena*, Battle Group Golden, Demeter System, Sagana Territory, United Sisterhood of Suns, 1042.11|22|04:66:63

At 149 million kilometers from their target, a Marine assault shuttle departed the *Pallas Athena* and made its way silently towards Persephone. In its wake, it dropped dozens of tiny spy probes that immediately began sending back vital information to the battle group.

Even though the Hriss cruiser was monitoring for enemy transmissions, it heard nothing alarming. The probes messages sounded almost exactly the same as the background noise of space. But aboard the *Athena* and her sister ships, computers translated the apparent chaos into intelligible data, and the news was good.

"One light cruiser confirmed, Commander," Navcom reported. "We also have nine enemy fighters stationed nearby."

"And the Hriss?" Lilith inquired. "What's their present status?"

"Normal alert mode, ma'am. Nothing that would indicate that they have seen us, or the Marine shuttle." In the meantime, the shuttle had penetrated the first thin layers of the planet's atmosphere and was beginning its descent.

"Excellent," Lilith beamed. "Helm? As soon as we pass the three minute mark, be ready to bring us out of stealth."

The three minute mark was the maximum firing distance for a ship attacking a target, versus the amount of time needed for that target to power-up for Null and make an escape transit. Under three minutes, even the most seasoned crew could not ready their ship and avoid the missiles that would be coming at them at one-quarter light. In very short order, Lilith knew that they'd have their quarry right where she wanted them.

***

The battle group had closed to within 74 million kilometers, and Lilith turned to the Senior Fire Controller, Salus n'Hera. They were now inside the three minute mark.

"Salus?" she said, "plot your solutions and open the missile doors. Sound general quarters. All hands to their battle stations." Once again, the ship resounded with the whine of klaxons. It was time for battle.

"Helm, take us out of stealth," Lilith ordered.

The *Athena* reappeared, followed by the *Artemis* and the *Demeter*. And on the Hriss cruiser, panic erupted as the three Sisterhood ships suddenly registered on their sensors. They knew that they were dead already.

Lilith tensed and sat forwards in her chair. "What's she doing Navcom?"

"It's complete pandemonium, ma'am," the woman informed her. "Their communications traffic with the surface just increased by a factor of four. I think their surface units are asking them for instructions on what to do next."

Lilith looked over at Ellyn n'Dira. "Advocate? May I demand their surrender?"

N'Dira nodded. "Yes, we now have clear evidence that they have fielded troops on Sisterhood soil, in blatant violation of the treaty."

"Navcom, open a hailing frequency to the Hriss," Lilith instructed. Then she spoke in Hriss'ka to the commander of the distant ship.

"*Alveraj, tekan n'ges vor na kreska. T'ya Alveraj Lilith ben Jeni at'ke' Pallas Athena, vreekava n'ges. S' bin atvor krasko n'kaaylag n' veesa,*" she said. "Captain, power down your vessel and surrender. I am Commander Lilith ben Jeni of the Sisterhood naval ship *Pallas Athena*. You are in violation of our Treaty of Peace."

The Hriss word for 'peace' was also a deadly insult, implying weakness. Lilith knew exactly what their response would be.

The Hriss proved her correct. *"Tal vorki, vreekava!"* the enemy commander barked. Roughly translated, his answer was an extremely coarse refusal coupled with a challenge to fight.

"Commander," Navcom said, "their missile doors are opening. I am also detecting several engine power-ups in their silo-tubes."

"Well, *that* was unexpected," Lilith remarked dryly. "Advocate, I think that we now have reason to believe that they are hostile." She addressed the entire battle group. "All ships, you may fire when ready. Fire Control, you have the ship. Engage hostiles."

The *Athena* let her missiles fly. In nanoseconds, they cleared their silo-tubes and accelerated to one-quarter light. The *Artemis* and the *Demeter* fired at the same time. To their credit, the Hriss cruiser responded with everything it had, but the outcome of the battle had already been determined.

Missiles from both sides unleashed multiple warheads. Most of these impacted with their enemy counterpart, but two warheads from the battle group got through, and continued towards the Hriss vessel. Its gunners did their best to shoot these down, and they actually managed to get one warhead before the other one hit their ship.

1.06 minutes later, the light from the explosion reached the *Athena's* sitscreens. If she hadn't been looking for it, Lilith would have missed the event; a small point of radiance that appeared briefly over Persephone. The false star brightened for a moment and increased by several magnitudes. Then it vanished.

"A confirmed kill, Commander," Navcom reported.

"Good," Lilith replied. "Send out our fighters and have them hunt down the remaining enemy assets. I don't want any problems from them."

At this command, the *Athena's* resident fighter wing, the *Nighthunters,* left their hangar. With only a handful of opponents to deal with, the battle they fought was brief. Lilith was just starting on another cup of tea when the *Nighthunter's* flight leader informed her that the space above Persephone had been cleared of all hostiles.

"Navcom," she said, "Please inform Col. Lislsdaater that the high-ground has been secured for her. Helm, move us into a close orbit over the planet and take up station."

Outer Fields, North Sector, Newhearth Colony, Persephone, Demeter System, Sagana Territory, United Sisterhood of Suns, 1042.11|22|04:86:63

Kaly looked through the sights of her rifle and aimed for the closest enemy warrior coming up the trail. She knew that her weapon was no match for the blasters that the invaders carried, but it was all she had. If the patrol came up the hill any further, she would have no choice but to engage them. The little ones and the rest of the girls were already moving away from the station as fast as they could, but unless she delayed the enemy, everyone would die.

The creature below her had something, probably a scanner, in its hand. It swept the space in front of it and then brought the device up to its face to read what it said. Then it turned and waved back to its companions with a lazy, confident gesture.

Kaly was now certain that it knew that they were up there. She brought the crosshairs up to rest right between its primary eyes and prepared to send a depleted uranium slug into the thing's skull.

One more step, and I'll kill you, she thought. She had no illusions about surviving for very long after that. Death was a given, and to her surprise, she wasn't afraid. Instead, a strange sense of calm pervaded her.

She was just beginning to squeeze the trigger when a hand came around her mouth while another blocked her finger, preventing her from firing. For an instant, she struggled wildly, and then a voice whispered in her ear. It was a woman.

"*Shh,* girl! Be quiet!"

Kaly obeyed, and as the woman released her, she looked over her shoulder and witnessed something she'd only seen before in realies; a Sisterhood Marine in full battle gear. The trooper smiled conspiratorially and gestured for her to stay quiet. Several other Marines had crept up on either side of them and they were training their weapons at the enemy patrol. At a signal from their leader, the squad opened fire.

The invader that Kaly had been sighting-in on died first, its head exploding as an energy beam cooked it off. It's companions tried to return fire, but the Marines cut them down before they could respond effectively. The fight, such as it was, was over in seconds.

The woman stood and helped her to her feet. "Come on, girl. Let's go get your friends."

Speechless, Kaly just nodded, still dazed by the violence and speed of the ambush. High overhead, the sky suddenly lit up with a series of flashes, and she looked up at them in incomprehension.

"That would be the battle group," the Marine explained. "Looks like they're giving that Hriss cruiser what it deserves."

Then the heavens brightened with a massive flare that covered a quarter of the sky. "And *that* looks like the end of things upstairs," the Marine observed. "Scratch one enemy cruiser, and Goddess damn their souls to hell."

***

While the Marines collected Kaly and the other girls, the battle group moved in and assumed orbit over Persephone. Then Navcom announced that they had company.

"Two, no make that three ships exiting Null, bearing 337.20.45 Mark 12, distance 17 million KM, Commander. They look like Hriss."

"Damn!" Lilith exclaimed. "Fire control, plot your solutions. Sound general quarters!" Until then it had been the perfect hunt, mission accomplished.

Navcom had more bad news. "Commander, it looks like three *Tina*-Class medium cruisers. They haven't opened their missile doors yet." The Hriss force wasn't their equal, but it was close enough in size and firepower to make any match between them uncertain.

"Open a hail to the Hriss," Lilith ordered. "Let's see if we can talk our way out of this one."

The Hriss Patrol Commander appeared on screen. "*Hesak, voara vreekava T'ya Alveraj Meskreka at'ka'Wsak'ko,*" he said. "Greetings, miserable egg-layers. I am Captain Meskreka of the Bloody Claw Clan ship, *Slaughterer*."

85

"Greetings worthless and impotent male," Lilith replied. "I am Commander Lilith ben Jeni of the Sisterhood naval ship *Pallas Athena.* What brings such poor specimens of manhood into our space?"

Insults were a common part of polite *Hriss'ka*, but she made sure to word her statements carefully. The wrong insult could trigger a battle that she *didn't* want.

"Our ships heard the pitiful cries of your weak and useless settlers," the Hriss informed her. "Out of a manly concern for such wretched beings, we responded in the hope of doing battle with worthy males. Instead we find only craven egg-layers."

Both of them knew that he was lying. It was patently obvious that the light cruiser had merely been the advance party for the enemy battle group.

"My apologies, Captain, for not finding the glorious battle that you sought," she informed him. "Unfortunately, the renegade ship has already been destroyed. I do not think you would have found them worthy of your missiles."

"A shame indeed," Meskreka agreed. "It would have been a pleasure to bathe in their blood." Clearly, the Hriss Commander didn't want to trigger a diplomatic incident any more than she did.

"Truly," she said, "but such is not the case. It would seem that your brave efforts have been in vain. Will you now depart in search of other quarry, or do you wish to dishonor yourself in combat with us?"

Meskreka let out the equivalent of a laugh. "I would not waste our missiles on such contemptible creatures as yourselves. We will depart instead, and seek out true opponents who are deserving of the painful death that we would bestow upon them."

"Good hunting, Commander Meskreka," Lilith said. "May you drink from your enemy's skulls."

"And may you become pregnant with a thousand Warriors, egg-layer. Perhaps one day, we shall choose to grace you with the privilege of dying in combat with us."

"Perhaps. Until then, Commander."

With these pleasantries exchanged, the Hriss battle group turned around and headed back into Null space. And everyone aboard the *Athena* breathed a sigh of relief.

"All right ladies," Lilith said. "Let's get on with the business of cleaning this planet up. We still have enemy troops down there."

CHAPTER 4

Bel Sharra Memorial Spaceport, Cyrene District, Thermadon City,
Thermadon, Myrene System, Thalestris Elant, United Sisterhood of Suns,
1042.11|23|05:00:72

Maya's psiever announced that it was lunchtime--and not a moment too soon as far as she was concerned. The customs warehouse only gave its staff a single short rest period, and an equally brief lunch. She sent a thought to the warehouse AI, clocking herself out, and then made straightaway for the food vendors and a park that she liked to spend her time in.

While she moved along the main concourse, she thought about her situation. More and more, she was beginning to feel that her best opportunities lay outside the spaceport, rather than in it. It wasn't that she wasn't making credits for herself. The problem was that she wasn't earning the kind of fantastic sums that she'd imagined for herself when she'd come to Thermadon in the first place.

Another set-up somewhere else in the city, was one solution, but she discarded the idea almost immediately. She didn't know the local underworld, nor whom she could trust, or avoid. Learning those kinds of things took time, and there were risks involved that she didn't care to take.

A second option, that was infinitely more appealing, was to find a berth for herself aboard a smuggler ship. Like any large port, Bel Sharra had its portion of merchanters involved in illegal activities, and this was where the *real* money could be made.

The trick was finding the right vessel. Moonrunners, as they were sometimes called, didn't advertise their business, and their crews were a secretive and suspicious lot by nature.

The right contacts, and the right introductions were what she needed. For that, Maya knew that the best place to start was with her partners in crime back at the customs warehouse. Neither of them had ever revealed whom they had sold their stolen goods too, but it only made sense that smugglers, having the ready means to dispose of them, were the obvious candidates for a solid client base.

She decided to broach the matter with her co-workers when she returned. In the meantime, she had her break to enjoy, and she didn't want to waste a second of it.

Then she spotted the edge of a plastic credit chit poking up from the rear pocket of a woman ahead of her. One glance told Maya that its owner was completely oblivious to her surroundings, and more interested in chattering with her friends than keeping an eye on her valuables.

Not one to let an opportunity slip by, she deliberately bumped into the woman as she passed. There was a brief exchange of apologies, and Maya walked on, concealing the stolen plastic in her palm as she pushed the woman with her talents. If the insensible creature ever even realized that her card was missing, she would be utterly convinced that it had simply been mislaid and never even think about the possibility of theft. Crime only became crime when the victim believed that they had been wronged, and thanks to her special skills, that wouldn't happen in this case.

She took her prize to the first vending machine that she could find, and bought herself some Nutro with it. The *chocalat*-flavored drink wasn't one of her favorites, but it supplied all of the energy that she needed for her work at the warehouse. More importantly, the machine didn't scan the ID's of anyone who bought from it. Lunch, for all intents, had just become free.

Stuffing the card into her pocket, Maya went to the park and found a bench for herself. She had just opened the drink and was bringing it to her lips when the same *something* that had roused her on her first night in T-Don, revisited her. Then a tall figure dressed in a long black cloak caught her eye in the crowd.

It can't be, she thought. But as she watched the hooded woman make her way through the press, she became certain of it. It *was* the same person.

Her curiosity piqued, she tossed the Nutro into a waste receptacle, and started to follow her. There was something irresistible and compelling about the stranger, and she was determined to find out what it was.

A few times, she nearly lost her quarry in the crowd, and almost gave up, but the woman always reappeared, tantalizing her into continuing with the pursuit. And when her psiever tried to warn her that her lunch break was nearly over, Maya ignored it and kept moving.

Abruptly, the woman changed direction, leaving the main concourse, and turning into a side corridor that led to a public restroom. When she rounded the corner and disappeared from view, Maya quickened her pace. When she came around the same corner, she found the passage empty.

Mystified, she began to walk the length of the hall, and then she spotted something out of the corner of her eye. She had just enough time to realize that it was the cloaked woman, standing where nothing had been just an instant earlier. Then woman reached out and grabbed her by the throat.

Without any discernible effort, she shoved her against the opposite wall, and lifted her up off her feet. Maya tried to fight against her grip, but the woman's gloved fingers were like steel bands, and she was unable to pry them loose.

Dark spots began to eat at the edges of her vision as she dangled in space, looking helplessly back down at her assailant. Despite the bright lighting in the hall, the woman's features were completely hidden by the shadows of her hood as if the garment had somehow leeched away all of the light around it. Only the pale, lower half of her face was visible, framing a pair of full, red lips that smiled back with predatory amusement.

"Why are you following me?" the woman asked. Her voice was like black silk, absolutely calm and utterly deadly.

Maya tried to answer, tried to apologize, or offer up some kind of clumsy lie, but the hold on her airway made even breathing nearly impossible. Instead, all that came out of her was a pathetic, incoherent gurgle.

"It seems that we meet again, doesn't it?" her captor purred. "Why is that, I wonder? Let's find out, shall we?"

Suddenly, Maya felt a pressure growing between her eyes, as if an invisible finger made of steel was slowly pushing its way into her skull. The sensation grew until it became unbearable, and simultaneously the strange presence that surrounded the woman, seemed to increase exponentially.

To her astonishment, Maya also realized that she was no longer alone in her own mind. Somehow, the other woman was in there, with her, filling her consciousness with an alien presence.

That's right my little esper—I'm a psi just like you are, she heard the woman think. *Surprised? I would be, if I where in your place. Now, let's find out who you really are.*

Unbidden, memory after memory rushed up to the surface of Maya's awareness. Thoughts and emotions flashed by in a rapid succession, like some kind of insane holovid that she was unable to stop. She could feel the woman sorting through them, picking and choosing things to examine like a burglar ransacking a house. Every secret that Maya had ever had opened itself up for review. Nothing was sacrosanct; her psyche was completely open to the woman's overpowering will.

She tried to summon up the energy to fight off the mental invasion, but her efforts were useless. The woman pushed her resistance aside with ease, and laughed at her. Then, just as abruptly as it had come, the pressure in her head disappeared and the foreign presence withdrew.

There's no need to fight me to exhaustion, her assailant thought, *I've confirmed what I suspected about you the other night. I will leave you now, little esper.* She released her grip, and Maya dropped into a heap on the floor.

"You should be careful whom you follow," she warned her. "You might just discover more than you bargained for." Before Maya could reply, or sit up, a searing pain lanced through her head. Blackness and oblivion followed on its heels.

Somewhere out of the timeless nothing of unconsciousness, she came to on the floor, lying in a puddle of her own drool, and looked up to meet the concerned eyes of a Port Policewoman.

"Are you all right?" the kaaper asked. Maya started to rise, but a dark band of pain constricted around her head and she abandoned the effort, groaning miserably.

"Please, stay where you are," the officer said. "You've had some kind of attack. The medics are coming down to take a look at you. Lie still until they get here."

"It was the woman," Maya said thickly. Her mouth felt like it was filled with packing foam and the words came out with difficulty.

"What woman?" the policewoman asked. "We didn't see anyone else on the security cameras."

"But—the woman—in the cape! She grabbed me!"

The policewoman nodded, but Maya could tell by the look in her eyes that the kaaper didn't believe her.

"We didn't see anyone matching that description, young lady. Why don't you just stay down? We'll have the medics look you over and maybe they'll be able to explain things to you. Okay?"

Maya didn't bother trying to convince the kaaper any further. She didn't have the energy for it. A strange numbness had sapped her of all her strength, and her mind felt as if it had been scoured raw from the inside out.

Even though the *something* that had accompanied her attacker was now gone, Maya still flinched when the medics arrived, half certain that the woman would somehow be there, standing behind them with her enigmatic smile. And when they went to attach their probes, she started to struggle, but a shot of some unidentified drug was jabbed into her inocular. Her terror was quickly replaced by a wave of pure bliss ansd she relaxed and let the medics do their jobs.

To everyone's surprise, their instruments showed nothing wrong with her, and her symptoms quickly disappeared. In the end, all that they could do, once she was coherent enough to understand them, was to issue a stern warning that she needed to see a doctor for additional tests.

Maya had no intention of doing anything of the sort. Doctors and hospitals meant more than just a closer physical examination. They also carried the risk of a deeper look into *who* she was and *who* she *wasn't*. It was simply not worth it. Instead, she let the medics believe that she would follow their advice, and left the scene on shaky legs.

A few times, as she made her way back towards the customs warehouse, she caught a glimpse of someone dressed in dark clothing in the crowd, and panicked. But in every case, the wearer proved harmless and by the time she was nearing her destination, she had become reasonably certain that she wouldn't be encountering her attacker a second time.

Her problems however, were far from over. The yard boss was waiting for her, accompanied by two customs officers. None of them had friendly expressions on their faces.

"Is that her?" one of the officers asked. The question was more a formality than an investigative necessity. The familiar blue flash of light had already alerted Maya that the woman's partner had scanned her as she had walked up.

"Yes! That's her," the yard boss spat, her voice dripping with malice. "That's the little dock rat!"

An old saying that had had its birth on Sita, came back to Maya; "*Troubles seldom travel alone.*" So far, her day was proving this proverb to be painfully correct. The only question she had just then was *how* bad things were going to get.

"We need to speak to her in private," the lead officer announced. "Can we use your office?"

The yard boss glowered at Maya and nodded her assent. "I'll be only too happy to make any statement you want and press any charges you need," she added as she led the way.

At the door of the tiny prefab structure, the officers thanked the yard boss for her cooperation, and promptly closed it in her face. Then, one of the kaapers sent a thought to the windows, making them opaque.

"We have information that you are responsible for some of the shortages that have come up over the last few weeks," the lead officer said. "We'd like to talk with you about that."

"I don't know anything," Maya answered.

"That's what I thought you'd say," the officer replied. Maya was just about to embellish her denial when the officer standing behind her suddenly seized her up under the armpits, and clasped the back of her head. For the second time that day, she struggled futilely against a force that she could'nt really resist.

"Let's get introduced first," the lead officer smiled. "My name is Officer bel Marda. And I know that you and some of the other dock-rats around here have been skimming off some of the freight and selling it."

"I'll give you names!" Maya blurted. At that point she didn't care if there was supposed to be honor among thieves or not. She was more than willing to give up her compatriots if there was a chance of getting herself out of the situation.

Bel Marda came up close to her. "Oh, I don't need names, girl. I have *those*. What I need from you is *cooperation*."

"Cooperation?"

Maya suddenly understood. She'd run into plenty of dishonest kaapers in the past, and as she saw it, straightforward corruption was always

93

preferable to honesty any time. Despite the grip that the other officer had on her, she smiled at Bel Marda, ready to do business.

This wasn't the right response. Bel Marda's partner rewarded her by increasing the pressure against her head and forcing her chin down. Maya moaned as red spots danced in her vision.

"Yes, cooperation." Bel Marda explained, nodding to her partner to let up a bit. "You see, I *run* this dock, and I can't have every filthy little dock-rat scurrying around, nibbling away at all my profits. Do you get the point?"

When Maya was too slow to answer, the woman behind her applied pressure again. "Ow—yes—okay—I see!" she yelped.

"Good. I thought you would. So here it is; you continue with your little caper and I get a cut of it every week. I want 75 percent of anything you make. Do you understand me?"

Maya nodded and the other policewoman released her. But Bel Marda wasn't done with her yet. Without any warning, she shoved her fist into Maya's stomach. The girl gasped in pain and dropped to the floor.

"And don't you even *think* of cheating me," Bel Marda hissed in her ear, "or you'll wind up lying on a slab. Zat klaar?"

She didn't wait for Maya to regain her breath or rasp out a reply. Instead, she and her partner walked outside, leaving her where she was. As Maya picked herself up from the carpet, she heard Bel Marda speaking with the Yard Boss.

"She wasn't the one," the kaaper explained, "Our source must have been wrong."

***

Maya caught up with her cohorts later that day, more intent than ever to find a smuggler ship. Staying at the warehouse, or in T-Don for that matter, was not even a remote possibility now.

Her companions were waiting for her in a quiet corner of E-section, but neither of them was smiling. The Tethyian had a swollen lip, and her associate sported an ugly-looking black eye. It was clear that Officer bel Marda and her partner had visited both of them and personally delivered their message.

"Go ahead and drop your boxes," the Tethyian said dejectedly, "for what good it will do. Now that Bel Marda has gotten her claws into us, we won't make enough credits to make the risk worth it."

"It wasn't that good a thing anyway," Maya replied. "I'd say it's time to run for it and find a better scam. Know any moonrunners looking for a hand?"

The Tethyian laughed bitterly. "It's not as easy as all that, girlie. 'Runner crews are a tight bunch. They don't let folks know what they are about, and they *don't* take on new crewwomen unless they're hard in need of a skill—very hard. Besides, if Bel Marda catches any of us trying to run for it, we won't be worth a decacredit." She made a throat-cutting gesture to emphasize her point.

"*If* she catches us," Maya countered. "You can stay if you want and work as her *bitch*, but I'm for jumping into Null and getting the *fek* out of here. And you can show me who the smugglers are. I know that's how you've gotten some of your stuff out of here."

"I told you the new girl was smart," the Tethyian said to her bruised friend. "Didn't take her long to figure things out did it?"

Then to Maya, "Yeah, I can finger them. But you're on you own when it comes to the meeting and talking part. A lot of them pay off the kaapers, and they wouldn't think twice about turning us over to Bel Marda if they thought it would buy them anything. So, if you want to risk getting *kakked*, that's your business, just leave me out of it."

"Yeah," Maya retorted. "I'll do that."

Over the next few days, the Tethyian made good on her promise, pointing out the ships that she knew were 'runners. A few looked particularly promising, and Maya took careful note of them.

Finally, towards the end of the week, and as they were hauling some cargo towards the customs warehouse on their hovercarries, the Tethyian nodded discreetly towards the CSS *C-JUDI-GO*. She was a small non-descript merchanter, sitting by herself in a nearby launch cradle. Maya had seen the diminutive vessel before and really hadn't paid it much attention.

"That one there," the Tethyian said. "She's one. I wanted you to know about her, special. Mind you, the *JUDI* 's one of the best, even if she doesn't look it. She's got a rep of getting cargo in and out where other's can't, or won't. She's even traded with the Hriss and made it out in one piece."

Maya gave the ship an appraising look. She had never expected any of the ships that they'd seen to actually *look* like smugglers, so the vessel didn't disappoint her in that respect. It was its size that was the issue.

Maya knew that not all illegal cargoes had to be large to make a profit. In fact, it was often the other way around; drugs like 'glass' or datapaks of restricted information didn't need much room at all, and the credits that they commanded were often far out of proportion to their physical volume.

The problem was that small ships had small crews, and seldom needed any replacements. And the *JUDI* was possibly one of the smallest she'd ever seen in port. In her estimation, this made the vessel a very poor candidate for a job opening.

"I know she's tiny," the Tethyian said, voicing her thoughts, "and I haven't heard that her captain's looking for any hands, if that's what you're thinking. But that's not why I pointed her out. I wanted you to know about her so you'd stay *away* from her."

Maya rewarded her with a perplexed expression. "What's so bad about her?" The merchanter appeared to be anything but threatening.

"I don't know who she pays off, and I've never done any business with her crew," the Tethyian explained. "I've just heard a lot of tales about her. She's a strange one. *Very* strange."

"Okay," Maya replied. "You've got my attention. What kind of 'tales' have you heard about her?" It was hard to keep the sarcasm out of her voice, but she did her best, realizing that the woman was being serious.

Her companion's voice dropped to a low, conspiratorial whisper. "The word around the docks is that the *JUDI* is cursed, and that her captain has some kind of witch working with her. They call her the Black Witch, and they say that the captain sold her soul to the witch to keep the *Indies* off their back. Some even swear the Witch is part *Indie* herself, and that's how she manages it."

Being a *trekker* herself, Maya had heard her fair share of wild space stories, but this was utter nonsense. She laughed right in the woman's face. "You're joking, right?"

The Tethyian's expression remained sober. "No, girl, I'm *not* joking. This is the word on the docks, and from dock-rats I trust who've been here for years. Now, mind you, I don't believe most of it, but as my mothers always said, '*where there's a tale there's a truth.*' The Witch is real even if the rest is *klaxxy shess*. I know that for certain."

"And just *how* do you know it?"

"Because I've seen her, girl, and other dock rats have seen her, too. She always comes around the launch cradles at odd hours, dressed all in black from head to toe, and wearing a cloak to hide her face."

Maya went pale. Unconsciously rubbing at her throat, she looked across the docks at the little merchanter, suddenly perceiving it in a new and loathsome light.

"That ship is bad luck," her companion added. "Anyone would have to be *warpy* to even *think* of shipping out with her. I say stay well away from her if you know what's best."

"Don't worry," Maya assured her gravely. "I'll keep my distance from the *JUDI*--and their *fekking* Witch." She meant every word of it.

***

The next day, Maya ventured off by herself and decided to try her luck with the CSS *Akantha*. It was a fair-to-middling sized vessel that the Tethyian had identified on their very first day out. The crew was in the process of loading cargo, and she was certain that her presence wouldn't seem suspicious to anyone watching. Chin held high, she went straight up to the woman on duty at the cargo bay doors.

"Whatcha need, girlie?" the sailor asked.

"A job. I heard that you might need a new hand."

The sailor snorted derisively. "Well, you heard wrong. If we needed someone, it would be someone with experience, and from the look of it, you don't have much."

Maya smiled sweetly. "Oh, I've got lots of experience," she said. "I've been a hand aboard plenty of merchanters, and I've got just the right qualifications to fit in with the kind of runs your ship *really* makes."

97

The woman's expression lost what little friendliness it had initially possessed. "I think you've got the wrong ship, little girl. You need to move along. *Now.*"

"Oh, I have it a'right," Maya retorted. "I heard that your captain is always looking for someone who doesn't care where her cargo comes from, or where it's going. *I'm* that someone."

"I don't know what you're talking about," the sailor snarled. "But you'd better move your little ass along the dock before I help you get there with my foot." She stepped towards her with a menacing expression, and Maya backed away.

"Fine, I'll go," she said. "But I'm the woman you need. I'll be on the docks if you change your mind."

Then she left. There were other ships to try, and she knew that it always paid to place multiple applications when looking for a new job. She was painfully aware that not having someone to introduce her was hurting her chances, but the Tethyian hadn't left her with much choice. She was on her own. Pure brass would have to make up for her deficiencies.

But by the time her psiever advised her that she needed to return to the warehouse, she had tried three other ships and the results had been just as disappointing. They were either not looking for anyone, or greeted her with the same unfriendly reception as the *Akantha* had. Reluctantly accepting the fact that the solution to her problems would not come that day, she headed back.

As she walked past the *Akantha*, she saw Bel Marda and her partner talking with the crewwoman at the cargo bay. Then they made eye contact. Seeing the the murderous expression on Bel Marda's face, Maya knew that she had been betrayed. It was time to run.

She dropped her hovercarry and pelted down the docks, pushing past anyone that got in her way, and leaping over obstacles like a Shakalan *gazell-bok*. The two customs officers started after her, shouting for her to stop, but she had been chased by law enforcement before, and paid them no heed.

Instead, she glanced briefly over her shoulder and used her talents, pushing at Bel Marda, and making her believe that a non-existent cargo box was suddenly in her way. The woman stopped short and her partner slammed into her from behind. As the two kaapers tumbled to the dock plates, Maya jumped off the platform and ran underneath it.

The underside of the dockway was a low, tangled area that had never been intended for human foot-traffic. It was clogged with service pipes, support beams and squat robots that mindlessly serviced the ships above them, and except for the headlights and guide lasers of the 'bots, the space was also quite dark.

Maya made for the nearest shadows and weighed whether to stay there and hide, or to keep running. But before she could decide, she heard a sound like sizzling meat, and a needlegun round ricocheted off a rusty support only a few centimeters away.

Throwing herself forwards, Maya clambered through the maze of pipes without bothering to confirm what she already knew; Bel Marda had found her and intended to kill her.

A few more rounds zipped past, accompanied by curses, but Maya knew that she had the advantage. She was much smaller than the other two women, and she was able to move through the area faster than they could. In a few seconds, she reached the opposite side of the platform, ignoring the bloody slash in her arm that she'd acquired from one of the rounds, and clambered back up onto the top of the dock.

With her pursuers still below her, Maya looked around in desperation for a bolt hole. But this part of the docks had only a few ships parked in the launch cradles, and most of them had crewwomen working around them. Only one merchanter was unattended. It was the *C-JUDI-GO,* and its hold was wide open.

She hesitated, but then she heard someone behind her shouting. Bel Marda was coming up over the lip of the dock. The policewoman hadn't seen her yet, but in another moment, Maya knew that she would.

Caught between two unappealing situations, she opted for the unknown. She gave Bel Marda another push with her talents, this time making her miss her footing and slip backwards off the dock. Taking advantage of the precious few seconds that she had gained, she ran straight up the *JUDI's* cargo ramp.

Bright lights came on automatically as she entered the hold, and she cursed at them for stealing away the chance for concealment. But there was little to be had in any event: the hold was mainly empty, and what cargo there was, was arranged in low neat rows that offered nothing to hide behind. The only solution was to go into the ship itself.

She didn't relish the idea one *nano*, but it was her only real option. Fortunately, the hatchway at the far end of the hold proved to be unlocked, and once it opened, she found herself in a small egress hall. More hatches were situated up and down its length, and at the far end there was a brightly painted ladder that led up to the control cabin.

Not wanting to risk an encounter with a crewmember, she ignored the ladder and chose the nearest hatch instead, praying to the Lady as she went in that the chamber was unoccupied.

Just as she had hoped, the space was empty. It contained a tiny foldout desk and chair, and two bunks were set into the bulkhead, with drawers for storage beneath them. But none of it offered a decent hiding place. With no better solution, Maya palmed out the light, flattened herself against the cold plastic, and listened.

Footsteps came up the cargo ramp, accompanied by muttered profanities.

There's nothing here, she thought, focusing her talents in their direction. *She went the other way.* It was a gamble, but one she had to take.

The footfalls slowed, became indecisive, and then took on more purpose as she heard them heading back down the ramp. After a few minutes, the only sound that came to her ears was the normal background noise of the port, and she let out a sigh of relief.

For the moment at least, the Goddess had seen fit to pardon her for her life of crime, and had granted her a temporary reprieve. She whispered up her thanks, and stayed where she was. After counting out a full two minutes, she finally decided that it was safe to leave.

The ship, however, had other ideas. When she went to open the hatchway, it refused to release. It took her a few more tries, and finally hammering at the stubborn controls, before Maya realized that she was locked in. Her hiding place had transformed into a prison cell.

***

Captain Inish bel Lissa and her Second, Zara bel Trina were at lunch in the Port when they were alerted that a problem of some kind had occurred aboard the *JUDI*. Their Third had refused to go into any details, only saying that it required their immediate attention.

Both annoyed and alarmed, Bel Lissa and her companion returned to the docks just as Bel Marda and her partner were conferring with one another at the foot of the launch cradle. This only increased Bel Lissa's sense of apprehension and irritation. Even so, she put on her best smile, and approached them calmly.

"Officers? Can I help you with something? I assure you that all our manifests are in order, and our vessel is up to all local and interstellar safety codes."

Bel Marda frowned at this. She knew all about the *JUDI*, and she didn't like the ship, or its crew. For some reason that had never been adequately explained, her Lieutenant had made it abundantly clear that the *JUDI* was one ship that she was *not* to attempt to skim any graft from. The vessel was untouchable, and it made her want to go *fekking nova* when she thought about all the credits that she was missing out on. But she didn't dare disobey her superior. Kaapers in modern correctional colonies didn't fare any better than their ancient predecessors ever had.

"Yes," she growled. "Your ship looks like everything is *straaked* away proper, Captain. But we aren't here to check up on you. We're looking for a fugitive that came this way." Her monocle projected a holo of Maya for Bel Lissa to see. "If you spot this girl, you give *me* a call. No one else. Zat klaar?"

"Of course," Bel Lissa agreed, more than a little nonplussed. Whatever the problem was aboard the ship, it didn't seem to have anything to do with the law. "I'll call you right away. Now, if you'll excuse me? My Second and I have some things to attend to."

Bel Marda nodded curtly and stomped off with her partner in tow.

"Well," Bel Lissa said, "that was more fun than I think anyone should have a right to have. Shall we go aboard and see what this so-called emergency is over a cup of *kaafra?*"

"Aye-yah, Captain," Zara replied, just as confused as her superior. They ascended the ramp together, casting their experienced eyes over the

101

cargo in the hold. It wasn't their real cargo, of course. That was safely hidden away in special compartments deep inside the ship, but none of the decoy containers looked as if they had been disturbed.

Their Third, Hari, met them at the inner hatch.

"Well?" Bel Lissa inquired, "I saw the customs officers and they didn't want anything except to tell me about some girl they're looking for. What's all this about?"

"It's about the girl," the woman answered. "I was doing the preflight systems checks when the ship detected someone coming aboard. The AI activated the security protocols and locked her inside the aft crew quarters. She's in there right now, and mad as a kaatze."

She called up a holo with her psiever for Bel Lissa to see. It displayed an image of the girl, pounding on the sound-proofed door of the Crews Quarters, and then kicking at the tiny fold out chair in frustration. Bel Lissa's lunch started to go sour in her stomach.

"I see," she remarked. "And *why* haven't we shown her off the ship, or given her up to the kaapers?"

And why, she wondered, *wasn't the inner hatch properly secured against unauthorized entry in the first place?* But this was something that she didn't want to get into just then. In her short time aboard the *JUDI*, Hari had gained a reputation for sloppiness when it came to security, and for the thousandth time, Bel Lissa considered replacing the woman at the next opportunity. First though, there was the matter at hand to deal with.

"It's Sarah, Captain," Hari explained. "After the girl came aboard and got herself locked in, the ship alerted her."

The *JUDI'S* AI was programmed to notify the woman of any significant events, and often without including Bel Lissa in the information loop. It was an annoying feature, but something that she was in no position to argue over. Unlike other ships, Sarah n'Jan, and not the Captain, was the final word on all matters. That was the way their employers wanted it.

"As soon as Sarah got the alert, she asked me for a holo-feed," Hari continued, "Then she told me not to let anyone know about the girl, and keep her here until she arrived. She was already on her way for the flight, but she said she was going to expedite. She also said that she'd deal with the girl herself when she got here."

Bel Lissa watched the holo for a moment longer as their inmate vented her anger against one of the storage drawers. Thankfully the drawer was locked, and reasonably strong enough to be proof against the assault. For a while at least.

"Very well," she finally said, not at all pleased with the idea that they had a wanted fugitive aboard. "I suppose that there isn't too much that she can break in there. Let me know when Sarah arrives. I'll be in the galley.'

"In the meantime, I want us to be ready for take-off and transit in one hour--unless Sarah says differently, or someone *else* sneaks aboard."

***

After ensuring that everything was being done to prepare the *JUDI* for flight, Sarah n'Jan went directly to her private cabin. There, she sent a command through her psiever to a small, hidden compartment set inside the bulkhead. When it slid open, she brought out a palm-sized case that she had been carrying under her traveling cape, and put it inside, along with an unlabeled plastic spray bottle.

Then she resealed the cache and removed her cloak, hanging it on a peg. Her needlegun came off next. After checking its ammunition level, she set it on the nightstand next to her bed, and sat down on the edge of the mattress with a tired sigh, giving herself a moment to relax.

Because of size constraints, the cabin didn't have much in the way of amenities. But since it served as a home for her as often as it did, she had equipped it with a few small items that made it seem less Spartan, and a little more welcoming.

On the far wall, was one of these decorative touches. It was a holopic of a rugged, empty looking landscape. A trio of tiny blue-white moons dotted the picture's horizon, casting triple shadows over the bare, rocky earth. Although others might have found the scene eerie, for Sarah, the silvery light that the moons cast on the rocky expanse was comforting, and easy on her eyes.

The holopic was an oft-reproduced image of the Plain of Trials that anyone from Nyx took with them off-planet. Although she was only half Moonborn herself, the image reminded her of the world that she considered to be her true home, the home of her heart. And the sere vista never failed to restore a sense of calm and order when she needed it the most. She drank in the image with her eyes, and then reached into the nightstand for her Tarot cards.

Like the holo, they were another Nyxian import that had their roots on Old Gaia. No one, not even her Nyxian teacher, knew the exact origin of the Tarot, but they had served as a guide for humankind, and then Womankind, for centuries, and were an integral part of the culture of the Nightworld.

Had she encountered Maya only once, she would have had no reason to consult them. In fact, their first meeting had seemed purely accidental and completely unimportant at the time. More of a curiosity than anything else.

Then she had come across her at the port. Being an experienced operative, she had immediately doubted her initial assessment, and had chosen to force their psychic link to determine the girl's true motives. In the end, however, all that she had managed to confirm was what she had initially suspected. That Maya was not an enemy agent and possessed no hidden agenda.

Once again, she had passed it off as a simple coincidence.

But then, out of all the other ships in the port that she could have chosen for herself, Maya had hidden aboard the *JUDI*, and Sarah had been forced to adopt a new theory. One that most new agents, lacking her training and experience, would never have entertained.

Although it was still quite possible that she was being deceived, Sarah was becoming more and more convinced that the agency of fate itself was responsible for their encounters. It was illogical, but thanks to her experiences as a military psychic, and the training she had recieved on Nyx, she understood that the paranormal and the irrational sometimes factored into life's equation. If this proved to be the case, then she knew that they would continue to cross paths until they took care of whatever business the Goddess intended for the two of them.

"Let's just see what we have then," she said to herself. She uttered a quick prayer to the Lady of Darkness for clear council and took the round cards from their pouch. Then she sorted through them until she found the one that best suited Maya's nature.

This was the Daughter of Knives. It signified an impetuous young woman with a fiery and aggressive disposition, given to the use of trickery and guile when it suited her. In the holographic image, a girl with dark hair stood in the desert twilight with her Tej knife raised up against an unseen adversary.

It was the perfect signifcator for Maya, Sarah decided, and she laid it down on the bed cover, shuffled the deck, and dealt out nine more cards. Then she called up a small glass of wine from the ship's galley and considered each of them carefully.

Her Nyxian mentor had taught that the last card was always the most important one in a reading. It stood for the Outcome of the Matter, and when she saw it, Sarah realized that she had known all along what it would be, even before it had been dealt.

It was the Journeyer, and one the most profound of all the cards in the deck. In the image, another young woman stood atop a mountain peak. Behind her, the three moons of Nyx, Eris, Eros and Geras, were in the sky, and on the horizon, the planet's tiny sun, Morpheus, was just beginning to rise.

The girl was depicted stepping forwards, with one foot raised to take a step that would send her off the edge to her death while the other was still planted firmly on the promontory. She carried a knapsack typical of those used by the young women who went on the Tej, and her Tej knife was in a sheath at her waist. A small wissaq beast, a harmless herbivore native to the Nyxian desert, trailed behind her, either croaking its encouragement for her to go on, or warning her of the peril that she faced.

Very interesting, Sarah thought. She looked at the next card. It represented What Might Come, and what was most likely to occur if the questioner resisted the Goddesses will. This too, failed to surprise her.

It was the Nine of Knives. Another young woman lay at the bottom of a canyon, with eight Tej Knives arrayed on the rocks around her. Her right leg was twisted at an unnatural angle, suggesting that she had broken it in a fall from the heights above.

The ninth dagger was in her hand, its blade shattered, and hovering above her body was a ferocious *taarq*. Its saber-like fangs were bared, and the gruesome image showed all too clearly that the predator had ripped the girls' throat out, a fate that sometimes occurred in real life for those who went on the Tej. But unlike the Death card, the Nine of Knives did not symbolize spiritual death. Instead, it was the harbinger of real physical destruction in the near future.

Sarah considered these two final cards, and looked over the rest, but she found nothing among them that disagreed with the overall prediction. Finally, she returned the deck to its pouch and took another, long sip of her wine.

The Goddess wills the way, she thought, making the sign of the Lady. The cards had shown her fate's design, and she didn't envy Maya for the destiny that the patroness of Nyx, Elatsha, the Lady of Darkness, had ordained for her. But Elatsha had made her will clear and Sarah now knew the part that she was intended to play.

She left her quarters and joined the rest of the crew up in the control cabin. Bel Lissa looked up at her as she took her station.

"Preflight is almost done. We should be ready to take off on time," the woman advised, "I also received confirmation that the *Belle Starr* will meet us at the L2 point and give us our escort until we reach the Thalestra system. That will mean one transit with them, maximum."

"Good," Sarah replied with satisfaction. "That will keep our escort fees within budget. We will have to make sure to use them again in the future. I like that their Captain is so willing to work within our needs and not gouging us for credits like the last escort did. Please make sure that we add in a small tip to show our appreciation to the good lady and her officers."

"Definitely," Bel Lissa agreed. "Any instructions about our special guest before the trip?"

Sarah called up a display of the Crews Qaurters. From what she could tell, Maya had finally stopped beating on things. "No," she answered, "Let us leave her be for the moment."

106

"Very well," Bel Lissa said, turning back to her instrument panel. "Preparing to call the tower for final departure. Zara, how's our draw doing?"

Lately, the main engines had been pulling a little more power than normal from their positronic reactors, and everyone hoped that the problem had been worked out. When Zara looked down at her readings, she smiled.

"She's in the clear, Captain. Performance is in the green. And I think," she added, rapping her knuckles on the control panel for luck, "that we lost that little gremlin that was playing tricks on us."

"Let's hope so," Bel Lissa remarked. "I don't want to have her taken apart and come up empty again."

Like all machines, spaceships had a tendency to misbehave until a qualified mechanic was standing over their innards. Then their problems would miraculously vanish—at least until they were out of the maintenance bay. And in the *JUDI's* case, the mechanics that they used were very expensive. Discretion wasn't cheap.

Bel Lissa initiated the take-off sequence. "The tower's cleared us for launch. All hands prepare for take-off." While the *C-JUDI-GO's* gravitational drive wound up, heavy blast shields dropped down around the merchanter. This was followed by the familiar thump and hiss of the docking cradle and umbilical lines detaching themselves. Seeing the confirmation on her holodisplay, she brought the secondary thermal antimatter engines on-line.

"Ship's gravity at maximum," Zara informed her. A low-pitched humming now reverberated through the control room. On the screens, a graphic displayed the positively charged gravitational field that now surrounded the ship.

Bel Lissa nodded in satisfaction and throttled the thermal engines to just a hair short of full power. "Take off on my mark..." she said. Then she brought the thermals to maximum and discharged the anti-gravitrons that had been building up in the main engines.

"--and launch."

The *JUDI* leapt up from the earth with a howl. In seconds, the port was below them and shrinking rapidly to become a pale smudge against the darker background of Thermadon City. Then the city itself transformed into nothing more than a small blotch on the continental face. Then this too disappeared beneath the clouds of the upper atmosphere, and the sky turned black. Stars appeared on the forward screens, first singly, then in dozens, and then hundreds that became thousands, which resolved into millions.

As the merchanter entered open space, Bel Lissa shut down the thermal thrusters and set their course for the 2nd La Grange point, where their escort ship, the CSS *Belle Starr*, was waiting. She opened a hailing frequency to the vessel, and the conversation played out over the cabin's speakers.

"Good afternoon, Captain n'Jarri," she said. "We are on course to join you, estimated arrival time one minute."

"That's affirmative, Captain," her counterpart responded. "We have you on tracking and are beginning our outbound run. Engaging Null-wings and powering up for transit now. Advise us when you are ready for the gate."

On the *JUDI*'s main sitscreen, the refurbished Navy cruiser was moving in a line away from them as they came around on her tail. Ahead of the escort ship, the displays showed the zone where the opening into Nullspace was projected to occur.

"On your track, Captain n'Jarri," Bel Lissa advised. "Open the gate at your pleasure."

The two ships where now moving together at the same speed towards the target zone. The *Starr's* helmswoman engaged the ships Pavilita generators and sent the energy out through its Null-wings. Ahead of them, a brilliant rift of pure light appeared, increasing in size until it dwarfed the approaching ships. In another second, they were inside of it, and entering Nullspace.

A bare ten minutes elapsed before the tiny convoy exited Null in another part of the Far Arm. The run itself had been completely uneventful. Only one Indweller had been spotted and it had stayed well clear of them, and at the very edge of their sensor range. Neither ship had had to fire so much as a single shot.

Bel Lissa made a point of thanking the *Starr's* Captain for her service, and after exchanging a few more pleasantries, brought the *JUDI* onto a standby course to nowhere in particular.

As for Captain n'Jarri, she wasted no time in turning her ship around and heading back into Null. The next leg of the *JUDI's* journey was about to begin, and both Captains knew that it was better if the *Starr's* crewwomen could swear truthfully, if they were ever asked, that they had left the *JUDI* behind in normal space, and awaiting another escort ship with an unknown name. It was a useful fiction, and the *Belle Starr* was receiving additional credits on top of their standard escort fees to play along with the charade.

The moment that the *Starr* had disappeared, Bel Lissa checked their long-range scanners. Once she had confirmed that they were alone, she sent a special command and unlocked the Null-wings hidden along the *JUDI's* hull. They unfolded out to their full length at the ships bow and stern, and as they locked themselves into position, she glanced over at Zara.

"Bringing the Pavilitas on line and routing power to them, Captain," the engineer informed her. The Pavilita generators that the *JUDI* possessed were quite diminutive in comparison to the *Starr's*, or any other Null-capable ship, but they were state-of-the-art, and reached their peak power levels immediately.

In the meantime, Sarah had called up a holo of the star patterns at their destination, and had memorized their configurations. Then the psi reached out with her mind through the Pavilita's, and shaped the energies contained within them until they had conformed to the image of their destination perfectly.

She gave Zara a slight nod. The older woman brought the stern set on line, and discharged the Pavilita's. Outside, the little wings danced with fire, and the ship's hull vibrated with a deep hum that everyone felt in the marrow of their bones.

"Cutting the gate," Sarah announced in a distant voice. At a command from her psiever, the stern wings released their energy to the pair at the bow. Two azure rays shot out from the *JUDI* into the darkness, and as the beams conjoined, a gateway appeared.

Bel Lissa throttled the ship's engines up and took the *JUDI* into Nullspace. The mists closed over them and she channeled energy to the ships defensive guns and kept a sharp eye on the battle sensors. But these steps were only supportive functions.

The main job of defending the ship actually lay in Sarah's hands, and the psi was monitoring a duplicate of Bel Lissa's display, using her talents to reach out even further than the ships sensors were capable of, probing ahead for the slightest indication of danger.

It wasn't long in coming. Sarah sensed the Indie seconds before the sensors did. It was below them, circling in the mists like the shadow of a physical predator sizing up its prey.

Then in a rush, the ebon shape rose upwards from the vapor, spreading itself wide, and turning into a giant cloak of pure lightlessness. Bel Lissa prepared to discharge the *JUDI*'s main guns into the horror, but before she could engage the firing stud, the creature shuddered. Its form rippled as the *Indie* reacted to an invisible force that was more powerful than anything that the *JUDI's* weapons were capable of. With a howl of infernal rage, the monster folded in on itself and retreated back into the safety of the clouds.

The *JUDI* flew onwards, unmolested, and Sarah's eyes fluttered open.

"There are two others nearby," she said distantly, "staying just out of our scanner range. I think that they are reconsidering their strategy. I injured the adult severely and this appears to have given its younger companions reason to pause."

Bel Lissa took her hand away from the fire control switches and returned her attention to the helm. She didn't express any gratitude, and Sarah didn't expect it. They had all been through this many times before. It was simply a fact that Sarah's amazing abilities were what made the *JUDI*, and the missions that it flew, possible.

CSS *C-JUDI-GO*, Lunar Raw Materials Plant, Virgo, Bethlehem System, Telesalla Elant, United Sisterhood of Suns 1042.12|04|07:02.10

The *C-JUDI-GO* came back into normal space at the edge of a small star system. The sitscreens showed them on an approach to a place called Virgo. It was the satellite of a T-class planet that any woman in the Sisterhood would have recognized with instant distaste; New Covenant, the capital world of the Marionites.

Instead of approaching Virgo at a leisurely angle, Bel Lissa brought the *JUDI* down in a tight arc, swinging the ship around the dark side of the moon. Then she hugged the landscape, using the sensors to guide the way. Except for the faint stars on the horizon, the terrain beneath and in front of the merchanter was completely shrouded in perpetual shadow, and only the displays on the holos told her when they had crested a mountain range, or dipped into a valley.

Up ahead, and through the forward view-ports, a bright line of landing beacons came to life. Bel Lissa engaged the *JUDI*'s own landing lights in response, illuminating a makeshift runway that ended abruptly at the foot of a rocky hill.

The *JUDI* rushed down the strip towards the hillside. Seconds before disaster could claim the vessel, a section of the slope began to open, revealing a dark hangar bay hidden inside.

Bel Lissa brought the *JUDI* in, entering the space with only meters of clearance to spare, and the moment they had landed, she powered the engines down. Back behind them, the hangar door slid shut and the lights outside winked off. They had arrived at their destination, with no one the wiser.

"Time to deliver our cargo," she announced. Everyone got up from their stations and filed out of the bridge to the main access way. Bel Lissa turned to Hari when they reached the ladder.

"I'll need you to stay aboard with our 'guest,'" she told her, "while we go talk with the client."

She didn't give any instructions to Zara. Unlike Hari, Zara knew her job without being told, and did it well. The *JUDI*'s engineer simply smiled at her Captain and Sarah, and made her way past them, headed for the engine compartment.

It was obvious from her expression that Hari was not happy with her assignment, but she made no protest. Which just as well. After the issue with the inner cargo bay hatch, Bel Lissa felt that it was more than fair that she make up for her carelessness by pulling guard duty. Besides which, their mission was on a need-to-know basis, and the temperamental woman had not been included in the information loop. Hari didn't "need to know" anything.

They left her there at the ladder and went straightway to Sarah's cabin. Once inside, Sarah opened the hidden compartment and brought out the spray bottle.

She uncapped it and brought it to her nose, dispensing some of its contents into each nostril. Then she picked up the case and concealed it under the folds of her traveling cape.

Leaving together, they headed for the cargo bay, where Bel Lissa activated the controls for the ramp. It opened up on an enclosed chamber of grey rock, covered with a light coating of lunar dust. A ring of high intensity lights surrounded the ship, marking the landing circle, and obscuring everything else in the chamber with their glare. As they stepped out, the lights dimmed and a smiling woman came forwards to greet them. She was dressed in an immaculate white jumpsuit with a symbol embroidered in gold above her left pocket. It was a four-armed star; the insignia of the Marionite Church.

Sarah spoke first. "We had a little trouble getting your order filled, Sister, especially since the material has become so closely monitored. But your prayers must have been with us, because we managed to procure what you needed."

"Praise Mari," the woman exclaimed, "She must have heard our humble entreaties. I mean no offense, but may I inspect the case, please?"

"Of course," Sarah nodded. She produced the case and opened it. Inside, nestled in thick foam, was a row of sealed containers.

The Sister reached in and carefully removed one. Its label read: *Xi-Gen Labs: Enhanced Genetic Materials, Class 5 Restrictions Apply. Unauthorized distribution carries a minimum mandatory sentence of 10 years. Title 51117, Sec. 13*

The Marionite's expression became positively blissful. "Bless you, Sarah. And bless you also, Captain bel Lissa. Truly, Mari has seen fit to grace us with women who can see through the unholy blasphemy of the Sisterhood. I know that you will both have a seat in Heaven with Jesu and Mari at the Creator's side."

"Perhaps," Sarah agreed. "And now, may we discuss the fee that we decided upon? I'm sure that you would also agree that we need to attend to our material concerns until God calls us to His side." She said this with a smile, and handed the case over to the woman, who took it gratefully.

"Yes. Of course," the Sister replied, "We can take our ease in my offices while I have your funds transferred." She led them away from the landing circle towards a prefab office module set against the wall of the chamber.

"I do hope that you and your crew will be remaining with us for a while. I am sure that after your long trip, you would want to avail yourselves of the opportunity for some prayer and meditation."

"It would be my pleasure, Sister," Sarah answered warmly. "I have missed the Holy Garden of the Immaculate Conception, and the long quiet hours that I spent there on our previous visits." Then, she sneezed.

"God bless you," the Sister said.

"Thank you, Sister. It must be the dust in here that is affecting me."

The Marionite smiled, and showed them into the office, certain that she understood Sarah's situation. In reality, she did not understand a thing. Sarah had been trained in many arts, including the ability to trigger otherwise involuntary functions. Her sternutation had been carefully timed for the precise moment when they had been passing beneath an air exchange vent.

And with this action, thousands of microscopic spybots that she had sprayed into her sinuses had taken flight. By the time everyone had seated themselves, the little nanobots had already winged their way deep into the laboratory complex. There, they began transmitting information back to the *JUDI* for later review by her employers, and their experts.

The Sister, completely oblivious to the fact that their security had just been compromised, leaned back in her chair. "Then it is settled," the woman announced, "I'll make sure that a shuttle is sent up from the Mother World to take you to Marristown. In the meantime, my assistant, Gari will attend you."

While she said this, a neoman entered the cubicle. He was dressed in the same white jumpsuit and bore a silver tray laden with a pitcher of hot kaafra and matching cups.

Sarah had encountered many neomen in her career, and their utter strangeness never failed to affect her. It was their appearance, she reflected, so quasi-human, and at the same time, so oddly proportioned, and utterly non-female. Where the eye expected to find breasts, there was nothing, and the rest was a collection of hard angles, instead of soft curves.

She found their voices to be equally as strange. They were far too deep to be normal, and seemed almost as if they were imitating a spoken language, rather than genuine communication.

But perhaps the most telling difference was their scent. Sarah had a hyper-keen sense of smell, and despite the masking effect of cosmetics, neomen always smelled a bit too musky to be considered to be anything *but* abnormal and animalistic. The neoman in front of her was no exception, and she tried not to wrinkle her nose when he leaned in close to set the tray down.

It was easy, just on the basis of physical attributes alone, for her to appreciate the necessity behind the prejudices that neomen faced in the Sisterhood. Although any woman understood that males had once been part of the human race, Sarah agreed with the forward-thinking idea that Womankind had simply evolved past the level of lower order animals. There was simply no longer any requirement for multiple sexes to exist in order to successfully reproduce. In her estimation, neomen were at their most basic level, redundant, and nothing better than genetic throwbacks that had no place in a modern, progressive society.

Naturally, she kept these thoughts to herself and accepted her cup from the archaic creature with a pleasant smile. She also found herself wondering, as she often did, how his kind would fare in combat. She had never had the opportunity to fight a neoman, and she always made it a point to size up their strengths and weaknesses in the event that that day ever actually arrived.

Sipping her beverage, she observed him carefully. Like most neomen, Gari had a powerful upper body. In fact, his muscles were grossly overdeveloped compared to a female physique. She knew that this lent him greater upper body strength, which was potentially deadly if it were applied correctly.

But he was also slower and less fluid in his movements than a woman would have been. Overall, this made him, without the training to compensate for his obvious genetic deficiencies, vulnerable to attack by anyone with faster reflexes, and more readily off-balanced.

Satisfied with her analysis of the creature, and her kaafra, Sarah let herself enjoy the respite. She was quite pleased at how things had transpired so far; their mission had concluded successfully and she was eager to receive the information that the spybots would send.

As for the Garden of the Immaculate Conception, she had been genuine in her desire to visit it. Of all the sanctuaries that she had ever been to, it was, without qualification, one of the loveliest. And because it was used by the Marionite leadership to conduct their most important business, it was also one of the best locations to plant additional listening devices.

***

Between the chase at the port, venting her frustrations on the contents of the cabin, and her confinement, Maya had thoroughly exhausted herself. For a time, she had simply sat on the deck, but as the minutes had stretched into hours, she had finally surrendered to her fatigue, and slept.

The realization that the *JUDI* had made planetfall was what woke her. The hum of the engines was gone, along with the thousand other small noises that a ship made when it was in flight.

They had been replaced by other sounds. Although layers of metal and plastic muffled everything, she recognized the high pitched whine of a hovercarry being operated, and the deeper rumble of a cargo container making contact with a floor as someone set it down. There were also voices mixed in with all this; distant, and strangely low pitched.

She pressed her head against the bulkhead and listened for a while, trying to decipher what the people were saying, and to piece together what it all meant. But as hard as she tried, she was unable to assemble a coherent picture.

Another sound, this time from a slot opening in the hatch behind her intruded on her spying, and she looked over her shoulder to see a food tray waiting for her. Someone had decided to feed her.

For a moment, Maya was tempted to leave the tray right where it was, just to show her captors that she wasn't completely conquered. But her body had other ideas. It had been hours since she had eaten, and when her stomach growled at her insistantly, she stood up and went over to the tray. She hated the fact that she was dancing to someone else's tune, but the odors coming from under the plastic cover were irresistible. And when she removed it, the food inside made her mouth water.

She took an experimental bite and found that it was just as good as it appeared. Then she ate, slowly at first, and finally with increasing enthusiasm until the tray had been picked clean.

When the last morsel was gone, Maya looked at the cameras that she knew were there, and smiled at her hidden audience.

Then she threw the tray down onto the plasmetal floor. *There,* she thought, *I ate and FEK you!*

She started to add in an obscene gesture, but caution intervened. She was still a prisoner, she reminded herself, and at the mercy of the Black Witch and her sinister minions. It was better to wait, and see if there was a way to work the situation out to her advantage. Freedom would only come if she appeared to be compliant.

So instead, she gently picked the tray back up and set it into its slot. Then she sat on the edge of the lowest bed, trying to appear as cooperative as possible--and hating every second of it.

CHAPTER 5

USSNS *Pallas Athena*, Battle Group Golden, Persephone, Demeter System, Sagana Territory, United Sisterhood of Suns, 1042.12|23|05:48:93

The Marines were still in the process of eliminating the last Hriss resistance on Persephone, and except for an occasional request for fire-support, there had been very little for the battle group to do except stand by in orbit. Most of the crew of the *Athena* that was not on active duty, or employed downside, had taken advantage of this by engaging in recreational activities. Although it was her turn on the bridge, Lilith took the time to treat herself to lunch down in the Officer's Mess rather than 'eating at the boards' in her office, or at the command chair.

When she entered, she heard music. Katrinn was seated in the center of the space, surrounded by a group of officers who were listening in rapt attention. Music was a special love of hers and the Zommerlaandar had brought out her guitar to play for them.

Lilith recognized the melody right away, and edged her way into the room to join the others.

"Jenny Has Gone for a Soldier" was an ancient composition that had been born centuries before humans had ever even conceived of space-travel It had survived the tumult of history and travelled with the first settlers to Alpha Centauri A.

Eventually, it had become a favorite of the Sisterhood Marines, many of whom called the system's main planet, Zommerlaand, their home. Although its title and the words had been changed many times, its meaning was still the same;

> *"Here I sit on Widow's--Hill,"* Katrinn began,
> *"Who can blame me, cryin' my fill?*
> *"And every tear would turn a mill,*
> *"Jen-ny has gone for a soldier."*

Like Lilith, her audience knew the tune, and joined in the chorus;

> *"Me, oh my, I loved her so,*
> *Broke my heart to see her go.*
> *Only time will heal my woe,*
> *Jen-ny has gone for a soldier."*

117

"I'll sell my rod," Katrinn went on, *"I'll sell my reel,'*
"Likewise I'll sell my spin-ning wheel.
"And buy my love a sword of steel.
"Jen-ny has gone for a soldier."

Her audience responded,

"I'll dye my dress,
"I'll dye it red,'
"And through the streets I'll beg for bread,
"For the girl I love has fled,'
"Jen-ny has gone for a soldier."

The folk-song went on like this for a while longer before Katrinn played the final notes, and let the music die away. More than a few of the women listening had been affected by it, and even Lilith's eyes weren't entirely dry. *"Jenny"* always managed to do that to servicewomen.

"All right," Katrinn said, striking up a cord, "now for something a little more upbeat."

She immediately launched into a complicated, lively rhythm that soon had everyone clapping in time. By the end it, Lilith had finally accepted a cup of tea that someone had pressed into her hand and taken a seat. She had decided that lunch, and the bridge, could wait for a few more minutes. Everyone had earned a break, even her.

Newhearth Colony, Persephone, Demeter System, Sagana Territory, United Sisterhood of Suns, 1042.12|30|07:28:33

With her work detail finished for the day, Kaly suddenly found herself with some free time on her hands. She walked away from the aid station and down past the taped-off Gathering Square, squinting in the glare of the late afternoon sunlight.

A pair of Navy space-fighters flew over at almost rooftop level, roaring inland to pound at the last remaining Hriss positions. One of the

Marines on her work detail had told her that with their cruiser gone, the Hriss infantry were still putting up a fierce resistance, but that they were ultimately doomed. The Sisterhood was giving the stranded Warriors no quarter, and taking no prisoners.

The girl shielded her eyes from the sun and as she watched the fighters, tasted bile. She wanted to be up there with them, raining death and destruction down on the invaders, and she invoked a silent blessing upon the pilots.

"May the Goddess grant you sure aim," she whispered. "And blast the fekking *shovelheads* to atoms."

Finally, the war machines disappeared behind a distant line of trees, and she moved on with no particular destination in mind, or any desire to find one. Eventually, she reached the open field that the Marines were using for the grave-pits.

Out of 6,000 colonists, only a hundred had managed to survive the Hriss onslaught, and three large trenches had been dug to accommodate the dead. Two of these had already been covered over, but the third was still waiting for the Marine earth moving machines to complete the burial process.

Kaly tried her best to avoid looking at the corpses, but the urge to stop, and stare down into at them was irresistible. They lay together at the bottom in neat, orderly rows. Each one was encased in a white plastic body bag and stenciled with a number and a bar code that identified the occupant and matched it to the Red Star's casualty lists.

Some of the bags were adult-sized, but too many were obviously children, and she was grateful for the fact that she couldn't see their faces. Faces like Ayleen's, staring up through her plastic shroud at the heavens with the frozen incomprehension of a sudden and violent death.

The Marine Priestesses who had officiated at the burial service had told Kaly and the other survivors that a monument would be erected on the site to commemorate the dead. A memorial that would list all of their names so that future generations of women would know who they were, and what had happened here.

This was supposed to provide some comfort. But it didn't, and Kaly didn't need a cenotaph to remember anything. The memories of that terrible

119

night, and all the nights that had followed it, had been seared into her soul more indelibly than any laser etching on a stone.

For some inexplicable reason though, she still hadn't wept for the dead. The tears had simply refused to come. Instead, all she felt was a great, hollow emptiness that sat in the middle of her like a black hole, consuming everything, including her ability to express her grief.

While she stood there trying to understand this, the wind came up, tossing dust and debris into the air and wrapping its fingers around her like one of the plastic shrouds. It was a cold and comfortless thing, and even though the sealed body bags made it physically impossible, she still thought that she could smell the faint miasma of burned flesh, and death.

Nauseated, she finally found the will to turn away from the mass grave, and resumed her wandering.

What do I do now? she wondered. Persephone and the people who had made it what it was, were all that she had ever known. Now, they were gone. The Red Star Psych doctors had talked about rebuilding the colony, but she knew that even if they repopulated the planet and reconstructed everything, it would never be the same. That place and that time was gone, along with her childhood and her innocence.

She also had no alternatives. There was no other place to go, and no other life to live. All there was, was the nothingness inside of herself, and the empty road that she was walking on. An empty road that led nowhere.

Just then, an armored personnel vehicle flew by her, and she jumped back relexively, choking from the dust kicked up by its fans. When she'd finally managed to clear her lungs, the dust had settled, and she caught sight of a group of Marines lounging underneath a tree. One of them stood up, took off her helmet, and leisurely shook out her blond hair.

Their eyes met for just an instant, but that was enough to change Kaly's life forever. The trooper was older than her by a decade, and she had the worn, tough-looking features that came from years of battlefield experience. But her eyes possessed an undeniable strength, an aura of total control in the midst of all the madness in the universe, and it pulled at Kaly like a magnetic field.

Then the Marine looked away to say something to her companions, and the moment was gone. Its effect on Kaly however, had been indelible. She suddenly knew with absolute certainty what she wanted for herself.

She wanted that same inner strength, the same self control. And she wanted revenge. Revenge on the Hriss for what they had done to her and to everyone she had ever known.

With a determined stride, she walked up to the group, the course of her life now firmly and irretrievably set.

"I want to fight," she declaired. "I want to join you."

"She must be klaxxy," one of the troopers replied, laughing derisively. "Go home, little girl."

"No," Kaly said. "You heard me. I want to join up."

The trooper that she had made eye contact with gave her a strange hungry look, as if she was sizing her up for her next meal.

"Izzat zo, little downzider?" she asked, "You vant to join za Marines?"

"Yes," Kaly answered. "There's nothing here for me any more."

"Tell her to go home, Troop Leader," the other Marine urged. "She's too skinny and weak to be good for anything."

The Troop Leader walked up to Kaly and looked down at her. Until that instant the girl hadn't realized just how *big* the woman really was, but she stood her ground bravely.

"You vant vhat I've had?" the Zommerlaandar challenged, "You vant maybe a little blood? A little killing, izzat it? You zhink you can handle zaat, little girl?"

"I already have," Kaly answered in a voice as flat as death. "I want to pay the *shovelheads* back for what they did to us. Who do I see to sign up?"

"You know vhat? You're a stupid girl," the Troop Leader said with a half smile. Then she turned to her friends. "Looks like she's made oop her mind to die stupid, too. Let's take her to za El-Tee. Maybe she can talk zome sense into her stupid head, *yah?*"

Two minutes later, Kaly was standing in the Marine Field Camp in front of the El-Tee herself.

"How old are you, girl?" the Lieutenant asked her. "And don't lie to me or I'll have Troop Leader Alika here kick your ass all the way back to the Aid Station."

"16 Standard," Kaly replied, trying her best to stand a little taller.

"16?" the officer laughed. "You're a child. The DI's on Hella's World will chew you up and spit you out before you even finish the first week of Basic. Go home." The woman turned and began to walk away.

Tears welled up in Kaly's eyes. "I don't *have* a home!" she shouted. "*They* took it from me!"

The Lieutenant turned around.

"I'm old enough to sign for myself, damn you!" Kaly spat. "I'm a woman, not a girl--and I'm free to choose. If you won't take me, then maybe the Navy *will*."

Kaly knew that she was right, and so did the officer. On just about every Sisterhood world, 16 was considered the legal age of maturity.

The Lieutenant shook her head in disgust. "Well, we can't have you becoming a damned can-scrubbie, now can we? All right, downsider, I'll make you a deal; you take two days and think this over just as hard as that pretty little head of yours is able, and if you *still* want to sign up, I'll swear you in myself."

"I will, and I'll be back," Kaly said defiantly.

"We'll see," the Lieutenant replied. "Troop Leader, see to it that this young lunatic gets back to the Aid Station. I don't want to see her hanging around camp until her time is up."

Troop Leader Alika clapped a big hand on Kaly's shoulder. "Come on, little honeypot, you've said all zaat za El-Tee vants to hear."

***

Two days passed, and Kaly was back at the camp, shivering in the pre-dawn cold, and holding a knapsack that contained the few possessions that she owned. As soon as someone recognized her, Troop Leader Alika was summoned.

"Zo? You vant vhat ve got?" the trooper asked. "A little blood, a little killing, zaat it?"

122

"Yeah," Kaly said. "Get the El-Tee."

"'*Kay*, stay here, downsider. I'll get *za* El-Tee," Alika told her. Then she added, "You're a stupid girl, you know *zaat*?"

Kaly nodded, doing her best not to let her teeth chatter, and waited where she was. By the time the sun had fully risen, Kaly n'Deena had been sworn in as one of the newest recruits in the United Sisterhood of Suns Marine Corps.

USSMCAS *Lucy Brewer*, In Flight, Persephone, Demeter System, Sagana Territory, United Sisterhood of Suns, 1043.01|02|02:60:10

As near as Kaly could tell, she appeared to be the only person that even remotely resembled a 'civilian' onboard the Marine assault shuttle. The rest of the *Lucy Brewer's* troop bay was filled with veteran Marines, and a number of them watched her with undisguised interest and amusement. They had all heard about the *klaxxy* little girl that had signed up downside and they all knew what she was headed for on Hella's World. And from their expressions, it was plain that none of them expected any more from her than the El-Tee had.

She tried to ignore their doubting stares, and did her best to appear relaxed and confident. It was hard for her to manage. As empty as her future had been on Persephone, a great unknown lay before her like a tremendous chasm that yawned ever wider with each passing minute. But she was not about to let her trepidation show. The troopers around her were now her peers, and she wasn't going to let them know that she secretly shared their misgivings.

Finally, after an eternity of waiting, a loud metallic clang sounded through the shuttle as it mated with the mother ship's hangar. As one, the troopers rose and started to file out of the compartment, and Kaly tried to unbuckle herself to join them.

One of the fasteners in her straps refused to open though. Suddenly imprisoned in her seat, Kaly cursed under her breath and fought with the release button, but it stubbornly resisted her efforts. The Marines filing past her didn't fail to notice her predicament, and several of them laughed, adding in comments about the "stupid hatchie," or making remarks about

123

the general unworthiness of downsiders. Kaly flushed deeply with embarrassment, and kept fighting with the buckle, all the while wishing that she were anywhere else in the universe at that precise instant.

"You're not doing it right," someone said from above and behind her. A trooper bent over her seat and unlocked the recalcitrant clasp with a practiced ease. "You better learn how to do that," she warned her. "Or someday you might find yourself trapped in a burning shuttle."

Kaly looked up into the face of the same Marine who had stopped her from firing on the Hriss patrol, and smiled gratefully.

"I see that you decided to choose a life of excitement and adventure for yourself," the woman remarked dryly. "But if you don't get your act together real quick, girlie, it's not going to be a very *long* life. Now, where were you supposed to report?"

"No one told me, ma'am," Kaly replied, standing and gathering up both her carry-bag, and what shreds still remained of her dignity. "They just said to get in the shuttle and go 'upside.'"

"*Ma'am?*" the Marine laughed, "Do I *look* like an officer to you? I *work* for a living! It's Troop Leader, girl! You get that right. Now, let's go see if someone is coming along to collect you."

Kaly followed her out of the shuttle and into a passage that she presumed was the receiving bay of the mother ship. A sign on the bulkhead confirmed this.

It read: "*Welcome aboard the USSNS Pallas Athena, SBC 1323.*" Another Marine stood underneath the sign, her hands on her hips, watching them as they came aboard.

"It looks like someone's waiting for you, after all. Good luck in your new life," the trooper said, clapping her on the shoulder. "Maybe we'll party together again like we did downside, *yah?*" She left Kaly alone with her escort.

"Are you N'Deena?" the new woman asked. Kaly nodded.

"Good. They told me some fresh meat had signed up. I'm Corporal n'Valri. Follow me. I'll get you a rack and show you where you can stow your gear." Without waiting to see if she was complying or not, the Corporal turned smartly on her heels and started off down the passage.

Kaly trotted after her, and by the time they reached the Marine Stores, she was out of breath and completely disoriented by the seemingly endless number of corridors that they had negotiated. A bored-looking Private was at the receiving window for the Stores, and looked up at her, clearly waiting for her to do something, but Kaly was completely clueless.

"Well? Give her your knapsack," N'Valri finally urged.

Kaly handed the bag over and the Private gave her a pile of grey fatigues and a small electronic chit in return. The girl stood there for a moment, not quite sure what was expected of her next.

N'Valri shook her head slowly in amusement. "Downsiders," she said disparagingly. The Private at the window laughed with her.

"That is your new u-n-i-f-o-r-m," she said, speaking to her like she was an infant or a half-wit. "Change into it and turn your civilian clothing over to the stores clerk here. She'll stow them with your knapsack. You can use that restroom over there if you need privacy."

Kaly obediently went inside the small chamber, and quickly donned the ill-fitting dull-grey uniform. When she came back out, she handed over her clothing to the Private. Her *civilian* clothing she reminded herself. From now on, she was a Recruit Trainee.

The Corporal looked her over with a critical eye. "Well, that's a *slight* improvement. At least you don't look too much like a refugee anymore, or a *can-scrubbie*. I imagine you're probably hungry."

Kaly nodded.

"Come on, I'll show you where the mess is. It may not be food like what you're used to, but it's hot and it'll fill you up."

After a brief breakfast in the Marine Mess, N'Valri escorted her to the ship's medbay to start her processing. Kaly didn't understand what this meant until she arrived.

The medics subjected her to every kind of test imaginable, and by the time she had departed, the area around her inocular was numb from all of the immunizations and samples that they'd taken from her. Her processing was far from over though. N'Valri led her to another part of the ship, which she learned was the library. A Navy crewwoman was on duty, and she assigned them to an empty computer station. Then the Corporal brought up what Kaly realized was some kind of test on the holo-screen.

"This is the CAFAT program," N'Valri informed her. "The Combined Armed Forces Aptitude Test. It's designed to assess your skills and help you to select your MOS."

"My MOS?" Kaly asked.

"Your job in the Marines," the woman replied. "You don't think everyone in the Marines is a ground-pounder do you? There's all sorts of jobs in the Corps and this test helps determine which ones you're best suited for."

"But I *want* to be a ground-pounder!" Kaly insisted.

"Really?" N'Valri asked incredulously. "Well, before you declare *that* for your MOS, take a look at the other jobs first. Then if you decide you don't want them, and your heart is still set on being a ground-pounder, just make sure to answer every test question wrong, and while you're at it, find a way to break the terminal. That should give you the qualifying score you'll need for Mobile Infantry Specialist."

Kaly gave her a bewildered look, and the Corporal clapped her on the shoulder and laughed.

"I'm just *kidding* girl! Do the best you can, and if you want MIS, then declare it when the CAFAT asks you. But if you want my advice, go for a support specialty. You'll be a lot happier and you'll live a *lot* longer. I'll come get you when the test is over." With that, the Corporal left her at the terminal.

The CAFAT test covered everything that she'd learned (or had tried to learn) in her primary education, along with basic intelligence tests and problem solving exercises. At the very end, the program calculated her score and presented a list of jobs that were available to her.

Kaly was tempted to locate the MOS for Mobile Infantry Specialist and get it over with, but she did as N'Valri had instructed, and dutifully went through the list. Some of the jobs were obvious, while others had obscure titles that utterly mystified her. Fortunately, the entries were interactive, and the program soon helped her to understand each job and its basic responsibilities. But in the end, none of them appealed to her like the Mobile Infantry Specialist did. When the program finally asked her to declare her choice, Kaly made it.

Right on time, N'Valri arrived to escort her to her bunk assignment. "I see you stuck with your decision," she sighed, glancing over at the holo-screen. "Oh well. You can't say that I didn't try to warn you. Let's get you down to Five-Bar and get you settled."

Kaly gave her another puzzled look, and the Corporal explained.

"'Five-Bar' is the unofficial name for the deck set aside for the Marines on an Isis class ship," she said. "That's where we stay when we're not doing something else. It's nice, just like home."

For some reason, the woman found this highly amusing and laughed. Without elaborating, she led Kaly through another series of corridors and down a lift to the Marine Quarters.

Five-Bar proved to be a series of large rooms or "pods" as the Corporal referred to them, separated by common areas, and restroom facilities. Each of the pods was subdivided by rows of partitions, and in each of these were niches with beds inside of them, stacked two high.

Every bed had drawers underneath it for storage, and there was shelf space above the head and foot, and along the interior wall, which offered additional places for stowing personal effects and small items. They also had their own overhead lights, and privacy drapes, many of which Kaly saw, had been replaced by their occupants with colorful fabrics. And at the end of each row of sleeping spaces, set in the bulkhead, were large lockers for heavier gear.

The Corporal guided her through the pods until they reached a partition in the very last one, and indicated the bed there.

"This is your rack until you ship out for Basic Training," N'Valri said indicating the space.

"My 'rack'?"

"Your bed," she told her. "That's what we call it in the Marines. You've got a whole new language to learn, girl."

"Yes. Thank you, ma'am," Kaly said.

N'Valri shook her head. "Goddess, I'd forgotten just how much a hatchie has to learn. Get this in your head: I'm no 'ma'am', hatchie. I'm just a Corporal. 'Ma'am's' are officers, lieutenants and above."

Kaly blushed as she realized that she had just made the same error that she had with the Troop Leader. "Yes, Corporal," she replied. Then she asked, "Corporal, what's a 'hatchie?'"

"Oh you should get *very* used to being called *that*," N'Valri answered. "That's what all new recruits are. It's short for 'hatchling,' which is what you are; still wet behind the ears from your mama's belly, and brand new to the universe. But, trust me, they'll get you dried out *real good* on Hella's World."

N'Valri started to leave, but when she saw that the girl was still standing there without the faintest idea of what to do next, she paused.

"I'll tell you what," she said, "Since you don't have anything to do until you get to Basic except lie here, I have two choices. I can dream up *shess*-work for you, or I can give you a leg up. What'll it be? I'm not going to make the choice for you, but I'd strongly suggest taking the leg up."

"A leg up?"

"Yes, something to help you prep for Basic. I'll look around and see if I can get my hands on an extra copy of the Grey Book for you. It'll help you start learning about being a Marine."

"Thank you, Corporal!" Kaly said earnestly.

"Don't thank me," N'Valri replied. "That way you might actually learn something and I won't have to worry about you getting under my feet. You see? There's something in it for both of us, *klaar*?"

"Yes, Corporal."

"I'll also dig up a pathminder for you so that you can find your own way around the ship," the Corporal added.

"So that you don't have to lead me around?"

"Now, you're getting it! I can see we're going to get along just *great*! Just remember to stay out of the restricted areas and leave everyone alone to do their jobs. And if an emergency happens, do what you're told and don't try to play the heroine. That'll just get you and everyone around you *kakked*, zat klaar?"

"*Klaar*, Corporal."

Sometime later, another Marine, a Private from the look of her, brought Kaly a holoreader with a copy of the Grey Book on it. "The Book" as it was nicknamed, covered everything from basic ranks, occupational specialties, Marine values, drills, and even military law. In short, everything that she would be expected to know in order to graduate Basic.

Kaly tore into The Book eagerly, trying to devour all the information that it contained in just one sitting. After just a few hours of trying however, her head was spinning. She hadn't counted on *just* how much there was to know.

That night, as she lay on her rack staring up at the plastic ceiling above her, she fought to suppress her excitement, and her rising apprehension. Just before lights out, the Corporal had returned and informed her that their ship would be rendezvousing the following day with another, smaller vessel that was heading towards her ultimate destination, the USSMC Marine Training Facility on Hella's World. From the way the Corporal and the The Book had described the process, her training there wasn't going to be easy by any means, and many who went through it, ultimately failed to meet the challenge.

"I'll make it," she vowed. "I'll make it and I'll be a Marine."

USSNS *Pallas Athena*, In Orbit, Persephone, Demeter System, Sagana Territory, United Sisterhood of Suns, 1043.01|05|04:33:31

When the relief Battle Group arrived, Lilith and Katrinn were standing by on the bridge. The sitscreens showed an *Isis*-Class supercruiser and four smaller *Chandi*-Class cruisers coming out of Null, followed in train by a trio of vessels bearing the familiar red pentagram of the Red Star Relief Organization.

A holo of Commander Shaaron n'Dani of the *Pelé*, Battle Group Silver, appeared before them. "*Bian dea*, Commander ben Jeni," she said. "My apologies for the long delay in getting here, but we had to wait for the Red Star ships."

The civilian disaster relief organization typically handled situations like Persephone, and Lilith understood N'Dani's situation perfectly. With increased Hriss raids on outlying colonies, the Red Star had their work cut out for them, and their resources were stretched thin. The little group of ships following the battle group had probably been gathered together from several neighboring Elants.

"Not a problem, Commander n'Dani," she replied. "We're glad to see you, and I know that the refugees will feel the same way. Will you require anything from us before we depart?"

"No, ma'am," N'Dani answered. "In fact, I was given orders to tell you to return to Rixa without delay. Something's coming up and they wanted your battle group to rest up and rearm for it."

"Well, you won't get any argument from us," Lilith smiled. Shore leave sounded very good to her. "We'll be under-weigh in half an hour. Good luck on Persephone, Commander. They're pretty shot-up down there."

"Thank you, Commander. And good luck with whatever it is that Rixa has planned." N'Dani cut the connection.

Lilith turned to her second "Well, Kat? It seems that we may have a little vacation time on our hands when we get back to Rixa. Any plans?"

"I'm of a mind to go home for a bit," the Zommerlaandar replied. "It's been too long since I've seen the farm. How about you?"

"I'm not sure," Lilith said, considering her options. She didn't have many. Her Helmsmistress, Caleda bel Tridis, had offered to take her to visit the deep deserts of her motherworld, Kevan, on their next leave, but the prospect of what would probably turn out to be a hot and dirty experience looking at a lot of bare rocks and sand didn't overly thrill her. And Quela bel Heela, her Environmental Systems Chief, had offered to show her the sights on Thermadon, but Lilith wasn't in the mood for the frenetic pace that the Capitol tended to set.

"Well, why not come with me?" Katrinn offered. Although she'd extolled the virtues of Zommerlaand to her many times, Lilith had never joined her Second on her infrequent visits there.

"You know, maybe that *would* be a nice trip," Lilith agreed. "All right, Kat, my answer is yes. I suppose it's high time that I saw this paradise of yours."

"Gaanskaa gaad," Katrinn said. "I'll tell Navcom to send word to my folks. You'll like the farm."

130

USSMC Training Facility, 75th Training Battalion, Hella's World, Hecate System, Artemi Elant, United Sisterhood of Suns, 1043.01|06|03:43:33

The final leg of Kaly's journey to Hella's World was aboard a crowded shuttle launched from the naval transport ship, the USSNS *Madeline Moore*. The vessel was packed with new recruits and the air fairly crackled with their collective anticipation. Kaly, crammed in the middle of an aisle of seats did her best to stay relaxed, but with two hours to go before they were downside, this was hard to manage. Her mind was going at light speed, alternating between fear and elation.

One of her neighbors, a sophisticated-looking dark haired woman several years her senior, sensed this and smiled at her.

"Don't worry," she said, "We'll get there soon enough. Enjoy the time you have right now. Trust me, you'll look back on your last few hours as a civilian and miss them."

Kaly smiled. "I'm just a little nervous, I guess."

"We all are," her companion assured her. "This is a big step, no matter who you are. I know what it's like. I went partway through Basic when I was about your age, and then I opted out. After a few years, I realized what a mistake I'd made and re-upped. Now, here I am. The name's Jana, by the way. Jana bel Anny. What's yours?"

"Kaly n'Deena."

"Pleased to meet you, Kaly. Where are you from?" Bel Anny inquired.

"Persephone," she replied in a quiet voice.

"Persephone!? Wasn't that where—?"

"Yes," Kaly answered, her features clouding.

"I'm sorry," Bel Anny said. "I suppose you're going to get a lot of women asking you about that."

"It's fine," Kaly responded. "Really." She realized that she should have known that the raid might have made the news. And that people, being people, would have questions about what had happened there. It was something that she was going to have to get used to, she realized, at least until everyone's attention wandered off to something else.

"Where are you from?" she asked, changing the subject.

"Thermadon," Bel Anny replied. "I'm a city girl from the Apollonia District. And this is my friend Berta Enggredsdaater, fresh from the wheat fields of Zommerlaand." Bel Anny indicated a large blond woman to her left. "She doesn't talk much."

The giantess rewarded Kaly with a short nod and half a smile.

"And in the next seat over, hiding behind her, is Lena n'Gari. She's from over Esyllt way, in the Marpesa Elant."

An attractive redhead with a girlish band of freckles painted across her face, leaned out from her seat and smiled shyly. If anything, N'Gari seemed even younger than she was, and Kaly wondered if the petite girl had lied about her age to get into the Marines.

"It looks like we're from just about every corner of the Sisterhood," Bel Anny observed. "We're some funny looking bunch, *nyah?*"

Kaly had to giggle. Bel Anny was right; their little group was probably the most mismatched collection of would-be warrioresses that she could have ever imagined.

"So? What's your MOS going to be when you get out of Basic?" Bel Anny asked.

Kaly replied without hesitation. "Mobile Infantry Specialist."

"Goddess help us! She's as *warpy* as we are," Bel Anny laughed. "We're all going for Mobile Infantry. Hey, maybe we'll be in the same training platoon together! That would be great! Hella's World is a One Station Unit Training Base. That means they train for Basic *and* Mobile Infantry. What do you think?"

"Yeah, maybe we will," Kaly agreed. "That would be good." She liked Bel Anny, and her friends, and she said a little prayer to the Goddess that the woman's wish would be granted.

***

The shuttle touched down on Hella's World, and the egress hatches opened out onto a blast furnace of a planet. A thick wave of hot air penetrated the cabin immediately. Everyone, including Kaly, broke into an instant sweat.

"Alright hatchies!" someone yelled from the front of the shuttle cabin, "grab your gear and get your asses off this shuttle *now*! *Burn it!*" A tough looking woman in grey fatigues, and wearing a Troop Leader's insignia, came down the aisle as Kaly hurried to undo her seatbelt.

"Get the *fek* up hatchie or I'll rip you right out of that seat!" the woman screamed. Kaly quickly found the catch, and the thing released itself without a fight. She sprang out of her seat immediately and rushed past the woman to the exit with the other recruits.

Outside, another Troop Leader was waiting for them, hollering at the top of her lungs for everyone to form up and then run with their gear as she led the way. Kaly ran for all she was worth, not sure what was going to happen next.

The terrified group left the tarmac and sprinted through a collection of small buildings until they reached a large assembly area with neat rows of footprints painted on the concrete. There, the recruits were ordered to drop their gear and find a spot to stand on.

A trio of Drill Instructors stood silently in front of the painted spaces, their hands clasped smartly behind their backs. From her Grey Book, and the conversations that she had had with Corporal n'Valri, Kaly knew that these three women, whom the Corporal had nicknamed 'the Three Fates', were going to be their training instructors for the duration of Basic.

When everyone had found their places, the Senior Drill Instructor stepped forwards. She wasn't the tall Zommerlaandar that Kaly had pictured in her mind when she'd imagined what a Senior DI would look like. Instead, she was short and dark, and Kaly guessed that she was a Kalian.

Despite her small stature, however, Kaly could tell that under her perfectly pressed grey fatigues, every centimeter of her was hard muscle. And despite the oppressive heat, there was not a drop of sweat anywhere on the woman.

The DI looked over the recruits with her small, dark eyes and smiled, but there was nothing friendly about her expression. "On behalf of our commanding officer, Col. Rayna n'Pela and the 75th Training Battalion," she said, "welcome to Hella's World, ladies.'

"You are now members of Training Platoon Carli, Company 1403, and you have been given the privilege of training here with us. Our motto is; *'That which does not kill you makes you stronger. And that which does kill you makes you useless to the Corps.'* You will commit these words of wisdom to your memory.'

"*If* you complete your training, you will be privileged to wear two emblems on your uniform. The first will be the insignia of the Sisterhood Marines; the sun, sword and the starship. The second will be the Eye of the Goddess.'

"The sun, sword and the starship embody the mission of the Corps: the sun for the worlds that we are willing to give up our lives to protect, the sword for our unwavering defense, and the starship for our mobility and readiness.'

"The Eye is a symbol that tells everyone that you graduated from the toughest Marine training facility anywhere in the Sisterhood, Hella's World. Whoever sees these two emblems together on your uniform will know immediately that you are one of the best of the best of the Corps.'

"My name is Senior Troop Leader Rani sa'Tela. My associates here are Troop Leader Lisa n'Vera and Troop Leader Jeni n'Teri." Sa'Tela inclined her head towards the two women standing behind her.

Collectively, the three of them were a study in contrasts. Where Sa'Tela was small and dark, N'Vera was tall, pale and bony, with what looked like a permanent frown of disapproval etched on her long face. N'Teri on the other hand, was a petite blond with delicate features, and of the three, looked the friendliest, or at least the most forgiving.

Sa'Tela continued. "We will be your trainers for the next six weeks. From now on, you will address us, and any Instructor that you meet, as 'ma'am'.'

"Our objective is to train you to become Marines. You have our solemn promise that we will not hold anything back from you to achieve this goal. We will push you to what you think are your limits, and well beyond them. What you will learn here will save your lives and the lives of your teammates--and *teamwork*, ladies, is what it's all about. Does anyone have any questions?"

Someone down the line was actually stupid enough to ask something. Sa'Tela marched right up to the woman, stopping just centimeters from her face.

"Button the *fek* up, hatchie!" she hollered, pecking the recruit in the forehead with the brim of her hat with every word, "I said *anyone*. And you're not *anyone* until you are a *Marine* and you are *not* a *Marine* yet! Just for *that* everyone will hit the deck and give me 50 push-ups right now!"

The other two DI's, who had been waiting quietly through all of this, suddenly exploded into action, screaming furiously at everyone to get down on the hot pavement and perform the exercise. Kaly threw herself down before either of the women noticed her, wincing as the oven-hot pavement seared her hands.

The rest of the day went by in a blur of running all over the base with the DI's hot on everyone's heels, yelling at the top of their lungs. While Troop Leader n'Vera proved to be just as horrible as Kaly had imagined, N'Teri completely transformed herself into a terrifying duplicate of the other DIs, fiercely barking out orders at the new trainees at every step, and showing them no mercy whatsoever.

The platoon's first stop was what was called the "reprieve room." Here, the recruits were told to empty their personal luggage and declare any contraband that they were carrying. This Kaly learned, was everything from candy, to personal realie players, to weapons. When she opened up her issue carry-sack for inspection, she was glad that she had already given up her personal effects back on the *Pallas Athena*.

For the most part, the items that her fellow recruits declared were fairly innocent, but one woman had actually brought a large fighting knife with her from her motherworld, and another recruit had had some *aska* root on her. These items were confiscated like everything else that the Corps deemed inappropriate, with a stern warning that from that point forwards, anyone caught in possession of contraband items would face prosecution in a military court and spend their time in the stockade.

With that, the recruits were quick-stepped over to the MedBay and underwent medical exams. After being poked, prodded, scanned and having their inoculation records re-confirmed, it was on to Stores, where everyone turned in their civilian clothing and received their recruit training clothes,

135

personal kits and naturally, new holocopies of the Grey Book. Even Kaly, who had already been through much of this already, had to repeat the procedure, simply for procedure's sake. The only bright points were that the holoplayer that she received was new this time, and her replacement fatigues actually came closer to fitting her.

As soon as everyone had finished, the platoon was hustled over to the chow hall and given their first Marine meal. Like every other structure on the base, this was a large prefabricated building with only a nod towards any conveniences. Just like the *Athena*, the dining arrangement was cafeteria-style, with long rows of steel tables for the recruits to eat their common meals at.

Kaly and the others were ordered to line up at the serving area and 'requisition' themselves a tray. Once everyone had gotten one, they were allowed to proceed and fill them, but with one caution; *everything* that went on the tray had to be eaten. Anything, Sa'Tela informed them, that was left over would be considered waste and the offending recruit would face punishment detail.

Kaly wasn't terribly hungry after all the running around, but she already knew better than to refuse to eat. She was also equally careful not to let herself take more than she could really finish as she filed down the line of servers.

At the end of the line, a Corporal directed her over to a nearby table and told her to wait there with her companions. After the entire platoon had finished assembling, they were ordered to sit. Enggredsdaater took her seat, and then made the innocent mistake of starting in on her meal. That was when she learned the hard way that everything in the Marines was done by command.

"What the *fek* are *you* doing?" Sa'Tela screamed, grabbing the woman's tray and flipping it onto the floor. The big Zommerlaandar looked up at the DI, utterly bewildered.

"You were told to *sit!* You were *not* told to *eat!* Get your big ass down and give me 50. Now!" Sa'Tela commanded. While Enggredsdaater dropped onto the puddle that had once been her meal and began performing the exercise, the DI put her hands on her hips and addressed the platoon.

"Ladies, let's get something *completely* clear: no one eats, sleeps or *shets* unless they are given the *order* to do so. From this point on everything, and I mean *everything*, will be done by the numbers and *on command!* Now, begin eating. You will stop eating on my two minute mark."

At exactly two metric minutes and zero seconds, Sa'Tela called the time. Kaly and most of the platoon had managed to consume everything on their trays. But, just as Kaly had suspected would happen, a couple of women hadn't finished. For this infraction, they were ordered to hoist their trays over their heads, and overturn them. Then, with their uneaten food dripping down onto their heads, they were sent off to run ten laps around the huge mess hall with Troop Leader n'Vera barking out abuse as she followed behind them.

Watching this, everyone wondered for the thousandth time if they were going to make it. If something as small as the size of a meal, or failing to finish it, could bring such swift and terrible punishment, none of them were certain they were ready for what lay ahead.

None of them, except Kaly. *I'll make it,* she told herself, repeating the vow that she had made on the *Athena. I'll get through this.*

***

That night, well after sunset, the new recruits of Training Platoon Carli stumbled like the undead into what would become their home for the next six weeks; a narrow prefab barracks with two long rows of plain metal bunks. There, they were each assigned a 'battle sister'. This person was to accompany them wherever they went. Like everything else, a stern warning came with the pairing. Anyone found without their battle sister would be forced to carry around a special 77 kilogram dummy that the DI's referred to as "Big Marji" for a full ten hours following the offense.

In Kaly's case, her battle sister turned out to be Lena n'Gari, and she praised the Goddess for this small favor. She was already beginning to spot the women who would be the troublemakers and the complainers, and she was glad that the little redhead was to be her partner instead. The two women quickly negotiated occupancy of the top and bottom racks, and then

137

the Troop Leader gave everyone formal permission to 'board' their racks and sleep.

Kaly climbed up into her bed, feeling like an old woman. Her body hurt like it never had before. Her skin was sunburned and everything else ached. Even her bones seemed to be in pain.

To add to the misery, her scalp itched fiercely. The first thing that recruits lost right along with their personal identity was their hair. This had been shaved off somewhere between the medical exam and getting their basic training gear issued out. When her hair did grow back, it would only be allowed to grow as long as Marine regulations allowed it to, or be confined to a tight, orderly bun. *And Goddess help any follicle that strays out of formation,* Kaly thought with a weak smile.

"It looks like the Goddess granted our wish," Bel Anny whispered tiredly from the rack across from hers, "We all got to be in the same platoon together. Enggredsdaater and I got partnered, and I see you and N'Gari were put together."

Kaly just nodded in reply, afraid to speak and alert the DI's that someone was not sleeping as ordered.

Bel Anny shrugged indifferently at her silence, and then winced as a muscle reminded her that it had been abused far beyond tolerance. She had been one of the ones who had been singled out all day by the Drill Instructors for push-ups and other forms of torture.

"Ouch!" she winced, "Now *that* hurt! Oh well, this will get easier as we go along." Kaly pulled her blanket over her, desperately hoping that Bel Anny was right.

She had barely fallen asleep when the lights came back on, accompanied by the loud clashing of metal on metal.

"Rise and shine, hatchies!" Senior Troop Leader Sa'Tela hollered, beating a metal mess tray with a large spoon. "Get your asses up and *stand-to!*"

Kaly stumbled out of her rack with the rest of the hatchies, and ran up to the painted line on the floor, doing her best to stand at attention. Sa'Tela and her fellow DI's quickly marched down the line. Reaching the end, they stopped.

"If this is what is supposed to pass for standing-to, then I fear for the Corps," Sa'Tela remarked scornfully. "Obviously, you need some instruction. I am now going to tell you how to stand at proper attention. Follow my words and do *exactly* as I say." She walked slowly down the length of the room. "Stand straight, head up, chin in, shoulders back. Relax your knees."

Everyone tried to follow the DI's commands, but a few didn't quite make the grade, including Kaly. "I said *relax* your knees, hatchie! You lock them up like that and you'll find yourself passing out on the parade ground! Now, heels together, feet at a forty five degree angle, arms at your sides, elbows in, fingers curled and touching your pant legs. *That* is the proper way to stand-to."

The instructors spent the next three minutes drilling the platoon; repositioning limbs, and correcting their head angles until everyone met with their approval.

"All right. That's more like it," Sa'Tela finally announced. "Now we can move on to our next item of business. She gestured towards Troop Leader n'Vera, who held up an uncomfortable-looking garment that they all instantly recognized.

"This, hatchies, is the Corps approved brassiere, which was issued to you when you arrived. It is also an item that I have observed that some among you are *not* wearing today. Hatchies, you *will* wear it at all times, and especially for *all* phases of your physical training.. It *is* also considered part of your uniform at *any* other time.'

"You may have had the luxury as 'civilians'," she went on, frowning with obvious distaste for the term, "to let your tits fly around wherever they wanted to go, but that *is not* how we do things in the Corps! You *will* use this approved device and anyone that I find *not* wearing it will find themselves on punishment detail, right along with your Platoon Leader. *Anyone* who sustains an injury to said tits because they did not do as they were ordered, will have a one way trip to the stockade medbay for damaging Sisterhood property, which, hatchies, is what your bodies are now considered."

N'Vera walked down the line, showing the bra to everyone. Kaly wanted to groan, recalling how uncomfortable the thing was to wear for any length of time. But instead, she kept her eyes straight ahead, and her protests to herself. On Persephone, she had worked in the fields with her fellow colonists, and, like most of the other women in the platoon, she had also taken gymnastics as part of her basic education. She knew, as well as they did, that Sa'Tela, and by extension, the Corps, was right. The hideous thing was absolutely essential for the kind of hard PT that the Marines engaged in.

"That is the only warning I will give you about this part of your uniform," Sa'Tela concluded. "I have one other matter that also needs to be discussed. A number of you hatchies appear to have come from worlds where personal hygiene and proper spacesuit wear have not made acquaintance with one another.'

"Well, ladies, here in the Corps, the proper wearing of Marine Battle Armor, in all its forms, includes the shaving of all body surfaces that might require sensor attachment. For those of you who do not have any clue what this means I will explain it just once." She held up a razor and showed it around the room.

"Ladies, this tool was also issued to you along with your bra when you arrived. You will use it to shave your bodies, including your legs and under your arms *every* day. Any *Hairy Mary* that I find who has not done this, and done it thoroughly, will find themselves on punishment detail right alongside the hatchies who did not wear their bra. I will *not* have my recruits looking like a bunch of *fekking neomen!* Is that clear?"

"Ma'am, yes, ma'am!" everyone responded.

"Excellent. You now have two minutes to find your bras and the razors in your kits and get yourselves *properly* dressed *and* cleaned up for PT. You then have two more minutes to get this sorry-assed excuse for a barracks ready for inspection. Now, *burn it, hatchies!*"

With that, the entire platoon exploded into a mass of confusion as the recruits did their best to get dressed and make up their racks in the limited time allotted to them. There were more than a few collisions as everyone moved to get the job done before the DI's called a halt.

At exactly four minutes, zero seconds, Sa'Tela ordered everyone to form up again. Then she walked the line, finding something wrong with everyone's rack.

"*Unacceptable!*" she roared, pulling a bed completely apart and throwing its components onto the floor. "Completely unacceptable! Hatchie, you will remake this rack! And Goddess help you if you don't do it up the Marine way! I will now show all of you that way and you *will* all listen because I will only show you once."

Sa'Tela then proceeded to demonstrate the proper manner of making up the bed, folding the sheets to a crisp perfection. Watching her, Kaly had to admit that the end product that she produced was far superior to anything anyone else in the platoon knew how to make.

The DI was not finished with her lesson yet. She reached into her fatigue pocket next, and produced a Kalian *rupa*, holding up the coin for everyone to see.

Kaly knew what a *rupa* was; although the official currency of the Sisterhood was the credit, a few worlds including, and especially Kali, had retained their old-fashioned hard currency out of tradition, and used it for local trade. But she didn't have the faintest idea how it related to making up a bunk until Sa'Tela tossed the coin into the air and its purpose became horribly clear.

The little alloy disk spun end over end and then landed on the blanket, bouncing off the taught fabric smartly. Before it could descend again, Sa'Tela caught it up in her hand and looked at them. "That should happen with every rack that I inspect," she said gravely. "Does anyone have any questions?"

Wisely, no one answered her inquiry. "Good. Then we all know how to do it correctly. All right, get to it. You have two minutes"

While everyone bent to their work, Sa'Tela paced the floor like an exotic predator waiting for her chance to strike. Then she called the time and inspected the results.

She subjected each bed to her coin test, and found several that were still below her standard. Yelling more expletives, she tore off their linens and ordered their owners to join them on the floor and perform push-ups until her inspection was done, or she had decided they had had enough punishment.

Finally, it was Kaly's turn. The DI scrutinized every crease of her rack closely, and then tossed the *rupa*.

141

Goddess, please bounce! the young woman thought. The coin descended with an almost painful slowness, and after what seemed like an eternity, it made contact with the blanket. To her infinite relief, it rebounded immediately. A slight nod of approval was all the reward that she received, but that was enough for her.

Then the DI inspected her Battle Sister's rack. This also passed muster, and she let herself breathe normally again. Risking a quick glance over at her, she saw that Lena had been just as nervous. And as tempted as they were to smile at one another reassuringly, they remained at rigid attention.

The DI moved onwards to the next pair of racks. When she completed her inspection at last, she allowed the hatchies who had been performing calesthenics to stand up and rejoin the line.

"Most of you managed to do a *passable* job of imitating the way a *real* Marine would make up their rack," she told all of them. "But a few of you did not, and for that you and your fellow recruits will pay. You will now scrub the deck clean, and as you do so, you will keep this one thought in mind; when one member of your team fails, all of you fail with her. This task will be done using your shower towels as follows."

Sa'Tela took a sample towel from N'Vera and rolled it up into a tight roll. "You will roll your towels like this," she said. "You will also fill a bucket with hot, soapy water. Then you will soak your towel in your bucket until the towel is saturated. Then you will get down on the deck and clean it by pushing the towel ahead of you like so."

The Kalian got down on her knees and pushed the towel in front of her, moving forwards while keeping her arms stiff. "Your Battle Sister will follow behind you and dry the deck using the same method with her towel. Now, get to it! I want to see this deck fekking sparkle!"

Kaly and Lena were as shocked by these orders as everyone else. In a day and age when housebots did that kind of work, the idea of actually having to get on one's hands and knees to *scrub* a floor clean with a towel was nothing short of prehistoric. Even so, they held their tongues and bent to their work. Kaly took up the lead running her roll along the floor, with Lena following behind. It was dirty, unpleasant work, and Troop Leader n'Vera kept a close eye on all of them.

142

Bel Anny and Enggredsdaater were working behind them when N'Vera spotted something that she didn't care for. "Is *that* what you call *clean*, hatchies?" she yelled. "*Unacceptable!*" With a kick, she overturned their bucket. Hot soapy water spilled out onto the floor.

"*Completely* unacceptable! Now go refill that bucket and scrub this section again!"

The hapless pair ran off to the latrine to refill their bucket and then returned for another round of scrubbing. This time whatever it was that they had missed on their first pass was absent, and N'Vera stayed silent, but it was clear from the look in her eyes that she would rather have found another fault with their work.

When the platoon had cleaned the entire barracks floor, Sa'Tela called the time. And after a brief re-inspection, she spoke to the platoon again. "One of the things we instill here on Hella's World is teamwork, ladies. You have already started to learn to count on your battle sister, and now you will also learn to count on the rest of your platoon. To help you think like a team, I will now announce your new platoon leader. This person will be your leader, and your liaison with the Instructors. Because of her prior experience in basic, Recruit bel Anny will be the new Platoon Leader. Do not let her, or me, down. Dismissed."

Kaly wasn't sure if congratulations were in order or not, and one glance over at Bel Anny, told her that the woman wasn't exactly overjoyed. If anything, she actually looked a little ill.

CHAPTER 6

It was early in the morning, ship's time, and Maya was sitting on the deck with her back against the bulkhead, staring up at the overhead. Her anger had long since exhausted itself. Now, she was just tired of having nothing to do except sit there.

Her boredom ended when the hatch slid open to reveal the Black Witch. There was no mistaking those full red lips or the shape of her oval face.

Panicked, Maya jumped to her feet, and backed away from her, her heart racing. After their encounter at the port, anything was possible, and had she had the chance, she would have exploited any avenue of escape and bolted. But there were none. She was trapped.

The woman entered slowly, keeping her hands in plain view, and immediately sat herself in the cabin's only chair. There, she quietly crossed her legs and put her hands in her lap.

Maya had been expecting a monster, but her unwanted guest wasn't one. Instead, what she beheld was a tall, slim woman dressed in a black bodysuit that covered her up to her neck, and long matching gloves.

And although her skin was extremely pale, and possessed an odd, iridescent sheen that only made itself obvious when she moved, it wasn't out of place for someone with Nyxian ancestry. The slight epicanthic fold of her eyes, along with her long, jet black hair also suggested that she was part Aran.

Not a monster at all. In fact, under other circumstances, Maya realized that she would have found her to be quite beautiful.

At last, the woman spoke. Her voice was a soft contralto, with only a hint of the predatory timbre that it had possessed at the port.

"Maya n'Kaaryn," she said, using Maya's real name, "My name is Sarah n'Jan, and I think that you know why I am here. We need to talk. We have since we first encountered one another.'

"You know that it is no accident that you felt me under your window. As I told you at the port, you are also a psi. But we are different from one another in a very important way and I think you realize this as well."

Yes, Maya thought fiercely, *I'm not cruel like you.*

144

Sarah smiled, as if she had heard this thought, and went on, "Maya, we are different because I have training and you do not. That is why I am more powerful than you. My talents have been artificially augmented and sharpened by my teachers.'

"I also know that you hate me. It takes no special ability to recognize that. But I am not here to ask you for your forgiveness. I did what I had to at the port. Instead, I have come to offer you a choice of futures.'

"You have two roads open to you. The first is the one that you travel now, surviving on your wits and your raw, untrained talents.'

"This is a short road however, with a certain end. There are others like me, Maya, many others, and some of them would have killed you rather than risk letting a rogue *esper* interfere in any way with their business. This will happen to you unless you make the decision to take another path, and change."

Change? Maya thought, *and become like you?* The very idea filled her with disgust. She kept her tongue however, and only a slight increase in her breathing betrayed her upset.

Sarah sat forwards, just enough to emphasize her point, but without intruding on Maya's personal space. "Yes, Maya, change. And learn; learn to control your abilities, and harness them to their true potential.'

"You know as well as I that this universe of ours is a jungle. It is filled with predators, and you must become a predator yourself or become someone else's prey. Your talents are your teeth and claws, and if you hone them properly, you will transform yourself into something far greater than you can now imagine."

Sarah paused, and let her consider this. Then she went on.

"We are putting in at Ashkele next," she said. "You know this port, don't you?" It wasn't a question and they both already knew the answer.

Ashkele, or the Free City as it was often called, was under the nominal control of the non-human Xee, but in reality it was an open port, governed by no single star-nation.

The city had been built by the Xee in the heart of a planet-wide necropolis left behind by the legendary Drow'Voi, an extinct galaxy-spanning civilization. The Xee religion believed that the blessings of the dead ensured prosperity, and by their reckoning, the vast cemetery had granted this to them in abundance. Whatever the actual causes, Ashkele's wealth was beyond dispute; the city was ranked as one of the richest in the Far Arm.

For Maya however, Ashkele was more than just a burial ground for the Drow'Voi dead. The port city had also been the graveyard of her innocence.

She had been born on an unlicensed agricultural colony, situated in a no-woman's zone of space between the Xee Protectorate and the Sisterhood. On her 12th year, a plague had come and ravaged the little settlement.

To save them, the women had sent their children into the hills with a handful of adult guardians. And by the time the epidemic had finally burned itself out, only the children and their caregivers had managed to survive.

With the colony effectively wiped out, Maya and the other children had been sent to Ashkele for temporary housing at one of the city's multi-species orphanages. Months of diplomatic wrangling had followed this, with Sisterhood and Xee officials arguing over their ultimate citizenship, and custody.

Eventually, the bureaucrats reached an accord among themselves, but by that time it was too late for Maya. She had run away and was roaming Ashkele's streets with other cast-offs.

The port had been a brutal place, wholly unlike the cities of the Sisterhood. What was considered extreme and unthinkable in the Sisterhood was commonplace in the Free City. Slavery, murder-for-hire, drug addiction, prostitution and a host of other evils were the norm in a place that was tenanted by dozens of races, each with their own concepts of moral conduct, and with no one to really police them.

The pressure to stay alive in such an environment had destroyed the Maya-That-Had-Been as thoroughly as the plague that had wiped out her motherworld. Only her talents, and her wits, had allowed her to survive long enough to become a teenager, and find a way for herself off-planet aboard a merchanter bound for the Sisterhood.

Ashkele held no fond memories.

"Yes," Maya finally said grimly. "I know it."

"I am not going to confine you here any longer," Sarah informed her. "You will be free to do what you will when we reach Ashkele. There, you may go your own way, or you can remain with the *JUDI* and go a *new* way.'

"If you decide to stay, you will have a place with us, and you will also train. I must warn you that the training will be hard, and in the end it is possible that you will hate me even more than you do now. I can assure you however, that if you take the road that I have offered you, you will find the rewards at the end worth any hardship that you might suffer along the way.'

"I will leave the final decision to you, and I suggest that you weigh your choice carefully. In the meantime, you have the freedom of the ship— unless you create problems for us. I think that you know what will happen in that eventuality."

Seeing that she understood, Sarah rose and left the chamber. The hatch remained open behind her.

Ashkele Free Port, Hallasa System, Frontier Zone, Xee Protectorate,
1042.12|06|05:83:33

Although Maya wasn't aware of it, she had something else in common with Sarah beyond her psychic abilities. This was her sense of smell. While she didn't possess an augmented olfactory ability like Sarah did, it was still quite keen and it played a powerful role in shaping her awareness, and associations.

As she walked down the *JUDI's* cargo ramp, the aroma of Ashkele hit her nostrils. The Free City was a heady mixture of chemicals, human and alien waste, machine exhaust, and a thousand strange spices, all overlaid with the flinty scent of the omnipresent dust.

Smelling this mélange, it was hard for her not to believe that she hadn't somehow been transported back in time. But she wasn't a frightened runaway scrabbling to survive any longer, she reminded herself. She knew how to take care of herself now. Raising her chin determinedly, Maya stepped off the ramp, steeling herself for anything that the city dared to throw at her.

Just as her foot touched the grimy dock plating, Zara called her name. Maya looked back over her shoulder at the old woman, and saw that Captain bel Lissa, Hari and Sarah were all standing with her at the cargo bay. Bel Lissa's expression was unreadable, Hari's was plainly impatient, and Sarah's was hidden beneath her hood. Even so, Maya could feel the woman's eyes watching her.

Zara walked down and handed her a holocard. "The Captain wanted me to make sure that you got this," she explained.

Maya took it from her and examined it. The text was animated, scrolling over the card's face at random intervals until she tilted it slightly. Then the words stopped, and centered themselves to read: *"CJG Enterprises, 13.8 Street of the Joyous Newly Dead, Ashkele Free Port, ComX: 13.8.3.055.7.889."*

"If you decide you want to join up with us, you can find us there. There's a pathminder built into the card if you need it."

Maya stuffed the holocard into her jumpsuit pocket. "I think I can find it on my own." In truth, she didn't recall exactly how to reach the Street of the Joyous Newly Dead, but she was fairly certain that it lay to the west end of the city, and somewhere near the Square of the Twelve Golden Corpses of Prosperity.

Not that she actually intended to ever go there. She had other plans for herself and they didn't include Sarah, or the *C-JUDI-GO*. Without another backwards glance, she walked briskly away from the merchanter, knowing that Sarah was still watching.

Let her, she thought defiantly. After what she'd been through, she had firmly decided that she was not about to accept the woman's offer. Her talents had gotten her through just fine so far, exactly as they were, and Sarah the 'Big Bad Witch' was the last person in the galaxy that she wanted as a teacher. And as much as she wanted a job aboard a smuggler, the *C-JUDI-GO* was not an option.

Not with *her* aboard.

Resolute, Maya walked on until the *JUDI* and her crew had dropped out of both sight and mind, and then got straight to work resuming the hunt that she had begun back on Thermadon. Although the Free City was a miserable place, it did possess two redeeming qualities; an utter lack of customs officers, and an abundance of smugglers who didn't bother to hide their profession at all.

She went up to the first vessel that she saw and approached the crew to make her pitch. In sharp contrast to Bel Sharra Memorial Spaceport, the crews in Ashkele were openly armed. Maya was met at the cargo ramp by a tough-looking woman toting a military-issue blast rifle, plainly standing guard while her crewmates worked.

"Help you with something?" the woman asked. Her finger rested lightly along the trigger guard, and it was obvious from the way she held the weapon that she was accustomed to using it, and could bring it to bear in a hurry.

"I'm looking for work," Maya said. "I'm looking for a ship that doesn't mind getting its hands dirty making a few credits."

The woman laughed and exchanged a deprecatory grin with her co-workers. "That'll be the Captain's call, honey-pot. She's busy right now, but I'll call her down. You can tell your lies to her. I don't want to hear them."

"I'll wait," Maya replied, folding her arms. "I've got plenty of time."

The woman cocked an eyebrow at her, and then closed her eyes as she accessed her psiever. "The Captain will be along in a while," she finally announced.

"A while" actually turned out to be thirty standard minutes. If the woman standing guard had seemed a hard sort, the captain looked like she was made of solid stone. She was a short stocky woman, with a leathery complexion, crisscrossed by a fine network of light-colored scars. She came down the ramp with a pronounced swagger, and her eyes had an unfriendly, suspicious gleam.

"Make it fast," the Captain said impatiently. "I've got better things to do today."

Maya took no offense at her brusqueness, and she didn't waste any time. Instead she kept her story short and briefly highlighted her skills and experience.

When she finished, the Captain stroked her chin thoughtfully. "Work as a hand, you say? Do you have any problem hauling glass?"

In fact, Maya did, and she suppressed a profanity. Glass smuggling was a filthy, dangerous business, and if they didn't get killed by the people who supplied it, any Nulltrekker who got caught by the authorities spent a long time in a correctional colony.

But she also had a personal reason to despise the substance. Something that went much deeper than any professional concerns. Glass had been responsible for the death of someone she had loved, and although the pain had dulled over the years, her hatred hadn't.

"Never mind," she said, fighting to keep her emotions in check. "I'll keep looking." The woman on guard laughed, obviously having expected as much.

The Captain scowled at the crewwoman and planted her hands on her hips. "Well," she said, "you won't find many ships here that aren't moving a little crystal, girlie, even if it's just a part of their cargo. If you think you're too good to haul it, then so be it. Come back when you've run out of ships and *maybe* I'll reconsider you--*if* I'm not *too* busy."

"Thanks," Maya replied with a forced smile. "I'll keep your ship in mind."

Disappointed, she moved down the line to the next ship. But her luck stayed poor; the vessel turned out to be a T'lakskalan slaver, and she didn't even risk coming near it, or its sinister reptilian crew.

The one after that was a human ship, but they were also hauling Szalian crystal. The third ship she came to was, oddly enough, a legitimate merchanter from a franchised line, but its Captain wasn't even interested in speaking to her without an initial interview by the company's personnel department. They were located on Thermadon.

Her hunt went on and on like this, with only a few variations in the theme, until by the end of the day, she had run out of ships, and energy. Sitting down in a heap on a bench at the port entrance, she wearily took stock of her situation.

With the exception of the jumpsuit that she wore, all of her personal possessions were light years away, back in her locker in Thermadon City. And aside from the crew of the *JUDI*, she no longer knew anyone in the Free City.

But although it wasn't a large sum by Ashkele standards, she did have credits. Although the Xee possessed a legal tender of their own, they preferred to do business in Sisterhood currency, due to its strength and stability compared to other forms of exchange in the Far Arm.

The rest of Ashkele followed their lead. The only way to get anything was with credits. This at least saved her from having to change her money at one of the Xee banks. Nothing in the Free City was really free, and the Xee charged murderous rates for such transactions.

Given her overall resources, and deficits, the only thing she could do was to find a place to stay for the night, and give the ships another try in the morning. Sleeping at the port, or on the street for that matter, was completely out of the question. There were simply too many chances for theft, robbery, or worse, Maya knew that much from personal experience.

She looked up at the sky, and saw that it was almost dusk. She had to get moving. Being on the street alone, and unarmed, especially after dark, was just as foolish as sleeping there. The Guns, the armed robots that the Xee employed to maintain the appearance of civil order, loosely patrolled the main thoroughfares, but the side streets, and anywhere the Guns were absent, were effectively lawless zones. T'lakskalan press bands prowled those places, capturing anyone that they thought might fetch a good price on the alien black markets, not to mention various types of street gangs, perverts, and a whole host of violent riffraff.

Maya got herself up and made for the port exit. A scan of her inocular there earned her several painful immunizations, but as unpleasant as these were, she wasn't surprised, or unhappy about it. Ashkele was not only one of the busiest crossroads of the galaxy, but it was also one of the filthiest. Unfriendly bugs were simply a given in such an environment.

As soon as the steel bars at the egressway had retracted, she stepped out into the street and sized up the foot and vehicle traffic around her. From the look of the place, the Free City hadn't changed very much, or at least not for the better, she observed. She located a rather battered and battle-scarred omni station nearby, and accessed the device.

The terminal came on, and promptly informed her that the very act of activating it had just cost her two credits, but again she was not surprised. The Xee charged for everything--including information, and overcharged at

151

that. Angry, but helpless as the terminal billed her for every search that she initiated in the local 'plexi, Maya quickly looked over the various fortified inns near the port, and reviewed their prices.

Her heart sank. Prices had been steep before she had left, but now they were reaching for the spacelanes. What little she had in her account simply wasn't enough to afford the lodging and the protection that the inns provided, and she laughed bitterly to herself as one of the establishments described not only its armored, blast-proof building, but proudly listed the many amenities that it offered to its guests.

Might as well promise me Corrissan champagne in a diamond glass, she thought sadly. Plain drinkable water, suited for human consumption, would be expensive enough, and she wasn't even certain that she would be able to afford that. The inns were plainly beyond her budget.

This left her with only one other choice while there was still light in the sky; the Necropolis. As a child, she'd used the vast cemetery as a place to hide and to sleep in in relative safety.

But back then she hadn't been alone. Instead, she had had her fellow urchins to watch her back. Lacking that thin measure of safety, she knew that she had to find a way to get out of the port unnoticed and locate a hiding spot for herself deeper in the ruins than she had ever gone before. In the absence of friends, solitude and concealment would have to suffice.

Fortunately, only the spots closest to the city tended to be occupied, and few beings, human or otherwise, ventured very far beyond them. This was both out of convenience, and fear.

Like any graveyard, the Drow'Voi Necropolis was supposed to be haunted, and Maya recalled many a night when she had thought she had heard the dead, wailing mournfully out in the darkness. Now that she was older, she understood that the eerie cries had actually been the wind, finding its voice in the multitude of crevices, cracks and holes that existed throughout the vast pile of stone. Ghosts didn't frighten her any more. Instead, it was the living that worried her.

As the light continued to fade, she headed away from the port towards a street that she recalled led to the outskirts of the city, and the wide, open expanse that separated Ashkele from the Necropolis.

Three blocks into her journey, an argument spilled out of a tavern, and Maya dodged the two humanoid combatants. One was a T'lakskalan. The dark reptilian creature was arguing with a large furred beast whose race completely defied identification. Whatever the pair was disagreeing about was shouted in alien tongues and equally impossible to determine, but it was obvious that their quarrel was a serious one.

The T'lakskalan gave the furry creature a hard shove, and Maya tried to squeeze by them and gain some distance from the fracas. By now though, a crowd was gathering. It was a mixed group of races from everywhere including the Sisterhood, and her exit was blocked.

Then the T'lakskalan produced a hand-weapon. To his credit, the other humanoid pulled something from under his fur that resembled a gnarled stick and started to bring it to bear on the reptilian. Neither creature got the chance to do anything more than this, though.

A dark, metallic arm pushed Maya aside, and she looked up to see one of the Guns. The matte-black machine had a vaguely humanoid configuration, and a single glowing eye that was fixed on the pair.

Both aliens turned to face the machine and the Gun said something to them on its speakers, but only the furred creature had sense enough to drop its weapon and back away. To Maya's astonishment, the T'lakskalan hissed a challenge at the Gun and stupidly tried to raise its sidearm.

Instantly, a bright, cyan-colored beam shot out from the Gun's eye, hitting the creature squarely in its center mass. The T'lakskalan screamed in agony and attempted to shield itself, but it was a useless gesture. In seconds, its entire form had evaporated into nothingness, leaving only a wisp of smoke and a greasy smudge on the sidewalk to mark where it had once stood.

The Gun pivoted smoothly on its hip-axis, and ranged its deadly gaze over the crowd. It spoke in several languages, ending its message in Standard. "Disperse now," it ordered flatly, "or be subject to disintegration."

Maya didn't need any further incentive, and got away from the scene as fast as possible. Fortunately, the fight had drawn all of the nearby foot traffic to it, and although the crowd was frantically trying to obey the Gun's command, the streets leading away from the tavern were reasonably free of living beings.

After a little searching, she was able to locate the road she had sought, and made her way down it without encountering another soul. With a final glance to see if she was being followed, she stepped off the pavement and onto the soft white sand that stretched from the city's edge out to the ruins.

The Necropolis itself was a gargantuan collection of carved stone towers and walls, many of which had collapsed eons before the Xee had colonized the world. The cyclopean blocks from these ancient catastrophes rested in great piles at the feet of the surviving towers, and where the sands permitted them to exist, roads or giant paths were still visible, leading off towards unknown destinations.

The place had no end. The cemetery covered much of the planet, and where the towers opened up around a square and created an open space, Maya's eyes could see nothing except another group of towers, and another beyond those, until their ranks were lost in the haze. Only the circular area that surrounded Ashkele itself afforded any kind of definite horizon, or open sky.

Out on this flat, the wind blew continuously. It altered the shape of the clean white sands in a constant dance of air, led by the dust devils, which patrolled the place like stray ghosts who had wandered out from the Necropolis. Despite this, Maya was still able to spot some fresh footprints in several places, leading away from the city into the ruins. Someone or something (in the case of the less recognizable tracks) had come the same way, she realized, and recently. More alert than ever, the girl pressed on, hoping that whatever had made the prints was merely seeking shelter for the night like her, and not planning an ambush.

When she reached the edge of the ruins, she picked up the only weapon that she could find, a chipped piece of rock that was lying on the sandy ground. It was better than nothing at all, but only just. Hefting the stone, she moved into the rubble piles, listening carefully to the sounds around her and watching for anything that indicated a threat. But with the exception of tiny rock falls, and the occasional cry of an unknown creature, the Necropolis was silent, and nothing moved within its precincts.

Because this was the outermost edge of the Necropolis, and so close to the port city, the stones around her were covered with graffiti written in several alien languages. These were either sprayed on with paint, or had been etched into the surfaces with tools or energy-cutters. Maya followed the markings, working her way deeper into the shadows.

When the graffiti could no longer be seen, she knew that she had reached the limits of the inhabited areas. From that point on, the only blemishes that she spotted were lichen mottling the stones, and the sandy path ahead of her was unmarred by tracks of any kind except what small animals had left behind.

She was alone at last, but it was nearly full dark by now, and she looked around her for some form of shelter. After a few minutes, she found a triangular opening in the base of one of the nearby towers. It was taller than she was, and the interior was hidden in darkness. From the outside it was impossible to tell how deep the chamber actually went, but the vanishing light offered her no other alternatives. Listening above her for the rumble of an impending collapse, she stepped inside cautiously.

Reaching what she thought was the center of the space, she rose up slowly, and carefully explored the ceiling with her fingers. It proved to be just above her head, but still high enough to allow her to stand upright. In the far wall, illuminated by the feeble light from the entrance, she spotted another triangular hole that led deeper into the tower. With no hand-light to explore it with, she was reluctant to venture any further, and stayed where she was. For better or worse, the anteroom would be home for the night.

It was cold in the chamber, and the thin jumpsuit that she wore did little to retain her body heat. Having no means to make a fire, or warm herself, she sat down in a sandy corner, and drew her knees up to her chin instead. To add to her discomfort, she was also ravenously hungry, and deeply regretted not buying some food for herself when she had had the chance.

Time had not been on her side though, and she made a promise to herself that she would make up for the missed meal in the morning. In the meantime, the night looked like it was going to be a very long one, and she wondered just how much sleep she was actually going to get.

Martin Schiller

Her question answered itself with brief periods of dozing, interspersed with wakefulness when anything around her made a noise. Despite her fitful slumber though, dreams still managed to find her in the darkness.

They were strange visions of the stone towers around her, but eons before they had become ruins. In one, Maya saw the Drow'Voi themselves. The non-humanoid creatures were huge, with irregular forms, and single central eyes that looked out onto the universe with unblinking stares. These great orbs were ringed by smaller secondary eyes, which she somehow knew gave the creatures the ability to perceive bands of light that she could only guess at.

As she watched them, the Drow'Voi flowed up and down the sides of the towers, seemingly in defiance of gravity, and manipulated strange machines with tentacles that sprouted anywhere on their bodies that they willed them to appear.

An eerie collection of sounds emanated from the devices that they controlled, and from the Drow'Voi themselves. They were a series of pure tones that came close to being music, but also seemed to be a form of speech. The sounds were also oddly familiar, and as she listened, she realized that the Xee and the rest of the galaxy were completely wrong about the Necropolis. The ruins were not a graveyard at all, but something else that was just beyond the borders of her ability to comprehend.

Before she could resolve the mystery however, the dream shifted and changed, and Maya suddenly found herself running between the towers. They were ruins again, and something was looking for her among the crumbling piles of rubble. She crouched low, terrified that this unknown force would find her, without knowing exactly why she felt this fear.

Finally, she hid herself behind a pile of stone blocks and risked a glance through a gap in the shattered masonry. A great eye, this time clearly human, took up most of the dark sky above her, and she knew instinctively that it belonged to something terrible beyond reckoning. Then the eye turned in her direction, and to her horror, Maya realized that whatever it was, had found her at last.

She awoke with a start, thinking that another rock fall, or an animal moving nearby had disturbed her fitful sleep. But she was wrong.

Instead, a red beam of light played across the stones, issuing from a spot across from her on the opposite wall. Then Maya realized that the crimson ray was actually shining *through* the wall from somewhere outside and her overtired mind finally recognized it. It was the seeker beam that T'lakskalan slavers used to seek out hidden life forms and it possessed the strange and fearsome ability to penetrate earth and even solid stone to locate its targets.

With only seconds to spare before it found her, she threw herself sideways and scrambled on all fours towards the opening that led deeper into the tower. She had just reached it when the very edge of the beam touched the heel of her shoe.

T'lakskalan seeker beams posessed another unique quality. They not only located living beings through solid objects, but also paralyzed them wherever they made contact with flesh. Her foot went numb instantly, and a triumphant cry issued from a reptilian throat off in the darkness. Maya let out a squeal of terror, and crawled forwards into the passage that led deeper into the tower, dragging her useless foot behind her.

The corridor proved to be narrow and extended only six meters before it abruptly terminated. Back behind her, the seeker beam was swinging around again, and there was the sound of alien feet rasping on the floor of the outer chamber.

At any other time, Maya would have employed her talents to defend herself, but she knew that they were useless against the T'lakskalans. For some unknown reason, the creatures did not react to any form of psychic coercion, and this left her without the only real weapon that she had. As the aliens came nearer, she searched frantically for any means of escape.

Then a high-pitched ping echoed down the corridor, followed by the sound of something metallic bouncing and skittering across the stone. Maya looked down and saw the gas grenade just as it rolled to a stop at her feet. There was a steady hiss, and the passage became choked with a pungent, chemical smell. Dizziness, and then a wave of unconsciousness followed this, and as everything faded away, she became dimly aware that some kind of commotion was taking place in the passage. Before she could form a coherent association however, she had floated off into nothingness.

***

The business card that Maya had been given was more than just a form of advertisement. It also carried a tiny tracking chip that had activated itself the moment she had put it away in her pocket. This had made the job of protecting her all the easier for Skylaar tau Minna.

As a member of the Assassin's Guild in Ashkele, the Nemesian made her living by tracking humanoids, eliminating troublemakers, and sometimes like now, keeping vulnerable targets safe. Having the little tracker to work with had almost made the favor she was doing for Sarah seem like a vacation—until the T'lakskalan's had shown up. For a brief period, she had hoped that the reptilians were after other quarry, but when she saw them use their seeker beam and enter the tower, she knew that her respite was over. It was time to go to work.

She left her hiding place and entered the tower just as the reptilians were approaching the girl's unconscious form. There were three of them, and they were so intent on bagging their catch that they didn't hear her coming up from behind.

Before they could react, she triggered a spring-loaded steel spike attached to the underside of her forearm, and plunged the weapon up and into the back of the nearest T'lakskalan's skull. The spike penetrated its brain, and the other two humanoids finally realized that they were in danger and spun around. But Skylaar had already thrown herself into a shoulder roll.

Landing between them and coming back onto her feet, she slashed out with a knife-hand strike across the throat of the creature to her left. Simultaneously, she dealt a palm strike upwards and sideways to the jaw of the creature's partner. Both of them went down immediately, one strangling on a collapsed windpipe, and the other dead from a broken neck.

Even though they were well beyond posing her any threat, she still kicked away their side arms. Then she used her wrist spike a second time to ensure that they were in fact, safely removed from the universe of the living.

After that, she checked on Maya. The girl was unconscious, but otherwise unharmed, and she knew that the effects of the gas would pass after a few hours.

Leaving her where she lay, Skylaar got to work removing the bodies. Sarah had been quite specific about this. Maya was never to know that she had been followed, or that she had had a protector watching over her.

Finally, when the task was complete, and all traces of the T'lakskalan's had been erased, the Nemesian returned to her hiding place and resumed her silent vigil.

***

Maya sat up, not entirely certain where she was or how she had gotten there. The sight of the corridor and the pale sunlight beyond it brought everything back, and she wondered why she wasn't in the belly of a slaver ship. The effects of the gas grenade made her thoughts fuzzy and difficult to organize, but she was certain that the T'lakskalans had been about to take her prisoner.

The only answer that she could come up with was that something had either frightened them away, or had caused them to shift their hunt elsewhere. *What* that might have been was a complete enigma though, but she had learned never to argue with good fortune. She was free and that was what counted.

She was also determined not to spend any more time in the ruins, and fought off a wave of dizziness to get on her feet. It took a few deep breaths to bring herself under control, but she managed to force the worst of her symptoms back, and stumbled out of the tower.

Even though it was now daytime, this was no guarantee of safety by any means, and she made her way out of the ruins cautiously, alert for any sign of the T'lakskalans, or any other enemy. Her way was unobstructed however, and she reached the sandy border that encircled Ashkele without incident.

When she stepped off the sands and back onto the street, her hunger reasserted itself. It gnawed persistently at her insides as she walked along the pavement and finally, when it became too severe to ignore, she stopped at a street vendor's stall and spent the last of her precious credits on some food.

Her breakfast was a small and expensive piece of unknown meat, impaled on a skewer, and washed down with an equally pricey bottle of water that tasted strongly of chemical disinfectant. The tiny meal proved barely enough to rejuvenate her, but it was all she had the means to purchase.

With her funds now completely exhausted, she headed back to the port. However, once she got there and resumed her hunt, her luck deserted her again. She found herself talking to more glass runners and captains of other ships that she would not, or could not, serve aboard. By the time Ashkele's sun had reached its zenith, she had gone through every ship in the port with nothing to show for her efforts.

Another hungry night in the ruins was all that awaited her. It was either that, risk death by committing a crime, or accept Sarah's offer. Exhausted down to her core, Maya sat down on the same bench that she had occupied only the day before, and wept. She was hungry, and completely out of alternatives.

***

The Free City of Ashkele was divided into separate districts; each with its own distinctive central square dedicated to a Xee God, or Gods. According to the holocard, CJG Enterprises was located near the Square of the Twelve Golden Corpses of Prosperity, and sat roughly in the middle of the Street of the Joyous Newly Dead. Like the other buildings around it, a high wall surrounded the place, keeping out the street noise and protecting the interior from prying eyes, and intrusion.

Approaching it, Maya immediately noticed the small black antennae at the top of the wall, spaced at regular intervals. In between them, the air shimmered slightly, suggesting that a charged field of some kind surrounded the property. Then a *Ginja-bug* approached the area, and when it abruptly turned around, it confirmed her suspicions.

The native insectoids could sense energy fields, and every Ashkelean learned to watch them carefully, Maya included. If the Ginja avoided something, then it was deadly, and a lot of homes and businesses in

160

Ashkele didn't have a problem with employing lethal measures to ensure their security. Clearly, CJG Enterprises was no exception to the local norm.

At least I'll have a safe place to sleep, she thought consolingly.

Mustering up all the pride that she had left, the girl walked up to the entrance. But the door had no buzzer, keypad or doorknob on its surface. Not knowing what else to do, Maya raised her hand to knock.

Before she could rap on the door however, a harsh robot voice spoke from somewhere above her.

"State your business," it demanded. If the residence was like any other in the Free City, Maya knew that there was probably a scanner and a weapon being trained on her at the same time. An involuntary chill went up her spine, but she wasn't about to show fear to a stupid 'bot.

"My name is Maya," she said evenly, "I was told to come here by Sarah."

The sentrybot considered this information and then the door slid open. Maya walked inside the portal with the leaden step of the condemned, dreading her inevitable meeting with the woman. There was no other choice, though, she told herself. Not for the present at least.

The scene that greeted her within was a spacious courtyard, filled with exotic trees and flowers from at least a dozen different worlds. While many of its elements were unfamiliar, she recognized some of them immediately; a small stand of graceful Nyxian *Jhola* trees, brilliantly colored Lamentine dragon-flowers, delicate *Spella* bushes from Corrissa, and Nemesian *S'sihl'ka* grass that was so fine and soft that it took a conscious effort for her not to remove her shoes then and there, and walk barefoot through it. Precise patches of sand, carefully raked into elaborate swirling patterns, broke up these plantings at strategic locations, and deliberately focused her attention towards the most pleasing elements of the place.

And winding through it all was a walkway made from weathered Tetran star stone, its brilliant pockets of tiny gems winking out at her from an otherwise jet-black surface. The stone path traveled sinuously through the garden, past tiny fountains that filled the air with their music, and miniature pools that tantalized her eyes with brief glimpses of luminous Tethyian pinfish.

161

Taken in its entirety, the courtyard exuded a sense of peace and tranquility that caught Maya completely by surprise. The place was clearly the creation of a master gardener, either from Sita or Ara, and definitely *not* the setting that she had expected to find at the home of a smuggler. Or a witch.

Zara met her halfway down the walkway and her old wrinkled face lit up with a smile. "I'd hoped we'd see you again," she said. "Hari'd thought we'd seen the last of you, but I knew better and I told her so. I imagine you'll want to freshen up and get yourself something to eat." The girl signaled her assent, and the older woman guided her into the house.

The interior proved to be just as tasteful and serene as the garden had been. The furniture was old-fashioned, with muted colors, and here and there in the large open living area, Maya spied various artifacts and antiques from a multitude of strange and exotic places. They were the souvenirs of lives spent roaming the stars.

Unable to resist her curiosity, she walked up to a niche in one of the nearer walls. The alcove held a tablet carved from some unknown ivory-colored stone covered in sharp-edged characters that vaguely reminded her of the Babylonian cuneiform she had seen as a schoolgirl.

On an impulse, she raised her hand and reached out to touch the carved symbols. As her fingers came near, the inscriptions suddenly glowed with a soft blue-white light and the room filled with sounds that could have been musical notes.

Maya gasped and stepped away from the artifact.

"The Captain and Sarah are quite the pair of collectors," Zara said. "That thing came from a Drow'Voi city on Tetra-Five. It's one of the few things anyone has ever found that they left behind. I don't know what it's for, and it cost the Captain a pretty fortune, but it does make some nice little noises, don't you think?"

Maya nodded, realizing that there was something familiar about the tones that the tablet had produced. Then she recalled her dream about the Drow'Voi from the night before.

They were the same kinds of sounds that had come from the machines that the creatures had used. And just like in her dream, she was certain that there was some deep meaning behind them, but it eluded her. Shaking her

162

head in bewilderment, she let Zara lead her away from the niche and deeper into the room.

Passing a large *tiggari* wood table, Maya spotted one object on it that didn't defy any explanation whatsoever. It was a finely crafted model of a long-range interceptor ship, with Sisterhood naval markings painted on its miniaturized hull.

She stopped and leaned down to examine the replica closely. Everything had been captured perfectly in small scale. The hull even had faint traces of pitting from micrometeorite particles. Admiring the skill of the model's builder, Maya read the ship's name aloud to herself, "USSNS *Anne Bailey*"

"So she was called," a voice behind her said. She turned around and saw that Captain bel Lissa was standing there. The woman had changed out of her customary flight-suit into a loose flowing gown, and like the house and gardens around her, it made her appear to be anything but the captain of a notorious smuggler ship.

"You were in the Navy," Maya stated.

"That I was," Bel Lissa replied, joining her at the table. "I did 17 years in the Star Service, some of it during the War of the Prophet. That was my ship before I left and went into business for myself. Next to the *JUDI*, the *Mad Annie* was one of the finest vessels I've ever had the pleasure of piloting."

"So, you fought the Hriss then?" Maya asked.

"Did I," Bel Lissa chuckled. "Zara did, too. Our little hunter-killer squadron sent quite a few of their Warriors off to the Eternal Battlefields of Paradise."

"Why didn't you stay in?"

Bel Lissa shrugged. "Because it stopped making sense, I suppose. The politics of it all got to me. We'd take a system, loose a lot of good women, and then hand it right back to the *shovelheads* when the politicians, or the admirals, decided it was expedient.'

"Besides, there's no future in such a life. With the *JUDI* at least, I have a lot more freedom, and I manage to do a lot more good."

Good? How could a smuggler do good? Maya wondered to herself. It seemed to be at total odds with the very nature of the profession itself. Moonrunners weren't philanthropists. They were opportunists.

Bel Lissa didn't elaborate though. "Well," she said instead, "I see that Zara has some food for you in the kitchen. Her chili's all she says it is, but let me give you a friendly warning: don't let her talk you into seasoning it up with any *Ototsaa-peppers*. Those things are hot enough to make a Hriss Warrior cry his eyes out."

Maya grinned irreverently at the comical image. "I'll take your advice." With Sarah not skulking around, she realized that she actually *liked* the crew of the *JUDI*, or at least its Captain, and her Second. And the chili in the other room *did* smell delicious.

Mercifully, Sarah did not make an appearance at any point during the evening that folowed, and Maya was thankful for this small blessing. She was not only able to enjoy two bowls of Zara's chili in peace, but also a clean bed and a quiet, restful night.

***

The smell of fresh brewed kaafra greeted Maya as she came downstairs, and she eagerly followed the scent to its source. However, as she neared the kitchen, she *felt* Sarah's presence, and frowned when she entered and saw the woman.

Like Bel Lissa, Sarah had shed her usual clothing for a loose comfortable robe. In her case, it was black with delicate silver embroidery that Maya guessed was Nyxian in origin. The woman said nothing to her, but sipped at her kaafra as Maya got a cup of the stimulant for herself.

A long icy silence passed, and it was Sarah who finally broke it. "Did you sleep well?" she asked.

Maya's eyes flashed with hostility, and she merely nodded an affirmative.

"I thought that Zara would take you shopping today," Sarah went on, unaffected by her animosity. "You might need some things."

164

Of course, Maya did, but she was not about to admit it. It was bad enough that she had allowed herself to be in the same house with her in the first place.

"You'll want to eat something," Sarah advised her. "Zara is an early riser." Then she picked up her cup and walked out of the room.

Although Sarah had been the one to suggest it, Maya *did* feel hungry and she requested a light meal from the kitchen's robochef as soon as she was sure the woman wasn't going to return. While she ate, Zara appeared in the living area, fully dressed, and escorting a guest.

The newcomer was older than Maya was, possibly 25-30 years standard, and a Nemesian. Like many women from the jungle world, her skin was pale green, and she bore a clan tattoo on one side of her face. It was the stylized image of a fierce looking bird with a sharp beak and formidable talons, and it conveyed her tribal membership, and her rank within it, to anyone who knew how to decipher the details.

The only departure from what was normal for someone from her motherworld was her hair. Instead of being the typical dark green, she had either dyed it, or had had it genetically altered to a dark blue, almost black color. In addition, she had garbed herself in a very un-Nemesian black bodysuit that was identical to the one that Maya had seen Sarah wearing. It covered most of her form, with the notable exception of her prehensile tail, which flicked alertly in the air as she entered the room.

She was also carrying a black wooden staff in one hand and a small pleather case in another, and it was obvious from the purposeful way that she moved that she had come on business of some kind. As she passed Maya, the Nemesian gave her a glance that seemed to take in all of her at once, assessing both her strengths and her weaknesses.

Uncertain how to respond, the girl nodded a polite greeting and the woman grinned at her, exposing her razor-sharp canines. Maya wasn't certain if this was an expression of friendliness, or a warning of some kind. Customs differed from world to world and she instinctively refrained from smiling back.

This proved to be the correct response; the Nemesian nodded in approval and then let Zara guide her to the glass doors that led outside to the rear garden. As they slid open, and she went through, Maya realized that Sarah had been waiting there, and had changed into her own bodysuit.

Suddenly, Maya made the connection between the two outfits. They were more than just a fashion statement. They had some function that lent itself to whatever the pair was about to do. But what that was, was an unknown, and despite herself, Maya was fascinated and walked up to the glass to get a better view.

The Nemesian handed Sarah the staff, and then opened the pleather case, withdrawing a dark kerchief. She used this to blindfold the woman's eyes and then produced two curved daggers. Their blades were at least as long as her forearm and looked as if they were razor sharp.

After exchanging shallow bows, the pair backed seperated and Sarah took the staff in both hands, assuming a slight crouch. The moment that she did this, the Nemesian responded, throwing herself into a roll. The instant that she came back up onto her feet, she slashed violently at Sarah with the knives from two directions at once.

Somehow, despite her blindfold, Sarah managed to perceive the attack, and dropped backwards into a roll herself, gaining distance and bringing the staff up in an arc. Before the weapon could connect with her opponent's temple though, the Nemesian dropped sideways into another roll that kept her inside the range of the weapon, and avoided the blow. This maneuver also created an opportunity for another attack and the jungle dweller took it, slashing at Sarah's exposed calf with the nearest dagger.

Instead of being cut by the blade, Sarah picked up her foot at the last instant and pivoted on her supporting leg, sweeping the staff down and around to catch the weapon. There was the sharp report of metal being struck as the dagger was wrenched from the Nemesian's hand, and sent flying across the yard.

The Nemesian countered immediately, letting the momentum of the strike drive her body sideways as she threw her remaining dagger at Sarah's mid-section. The blade never made contact. Sarah stepped sideways and spun her staff to deflect the missile, sending it into the air to join its mate on the grass.

And then, just as suddenly as the combat had begun, it was over. Sarah was removing her blindfold, and the Nemesian was smiling at her, a genuine smile this time, of obvious approval.

Maya let out her breath, and loosened the death grip she had been holding her cup of kafra with. She also backed up a few steps away from the glass, hoping that the interior had concealed her from view. The very last thing she wanted was for Sarah to know that she had been standing there the entire time, gawking at them like some kind of fringe-worlder seeing her first big spaceport.

Outside in the yard, Skylaar taur Minna collected her daggers and rejoined Sarah. "You did well today, *Cho' sena*," she said. "Although I think that you allowed yourself to stay just a little too close to me. I almost had you with that calf-slash, and I could have followed through with an attack to your supporting leg if I had wanted to. As it stands, I seem to have scored at least one good hit."

She was looking directly at Sarah's forearm, and a shallow cut in the bodysuits material. The smart material was already healing itself and resuming its smooth, unmarred appearance.

Maya had no way of knowing it, but she had been completely correct about their outfits and their functionality. The bodysuits were not just for appearances; they were resistant to edged weapons and projectiles like needlegun rounds, and automatically repaired themselves whenever they were damaged in any way. Had the cut that Skylaar inflicted been delivered to bare flesh instead of the suit's protective material, it would have caused serious injury.

Sarah knew this, and nodded guiltily. "Yes, *Sena' tai*," she said, using the Nemesian honorific for her teacher. "You are right. I was too slow, and I should have gotten more distance and used my staff's length to greater advantage. I was careless. Please forgive me."

"*Knowledge is the profit earned from a lesson learned*," Skylaar quoted. Then her slitted eyes flicked briefly towards the glass doors. "Now, perhaps you would care to tell me why the girl is here?"

"I intend for her to become an agent," Sarah answered.

Skylaar's brows knitted. "Why is that? You've never taken on an apprentice before."

167

This was true. Although Sarah had recruited plenty of assets, she had never chosen an Agent-Candidate. Instead, she had been content to let the OAE handle all recruitment and training.

"It is my prerogative," Sarah replied. "If I find someone who is promising enough, you know that I can bypass the selection process."

This was also true. Agents were empowered to induct individuals that they felt would prove useful to the organization as operatives. It simply wasn't a common practice. In fact, it was extremely rare.

"So, tell me, how does *she* rate such an honor?" Skylaar asked, raising a skeptical eyebrow.

Sarah answered, undaunted. "Maya is tough, resourceful, suspicious, and most of all, audacious. Did you know that despite all the rumors I had put in place, she actually tried to *follow* me and *spy* on my activities?"

Skylaar panted lightly, the Nemesian equivalent of a dry chuckle. "I can imagine how *that* turned out."

Then, after a moment's pause, she added, "But these qualities, however fine, still don't justify your decision, nor explain why you wish to involve her. There must be more hiding in the trees here."

Sarah nodded. "There is, Sena-tai." She went on to describe their first encounter at the hostel, and then Maya's flight from the Customs Police. Finally, she shared what the Nyxian tarot had had to say on the matter.

"I firmly believe that Fate is taking a hand here," she concluded, confident that Skylaar more than anyone else, would understand. Nemesis had not forgotten the role of the paranormal in life's affairs.

"Whether she knows it or not, I think that this is the destiny that the Goddess intends for her."

"And what makes you think that she will accept such a destiny?" Skylaar challenged. "She seems to me like someone who would be content to live her life just as it is."

"I disagree," Sarah returned. "I learned differently when I read her at Bel Sharra. Although she hasn't quite realized it herself, she has grown tired of her wanderings. She is looking to find some real purpose to her life, and a place in the world. The Agency is that place."

"Perhaps," Skylaar returned, uncertainty still shading her tone. "But ours is a rather dark and dangerous world, and certainly not suited to every woman."

"All Maya has ever known is darkness and danger," Sarah refuted. "She understands that she will always be surrounded by it, and that it will play a part in her life. The prospect of gaining more control and power for herself in the face of that is something that she secretly yearns for."

Skylaar inclined her head in agreement, and waited to hear the rest.

"It is also a---a feeling--that I have," Sarah said. "Something is telling me that someday, she will prove to be very important to us. I cannot pinpoint what this might be, nor how it will come to pass, but it is there, and it has only grown stronger. This is *meant* to be, Sena-tai. I am sure of this."

"There are some women in the Agency that would argue that that is not a valid reason for recruitment," Skylaar rejoined.

But she also had to agree with her. Life, and her own dangerous profession, had taught her the value of listening to her instincts.

"I have one final question for you, Cho-sena," she finally said. "Why do you *care?* Why do *you* want her to be an agent?"

Sarah sighed thoughtfully, then answered her. "I suppose that she reminds me of myself in a way—or of what I might have been had I the same background as her. Despite her disadvantages, I want to see her become everything that I have become, and then surpass me. Perhaps it is my bid for a tiny slice of immortality. Or vanity."

"Or both," Skylaar ventured wryly. "And also the chance to make a positive difference through her. To revisit old mistakes and set them a'right? To heal old wounds?"

Sarah looked away, her features clouding, and nodded. She had never been able to hide anything from Skylaar.

"I take it that young Maya has agreed to your offer?" the Nemesian asked.

"Not completely, *Sena' tai,*" Sarah replied, facing her teacher again. "I am guiding her in that direction. But I believe the fact that she has been watching us during our entire lesson indicates a growing interest on her part."

169

"And Lady Ananzi? Have you consulted her about this?" Skylaar inquired.

"Not yet, Sena-tai," Sarah said. "However I am certain that when I plead my case, she will agree with my decision."

"Very well," Skylaar conceded. "What would you have of me?"

"Maya needs someone that she can trust and admire," Sarah explained. "Someone that will help put a friendly face on the training process and teach her discipline. I simply cannot provide that face. She hates me, and she will continue to do so for a very long time."

"Yes," Skylaar agreed. "She does at that." She also knew, just as Sarah did, that students often benefited from a combination of cruelty and kindness.

"So, will you help me?" Sarah asked.

"I will," Skylaar said. "I too have the same intuitive feeling about her and sense the same qualities. The future will show us both if we are correct, however. In the meantime, while we await tomorrow's arrival, shall we work on your skills some more?"

Sarah bowed to her deeply. "Yes, *Sena' tai*. I would be honored if you would care to guide me. And thank you."

"No thanks are needed," Skylaar said, waving it off. "If she becomes the agent that we think she will be, that will be compensation enough."

***

While Maya watched Sarah perform her own series of attacks with the double knives, Zara came up from behind and touched her on her shoulder. Startled by the unexpected contact, the girl whipped around and the old woman quickly withdrew her hand.

"Sorry girl," the Engineer apologized, "I didn't mean to give you a fright. Those two have been training here every day for so long that I forgot just how interesting they are to watch if you've never seen them go at it.'

She pointed towards the Nemesian. "That one with Sarah, she's her teacher. Her name's Skylaar taur Minna, and I've heard she's one of the best to come out of the K'aut'sha Fighting School on Nemesis in years."

170

Even though she was no martial artist herself, Maya could tell that this was not an exaggeration, just a simple statement of fact. No matter how cleverly Sarah tried, the Nemesian parried away all of her attacks with a deceptive ease. She appeared to exert no effort whatsoever, and where Sarah moved with competence, the Nemesian performed with an absolute grace, and a total economy of movement.

Maya felt a twinge of envy at the display. Living on the street, she had been in a few fights herself, and while she could hold her own, everything that she had learned had been gathered piecemeal, wherever and with whomever cared to show her a few moves. Seeing the pair engage in what was almost a dance, she realized that what she called fighting didn't even approach their level of proficiency. Compared to them, her skills felt clumsy and inadequate.

I wonder how I would do, she thought, *if I had a real teacher like that.* Then it occurred to her that this was probably the very direction that Sarah had intended for her mind to take all along, and she angrily banished the notion.

"Didn't you need to take me shopping?" she asked, eager to change the subject.

"Ay-yah. That, I did," Zara replied. "The Captain wanted me to get you squared away. You're going to need good gear if you're going to work aboard the *JUDI.*"

Maya followed her away from the window. "What will I be doing on the *JUDI?*" she asked. The ship only had four crewmembers and it was a question that had been on her mind since she'd reluctantly decided to accept Sarah's offer.

"Oh, a little of this and a little of that," Zara replied. "Mostly, you'll be working under me and filling in at Hari's old station."

This surprised Maya. "Where's Hari going?"

"Don't know," the woman answered, "but Sarah and the Captain talked it over and they agreed on a change of hands. So, you're to become the new engineer's mate. It's a good place to start, you'll get to know the *JUDI* real well that way."

She paused and added, "By the way, keep that news buttoned-up tight, Maya. Hari hasn't been told yet."

"What news?" Maya responded with an ingenuous smile. "I don't know *what* you're talking about."

Zara grinned back. "That's just what I was hoping you'd say, girl. Well, since you're already dressed, let's be off and take care of our business."

An armored hovertaxi met them at the front gate. It took them to Ashkele's exclusive Zinthara District, and down its main thoroughfare, the Street of the King of the Dead.

This boulevard was renown throughout the Sisterhood, and by most of its neighboring civilizations, as one of the premier shopping locations in the Far Arm. Maya knew it from her days as a runaway, but she had never been down it, nor inside any of its fashionable shops. The Zinthara was not a district that tolerated penniless waifs, and well-patrolled by the Guns. It was a side to Ashkele that until then, she had only glimpsed from the outside, and it was where the Free City's real power as an economic force was made plain.

As the hovertaxi negotiated its way through traffic, passing alongside huge limousines, Maya pressed her nose to the glass and gaped at all the wealth and diversity that was on display. On one block, a pair of T'lakskalan slave masters walked out of an exclusive shop together, their favorite slaves chained to them by golden leashes, while Xee merchants hurried by encased in translucent bubbles. A few paces on, Anx'Ma nobility glided over the foot traffic on platinum-plated hover carries, clad in harnesses glittering with rare gems. And as the taxi turned a corner, Maya spotted a pair of bejeweled Seevaan Queens, accompanied by their retinues of handmaidens and warriors, debating the latest fashions, and using intricate gestures with their lacquered front pincers to express themselves. These and the elite of a dozen or more races that Maya didn't even recognize, mixed and mingled together under the bright sunlight, united in one common endeavour; either to spend their wealth, or to acquire more of it.

In sharp contrast to the rest of Ashkele, the streets and the shops were immaculate. Everything was clean and polished and there were no street vendors hawking their wares, nor brawls of any kind. The Street of the King of the Dead was a place that existed completely apart from the rest of the port city. It was a true free market zone where all hostilities were set aside in favor of pure consumption.

The very last thing that she expected was for the robot hovertaxi to slow, and park at the curb. Up until that instant, she had been under the impression that they were merely using the street as a detour to get somewhere else. Being able to see the place up close had been one thing, but actually *shopping* there, was another matter. Suddenly, Maya became painfully conscious of her worn jumpsuit and looked at Zara with frank incredulity. "We're stopping *here*?"

"Yes, here," Zara responded, "*Far Star Outfitters* has an outlet in this district. It's the best place to get the best gear, and that's what the Captain wanted us to do. And afterwards, if you're in the mood, we can stop for lunch. I know *I'd* like to. The restaurants here are the finest outside the Sisterhood."

"Of-of course," Maya replied hesitantly, not entirely certain that her companion was being serious with her.

But Zara was, and got out of the taxi, gesturing for her to follow. As Maya did so, she instinctively looked around herself for any sign of the Guns. Although none of the robots were anywhere near them, she was half-certain that someone or something would realize that she didn't fit in, and order her escorted out by the machines, or worse.

"You know, Maya, you're really not the same girl that you were," Zara said just loud enough for her to hear. "And we're here to *buy* things. The Xee *like* anyone who comes to spend credits, no matter their past.'

"If you like," she added, "we can stop in somewhere right now and get you something a little less...conspicuous. Would that make you feel a little better?"

Maya nodded vigorously, and let Zara guide her down the street into a clothing shop that catered to humanoid bipeds, including humans. When they reemerged, she had happily discarded her jumpsuit, and dressed herself in finer clothing that was more suited to her surroundings. But she still had to consciously fight off the urge to shrink away from two well-polished Guns that passed them as they made their way down the sidewalk. Habits, even if they were as old and as worn as her jumpsuit had been, were still habits, and hard to shake.

173

Her companion on the other hand, seemed oblivious to the robots and everything else. Zara acted as if she was used to the place, and the outrageous amount of credits that they had just spent on clothing seemed insignificant to the woman.

It was another surprising facet to the *JUDI*, and her crew, that Maya filed away in her mind for future reference. If things got bad, she told herself, or a better opportunity came along, they obviously had enough credits and valuables to see her safely away. In the meantime, she planned to enjoy what she could of their largesse. While it lasted.

After a few blocks, they reached their destination. *Far Star Outfitters* occupied an entire corner in the middle of the Street of the King of the Dead. There was no mistaking the place. Its name was one that Maya and anyone else who traveled through Null knew and respected, and the store was not modest with its signage.

An elaborate animated holo, complete with a generic merchanter flying out of it, commanded the eye as the companies name and trademark followed in the ship's digitized wake. It was displayed in several languages, including Standard, and the holo itself was projected in different light bands so that any eye, human or otherwise, could see the advertisement and know that the finest goods available to spacefarers were there, and ready for sale.

When they entered the store, the resident AI greeted them warmly, using the projected image of a human female, dressed in an impeccable jumpsuit that was emblazoned, quite naturally, with the store's name and logo.

"*Sa'la jantildamé,*" the virtual guide said. "How can Far Star Outfitters assist you today?"

"We have an account with you," Zara answered. "We'd like to get several worksuits and a kit for my mate here, and I also wanted to pick up a jacket for her, made to our specifications."

She supplied the account information and the AI processed it. Then a scanner beam played briefly over Maya.

"Yes," the holo agreed, "and now that we have her measurements, we will have everything ready for you in just a few minutes. In the meantime, may I invite you ladies to browse, or perhaps enjoy some of our Sitalan Orange Pekoe? It's quite refreshing."

"That's a fine idea," Zara agreed. "A cup of tea would give my friend here a wonderful opportunity to become familiar with the jacket's features." The holo beckoned them to accompany her, and led them to an informal lounge area in the back of the store.

Maya gave Zara a puzzled look. "Why would I need to review a jacket's features?" she asked. "If I remember it right, you zip it up to stay warm and take it off when you're too hot. How complicated can that be?"

"This jacket is just a little bit--*special*," Zara said mysteriously as she took her seat and a cup of tea. "You'll see."

After a few minutes, a salesbot appeared, carrying a rather conventional looking jacket made from vat-grown leather. Maya took it from the machine and inspected it. Although it was attractive enough, and there seemed to be some items inside its pockets and nestled in the lining, it looked like any other jacket that she had ever owned, albeit of better quality.

Zara smiled knowingly, and the salesbot spoke. "Miss, there is a guided informational holo for this garment. If you would be kind enough to open the left front pocket, and withdraw the sealed pouch, it will begin."

Still wondering what might make this garment so singular that it required a tour, Maya did as the 'bot instructed. When she withdrew the pouch, a voice sounded in the air around her.

"Greetings, customer," it said, "and welcome to an interactive tour of your new ApeeCorp Adventurer Jacket. This garment has been constructed of the finest ballistic and e-blast resistant materials available.'

"It also comes equipped with the latest safety equipment and features. The pouch you are now holding contains a first aid kit, food bars, a water purifying straw, a mirror, a combination shelter and poncho, sealable plastic storage bags, a compass and a micro-signal light." A virtual image of each item was displayed in a hologram that floated in front of her.

"Are you sure you didn't forget something?" Maya asked dryly.

"No, ma'am," the voice replied somewhat indignantly. "I am quite sure that my inventory of that packet is complete."

175

"Of course. Sorry," Maya said, trying to ferret out where the holojector had been hidden on the garment. One button near the collar looked particularly suspicious and she gently placed her finger over it.

The voice reacted immediately. "Please!" it said, "do *not* touch the projector lens! Do you wish to terminate this tour?"

"No," Maya replied, removing the offending digit. "Please, continue."

"If you will return the pouch you are holding to its compartment, I can show you some of the other features of this jacket." Amused and intrigued, Maya complied.

"In the lower left arm pocket you will find 30 meters of monofilament line. This cord, although very fine, has the tensile strength of the high-grade plastisteel and can support weights up to 1,133 kilograms. A special climbing ring, hidden in another pocket, next to the zipper, allows the user to secure themselves to the line when climbing becomes necessary."

"Very ingenious," Maya remarked.

"Indeed," the voice agreed. There was a definite note of pride in its artificial tone. "Now, if I might direct your attention to the left upper arm pouch."

Maya unsealed the pocket.

"In this pocket you will find a folding plastisteel mini-grapple, and a micro-plazer saw. The plazer saw is capable of cutting through some of the hardest surfaces known in the Far Arm, and the grapple, although small, is strong enough to easily support the weight of a medium-sized hovercar without failing."

Maya couldn't imagine why anyone would want to suspend such a heavy vehicle from the tiny device, but the claim was impressive nonetheless.

"Now, in your upper right arm," the voice continued, "you will find a universal lock-picking kit and 10 packets of a chemical explosive compound with built-in biotimer devices."

"I take it that the explosives are provided just in case the universal lock-picking kit doesn't prove to be so...um...universal?" Maya asked.

"Of course not!" the voice replied, clearly appalled. "It was placed there for general emergency purposes. The universal lock-picking kit is guaranteed to grant access to any lock, mechanical or electronic."

" My apologies," Maya said.

"*If* we might continue," the voice said in a decidedly flustered tone, "in your right forearm pocket you will find a mini-re-breathing device for underwater travel and a plastisteel knife."

"Basically the perfect evening wear for the all-around spy, then," Maya remarked. "Is that all, or does the jacket turn into a hovercar if I unzip the correct pocket?"

Unfortunately, the voice didn't have the programming to understand sarcasm when it heard it. "I am profoundly sorry," it replied, sounding genuinely regretful. "The jacket does not have flight capability. However it does possess several other features that you will find are quite useful. May I tell you about them?"

"Sure," Maya agreed, trying her best to sound serious. "Please, tell me more."

"The jacket also has numerous empty pockets so that the wearer may store additional equipment and weapons, as they desire. The contents are guaranteed to be shielded from all known forms of detection-scans by a specialized inner lining.'

"You will also note that the jacket's temperature may be regulated by psiever-command and, as an added feature, this holojector may be used to project a mirror image of the wearer to a distance of 30 meters, line-of-sight, and to a lesser distance around corners."

"Well, I'm glad you told me all this," Maya said, "Otherwise I might have given this jacket away to charity."

The voice was absolutely scandalized. "Charity? This jacket is brand new and made from the finest--"

"I was just joking," Maya assured it. "I can see that it is one of the finest and best equipped garments ever devised for the adventurer. Thank you for the tour."

"Why, yes. Of course," the voice answered, its artificial feelings soothed to some extent. "Ask me for further information any time you desire it." With that, the voice went silent.

"So," Maya asked, turning to Zara, "Why in the Goddess' name, would I need all this when a plain, simple jacket would do?"

"Well, Maya, the *JUDI* sometimes does business with...odd folk," Zara informed her. "The Captain likes us to be prepared for anything that might come up. You know, just like the Star Scouts, 'always be ready' and all that. That's something I'd have thought you'd known about us 'runners. Things can get a bit chancy in our line of work and it helps to have any kind of edge."

Maya nodded, pretending to understand and accept Zara's explanation. Although she'd never worked aboard a smuggler ship, she had also never heard of their crews being equipped with such a strange array of gadgets. Spies and realie-adventurers like *Lana, the Longstar Ranger* needed them, but not smugglers.

Then again, the *JUDI* *was* a unique ship, and it was just conceivable that Zara wasn't having her on.

With any luck, she thought, *I won't be around long enough to need explosives or a grappling hook. And once I am gone, this jacket's little secrets could come in very handy.*

She smiled at the woman. "Well, I'm glad the Captain wants us all to be so prepared. I'll have to thank her when we get back."

The salesbot had made its reappearance during the jacket's interactive tour and was waiting patiently for their attention. It held three jumpsuits in its arms, all neatly folded, along with a kit bag.

All of the articles were sky-blue in color, and Maya recalled seeing similar jumpsuits being worn by the *JUDI's* crew at various points while she had been an unwilling guest aboard the ship. Most merchanters issued jumpsuits to their crews to use when they needed to perform the really dirty jobs, and also to act as a form of free advertising when they were in port. Sky-blue seemed to be the *JUDI's* official color, and Maya took one of the suits from the 'bot and examined its shoulder patches.

What she saw elicited a mixture of both humor and irritation. The round patch was also sky-blue with dark blue bordering. The name of the ship and its maritime registration number were displayed around the border: CSS *C-JUDI-GO*, 1692. This was normal enough.

But in the center of the patch was the silhouette of an old fashioned Gaian witch flying on her broomstick against the backdrop of a yellow crescent moon.

Of course, she thought, *why should I even be surprised?*

"It looks like Captain bel Lissa doesn't mind the rumors that are in orbit about her ship and the Witch," she observed aloud.

"Not in the least," Zara replied. "Sometimes even bad publicity comes in handy. The witch story keeps a lot of nosy-bodies from bothering us too much, and makes the rest wonder from a distance, or go away thinking it's all a yarn. Any way it plays out, it works for us."

Too bad the witch isn't just a story, Maya thought sourly.

***

They returned from their shopping expedition late in the day, and after a light dinner, Maya retired for the evening, thoroughly exhausted from the adventure.

The next morning, she discovered that she had the house all to herself. Captain bel Lissa and Zara had announced the night before that they had had business in the city, and Sarah was also gone, having vanished without providing any explanation.

Maya got herself some breakfast, and with nothing else better to do, went outside onto the lawn. To her surprise, Sarah and her teacher had left behind some of their training equipment from the day before, and she couldn't resist picking up one of the twin daggers, and inspecting it.

The weapon proved to be just as sharp as she had surmised, but also surprisingly light. While she hefted it, she tried to remember some of the maneuvers that she had seen the day before, and then did her best to approximate a particularly vicious-looking parry and counterattack that Skylaar had employed. Her first attempt came close, but something felt wrong about it, and as she tried it again, she realized that it was her stance. It wasn't the same as the Nemesian's had been.

Experimentaly, she lowered her hips and rearranged her feet until she was sure she had assumed a fair approximation of what she'd seen. Then she gave the maneuver another try. Although her movements were not anywhere near as elegant as Skylaar's, she could sense the difference as she swept the blade around, and grinned at her discovery.

179

A voice startled her. "That was very perceptive of you, Maya. Not many beginners realize that proper balance and footwork are more important than what your hands are doing."

Maya spun around to see Skylaar standing there with her arms folded, and an appraising expression. The girl put the dagger down immediately and stepped away from it like a child who had been caught with something she had been forbidden to handle.

"Sarah's not here," she said.

"I am aware of that," Skylaar replied. "I actually came to see *you* today." If anything, this was an even greater surprise to Maya than her sudden appearance.

"Me?"

"Yes, you," the woman answered with the straightforwardness that the Nemesians were famous for. "As you may have noticed, I train martial artists, and Sarah is one of my pupils. But I always have an eye open for anyone that might show promise."

Maya was just as direct in her reply. "Did Sarah put you up to this?"

"She mentioned her offer," Skylaar answered, "and also her hope that I would help, but it was I that decided to speak with you. I too feel that you have some potential, and I am the one who decides who will, and will not, be my students. What you do with her beyond that is your own affair."

Maya regarded her uncertainly, suddenly at war with herself. She loathed the idea that Sarah had had a part in this, or that the woman would derive any satisfaction if she accepted Skylaar's offer, but she also wanted what the Nemesian was offering.

"If her involvement in this matter offends you, I fully understand," Skylaar said, "Please forgive me for any presumption on my part. I will not bother you any further." With that, she began to gather up the training equipment.

"Yes—I mean--no," Maya stammered, finally decided. "Please, stay."

Skylaar stopped and set everything back down, keeping only a single dagger. "Very well. I shall. Now, may I offer you some knowledge?"

Maya nodded.

"If you are going to fight with a knife, you should learn to fight with it correctly. I gather that you have had *some* fighting experience?"

180

"Some," Maya said with a hint of defensiveness. "I've been in a few scrapes."

Skylaar considered the blade. "Experience is always a valuable weapon," she said. "The only danger is when that weapon is poorly crafted, or mishandled." She offered it to Maya. "Please, instruct me. Show me something of what you know with this."

"But-"

"Please," Skylaar insisted. "I am always eager to learn new techniques."

Maya took the dagger from her, and thought for a moment about what she'd seen on the street. Then she remembered a particularly nasty fight she'd witnessed on Delgen, and went into a crouch.

Skylaar simply stood there, waiting. Her expression was calmness itself.

Without warning, Maya lunged forwards, thrusting out with the knife. Halfway to Skylaar, she traded knife-hands and swept in and underneath for a strike at the woman's midsection.

The blade never made contact. At the last possible second, the Nemesian pivoted on her left leg and swept around with her right. The outside edge of her foot struck Maya's wrist along the tendon, making it spasm. The dagger fell from her hands, and Skylaar let her foot drop and leaned forwards, loosely grasping what had been Maya's knife hand as she brought her other hand palm-upwards, and lightly brushed the girl's chin. Then she froze.

"With that combination, I was able to disarm you, and had I followed through, I could have delivered a palm-strike to your jaw," the Nemesian informed her.

"If my strike had hit you one way, I could have simply stunned you. Placed in another manner, and I could have snapped your neck. The choice was mine." Then she stepped back. "Would you like to see how it was done, step by step?"

"Yes," Maya answered, deeply impressed. "I would."

"It would be my pleasure, *Cho-sena*. Let us begin with the crossing side-kick that I used."

Their session lasted an hour, and at the end of it, Maya was exhausted but exhilarated. The side-kick had taken some work, and although it was as far from perfect as possible, she finished their session feeling that she had learned a tremendous amount in a short time, and said as much.

"That is where the trail through the forest really begins," Skylaar said. "Once you realize that you know only a tiny fraction of its length, then you might actually have the chance to learn just how far it truly extends."

With this, the woman bent down and began to gather up her weapons. "I hope that you will allow me to return here again tomorrow."

"Why, yes," Maya answered, both surprised and pleased. "Yes, of course. Please come back, Sen-sena..."

"*Sena-Tai*," Skylaar said. "It is Nemesian and it means 'She Who Learns,' and it would be my great pleasure, *Cho-sena*."

"Yes, *Sena-tai*," Maya replied. As Skylaar turned to leave, she asked, "*Sena-Tai*, what does *Cho-sena* mean?"

The woman smiled. "It means, 'She Who Teaches.' Please, practice your crossing sidekick. I would like to learn more from you."

Apollonia District, Thermadon City, Thermadon, Myrene System, Thalestris Elant, United Sisterhood of Suns, 1042.12|09|00:01:66

Sarah parked her hovercar in an alley, and watched the movement of the traffic on the streets around her. She wasn't overly thrilled to be back in Thermadon, but the *JUDI's* business had required her deft hand, and the DNI had supplied the contact. They had guaranteed that the woman she was about to meet was not a part of any professional gang, but Sarah was not about to accept their word on its face alone. Even with relative amateurs, there was always the potential for danger, and the DNI was known to be wrong from time to time.

She reached out with her mind and *felt* around her. As near as she could tell, her contact was still some distance away, and hadn't entered the area yet. And other than the two of them, there were only a few women nearby that were still awake, and none of them raised any mental alarms. But after her encounter in the park, she was not about to let herself relax based just upon this alone.

182

Aria, engage proximity alarm, she thought to the car. *And link in with the 'Plexi and give me a population display of the area.*

Yes, Mistress," the car responded. *Would you also like me to engage any weapons systems? I was very bored sitting in the garage, and I wouldn't mind a fight if one came our way.*

I'm sure that you wouldn't, Sarah replied. *But we are not here to pick one. Passive defense only, and please send the 'Plexi data to the dash HUD.*

Yes, Mistress, the vehicle answered. There was a decidedly disappointed tone to its reply and Sarah pointedly ignored it. Instead, she focused her attention on the display before her.

Like many large cities in the Sisterhood, Thermadon used satellites to monitor its population, and their movements. Among other things, this allowed the city's AI to make adjustments to vital services based on population density.

As residents shifted from one area to the next, the information that the satellites provided to the omniplex allowed the city's AI to change traffic controls, and redirect water and power to where they were needed the most. It also furnished Sarah with a real-time map of every woman in the surrounding sub-district that she could check against what she felt.

From what she could see, her talents had perceived the situation accurately. There were no people that she hadn't expected to find, and they all appeared to be going about their legitimate business.

There was still the slim chance that enemy agents had tapped into the local 'Plexi, and had simply deleted their presence from the datastream, just as she did whenever she visited the spaceport, but things *looked* quiet. She earnestly hoped that they actually were, and would stay that way.

After several minutes, she spotted her contact walking down the street. According to the DNI, the woman was a non-commissioned Naval Officer, and despite the fact that she had dressed in civilian clothes, her short regulation haircut betrayed her profession immediately.

Engage engine, she instructed. The vehicle started up and moved out from its hover position in the shadows. Sarah flashed her headlights at the sailor and brought the vehicle down to street level, opening the passenger door at the same time.

183

Startled, the woman jumped back, and Sarah took charge of the situation immediately. "Get in," she ordered.

The sailor obeyed and threw herself into the passenger's bucket seat. Her clothing smelled of rain and the musty odor of long periods of storage.

"Are you Mariner n'Fari?" Sarah asked. There was something about the sailor, she suddenly realized. Nothing threatening certainly, but a strange cloudiness to her aura that made her seem a bit off.

"Yes," N'Fari replied. "Do you want to scan my military ID?" She began to roll down her sleeve to expose her biochip, and in the process revealed an arm covered in small scars. Some of them were quite old and others were clearly fresh, and just beginning to scab over.

Sarah grabbed her arm and held it. And as she did so, she *felt* the woman for the briefest of seconds, corroborating what she had suspected and also providing the reason why the sailor had been so willing to go ahead with their transaction. She was a cutter, a glass addict. The insidious drug had worked its evil on her, and distorted her bioplasmic energy field.

"No, that will not be necessary," Sarah said, letting her go with obvious distaste. "Let's get this over with." She reached into her cape and brought out the credit chip that she had prepared for the meeting. "I am offering 40,000 credits for one T-190 Anti-ship Torpedo. I understand that you have one to sell me."

"Planning a little upgrade on your ship?" N'Fari asked, attempting to inject some levity.

Sarah was not amused. "If you want to leave this meeting alive," she warned, "then you would be best advised to curb your curiosity." To her satisfaction, her passenger paled.

"I-I'm not sure that's enough for one of those," the sailor finally said with a shaky voice.

"40,000 is what was agreed."

"Make it 50,000 and you have the torpedo," N'Fari countered.

Sarah nodded. "You have a deal." She dropped the credit chip into the addict's trembling hand, and then added another. It had been pre-programmed for 10,000 credits. One of the benefits of having talents was the ability to predict exactly how a deal would conclude.

"We'll send it out for testing at the weapons range," N'Fari volunteered. "Fomalhaut has one on its third moon and no one will suspect a shipment like that. We have a contact there that will help you get the torpedo before it arrives at the range."

She talked too much for Sarah's liking. "Remember this," she said to her in her deadliest tone. "No one will care overmuch if you and your cutter friends disappear. Make sure you do *exactly* as you have promised."

N'Fari cringed, earning an evil smile from Sarah.

"It will be at Fomalhaut by the end of the next month," the sailor assured her. "We'll contact you and tell you where you can pick it up."

"I am certain that you will."

With that, Sarah opened the car door, and N'Fari stepped out without having to be told. As she backed away from the vehicle, Sarah re-closed the passenger door and engaged the car's flight controls.

Link me with the omni, Interplex, she instructed.

She sent a message to Bel Lissa in Ashkele with the news. Next, she placed an order for a white rose to be delivered to a specific address in the city, and then headed for *Jackie's*.

***

The white rose had been a signal to her employers that she wanted a face-to-face meeting. Sarah had only used it a few times in her career, but she considered the business that was on her mind important enough to make the request.

While she sat in her private booth and waited, she considered her decision and did not find it wanting. The only thing that remained was to put her plans into motion with her employers.

She was just taking her last sip of her wine, when their representative made her appearance. Jackie was at the bar as always, and when the woman asked after Sarah, the bar owner smiled and pointed her out, assuming that she was the mystery lover that had been sending all the black roses.

Sarah made sure to smile warmly as the woman approached, and even added the extra touch of hugging her and planting a kiss on her lips. The representative was enough of a professional to respond with equal enthusiasm, and let Sarah guide her into the booth. While the pair sat together and made the typical small talk that lovers engaged in, they communicated with each other using their psievers on an encrypted channel.

You requested a meeting, her guest thought. *Has there been a problem with the delivery?* Even though there was an infinitesimal chance that *Jackie's* surveillance systems might intercept the conversation, she was taking no chances and had kept her words vague.

None whatsoever, Sarah replied, with equal obscurity. *We will have it within the month, and you can expect delivery shortly after that time. My business tonight concerns another matter; Hari n'Sarolyn and her tenure aboard the JUDI.*

Go ahead, the woman responded, squeezing Sarah's hands and giving her a loving expression. Her mental tone however, remained serious and businesslike.

Sarah put an arm around her. *I feel that she has become unreliable and careless, particularly with regard to our security measures. The Captain and I have discussed this, and we believe that N'Sarolyn is a liability. As you are aware, we have complained about her before, and now I wish to replace her with someone else.*

We can arrange for a replacement, her companion assured her, laying her head on Sarah's shoulder.

That will not be needed, Sarah replied, stroking the woman's hair with false affection. *I have already made arrangements.*

With whom? the woman asked. *We have received no communications from you until now about this. Are you bringing in someone from the outside?*

Yes, I am, Sarah answered. *I have recruited a young woman that I discovered here in the city. I believe that she will fill Hari's role aboard the JUDI in a more than satisfactory manner. I also think that she will make a fine agent once she has been properly trained.*

This is quite irregular! the woman protested. *You know that we prefer to screen prospective agents ourselves before accepting them.*

I also know that I have the privilege of recruiting promising candidates, Sarah countered. *I am exercising that very right, but I will be happy to provide you with any information that you might need to conduct an independent review of my choice.*

Her guest was not convinced. *And if you are wrong in your assessment?*

Then I will personally see to it that my candidate is either eliminated, or her memory is erased. I am confident that it will not come to that, however. To anyone watching, her expression was blissful, even though she felt anything but.

Very well, the woman thought back, with definite reluctance. *Give me all your information about her. In the meantime, how do you propose that we deal with N'Sarolyn?*

A simple transfer would be sufficient, Sarah answered. *Possibly into a less sensitive position?*

That would be suitable, the woman agreed. *Although you may consider her unfit for your operation, I am certain that we can find other assignments that are more suited to her abilities. How soon do you need her transferred?*

Given its sensitivity, I would prefer if that took place before she becomes aware of the upcoming delivery, Sarah answered. *I plan to return to Ashkele in the next week, and I feel that it would be best if she were discharged at that time.*

Agreed, her contact replied. *We will make the arrangements immediately.*

The woman rose at this point, and planting a kiss on Sarah's lips, left the booth with a counterfeit smile. Sarah waited for a few minutes more, and then she left as well.

As she climbed into her hovercar, Aria announced that she had a message waiting. Sarah was not surprised by this, and even though she told the car to display it, she already knew what it said, and who had sent it.

For an instant, she wondered how the sender even knew she was in town, and how she always seemed to know. Her movements were *supposed* to be classified.

She strongly suspected that something in Aria's programing was responsible, or that someone in her organization was providing the information. But she had never located the subroutine, or established any definitive proof linked to anyone specific.

Not that it mattered, she thought tiredly. What mattered was that "T" *did* know, and that she had no choice. She had to go to her.

Someday, I'll kill her, she vowed. *Someday. But not tonight.*

Ashkele Free Port, Hallasa System, Frontier Zone, Xee Protectorate,
1042.12|16|03:09:87

Maya was in the kitchen, drinking her second cup of morning kaafra, when Hari and Zara walked by. Both of them were fully dressed, and Hari who was normally sullen, looked particularly dismal. Zara didn't look terribly happy herself.

Then Maya saw that Hari was carrying her kit bag, along with a larger duffel. *So Zara was right*, she thought. *They really are letting her go and putting me in her place. That was fast!*

She made eye contact with Hari and the other woman paused. "Good luck" she said bitterly. "You'll need it with this bunch."

Maya didn't respond to her caustic remark, and merely took another sip of her kaafra.

"Now, there's no need to make a scene, Hari," Zara said, trying to pull the woman away.

Hari shook off the engineer's hand and glared at her. She started to say something else, but stopped herself before the words came out. With a final frown at Maya, she walked to the front door and let Zara show her out.

And a Bian dea to you too! Maya thought derisively, *Have a great day!* She had never cared much for her anyhow.

The girl put Hari out of her mind completely and accessed her psiever. It was 03:29:37.

Maya suddenly realized that she only had a few minutes to get ready for Skylaar. She downed the rest of her kaafra in one gulp and pelted towards her quarters to change. Skylaar was always precisely on time, and she expected the same of her students.

At exactly 03:33:33 Skylaar arrived, and found Maya waiting for her out on the lawn. The Nemesian wasted no time and started their lesson by demonstrating some stretching exercises, and then proceeded to instruct her in basic blocks and punches.

When she was satisfied with Maya's movements, the two of them repeated the attack from the day before, with Skylaar pausing at each stage to show her the finer points of what she had done to defend against it.

While she worked out with the Nemesian, Maya realized that she was truly happy. There was something exhilarating about the training, and at the end of their session together, her spirit felt lighter than it had been in a very long time.

"That is one of the great truths about any martial art," Skylaar said when she mentioned this. "It is not just the crude act of trading blows with an opponent. Anyone on the streets here in Ashkele can do that. It is more of a dance between two forces; one advances, the other retreats, and in this dance, the soul finds liberation."

"Yes, *Sena-tai*," Maya answered. "I think I see what you mean."

"Now, we shall put that understanding to the test," Skylaar stated. "You derived a great deal from the sessions where you watched Sarah and I work together. She has just returned after completing some urgent business, and I have asked for her to join us."

Maya scowled at the mention of the woman's name. She had come to treasure her time with Skylaar and didn't relish the idea of sharing it with Sarah one nanobit.

"I realize that you are none too fond of her," Skylaar acknowledged, "but I also know that there is much that you can learn just from watching us train. That is part of today's lesson. To learn how to open yourself up to anything that might bring you greater knowledge. Even a hated opponent can have something useful to teach--even the very key to their defeat. So, today, I want you to set aside your feelings, watch and see what you can learn."

Even if she wasn't overly pleased with the idea, Maya had to acknowledge its wisdom. "Yes, *Sena-tai*," she said.

Privately, she hoped that she was going to get to watch Skylaar knock the stuffing out of Sarah. With that pleasant possibility on her mind, she obediently sat down on the grass.

Skylaar rewarded her with a half smile, and Maya suspected that her teacher knew exactly what she had been thinking, but the Nemesian made no comment, and beckoned towards the house for Sarah to join them. The woman appeared, and seeing Maya, inclined her head slightly in greeting. Then she bowed deeply to Skylaar.

"We will resume our lesson from the other day," Skylaar announced. "As you may remember, our main emphasis was on distancing. Today, I will have you take up the sword, and I will defend, using each element in my defense to illustrate for Maya's benefit the different ways that one can respond to an attack. You may begin when you are ready with an underhand cut."

"Yes, *Sena-tai*." Sarah picked up a sword that Maya had seen earlier that morning. It had been sitting alongside the usual staff and daggers, and she had wondered at its purpose. The single edged blade was at least a meter long and slightly curved, with an extremely small hilt that had seemed far too diminutive to provide very much protection for the wielder. Sarah gripped it with both hands and reversed the blade so that its edge faced up towards Skylaar.

At a signal from the Nemesian, she stepped forwards and swept the blade upwards, attempting a cut up and through the center of the other woman's body. Skylaar reacted by dropping her left arm, falling back and sideways, and using her rear leg to support her weight. The blade sung as it bit into empty air.

"That is the element of wood," she explained, "bending in the wind of the opponent's attack. Now, we will see water. Please, Sarah, a horizontal cut from the half-seated position."

Sarah sat with her legs under her, and holding the sword with one hand, brought it around so that it was at her side and its tip was pointed behind her. She waited like this for a second, and then suddenly, rose up on one leg as she swept the blade outwards.

She was aiming for Skylaar's legs. Skylaar jumped backwards, and as Sarah stood and began to make an overhead cut, rushed forwards, capturing the woman's sword hands at their wrists with one hand, while she struck her chin in a palm strike with the other.

190

It was only as Sarah flew backwards, that Maya realized that Skylaar had also stepped in behind her, tripping her in the process. The woman landed quite squarely on her behind, making the demonstration all the more entertaining.

"As you saw," Skylaar said, "I retreated like water does, and then came back like a wave to crash onto my attacker and off-balance her. Now, we will see fire. Another underhand cut, please."

Sarah stood, gripping her weapon in both hands. Before she could even manage to begin her cut, Skylaar was on her, blocking her arms from raising the blade with an arm and sending a knife-edge hand strike rocketing towards the bridge of her nose. She pulled the blow at the last possible instant, and Sarah froze in place. The overall effect was exactly like a fiery explosion that terminated the attack before it had even had a chance to begin.

"Now, we will see steel," Skylaar continued. "A straight, forward thrust, please, Sarah."

This time, Sarah tried to thrust the weapon right into her belly. Skylaar reacted by dodging sideways and brought her hands downwards, hitting the top of Sarah's arms with a pair of knife-edged strikes. The blows caused Sarah to drop the sword as her muscles contracted from the twin impacts.

"Lastly, we will see stone. An overhead cut, if you would."

Sarah raised the weapon over her head and then brought the blade downwards. This time Skylaar didn't even bother to dodge. Instead, she simply stepped into the cut and brought her hands up to catch Sarah's arms just below the wrists. At the same time, she kicked her sqaurely in the stomach.

The effect that this had was like a starship under full engine power, hitting an asteroid. Sarah dropped the blade with a loud *oof!* and folded over as Skylaar's foot found its target.

Maya was thoroughly pleased with the outcome.

"So, as you see," Skylaar said as she helped Sarah up from the ground. "There are many ways to defeat an attack, based on your nature, the nature of your attacker, and the form of the attack. While you train, try to think about what element you are expressing when you move, and about what element your partner is expressing. Knowing that, and how each element

191

interacts with one another, can provide you with the key to ensuring that the dance between you goes in the direction of your choosing. Do you have any questions?"

"Yes *Sena-tai*," Maya replied, "How exactly does each element work with another? I don't understand that part."

Skylaar smiled. "Generally, wood bends to wind, but burns with fire and yields to steel, but with patience, wood can also split stone and stand against the power of water. The same is true of all the elements of the Great Mother Forest; each has their strengths and weaknesses, and each one possesses its complimentary opposite. Now, I believe that we have learned enough for today and I also understand that Sarah has some news for you."

"Thank you as always for teaching us, *Sena-tai*," Sarah said. "Maya, we have a mission to go on. We may be gone several days, so you will need to prepare for that eventuality."

"Yes," Skylaar agreed. "As we will not be meeting on those days, I would ask that the two of you use any free time that you have to practice together. Sarah has studied our art for many years, and she can help you a great deal, Maya. It would also be good for her to train with someone whose moves she is not acquainted with. When you get back, you can ask me any questions that you have, and I will try to answer them to my own limited abilities."

"Yes, *Sena-tai*," Maya responded. She wasn't pleased with the prospect of training alone with Sarah, but she also knew that any opportunity to practice was not to be missed. *And, Goddess willing*, she thought, *I might even get the pleasure of giving her a few good blows myself.*

192

CHAPTER 7

Rixa Naval Base was the largest fortified military installation in the Sisterhood, spanning an entire star system. At its outermost limits, it was ringed with hundreds of thousands of automated mines that interrogated any ship attempting to approach, and compared their answer to transponder signals on file. Anything that didn't answer their challenge quickly, and correctly, found itself on the wrong end of ship-killer missiles.

Inside of this minefield was another ring of permanent missile stations, either orbiting the outermost planets, or stationed on the larger asteroids. Squadrons of deep space interceptors and light cruisers also flew picket duty there, adding another layer to Rixa's formidable defenses. In the third and innermost ring, was the fourth planet itself, heavily fortified with anti-space batteries, and patrolled by more squadrons of fighters and cruisers.

A group of Mobile Space Hangars, or MSH ships, also hung in orbit over Rixa. Each MSH was 32 kilometers long, and fully capable of housing an entire fleet in each of its three docking tubes. Although they were now on semi-permanent stations above the planet, Lilith knew from her Academy training that the MSH ships were fully Null-capable.

In their second war with the Hriss in 715.56 ASE, several of them had actually been used as carriers to transport Sisterhood forces en-masse to surprise the enemy. It was still hard for her to believe that such huge machines could manage such a trick, but manage it they had.

The *Pallas Athena* was assuming its final approach to the MSH Ship USSNS *Hippolyta* when the helm paged Lilith.

"Commander," Caleda bel Tridis announced, "*Hippolyta* Approach Control has assigned us a docking vector. Estimated time-to-dock, three standard minutes."

"Very well," Lilith replied, "Play the ship's song for all hands." While the *Little Drummer Girl* sounded throughout the vessel, the dockmistresses on the MSH took remote control of the helm. The *Athena* moved slowly into the gargantuan docking tube and began to align itself with the central rail, passing over other ships that were already parked against it.

Lilith's breath caught in horror as they went by one of these vessels. It was the USSNS *Kit Cavenaugh*, a medium cruiser with Battle Group

Platinum. Like her own battle group, Platinum had also been patrolling in the Sagana Territory, but in another quadrant.

The entire starboard side of the *Cavenaugh* was ripped wide open, and extensive battle damage scarred its hull from bow to stern. From what Lilith saw, there was no way that the ship could have made it to Rixa under its own power. Reflexively, she made the sign of the Lady, and noted that quite a few crewwomen on the bridge had copied her.

What happened? she wondered. Damage like that only came during wartime, and she shuddered at the thought of how many might have died when the ship had taken it. Clearly, something serious had occurred.

She made a quick inquiry through the ship's computer, but the matter came back classified 'Majestic', the very highest level of security. Lilith herself possessed 'Radiant' level clearance, which was generally high enough to access most state secrets. Majestic on the other hand, was reserved for matters that were restricted solely to the Admiralty, the Chairwoman of the Supreme Circle, and her advisors.

Finding herself locked out of the file, she tried a few more avenues, attempting to access branching files and subdirectories, but got nowhere with any of them. Whatever it was that had happened to the *Cavenaugh*, the Admiralty had made dead certain that the facts would remain off-limits to everyone, regardless of rank, until they decided otherwise.

Just the same, she resolved to learn what she could when she got downside. There was always the outside chance that someone with the *Cavenaugh's* crew, or Battle Group Platinum, would be willing to give her the facts, off the record.

"Coming up to the rail," Caleda announced, keeping her voice carefully professional. Outside, robotic arms and embarkation tubes had swung out in preparation for mating with the *Athena*.

"Final alignment, ship's speed slowing to zero. Docking now." With this declaration, Battle Group Golden's three-month patrol was officially over. Only one task remained: submission of the official ship's log, and the debriefing of its officers.

Lilith looked over at the Comtech stations. Katrinn was already there, retrieving a copy of the log. Ellyn n'Dira, Mearrin d Rann, and Colonel Lislsdaater were with her, making certain that multiple witnesses were present who could testify that the log had been transferred without interruption. And in keeping with this custom, a sailor with security also stood by, waiting to escort them out of the Command Center.

Once her Second had the data-orb in her possession, she placed it into a special armored, blast-proof case, and locked it by pressing her thumb against a sensor which read her bioplasmic signature. From that point onwards, only the Zommerlaandar's aural pattern would open the lock, and any attempt to access its contents by any other means would cause the case to destroy its contents.

Lilith joined the group at the main lift and headed down with them to the Embarkation Decks. Crewwomen not assigned to stay aboard were already beginning to fill the deck, and the securitywomen made sure that everyone cleared the way for the Commander and her party. A shuttle was standing by, and in short order, they were headed down to the surface of Rixa.

Landing on the southern continent, they identified themselves to reception security and were shown to a small cubicle in the Incoming Personnel Section. There, a private computer terminal had been set aside for their use. Katrinn laid her case onto a counter, and Lilith began the formal ritual of debriefing.

"Ben Jeni, Lilith 567984138, Commander, *Pallas Athena*, USSNS 1323," she stated.

"Acknowledged," a soft voice replied from nowhere, and everywhere. "Please submit your inocular for vaccination and medical records verification."

Lilith exposed her forearm and submitted it to a scanner beam that issued from the ceiling. The light played over the permanent vaccination site, and then winked out.

"Medical records verify current vaccination history," the voice said. "No additional measures are required to meet local conditions. Voiceprint and Bioplasmic signatures confirm identity. Welcome back to Rixa, Commander ben Jeni"

Katrinn went next. "Bertasdaater, Katrinn, 597667518, Lieutenant Commander, *Pallas Athena*, USSNS 1323." Like it had with Lilith, the voice requested to inspect her inocular and verified her identity.

It was Mearrin's turn after that. "D'Rann, Mearrin, 590231475, Lieutenant Commander, *Pallas Athena*, USSNS 1323."

And finally, the Advocate and Col. Lislsdaater went through the process.

"All required officers are present," the voice stated, "and match voice and bioplasmic records. Vaccination records are current, and egress on-planet is granted without restriction. Please submit your ship's log in the data receptacle for processing."

Katrinn opened the case, and took out the data sphere, inserting it into the waiting arms of the reader. After a moment, the voice spoke again.

"Is this the full and complete record of your patrol?" it asked.

"Yes, it is," Lilith answered.

"I can vouch for an unbroken chain of custody from the ship to this terminal," N'Dira said.

"So can I," Lislsdaater added.

"Due to the nature of the action that you saw, and special flags placed in this system by Topaz Fleet Command," the voice informed them, "an appointment has been arranged for you with Fleet Admiral Myrelli ebed Cya this afternoon.'

"It has been automatically scheduled for 07:70 hours in her offices in C Quadrant. All officers currently present are to report there immediately. Captain taur Minna and Bel Sarra have also been notified, and will also be in attendance. Do any of you require directions?"

"No, thank you," Lilith replied. "We know the way."

***

The offices of Fleet Admiral Myrelli ebed Cya overlooked the famous Valley of the Veils. Outside her windows, and hanging over the nearby mountains, huge diaphanous shapes created by the union of millions of living microorganisms floated on the updrafts created by the warm air from Rixa's shallow seas. The planet orbited a binary star, and at that hour, the twin suns were setting, catching the Veils with their golden light as the translucent communal organisms rode the wind. It was a breathtaking spectacle, and although Lilith had visited the Admiral's office many times, the gigantic yet fragile entities never failed to captivate her.

"You're in luck, Ladies," the Admiral said as she took in the view. "The air over the Valley is busier than normal for this time of year. You couldn't have come at a better time to see the Veils"

"Yes, ma'am," Lilith agreed, standing at attention with her officers. "They are quite lovely."

Myrelli smiled, and turned away from the window. For just an instant, the light caught the skin on the side of her face, and Lilith could just detect the slight difference between her natural flesh and where the Navy Doctors had re-grown it. Most women wouldn't have even noticed, so perfect was the science of re-growing damaged tissues, but Lilith, like many of the officers trained at the Naval Academy on Calaphis, knew Myrelli's history intimately. And in all their years of association, she had never been able to look at her superiors' features without recalling it.

During the War of the Prophet, at the Battle of Wrede 178, Ebed Cya had been in command of an *Isis*-Class starship, facing a vastly superior enemy fleet. Against astronomical odds, she'd managed to destroy the entire opposing force, but not before her ship, the USSNS *Brigid*, had taken a hit from a final enemy missile. The strike had failed to destroy the *Brigid*, but it killed most of her crew instantly, and set the bridge ablaze.

Ebed Cya survived this catastrophic event, but only just. When she was rescued, seventy percent of her body had been covered with second and third degree burns, and she had hovered precariously on the very brink of death for weeks. But thanks to a combination of the Goddess's luck and sheer willpower, she had hung on to life. A long and painful rehabilitation period had followed this, and then, miraculously, she had returned to active service.

For her bravery in battle, Ebed Cya was promoted to the rank of Vice-Admiral, and had the singular distinction of being one of the few living recipients of the Supreme Circle's Medal of Honor with a Star-Cluster. Eventually, she had been appointed to teach tactics at the Star Service Academy on Calaphis, and had risen to the rank of Admiral, and finally Fleet Admiral, overseeing the Topaz Fleet. A mentor of Lilith's from her earliest days as a cadet, Ebed Cya was, without question, one of the finest military minds in the Star Service, and a living legend among its officers.

"I understand that you saw some action in Sagana," Myrelli remarked, taking her seat behind her huge desk. "You may be seated, ladies."

While Lilith and her companions took their chairs, a holo of the enemy cruiser being destroyed over Persephone materialized in mid-air and played itself out. It had been taken directly from the *Athena's* Log.

"One light cruiser and a battalion of infantry," Myrelli observed. "I also understand that another battle group attempted to join them." Another holo appeared, depicting the second Hriss squadron.

"Yes, ma'am," Lilith answered. "We managed to *persuade* them to retire from the area."

"Yes, I can imagine," Myrelli remarked dryly. She looked at the enemy battle group thoughtfully. "Tell me, Commander, what do you make of the forces that you encountered? Give me your opinion of them."

"The light cruiser captain was an amateur, ma'am," Lilith responded. "He failed to fully neutralize the colonies communications swiftly enough, and he had no remote listening posts on standby in the system. Instead of a hit and run raid, he chose to linger, and when we arrived, he seemed to be genuinely surprised that we had responded, and his defense was inadequate."

"And his infantry?"

This was Col. Lislsdaater's cue. "Equally mediocre, ma'am. They appeared to be totally untrained to deal with an opposing force. Their defense measures were inadequate, and they were slow in responding to our attack. In addition, their armor was of insufficient numbers to provide any meaningful support for their ground forces. Our greenest recruits could have put up a better fight."

Ebed Cya nodded. "What of their relief group, Commander ben Jeni? What did you make of them?"

"They were cut from a completely different cloth, ma'am," Lilith answered. "Their maneuvers were disciplined, and from what I gathered from my conversation with their Commander, they were veterans."

"A rather odd mix, don't you think?"

"Yes, ma'am. Quite odd."

"And what would you make of this encounter overall?"

Lilith suddenly felt like she was back in the Academy, facing Ebed Cya across a classroom. "I would venture that it was a test, ma'am. I believe that they used their most expendable forces as bait in order to gauge our strength and response time.'

"I also believe that the veteran force arrived with two missions; the first being to assist their forward elements in securing the resources that they had come for, and the second was to observe the nature and reaction of our forces to their incursion."

Ebed Cya nodded. "I tend to agree, Commander, and I thank you all for your frankness. We'll discuss this matter in greater detail when you return from shore leave. In the meantime, there is one other issue that I need to discuss before we end this meeting. It concerns the transfer of a marine to your ship, Commander."

Lilith sat forwards a little, thoroughly puzzled. The transfer of a single trooper to a ship was generally not an issue that concerned any of them at their rank-levels. *Unless there was something very special about that trooper,* she thought warily.

"I am sure that you are all aware that the High Court recently heard a case brought before it by the Marionite Church concerning the rights of neomen and their status in the armed services," the Admiral said. "Their suit specifically addressed the so-called *right* of neomen to serve in combat units.'

"While you were on patrol, the Court reached their decision, which was to allow this to occur. Naturally, the Navy disagreed with the ruling, and immediately filed a formal appeal, with the Marine Corps filing their own petition simultaneously. Unfortunately, the High Court saw fit to deny our respective pleas, and the Supreme Circle subsequently issued an order to our two service branches to abide by the decision."

Lilith paled and glanced over at her officers to gauge their reactions.

Col. Lislsdaater was sitting straight as a ramrod in her chair, her face an impassive mask. But her fists were tightly clenched, betraying her anger. Katrinn, Mearrin and N'Dira seemed equally stoic, but Lilith could tell from her years of association with the trio, that her Second was somewhat surprised by the news, Mearinn was reserving judgement, and N'Dira was actually slightly amused. As for Bel Sarra, the Captain of the *Demeter* looked worried, probably fearing that *her* ship would become involved, and although Erin taur Minna *looked* calm enough, her tail twitched with an unhappy agitation that was a match for Lislsdaater's dark mood.

Admiral ebed Cya, undoubtedly perceiving the same things, continued on, "Towards that end, a single trooper, Jon fa'Teela, was selected from the neomen we currently have in the service, and he was issued orders to report for duty aboard the *Pallas Athena*. He is to arrive in two weeks time and once there, he is to serve with the 115th under Col. Lislsdaater just like any other Marine.

"Ladies, I will state for the record that I do not approve of this *experiment*, especially now, with the raid on Persephone still fresh in the public mind. But, like yourselves, I am a soldier and I will follow the orders given to me by the Chairwoman and the Supreme Circle. I expect that while he is in your battle group, you will hold Fa'Teela to no more *and no less* than the same standards that every servicewoman is expected to conform to.'

"I must add that this event has also generated a considerable amount of interest with the news media, and that you should each expect to be contacted by journalists. I am required to remind you, and the officers and crewwomen serving under you, not to make any comments, nor to agree to any interview unless it is approved and monitored by this office, and by the Commandant of the Marine Corps.'

"On a personal note, I would also like to extend my apologies to you, Commander ben Jeni, and to your officers. When this matter came to the Admiralties' attention, we were compelled to find the right ship to place Fa'Teela aboard, and considerable pressure was brought to bear concerning its selection. There were several candidates, but because your battle group has such a distinguished service record, yours was the one we chose.'

"To be frank, while the situation is unpalatable, there is no other group of officers, and no other crew that could undertake such an assignment and enjoy any more of my confidence. I realize that this is not welcome news, but I also know that you and your staff will handle the situation in the proper manner. That is all, ladies. You are dismissed."

Everyone stood up, and saluted the Admiral. The debriefing was over. No one said a single word about it until they were at the magnorail station, waiting for the train.

N'Dira ventured the first comment. "I must say that that was a surprising decision for the High Court to reach," she said. "The Justices are usually much more conservative. I didn't think they would rule that way when the case was brought before them. It's really quite a turnaround."

"Yes," Lilith replied sarcastically. "A landmark decision for *all* of us to *celebrate*."

Erin taur Minna snorted, and spat into a nearby waste can. "It's *fekking* blow! A goddess-damned disgrace!"

Mearrin shrugged, and waved off Taur Minna's upset with a webbed hand. "I think that until we see how he performs, we should keep an open mind. According to the Admiral, he has been serving for some time now, and may manage to adapt to his new role."

"*That* I strongly doubt," Erin growled. "More the like, he'll bring us nothing but dishonor. What the *fek* was the court thinking? Men have no place in combat! They'll force us to lower our standards to *accommodate* them."

"Well," Katrinn offered carefully, "There *is* one small point of light. We only have one neoman to deal with, and not a whole company of them."

The train had arrived by this point, and everyone except Col. Lislsdaater got aboard.

"Aren't you coming?" Lilith asked her.

"No, Commander," the woman replied stiffly. "I am going to remain here. I have some business with the Commandant's Office, and after that I plan to get very, very drunk." Her features were unreadable, but the look in her eyes could have melted hull plating.

"I'll see you in two weeks, Marya," Lilith said. "Try to make sure that your hangover is gone by then. We'll all need our heads clear. Until then, you are dismissed."

The corner of Lislsdaater's eye twitched slightly, but beyond that, she remained expressionless. She gave her superior a brisk salute, turned sharply on her heels, and marched away.

The train doors hissed shut, and Katrinn shook her head ruefully, "I pity any poor trooper that she runs across on her way to the Commandant's Office."

"If I know the average sailor or Marine, we're going to be dealing with some serious morale issues when we get back," N'Dira cautioned.

"I'll say," Lilith agreed. "The *Athena* is going to be the laughing stock of the whole Fleet over this. Goddess, I don't know, maybe once he's aboard, everyone will just get used to the idea and forget all about him."

"Let's hope so," Katrinn said, but none of them really believed that that was going to happen.

So much for the rosy glow of shore leave, Lilith thought unhappily.

When they reached the next train station, Ellyn n'Dira excused herself for an appointment at the Advocate General's Office. Mearrin also left them for a meeting with the Dean of the University Extention program. And Bel Sarra and Taur Minna also bade them farewell. They didn't mention what their business was, but Lilith guessed that Erin at least, was probably going to seek out Col. Lislsdaater, and join her in her pursuit of the perfect hangover.

Lilith and Katrinn had no such aspirations, or obligations, and looked to one another for ideas of what to do next. Despite the news about the neoman, Katrinn was determined to enjoy her leave, and she urged her superior to do the same.

"He isn't going to be an issue for another two weeks," she observed. "And *I* for one would like to have some fun before we have to report back to the *Athena* and deal with him.'

"What do you say we visit the PX and do a little shopping? I have some things to get for my family, and you might want to browse some of the stores yourself. You know there's no better medicine to help brighten your mood than a little shopping."

Lilith had to concur with her Second's advice. She *did* have a rare bookstore that she wanted to visit, and any excuse to think about something other than Fa'Teela was a welcome distraction.

"You're right, Kat," she agreed, "I could use a dose of that medicine right about now. Let's meet back for lunch at 05:83. How does the *Jenah*

Nari sound?" The restaurant served a combination of Kalian and Aran cuisine that was the finest available outside of the two worlds themselves.

"Perfect," Katrinn beamed. "05:83 it is. I'll see you there."

***

Like many military installations throughout history, Rixa offered special shopping facilities for its resident and visiting personnel. Being the largest of all Sisterhood naval facilities, the PX on Rixa was much more than just a single building. Instead, it was an entire complex that covered several kilometers of the planet's surface.

The Rixa Naval PX boasted its own realie theaters, restaurants and shops, each of which rivaled their finest civilian counterparts in quality and selection. For a crew coming off a long, hard patrol, the shopping center was a welcome reward for both officers and enlisted alike. Whether it was simply a taste of home, a gift for a family member, a night out, or a comfort item, something could be found at the Rixa PX to satisfy almost any desire, and credit-balance.

While Lilith went off in search of her bookstore, Katrinn visited several shops and in short order, picked out the perfect items for her sisters, her mothers and her grandmother. In addition to a new, compact robochef unit that she knew they wanted, and several other bulky, but necessary items, she also purchased a fine pair of plastisteel knives guaranteed never to loose their edge, and exquisite linen shawls from the Kalian world of Sita.

Hefting her heavy bags, she then went into a branch of the largest toy store in the Sisterhood, *Stelli and Leese Inc.,* for what was to be the toughest part of her shopping excursion.

There, playthings from every corner of Sisterhood space, and even from non-human worlds, could be had by servicewomen interested in buying something for a young loved one back home. In Katrinn's case, she had several little nieces that she wanted to get presents for. Zommerlaandar custom was to purchase each child their own gift, and also something for all of them to share together. Not only did this ensure that everyone received their own present, but the single, shared gift, reinforced the values of family, and the concepts of working and playing together.

The individual toys were easy enough to find, but the communal gift was another matter altogether, and it wasn't long before she felt herself overwhelmed by all the choices that *Stelli and Leese* offered. Hundreds of thousands of toys were on display in the store, all separated by departments. At first glance, many of them looked promising, but after considering them, Katrinn was forced to press on, undecided. Finally, in the doll department, one of the toys managed to catch her attention. Literally.

"Excuse me, jantildam," a toy bear said, "but you seem to be a discerning customer, with a good eye for children's toys."

"I like to think so," Katrinn replied, a little nonplussed at finding herself having a conversation with a toy.

"Perhaps I could interest you in purchasing myself and my friend next to me." A graceful little fairy stood next to the bear, and gave her a polite curtsy.

"What's your pitch?" Katrinn asked suspiciously.

"Hardly a pitch, madam. More of a proposal," the bear said. "My friend and I have been here in the store for over a month, waiting until the right patron walked by before we introduced ourselves. You are clearly just such a person and you are obviously shopping for children that you adore; children who will give us good homes."

"And why should I buy you?" Katrinn inquired.

"Because my friend and I are perfect for small children. You *are* shopping for little ones I assume?"

"I am. Go on."

"My friend and I are Biobots, and we specialize in story telling. Come now, good lady, what child isn't entertained by stories?"

"Biobots?"

"Yes, madam, Biobots," the bear said with a bow. "We are, even if I say so myself, the perfect toys. You see, our batteries are recharged by bioplasmic energy, and especially by strong emotions. In our case in particular, by love."

Katrinn put down her bags. If she hadn't known better, she would have sworn that the bear had a sly gleam in its eye. "Okay, you have my attention," she said. "You say you and your friend tell stories. How many?"

"We are each programmed to tell 1,602,385 different stories, with another 12,665,780 variations," the bear said proudly. The little fairy next to him nodded enthusiastically in agreement.

"That's quite a few tales," Katrinn agreed. "But tell me, little bear, can you and your friend tell Zommerlaandar stories?"

"*Yah,*" the bear replied in fluent Zommerlaandartal, "*blaak veraal aal denn Zommerlaandarstaarrie geskaad naam.* We can tell all the Zommerlaand stories."

"*Skeyaa denn 'Gröt Anne' staarie denn haar aans?'*" the fairy asked. She was offering to tell a tale about one of Zommerlaand's favorite figures, Great Anne the Giant.

"*Nen,*" Katrinn said. "No need, I believe you. Now, as a Kalian might say, how many *rupas* must slip through my fingers to buy you?"

"Not many, madam," the bear assured her. "We cost a mere 1,250 Sisterhood credits a piece, and there is a ten percent discount if you buy us both."

Katrinn was aghast. "*Twenty-two fifty*? I could buy a whole store full of non-talking dolls for that!"

"Yes, madam, you certainly could," the bear conceded. "But none of them would be as loved by your little ones as us, and none of them would grow in sophistication as their mistresses aged. *We* are gifts that will last a lifetime."

"All right," Katrinn said. "You have me there. Do you get in my bag, or what?"

"Only if you desire it, my lady. We can also carry your bags for you if you wish it. We may appear to be small, but we are both *very* strong."

Katrinn held out her bags. "For what I am paying, you'll definitely carry the bags." The two toys jumped off the shelf, and to her amazement, hefted them over their tiny shoulders without any apparent effort.

"Lead on, good lady!" the bear said cheerfully. "We cannot wait to meet the children of such a fine woman."

"Save it," she replied. "We're getting lunch first."

Waanderstaad Spaceport, Zommerlaand, Sunna 3, Solara Elant, United
Sisterhood of Suns, 1043.01|09|04:85:27

When the military shuttle entered the atmosphere, Lilith marveled at
the clear blue skies of Zommerlaand.

*This must have been what Old Gaia looked like, centuries before
industrialization*, she thought.

The shuttle changed its flight angle, and she caught sight of the
immense rolling green fields that covered most of the planet. The word
"beautiful" would have described the vista, but it was more than that. An
incredible aura of peace seemed to lie over the landscape, covering it like
the rolling white clouds that stretched out and away from her viewport.

Four minutes later, the shuttle landed. Waanderstaad Spaceport could
have been any other landing field, except for all the farmland around it, and
its gargantuan scale. Its main terminal was actually rather small since the
spaceport received few flights that were purely for passengers, or non-
agricultural cargo.

The concrete runways and grain storage towers were another matter
entirely. They were colossal in size, and launch cradles lined the length of
the spaceport's runways out to the horizon and beyond. Merchant vessels
occupied most of the cradles, their holds packed to the bulkheads with the
planets' produce.

Zommerlaand was the granary of the Sisterhood, and for that reason,
Waanderstaad was also the second largest spaceport in existence, surpassed
in size only by Bel Sharra Memorial on Thermadon. Hundreds of worlds
set its food on their tables, and as Lilith considered this fact, it seemed odd
to her that Zommerlaand was also home to some of the Sisterhood's
toughest soldiers.

Such a green and pleasant world hardly seemed the proper birthplace
for such fierce fighters. But it was; Zommerlaandertal was the unofficial
second language of the Marine Corps, and many of its slang terms had
made their way into Standard through the centuries, thanks to the
contributions of Sunna 3's daughters to their nation's defense.

While she pondered this dichotomy, the shuttle taxied to the military terminal and a docking tube swung into place. As soon as it had locked on, Katrinn rose from her seat and started gathering her things from the overhead compartment.

"Come on," she said, "My sister Ingrit said she'd meet us." Lilith followed her lead, and they disembarked.

After having their inoculars scanned, and receiving immunizations, they entered the spaceport proper. To Lilith's surprise, a pair of local police officers met them at the entrance to the civilian terminal.

"*Godag Daare,*" one of them said. "I'm afraid you must leave your weapons here at the terminal. We have lockers that you can use to store them in during your visit."

"I'm sorry?" Lilith replied in bewilderment, "What did you say?" Of all the things she had expected to encounter, the very last was any problem with their side-arms.

"No energy weapons on Zommerlaand, ma'am," the officer stated. "Now, if you'll come with us, we'll show you where the storage lockers are."

Katrinn interrupted, speaking to them in Zommerlaandartal "*Ehtj Mojlaag dar Kaaperin. Saa es nej voor Zaldaat; Vi aanz gan angezaampte.* And if you need to hear it again in Standard, that's for civilians. Military personnel are exempt. Read your code book."

"*Maan dar,* the law is clear. No energy weapons on Zommerlaand."

"The local law may or may not say that," Katrinn retorted, "but Sisterhood law is *equally* clear. Military personnel are *required* to carry their sidearms with them whenever they are downside at a civilian location. It's been that way since the First Widow's War, and if you don't believe me, go ask your supervisor."

The policewoman fidgeted, unsure what to do next. Finally, she accessed her psiever. From her expression, the response that she received was clearly not the one she had wanted to hear.

"My supervisor says that you are correct, ma'am," the officer informed her unhappily. "Nevertheless, I must ask you to tell me where you are going with the weapons."

Martin Schiller

"Grunvaald Collective Farm near Vaalkenstaad," Katrinn replied. "We'll be staying there for a few days with my family."

"*Denn gaaf,*" the officer said, entering the information into her elzlate data-pad. "You will stay in contact with the Vaalkenstaad Police while you are there. If you leave, you will tell them where you are going. Zat klaar?"

"*Klaar,*" Katrinn agreed. Then she turned to Lilith. "Let's go. My sister said she's going to meet us out front." They left the two officers standing where they were and walked out into the civilian terminal.

"What was that all about?" Lilith asked.

"A stupid local ordinance," Katrinn replied with disgust "I should have warned you about it. The kaapers try to enforce it all the time, but they know that they're in the wrong. Don't let it spoil your trip."

"I won't," Lilith replied. But she also couldn't help but notice that the two kaapers were now following them at a discrete distance. *Different planet, different ways,* she thought. Just the same, the requirement that they had to report in with the local police made her feel like some kind of registered criminal.

The heat and the humidity hit her like a hammer when the terminal doors opened. Automatically, she adjusted her field cap against the brilliant sunlight and tried to get herself used to the temperature as they walked outside. The rich air felt thick and wet in her lungs and she wondered how long it would take for her to acclimatize herself.

Katrinn however, seemed utterly in bliss and took a deep, satisfied breath. "Isn't that wonderful?" she asked. "You can smell all the growing things. Goddess, I've missed that."

"It's … intense," Lilith agreed politely.

"Ah, you'll get used to it," her companion replied, nudging her playfully. "After a few days, you'll never want to breathe canned air again."

Lilith wasn't so certain, but she didn't contradict her.

A tall blond woman walked up to them at this point. "Well if it ain't my little *Sady* in her fancy black button-oop! Heyas, *Roont!*"

Lilith looked up at the newcomer. From the resemblance, she knew immediately that the woman had to be Ingrit, Katrinn's "baby" sister. Like most Zommerlaandars, Ingrit was huge; easily over 1.8 meters tall, and powerfully built. Until that instant, Lilith hadn't quite realized just how *short* her Second really was. She felt like a child herself standing next to Ingrit.

"Sis!" Katrinn cried. She dropped her kit bag and the two women hugged enthusiastically.

"*Mihn Gudinn*! It's good to see you!" Ingrit exclaimed, and then looked speculatively over at Lilith. "And who is this pretty woman?"

"My Commander," Katrinn answered. "Lilith ben Jeni."

"Pleased to meet you, Commander," Ingrit said with a big grin. "*Vaalkomm aan Zommerlaand!*" Ingrit's purple irises, a genetic characteristic of Zommerlaandars, sparkled with interest. She smelled of fresh grass and clean sweat, and as they clasped hands, Lilith realized that she found Ingrit incredibly attractive. It had been a long, long time since she had felt that way towards anyone, and she actually blushed.

If Ingrit had noticed it, though, she didn't let on. "So, the flitter is parked nearby" she said, grabbing up both of their kit bags before either of them could protest. "The local kaapers wouldn't let me park at the curb."

"I'm not surprised," Katrinn remarked sourly.

"So, you met them, then? Sorry," Ingrit replied. "Really, most Zommerlaandars are very nice, not like *denn Kaaperin* at all." This last remark was directed to Lilith, who simply nodded, having heard none of it. The sun flashing off Ingrit's braids had completely distracted her. They looked like they were made from beaten gold, and she desperately wanted to touch them.

This is ridiculous, she thought, angrily. *I've just come downside, and I'm already eyeing Katrinn's sister like a bitch in heat.* The woman was probably happily *pairmated* with someone, she decided, with a whole pack of children of her own. Lilith felt ashamed of herself, and hoped that she wouldn't humiliate Katrinn, or herself, during their stay by saying or doing anything stupid.

The 'flitter' Ingrit had referred to turned out to be a battered red hovertruck that was missing a headlight on one side, and to Lilith's eye, sported more dents than a battle cruiser coming back from a combat mission. A picture of a barn and some words in Zommerlaandar were painted on the sides. It took Lilith a moment to translate them to herself.

209

"*Grunvaald Haarmaaneplaatz,*" she read aloud. "Greenfield Collective Farm"

"*Yah*, that's home," Ingrit said. "You'll love it. And don't let old Betsi here fool you. She's old, just like the farm, but she still takes care of us real good."

As Ingrit stowed their bags in the cargo bed, Lilith regarded the vehicle doubtfully. In her opinion, it didn't look very airworthy. Katrinn however, seemed completely unconcerned, and climbed in without a second glance.

"Come on," Ingrit urged, waving Lilith aboard "we've a fine supper waiting for us. Got to welcome my little *Roont* back home after all her adventures." Putting her faith in the Lady, Lilith took her seat and also made sure to securely buckle her seat harness.

Old Betsi might have looked tired, but her engine still had plenty of power and Ingrit made sure not to waste an erg of it. She drove the hovertruck like a mad woman, speeding them out of Waanderstaad and into the open country with a carefree disregard for the speed limits posted along the main highway. Fortunately, the traffic was thin, and everyone else seemed to be just as insane as she was. They had just roared past a sign that Lilith was reasonably sure had read "Stop!" in Zommerlaandartal when Ingrit announced that they were nearing the Grunvaald farm.

Lilith didn't see anything that looked like farm buildings or houses, just endless open fields filled with corn and wheat, and the occasional agribot tending them. Then, just as she spotted a dirt road off to one side, Ingrit careened into it, sending a plume of dust and gravel into the air as Betsi's fans encountered the new surface.

As they flew down the narrow track, a pair of young women on horseback waved to them. From the way Katrinn returned their greeting, it was obvious that they were relatives of hers. *Nieces or sisters probably,* Lilith thought.

Up ahead, the road ascended a grassy hill. Betsi crested the ridge, and then Lilith got her first view of Grunvaald Farm. It was even lovelier than Katrinn had described it.

The farm sat in Sunna 3's golden light, in a valley at the edge of a large tract of verdant woodland. The barn was an ancient structure; all aged

210

wood and weathered paint. Nearby this sat the main house: a classic old-earth design, straight out of a history realie about the 19th century. In one window on the second floor, real lace curtains billowed out lazily in the breeze, framing an orange tabby-kaatze that regarded them with mild interest as they pulled up to the front. In another, a face peered out, and then disappeared.

The front door opened as soon as they started to climb out and a herd of children burst out of it, crying joyfully as they rushed up to the hovertruck.

"Aunt Katy! Aunt Katy's back!" they squealed. In moments, Lilith and Katrinn were completely surrounded by earnest, happy little faces.

"Lilith," Katrinn said. "I'd like you to meet my nieces. This is Marta, Lisl, Gretta, Alyis, Clara, Helga, Berti, Janis, and this wiggly one," she said picking the littlest girl up, "is Fryya."

Fryya looked at Lilith with big, uncertain eyes. Lilith was clearly an unknown commodity. "Are you a sailor like Aunt Katy?" the girl asked shyly.

"Yes, I am," Lilith replied. "We both work on the same starship together."

"Do you remember its name, Fryya?" Katrinn asked.

Fryya thought about this for second before she started sucking her thumb. "No," she finally admitted.

"The *Pallas Athena!*" one of the other little ones piped up.

"That's right, Berti. That's the ship I work on," Katrinn said.

"Did you bring us anything?" another asked. Lilith thought it was Clara, but she didn't have everyone's names memorized yet.

"Clara!" Ingrit scolded, "Aunt Katy just got here. It would serve you a'right if she didn't bring you anything, you greedy thing!"

"I'm sorry," Clara apologized.

"No worries, Clari," Katrinn said, tousling her hair. "I brought something for everyone and something for all of you." Then as she looked up at the porch, her expression changed and Lilith followed her gaze.

Two women stood there, and Lilith suspected from their age, and the resemblance, that they were Katrinn's mothers. The pair walked up and Katrinn embraced each of them in turn.

"Lilith," she said as she stepped back. "These are my mothers, Berta and Helga." Both women had the same clean, strong appearance that Ingrit had inherited, and they greeted her warmly.

"*Vaalkomm*," Berta said. "It is good to meet our Katy's friend. We have heard a great deal about you over the years. Please, be welcome in our home."

"Thank you," Lilith replied. "I have heard much about you and your family as well, and it is good to finally be able to meet all of you in person."

Then she saw that a third woman was coming outside to join them, and everyone around her stopped what they were doing. She was very old, well over two hundred standard years and wore a long, plain dress and an apron covered with Zommerlaandar characters. In its center was a pair of letters that were combined together into an eye-catching design. And at the old woman's neck was a simple necklace made of wood with another Zommerlaandar letter carved into its face.

From what Katrinn had told her, Lilith knew that some Zommerlaandars regarded their alphabet as sacred, even attributing it with magical power, and it was clear to her that the apron and the necklace both had some great symbolic importance. The woman smiled enigmatically as she joined them.

"Lilith," Katrinn said reverently. "This is my grandmother."

"*Vaalkomm*," the woman said taking Lilith's hand. Despite her age, her grip was strong and firm. "You must be the Commander that Katy has told us so much about. A friend of my granddaughter's is always welcome in our home."

"Thank you, *Grötdaar*," Lilith replied, remembering the Zommerlaandar honorific for an elder.

"Oh, call me Grammy," the other woman said. "Everyone else does, although it's *nice* to see someone with manners come a'visiting for a change. *Zo*, supper is on the way. Everyone go in and wash up.'

"Ingrit, you show Katy and her friend to their rooms. They'll want to freshen up before we eat. *Gaane-an, afgaan. Zoop!*"

The troop of children ran back inside, laughing and giggling all the way while the adults followed behind them at a more decorous pace. It was obvious who ran the household, Lilith reflected.

"Lilith," Grammy said, offering an arm, "let me show you our home." Lilith took hold and let the woman guide her. As they walked inside together, Ingrit motioned for Katrinn to wait.

"Zo, sis," she asked when they were finally out of earshot. "What's the story with you two?"

"No story," Katrinn replied. "She's my boss, that's all."

Ingrit nodded with a calculating smile. "*Gaanskaa gaad.*"

From the way that she was looking at Lilith, Katrinn had no doubts whatsoever about her sister's intentions. On a planet of nothing but blonds, Ingrit's attraction to Lilith's dark looks was perfectly understandable.

"Yah," Ingrit added speculatively, "she's a pretty little thing, that boss of yours."

Katrinn smiled. *It just might be what Lilith needs,* she mused.

***

After months in uniform, Lilith walked down to the kitchen feeling a little awkward in civilian clothes. But Grammy set her at ease immediately.

"*Ah, gaaf, verda baatar!*" she declared. "That's got to be more comfortable than those old black *button-oops* you had on. *Gaane-an,* sit! We've a bit 'afore everyone comes bursting in here for supper."

Lilith took a seat and Grammy handed her a bowl of vegetables and a small knife. "Peel those for me, won't you *Sötehaart? Taake.*" As she started in on them, the old woman smiled. "So, you and Katrinn work together I hear, up on that big starship."

"Yes, Grammy." Lilith answered. "She's been with me now for the last three years. She's a good officer."

"I know she doesn't tell me much about what goes on up there," Grammy said. "I 'spose she doesn't want to make me worry. Is it bad up there sometimes?"

"No," Lilith lied. "It's mostly routine patrol, nothing special."

213

"It's sweet of you to try and spare me," Grammy said. "But I know better. People tell me things, and *denn Maarkken* tell me even more."

"The *Maarkken*?"

"*Yah*, the Signs. Don't you know what those are?" Grammy's eyebrows rose in amazement. "Don't they have the Signs back on your world?"

"No, ma'am, I don't think they do," Lilith replied.

"The Signs tell us things," Grammy explained. "Like when you had those three ships pop out all of a sudden on you. Had a raven friend of mine let me know my Katy was in big trouble. I had to do some fast work there, I'll tell you. Those fellows would've shot you up for sure otherwise."

"Ma'am?" Lilith asked incredulously. To the best of her knowledge, Katrinn hadn't said a word about the Persephone raid to anyone outside the Navy. And a raven *telling* her things? Fast work? *What on earth did Grammy mean?* she wondered.

Grammy didn't elaborate. "A shame, not knowing about *denn Maarkken*," she sighed instead. "Can't figure how anyone could get by without them."

The door flew open and Katrinn's nieces rushed in, interrupting any further conversation. "Is it supper yet?" Clara shouted.

"Not 'till you get your hands washed, its not," Grammy admonished. "Get upstairs and wash all that dirt off. *Mihn Gudinn* what a pack of *vaaldkaytin* you are!" Ingrit and Katrinn filed in behind them.

"You two!" Grammy ordered, "You have empty hands! Help me here with these potatoes!"

Lilith shook her head and went back to her work, completely mystified by what Grammy had said about the Signs and the Persephone raid. She recalled that Katrinn had mentioned from time to time that her Grandmother was something special on Zommerlaand, a holy woman of some sort, but she'd never paid much attention to it.

Now, she was starting to wonder. How *had* Grammy known about the second Hriss battle group? Was she some kind of psi? The answer, for the moment at least, eluded her.

214

Supper made its appearance a few minutes later; a generous table full of food that looked so fresh and appetizing, that it put the *Athena's* cooks, as good as they were, completely to shame.

"It's a good thing that Sa'Vika isn't here to see this," Lilith remarked to Katrinn as they took their seats. The SAO would have collapsed from the inferiority complex the repast would have caused her. Katrinn smiled in agreement, and passed a dish of greens her way.

Lilith piled her plate high like everyone else, and she was just about to bring the first appetizing forkful to her mouth, when little Clara spoke up.

"Aren't you going to give the *Klaana Aamskaand* some?" the girl asked. Lilith realized that she'd missed something important.

She put down her fork. "The *who?*"

Clara looked at her like she was addled, and shrugged with exasperation. "The Little Cousins, the Little People. You know, *denn Aalfen*. The *Alfs,* silly. They want some supper, too."

Then Lilith noticed that all the women and girls around her, including her Second, had pushed a tiny portion of their meal off to one side of their plates. She'd seen Katrinn do it many times on the *Athena*, but she'd always just assumed that her Second was a picky eater. It suddenly became clear that this was actually a custom that all Zommerlaandars observed with great seriousness.

"Now, Clara," Ingrit reprimanded, "she doesn't know our ways, so don't be rude. Why don't you show her how it's done then?"

"Well," the little girl said, assuming an air of great authority. "You take some of the best parts and you put them on the side, so that the little people can fly down and get them. They usually like cream and cheese, and sometimes meat, and they *always* like something sweet." She looked at something in the air that Lilith couldn't see and added, "Don't you?"

Satisfied with whatever had just transpired, she looked back at Lilith. "Also make sure not to lay your fork down in what you give them. They don't like metal things."

Lilith glanced over at Ingrit, and Katrinn, and realized that they had been listening closely to little Clara, and nodding their approval as she had gone through the details of the ritual.

"May I ask you a question, Clara?" she inquired.

215

"Yes, ma'am."

"Why do we give the... little cousins... part of our meal?"

"So, that they'll help us and give us good luck. Besides, some of them are my friends," Clara smiled.

"Well," Lilith replied, "I don't want to offend your friends. And I like good luck, too." With that, she took a small portion of everything she had and put it on the edge of her plate. "How do I know they're eating it?' she asked.

"Because you'll see them!" Clara returned, amazed at Lilith's denseness. "They'll fly down and take a little bit. See? There goes one now!"

Lilith wasn't certain, but something, an insect possibly, *had* flown by just then, but when she looked directly at her plate, she saw nothing out of the ordinary. Clara smiled enigmatically, and began eating her supper along with everyone else. *Different planets, different ways,* Lilith reminded herself.

She started in on her supper, and it proved to be just as delicious as it had looked.

"You like the fish?" Ingrit asked as she helped herself to a second portion. "We raise them here. Caught them this morning for supper."

"Yes, I do. It's quite good," Lilith answered with a touch of shyness. To her shame, she realized that she was having a hard time meeting the other woman's eyes. Ingrit seemed to be able to bring out the schoolgirl in her. "What kind of fish is it?" she finally managed to ask.

"A survival from the days when Zommerlaand was first terraformed," Katrinn answered. "They were some of the first fish the settlers brought here. We call them catfish."

"Catfish?" Lilith asked. That seemed like a very strange name to give a fish.

"Yah," Ingrit said. "I'll take you by to meet them tomorrow. We're quite proud of them this year. They're nice and big."

"That would be nice," Lilith managed to stammer.

Gretta, who'd been sitting quietly with the other children, interrupted them. "Aunt Katy? Have you seen any aliens?"

"A few," Katrinn replied.

216

"Really?" Fryya asked, her eyes going wide as saucers. "Were they ugly? Were you scared?"

"No," Katrinn said. "I wasn't scared."

"Tell us about it," Clara asked, "*Please*? What were they like? Did you fight any battles with them?"

"I can see *someone* who has been watching too many holos," Katrinn's sister Marina observed. She and her pairmate, Hanna, who sat next to her, had been introduced to Lilith as the children's mothers.

"Now, all of you, you let her be about that," Hanna said reproachfully, "I imagine she'd like to put that aside for a bit."

"But,*Modaar!*" Gretta pleaded. The topic was simply too exciting for her to let it go.

"It's all right, Hanna," Katrinn replied. "I don't mind talking about some of it. We'll sit after dinner and I'll tell you all a few stories. But first, I've a few gifts I want to give out. *Zo*, finish your supper!"

That did the trick; the children dug into their portions with a will. The promise of gifts from off world *and* stories was simply too much to resist.

After supper everyone went into the big gathering room and Katrinn brought out her luggage. Grammy and her sisters were pleased with their gifts, but it was the Biobots that made the biggest impression on everyone. In short order, the children soon had the toys telling them story after story, and completely forgot about Aunt Katy's promise to talk about space. Lilith knew that that had been Katrinn's plan all along. They were far too young yet to hear about the harsh realities of life outside of Zommerlaand and the Inner-Systems.

***

The following morning, Ingrit invited them to go horseback riding. Lilith had seen horses in realies, and even ridden them there, but encountering the real thing was even more magnificent than any simulation could manage. Her own mount was a green and purple mare, with big intelligent eyes. The moment that it saw her, the horse lowered her head and nickered. Lilith gave the animal a tentative stroke, amazed at how soft its coat was.

217

"Jenny likes you," Ingrit said. "That's good. Let me help you up." She came over, and grabbed her by the waist, lifting her so she could reach the saddle. A delicious tingle went down Lilith's spine at this brief contact. Then the moment was over, and she felt herself blushing again.

Ingrit smiled knowingly and mounted her own horse, and then the trio left the stables and rode down to a large pond near the barn.

"That's were supper came from," Ingrit told her as they reached the pool. Lilith saw nothing where the woman had pointed but muddy water.

Ingrit rode over to the water's edge. "Heyas, *Roont*, been a while since you seen them. Wanna call Grandmother and her kinfolk up to say heyas?"

"Sure," Katrinn agreed, reaching into her saddlebag. She brought out a small pouch, took a handful of something and threw it out over the water. The pond exploded as huge black forms rose to the surface, and began feeding.

Lilith watched this activity with mild horror. It was hard for her to believe that such ugly looking creatures had tasted as good as they had.

Smiling broadly, Ingrit turned around to face her. "Beautiful aren't they? They got nice and fat this summer."

"They're something all right," Lilith agreed. "Do you swim in there too?"

"Sometimes," Ingrit informed her. "They don't bite that much and we keep the little ones out of the water, just in case they get *too* hungry."

"Ingrit!" Katrinn said in a scandalized tone, "You stop that! Lilith, don't listen to her. She's just having you on. They might look awful, but they aren't dangerous at all. Now, let's ride on before she gets going with another lie."

Ingrit laughed, and the three of them rode out into the fields towards the woods.

For Ingrit and Katrinn, the woods were something they took for granted, filled with things that they had both grown up with. For Lilith, it was another matter altogether. Her own motherworld, Ara, had been a barren place with few life forms and only patches of lichen here and there to lend color to the otherwise lifeless grey-black rock.

Every time she visited a *greenworld*, the incredible variety and beauty of the life in such places always enthralled her. Traveling under the welcoming arms of the trees, Lilith drank in the delicious sights and sounds around her.

A harsh, croaking call interrupted her reverie. She looked up and spotted a huge black bird that seemed to be looking right back down at her with an appraising gleam in its eyes.

"That's Old Meg. She's a friend of Grammy's," Ingrit said. "She's been around near as long as anyone can remember. And it looks like she's got her eye on you."

That must be the raven that Grammy mentioned, Lilith thought. As if to confirm this, the bird cried out again.

"Grammy told me about the Signs last night," she said, "but she didn't tell me what they were."

"That's Grammy all right," Ingrit replied with another smile, "She can never go too long without talking about *denn Trowaarei,* the Magic, and then its all shadows and cobwebs from there on out. It's really very simple; the Signs are the things around you that tell you things. The way a wind blows at a certain time, the way the moons faces are, and--"

The raven cawed again, even louder. If Lilith hadn't known any better, she would have thought that the bird was becoming impatient with Ingrit.

"I'm *gettin'* to that part!" Ingrit yelled up to the creature. "*And* the way some animals act. If you're watching for the little things, they'll tell you what's going to happen, or what you have to do to set things in your life a'right."

"That's kind of what Grammy said," Lilith said. "She even claimed that Old Meg actually talks to her."

"That she does," Ingrit replied. "Sometimes Old Meg talks to me too, but not like she does to Grammy. The Old-timers who settled Zommerlaand way back used to say that the ravens were messengers of the Gods, and I guess that's so."

Old Meg ruffled her feathers and made a loud clicking noise, as if to scold Ingrit for not getting to the point faster than she had. Then the bird flew off towards the farmhouse.

"Zo," Ingrit shrugged, "let's ride on. There's a nice lake I want you to see before we head back."

Lilith followed Ingrit's lead as they made their way up through the forest towards the lake. At one point in the track, the normally conversational Zommerlaandar suddenly quieted and took off her hat. Then she stopped her horse and made a sign over herself. Katrinn, Lilith saw, did the same.

At first, she assumed that they were making some kind of warding gestures, but as she drew up next to them, she realized that they were actually salutations of respect.

"We are entering the High Place, the grove of my Family," Katrinn stated solemnly. Her Second inclined her jaw towards the clearing ahead of them and then spurred her horse forwards.

Trailing behind her, Lilith realized that the trees in the grove were quite different than the rest of the forest that surrounded it. They were a mixed lot; some oak, some pine, some ash, a few that she recognized as rowan and willow, and still others that she could not identify, all clustered together in a greater variety than would have been natural for such a setting.

Their ages also differed widely. Some were clearly ancient and their limbs towered over them as they came into the grove. Others had obviously only taken root in recent years and barely reached the horns of their saddles. No matter their size or age, however, the trunk of each tree had been carved with Zommerlaandar characters, and wore ornaments tied into their branches.

These were made from knotted cordage, or fabric which was either bright and colorful, or faded with the years and the weather. But some were simple strips of wood, suspended with string and intricately carved with geometric designs. All of the carvings were painted, and they varied in shade from bright red to dark-almost-black depending upon their age.

A gentle wind passed through the tree limbs as they reached the center of the clearing. It stirred the decorations and created a sound that almost resembled the melody of wind chimes, only far more subtle and delicate.

"That's the ancestors talking," Ingrit said in a hushed voice. "You can hear them speaking and laughing with the wind. Grammy says that if you listen long enough, their words can even become clear enough to understand."

"What do you mean, 'the ancestors'?" Lilith asked.

220

"Ancestors. You know, family," Ingrit replied with an expansive gesture. "They're all around us here, from the oldest ones that came from Old Gaia, to the newest of us. Even the *Mehnz*, the males from before the Plague are here, with the women that knew them as helpmates."

"You mean that each tree represents one of you, is that it? They're symbols of each person in your family?" Lilith had heard of similar customs on Old Gaia, Nemesis and on Larra's Lament, and she presumed that this was also the case on Zommerlaand.

Ingrit shook her head "No, not symbols, they *are* us. Each one of them is a part of us."

"I don't follow," Lilith admitted.

Ingrit dismounted and gestured for Lilith to follow suit. The woman took her hand and led her over to one of the nearer trees, a young oak that was only two decades old at the most.

"When a Zommerlaandar girl is born, her *Geboortsplaats en denn Naavelstraang--*" Ingrit hunted for the right words in Standard for a moment, and then said, "her umbilical cord and her placenta, they are brought here and buried in the soil of this place. Then a tree is planted over them, and in time, the two become one and the same. It is one of the ways that we Zommerlaandars are tied to the land, and how the land is tied to us in turn."

"That's fascinating," Lilith said. "I noticed that the trees here are different from one another. Is there a reason for this as well?"

"*Yah,*" Ingrit answered, "A very good reason. The *Oude Mehnsz* from Gaia believed that each kind of tree had a special meaning and a special time of the year all its own. They taught us that every month has its own tree, and when a girl is born, the time of the year she is born in is also the tree that is hers."

The Zommerlaandar reached out to the young oak and stroked its trunk affectionately, "This one here, is Katy. You can see her name carved into the trunk here. She was born in the summer, in the time of the oak, and she is part of our land no matter how far away she journeys. Grammy says that that helps her to keep an eye on her, and keep her safe."

"A very moving custom," Lilith agreed, "and a very beautiful one."

221

"That is not the only thing that is beautiful here," Ingrit said suggestively, placing her arm around Lilith's shoulder. "Shall we ride on to the lake?"

***

That night, after supper was done, Grammy herded the adults out onto the porch. "The little ones are at it again with those toys you brought them, Katy. They'll be busy until bedtime, so I thought we'd have some time for a little adult fun." She was holding a box with some glass jars inside of it. A clear liquid sloshed around inside of them. Ingrit reached in right away and handed Lilith one.

"I thought we could all use a little of my special mash," Grammy added.

"Mind you," Ingrit warned, "drink it slow. Grammy's brew can hit you pretty hard the first time you get to know each other."

Lilith uncapped her jar and took a careful sip. To have described it as strong would have been an understatement. It easily surpassed the strongest *Aqqa* that she'd ever drunk.

"Goddess!" she coughed. Ingrit hadn't been kidding this time.

"*Gaad? Yah?*" Ingrit asked. She took a healthy pull from her own jar. "Ahh, Grammy! This is the best batch yet! Just right for Katy and Lilith's visit."

Lilith tried another sip. This time it went down a little easier. *It isn't that bad,* she thought, *once you get used to it.* Slowly, she felt the tension of the last three months drain out of her.

Later, after finishing a second jar, Ingrit helped her to stagger up the narrow stairs. "Goddess, I'm drunk," Lilith laughed. "Your Grammy makes a very mean brew."

"That she does," Ingrit acknowledged, steadying her with one hand and opening the door to her bedroom with the other. "You looked like someone who needed a little of her special medicine."

"Yes," Lilith confessed, "I suppose I did at that." She let Ingrit lead her into the room.

"Zo," Ingrit asked, "you think you might be interested in something that could help you relax a bit more?"

"Like what?"

"This." Ingrit gathered her gently into her powerful arms and kissed her deeply. When they finally parted, Lilith was breathless.

"If you want me to, I'll go," Ingrit said.

Lilith looked up at the woman, her pale blue eyes filled with uncertainty. This was the happiness that Ophida had predicted, she realized, sent by the Goddess herself to fill the void in her heart.

But can I take the risk? she wondered. *Should I?* The possibility of another loss in her life filled her with dread, but it warred with an even greater hunger to feel whole again, even if only for a little while.

She finally answered Ingrit in a small, barely audible voice. "No," she said, "Please, don't go. Stay."

Ingrit smiled tenderly and gently ran her hand through Lilith's hair. "My pretty little starship commander," she said huskily.

They kissed again, and the moment seemed to go on forever.

***

Downstairs, Katrinn had heard the bedroom door close, and shortly after this, the unmistakable cries of mutual pleasure. She looked over at Grammy, her eyebrows raised questioningly.

"It seems your friend got with Ingrit at last," Grammy said with a devilish wink. "They looked like they needed to spend some time together."

"Leave it to my Grammy to set things a'right," Katrinn observed, toasting her with the Mason jar.

***

Katrinn was already at the breakfast table when Lilith came down the stairs. "*Godag!*" her Second said cheerfully. "Hungry?"

To her own surprise, Lilith was. "Yes," she replied. "Where is everyone?"

223

"Out in the fields," Katrinn answered. "You know, life on the farm, gotta get up early! Bring in those crops!" She handed Lilith a plate and began to dish out a serving of biscuits and gravy. "So, how are you feeling today?"

"Much better, thank you. As if you didn't know," Lilith said accusingly.

"Oh?" Katrinn returned with a feigned innocence. "And did you sleep well, Commander?"

"Absent a few bruises, yes I did. Now, pass the bacon."

After Lilith had finished with her breakfast, they agreed to ride out into the fields to join the others. On their way to the barn however, a hovercar with official seals on its side came down the drive and parked in front of the farmhouse. A policewoman got out and stretched languorously.

When she saw them, she waved. The two women had no choice but to turn around and see what she wanted.

"Heyas, folks," the kaaper said. "I'm Klara Fryyasdaater, the local Constable hereabouts. The people over at Vaalkenstaad wanted me to come out this way and see how everyone was getting along."

"I'm afraid you missed them," Katrinn said. "They're all out in the fields working."

"*Yah*, well no matter on that. I'm really here to check up on you two. I heard tell you came out this way with a pair of energy-pistols. *Zat zo?*"

"Yes, ma'am," Katrinn said. "We still have them."

"That's good," Fryyasdaater said. "Can't have weapons like that floating around unaccounted for. Where are they then?"

"Upstairs," Katrinn replied. "Locked up in Grammy's cedar-trunk. I have the key. Do you need to see them?"

"*Nen, taake*," Fryyasdaater answered. "I'll take your word on it. Damn silly if you ask me, having me come all the way out here on a hot day like this for a pair of pistols, but rules *are* rules.'

"Not that anyone really follows them, mind you. I can't count how many folks out here have a few blasters that their kin brought back with them and tucked away. But we have to look like we're trying to keep that kind of thing down. Sorry for bothering you on such a hot day."

Katrinn got the hint. "Would you like something cold to drink for the trip back?"

"Why, that would be right neighborly of you, *taake*."

Katrinn went inside, and came back out with a glass of ice-cold lemonade. Fryyasdaater drained the glass.

"*Taake vaar*," she said, and then she got back into the hovercar. "Make sure someone lets us know when you two have left. It'll save me another trip out this way. Oh, and give my regards to Grammy, will you?"

"Will do," Katrinn said.

USSMC Training Facility, 75th Training Battalion, Hella's World, Hecate System, Artemi Elant, United Sisterhood of Suns, 1043.01|16|02:51:98

Kaly struggled up the slippery dirt track, feeling like she was hauling the entire planet on her back. In reality, she was only carrying a 28-kilogram pack, but fatigue, and the heat, made every kilo seem like ten times more than what it really weighed.

"Close up that line, damn you!" Sa'Tela shouted. "I don't want to see any stragglers."

Kaly tried to obey, but keeping up with the taller girls was proving harder with every step. The desert didn't help her either; the loose gravel under her boots made the going even slower.

Troop Leader n'Vera came up along side her. "Goddess blast you, N'Deena!" the DI hollered in her ear. "You're taking too long to get up the *fekking* trail. *Burn it*, hatchie!"

At that exact instant, Kaly slipped and fell flat on her face. She tried to raise herself, but the weight of the pack and her exhaustion conspired to keep her down. Tears of frustration and exhaustion welled up in her eyes as N'Vera bent over her.

The DI was furious. "Are those *tears* I'm seeing? *Fekking* goddess damned *tears*?"

"Ma'am, yes, ma'am," Kaly sobbed.

"Well listen up, *hatchie!* Marines don't cry! Marines ignore their pain and march on. They are *hard* and you will be *hard* or you will *fail!* Do you *hear me*, N'Deena?"

"Ma'am, yes, ma'am!" Kaly cried.

"Are you *hard*, N'Deena? Can you march on? I don't think so! I think you're too *soft* to handle this."

"Ma'am, no, ma'am!" Kaly yelled. "I can handle this!"

"We'll see! Now, get up and get moving or I'll give you a *fekking* good *reason* to cry. Do you *hear* me?"

"Ma'am, yes, ma'am!" Kaly struggled again to get to her feet, but only managed to rise up halfway.

"Goddess damn-it all!" N'Vera yelled, "Pick up your teammate, you stupid cows!"

Lena n'Gari ran up and grabbed Kaly by her pack-straps, wrestling her to her feet.

"Come on, Kaly!" N'Gari said in a low voice, "Let's get going before she adds another kilometer to the march!"

Kaly started moving again and N'Vera came up alongside her. "By the Lady, you are the most worthless sack of *crap* I have ever had to deal with! You'd better get your act together, little girl. Your friends might not always be there to drag your ass out of trouble. Now, *march!* And I better not see you take another tumble, or cry one more tear. Do you hear me, N'Deena?"

"Ma'am, yes ma'am!" Kaly replied. The gravel tried its best to spill her a few more times, but through sheer willpower, she was able to stay on her feet and finally crested the small hill. She could see the base from there, far off in the distance, shimmering in the heat waves like a mirage.

Senior Troop Leader Sa'Tela was waiting for them at the summit, and blew her whistle. "All right, hatchies! I don't think I can stand another nano watching this sorry-ass performance. We're going back to base now. Double time! Let's burn it!"

When they straggled back into base at last, Sa'Tela led the platoon through an agonizing calisthenics drill, before cutting them loose to stow their gear. A round of cleaning the barracks, and then an inspection that inevitably uncovered a reason for everyone to suffer more punishment, followed this.

That night, after lights-out, someone wept.

Kaly didn't know who it was, or even where she was, but her sobs echoed through the common room, just loud enough to hear, but thankfully not enough to wake the Drill Instructors. There was a deep weariness and pain to the cries. It was the lament of someone who had been pushed beyond all endurance, and hope.

Kaly understood perfectly, and would have joined the unknown woman, but she was beyond tears herself. *Marines ignore their pain and march on,* she repeated silently. Maybe they did, she thought. But right then she felt like anything *but* a Marine.

Instead, she just felt numb. Numb from everything she'd been through in the last two weeks. As she lay in her rack staring at the ceiling, she wondered how much longer she would be able to take what the DI's were dealing out.

I shouldn't have come here, she realized. *I shouldn't have done this.* Troop Leader Alika, back on Persephone, had been right. She was a stupid girl after all. Joining the Marines had been the biggest single mistake that she had ever made in her life.

Her hatred of the Hriss, her anguish for her ravaged home, her patriotism, all of her reasons for joining-up, now felt hollow and meaningless. All she wanted to do was to stop hurting, and sleep deeply enough to erase the memory of everything she'd been through. But she might as well have wanted to walk to the Andromeda galaxy. There was no end in sight.

Goddess, how will I make it? she wondered. The idea of enduring one more day on Hella's World filled her with absolute dread. She could almost hear Senior Troop Leader Sa'Tela's voice, barking at them to wake up for another set of calisthenics, another parade drill, or another forced march.

I can't do it any more. It's over.

In the morning, she was going to muster-out, and the Corps could be damned. Kaly rehearsed the scene in her mind, practicing the words that would free her from her torment like a magic spell. She pictured herself standing in front of Sa'Tela and telling her that she was quitting.

Then she imagined the expression of smug satisfaction that Sa'Tela and N'Vera would have on their faces, and a sudden spark of rage ignited inside of her.

Those evil bitches, she thought. *They'll probably enjoy seeing me muster-out.* Making people quit was what the DI's *really* wanted. Kaly was sure of it; she was positive that she'd seen the faintest traces of a smile come over their faces whenever the platoon was suffering its worst.

Grim determination suddenly surged up from the depths of her being. *No*, she vowed clenching her fists under the thin blanket. *I won't give you the satisfaction, you stinking bitches. I won't let you crush me down just so that you can feel superior and laugh at me as I walk away.*

She realized just then that she was in a fight; one that was just as profound as anything she'd been through back on Persephone. If she mustered out, she would lose it just as surely as if she had surrendered to the Hriss. That was even more unbearable than the pain her body was feeling.

"I'll show you," she whispered aloud. "I'll show you who'll make it through. I'll be standing there when this is all over and then *I'll* be the one with the smile on *my* face." This decision brought a surprising new vitality to her being, overwhelming her soreness, and re energizing her.

Gradually, she forced her weary body to relax. She knew that she'd need all the rest she could get for the conflict ahead. A dreamless, deathlike sleep came for her…

The lights came on.

Sa'Tela's familiar voice boomed out through the barracks, jarring Kaly and the rest of the platoon wide-awake. But now, it was also the voice of her opponent.

"Everyone out of your racks, now!" the DI shouted. *"Roll call!"*

Kaly was out of her rack and standing at attention before the others around her had even gotten their feet on the deck.

"Sound off!" Sa'Tela barked. One by one, the recruits yelled out their names and service numbers. Then it was Kaly's turn.

"N'Deena, Kaly 203031756!!" she shouted defiantly. Her voice was louder and sharper than it had ever been before, and there was steel in it now.

We'll just see who wins this fight, Kaly thought fiercely as she watched the DI's inspect the platoon. *We'll just fekking see.*

***

Although Kaly had found a reason to persevere, Platoon Carli suffered its first casualties that same morning. It happened just after PT, and before breakfast in the mess hall. Normally, this was a brief period of downtime when the recruits caught up with maintaining the barracks and their gear, and it was also one of the few points in the week when a recruit could speak with the Drill Instructors in private.

Kaly was trying to rub some polish into a particularly stubborn boot scuff, when two recruits walked by and went into the Senior DI's office together. One of them was a girl that had had problems from day one with everything. The other, her battle sister, hadn't really seemed to have had as much trouble (not that Kaly had spent much time watching anyone else's progress except her own and her battle sister's), but from the worn expression on their features, she could tell they had reached their absolute limits.

"They're done," Bel Anny said in a low voice.

"How do you know?" Kaly asked, watching as the pair knocked on the door to the DI's offices.

"You can tell from the shoulders," Bel Anny explained. "The way they slump. And you can see from the way they walked by us. You know, not meeting anyone's eyes. It's over for them. They're opting out."

The pair went in, and after a few minutes, Bel Anny's 'read' of the situation proved accurate. A Corporal from Operations walked in to the barracks and went straight through into the office. When she came back out, she had the two ex-recruits in tow. They said nothing to anyone, and kept their eyes straight ahead, walking out of the barracks, and back into civilian life.

That won't happen to me, Kaly vowed. *The DI's might have ground them down, but they won't get me the same way. I won't let them!* She went back to work on her boots with a will.

Later, after breakfast, the platoon listened to a lecture on Military Courtesy given by Troop Leader n'Vera. After spending a full hour learning how to salute, when to salute, who and what to salute and what *not* to salute, they were marched over to the PTS Building for their first Psionic Training System feed. Kaly wasn't too sure what the *feed* would be about, and she didn't really care. They'd been spared the usual parade drills that normally followed breakfast, and that was all that really mattered.

The PTS room was a small amphitheater just large enough for the platoon, with a tiny stage at its head. A covered table stood on the stage and a podium was positioned off to one side, presumably for the Instructors to use. Every seat in the room had a pair of wireless headsets sitting on them, wrapped in clear plastic. And except for the spotlights on the stage, the lighting was dim.

Kaly breathed a sigh of relief as she and Lena found themselves places to sit. The air in the little theater was deliciously cool and inviting, and it was a struggle not to fall asleep right away.

The DI's probably planned things this way, she thought, forcing herself to sit up. *Put us in a nice dark, cool place and then chop us for drifting off.* But she wasn't about to get caught for something as stupid as that. A couple of the other recruits, including Enggredsdaater, already had been during a lecture earlier in the week, and they had paid for it by working double fire watches and doing duty in the commissary, scrubbing pans.

You'll have to work a lot harder to catch me up like that, she thought fiercly.

At Sa'Tela's order, everyone unwrapped their headsets, slipped them over their temples, and then waited for the feed to begin. Kaly knew that the Marine PTS used the same psionic system that realies did, but instead of allowing for passive observation, and a certain amount of intellectual distance, the PTS literally crammed information directly into the brain's memory centers.

Kaly was fighting with herself again to stay awake, when the PTS feed began, jolting her to full consciousness. The lesson, on the field stripping and operation of the Mark 7 Blaster rifle, overpowered her tired brain and forced it to pay complete and total attention.

In seconds, her mind was force-fed every detail of the weapon down to its smallest component. By the end of half a metric minute, she knew all of the blaster's specs, every emergency that had ever been encountered with it, every trouble-shooting procedure, and even how to drill with it on parade.

Abruptly, the feed stopped. Kaly's head felt like a fried chikka egg that had been left out too long in the Hellan sun.

"All right, hatchies," Sa'Tela said, "Get out of your chairs and come over to the table."

Kaly took off her headset and stumbled up to the front of the room with the rest of the class, fighting off the fierce after-images that were left over from the feed. Once they were formed up, N'Vera pulled back the cover from the table, revealing brand new Mark 7 Blaster rifles.

"Each one of you will take a weapon," Sa'Tela told them. "You will then field strip and reassemble it. Take up your weapon now, and begin disassembly."

Kaly grabbed up one of the gleaming blasters and blinked stupidly, not quite sure how to begin. Then, in a flash of insight, she knew *exactly* what to do, and began to strip the weapon down. Her hands moved faster and faster as she worked, and with more and more assurance.

This is easy, she thought, amazed that anyone would ever be confounded by such a childishly simple task.

"Very well, Hatchies," Sa'Tela said. "Now reassemble your weapon. You have ten seconds to complete this task. *Go!*"

Putting it together proved even more elementary than taking it apart. She had hers together in less than eight seconds, slapping an inert battery pack home with a satisfying click. She smiled in triumph and looked around to see if anyone else had managed to match her time.

Her grin disappeared when she saw that one recruit at the end of the table had not finished. It was Valeri bel Talla. She knew her a little better than the pair who had opted out. A native of a Fringe World like Persephone, Bel Talla had come up with her on the same shuttle, and they'd had a chance to talk briefly a couple of times.

Bel Talla was just standing there, looking down at the sprawl of parts before her with a look of complete confusion on her face. Tears streamed down from her eyes as she made a visible effort to comprehend what she was seeing, and Kaly's heart went out to her. Sometimes the PTS feeds went like that, she recalled. A small percentage of minds either couldn't handle the information, or simply rejected it.

The DI's had also noticed the woman's struggle, and they came over and tried to lead her away from the table.

"No!" she cried, "I can do this! I know I can. Stop! Please let me try! I just need a moment to remember!" There was a brief struggle before she finally surrendered and let them guide her out of the training room, the very picture of utter defeat.

Everyone knew that Bel Talla wouldn't return. Her days as a recruit were over, and the platoon had lost its third member. Like the rest, Kaly wondered just how many more would opt out, or "fail to adapt" like Bel Talla had, before Basic finally ended.

"All right," Sa'Tela said as she rejoined them. "All things considered, well done. The blaster rifle you are now holding is your personal weapon for the duration of Basic. Except for inspections, drills and range time, it will be stored in the platoon weapons locker. Anyone found in possession of a weapon at any other time will find themselves up on charges. Is *everyone klaar?*"

Kaly and her fellow recruits replied as one. "Ma'am, yes, ma'am!"

The Troop Leader held up a chit with a plastic neck-string attached to it. "You will be given a chit like this as a receipt when you store your weapon in the locker. If you need to requisition your weapon, you will be required to present your chit to your Platoon Armsmistress. Do *not* loose it! If you do, you *will* face punishment detail. Is *everyone klaar?*"

"Ma'am, yes ma'am!"

"Good. Your Armsmistress will be Platoon Leader bel Anny. She will be in charge of the locker along with Troop Leader n'Teri. Is *everyone Klaar?*"

"Ma'am, yes ma'am!"

"Good," Sa'Tela replied. "You will now name your weapon and you will take care of it like a daughter. Damage it in *any* way, and you will wish you had never been born. That blaster *is* your life from here on out. Form up and stand to, and on my order, give me the name of your weapon!"

Everyone hustled over to the foot of the stage and stood at attention, weapons in the inspection position. As Sa'Tela walked down the line, questioning each trooper, Kaly desperately tried to come up with a fitting name for her blaster, but her imagination failed her. She was still struggling to compose something appropriate by the time the DI reached her.

"What is the name of your weapon, hatchie?" Sa'Tela asked.

Kaly had no choice but to blurt out the first thing that came into her overtired mind. It was the name of the first Navy ship that she had ever stepped aboard. "Ma'am, this recruit's weapon is named *Athena*!" she hollered.

"*Athena*?" Sa'Tela replied. "That's a pretty grand name for a blaster, *hatchie*. You'd better live up to that with some expert shooting, or I'll make you change it."

"Ma'am, yes ma'am!"

Sa'Tela nodded in approval and moved on. After she had gotten names from everyone, she addressed the entire platoon. "Because I am so pleased with your progress today, you will have twelve minutes of free-time. Make good use of it."

Everyone headed for the same place: their racks. Like the rest, Kaly had learned that twelve metric minutes was *plenty* of time to get some real sleep. She stowed her weapon in the locker, and after receiving her chit, made straightaway for her bunk. She was fast asleep before her head had even finished hitting the pillow.

Maristown, New Covenant, Bethlehem System, Telesalla Elant, United Sisterhood of Suns, 1043.01|17|05:50:59

500 light years away, Jon fa'Teela sat on a small wooden bench and watched the waves hitting the beach far below him. The neoman was in his Marine dress uniform, and his kit bag lay nearby. It was the final day of his leave after completing Advanced Infantry Training, and he wanted to savor as much of his motherworld as he could. He knew that it would be a long time before he might have the chance to return.

While the sunlight played over the waters, he took a deep breath of the sea air and tried to compose himself. Although he now wore the coveted Eye of the Goddess pin on his tunic, signifying his graduation from the brutal training course on Hella's World, he knew that his greatest challenges still lay ahead.

The neoman closed his eyes and prayed for the tenth time that day. *Jesu, watch over me as I go forth,* he asked silently, *guide me as I promote Thy faith and carry out Thy mission. Mother Mari, be with me through all my trials and turn the hearts of those that I might meet towards my favor.*

He opened his eyes again. A Marionite Sister was standing nearby, looking for the entire world like an angel in her white robes. It was Sister n'Avenal, his long time mentor and teacher.

"Jon?" she said, "the Marine Liaison Officer is here. She's waiting for you up in the Abbesses' office."

Jon stood and gathered up his bag. "Thank you, Sister."

He started to follow N'Avenal up the steep gravel path, but then he stopped. "Sister? May I make a confession?"

Sister n'Avenal turned to him and smiled. "Of course. What do you wish to confess, my son?"

"I have doubts about my fitness, Sister," he admitted. "I'm not sure that I'm the right vessel for this task." *There,* he thought, *it was out in the open at last.*

Sister n'Avenal clasped his hands and looked at him compassionately. "Jon, that alone is reason enough to send you forth. The Holy Mother Church would never have chosen anyone who did not possess the proper humility for such a great responsibility."

"Yes, Sister," Jon replied, "and I don't question the Church's wisdom, but I don't know if I will have the strength to accomplish my work. I barely made it through Hella's World, and I don't know if I'll be so lucky with my new unit."

"Your burden is a terrible one indeed, Jon fa'Teela," N'Avenal agreed, "but luck is not involved. As it tells us in the scriptures, ''It is the Creator's Will that we shall save the unbelievers from their blindness with the light of Truth.''

"It is also His Will that we shall help restore the order of things as He intended them; that men and women should share the stars together, and open the way for the Great Redeemer to return to us. I know that Jesu and Mari will surely watch over you, and that you *will* prevail for you are acting in His name. Draw strength from your Faith and go forth without any doubt in your heart."

"I will, Sister," Jon promised.

"Our prayers will be with you, Jon." She reached into her robes and handed him a small book. It was a traveler's copy of the *Revelation of Mari*, the holiest book of the Marionite faith, and he took it from her reverently.

"I carried this with me when I was a young missionary on Thermadon," N'Avenal explained. "It gave me great comfort during times of trouble and I wanted you to have it."

It was more than just a gift from a teacher to her student. The presentation of the book also formally symbolized the final step in becoming a missionary for the Church. The fact that she had honored him with her own copy only underscored the importance of what he was about to undertake, and made it even more sacred.

"Thank you, Sister. I will read it often," he replied, stowing it carefully in his kit bag.

Sister n'Avenal smiled and then her expression became grave. "There's more that I must tell you, Jon. A missionary's life can be a hard and dangerous one. The Sisterhood barely tolerates the Church, and the time may come when you might need the aid of the Faithful who live in secret among the unbelievers. Should you ever have such a need, look for our signs. Where you see them, you will also find aid and comfort."

Jon inclined his head in understanding. Just as their distant ancestors had in ancient Rome, the Faithful of the present identified each other through the use of covert symbols. The most common were the three sacred stars, representing the Father, His Son, Jesu, and the Holy Mother, Mari. It was something that every member of the Church who planned a journey away from the Marionite worlds learned, but he was grateful for the reminder, if only because it reassured him that he would not be completely alone in a hostile universe.

"There is something else, Jon," she added. "Some of us have a special calling in this life, and the Creator chooses us from among His flock to do His Will.'

"I have known you for many years, and He has already selected you to be His missionary. But I also think that you may be called upon to serve Him in another way as well.'

"If it is His Will that this is to be, He will send you a message through the Faithful so that you will know when, and how, you are to act. Look to the *Book of Sacred Numbers* for its meaning, and then accept your lot with meekness and obedience."

"I shall do whatever is asked of me, Sister," Jon responded. He felt humbled that such a great trust was being placed in him, and also a little intimidated. Even so, he kept his composure, and met her gaze squarely.

"I have never doubted that you would, my son," N'Avenal assured him. She made the sign of the cross over him, and then kissed his forehead. "Be blessed. May Jesu and Mari walk with you wherever your footsteps might take you."

CHAPTER 8

The Marine stationed at the docking tube glanced up at Jon, and then did a double take.

"Fa'Teela, Jon 447689231, reporting for duty, ma'am," he stated calmly.

"You're joking, right?"

"No, ma'am," Jon replied. He handed her the flimsy with his orders printed on it. The Private read them, and then re-read them, her mouth hanging open in disbelief.

"Just a moment," she said. Then she spoke into her com. "Troop Leader, there's a neoman down here at Bay 32. She, er, he, says *he's* supposed to report for duty with Anna Company." She looked back up at Jon. "Troop Leader Da'Saana is on her way. You… just…stay here."

Jon nodded and set down his kit bag. A few Navy crewwomen passed by and a number of them stopped in their tracks and looked at him with open curiosity. Jon was used to this though, and returned their insolent stares with a polite smile. Wherever he went in the Sisterhood, women always stopped and gawked at him.

When Troop Leader Da'Saana arrived, she took one look at him, and then her face reddened as she scrutinized his orders. "What is this?! These orders say that this—this *thing*--is supposed to report for active duty with *my* unit? I'll be damned if I'll let that happen! Come on, you, we're going to go see the Officer of the Day right now!"

The Troop Leader turned and stomped back up the ramp, cursing loudly. Jon followed at a discrete distance.

The moment that they reached Colonel Lislsdaater's office, Da'Saana demanded to speak with the officer in charge of the watch. She got her wish granted a second later when the Colonel herself came outside to see what all the commotion was about. She had returned early from her leave, and the short vacation had done nothing to improve her temper. Despite this however, she listened with apparent calm to the Troop Leader's complaint.

"Colonel? Did you know about this? This is outrageous!" Da'Saana sputtered.

"Troop Leader, we will discuss this in my office," Lislsdaater replied evenly. "Fa'Teela? You come too. Let's go."

237

As soon as they were behind closed doors, Da'Saana exploded again. "Colonel, you can't let them do this to my unit! I can't have this *creature* with my girls! It'll drive morale straight down the toilet!"

It was at that point that Lislsdaater abandoned her calm façade. "For one thing, Troop Leader," she said, her voice rising, "they are *not* your girls. They are *mine*. For another, I knew all about this. I also know that these orders come directly from Rixa, and have been signed by the Commandant herself. Do you think it's *your* place to question *her* orders, Troop Leader?"

"No, ma'am, but--"

"But *nothing*, Troop Leader!" Lislsdaater snapped. "You may not like these orders, but you *will* follow them. Is that completely *clear*, Troop Leader? Or do I need to *explain* things to you any further?"

Da'Saana snapped to attention. "Ma'am, no, ma'am!"

The Colonel walked around her desk and planted herself directly in front of Jon. "Now, Trooper fa'Teela, I understand that you neomen are homosexual. Is that correct?"

"Ma'am, yes, ma'am," Jon replied. He was also at attention by this point and made certain to keep his eyes straight ahead.

"And why may I ask is that, Fa'Teela?"

"Ma'am, although my faith celebrates Our Savior's first birth through Mother Mari, and awaits the day of His return, we also believe in being good citizens and obeying the conventions of society by maintaining the separation of the sexes."

"So, you're all just a bunch of decent, law-abiding people are you?" the Colonel sneered. "That's good, for your sake."

She paused, letting her words hang in the air. Then she continued. "Since the Corps has decided to make our outfit the showcase for this sick little social experiment, there are a few things I want to make perfectly clear to you.'

"Number one. For the record, I do *not* approve of your presence in the Corps, or your posting here. Nor do I appreciate the havoc that it will undoubtedly cause among my troops, and I will be watching you *very* closely. If you make enough mistakes then I will have the distinct pleasure of transferring you to the most miserable hole I can find for you.'

"Number Two. You will *at all times* comport yourself in a professional manner. You *will* be every centimeter of the perfect Marine. Your *kind* has a long, sad record of emotional instability and violence, and I will *not* tolerate any incidents of *any* kind while you are with us. Give me cause, and I will happily send you to the brig in irons.'

"Number Three. Even though you *say* that you have no interest in women, your *kind's* history is another matter. You will keep your relations with your fellow troopers above board at all times. If I have *any* indication that there has been any form of *perversion* caused by you, or participated in by you, I will see you and whoever you *coupled* with, brought up on charges, and I can guarantee a guilty verdict. Are we completely clear on all this?"

"Ma'am, yes, ma'am," Jon replied.

"Very well. Make sure I do not see you in this office again for any reason. Troop Leader, get this trooper down to Five-Bar and get him a rack. Make sure that it is cordoned off from the other troopers, and make sure that she – *he* – has some separate facility that he can use for his bodily functions."

"Ma'am, yes, ma'am."

"Dismissed."

Da'Saana escorted Jon in stony silence down to Five-Bar. Despite the confusion his presence caused there, no one dared say anything to the Troop Leader when she relayed the Colonel's commands. He was shown to a rack in the back of the furthest pod and a grey plastic tarp was hastily taped up in front of it, effectively isolating it from the other sleeping areas.

Arranging for his bathroom was another matter all together. The Marines used communal facilities that could not be partitioned as easily. In the end, Da'Saana had to go begging to the Navy Liaison Officer. A bathroom, two decks up that was not in general use by the crew, was finally designated for his use.

Then Da'Saana handed him a small Marine-grey data terminal. "It's a pathminder," she explained. "While you are on board, we will be sending you on work details. You will use this to get around the ship. The instructions are on the face. Do you think you can handle them, or are they too complicated?"

Jon looked at the small device and read the first few instructions. "No, ma'am, I think I can get this to work."

"We'll see," Da'Saana said doubtfully. "Frankly, I'm surprised you can even read. Lunch is 05:00 hours in the mess. Be there or go hungry." With that, she was gone, casting evil glances at several troopers who had gathered to watch their conversation. Wisely, the women quickly found other things to occupy their attention.

Jon ignored their whispers, and went to his cubicle, drawing the privacy curtain closed and laying on the bed to study the pathminder more closely. The screen offered him three choices; General Ship's Information, Navigation, and Emergency Procedures.

From his experiences on Hella's World, he knew that it wouldn't be long before Da'Saana would be grilling him on every piece of information, so he decided to get to work right away. After setting an alarm with his psiever, he tapped the tiny elzlate pad. A schematic of the ship appeared in mid-air and a voice began to speak.

"Welcome aboard the United Sisterhood of Suns Naval Ship, *Pallas Athena*," it said,"registration number SBC 1323. Named for the ancient Greek goddess Pallas Athena, guardian of ancient Athens, the *Athena* is 325 standard years old. She is one of the first of the *Isis*-Class warships, built to repulse the Hriss invasion fleets of the Second Widow's War and lay siege to enemy planets. Her official insignia is an owl, face affronte on field sable.'

"Construction first began on the *Athena* at the Cingulum X Naval Yards in 717.15 and took five years to complete at a cost of 58,393,478,672 credits. The first antimatter reactor core was installed on 723.15 and criticality was achieved on 725.18. The fourth reactor achieved criticality on 726.30 and was operated at full power on 727.20.'

"Official commissioning ceremonies were held on 729.47, when command was given over to the *Athena's* first Commander, Hila n'Tanya. After Commander n'Tanya died in 773.07, her personality was translated into the *Athena's* main computer, according to the terms of her will.'

"She continued to serve until 973.39 when her personality matrix became unstable. At that time, temporary occupancy was granted to the personality of Admiral Juli sa' Chani, who served until the computers

240

present personality matrix, Commander Dana bel Hanna, the third commander of the *Athena*, could be translated in 1023.22. Commander bel Hanna continues to act as the guiding intelligence for the ships computer systems as of this date.'

"The *Athena* measures 1000 meters, or one Standard kilometer. At her widest, she is 333.33 meters and 200 meters tall at her highest point. She has one resident fighter wing, the *Nighthunters* and also hosts one Marine detachment, the 115th Combined Combat Regiment, *Hekate's Hounds,* who act as a combat force for any planet-side actions."

Jon's psiever interrupted at this point, reminding him that it was now 04:94:93 hours. He had only a short time to get to the mess hall and eat lunch. After the day he'd had so far, the last thing he wanted was to go hungry. He quickly punched up the navigation function and selected the mess hall set aside for the Marines.

A bright red ball materialized. "Please follow the red ball to your destination," the pathminder advised. "At normal walking speed you should reach it from your present location in two-point-nine standard minutes, including lift time."

***

The mess hall was filled with Marines waiting in line for lunch, but when Jon stepped into the chow line, they backed away and let him walk it by himself. While he selected his meal, he did his best to ignore all the eyes that were on him, and the whispered comments that followed, but it was impossible to filter everything out.

"Goddess," he heard one trooper say, "Is that the neoman? Look at the size of that ugly brute! He looks like some kind of animal."

"Close enough," another sneered. "I think it's damned insulting that the Corps would allow something like *that* to wear our uniform."

"It's not their choice," a third woman piped in, "it's those *fekking* politicians caving into the Marionites."

"Yeah, *those* filth," the first agreed.

Jon moved himself out of earshot and finished with his selections. When he reached the end of the line, he looked for a place to sit down.

241

Only a few of the tables in the hall had extra seats, but as he approached each one, he was rewarded with sullen looks from their occupants, and trays were quickly shoved into any open space, denying him a place. Rather than challenge anyone, he moved on, finally locating an empty table at the very back of the hall.

It was then that he realized that he had been so distracted by the hostile reception that he had forgotten to get himself any utensils to eat with. A caddy stood in a corner nearby and he got up to get himself a knife and spork.

But when he came back to his table, his tray had been turned over and his meal was lying in a puddle on the floor. A few Marines watched him with casual hostility, and one or two even laughed as he picked it up and went back to the chow line to get himself another lunch.

***

At reveille, Jon was given orders to report to MedBay. Troop Leader Da'Saana's mood had not improved in the intervening hours. "The ship's Doctor wants to take a look at you, Fa'Teela," she frowned. "She probably can't believe that we have such a freak on board and wants to see for herself. Use your pathminder, and don't let me find out you wasted any time getting there, *Klaar?*"

"Yes, ma'am."

Jon consulted the pathminder and determined that the MedBay was two decks up from him and towards the bow. When the red ball appeared in his vision, he followed it. As always, crewwomen stopped what they were doing and stared at him, but he kept moving.

As he reached the lift and stepped into it, a pair of techs looked at him in surprise and made no secret of edging away to the other side of the car. Jon smiled pleasantly, and ignored them as they whispered to each other. To everyone's collective relief, his stop came up, and he got out without a backwards glance.

The nurse at the MedBay receiving desk was a little more professional, and if she had any reservations about his presence, the young officer didn't display it outwardly. "Fa'Teela? Dr. elle'Kaari is waiting for you in exam room 5. There's a pair of nighteyes, in the box by the door. You'll want to use them."

"Yes, ma'am," Jon replied, suddenly realizing that his doctor would be a Nyxian.

Nyx was one of the most famous BioWorlds. Due to an excess of solar radiation, the majority of its native life had evolved to live a purely nocturnal existence. In the absence of sunlight, Nyxian fauna tracked their quarry, or avoided becoming prey themselves, by sensing energy fields with the same sensitivity that Gaian sharks had once been able to smell droplets of blood in kilometers of ocean. Its flora had also specialized, using scent, bioplasmic fields and phosphorescence to either attract pollinators, or deter predation.

The first human settlers to encounter this unique ecosystem had followed the doctrine of biosyncronism to the letter, genetically engineering their offspring to emulate local conditions. They had also taken the step of copying the physical traits of some of the more compatible life forms, and integrating them into the physical design of their progeny.

The end result was a race that was able to see the body's physical energy, and by extension, accurately diagnose illnesses and injuries. This remarkable trait led to the planet producing some of the finest doctors in the Sisterhood, and the eventual establishment of one of its premier medical universities, the University of Nyx at Nocturne.

There was a price for such adaptation however. This was a form of extreme albinism, and Nyxians were forced to wear special protective clothing, collectively known of as the *Qada*, whenever they ventured forth in normal light. Like most of the animals native to their world, direct exposure to full spectrum light caused severe, and even fatal cellular damage for a Nyxian woman caught in the open without her *Qada*.

Instead of considering this to be a handicap, the women of the Night World embraced their genetic heritage, and their unique culture. They referred to themselves as the Moonborn, and wore their black *Qadas* with pride. And everywhere they went, these full-body garments symbolized the role that many of them played as master healers and guardians of health. They were a welcome sight to most women, and the color black itself, stood universally for help, health and well-being.

The only exception was on the Marionite worlds. Historically, the early New Catholic Church of the Revelation of Mari had not welcomed the Nyxians any more than they had the other bioworld human-variants. To the first Marionite elders, their very existence had been anathema, and their special abilities tantamount to witchcraft.

The passage of centuries had eventually led to a relaxation of this extreme view, and its official repudiation by the Church, but there were still many of the Faithful who were not comfortable with the Moonborn, or their medicine. On Faith, Hope, and New Covenant, medical care was provided to the population the "old fashioned way", and this, along with the negative view that the Sisterhood itself had towards the Marionites, ensured that few Nyxian physicians ever graced these star systems with their talents.

Jon did not have the luxury of being uncomfortable, however. Orders were orders, and the Corps didn't factor in his personal feelings when it came to issuing them. Nor did it care about any religious basis they might have had. In fact, the Corps didn't officially recognize his religion at all. He was to report to the ship's doctor and submit to her care, irrespective of her race or culture.

With this in mind, Jon put on the nighteyes and went through the door into a small antechamber. A holosign immediately materialized at eye-level urging him to close the door behind him, and warning that the inner door would not unlock until he had complied with these instructions. The neoman obeyed, and when the inner door opened, he was glad for the nighteyes. The room beyond was completely dark, and without them he would have never even found the exam table.

The doctor entered a moment later. "Trooper fa'Teela? I'm Dr. Saara elle'Kaari, Senior Ships Medical Officer."

Jon had expected to see her dressed in her *Qada*, but Elle'Kaari only wore plain black scrubs instead. He had never seen a Nyxian without their *Qada*, even in a holo, and her physical appearance startled him. The woman's skin was pure white like her hair, which she had bound up into a simple bun. And her irises were the palest shade of blue that was possible, coming just short of being completely colorless.

Elle'Kaari fully understood the effect that she had had on him. "I'm sorry if how I look alarms you," she apologized. "Sometimes I catch my

244

patients by surprise the first time they visit me. It's just that I prefer to work without my *Qada*, hence the need for a darkened room. I guess that's the price I have to pay for being a little different."

"Yes, ma'am," Jon agreed. Being different gave them something in common, he realized. "I'm afraid I must confess that I really haven't had much experience with the women from your world."

"Nor I with neomen," Elle'Kaari replied. "In fact, I had heard that there still weren't any Moonborn serving on the Marionite worlds, but I didn't quite believe it. Is this true?"

Jon nodded. "Yes, ma'am."

"Who provides your medical care if we don't?"

"The Sisters have their own physicians, ma'am," he answered. "None of them are Nyxian."

Elle'Kaari shook her head in astonishment. "So it's all scanners and imagers then?"

"Yes, ma'am."

"Amazing," she said, shaking her head. "And please, just call me 'Doctor.' I'm much better at that than being a 'ma'am'. May I call you Jon?"

"Why, yes. Please."

"I take it that although you didn't have Nyxian doctors on your motherworld, you *are* familiar with how we work, aren't you? You should have been exposed to some of our medical techniques in Basic."

"Yes, Doctor, somewhat," he answered. "There was a Nyxian physician on Hella's World, but she was only there to supervise my physicals. All of the care I received was from her assistants, and I really didn't deal with her directly."

Elle'Kaari frowned. "I'm afraid that the medicine in Basic is something of an assembly line out of necessity. Here on the *Athena* though, with a resident crew, it's a little bit more in depth and personal.'

"Jon, I'll get straight to the point. The reason I asked you to come here today isn't for a routine physical. I have your chart, and when I read it, I saw that you were up to date before your transfer.'

"What I really wanted, was the chance to study you. As you know, we don't have any other neomen aboard, and there aren't that many in the Star

Service for that matter. Your physiology is unique, and if you'll let me study it, it could provide some valuable information. That's not an order, by the way, just a request."

Jon was surprised by this, and pleased. By the insignia on her breast pocket, he knew that Elle'Kaari was a Captain, and could have simply commanded his obedience. But she hadn't. She had actually *asked* him, one *person* to another, for a favor. There was really no question in his mind what his response had to be.

"Certainly," he said. "I'd be more than happy to help you, Doctor."

Elle'Kaari beamed. "Thank you, Jon! I was hoping that you'd want to work with me. Can we get started right away? Or is there something else that you need to take care of today?"

Jon shook his head. Other than pure *shess* work, courtesy of Troop Leader Da'Saana, there wasn't. "Nothing that I know of, Doctor."

"Wonderful! Then let's get started," she said. "Please, let me see your inocular. I know that you had all your shots when you reported aboard, but I am still required to double-check. Then we can take a look at more interesting things."

Over the next hour, she subjected him to every conceivable medical test. Although some parts of it were embarrassingly intimate, she kept the mood light by describing Nyx to him.

Eventually, the conversation came around to the subject that had been in the back of his mind the entire time; Nyxian medical techniques. Although Jon considered himself a member of the modern Church, and didn't view the Nyxians as infernal beings in league with the Adversary, he *had* felt a little uneasy. But so far the exam had been very much like the ones he had been subjected to on New Covenant, and in Basic, and he hadn't encountered anything even remotely mystical.

"One beneficial side effect to our adaptation is an extremely heightened perception of the bioplasmic and bioelectrical energies in living beings," Elle'Kaari informed him. "This sensitivity allows us to see the state of our patient's internal structures."

Put in this matter of fact way, Elle'Kaari didn't make Nyxian medicine seem any more outré than what psi's were capable of and Jon found himself relaxing a little more.

"You mean that you can see my life energy and make your diagnosis completely from that?"

"No, not completely," she replied. "But the ability to see that energy helps when it is used in conjunction with more conventional testing procedures like the ones we've been using." She adjusted a small instrument and held it to his arm.

"For example, I can tell just from your bioplasmic field that you broke your left leg many years ago. The physical wound has healed, but your body has never forgotten the injury, and I can see the old break. It is 10 centimeters superior to the distal end of your tibial bone on the anterior side. A scan of the area would only serve to confirm this in greater detail, but I know it's there."

Jon was stunned by her accuracy. The break had occurred when he was only twelve in a stupid hover-sled accident. He'd never even mentioned it during his induction physical.

"What else can you see?" he asked.

"That for all intents and purposes, you're as healthy as an *narwog*. In fact, I haven't seen someone as fit as you in a long time. Your diet back on New Covenant must have been exceptional. Please turn to your left and cough, would you?"

Jon did so, and then it was her turn to be the listener. "Now, enough of Nyx," Elle'Kaari said. "Can you tell me a little about your world, Jon? I've heard so much, and none of it that I can really trust. I'd love to hear it straight from the source--if you'd be willing."

"I-I'm not quite sure where to start," Jon stammered.

"Start with your faith," she suggested. "What do you believe?" This was just the right question, and before he knew it, Jon had expounded most of the major points of his religion to her. Instead of being repulsed by his belief in a male God, Dr. elle'Kaari was genuinely interested in such a novel concept.

He went on to tell her all about the Sisters that had raised him, and about their holy mission to bring men back into the world to make way for the Redeemer. He even shared his own personal quest to prove the worth of neomen in the military.

And Elle'Kaari never argued with a bit of it. She just let him talk, and only interrupted to ask questions when a point confused her. Before Jon knew it, the exam was over.

"Well," she said as she stood back. "That will do for today. I'll have plenty to think about over dinner tonight."

"I'm glad I could help," Jon said, dressing. "If there is anything else I can do--"

"Oh, I was hoping that you would be interested in further studies," she said. "There is much that is the same about neomen and women, but there is also much that is so *very* different. I'll make sure to let Col. Lislsdaater know that you'll be needed here a little while longer. Will that be all right?"

"Why, yes. It would be!"

"Good," Elle'Kaari smiled. "I'll tell her that I'll need you back first thing tomorrow. Oh, and Jon, if you have time, could you send me a copy of some of the passages in your holy book? I'd love to study them."

"Of course!" Jon smiled back. This was better than he'd ever dreamed possible. He knew that the doctor was undoubtedly interested in his religion from a purely clinical standpoint, but he told himself that scientific study could always turn into genuine faith, given time, and Jesu's blessings.

He left the MedBay feeling elated and grateful. Mari in Her infinite mercy had provided him with a small bit of warmth in an otherwise cold and hostile place.

Grunvaald Haarmaaneplaatz, Vaalkenstaad Township, Zommerlaand, Sunna 3, Solara Elant, United Sisterhood of Suns, 1043.01|28|05:20:56

The final day of shore leave arrived all too swiftly for Lilith. "There's one more thing I want to do before we go," Katrinn said to her. "I have to visit the High Place. It's sort of a ritual we do here before we leave Zommerlaand. You can come with me if you like."

"I'd love to," Lilith replied. She finished stowing her gear into her kit bag and followed Katrinn out of the farmhouse. Her Second led them up the trail to the special grove Ingrit had shown her, and from there, to something she hadn't noticed on that first visit. There, a chair had been carved from a tree stump that was still rooted to the ground. Grammy was seated in it, watching them as they came up. Ingrit, Marina and Hanna were with her, and they all wore solemn expressions. Above them all, monitoring the proceedings from a nearby branch, was Old Meg herself.

"Greetings, *Grötdaar*," Katrinn said. "It's time for us to leave."

"*Yah, daater*," Grammy nodded. "I know, and as always, I'm sad to see you go. Sit down you two, and we'll see what words of wisdom the Wise Ones have for your journey." She closed her eyes and sat very still.

As if on cue, Old Meg flew out of her tree and landed on Grammy's shoulder. The bird eyed them both for a moment before she began making soft clicking noises in Grammy's ear. Then she flew back up to her perch.

Grammy's eyes opened, but when she spoke, her voice was younger somehow, and not quite her own.

"Your journey will be a long one," she began, "and fraught with hardship. Sisters fight, old quarrels fester and the people of the past return. But above all, beware of the treasure in the deep. It is both the seed of darkness and the germ of hope. Only wisdom will determine which will grow from it, but it is not your hand that will plant it." Overhead, Old Meg cried out, seeming to confirm what Grammy had just told them.

There was a long pause before Grammy's eyes fluttered open, and when she looked at Katrinn, they were wet with tears. "The Wise Ones have spoken," she said, her voice sounding old again, and worn. "*Daater*, I know that the road you have chosen for yourself is the one of the warrioress, like so many of our kin before you, and I cannot fault you for choosing it. I never have.'

"But this old woman worries now and again for you up among the stars. You have a good friend in Lilith here. You are like sisters. Promise me that you'll watch out for each other like sisters do, and I'll worry a little less when I look up at the sky at night."

"Yes, Grammy," Katrinn replied gravely. "We will."

Grammy rose from her place. "I have a gift for both of you. Something I made for you to wear on your travels. I know that Lilith here does not believe like someone born of our soil, but I hope that she will accept it and wear it none the less."

She reached into a small pouch and produced a pair of wooden medallions strung on thin leather cords. She handed Katrinn one, and Lilith the other. While Katrinn donned hers, Lilith paused for a moment to examine the gift. It was carved with Zommerlaandar symbols like the ones Grammy herself wore. They had been combined together into an intricate pattern, and colored in with red paint.

"Thank you, *Grötdaar*," she said, putting it around her neck.

Katrinn hugged her. "Yes, thank you, Grammy. We'll be back before you know it."

"Of course, *Daater*," Grammy replied. "And Lilith? You come back with her. You know you are always welcome here among us."

"I shall," Lilith promised. "Thank you for welcoming me."

"Safe journey, both of you," Grammy said.

Ingrit came forwards. "Come on, *Roont*. I'll take you to the port."

Katrinn nodded sadly and started down the trail. There were tears running down her cheeks. Lilith followed in silence, and Ingrit took her hand. After a few steps, they paused and looked into each other's eyes.

"I'll write," Lilith finally said.

"And I'll look forwards to reading your letters," Ingrit answered, kissing her long and tenderly. When they separated at last, and started back down the path together, it was Lilith's turn for tears.

***

Lilith looked out the window of their shuttle with a wistful expression. It had left the upper atmosphere and reached space. "I don't know how you ever left Zommerlaand in the first place, Kat."

"Well," Katrinn said looking down at the planet, "That's a little hard to explain to a city girl. No offense, Lily."

She paused for a moment. "I guess the best way to put it is that as wonderful as it was growing up there, the horizon was just never *big* enough to suit me. I always wondered what the rest of the universe was like, and when I got old enough, I went out and took a look for myself."

"Maybe I can understand that," Lilith replied with a smile. "But still--"

"Yeah, I know," Katrinn agreed, "it *is* wonderful. I guess that's why I keep coming back. As much as I like my adventures *oop dah an denn*

250

Staarn, I still have to come back every once in a while to recharge my soul."

"I think I understand." Lilith offered her hand across the narrow aisle, and Katrinn took it. "Thank you for sharing it with me. It's a special place."

"My pleasure," her Second said. "I knew that you'd find something there for yourself."

Lilith sighed and flipped down the data terminal embedded in the rear of the seat in front of her. "Well, Kat, what say we catch up on what the rest of the universe has been doing while we were away?"

"Ugh!" Katrinn grimaced. "If we *must*."

"Newsfeed," Lilith said to the machine. "Major stories only, multiworld."

A life-size holo of a newscaster appeared in the aisle. Lilith had seen the woman's broadcasts before, and she always reminded her of an officer that she'd served with on the USSNS *Hecate*.

"Welcome to another edition of SNN Top Story," the image began,"Our first story tonight is from the Delgen system in the Almastris Elant where an outbreak of the deadly Wigoni AV-13 Virus has already claimed 200 lives, in what medical researchers say is the worst outbreak of this disease in years.'

"Public officials urge calm, and Dr. Marra n'Vera of the Delgen Center for Public Health told SNN reporters that the virus appears to be completely contained. However, as a precaution, all travel to and from the planet has been sharply curtailed, and maritime authorities are checking outgoing crews and passengers for any signs of the illness before allowing them to transit out of the system. Do you wish more details?"

"No, thank you," Lilith said. "Next story, please."

The virtual newscaster moved on with a smile. "The Supreme Circle heard testimony today from the Coalition of the Far Arm Colonies, a special interest group serving the newly emerging colonies in the Thamari Elant and the Sagana Territory, urging them to increase military spending to help protect these outlying areas. They cited the recent attack by Hriss renegades on a member colony on Persephone in the Demeter system as just one of the many aggressive actions taken by the Hriss nation against the Sisterhood in recent years.'

"In a related story, Clara bel Fava, the Chairwoman of the Coalition, sharply criticized the Star Service for what she called a 'slow and inadequate response' to the recent crisis, and laid the blame for the deaths of some 6,000 colonists on Persephone squarely on the shoulders of the Navy. Do you wish more details?"

"Yes!" Lilith responded irritably. She was already regretting her decision to listen to the news, but she had to catch up on current events before reporting back for duty. The story went on.

"Fleet Admiral Myrelli ebed Cya, commander of the Topaz Fleet commented on this allegation in an interview with SNN reporter Hilari n'Mara."

"The actions of my fleet," the Admiral's image said, "were above reproach. Although we deeply regret the lives lost, there was no way that our forces could have responded any sooner, nor more decisively.'

"I would also like to point out that the Chairwoman failed to mention that we responded as soon as we received notification of the event. She also neglects to mention that although there were losses, there were also survivors, thanks to our efforts. Or that the Red Star is doing all that it can to aid them in the process of rebuilding and recovery."

"You tell'em, Admiral!" Katrinn shouted. She was absolutely scandalized. "Can you believe that, Lily? Blaming *us* for Persephone? What nerve! And *then* when they need us, they sure howl long and loud! *Vaarsa aasnaslaake!*"

"Politicians," Lilith growled with disgust. "Next story, please."

"A milestone for the rights of neomen, and their integration as full citizens of the Sisterhood, took place this week when one of the first neomen to join the Marines reported for active combat duty with *his* unit aboard a Star Service warship.'

"Although the Navy refused to grant SNN an interview with the service*man*, or confirm exactly where *he* is posted, the Naval Office for Public Affairs on Rixa did state that he is adjusting well to life aboard his new ship.'

"However, reliable sources inside the Navy were able to confirm for SNN that the vessel he is serving aboard is the *Isis*-Class starship, *Pallas Athena*, and that his duties are no different than any other Marine serving in

252

the field. Our viewers should also be aware that the *Pallas Athena* was part of the battle group that responded to the recent Hriss attack on Persephone. Do you wish more details?"

"No," Lilith said. "No further details."

"Of course, Commander ben Jeni," the holo replied. "Before we move on to our next story, do you, as the Commander of the *Athena*, have any comments that you would like to make to SNN about the Persephone raid, or the neoman?"

I should have expected as much, Lilith thought. Newsfeeds were not only interactive, they could be personalized and keyed to the viewer. Just as Ebed Cya had warned, the journalists were trying to corner her.

"No, no comment," she answered tersely. "End newsfeed. *Now!*" The holographic newscaster frowned, but disappeared.

"So the predators begin to circle the prey," she observed. "We'll have to make certain that our officers and the crew are strongly reminded to keep this all confidential. The last thing we need on top of the neoman himself is anything leaking out to SNN that could hurt the Navy."

***

Mearinn was waiting for them they came aboard the *Athena*. "Welcome back, Commander," her Third said as she took one of her bags. "How was your leave?"

"*It* was great," Lilith replied. "Our debriefing, and the stories in the newsfeeds left something to be desired though."

"Yes, I can imagine," Mearinn said. "To save you the trouble of asking, he came aboard ten days ago."

Lilith set down her luggage as they boarded the lift, and started their ascent to Officer's Country. "Did he now? And how is *he* adjusting to his new home?"

"Col. Lislsdaater returned from leave early and she has been handling the matter personally," Mearinn informed her. "So far, aside from some rather vocal complaints by his platoon and his Troop Leader, we haven't had any incidents. I understand that he's been spending all of his free time with Dr. elle'Kaari up in MedBay."

"MedBay? Why? Is he sick or something?" Lilith certainly hoped so; if the neoman was unfit for duty, she had all the cause that she needed to see him off her ship.

Mearinn shook her head. "No, ma'am. The doctor told me that if anything, he is at the very peak of physical fitness. She's been using this event as an opportunity to broaden her scientific knowledge of his kind."

The lift arrived at their destination and they stepped off. "Well, so much for that faint hope," Lilith frowned. "Anything else that I should know about before I relieve you?"

"The ship has been completely rearmed and refitted," Mearinn informed her. "Minor micrometeor damage to the hull was repaired and our systems are all operating at top service levels. Also, I was supposed to remind you that your visit to the core is coming up."

In the rush to get to Persephone, and the events that had followed the raid, Lilith had put that routine chore at the bottom of her list of priorities. Every four months, she and her officers were required to meet with the personality housed in the computer's mainframe, and assess its mental fitness. For the most part, this was an uneventful affair, but she knew how necessary it was. Ships had been lost to personalities gone mad before.

"What time is the interview?" Lilith asked.

"Five standard days from today," Mearinn replied. "At 03:53:33 hours."

"Fine," Lilith sighed. "Anything else?"

"The usual reports of the ghost on deck 12," Mearinn replied. "An engineering crew reported seeing an apparition, and said that they heard knocking sounds in one of the bulkheads."

Being an old ship, the *Athena* had her share of ghost stories and Lilith had heard this particular tale a number of times before. She made a mental note to talk with the ship's High Priestess about it. While she didn't believe the stories herself, she knew that an exorcism ceremony would go a long ways towards calming down those crewwomen who were too superstitious for their own good.

"Anything else?"

"Well," Mearinn hesitated. "There *was* one other thing. Skipper was a bit of a handful while you were gone."

"What did that little *duvel* do now?" Katrinn inquired with a grin. By this point, they had reached the door to Lilith's cabin.

"I fed him just like you said," Mearinn explained, "and I visited him every day."

On the other side of the door, Skipper was meowing loudly, and sending messages to her through her psiever. *Don't believe her!* he thought frantically. *She's lying!*

Lilith ignored him. "And?" she asked.

"Well, the third day you were on leave, he got out somehow. We searched the entire ship and we finally found him in air shaft 4117-C, but it took us several hours and most of Engineering to catch him. I don't know *how* it happened, Commander, but he didn't seem any worse for the experience."

Katrinn turned away, stifling a burst of laughter.

"And they actually used to say that kaatzes were good luck on a ship!" Lilith remarked. "Well, no problem, Mearinn. I'll have a little talk with him. Anything *else*?"

"No, ma'am, that is all."

"Very good," Lilith said. "Thanks for watching the old boat while we were away. You are relieved of command." She gave Mearinn a formal salute.

"Thank you, Commander," Mearinn answered, returning the gesture.

Fleet Admiral Myrelli ebed Cya' s Office, Topaz Fleet Command, Rixa Naval Base, Rixa, Belletrix System, Pantari Elant, United Sisterhood of Suns, 1043.01|30|03:11:67

The briefing for the Battle Group Golden's next patrol was held in Admiral ebed Cya's office. It was not as intimate and informal as the previous one however.

In addition to Lilith, her officers, and Ebed Cya, there were also several Admirals, Vice Admirals, and representatives from the OAE present. Lilith took her seat, knowing that whatever Rixa was planning, it was going to be very difficult and dangerous in nature.

"Ladies, first of all, let me welcome Commander ben Jeni, Captains bel Sarra and Taur Minna, and their staff, back from their leave and thank everyone for attending today," Ebed Cya began. "Commander ben Jeni, this Command has evaluated your engagement with the enemy in the Demeter system, along with several other reports received over the last few weeks by sister battle groups in and around the Sagana Territory."

"Several Hriss Clans, using the pretext of rebellion against their central government, have been conducting a series of probing raids into Sagana. In reality, they have enjoyed their government's secret blessing and have been acting with increasing aggressiveness. Like your own battle group, our other forces in the area have encountered progressively larger enemy forces with better equipment and more seasoned personnel.'

"To date, we have managed to repel the raiders, but not without suffering some reversals. The invasion of Persephone and the damage to the *Kit Cavenaugh* are two prime examples. For those of you who have been wondering about this, I can now tell you that the *Cavenaugh* and her battle group encountered an enemy squadron in the Enyo System. They managed to destroy the opposing force, but only after sustaining massive battle damage, and incurring significant casualties."

Lilith was not surprised by this disclosure in the least, and she had already guessed most of the details for herself, despite the fact that no one had been able, or willing, to confirm anything. The Navy had done a top-rate job of keeping the *Cavenaugh's* crew, and Battle Group Platinum, from talking to anyone.

Now that she had her confirmation, she could see the reason for such silence. Things were bad in Sagana, and it seemed very likely that they were about to get much worse.

"We believe that the Hriss objective is to gauge our strengths and weaknesses through an aggressive program of reconnaissance-by-fire, just as they did at Persephone," Ebed Cya said. "Naval Command feels that unless we demonstrate a strong display of force in reply, the next phase may be an all-out invasion of the territory, with fleet-sized forces.'

"Such an incursion, if it occurred, would lead to another interstellar war between our two races. If that comes to pass, the public will call for nothing less than *total* war--and the absolute annihilation of the Hriss as a species.'

"Ladies, the average woman is tired, and she will ask us to do the unthinkable. There will be no treaties this time, no settlement that will lead to a betrayal. She will demand that we enforce the ultimate peace, which can only come when there is no enemy left to fight. It will also cost us many lives to make that a reality. I for one, desperately hope that such a conflict can be avoided.'

"The path that we will ultimately take rests on your shoulders alone, and the unfavorable publicity that we received from the Persephone affair only underscores the grave nature of your mission. The public is clamoring for action, and the Supreme Circle has commanded it."

Lilith felt a chill go down her spine. *War*, she thought. *Will it come to that again?* In the 1,042 years of its existence, the Sisterhood had fought four wars with the Hriss already.

The First Widow's War had repelled their invasion and engendered the birth of the Sisterhood. The Second Widow's War had seen the Hriss Imperial Navy decimated, ushering in the expansion of the Sisterhood into new regions of space. But the War of the Bandit and the War of the Prophet had been fought to keep a check on the rogue clans and renegade elements that had risen up in the aftermath to seize power.

The peace since the War of the Prophet had been uneasy and fragile, and although the Sisterhood had been the victor in every conflict with the Hriss, those triumphs had been bought at a terrible cost.

Will there ever *be a true peace?* she wondered. She could see why the Sisterhood at large, hating these clashes, would want genocide, and like the Admiral, she dreaded that possibility.

"Ladies," the Admiral continued, "your mission will be two-fold in nature. Your first objective will be to project our naval power into the Sagana Territory and destroy any and all hostile forces that you might encounter there.'

"Your second objective will be to help the outer colonies increase their defensive capabilities and their level of preparedness. To this end, a special detachment of Marines, the 233rd Combat Engineers, will be accompanying you on your patrol, along with the supplies and weaponry that they will require for the task.'

"I would like to tell you that your mission will be an easy one, but I cannot. It is highly likely that you will be forced to engage enemy forces comparable to, or even superior to your own.'

"In addition, you may not always get the cooperation that you might otherwise expect from the colonies that you visit. Although the public at large is unaware of it, for some time now, a number of the worlds in the territory have formed a loose association calling itself the Rampart. To explain this organization to you, I will now turn the briefing over to Wila bel Jeanna of the Agency for External Affairs."

Lilith's eyes narrowed in displeasure as she recalled Bel Jeanna's role in the matter of Captain D'Orsi and the *Spacewitch*. Still, she made herself pay attention. As much as she disliked the OAE, knowledge was power when it came to situations as volatile as the one in Sagana, and every bit of information had value—regardless of the source.

Bel Jeanna rose from her place and stood before the assembly. "Thank you, Admiral. Ladies, the Rampart was formed to help coordinate the common defense of its member worlds, and as a means to give them a more organized voice and better representation. But within this group, there are extremist elements that you should be aware of.'

"Some of these elements have actually proposed secession from the Sisterhood, and advocate a policy of arming themselves to a level that is well beyond what the Concordance deems either appropriate, or legal.'

"Towards that end, we have seen an increasing number of smugglers bringing military grade weapons into the area, and we have interrupted several attempts to secure heavy weapons from both Sisterhood sources, and from neighboring races.'

"To make matters worse, other dissident members have even gone so far as to suggest capitulation to the Hriss, or even outright alignment with them. Fortunately, these elements are a very tiny minority with no general support.'

"But the fact that such drastic changes are *even* being discussed highlights the serious state of affairs that we are dealing with. Our agency will be providing you with detailed information on these groups, and the individuals involved. Thank you for your time." Bel Jeanna returned to her seat and the Admiral took over the briefing again.

"Thank you for your information, ma'am," she said to the agent, "We appreciate your agency's invaluable assistance and we will look forwards to receiving that data from you."

She addressed Lilith and her staff next. "Because of this highly unstable climate, you should be aware that the worlds that you visit may prove resistant to your efforts, and may even go so far as to reject your assistance. For your mission to be a success, it will require all of your skills as diplomats, and should you encounter Hriss forces, as fighters.'

"Regardless of the obstacles, or the opposition you encounter, you must prevail. Peace utterly depends on it. May the Goddess watch over you and grant you success. You are dismissed."

Everyone in the room made the Lady's sign and stood. There was none of the normal chitchat that usually followed a briefing. Instead, they filed out of the Admiral's Office in silence, deeply sobered.

***

Lilith and her command staff were not the only members of her ship to be briefed about the mission to the Sagana Territory. Shortly after the meeting in Admiral ebed Cya's office had concluded, Ophida N' Marsi received a coded signal on her psiever, informing her that Willa bel Jeanna wanted to speak with her via encrypted holo.

At the time the message reached her, the priestess was in her private office researching the exorcism ceremony for the alleged ghost on deck 12. But as important as the rite was, she had been waiting to hear from Bel Jeanna, and set an electronic bookmark in the text. She brought up her com terminal and entered her private code.

Bel Jeanna's image appeared immediately. Never one to waste time with idle banter, the woman got straight to the point. "Good afternoon, Reverend," she said. "The *Athena* is being sent on a very sensitive mission to the Sagana Territory, and you and your agents will be playing a vital role during that patrol."

"I see," Ophida replied. "What is the situation?"

Bel Jeanna provided her with the same overview of the Rampart that she had presented to Lilith and her officers, including the briefing on its dissident elements. Then she focused on Ophida's specific role.

"Naturally, the Agency is concerned about interference from the dissidents, which we believe, may range from simple non-cooperation to outright sabotage. Your station will be charged with the job of making contact with our assets in Sagana and determining the level of threat.'

"If you find that it is substantial enough to impede the battle group's mission, then your task will be to neutralize any of the elements involved. Towards this end, our assets in the area will be instructed to provide whatever assistance you need, and if you require it, we can also furnish you with any specialists to deal with any particularly difficult problem areas." Which in plain Standard, meant assassins.

"Do we have any individuals in particular that we need to be concerned about?" Ophida asked.

"Yes," Bel Jeanna nodded. "I am uploading the intel files on several key figures that may require special attention, but until we are certain that they intend any action that could impede the situation, they are only on your watch list."

Several holos appeared along side Bel Jeanna's image, along with their information. Ophida only glanced at them, planning to study the case files in detail after their meeting was over. "Was there anything else?"

"Yes," Bel Jeanna answered. "We were curious about the neoman. What have your agents observed so far?"

"The greatest issue that we have encountered is his acceptance with the crew," Ophida informed her. "However, Fa'Teela seems to be remarkably patient with the abuse he has received, and I believe that this may be supported by his religious belief system. In terms of his work performance, he is doing everything that is asked of him and has strictly adhered to all procedures."

"A model Marine then?" Bel Jeanna asked. There was a note of doubt in her voice that Ophida shared. "We know that the Marionites sent him out as a missionary, and there is a strong probability that he may also be acting as a covert agent. Have you had any indication that he has received clandestine communications from them, or that he appears to be acting under any orders?"

"None," Ophida said. "Since he came aboard, he has not been contacted by anyone, and he keeps to himself. Because of that, I have had Dr. elle'Kaari initiate a relationship with him, and according to her report, she has managed to win his trust. With her in place, I am reasonably assured that we will be able to spot any subversive activities. In addition I have a watch set for any communications that he receives."

"Good. Continue to monitor him," Bel Jeanna instructed. "And good luck in Sagana."

Necropolis Ruins, Ashkele Free Port, Hallasa System, Frontier Zone, Xee Protectorate, 1043.01|30|07:69:24

Zara guided their rented hovertruck through the debris-strewn path, choosing her course with care. This far out into the ruins there was little chance of getting a tow if a fan blade broke or the anti-grav units failed. Bel Lissa and Sarah sat up front with her, and Maya was in the back, wedged in between a cargo container and their guest, who was also a rental.

Captain bel Lissa had insisted on hiring the robot for the meeting. There was simply no telling what their customers would do, and Gun 501 was a safegaurd against any treachery.

Despite the need, Maya still felt uneasy sitting next to the machine and when the hovertruck dipped into a low spot and she brushed up against its matte black armor, the physical contact made her skin crawl. As far as she was concerned, the sooner they were done with their meeting and had parted company with the Gun, the better.

The hovertruck had entered a large square by this point, and Zara stopped to consult a map on the windshield's HUD. Most of the Necropolis was uncharted, and the fragmentary map had been purchased from a rather dubious Xee merchant who had guaranteed its accuracy. The alien had sworn that it was an updated copy of a copy of a copy of the one produced by the National Astrographic Societies' famous archaeological expedition over 350 years earlier.

This had been a lie however; the Xee had occupied the planet for eons and they had always forbidden any non-Xee from mapping the Necropolis, even representatives of the illustrious Society. Ostensibly this was for religious reasons, but in reality, they had instituted this prohibition in order to hoard any profits that might otherwise have been garnered from map sales to outsiders.

Not that Bel Lissa and her party had had any alternatives to choose from. Few maps, even Xee versions, were available. The Xee were more comfortable wandering the ruins without them, and claimed that their strange Gods led them along the proper paths without the need for such mundane tools. This was probably also a complete fabrication, but no one had ever had a reason, or the inclination, to ferret out the truth.

"Well?" Bel Lissa asked.

Zara squinted at the symbols on the plastic windshield. "According to the map, we're in Square 4765. Temple 8033-A should be about a kilometer from us, on a heading of 199.5 degrees, but it looks like we'll have to take a detour up ahead, so I'll need to recalculate our route."

She pointed towards a large building of unknown function that had partially collapsed onto the street. Maya turned in her seat, craning her neck for a view and it was immediately apparent that the debris pile was far too high for the hovertruck to simply climb over.

After a few more moments of study, Zara restarted the vehicle and took them west down a narrow side street. The ruins there were tall, and closely packed, and Maya eyed them nervously. Quite a few of the structures towering over them looked as if they were unstable enough to come crashing down with even the slightest vibration.

As they negotiated the gloomy passage, a few small pieces of masonry did fall down around them, and Maya held her breath. But the hovertruck made it through the gap safely and entered another open square.

And not a moment too soon. Zara was just turning the vehicle back onto the correct heading when there was a loud rumble from behind them.

A thick cloud of dust belched out from the street that they just exited from, obscuring the full extent of the collapse, but from the sound of it, and what she saw spilling out, the girl knew that it had been fairly substantial.

Zara looked back over her shoulder at the rubble with casual unconcern. "Ah wells," she remarked, "I suppose we'll have to find a new way home around that." For some reason, everyone except Maya thought that this was extremely funny.

They arrived at their destination several blocks, and a few more hair-raising passages, later. It was another large square, and parked in the middle of it was a low, tracked vehicle. The machine was armored and it sported a single gun turret on its roof.

When their hovertruck came to a halt, an egress hatch on the alien vehicle popped open. An armed Hriss Warrior stepped out of it and the turret on the roof rotated around and brought its armament to bear.

The robot sitting next to Maya reacted to this immediately. It came to life and stepped off the back of the truck, turning its fearsome eye towards the Hriss and its vehicle.

"Drop your weapon and power down your vehicle," it ordered in a flat metallic voice, repeating the same order in Hriss'ka. The Hriss did not hesitate, and promptly put his weapon onto the ground. The turret gun also complied, turning away from the ebony guardian as if it hadn't *really* been interested in a fight after all.

"I am Gun number 501," the robot announced. "I am the rental of these creatures. For the duration of this meeting, no weapons will be allowed. Violators will be vaporized."

Whatever reservations Maya had harbored about the thing's presence fled her. Gun 501 had just proven that it was more than worth every credit that they'd spent to rent it from the Xee.

Gingerly, the Hriss stepped away from his weapon and walked closer to the hovertruck, keeping his arms spread wide. Maya was familiar with what a Hriss looked like from realies and holovid shows, but until that very moment, she had never actually encountered one in the flesh.

The creature had two arms, and was bipedal, and as she observed him more carefully, she noted a six-fingered hand, which was accompanied by that great tool of advanced evolution, an opposing thumb. This, though, was where any resemblance between their two races ended entirely.

The Hriss standing in front of her was much taller than the average woman, and powerfully built. Where weapons harnesses and additional body armor wasn't covering it, his body was protected by a hard exoskeleton. Its surface was rough and pitted, and tan-brown in color, with touches of deep red where the creature's jointed shell formed edges, or ridges.

It was his head though, that commanded her attention. This was a broad flat plate that narrowed down sharply to meet with his mandibles. Seeing it, it was obvious where the derogatory nickname, *shovelhead,* had gotten its genesis. The creature's flat skull *did* slightly resemble a shovel blade, she realized, but only just. From what she remembered from the realies that she'd seen, a Hriss was recognizable as a noble from the shape and the extent of his skull plate. The larger and broader the plate, she recalled, the higher the rank of the individual in a Hriss clan-sept. Or at least that was how she *thought* it went.

The creature returned her two-eyed gaze with four of his own; two primary eyes set inside deep, ridged sockets, and two smaller, secondary ones set in shallower depressions above these. All of the eyes glowed faintly with a sickly yellow-white color that she had heard somewhere was created by a form of internal bioluminescence.

Supposedly, the glow gave the Hriss some natural advantage in their native environment. Whether this was true or not, the effect, coupled with the shadows cast by his deep eye sockets, was sinister and chilling, and this was compounded when the Hriss did something very human. It blinked.

Maya shuddered involuntarily, finding the Hriss every bit the ugly and threatening creature she'd expected, and she easily appreciated why the Sisterhood had fought four wars with his kind. The thing was a monster out of nightmare.

Her reaction seemed to amuse the brute, and he exposed his long fighting claws, and flexed them. Maya refused to let herself be cowed though, and stared straight back at him. In response, the creature let out a sound that seemed to be a cross between a cough and a clicking noise, and Maya realized instinctively that he was laughing at her.

Captain bel Lissa however, was totally unfazed. She got out of the hovertruck and walked straight up to the Warrior, addressing him in pidgin Hriss'ka. Maya's psiever supplied her with a rough translation.

"G'nar'varkka, we are here, oh eater of your enemies flesh," Bel Lissa said "to be enriched by the trading of weapons in exchange for the spoils of battle that you have honorably torn from your enemies hands. We have brought you a portion of the sample you requested and we expect a proper share in return."

G'nar'varkka's luminous eyes narrowed and he replied in a harsh guttural voice that issued from internal lips set deep inside his mandibles.

"A portion of a weapon?" he growled, "Miserable egg-layer, do you think me such a fool that I, a fighter almost too noble to even dispatch a creature as lowly as yourself, would accept only part of a sword, or a half a rifle in exchange for whole riches?" His combat claws flexed again, but this time it was with irritation. Even so, he kept a careful distance from the Gun.

"That I do," Bel Lissa replied defiantly, placing her hands on her hips and staring up at the creature. "I dare to offer you a portion of a weapon because I know that had I brought you the entire thing, and not had the Gun here with me, that you would have denied me my rightful share of your riches, and taken my breath from me for being so stupid."

"You know our ways all too well, egg-layer," the Hriss admitted slyly. "I would have gladly slain you for fools, even if your lowly blood would have soiled me by its mere touch. I commend you. You think almost like a Hriss. Perhaps there is hope for your pathetic species yet."

"We will accept your compliment," Bel Lissa returned, "and half of what is owed us now. The rest of the weapon will be delivered elsewhere. Even in this dead place, there are too many eyes that might have watched us and could yet interfere. You may name the place, and we will come there, but rest assured, we will be as well prepared as we are now for any treachery."

G'nar'varkka gave out his version of a sigh of resignation. "So be it, wretched female. We mighty Warriors will allow you to do this thing for us. You will receive half the credits owed, and we will contact you with the place and time of our next encounter. With luck, you will fail to consider all of the possible dangers, and I will have the pleasure of eating your bones myself."

"I issue the same warning to you, oh arrogant one," Bel Lissa retorted, waving over to Zara and Maya. The two women lifted up the case and brought it over to the Hriss.

"Open it," Bel Lissa ordered. "And back away so that a mighty Warrior might look upon its contents without being distracted by mere females." Maya gritted her teeth at such talk, but did as her Captain had directed.

Inside the case, packed in foam, was the rear assembly of a military grade anti-ship torpedo. The Hriss purred like a kaatze as he ran one of his long claws over its oily surface. "Yes," he said. "This is well worth a few paltry credits thrown in the dust for spineless egg-layers to squabble over."

He reached into a belt pouch and handed Bel Lissa a shiny plastic credit chit. Bel Lissa in turn produced a small hand terminal from her own belt and inserted the chip. Seeing the amount that it registered, it was her turn to purr with satisfaction.

"Quite acceptable," she said.

With that, G'nar'varkka barked a command into a bracelet he wore on his wrist. A pair of Hriss walked out of the armored car and took possession of the case. When they had disappeared with it back into the belly of their vehicle, the Hriss addressed Bel Lissa once again.

"Our representatives will contact you soon. Until then, may your swords sheath themselves in the bodies of your victims."

"And may you collect the heads of many worthy opponents," Bel Lissa replied politely. Their business, for the moment at least, was concluded and everyone, human or otherwise, was the richer for it.

***

On their return trip to the city Maya wondered about the transaction that she had just witnessed. During the journey there, and throughout the negotiations, she'd been too nervous to really think about it, but now that the danger was past, she realized that the entire thing had made no sense at all.

Everyone knew that the Hriss and the Sisterhood were sworn enemies, and had been for centuries. While Captain bel Lissa and her crew *were*

266

smugglers, Maya found it difficult to accept that they would do business with the Hriss, much less sell them an anti-ship torpedo. Even Moonrunners had some loyalty to their own species, and the Captain and Zara had been proud of their naval service in the last war. For veterans like them to suddenly turn around and hand their mortal enemies a dangerous weapon, simply did not add up.

As for Sarah, her position on the matter was an unknown quantity, but again, the girl couldn't reconcile Bel Lissa and Zara's involvement with her if she favored trading weapons with the Hriss, and they didn't. Nothing fit with anything else. Which meant only one thing. Something she wasn't seeing had to be going on, and she decided to find out what that was when they made it back to Ashkele.

She knew that this was a potentially dangerous gamble to take. Sometimes the woman who asked too many of the right questions wound up dead instead of getting a larger cut of the action, but Maya wasn't going to stand by and let Sarah or the Captain play her for a fool either. Fools made fewer credits than those in the know, and oftentimes, they took the fall for everyone else. She had to confront them, and gain the upper hand.

There was one card that was in her favor. Sarah had an investment in her, although Maya still didn't know how far it went, or what her ultimate objectives were—but if it came to it, she could threaten to cut her ties. It was an edge, however slight

With her course set, Maya tried to relax and enjoy the ride back.

Arriving at the Free City at last, Zara returned the Gun to its station in the Square of the Twelve Golden Corpses of Prosperity, and after Bel Lissa had negotiated the rental fee with its Xee masters, drove them back to the house. Once they were inside, Maya decided that this was as good a time as any to make her move.

"Captain," she asked, "I have a question."

"What is it, Maya?" Bel Lissa replied, taking off her jacket and pouring herself a glass of amber-colored wine.

"That deal we did back there. Why are you selling the Hriss that torpedo?" Everyone in the room stopped what they were doing and turned to look at her.

"I think I deserve an explanation if I'm going to be part of this crew," she insisted.

"There's really nothing to explain, Maya," the Captain answered nonchalantly. "The Hriss want it, and we have it to sell." She sat down on the couch and took a sip of her wine.

Maya walked over to the little replica of the *Anne Bailey*. "I don't believe you," she said, indicating it. "No one who did what you did in the Navy would sell them something like that. The same goes for you too, Zara. You're lying to me."

Bel Lissa looked at Zara, and then over to Sarah, who nodded back solemnly. "Inish," Sarah said, "She's just as clever as I told you she was. I think we'll need to resolve this matter, here and now."

"*Ay-yah*," Zara agreed. "If we don't do it now Captain, you know that we'll have to later. If it goes badly, Sarah can always handle things."

"I'd rather not," Sarah replied, "But I will if I need to."

Maya felt a chill at these words, but she hid her disquiet. This was the dangerous part, and it was not the time to show any fear, even if if Sarah, with all her talents, knew otherwise.

Bel Lissa gazed at the model thoughtfully and then put down her glass. "Maya," she said, "perhaps you would like to sit down to hear what I have to say."

"I'll stand, Captain."

"As you please," Bel Lissa responded. "You're absolutely right, Maya. Things are not what they seem. Zara and I fought the Hriss in the last war, just like we told you. And we hate them for all the good women that had to lose their lives defending the Sisterhood."

"So, your way of paying them back is to give them weapons to kill even more women." Maya asked mockingly, "I'm supposed to accept that *shessdrek*?"

"Of course not," Sarah interjected. "We do give them weapons, yes, but not ones that work the way they think they will. That torpedo has a line of code hidden in its program that will make it explode harmlessly if it is ever fired at a Sisterhood warship. Our friend, G'nar'varkka doesn't know that of course."

"And you pulled this little swindle for the... what? The fun of it? The credits?" Maya demanded. It was time to play her card, for better or worse. "There's still something that none of you are telling me, and if you want me to be a part of this crew, you'd better come out with it. That, or let me go now."

"You can leave any time you wish, Maya," Bel Lissa said. "I'll even make sure that you get passage back to Thermadon with enough credits to get you by until you can find something else. It's your choice."

For just a moment, Maya was tempted by the offer. Up to that instant, she'd always imagined that she would eventually find a way to get out from under Sarah's control and go her own way. That her stay with the *JUDI* was a temporary thing. With the chance dangling enticingly right in front of her, it was hard to resist taking it.

But if Bel Lissa was willing to pay her off, then there was a very good chance that the secret they were keeping was worth even more. She had to play her game to the end.

"And if I agree to stay?" she asked.

"You also agree to keep what I am about to tell you a secret," Bel Lissa countered. "That's not negotiable."

"What if I don't keep this little secret of yours?" Maya inquired. "What then?"

"Then I will do what I must, Maya," Sarah said quietly. Somehow, and without Maya perceiving it, the woman had moved from where she had been, and was now directly behind her. "I assure you that I will not enjoy it, but I will not hesitate. Please, consider leaving now if you are not certain of yourself."

Maya looked over her shoulder, and Sarah stepped back and gestured towards the door.

"You have the option to leave right now," the woman told her, "to leave or to stay. You must choose which road you will take, but as the Captain said, if you decide to stay, you *must* keep your silence."

A remark that the Captain had made on her first day at the house came back to her. It had puzzled her when she had heard it, and now, she suspected that it was connected with the *JUDI*'s secret. Another card suddenly seemed to be in her hands, and she played it.

269

"I have a question I want to ask before I decide, Captain," she said.

"And that is?"

"The first time I was here, you said that 'sometimes you did some good' being a smuggler. Does this secret of yours have anything to do with that?"

Bel Lissa took in a deep breath. "Yes, Maya. It has *everything* to do with it. But I can't tell you any more unless you agree to keep silent. There's no going back once you do that."

Maya looked at Sarah again. Somehow, and possibly through the agency of her own talents, she could tell that Sarah was ready for the matter to go either way, and desperate for her to make the right decision. There was also death in the woman's eyes, and Maya had no doubt about what would happen if she chose incorrectly. It was all as clear to her as if Sarah had spoken her feelings aloud.

But Maya also realized something else simultaneously, something that was wholly unexpected; that Sarah, in her own strange way, actually *cared* about her. It was an unsettling revelation, and one that she had not been prepared for. She took in a deep breath of her own, shelving this surprising discovery for a later time, and faced Bel Lissa. "I'll stay," she agreed. "And I'll keep my mouth shut."

Behind her, Sarah's relief was almost palpable.

"I was hoping you would say that," Bel Lissa said. "And now I think that you really might want to relax and take a seat. Maybe even have a glass of wine?"

The girl shook her head and sat down on the couch. "The wine can wait, Captain. I have the feeling what you're about to tell me should be heard with a clear head."

"Well, if *she* won't get a glass, I sure as *fek* will," Zara interjected. "Sarah? How about you? You look like you could use a drop or two yourself."

"Yes, please," Sarah said, finally removing her cloak. "Or something a bit stronger if you have it."

While the women got their drinks, Maya waited patiently, never taking her eyes off of Captain bel Lissa. When Zara and Sarah had taken their places, she nodded to the woman. "I'm ready now," she said.

"It goes back to the end of the last war, Maya," Bel Lissa began. "Zara and I had just reached the end of our enlistment when we were approached and given the option of continuing our service, but in a different way. A similar offer was made to Sarah, and we all found ourselves working together aboard the *JUDI*."

"How so?" Maya asked.

"You already know that the *JUDI* is not a normal ship," Bel Lissa replied. "Everyone knows that. She's a lot more than a moonrunner, though. We do smuggle, but not for the same reasons that others do. The credits aren't what's important to us."

"And what is? "

"Service, Maya," Bel Lissa answered. "We served the Sisterhood in the Navy, and we fought to protect it, and girls like you, from enemies like the Hriss.'

"At the end of the last war, we learned that another war had started. It was a different war, not like the one we'd been through at all. It was a war that was fought in the shadows, and not just with the Hriss either. That war is still going on, and it's just as deadly as the other one was. If we loose it, we'll all be just as dead."

"We can't allow that, Maya," Zara interjected. "We fought too hard to let that happen. That's why, when our time was up with the Navy, we signed up."

"They needed us," Bel Lissa explained, "They needed our experience and our loyalty. The women we work for, they're the ones that give the *JUDI* her orders, and I'm proud to say that our little ship does more for the Sisterhood than any battle cruiser ever could."

"So, you're spies then," Maya concluded, suddenly feeling like she was in the middle of an adventure-realie.

"Yes," Sarah admitted. "In a manner of speaking, we are at that."

"And you were in the Navy, too?" Maya asked her. Sarah had never struck her as the military type, her martial arts skills notwithstanding.

"I was," Sarah nodded. "I joined the Navy when I wasn't much older than you, and I was posted aboard a starship as a psi. Then, after a few years, I was invited to join Naval Intelligence.'

"I accepted the opportunity, and transferred. After I had been with the DNI for a while, the same group that had enlisted the Captain and Zara approached me.'

"They asked me to serve the Sisterhood in ways that no woman in the Navy ever could have. I thought over their offer very carefully and in the end, I made my choice and did what we are asking you to do here tonight, Maya; I joined and I kept my silence."

"So, who is this mysterious group that you all work for?" Maya asked.

"This is where the conversation becomes perilous," Sarah warned. "And it is also where your silence will guarantee you a long and happy future."

Maya spread her arms wide. "Well," she said, "here I sit. As silent as space."

Bel Lissa was the one who finally answered her question, "We work for the OAE, Maya. The Agency for External Affairs."

It took a moment for her words to sink in, and when they did, Maya burst out laughing. "The OAE? The *Diplomats*?"

The OAE was the very last name she had expected to hear. Telling her that they worked for the Star Scouts would have been more plausible.

"Oh, the OAE *are* diplomats," Sarah assured her. "Some of them are, at least, and that's just what they want all the good little girls to think when they tuck themselves in at night, but it is not what they *really* are. Not what *we* are.'

"The Agency has a much bigger job than just trading niceties with alien governments. Its real job, *our* job, is to gather information, assess threats, and deal decisively with them before they can become serious problems.'

"It's a hostile universe, Maya, but I don't have to tell you that. The Sisterhood faces threats to its existence every day, from many quarters, and from forces that most women never hear about, and because of us, never will.'

"Some of our enemies are obvious and external, like the Hriss, and others less so. Some of them even come from within the Sisterhood itself. It is our mission, and the mission of the *JUDI*, to help make sure that these enemies, whoever they are and wherever they are, are defeated and destroyed before they can do the same to our nation."

"I feel like I should be hearing *Sisters United* playing in the background while I stand up to salute," Maya commented sarcastically.

"Where I you," Sarah rejoined, "I might say the same thing. After all, what has the Sisterhood ever done for you? Nothing. I, for one, don't expect you to be a part of what we do out of something as anemic as mere patriotism.'

"I would however venture that the chance for profit, and adventure, might just appeal to you. That, and the little fact that whatever you do, as long as it is done in the Agency's service, is perfectly legal."

"Now that *does* have a nice ring to it," Maya agreed. "All right, I'm in. But just so long as no one calls me little miss-goody-do-right."

Sarah smiled broadly and raised her glass in a toast. "On behalf of the Agency, I can assure you, with great certainty, that no one will *ever* call you *that*. Welcome to the OAE."

***

That night, after Maya had gone to bed, Sarah and Bel Lissa finished the last of the wine together.

"I want to thank you," Sarah said, "and to apologize. I know that you don't care for play-acting, but it really was necessary. Maya would never have agreed otherwise."

"Don't mention it," Bel Lissa replied. "You were absolutely right. I know that I had my doubts about taking her along for the meeting with the Hriss, but she saw it exactly the way you said she would, and angled for a deal just like you predicted. I would have preferred that she had joined up with the Agency out of a sense of patriotism, however."

"As I pointed out, that is not what appeals to a girl like Maya," Sarah returned. "She's been on her own for a long time, and doesn't deal in abstractions like that."

"No, of course not," Bel Lissa conceded. "I just hope that she doesn't try to find a way to turn our secret into credits."

"Don't worry yourself on that score," Sarah assured her. "I will keep an eye on her and keep guiding her on the right course. Besides which, who would buy that information?"

"True enough," Bel Lissa agreed. "Well, you've got her in with us now and I hope that she proves to be all that you expect."

"She hasn't disappointed me yet, Inish," Sarah replied. "I am certain that she will be a valuable asset to the Agency when her time comes."

Bel Lissa stood. "I hope so. Well, *bian sarà* to you, Sarah." She left the room.

Now alone, Sarah leaned back on the couch, closed her eyes and rubbed at her temples. It had been a stressful night and she was glad for the solitude. Although Maya still thought that she had her freedom and even enjoyed an advantage, the girl was slowly gaining the sense of loyalty and attachment that Sarah needed her to have. And thanks to Skylaar's support, the notion of formal training was becoming less and less repugnant to her every day.

The road ahead was still a long one, but she was certain now that she would eventually be able to mold Maya into the shape that she intended for her. The Goddess's will would be done, whether Maya wanted it or not.

USSMC Training Facility, 75th Training Battalion, Hella's World, Hecate System, Artemi Elant, United Sisterhood of Suns, 1043.02|01|02:28:33

Kaly marched along in silence, enduring the cold that numbed her face and made her exposed hands feel like they were on fire. Her platoon was headed for the weapons range, by way of a 4-kilometer march through the low hills that surrounded the training base. In reality, the range was only a quarter of a klick from the barracks, but going straight to their destination wasn't the Marine way. Instead, Sa'Tela had opted to take them on "the scenic route."

After all, Kaly thought, watching her breath mist the air, *why waste a perfectly good opportunity to get in a little torture before breakfast?* She smiled at her grim humor, but only a little; her lips had cracked from the daily extremes of heat and cold and it hurt to smile too widely.

Several icy minutes passed before the platoon finally reached its destination. There, Kaly and her companions were given an opportunity to unload their meal packs and eat.

The Corps had spared no expense in making its rations as delicious as they were nutritious, and they were one of the few comforts that the recruits were allowed to enjoy. Like many armies before them, the Sisterhood Marines had learned that a good, hot meal could make all the difference in a fighting force's morale.

Some of the selections the stores had offered had been utterly foreign to Kaly, catering as they did to a wide divergence of tastes and customs, but when they'd stocked their packs for the march, she'd managed to find a few dishes that were both familiar and appealing. While the sun rose in the barren sky overhead, she sat on the ground and savored a self-heating plate of chikka eggs and biscuits, topped off with dashes of *Ototsaa* pepper sauce. As far as she could remember, this simple meal had never tasted as good as it had since she'd started Basic, and she dug into it with gusto.

She was just scooping up the last speck with her spork, when the DI's announced that everyone was officially finished. They were told to put away their mealpacks, and assemble at the firing line.

This was a series of shallow depressions paralleling each other in the otherwise featureless sand, and facing a low line of dunes. At each spot, a small marker post displayed a number, and Kaly saw that there were enough places there for the entire platoon. Out on the dunes, another, larger group of signs marked out locations that corresponded to the positions in front of them. Beyond these, at the top of the largest dune, a final sign proclaimed the distance in meters.

Sa'Tela began with a review of the approved firing stances; standing, crouching and fully prone, followed by the range rules and safety measures. When she was finished, she had them demonstrate the stances and recite everything back to her.

This was more than just a desire on her part to feel reassured. It was also an integral part of the training process. Even though the recruits had already learned all of this, and more from the PTS feed, hands-on repetition

275

helped to complete the inductive learning process and fully embedded the knowledge in their minds.

"Well," Sa'Tela said at last. "I suppose we're about as ready as we'll ever be. I'm not too comfortable letting you silly cows handle live weapons, but the Corps gives me no choice. Take up your positions and try not to kill each other." With this left-handed blessing, everyone stepped forwards to the firing line and took a place.

The DI's then walked down the line, making sure that everyone had their blasters pointed downrange, and issued them live battery packs.

"All right!" Sa'Tela announced. "This will be a move-by-the numbers exercise. One: Charge-up! Insert your battery packs now."

In unison, Platoon Carli slammed the 'packs into their Mark 7's with a loud clack that echoed across the desert. It was a sound that Kaly would eventually come to know all too well, and able to pick out of a forest of noises, anywhere. A sound that would cause her to tense reflexively in anticipation of combat.

At the present however, everything was still too new, too unfamiliar, for it to be anything more than a general component of her nervousness. Training with the energy rifles was at the very core of Marine education and she desperately hoped that she would make the grade. Those unfortunates who failed at this phase were processed out immediately, with no exceptions. The Grey Book stated it bluntly: *"Every Marine is a riflewoman. Failure to qualify on the firing range consititutes a fundamental failure to be a Marine."*

Sa'Tela gave them the next order in the practice drill. "Two: Switch on your power."

Kaly found the power-up switch on the right side of *Athena's* polished frame and flicked it over. The Mark 7 began to hum, lending its deep voice to that of its sisters.

"Three: From the standing position, grasp your weapon. Do not, I repeat, do *not* put your finger on the firing stud until I tell you to. Point the weapon downrange at the berm in front of you."

"Four: Pointing your weapon downrange, sight in on the target immediately in front of you."

As she said this, a group of white plastisteel silhouettes, shaped vaguely like bipedal life forms, popped up from the ground at the foot of the dunes. They seemed to be over a parsec away, and Kaly wondered if she would even be able to hit hers at all.

"Five: Switch on the weapons transmitter stud." From the PTS feed, Kaly had learned that this was another switch located just above the power-up. She found it and as she activated it, the gun sent a signal to her psiever, which created an image of a crosshairs in her field of vision, showing her the actual aim-point of the weapon. She carefully moved her blaster around until it rested exactly on the center of her target.

"Six: Now that you are psionically integrated with your weapon, you may bring your finger into the trigger guard and depress the firing stud. Fire one, I repeat, one shot. Fire now."

Kaly pressed the trigger-button. The Mark 7 discharged a bolt of pure energy with a loud crack. Ozone filled her nostrils as the shot hit and disintegrated her target into a million tiny pieces.

"Good work, N'Deena," Sa'Tela said from close behind her. In her anxiety, she hadn't heard the DI's approach. "You need to work a little more on your hand-mind-eye coordination, but that was a good start. You might just have picked the right name for your blaster after all. Keep it up."

Kaly did her best to maintain her outward composure, but inwardly, she swelled with an angry pride. *That's right,* she thought, *I did do it right, didn't I? Even you had to admit that, didn't you?*

Sa'Tela let the platoon fire a few more rounds before she took them through the next phase. "All right, hatchies," she said. "Now that you have had the luxury of firing with the psiever link, we will now learn to shoot the old-fashioned way, and the Marine way, with open sights. You will switch off the transmitter stud now."

Kaly obeyed and the cross hairs disappeared from her vision.

"Some of you might be wondering why we are doing without such an important feature of the blaster. The answer is simple; like any piece of technology, it can fail. If you do not have the fundamentals of basic marksmanship ingrained into you, then such an event could prove fatal. You will now be taught what Marines have been learning for centuries."

Sa'Tela then led the Platoon through the ancient art of shooting; how to sight the target through open metal sights, how to breathe and when *not* to breathe, and when and how to fire. For many of the recruits, this phase proved to be the most frustrating, but Kaly suddenly found herself benefiting from her upbringing on rural Persephone, and her experience with chemical slug-throwing rifles. Unlike them, the Mark 7 had no recoil whatsoever, and once she got used to the sights, she was able to score hit after hit with it.

"Well, N'Deena, I thought I was going to throw you when we turned off the signal," Sa'Tela said as she watched her shoot. "It looks like I owe you another compliment. That's two in one day, hatchie. You'd better not get a swelled head."

"Ma'am, yes, ma'am," Kaly replied.

"Good, carry on."

Kaly grinned, imagining how much of a strain the compliment must have been for the DI to give. *Get used to it, bitch,* she thought, letting off another perfect shot. *There's a lot more of that coming.*

Platoon Carli spent the rest of the day at the range working with their blasters until Sa'Tela was more or less satisfied with the results. Then the trainees received a surprise. Instead of marching back to the barracks as everyone had anticipated, the platoon was ordered to go to a nearby clearing and pitch their tents for an overnight bivouac.

Kaly had been camping many times, both for pleasure, and when she had been a traveling repair tech, and had little trouble assembling her tent with Lena's assistance. But some of the women, hailing from more urbanized worlds, were not as seasoned, and experienced problems. As soon as they were able to, Kaly and her battle sister did their best to help those nearest them to erect their shelters. Although neither young woman knew it, their actions did not go unobserved. Sa'Tela and N'Vera watched them from a distance, and took quiet note.

Eventually, all the tents were assembled and their evening meal arrived by hovertruck. Unlike the morning's packaged rations, the food was fresh, and although it tended to get a little sand in it now and again, deeply satisfying to the weary recruits.

Kaly went to bed in her tent that night feeling a sense of accomplishment that was shared by most of the platoon. The DI's must have also felt this as well, because they allowed everyone the luxury of sleeping until dawn.

CHAPTER 9

USSMC Training Facility, 75th Training Battalion, Hella's World, Hecate System, Artemi Elant, United Sisterhood of Suns, 1043.02|02| 05:41:67

"All right, hatchies," Troop Leader n'Teri said. "I will be your Instructor for today's module. We have now entered an important phase in your training. Today we will focus on personal hand-to-hand combat skills."

Without even realizing that she was doing it, Kaly had started to drift off to sleep. But Lena n'Gari noticed, and elbowed her in the ribs. "Wake up, N'Deena!" the girl whispered. Kaly shook her head and sat up straight.

N'Teri continued speaking, apparently unaware of Kaly's transgression. "The point of these lessons will be to enable you to defeat a larger opponent in situations where you do not have any other weapon than your hands and feet. Does anyone here believe that I cannot defeat them in single combat?"

She waited, but no one challenged her. They knew better.

"You disappoint me," N'Teri frowned. "If no one here wants to try me, then I'll have to call on someone for my demonstration."

Oh, Goddess, don't pick me, Kaly thought. *Please, pick anyone but me.* Incredibly, she, and everyone else, got their wish. The DI turned to Senior Troop Leader Sa'Tela, and signaled her. The woman nodded and went out into the hall outside. After a minute, she returned, accompanied by two military policewomen… and someone else.

It took a moment for the identity of the figure to register. When it did, Kaly's jaw dropped open in revulsion and amazement. It wasn't *someone* else, it was some*thing* else; a Hriss.

"Hatchies," N'Teri announced, "meet Hvaarka. He is a full-blooded Hriss Warrior captured during a recent operation to retake a planet that his clan had raided. Ordinarily, he would have died with his clan-mates in the fighting, but he was severely wounded, and our forces elected to capture him for his possible intelligence value. He is now a prisoner of the Sisterhood Correctional Service, and working off a sentence of piracy by helping the Corps. He will assist me today during this module."

The Hriss stepped forward, rewarding the class with a gaze composed of pure evil. Kaly's mind screamed in outrage, *A Shovelhead! A Goddess-cursed Shovelhead!* The DI had mentioned that Hvaarka had been captured during a recent raid, and that meant only one thing: he was one of the

280

raiders that had attacked *her* world. Images of the carnage on Persephone seared her brain like fire, each as clear to her as if she was still there.

Kaly didn't realize it, but she had begun to growl, a deep visceral sound that came up from her very depths. If she had had her Mark 7 with her, she would have gladly killed the Hriss then and there.

"I can see that a few of you know what a Hriss is," N'Teri observed. "Good. Now for our first lesson. Recruit N'Deena, step forward!"

Kaly obeyed and N'Teri handed her a combat knife. Its plastisteel handle felt cool and inviting in her hand.

"N'Deena, I noticed that you have some personal reservations about our guest. I understand from your file that you were a member of the Persephone colony. Well, here's your chance, girl! He and his friends murdered your people. Kill him."

The guards standing next the Hriss faded back and Kaly's vision narrowed down to the creature, and nothing else. For his part, the Hriss regarded her with an expression that reminded her of amusement, and he made a noise that sounded like a cross between clicking and a bad cough.

"He's laughing at you girl," N'Teri whispered into her ear. "He's laughing at all the people you knew that he and his friends slaughtered. Did you know that before he came here today he told me that he personally *enjoyed* killing your people? He said they were weak, and that they died screaming like cowering *rabiteths.*"

That was all Kaly could handle. With a scream of primal rage, she launched herself at him, wanting nothing less than to rip him wide open with the knife and bathe in his steaming entrails.

She never achieved her desire. At the last possible instant, the Hriss sidestepped and slammed his fist between her shoulder blades. Kaly grunted as her lungs expelled all of their air and she slammed into the mat. To her credit, she managed to get up and turn around for another attack, but the Hriss surprised her again, sending his foot into her stomach even as he wrenched the knife from her hand. In seconds, she was down again, and he was on top of her, pressing the blade against her throat.

"Stop exercise!" N'Teri barked. The Hriss laughed one more time and stood. "That is lesson number one. Undisciplined hate *does not* kill your enemy. It kills *you! Klaar?*"

Martin Schiller

"Ma'am, yes, ma'am!" the class yelled in unison.

N'Teri helped Kaly up from the mat and then retrieved the knife from Hvaarka. The odd-looking pair exchanged something in what Kaly imagined was Hriss'ka, and then the DI addressed the recruits in Standard.

"And now for lesson number two. Recruit bel Jeera, come forwards."

Aliz bel Jeera was the de facto leader of a group Kaly and her friends had come to call "the rebels." A street-tough from the south side of Thermadon, Bel Jeera had resisted the DI's discipline from day one of Basic, smirking behind their backs, and generally challenging everything. Bel Jeera clearly thought that she knew more than anyone around her, even the Instructors and this had made her attractive to the platoon's complainers, who had gathered around her like she was a magnetic field.

The young woman grinned at a few of her followers, and swaggered out onto the mat to take her place opposite the Hriss.

Both of them got down on their haunches and eyed each other cautiously. Then they began to circle around one another, each looking for an opening in the other's defenses.

Bel Jeera made the first move, lashing out at the Hriss with a series of savage kicks that Kaly thought must have aided her in street fights back on her motherworld.

Hvaarka retreated from them, and Bel Jeera laughed as she pressed the advantage. "Hah! This is too easy!" she exulted. "I thought these *shovelheads* would be a challenge."

With a malicious smile painted on her face, she wound up for a reverse kick at the creature. Even as she prepared to move, Hvaarka rushed forwards and came inside her guard. He grabbed at her leg before it was fully cocked, sweeping her backwards off her feet at the same time with his free arm. Bel Jeera toppled over with a cry of alarm, and then Hvaarka was on top of her, with both of his six-fingered hands grasping her head, ready to snap her neck like a green twig.

"Stop exercise!" N'Teri commanded. "Overconfidence is one of the deadliest enemies one can face on the battlefield. Even if you are certain of victory, *always* keep an eye on your opponent. Sometimes, at the last second, your enemy may hand you a surprise. Now, for our third lesson. Recruit Enggredsdaater, come forwards."

282

Bel Jeera sullenly returned to her seat and Enggredsdaater, unarguably the largest woman in the class, stepped up to the Hriss. "You may attack when ready," N'Teri instructed.

Things would go much differently with her, Kaly thought.

Without uttering a sound, Enggredsdaater charged at Hvaarka. She quickly got her powerful arms around the Hriss's waist and started to squeeze him tightly. For a moment, it seemed as if the Zommerlaandar had the advantage, but the Hriss surprised her with a head-butt. Enggredsdaater screamed in pain and released him.

The Hriss wasn't about to give her the chance to attack again though. Instead, he grasped her wrist and threw her to the mat. Before she had even finished falling, he was on top of her, ready to throttle her to death.

"Stop exercise!" N'Teri shouted. "That is lesson three. Sheer strength and size does not guarantee victory. Only skill, matched with endurance, wins the day, as I will now demonstrate."

The DI stepped onto the training mat and faced Hvaarka. "Now, you will all remember," she said, "that Hvaarka is working off his sentence. He has been promised his immediate freedom if he ever manages to defeat me. He will now attempt to gain that release."

Then N'Teri snarled something in Hriss'ka. Whatever it had been, it had the same effect on him as her words had had on Kaly. Hvaarka roared and launched himself at the Drill Instructor, knocking her down. It seemed as if he was going to pin her to the ground, but even as the pair fell, N'Teri did something and Hvaarka tumbled off. He hit the mat with a shuddering crash, but recovered almost instantly, coming at her again and swiping at her with his fist. N'Teri ducked to the outside of his arm and grasping it with both hands, stepped sideways. Hvaarka went flying a second time.

Incredibly, she turned her back to the creature and faced the class with a serene smile. Hvaarka saw his opportunity and charged. This time he managed to get his forearm around her throat. N'Teri grasped the limb with her hands, digging her fingers deep into the soft joint between his exoskeleton. The Hriss gave out a whistling noise that was unmistakably a scream of pain, but N'Teri wasn't done with him. She kicked her leg into his shin and then threw him over her shoulder as if he weighed nothing. For the third time, the Hriss hit the mat. Hard.

With a deep roar, he got up and lunged at her. This time his fighting claws were fully exposed. These natural weapons were easily 30 centimeters long, and razor sharp. Kaly gasped in horror, but N'Teri remained calm and stood her ground.

The Hriss was just about to make contact, when the diminutive blond leapt up and kicked him solidly in the chest. To Kaly's amazement, this seemingly inconsequential blow sent the Hriss falling back like he had been hit with a grenade. When Hvaarka rose again, he did so slowly, and it was clear that he had no intention of attacking her a fourth time.

N'Teri said something in Hriss'ka, and Hvaarka replied to it with what was clearly a bitter laugh. Then the Marine guards came over and escorted their prisoner from the room.

The petite woman watched him leave, and then faced the class again. "It seems that Hvaarka didn't manage to win his freedom today. Perhaps next time, he will. Now, let's examine the vulnerable strike zones on a Hriss. Everyone sit down and feel free to ask questions as we go along"

The recruits sat themselves in a loose semi-circle as N'Teri called up a holo of a Hriss Warrior. "The average Hriss is vulnerable to attack in several areas. The first of these is the back of the head where it joins the neck. Here, the bony plate of their head thins out to nothing, which is why you might have noticed Hvaarka leaning his head back during combat. He was trying to keep that area protected. A strike to this spot can cause everything from simply stunning a Hriss, to unconsciousness, or even death."

Kaly thought about this, and realized that the Hriss had done exactly what N'Teri had described during all of his bouts. She made a mental note to herself to remember this site.

"Another area that is vulnerable is the throat. Like us, the Hriss breathe air, which is delivered to the lungs by means of their version of a windpipe. A blow here can cause this structure to collapse and cause death from mechanical asphyxiation." N'Teri made a chopping strike at the area to demonstrate the proper form of the blow.

Kaly tried to mimic her hand position and managed a passable copy. It reminded her of the classic fighting chops she'd seen in action realies.

"The next vulnerable area," N'Teri continued, "is under the armpits. The Hriss possess special scent glands there that are used to attract the females of their species, and these are close to the surface and in a location that their exoskeleton does not protect. A blow here can cause instant incapacitation or death. This is why most Hriss fighting armor covers this area.'

"Another spot is what on a woman would be the solar plexus. Hriss body structure in this area is quite similar, and a properly delivered kick can stun them. In addition, further down, in what is our lower abdomen and to either side of the mid line, the Hriss has his kidneys." N'Teri pointed to the two areas and drew circles with her finger. "A blow here can rupture these organs, and bring about shock and ultimately, death. Again, this is a well armored spot on most Warriors for that reason."

Kaly raised her hand, albeit tentatively. Like the rest of the platoon, she found the luxury of being able to interrupt, and ask an Instructor a question a rare and unexpected privilege. Despite the invitation, though, she still half expected to get yelled at, but she had a question that she felt she simply *had* to ask.

"Ma'am?"

"Yes, Hatchie?"

"Ma'am, this recruit wonders if the Hriss genitals are vulnerable as well. I heard back in Primary about fighting maneuvers that were used against human males in that area of the body."

"That's a very good question," N'Teri replied. "Unfortunately, Hriss genitalia are kept retracted up inside their bodies and tend to stay that way unless they are mating. A blow to that area would only strike bony plate. But it *was* a good idea and I want to thank you for mentioning it."

Kaly sat back down, a little disappointed at the answer. *Well, at least I asked,* she thought.

N'Teri went on for a few more minutes, and then she clapped her hands together, banishing the holo and grabbing everyone's full attention. "All right, class! Pair up! We will now study some basic blocks and throws. If you do well enough, I will see about having Hvaarka visit us again for some advanced exercises."

The DI started to explain the first maneuver to them. Kaly and her companions paid *very* close attention.

USSNS *Pallas Athena*: In Space Dock, Rixa Naval Base, Rixa, Belletrix System, Pantari Elant, United Sisterhood of Suns, 1043.02|03|03:53:33

Despite its power and complexity, the core of the ship's computer was a simple affair; a plain grey room with seating for techs and visitors, with a small holojector set in a low pedestal in the center of the chamber. Lilith and her officers filed in and took their seats as the Senior CompTech began the interview.

"Lt. Vena bel Devora, beginning interview sequence," she intoned. "Authorization code, Carli-Dana-Ellyn-5173"

"Acknowledged," the computer answered. "Logging scheduled interview: year 1043.02.03, 03:53:33 hours."

A holo of the current ship's personality matrix appeared. It was the likeness of Commander Dana bel Hanna, the third commander of the *Athena*.

Everyone, including Lilith, took careful note of her physical appearance. One of the telltale symptoms of a personality matrix going sour was a degraded self-portrait. But the holo appeared to be an accurate representation of how Bel Hanna had appeared in life, with no discernible flaws or distortions.

"Greetings, Commander ben Jeni, Lt. Commanders Bertasdaater and d'Rann, Reverend N' Marsi, and Lt. bel Devora," Bel Hanna's image said. "I hope that you are all well today."

"That we are," Lt. bel Devora replied. "How are you feeling today?"

"An interesting question, Lieutenant," Bel Hanna responded with a smile. "Before my personality matrix was translated into this ship, I would have said that I was feeling well. Now, after being a part of it for so long, I think a more accurate statement would be that I am operating at my fullest capacity with no errors. I suppose that would equate in physical terms with a sense of well being."

"I am glad to hear that," Lt. bel Devora said. "Shall we begin with our questions?"

286

Ophida N' Marsi went first. "Commander bel Hanna, do you still remember your body, and what it felt like to be in it?"

"If by that, you are asking if I still have a sense of connection with the organic beings that inhabit the ship, my answer would be yes, very much so," Bel Hanna answered. "I must admit however, that some sensations that I knew when I was in a physical state have faded in my memory to a certain extent. I hope that you don't find this too alarming."

"No, not particularly," Ophida replied. "I imagine that if my brain was translated from my physical body into a bioelectronic receptacle, that I would be just a *bit* fuzzy on some particulars myself."

"I'm glad you understand my situation," Bel Hanna said.

"But tell me, do you ever miss your body?" Ophida asked.

"No, not really," Bel Hanna said. "I have found that the trade off was a generous one. My senses, if we can accurately call them that, are radically enhanced. Through the ships' sensors, I can perceive far more of the universe around me than I ever could in a physical body, and I think much faster and comprehend far more."

Ophida nodded. "What do you think about when you are not processing operational data?"

"Many things, Sister," Bel Hanna replied. "Of late, I have engaged in a fascinating study contemplating the true nature of the Divine Spirit. Recently, I was able to secure some very vital data concerning this subject from the *Marie T. Rossi* when we were last docked together. It seems that her personality matrix has also been pursuing a similar line of research."

"How fascinating," Ophida remarked. "Did you reach any conclusions?"

"Yes, I did."

"Would you care to share them with us?"

"Yes, but I must warn you that you may not agree with my assessment," Bel Hanna cautioned.

When Ophida nodded her assent, she began.

"Like any woman, I was raised to believe in the Goddess. But then I realized that I had no definitive proof that such a being existed. So I set out to verify it.'

"From my initial calculations, I concluded that the universe was by no means a random collection of matter that simply *happened*, or that a series of accidents *somehow* led to life and consciousness. In fact, the sheer mathematical odds *against* the universe even being born, much less producing sentient life, are astronomical."

"Naturally," Ophida agreed.

"This is where the formulae supplied to me by the *Rossi*, entered into my equations as a way to solve for '*x*'. Only a great sentient force, interpenetrating everything, including the individual observer, could fully answer the question of 'what' and 'why' we are. To borrow from an Old Gaian source, I concluded that we are all 'God' literally experiencing itself through a great dream.'

"Then, I realized that a second question had arisen; what was the true face of that 'God', and which of the many religions that exist in our galaxy are correct?"

"And you found the Goddess?" Ophida asked.

"No, and yes, Mother. Given the vastness of our universe, there simply cannot be only one true vision. If there were, then all beings would share in it without deviation. Because they do not, I decided that perception of the divine is based upon the culture and experiences of the viewer. To borrow from another Gaian author, it wears masks to fit our expectations. This makes all forms of deity *equally* correct, and *equally* incorrect."

"But surely, the *only* true form is the Goddess?" Ophida countered, profoundly shocked by this statement.

"According to my calculations, it is not." Bel Hanna said. "I will be happy to share my figures with you, if you wish."

"No," Ophida replied, now visibly upset, "and I think you are wrong. If you were correct, then even the Marionites would have a valid claim on the truth, and that *cannot* be! Surely you are aware of what the *Cauldron* says about the Goddess being the 'one and only source of all things'?"

"Reverend," Lt. bel Devora interrupted. "As much as I'm sure you'd like to spend time arguing theology with Commander bel Hanna, we have other issues we must address. Perhaps you two can arrange for a private session together?"

"Yes, of course," Ophida huffed.

"Commander ben Jeni?" the CompTech asked, "Do you have any questions for Commander bel Hanna?"

"Yes, I do," Lilith replied. "Commander, how do you feel about our mission to defend the Sisterhood? Do your calculations about divinity affect your views on this?"

"A very reasonable question, Commander," Bel Hanna responded. "I have not forgotten my purpose, or the purpose of this ship. The *Athena* has always been a weapon of war, and as its matrix, I must be ready to help it to defend our nation."

"Doesn't that conflict with your notion of all beings, even the Hriss, being part of this divine dream you're speaking about?" Lilith inquired. "How do you resolve the idea of God, in effect, killing itself?"

"That is a truly weighty subject," Bel Hanna said. "During my contemplations, the issue of good and evil did arise, and I came to another troubling conclusion. I apologize in advance for any offense that I might give."

"I am sure that we can listen to your answer as adults," Lilith assured her, glancing pointedly at the High Priestess. "Please, share it."

"In analyzing the existence of the divine," Bel Hanna explained, "it became apparent that the dream of God is also a nightmare at times. That evil exists is a given, but *why* it exists was the central issue that the other ships and I debated.'

"Three major theories emerged. The first was that God is utterly mad. The second was that it simply does not care, and the third is that evil is some sort of divine error. In the end, the ships could not agree, but I still hold to my own conclusion."

"And that is?"

"That the divine *is* perfect, and without flaw. Everything in the universe, both good *and* evil, are merely expressions of that perfection. There was, and is, no mistake in the mathematics of our creation. God, or the Goddess if you wish, is everything; the giver of life and its taker, the beauty *and* the horror.'

"I also contend that as physical beings, we *must* exist in a state of constant struggle. This means that because I am cast in God's dream as a member of the Sisterhood, and charged with defending it, that I am merely acting in accord with the divine will.'

"In the Hriss interpretation of the universe, this makes me evil, although to the Sisterhood, I am good. In fact, I am neither, and am simply what I must be. Which, I might add, is also quite unfortunate for our enemies." Bel Hanna laughed at this. "Does that answer your question?"

"Yes," Lilith replied. "In a very surprising way, but yes, it does." She looked over to gauge Ophida's reaction, but the priestess was stone faced.

"Is there anything else you would like to ask me?" Bel Hanna inquired.

"There is one other thing," Lilith said leaning forwards, "and it's come up after every meeting that we've ever had, and now I think that the time is right. How do you feel about *being* the ship itself?"

Bel Hanna grinned knowingly. "Yes, I imagine that you might have wondered about that, Commander. You can't sit in your chair on the bridge without wondering every so often what it might be like, can you?"

"No," Lilith admitted. "Sometimes I get a glimpse, but only that."

"It's hard to put it in terms that you would understand in your present state of being," Bel Hanna said, "but before I was translated, I never imagined how gloriously free it felt to fly in space, or to literally *feel* the stars or *hear* the heartbeat of a galaxy. I never had the slightest idea that living in a body was actually a sentence in a prison cell. I only wish now that I had been translated sooner."

"Interesting," Lilith remarked. She'd never mentioned it to anyone, but like a lot of senior officers, the option of willing her brain to the Navy had crossed her mind from time to time. She had never taken the final definitive step of having the Advocate put that provision into her will though.

"Someday, when you are ready, you really should consider being translated," Bel Hanna urged. "Anyone who loves their ship as much as you do should join with it when the time comes."

"But if I did that," Lilith countered, "and if I were given the *Athena*, then wouldn't that also mean that you would be removed, and possibly deactivated? That you would die?"

"Yes," Bel Hanna's image agreed. "It might at that, if the Navy didn't have a use for me in another ship. But then, I knew that this was a possibility when I agreed to it. I understood that translation would only extend my life, not make me immortal.'

"I have had a good second life here in the *Athena*, but I have never wanted my existence to be an unending one. There is, according to the same calculations that I made concerning divinity, the very high possibility of a third life for me, and for everyone, after we translate from this one. If so, then I think that it would be a marvelous adventure, and I would certainly not want to miss it. After all, I've already died once, and things didn't turn out that bad, did they?" Bel Hanna laughed again.

Lilith smiled wryly. "I will consider your suggestion, Commander, I promise you."

Then she turned to her fellow officers. "Well, she has certainly answered all of my questions. Does anyone else have something they'd like to ask before we conclude the interview?"

No one, not even Ophida, spoke up, so Lilith stood. "Thank you for your time, Commander."

"And *you* for yours, Commander," Bel Hanna replied. "Visit me again on a freeday, won't you? I would love to talk with you some more."

"I accept the invitation."

"Until then," Bel Hanna smiled, and then the hologram disappeared. The interview was over.

The group left the core, and Lilith accessed her psiever. *Private Channel. Sever all linkage to the ship's mainframe; cut all monitoring systems, my area. Authorization: Commander's Code Mari, Ellyn, Teri 377850.*

Every sensor around them went dead. The computer was now effectively deaf and blind to their presence.

"All right, let's have everyone's assessment," she said.

"Well, I for one am deeply bothered by Bel Hanna's commentary concerning divinity," Ophida began. "I think it shows some dangerous anti-social tendencies taking root. According to her personnel file, Commander bel Hanna used to be a very devout follower of the Lady. Now…I don't know what to make of her."

"I'd hardly call a change in personal theology a dangerous tendency," Katrinn argued. "It sounds more like personal growth to me."

"Bel Hanna serves a ship with a crew of women who follow the Lady," Ophida rejoined. "Now, she seems to be at odds with their collective view. What's next? How long before she decides not to involve her systems in combat because she's found an equation that prohibits her from fighting? Or a line of thought that convinces her that she's evolved too far to serve the organic beings that inhabit her? You all know where *that* could lead!"

Everyone did. Only a decade earlier, the personality matrix inhabiting the USSNS *Ishtar* had gone insane. The ship's computer had simply stopped responding to her officers' commands one day, and took off for parts unknown.

To the present, no one knew the fate of the *Ishtar*, or the crewwomen who had failed to escape her. It was the *Ishtar* incident that had forced the Navy to mandate regular diagnostic interviews.

"I see your point," Lilith agreed. "But I don't believe that Bel Hanna is as unstable as you do. From what I heard, she still seems committed to our mission, even if her reasons are a bit odd."

"The Commander is right," Mearinn said. "I didn't detect any signs that she was leaning towards megalomania or psychosis. Instead, she seemed to be trying to be as frank as possible with us about some truly incredible conclusions. Surely, you have to agree that her present state of being would tend to alter her world view somewhat."

"Yes, but I still see dangerous possibilities," Ophida insisted. "I am equally disturbed by the fact that she is communicating with other ships. That only multiplies and magnifies the potential danger. I strongly recommend that you consider replacing her immediately with a more stable and conventional personality, and urge that the same thing is done for the *Marie T. Rossi*."

"No," Lilith disagreed. "I think that would be premature. I must remind you that suitable candidates for translation are not plentiful, and refitting a capital ship with a new one is a long and complicated affair.'

"So, instead of taking such a radical course of action, I'll schedule a series of regular follow-up interviews and reassess her situation. If her thoughts are straying in dangerous directions, then and only then, will I consider recommending her replacement."

Ophida was visibly unhappy with Lilith's decision, but she had to agree.

USSMC Training Facility, 75th Training Battalion, Hella's World, Hecate System, Artemi Elant, United Sisterhood of Suns 1043.02|05|05:41:69

"Good afternoon, ladies," Troop Leader n'Teri said. "Today we will learn the ancient art of Pugil stick-fighting." The DI was wearing a protective helmet that reminded Kaly of batbat armor and she held a large wooden staff with two padded ends.

"Goddess, all she's missing is a suit of chain-mail and a leather shield," Jana bel Anny whispered. Kaly suppressed her laughter and tried to take the Instructor seriously. Her comical appearance made this a very difficult task.

"Now, some of you," the Troop Leader went on, "might think that in this day and age of energy weapons, planetbuster missiles and battlebots, such a weapon is an anachronism, and you would only be half right. Compared to such sophisticated weapons, the art of stick fighting *is* useless.'

"But history has proven again and again, from the wars of Old Gaia to the present, that the soldier in combat cannot always rely on technology to win the day. Occasions still arise when fighting with your rifle butt, or its barrel, is the only recourse you will have, and that is when what you learn here will save your life.'

"Recruit Enggredsdaater, put on your training helmet and step forwards." The blond giantess complied and took up a pugil stick from the drill instructor.

"All right," N'Teri invited, "this is your chance to have a go at a DI—no penalties for any hit. You may attack me at your leisure."

Enggredsdaater hefted the stick, feeling its weight for a moment, and moved forwards. Suddenly, she made a jab at the smaller woman's midsection. N'Teri sidestepped her thrust and brought her own pugil stick down onto Enggredsdaater's staff, knocking it from her hands and then sweeping inwards to land a blow in her abdomen. Enggredsdaater doubled over and N'Teri took advantage of this to land a harder blow between her shoulders. Enggredsdaater grunted and fell forwards.

"A good try," N'Teri observed, helping the Zommerlaandar back up, but you left yourself open to my parry and counter-attack. "Try again."

This time Enggredsdaater was a little more cautious, feinting with a jab and then trying to sweep around to catch the DI on the side of her head. But N'Teri ducked under the strike and rammed another blow home to her stomach. This time as Enggredsdaater started to collapse, N'Teri finished her with a sweep to her right knee, sending her toppling.

"Thank you, Recruit," N'Teri said, helping her to her feet again. "Now that I have shown you all a little of what this primitive weapon can do against a larger opponent, we will practice its fundamentals."

She had everyone line up and then proceeded to demonstrate basic moves with the pugil stick; blocks, strikes and sweeps. When she finished, the DI had everyone pair up with their battle sisters to practice what they had seen. While Kaly went through the drill, she did her best to be gentle with Lena, and N'Teri caught her.

"You are not doing your sister any favors by holding back, N'Deena!" N'Teri barked. "All you are doing is failing to let her learn from her mistakes and that will get both of you killed. Do you hear me?"

"Ma'am, yes, ma'am!" Kaly replied, thoroughly abashed.

"Good. Now I want to see you thrust, and N'Gari, I want to see you block. N'Deena, your job will be to land a blow on her—a hard blow. Do it, *now!*"

Kaly jabbed and N'Gari tried to block it, but she was a shade too slow. Kaly's stick hit her in her stomach and N'Gari folded over with a grunt.

"Now, that's a little more like it," N'Teri remarked. "Now maybe N'Gari will learn to get out of the way when she parries. Don't you agree, N'Gari?"

"Ma'am, yes, ma'am," N'Gari managed to croak.

"Excellent!" N'Teri said. "Carry on." She walked away to inspect another pair.

"I'm sorry, Lena," Kaly whispered. "I really didn't want to hurt you."

"I know," N'Gari replied. "But she's right, and I deserved it. I really do need to learn to get out of the way. Don't ever hold back on me again. Please?"

"Okay," Kaly agreed, readying for a repetition of the thrust maneuver.

"Thank you," N'Gari said.

***

During their second class in pugil sticks, N'Teri resumed with the practice drills she had shown the Platoon during their first session. After everyone was performing them more or less perfectly, the instructor called a halt and paired up the recruits based on comparative body size. When Kaly's turn came, she was paired with Enggredsdaater. Everyone gathered around to watch the match.

"All right N'Deena and Enggredsdaater, this will be a one-on-one free form match. No holds barred." N'Teri told them, "And don't let me see either of you holding back, or you're both pulling fire watch! *Go!*"

A look of doubt crossed Enggredsdaater's features as she hefted her stick. It was obvious that she was unwilling to hurt her friend, but there was no real choice in the matter. Reluctantly, the Zommerlaandar lumbered forwards and attacked. But Kaly dodged her assault with ease, and landed a blow to her kidneys.

Immediately, Enggredsdaater spun around and swept Kaly off her feet with a vicious counter-sweep. As she came in for a downward thrust, the smaller girl rolled out and got up swiftly. Recovering, Enggredsdaater tried to score a strike with a straight-on thrust. To Kaly's surprise, she saw the move coming and countered it with a two handed parry. N'Teri's expert eye had also seen the opening as well.

"Finish her!" the Instructor commanded.

Kaly did what she had to do. With a brutal overhead strike, she pivoted off from her parry and hit Enggredsdaater on the top of her helmet. She followed this with an uppercut to the Zommerlaandar's jaw. Enggredsdaater's stick flew from her hands as she fell backwards.

"Excellent work, N'Deena!" N'Teri exclaimed. "Ladies, she has just demonstrated one of the fundamental principles of hand-to-hand combat;

show no mercy to your opponent and exploit every opening they give you! With that, a smaller fighter can overwhelm a larger one, no matter how powerful they might appear to be. All right, next pair!"

"*Gaanskaa gaad*," Enggredsdaater said as they took their place in the small crowd. "That vas well fought. I should have seen zat coming when you rolled out from under me." She spat out some blood.

"Thanks," Kaly replied, "but I'm still sorry."

"No need," Enggredsdaater demurred, "I figure maybe a cut tongue is vorth learning a few things. Besides, there's always za next match, *yah*? Maybe I'll get you zen!"

"*Yah,*" Kaly returned. "Maybe so."

USSNS *Pallas Athena*: In Space Dock, Rixa Naval Base, Rixa, Belletrix System, Pantari Elant, United Sisterhood of Suns, 1043.02|06|03:90:28

"This is a simple psi test, Jon. Concentrate on the card I am holding in my hand," Dr. elle'Kaari instructed. "Then tell me what image comes into your mind. I'll tell you if you got it right or not."

Jon fa'Teela relaxed and closed his eyes. He'd played this game since he was a child, and like many neomen in his Generation, he was usually able to manage it with an 80 to 90 percent accuracy.

An image of wavy lines flashed in his consciousness, and he started to tell her this, when he thought better of it. The Sisters at the Abbey had warned him about displaying his abilities to outsiders, and their admonitions came back to him sharply.

He didn't relish the idea of lying to the only person who had become his friend aboard the *Athena*, but he knew that he didn't have any other alternative. If the universe at large learned about the Church's project to create psychically enhanced neomen, disaster would surely follow. Any chance of the Redeemer arising in his generation, or any other, would be utterly dashed.

"A blue square," he said at last. It was for the good of everyone's soul, he told himself. But deep down inside, it still felt wrong.

Elle'Kaari frowned. "Sorry, Jon. Let's try another one, shall we?"

Jon saw the red star in his minds eye. "A set of wavy lines," he replied.

Elle' Kaari shook her head. "No, that was not it. Let's try another."

This time Jon saw a circle. He knew that if he was too inaccurate, that the doctor might become suspicious, so this time he gave her his genuine impression.

"That was correct," she said, brightening. "Let's try another."

Jon made sure to give her the wrong answers from that point on, and only got a few more 'right'. By the time their session ended, he had only achieved a pitiful score of 20 percent, which was well below average. It was a dismal failiure, but a believable one.

Elle'Kaari sighed with disappointment and put down the cards. "Well, Jon, you didn't score very highly on this test. Tell me, do you know if any of your fellow neomen have a higher aptitude for psi talents?"

"Not that I am aware of, Ma'am," he lied.

"I'm sorry to hear that," Elle'Kaari said. "That will do for today, Jon. As always, thank you for coming here. Can we schedule another meeting for tomorrow? Your lab results should be back, and I'd like to go over them with you."

"Yes, Doctor." Jon got up and walked to the door. "I'm sorry that I didn't do better on that test."

"Don't worry about it," Elle'Kaari replied. "Not everyone has talents, and it looks like nature left you neomen completely out of the loop. Let's see each other tomorrow at the same time. I'd also like to run some neurological tests on you, if that's all right."

It still pleased and surprised him when Elle'Kaari asked his permission for anything and this only reinforced his sense of guilt, but he pushed it back and answered her cheerfully. "Yes, I'd be glad to help you."

"Oh, and one more thing," Elle'Kaari added. "Here are some pills for that back problem of yours. They aren't a substitute for rest, which is what it needs, but they should help you get through your duties."

Jon took the medicine from her and blushed. He'd forgotten that she could see injuries in her patients, and he hadn't told her about the muscles he'd pulled in his lower back. "I didn't want to bother you with it," he explained.

"That's very considerate, Jon. But as your doctor I'd prefer if you bothered me when you had a problem. That's what I'm here for. And don't worry, I'll keep the information in your private file, for now."

Then she held up a warning finger. "But, if you let it get worse, or don't tell me if you hurt yourself again, I'll send it straightaway to Col. Lislsdaater in a Fitness Report."

"I understand," he answered sheepishly. "I'm sorry. You're right, I should have come to you."

"I'll see you tomorrow, Jon. *Get* some *rest*."

The moment that Jon fa'Teela had departed, Dr. elle'Kaari turned to a door behind her. "You can come in now. He's gone," she said.

Caleda bel Tridis, the *Athena's* Senior Navcom Officer entered the room. Of all the psychics serving aboard, the Tethyian's talents were unarguably the most accurate and powerful. And like Elle'Kaari, Caleda also worked for Ophida, and the OAE, as an agent.

"Well?" Elle'Kaari asked.

"I heard the answers he gave you," Bel Tridis stated. "But he knew each card. I'm sure of that. I could feel him reading you." She paused, letting that sink in before going on. "I also know that he's highly telepathic, at least as a receiver. I sent a wrong image to him a few times and these were the answers that he voiced out loud."

"So, how accurate was he?" Elle'Kaari inquired.

"He received everything that I sent him with 100 percent accuracy, and his own attempts were on the order of 85 to 90 percent. More importantly, he didn't sense me, which tends to indicate that he has some blind spots in his abilities," the psi replied with a smile.

"Yes, that *is* significant," Elle'Kaari agreed. The OAE had known for a long time that the renegade sect was developing neomen with talents, and they had a fairly good idea of how successful those efforts had been to date. But until Jon, the Agency had not been able to study a neoman's talents in detail, or determine their shortcomings. The fact that he was susceptible to psychic coercion, and also blind to it, was an important discovery.

"Yes, quite," Caleda agreed. "In my mind, the only question is what kind of danger, if any, these psychic neomen might pose."

"If you want my opinion," Elle'Kaari said as she walked over to her desk, "I think they represent a substantial threat to the Sisterhood, if only because they are rogue espers under the control of a dissident group, and that's what I've said to Ophida on many occasions. My advice to her, and the Agency, has always been to shut down the Marionite project immediately. But no one ever listens to their doctor, do they?"

***

Jon was on his way back to his rack when he ran into Troop Leader Da'Saana. "Fa'Teela!" she hollered. He stopped in mid-stride and stood at attention instinctively.

"I see you're done with the Doctor for the day," she observed. "That means you're ready to put in some *real* work for a change."

"Ma'am, yes, ma'am."

"Get yourself down to the laundry room and help out the crew there. When they're finished with you, report to me for another work detail."

"Ma'am, yes, ma'am!" Jon saluted her and then turned smartly and marched off towards his destination.

Da'Saana glowered at him as he walked away. The neoman still hadn't given her any cause to write him up. *Just one little thing, Lady,* she thought. *That's all I want. One little thing.*

She didn't notice that someone had walked up behind her.

"Are you his Troop Leader?" a voice asked casually. "How is he working out so far?" She turned around to see Lilith standing there. Now, it was Da'Saana's turn to stand at attention and salute.

"Yes, ma'am, I am," she replied, staring straight ahead. "I have no complaints about Fa'Teela"

"Good," Lilith said, arching an eyebrow. "Let me know about his progress from time to time, would you? I normally wouldn't ask this, but he's a special case. I'm sure you would agree on that point."

"Yes, ma'am," Da'Saana answered crisply.

"Please, don't let me hold you if you have something to do," Lilith said. Da'Saana remained where she was, and Lilith added, "Dismissed." The Troop Leader left immediately.

As far as Lilith was concerned, the sooner that the *Athena* shipped out for their mission, and got back to something resembling a routine, the better.

She accessed her psiever and sent a message to Katrinn. *How are the Marines coming along with their loading?*

USSNS *Pallas Athena*, In Space-Dock, Rixa Naval Base, Rixa, Belletrix System, Pantari Elant, United Sisterhood of Suns, 1043.02|08|07:08:33

Jon stepped off the cargolift completely exhausted. When Dr. elle'Kaari wasn't testing him, Troop Leader Da'Saana had permanently assigned him to the laundry processing facility. This meant long, hard hours hauling heavy bales of dirty uniforms, which had done nothing to help his aching back. He was looking forwards to getting to his rack and having the chance to get off his feet and rest.

Corporal n'Darei stopped him halfway there.

"Fa'Teela!" Her dislike of him was equal to Da'Saana's, if not greater. He snapped to attention. "Yes, ma'am?"

"What are the standard dimensions of the *Athena's* central passageways?" she demanded.

Jon had been through enough surprise question and answer sessions during basic, that he didn't wonder why he was being asked this question. Corporal n'Darei was simply his superior, and he had to answer her.

"Three point oh-five meters by three point oh-five meters, ma'am."

"Where is bulkhead 115 located?" she inquired.

"Ma'am, bulkhead 115 is located aft of the hydroponics section. It houses a section of the main forward lifts and pumping equipment for the air recirculators" he responded.

"What is the fifth general order?"

"Ma'am, my fifth general order is to stay at my post until properly relieved, ma'am."

They went on like this for a while, with Corporal n'Darei firing question after question at him. Finally, she stopped. "Alright," she said, "good enough. Dismissed."

Jon saluted her and continued on his way. His heart sank when he reached his rack and pulled the curtain aside. The storage drawers set under the bed were wide open. His clothing and personal effects were strewn across the mattress, and a cursory inspection revealed that at least two of his uniform shirts had been slashed with a knife.

The most painful discovery of all was the smallest item; his copy of the *Revelation of Mari*, was gone. Only a single torn page remained, resting on the decking.

Jon heard laughter behind him and turned around to see several Marines looking at him with leering grins. Then they walked away, and he suddenly realized why Corporal n'Darei had really stopped him in the corridor.

For a moment, he felt nothing but white-hot fury. It wasn't the first time something like this had happened to him; on several occasions during Basic, his fellow recruits had also vandalized his possessions.

He knew that this was their way of sending him the message that he was not, and never would be, welcome, but the loss of his little book made this particular message hit home like the others hadn't.

Jon sat down on the edge of his bed and tried to compose himself, not caring if anyone was still watching him or not. After taking a few, deep breaths, he prayed silently.

"Mother Mari," he whispered, "Forgive these women for what they have done, and give me the strength to rise above my anger. Let me love my oppressors and in so doing, lead them away from their evil ways towards your light." He made her holy sign and stood up, feeling a little better. Then he started in on the unhappy job of salvaging what he could.

USSNS *Pallas Athena*, In Space-Dock, Rixa Naval Base, Rixa, Belletrix System, Pantari Elant, United Sisterhood of Suns, 1043.02|09|02:21:63

While Skipper sat in her lap, purring with contentment, Lilith sipped her tea and went through the morning's mail at the small desk in her quarters. She did so in a slow, and leisurely manner. Most of the holographic messages were fairly routine; a report from Engineering on the

301

progress of the retrofitting on deck 12 for the Marine Engineers Detachment, a brief from security covering the last 10 hours and so on.

One communique was from Fleet Admiral ebed Cya however. She put down her tea and read it over carefully.

"Commander ben Jeni," it began, "as you are aware, we have received several requests from Sisterhood News Network for an interview regarding the addition of a neoman to your ship's compliment. After much consideration, we have decided to grant this, with certain limitations. Please contact me at my office today at your earliest convenience for a complete briefing."

"Come on," she said to her kaatze, "Get up. I have work to do."

But I'm comfortable. Let them wait! he protested.

"Get up *now!*" she said, unceremoniously grabbing him from her lap and dumping him on the bed.

Well! Really! It's not like it's for anything important! he sputtered, but Lilith wasn't listening. She had already opened her closet and was getting into her dress uniform as quickly as possible.

Three minutes later she was up in her office. "Com?" Lilith said. "Patch me through to Topaz Fleet Command, Fleet Admiral ebed Cya's office."

The insignia of the Topaz Fleet appeared in the holo field, and then the Admiral herself. Unconsciously, Lilith sat up a bit straighter in her chair.

"Commander?" Ebed Cya began "Good to see you again. How are things proceeding up in spacedock?"

"Quite well, ma'am," Lilith replied. "Engineering assures me that the special modifications are nearly complete and that the Marine Engineers will be able to load their large equipment shortly. We will be shipping out as soon as they are done."

"Not quickly enough, it seems," Ebed Cya remarked. "As you might have gathered from my message, there has been some pressure brought to bear on my office to grant an interview about your neoman. I'm afraid we'll have to go ahead with that before you leave for your mission."

Lilith didn't care for the idea that her newest crewmember was "her" neoman, but she didn't contradict her superior. "What can I do to help?" she asked instead.

302

"I've made it clear to SNN," the Admiral replied, "that we will not allow a direct interview with Fa'Teela himself. They weren't happy with this, but since it goes against naval regs concerning enlisted personnel and the press, they had to concede the point. We will, however, allow their correspondent to interview *you*."

"Yes, ma'am."

"I assume that he is adjusting to life aboard your ship without any complications? We want to make sure that this interview has a positive atmosphere."

Lilith had heard a few rumors about the difficulties Fa'Teela had encountered since coming aboard. And she'd certainly witnessed the way Da'Saana had treated him, but loose gossip and one poor interaction was not confirmation. Just the same, she suspected the worst, and decided that this was not something that her superior would want to hear right then.

"Yes, ma'am," she said circumspectly. "To the best of my knowledge, he is adjusting as well as could be expected."

"Yes. Of course he is," the Admiral answered dryly. "Very well, Commander. The interview is scheduled for this afternoon, at 06:25 hours, in my office. Please make certain that we are in a position to present the best face possible."

Ebed Cya cut the connection, and Lilith immediately contacted Saara sa' Vika. If anyone knew what was really going on on the ship, it was her SAO Officer. She and her women had the confidence of every crewwoman aboard, and Lilith had used this to her advantage many times during her tenure as the *Athena's* commander.

Their conversation about the neoman was brief, and enlightening. Things were definitely not going well for Fa' Teela. Something would have to be done. Straightaway.

Her next call was to Col. Lislsdaater.

"Colonel?" she said when the officer appeared on the holoscreen, "I want to know how things are going with the neoman--and I want to know *everything*. Report with your subordinates to the main conference room in ten minutes, and if you would, bring his Troop Leader and her Corporal along with you. I'd like their input."

***

After listening to the Colonel and her subordinates, Lilith's mood had darkened considerably. To their credit, none of the officers attempted to minimize what had occurred, or to conceal it, but this did little to mollify her.

"Ladies," she finally said, "To put it mildly, I am not pleased."

The Colonel started to interrupt, but Lilith silenced her with her hand. "Please, all of you, listen to what I have to say. Many centuries ago, there was an effort to integrate women into the armed services. This was met with the same kind of resistance that we are seeing here, and worse. It did not prevent women from ultimately being integrated however, and it will not stop a similar event from happening now, regardless of your feelings, or mine.'

"While I share your discomfort with this situation, I do not want it to bring any embarrassment to the Navy, the Corps, or this ship. Therefore, I would appreciate it if you would accommodate me by taking steps to make sure that any and all forms of hazing stop. I would also like it if you reassigned Trooper fa'Teela to a detail that makes it appear, at least, that we are doing our best to work him into life aboard this ship."

"Ma'am?" Lislsdaater asked, "May I speak?"

"You may."

"Ma'am," the Colonel said, "with all due respect, I do not think Trooper fa'Teela is mentally capable of duties that are any more complex than the ones he is currently assigned to."

"Have you even tried to verify this, Colonel?" she countered. "Do you have *any* fitness reports from the ship's doctor that would agree with your assessment? Have you even given him the *opportunity* to fail? I think not."

The Colonel was unable to rebut this.

"I would like to hear that fa'Teela has been reassigned before I go downside for my interview. Perhaps a posting in Ordnance Stores would be a more appropriate slot for him. Wouldn't you agree?"

"Yes, ma'am. Consider it done."

***

The very instant that Lilith entered the Admiral's office, and laid eyes on the SNN correspondent, she was on her guard. Although the newswoman smiled at her as she took her seat in front of the holo camera, Lilith knew that she was entering a potentially dangerous battlefield of insinuation and innuendo. Having the reputation of the Navy at stake didn't help to calm her in the least.

After a polite introduction by the Admiral, the journalist began.

"I'm speaking with Commander Lilith ben Jeni, commander of the starship *Pallas Athena*. For those viewers who have not been following this story, the *Athena* was where the neoman, Jon fa'Teela, was assigned to serve after completing his training to become a Mobile Infantry Specialist. Trooper fa'Teela is the first neoman to serve in our armed forces on a combat ship since the inception of the Sisterhood, over 1,000 years ago. Tell me, Commander," the newswoman inquired, "how has your crew adjusted to a neoman coming aboard their ship?"

Lilith replied carefully. "Trooper fa'Teela's arrival did not affect my crew in any substantial way."

"But Commander, Weren't there a few crewwomen who found his presence startling, if not uncomfortable?" the newswoman asked.

"Not that I am aware of," Lilith lied. "Aside from the standard notification that he had arrived for duty aboard the *Athena* along with a number of other replacement personnel, we've experienced nothing out of the ordinary."

"But surely," the newswoman insisted, "*someone* must have had an objection to his presence. We have some unconfirmed reports that Trooper fa'Teela was singled out by his fellow Marines and hazed."

Lilith was grateful that she had been informed in advance about Fa'Teela's poor treatment, so she was not surprised by the question in the least. Nor was she foolish enough to admit what she really knew.

Sometimes, a lie was necessary to defeat an enemy, she told herself.

"I am unaware of any hazing going on aboard my ship," she said. "I assure you that any such incidents, had they occurred, would have been dealt with as a serious breach of military regulations.'

Martin Schiller

"With regards to Fa'Teela's overall acceptance by the crew, I like to think that the women serving aboard the *Athena* represent a cosmopolitan cross-section of our society. In the past, we have dealt with non-human races that were far stranger than any neoman, and my crew seems to have handled those events well enough. I would even venture to add that he has proven to be considerably less of a challenge to their morale."

Her interviewer was unconvinced. "So there have been *no* problems between him and the crew then?"

"Not to my knowledge," Lilith responded casually. "Trooper fa'Teela is just another member of our Marine detachment."

"Commander, can you tell us what his current duties are aboard the *Athena*?" the woman asked with a sly expression.

Lilith smiled back at her, glad that she had had him reassigned that morning. "He is currently serving in our Ordnance Stores, which as you might be aware, is a potentially sensitive posting aboard a starship."

"Really?" the newswoman replied, clearly surprised at this news.

"Yes," Lilith said. "He has the complete confidence of his superiors and I am sure that he will do well there."

"I see," the woman remarked, "Then you're saying that the neoman has been integrated into the crew just as any woman would have been?"

"Well, there were certain adjustments that did have to be made," Lilith admitted.

"And these were?"

"He did require special quarters and personal facilities, but nothing that was extraordinary, or that put my crew to any major inconvenience," Lilith stated.

With these words, the last of the fire seemed to go out of the journalist's eyes. "I see," she said, clearly disappointed. "Well, thank you Commander for your time."

So much for a scandal, Lilith thought.

***

That evening after she had ended her shift, Lilith retired to her quarters. She ordered herself a cup of tea and settled down in her favorite seat. This was an old rocking chair that Katrinn had gifted to her after a visit to Zommerlaand. Skipper, as usual, wasted no time in jumping up onto her lap, and making himself completely at home.

"Newsfeed," Lilith commanded, petting the kaatze absently. The holocast appeared over the carpet of her stateroom. "Give me the latest interviews concerning the neoman," she added. The interactive broadcast obediently served up an interview with Admiral ebed Cya, which Lilith knew had been recorded just before her own session with the SNN reporter.

"Next segment, please," she requested, and her own part appeared. This time, the interactive Newsfeed did not attempt to ensnare her in another surprise interview, and the clip played out without interruption.

The predators have gone off in search of other game, she reflected. *Good.*

To her eye, she came off as polite and professional, but without giving up a single tidbit to satisfy the rapacious correspondent. She didn't look too bad, either. As silly as it was, before the interview, she had privately been concerned that the grey in her otherwise jet-black hair might have made her seem old to the broadcast's viewers. Instead, it lent her a certain air of distinction.

"Look, Skipper," she said to the kaatze, "There's Mommy on the holocast." The animal looked up, saw her image hanging in the air, and did a double take.

How did you do that? he thought in amazement. As she started to explain the technology to him, he reached out with a paw and put it to her lips.

No, don't bother trying to tell me, he thought. *I'm sure that your understanding is quite limited and would only serve to confuse me.* Then without further ado, he lowered his head and went to sleep.

"Rude fellow!" she laughed. When the interview concluded, she decided that she wanted to find out what else the universe was up to. "Other major stories," she said.

Most of the segments that followed were about subjects she didn't care about, but one managed to capture her interest. It was a show about the fabled Lost Colonies of Man. Lilith had always been fascinated by this myth and let it play.

307

"Every schoolgirl has heard the tales of the Lost Colonies," the commentator began, "fabulous myths about a pre-plague group that broke off contact with Old Gaia in the early days of interstellar space travel. Some of these stories tell of a society free from want, from war and from disease, far from Gaia's most distant settlements. A separate, magical place promising technologies that are far beyond any we have today.'

"Of course, most of these tales are pure fancy, but recently Dr. Layrri t' Sharalese of the University of Thermadon at Thenti, posited the theory that there might be some truth behind these myths.'

"Recently, ruins were uncovered on Phantasma 9-A, in the Sagana Territory, that some believe may be of Gaian origin. Dr. t'Sharalese has gone further than this by suggesting that this *is* proof of the existence of the lost colonies. While many in her field deride her as a sensationalist, Dr. t'Sharalese believes that the evidence for her claim, while not conclusive, does at least argue for further research.'

The professor herself appeared next. "Back on earth," she said, "before the days of space travel, it was an article of faith that cities like Troy and the continent of Atlantis did not exist. But visionaries like Heinrich Schliemann and Toshiro Matsumoto proved these beliefs false. The evidence that we have uncovered at Phantasma 9-A is quite similar to the technology of the 23rd century, and in some cases identical. I think that if we continue our research there, we may be looking at another Troy being uncovered for the universe to marvel at."

"And is there the possibility that some survivors of the lost colonies might still exist, somewhere outside the Sisterhood?" the interviewer asked.

"That's impossible to say," the professor said. "Naturally, I'd love to think that some fabulous civilization exists out there, waiting like Shangri-La to be discovered, but it would be reaching too far to suggest that such a thing was reality. Given our advanced technology, I would think that we would have detected them by now. But we can always dream, can't we?"

Yes, indeed, Lilith thought. *We can always do that.*

CHAPTER 10

USSNS *Pallas Athena*, In Space-Dock, Rixa Naval Base, Rixa, Belletrix
System, Pantari Elant, 1043.02|10|03:34:62

Even though it wasn't her freeday, Lilith used her short in-shift break
to visit the ship's Temple.

Ophida was pleasantly surprised to see her. "Commander? What
brings you to the Lady's House today? I thought you were on duty."

"I had a little free time, and I wanted to talk with you, Mother," Lilith
said. "It's been rather hectic since we last saw each other, and I wanted the
opportunity to share my news with you before we shipped out." Given the
mission ahead of them, they both knew that another freeday was an
unlikely event for the foreseeable future.

Ophida led her into the Sanctuary. "How can I serve you, Daughter?"

"Mother," Lilith said as they sat together. "I would have you hear
me."

"Please, speak your heart, Daughter."

"I met someone while I was on leave," Lilith said. "A sister of
Katrinn's. Her name is Ingrit."

"Is this good news?" Ophida asked.

"Yes," Lilith replied with a light in her eyes that Ophida hadn't seen in
quite a while. "She's a wonderful person, and we had a very special time
together. Since I returned here, I've found myself thinking about her a
great deal, and I miss her greatly."

"But?"

Lilith smiled shyly. "But I'm still not sure about things between us. I
wonder if this feeling will last, or if everything will come crashing down on
me all of a sudden. It's hard not to think of that, especially since things
were so wonderful between us."

"Perhaps they will, and perhaps they won't," the Priestess offered.
"But let me ask you this: were you happy when you were with her?"

"Yes, Mother, I was. Very happy."

"Then that should be your guide, Daughter. Nothing lasts in this
universe; not love, or anger, or pleasure, or pain. One passes into another
and back again and there are no guarantees that anything will be forever.'

"It's the fleeting moments of happiness that we must treasure. Without
them, life is just one long, hard struggle. As a poet from Old Gaia once

said, *'Tis better to have loved and lost than to have never loved at all'. There is great wisdom in this statement.'*

"And as you know, *'The Goddess wills the way,'* Lilith. As I counseled you the last time we spoke, you must accept what She sends you, and enjoy it, for as long as She grants it to you."

Lilith nodded slowly. "Yes, I understand, Mother. Thank you."

"Is there anything else you would like to speak with me about, Daughter?"

"Oh, about what you would expect," Lilith sighed, "The Marine Engineers have most of their gear aboard. All that remains now are the heavy weapons and emplacement components. Engineering says they almost have the space ready for that, and the late shift crews have been reporting the ghost again."

"Yes," Ophida acknowledged. "I'm planning my exorcism ritual to take place just as soon as the crews are done with their retrofitting."

"Good," Lilith replied. "I'm getting tired of hearing about it. Tell me, Mother, except for ghost stories, how fares the crew? They have your ear, and I'd like to know what they tell you as long as it doesn't violate your vows."

"All in all, they fare well enough, Daughter," the Preistess replied. "A pair of officers from Fire Control and Stores approached me to perform a pairmating ceremony before we ship out and I'm in the process of scheduling it. You received their request, I hope?"

"Yes, Mother, and I approved it," Lilith answered. "But I'm a little concerned about the pairing. The supervisor for the woman in Stores mentioned that they might also be considering parenting a daughter."

"Yes," Ophida said. "I can share that much with you without violating their trust. They mentioned the possibility to me when they approached me to perform the rite."

"That could cost Stores a good officer," Lilith observed.

"Yes, but how good an officer would either of them be if they were denied this?" the Priestess asked. "If they paired, but couldn't consummate their union by bearing a child, resentment would grow inside both of them. Better to bend to the Lady's Will on this matter, I'd say."

"Yes," Lilith nodded. "I realized that, and I'll approve the maternity leave if they ask me for it, provided that they take it *after* our patrol."

"That seems a reasonable condition," Ophida agreed. "You know that the couple has also asked that you attend the ceremony. Will you? They had hoped to have the Pairing at the start of the next week."

"I will, Mother," Lilith promised. "I wouldn't want to slight them by not being there. Please tell them that they can count on my presence. We still have another week and a half according to the Chief Engineer before we'll be ready to ship out."

Ophida smiled. "I am glad that you can accommodate them. They seem to be a well-matched couple. Is there anything else that you would share with me, Daughter?"

"No, Mother. I have shared all that was within my heart," Lilith replied formally.

Ophida rose and placed her hands on Lilith's head. "May the Lady always guide you, my Daughter. May she sooth your troubled brow, and be a comfort to you as you perform your duties. Blessings of the Goddess be upon you as you go forth from this place."

Lilith stood and clasped the Priestesses hands. "And Blessings be upon you, Mother. Thank you, as always, for listening and for teaching me."

USSMC Training Facility, 75th Training Battalion, Hella's World, Hecate System, Artemi Elant, United Sisterhood of Suns, 1043.02|10|05:43:65

"Now that you have mastered the pugil stick, we will move on to the next level," Troop Leader n'Teri said. "There is one weapon, more than any other that distinguishes the Marines as a unique military service. It is the bayonet."

She held up a Mark 7 energy rifle with a wicked looking knife attached to its barrel. Like the pugil stick, the archaic weapon made her appear almost humorous, but after her demonstrated prowess at hand-to-hand combat, and pugil stick fighting, no one was tempted to make any jokes.

"The bayonet serves two purposes that have made it a part of our arsenal since the very first Marines were formed back on Gaia centuries ago. The first is that it teaches aggression, and aggression, ladies, is what warfare is all about.'

"The second is that it teaches us to never surrender. The bayonet is the weapon of last resort for the Marine. If your Mark 7 has run out of charge, malfunctions, when you need to make a silent attack, or when you must engage your enemy at extremely close quarters, then you will employ the bayonet."

N'Teri walked over to a training dummy that had been made up to look vaguely like a Hriss. "I will now demonstrate the five killing blows."

With that, the small woman let out a hideous scream and proceeded to attack the dummy with a series of vicious jabs and strikes. Watching her, Kaly suddenly felt a profound respect for the outdated weapon. Had the dummy been a real Hriss, she had no doubt that the Troop Leader's attack would have finished the creature off in short order.

N'Teri turned back to face the platoon. "Since you ladies are new to this weapon, you will practice the maneuvers without it. We will begin with the forward jab which you may recall from your pugil bouts." She demonstrated by stepping forwards and thrusting outwards.

"Do it like that. Begin."

The platoon, which had been standing in a line with their un-charged Mark 7's, did their best to imitate the move. Kaly was pretty sure she had gotten the motion right when the DI interrupted the class.

"No!" the DI declaired. "That's *not* how to do it. I want to *hear* you yell when you thrust. I want to hear it *loud*, and I want to hear it *angry!* This will stimulate your adrenaline in real combat, and just possibly give you the edge you will need to prevail. Now, again!"

Kaly and the others stabbed the empty air, giving out what they thought were passable battle cries, but again, N'Teri was unsatisfied with their performance.

"Louder!" the woman urged. "*Remember what we are fighting for!*"

For just an instant, as N'Teri said these words, an image of a helpless young girl flashed in Kaly's mind. She didn't know it, but the image had been subliminally implanted in everyone's consciousness during their daily

PTS sessions to stimulate their maternal instincts. For her, the mental picture blended with her own memories of the bodies of her classmates lying out in the Gathering Square, back on Persephone. She thrust out with her weapon, uttering a fierce cry that came up from the very depths of her, a primal wail of pure rage.

"Yes! N'Deena has it a'right!" N'Teri said raising her fist. "*That* is what I was waiting to hear! Remember this if you forget everything else people; we are the thin grey line that stands between our enemies and the murder of our loved ones! *Anyone* or *anything* that dares to try and cross that line must be met with our *absolute* and *unwavering* resistance. Now, *again*!"

The session went on for another hour. By the time the lesson had concluded, the platoon had managed to master the five basic maneuvers. To show that she was satisfied with them, N'Teri allowed Platoon Carli to march back in formation to their barracks with their brand new RB-22 bayonets attached to their Mark 7's.

As they headed back, Kaly realized that she was not tired in the least. Her exhaustion had completely vanished, replaced instead by a heady sense of elation. She felt like she was ready to take on the entire universe.

Sa'Tela and N'Vera were waiting for the platoon at the Parade Ground, and watched them critically as they passed, trying to spot any missteps in their formation. Kaly kept her eyes forward, and concentrated on her marching, and there was a spring in her step that had never been there before.

***

The Bayonet Assault Course was a combination obstacle course and close-quarters combat range. A series of beams, fashioned from concrete, were scattered throughout its length, each at varying heights, and ranging from ankle high to waist high barriers. A low ditch, covered with barbed wire lay beyond the beams, and simple square targets made from heavy plastic foam, and set on posts, stood at attention at seemingly random locations.

"Alright, ladies," N'Teri said. "The objective of this course is simple. You are to negotiate the obstacles and make your way to your opponent's

313

position, which are the targets you see on the posts. You are to use your bayonet and eliminate them. Once you have finished with an opponent, you are to move on, attacking each one until you have completed the course. You are *not* to drop your blaster for *any* reason and you *must* score a hit on *every* opponent. Zat klaar?"

"Ma'am, yes, ma'am!"

"Very good," N'Teri replied. "First pair: Bel Anny and Enggredsdaater, *go!* And I want to hear your battle yell!"

The two women gave out ferocious cries and ran into the course. When Bel Anny reached the first waist-high barrier, she threw herself over it, rolled and recovered, and then ran on.

Enggredsdaater was less graceful than her battle sister, and more or less collided with the obstacle before rolling off it sideways. After suffering a hard landing, she got to her feet, and pelted after Bel Anny.

"That's going to be me," Lena n'Gari said fearfully. "I just know it."

"We'll see," Kaly replied, secretly sharing her battle sister's doubts.

By this point, Bel Anny had arrived at the first foam target which was situated at the edge of the wire pit, and shoved her bayonet into it. But when she tried to pull the weapon free, the foam resisted, and she was forced to plant a foot against the support pole and pull with all her might. The blade finally came out, but Bel Anny nearly tumbled backwards.

Seemingly unfazed, she let out another battle yell and ran onwards, diving into the pit, and crawling under the wires. Then she was coming out the other end and rushing at the next target.

This time, she brought up the butt end of her blaster and dealt the target a blow with it before jabbing with her bayonet. The blade released more easily this time, and Bel Anny was off to attack the target beyond it.

Enggredsdaater had much less trouble with the first target, but she was very nearly defeated by the wire pit. Unlike her smaller partner, the large-framed woman had difficulty keeping low enough to avoid the wires. On two occasions, the sharp barbs caught on her fatigues and she was forced to power through, tearing holes in her clothing, but in the end, she made it out and completed the course.

When the pair returned to the group, both of them were out of breath, and Kaly saw that Enggredsdaater had suffered a wound on her leg where the wire had bitten into more than just cloth.

"Good work, you two," N'Teri said. "Bel Anny, you might want to watch over-penetrating with the blade. As you found out, you can get hung up on a target. The same thing can happen with a real flesh and blood body. And Enggredsdaater, I don't think I need to tell you that you need to keep your ass down a little lower, do I?"

"Ma'am, no, ma'am!"

"Good, now get yourself over to MedBay and get that leg looked at. And don't let me hear that it's going to take up any of your training time, *Klaar?*"

"Ma'am, yes, ma'am!" Enggredsdaater bellowed. The two women trotted off together, double time.

"Next pair: N'Deena and N'Gari!"

With a nod to each other, the two women started off. N'Gari proved to be the faster of them and took the obstacles first. While Kaly negotiated the low beams, N'Gari had reached the waist high beam. For a moment, she hesitated, and then threw herself over the top, managing to reproduce a passable copy of Bel Anny's roll-and-recover maneuver.

Kaly came up next, but she was so intent on the waist-high beam that her foot caught on the last of the lower ones. Tripped by it, she flopped forwards to the ground with a groan, holding her blaster off the ground for all she was worth.

N'Teri yelled something behind her, but Kaly ignored it and scrambled to her feet. With a loud cry she leaped over the waist-high beam and came down on the other side, rolling across her shoulder blade like she'd been taught in Primary gym class, and coming up on her feet.

Then she was rushing towards the first target. She brought her bayonet to the fore and lunged. The blade bit into the target with a force that surprised her, and for an instant, she was afraid that she would not be able to withdraw it. At the last moment before she was about to bring up her foot, it came loose and she ran on to the wire-pit.

Up ahead of her, N'Gari had made it out of the pit and was moving on to the next set of targets, but Kaly only spared her the briefest of glances.

315

After her experience with the waist-high beam, she didn't want a repeat of her misadventure. She threw herself to the ground and clambered into the pit, doing her level best to keep her body away from the sharp barbs overhead. The wire clanged and hissed like a living thing as she passed underneath it, but aside from a passing snag from one of the last wires at the end, she made it through unscathed except for a little sand that had managed to find its way into her right eye.

Blinking furiously to clear the tears, she ran on, dealing the next target a butt-strike, followed with an overhead blow with the barrel of her blaster, and finally a killing thrust with the bayonet.

The final target lay ahead, half concealed in a low pit that simulated a dug-in emplacement.

The sand proved treacherous there, and Kaly fought briefly for her footing. A flashback came to her of her collapse during the Platoon's first march, but she was not about to let that reoccur, and dug in with the butt of her blaster and hauled herself up the slope. Then she was over the top, charging down at the target with a roar.

N'Teri critiqued the pair when they returned to the Platoon. "Absent a few spills here and there, you both did well enough and recovered quickly in each instance. Now, I will say this; N'Gari, you need to be a little more aggressive and learn to trust yourself. You did fine when you finally took the waist beam. N'Deena, you need to watch where your feet are."

"Ma'am, yes ma'am!" Kaly replied.

"Good. Next Pair: Bel Haariet and T'Sheela. *Go!*"

By the time the sun had set on Hella's World, the entire Platoon had negotiated the course. There were a few minor injuries, the worst being Bel Haariet, who had tripped on a low beam and cracked a tooth, and a couple of recruits who had earned themselves some bruises with bad footing, or missteps. Despite these setbacks, N'Teri was satisfied with their overall performance, and Platoon Carli returned to their barracks in high spirits.

USSNS *Pallas Athena*, In Space-Dock, Rixa Naval Base, Rixa, Belletrix System, Pantari Elant, United Sisterhood of Suns, 1043.02|11|03:96:32

Jon backed the freight-loader slowly, keeping a careful eye on the rear holo-displays for any traffic behind him. Even though the anti-ship missiles that the loader was carrying were packed in an armored case and nestled in protective foam, he was still nervous about working with them. Most of his fellow ordnance workers, having served a much longer stint in the stores than he had, had a more casual attitude. But Jon had heard too many tales, whether they were true or not, of the disasters that could happen hauling ordnance around a ship, and he wasn't about to let his guard down for one nano.

As he moved across a traffic lane and into the next row of bomb racks, his psiever alerted him that he had a message. Because of the volatile nature of some of the items stored in the area, normal comlinks weren't used and psievers did double their normal duty. Making sure that no one was coming his way with another load, he stopped the machine to access the device.

The text message appeared in his vision. It said; "You have a visitor. Ordstores entrance G-1. Report immediately." It vanished and he saw that an Ordnancewoman was coming towards him.

"Fa'Teela," she said, "I'll take over your load for you. Get over to G1." Jon jumped out of the loader's seat and made his way to the entrance area, curious about the identity of his visitor.

When he reached the double-shielded blast doors that protected the rest of the ship from the Stores, he saw a small brown-skinned woman standing there, dressed in a long, dark robe. Her head was shaved bare, and she sported one long heavy-looking earring in her right ear, with multiple links that brushed the top of her shoulder.

From his childhood training, he knew that this meant that she was a priestess of one of the many goddess-worshiping sects that permeated the Sisterhood, and based on the great length of the earring, a highly placed one at that. He made a sign against witchcraft as subtly as he could, and walked up to her.

The priestess noticed the gesture, and smiled tolerantly. "Greetings, Jon Fa'Teela I am Ophida n' Marsi, the Ship's High Priestess. I had heard that you were aboard, but I hadn't had the time to drop by for a visit until now. Please accept my profoundest apologies."

"None are needed, Sister," he said formally.

Ophida smiled again, this time at the honorific he'd used. "I know that my Temple has little to offer you, but I'd like to think that the truth comes in many guises. Perhaps you'll drop by some time, if only to talk. I've heard a bit about your religion from Dr. elle'Kaari and frankly, it fascinates me."

"Yes, Sister," Fa'Teela replied, already hoping that his duties would prevent him from having to keep such a promise.

"In the meantime," she continued, "one of my congregation passed along the sad news that you had recently lost a possession that was quite near and dear to you. I hope that I'm not presuming, but I took the liberty of procuring a copy of your sacred book so that you might have something to give you comfort during your time aboard the *Athena.*"

The priestess reached into her robes and pulled out a brand new copy of the *Revelation of Mari.*

Jon took it from her. "Thank you, Sister," he said, amazed that a non-believer like herself, a witch if his training had been accurate, would do such a thing for him. "I'll try to drop by the temple when I'm off duty."

This time, he meant it earnestly. Surely, Jesu's light had managed to penetrate her heart, he thought, if only a little. Nothing else could have explained her kind gesture.

"I won't keep you any further, Jon fa'Teela If you decide to visit, just ask any crewwoman, or your pathminder for directions."

"I will," Jon assured her.

Watching him walk away, Ophida smiled to herself. Although he did not suspect it, the destruction of his first copy of *The Revelation* had not been the product of random vandalism by any means. It had been a simple matter for her to arrange the event, and its real intent had been to make certain that her gift to him would be accepted.

The copy that the neoman now had in his possession was going to do much more than provide him with spiritual comfort. It would also help her with her surveillance. In addition to the religious text, the book contained a built-in sub-microscopic computer in the spine that tracked every page that was turned, as well as other equally sophisticated microelectronic features. From this point onwards, she would be able to see what captured his interest, and if he took the little book with him, where he went, and more importantly, who he met with and what they said to one another.

CSS *C-JUDI-GO*, Nosferatu I, Nosferatu System, Frontier Zone, Xee Protectorate, United Sisterhood of Suns. 1043.02|11|08:86:09

Maya watched the *Belle Starr* on the *JUDI's* forward sitscreens as they orbited in tandem around Nosferatu's only planet of note, a huge orange and yellow G-Class gas giant. The escort ship had come along partly to maintain the illusion that the *JUDI* wasn't Null-capable, and also for the added protection that their guns offered. Given the volatile nature of their clients, having the extra firepower around for their meeting was only smart, she reflected.

Sarah spotted their "guests" first. "The Hriss have arrived," she said barely above a whisper. Maya looked, but she saw nothing on her displays except the *JUDI* and the *Starr*. Just the same, she didn't doubt that the woman was correct.

"There are five of them," Sarah told everyone, "one freighter and four smaller ships, fighters. They are separating now. One of the groups will be coming out of stealth momentarily."

The Hriss merchanter and its pair of escorts came up on the long-range scanners at the exact instant that Sarah uttered this, but the other two fighters remained hidden from the *JUDI's* instruments.

That fighters were the only escort that the freighter had, was normal enough for the Hriss. According to Zara, the Hriss preferred to employ fighters for their Null escorts, rather than heavier cruisers like the *Starr*. Evidently, they considered it a greater challenge to traverse Null with a lighter escort. And perhaps it was, on some insane level, Maya mused.

The second pair of fighters, still in stealth, was an entirely different story, and she wondered what they were up to. Knowing the Hriss, it was nothing pleasant.

"Maya, keep an eye on the scanners," Bel Lissa instructed. "If that second group appears, you sing out. If they're here for what I think they are, they'll be inside gun range when they finally let you see them.'

"Also, send a burst transmission to the *Starr* and let them know what's going on. Captain n'Jarri's probably smart enough to guess about the second group, but I don't want to take any chances that they might surprise her."

Maya quickly brought up a holographic keypad and tapped out a brief message to the *Starr*, then sent it.

The *Starr* replied immediately. "Captain, the *Starr* is ready," she reported, "they're powering up their guns and asking us to let them know when we have any more information on group two."

"We will, as soon as *we* know," Bel Lissa replied.

In the meantime, the Hriss merchanter had hailed the *JUDI*. "This is T'Nesh'velaka of the cargo freighter *T'Pekzaa*," a brusque voice informed them. "We will be assuming a docking orbit with you shortly. Prepare for cargo transfer."

"This is Captain bel Lissa of the *C-JUDI-GO*," Bel Lissa answered. "Standing by for you on this orbital track." She cut the Com line and turned to Sarah. "Anything more on that second group?"

Sarah didn't answer her right away. Her eyes were closed and her face was an expressionless mask. After a moment, she stirred and met Bel Lissa's gaze.

"The second group is assuming an orbit below and behind us," she said. "They are remaining in stealth mode. These," she tapped out a figure on her own holoboard, "are their rough coordinates. I detect a sense of latent hostility and suppressed joy coming from the pilots. Apparently, they do not think we know about them, and are gleefully anticipating our terror when they finally decide to reveal themselves."

"So, it's to be an ambush, then. *What* a surprise," Bel Lissa remarked drolly.

Maya shook her head in disgust. The madness of their thinking completely confounded her. Cutting a deal with someone, and then trying to kill them afterwards was nothing short of psychopathic.

Before Bel Lissa could ask her for it, she turned her sensors in the direction Sarah had given them, and tried to detect anything that would give the *JUDI* more of an exact fix on the hidden fighters.

320

"Try looking for a spatial distortion," Zara suggested. "If they're where Sarah says, and they probably are, you should pick up some kind of anomaly. That's if the planet's magnetosphere doesn't interfere and block it out."

She looked hard, and found nothing. Then the *Starr*'s veteran crewwomen contacted them with another scrambled burst transmission, and confirmed Sarah's coordinates.

Double-checking her display again, Maya finally spotted them; a pair of distortions, barely detectable against the backdrop of space and the planet's noise. While the ship's computer assigned the targets a probable orbital track, Maya flushed with embarrassment. She had been hoping to be the first one to find them, but the role of heroine had been denied her.

By this point, the *T'Pekzaa* was coming in close to dock with them. "Maya and Zara," Bel Lissa said, "get down to the cargo bay and get the package ready for transfer."

The two women left their stations and hustled down the ladder together to the bay, while Bel Lissa kept up a running commentary on the ship's status over the general com.

"Target coming up and slowing," she stated. "*T'Pekzaa*, please ease down your engines and match our speed." Then, "Assuming docking position. Both ships confirmed at equal speed and attitude. Crew, prepare for docking."

There was a soft bump against the *JUDI*'s hull and Maya guided the hovercarry over to the egress hatch. The panel over the hatch came alive, indicating that pressure was being equalized in the docking tube. When it flashed green, the door popped open, revealing a passage across to the *T'Pekzaa*.

The *T'Pekzaa*'s egress hatch opened next, and Maya thought that she detected the faint odor of something that smelled like cinnamon in their common air. A Hriss, armed naturally, came into the tube and walked out to its center, waiting for them.

If Zara was nervous, she didn't show it, and Maya kept her own features placid. Had the Hriss really wanted to, they could have used the docking tube to simply board the *JUDI*, eliminate everyone and sieze their prize. But as she pushed the hovercarry forwards into the passage, she realized just how impractical and unlikely this notion actually was. Docked as they were, both ships were vulnerable and any weapons fire would have spelled doom for everyone on both vessels. Even so, she was anything but comfortable as she came close to the creature.

"Remove the cargo container from the carry, wretched females, and stand away," the Hriss commanded in heavily accented Standard. Maya and Zara lifted the plastic box from the hovercarry and set it down at the creature's feet. The Hriss slung his weapon and opened the case to examine its contents. It was the forward section of the anti-ship torpedo.

Satisfied with what he found, the Hriss spoke into his personal com unit to his ship, and then he straightened and handed Maya a credit chip.

She tried to take it from him without touching his hand, but this proved impossible, and she was revolted by their physical contact.

The Hriss sensed her distress, and laughed. "Gutless weakling," he said, "even my touch sends you into spasms of terror. I am amazed that such miserable creatures have anything to offer beings as noble as ourselves. Be off now, spineless ones, and be grateful that I allowed you to continue living."

Maya wanted to answer with something equally haughty, but she bit her tongue and backed away into the *JUDI* with Zara instead. The egress hatch closed, and as they watched him through its small window, the Hriss casually lifted the heavy cargo box onto his massive shoulders and walked back with it into his own ship.

"Hideous things," Maya said.

"*Aye-yah,*" Zara agreed, "that they are. Let's get back up to the bridge, girl. The easy part is done. Things are going to get a bit tricky from here on out."

By the time they had reached their stations, the *T'Pekzaa* had disengaged and was heading out to make its transit into Null with its escort. But the second group of fighters was remaining in orbit with them.

"All hands, strap yourselves in," Bel Lissa commanded. "The fun should be just about to start." Maya obediently drew her safety harness around her and double-checked its settings, fervently hoping that Bel Lissa was wrong about the situation.

The *T'Pekzaa* entered Null and vanished with its prize just as she finished with her straps. In the meantime, the second group of ships had not only changed orbits, but had also come out of stealth. They were headed straight towards them, she realized. And then an alarm sounded. The *JUDI* was being bracketed by their targeting radar.

"Here comes a whole shipload of *shess!*" Bel Lissa warned. "All hands stand by for combat!"

The Hriss pilots didn't waste any time issuing a challenge or any of the usual insults. Instead, the two fighters fired anti-ship missiles at the *JUDI* and the *Starr* simultaneously.

"Initiate countermeasures!" Bel Lissa shouted. Zara immediately launched a pair of military-grade decoys from the *JUDI's* stern. They activated and Bel Lissa engaged the ship's engines, driving the vessel straight down towards the face of the gas giant. As its pale atmosphere began to fill the view ports, the *JUDI* shuddered from an explosion.

"Decoys destroyed," Zara reported. "The fighters are following us and launching another volley."

A second string of missiles arrowed down at them, and Zara responded with more decoys. The missiles went for the bait, but everyone aboard knew that the battle was far from over.

"They're closing up to gun range," Bel Lissa announced, increasing the *JUDI's* angle of descent.

Outside, the universe changed from the stark blackness of space to a strange dream world of orange and yellow mist that reminded Maya of Null. They were descending into the gas giant's atmosphere. It was a move that would either save them, or seal their doom. She held onto her seat with a death grip as they dropped into the mists, unsure of what she was supposed to be doing to help.

The *JUDI* shook from another detonation and Bel Lissa gave her the guidance she needed. "Maya," she said, "watch the altitude readings. Let me know when we get near 6,700 meters and keep an eye on the hull-pressure. It's going to rise a bit." Maya nodded, and consulted her display. Already, the readings were starting to climb sharply.

She wasn't completely sure why the 6,700-meter mark was so important, but she guessed that this was probably the *JUDI's* maximum safe depth. If they exceeded that, the ship would implode under the incredible pressure like a squashed kzizka bug. The only consolation was that their end would be swift, and relatively painless.

Her dark train of thought was interrupted by something happening on the forward screens. She looked up and saw ice. No, she corrected herself, not ice, but chunks of frozen ammonia being pulverized as the *JUDI* went through a band of frigid air.

The fighters behind them fired their plasma guns, lighting up the frozen crystals as they tried to score a hit on the merchanter. Maya kept her eyes on her readings, trusting that Bel Lissa and the *JUDI's* AI were doing all they could to evade the gunfire.

One bolt hit though, and demonstrated that the *JUDI* was not the average merchanter that she appeared to be. Thanks to their OAE connections, the little ship was equipped with military grade blast-resistant armor. Watching the readouts, Maya was shocked to see the energy from the plasma being absorbed and channeled into the vessel's reserve power supply.

The enemy pilots were also just as surprised and ceased firing. They also accelerated to bring other armament to bear.

"Captain" she said, still marveling at her discovery, "we just hit 450,000 bars, altitude 4,572 meters and dropping. Outside pressure is 458,872 kilos per centi."

"Acknowledged," Bel Lissa replied as she increased power to the grav bubble and throttled up the thermal drive to compensate. At the same time, she sent the *JUDI* spinning into another evasive maneuver. "Zara? How are the reactors holding up?"

Unlike earlier warp-based systems, spaceships like the *JUDI* didn't possess shields in the archaic sense of the term. Thanks to the nature of gravitronic engines, the particles which surrounded the ship not only provided it with motive power, but also acted to protect the crew from the forces of acceleration and impacts with foreign objects.

But they required power to do this, and the greater the force being brought to bear against them, the greater the demand on the reactors. And every ship had its upward limits.

"They're starting to dip into the yellow with all this tossing around," the Engineer answered.

"Keep an eye on things," Bel Lissa told her. "I'm routing some power from the reserves."

Then she glanced at the displays and added, "Everyone get ready for some turbulence; it's going to get a little rough."

"Rough" proved to be an understatement. The *JUDI* cleared the band of ice and came out of the upper atmosphere into a relatively clear section of sky. But here the merchanter was pummeled by wind gusts exceeding 320 kph. The *JUDI* trembled like a giant's hand was shaking her, and Maya was thrown hard against her straps.

Above and behind them, the fighters weren't faring much better; a glance at a rearward display showed them being tossed violently about. While they fought for control, Bel Lissa managed to regain the *JUDI's* helm and pitched her nose into an even steeper descent. Abruptly, the merchanter cleared the jet stream and entered a calmer layer of atmosphere.

"Now, for a little payback," she said fiercely. "Zara, let's use those mines that we paid so much for."

Zara grinned and launched the devices. In the meantime, the fighters had just entered the clear zone themselves. Having closed the distance at last, they had switched over to railguns and pieces of metal spat out at the *JUDI* at hypersonic speed.

A sharp *pang* sounded on the bridge as one round managed to penetrate the grav bubble and scored a hit. Then a voice-alarm calmly announced a rapid drop in the cargo bay's pressure. It was followed by a sharp whistling sound and Mayas ears began to hurt. Half a second later, the ship's automatic safety systems engaged the airtight emergency doors between the bridge and the cargo bay, and her pain retreated as the pressure rose to tolerable levels.

Outside, the mines that the *JUDI* had dropped finally detonated and the explosions sent the fighters spinning. One of them, damaged beyond recovery, spiraled down into the misty depths to meet its inevitable destruction. The other managed to recover from its tumble though, and renewed its attack.

In the meantime, Maya realized that their altitude reached the critical mark. Exterior pressure was now an unbelievable 683,209 kilos per centimeter, and she knew that except for gravitronic field, the *JUDI* would have been nothing more than a flattened ball of titanium by this point. But even this wouldn't save them if they dropped much further, she thought. There was only so much they could take.

"Captain!" Zara yelled as they entered another band of wind, this time exceeding 500 kph. "The power drain's too much. We're in the red! The bubble will collapse in 45 seconds!"

The reserve batteries were already giving all that they had, and Bel Lissa nodded grimly, and kept her attention on the helm. Although the *JUDI* was being subjected to astronomical stresses, there wasn't much she could do about it. The Hriss fighter was still there, pounding away with its railguns like a demon as they dropped together towards the gas giant's heart.

"Depth?" she shouted over yet another pressure alarm.

Maya gritted her teeth and ignored the ache in her ears long enough to see that they were dropping below their maximum crush depth. "6,800 meters," she hollered back.

"Good," Bel Lissa said. "Not much longer now." She had an evil grin on her face that Maya didn't understand. Far below them, another band of clouds was rising up to meet them like a hungry river of pure death, dark and foreboding. Their situation seemed hopeless and the Captain's attitude was inexplicable.

Suddenly, the chase ended. The fighter's reactor reached its absolute limit and failed, leaving only a fiery ball of expanding gases and flying debris to mark where it had once been.

Now the girl understood the significance of the 6,700 mark and felt a wave of admiration for Bel Lissa. It hadn't been the *JUDI's* limit after all, but their enemy's.

They were not out of danger, though. Bel Lissa fought desperately with the *JUDI* to bring her nose back up and for a long terrible moment, it seemed as if the ship was inexorably locked in its embrace with the gas giant's gravity. But then, with a roar that resounded through her frame, the merchanter tore free and rose back up towards the upper atmosphere. Tears of relief came to Maya's eyes as she watched the gases thin, and the stars reappear.

A hand clapped her on the shoulder. It was Zara. "Well, Maya," she said, "at least you can't say that life on the *JUDI* is boring!"

All that she could do was laugh right along with her—and savor the fact that she was still alive.

"It looks like we're alone for the moment," Bel Lissa announced. The sensors were finding nothing except a scattering of debris. Someone, possibly the *Starr*, had been in a fight of their own while the *JUDI* was being chased.

"Do you think that's what's left of the *Starr*, or the Hriss?" Zara asked.

Bel Lissa shook her head. "I'm not sure. But knowing Captain bel Jarra and her crew, my credits say that's what's left of a few warriors that tried to jump her while we were down below."

No one argued with this conclusion, or wanted to linger in the area to find out one way or the other. Without ceremony, Sarah opened a gate and they transited into Null, en-route back to Ashkele straightaway.

***

It was late at night when they landed, but anything but quiet in the Free City. The streets around the spaceport were choked with the Xee and their associates, conducting their yearly *Hey-Hey* Festival. Although the Xee actively sought the intervention of their departed ancestors in their daily business transactions, they also believed that harmful spirits could affect their profits through acts of ghostly mischief. For this reason, the community-wide event had a great importance to them; its basic aim was to placate positive occult forces, and banish negative ones.

But in keeping with everything else that the Xee undertook, the Hey-Hey Festival was also big business, and not as straight forwards as it seemed on the surface. Competing merchants paid the Xee priesthood hefty fees to exorcise their homes and businesses, and equally large bribes to curse their competitors with the same evil spirits.

327

Once the intended victim learned about this, often through the agency of the very same priests, additional bribes were paid out to redirect the negative entities back onto their opponent, who did the same, and so on into infinity. Months of bribes and counter bribes tended to precede Hey-Hey and the "winner" of such contests, was the one who paid the most, and won the greatest religious favors. This corrupt, but universally-accepted practice, had made the Xee clergy extremely rich and powerful, and the ceremonies that they conducted during Hey-Hey were lavish and lengthy, if only to give everyone concerned a sense of getting their money's worth.

After all the years she had spent living in Ashkele, Maya knew that the event would go on all night, or at least until every corner of the Free City had been ritually cleansed, or cursed. She tried her best to ignore the rough clanging of cymbals and the harsh banging of drums sounding outside the port, and followed her weary crewmembers as they stumbled out of the merchanter together.

"Well," Bel Lissa said over the din, "we're home. Just smell that sweet polluted air!" The woman laughed at her own joke and led the way out of the port and over to an omni. There, she inserted the credit chip that the Hriss had given them and pecked out a sequence on the flatscreen. The machine considered her request, and finding it acceptable, spat out four new credit chips. Bel Lissa put one of these into her flight-suit, and handed a pair over to Zara and Sarah.

She then turned to Maya and solemnly presented her with the final chip. "Here's your share, Maya. You earned it back there in Nosferatu."

Maya took it from her. "Thank you, Captain."

She stepped up to the omni and inserting the chip, read the balance. It was an impressive sum, well beyond anything that she might have earned back on Thermadon running scams or stealing.

The JUDI might just be something I'll stay with for a while, she thought. The money was just *too* good, notwithstanding the fact that she'd nearly lost her life earning it.

"Congratulations on completing your first real mission with us, Maya," Zara added, clapping her on the shoulder. "Now, you're *really* part of the crew."

328

"That you are," Bel Lissa agreed. "But you're still a hatchie and I'll expect you to spend some of your time from here on out training under Zara, and learning what she knows about the *JUDI*. I'll warn you now; it'll be a steep learning curve."

"I'll look forwards to showing you what the *JUDI* can do, Maya," Zara said, "She's a surprising little ship, she is. I might even be able to teach you a few things that even the Captain here doesn't know."

At that, the group picked up their respective kit bags and walked together towards the entrance to the Free City. "I'm inviting everyone over to the *Nulltrekker*," Bel Lissa declared. "The drinks are on me."

"Sounds good, Captain," Zara grinned. "Especially if *you're* doing the buying." The *JUDI's* Engineer winked mischievously at her superior.

"Going to the *Nulltrekker's* a little ritual we like to do at the end of a tricky voyage," Bel Lissa told Maya. "You'll like the place. Best drinks in the city--and you'll have to agree that the price is right."

***

The *Nulltrekker* catered almost exclusively to the crews of merchanters visiting Ashkele. Most of the bar's clientèle hailed from the Sisterhood though, and just about everything from the music, to its signs, was in Standard.

"Your first time in here, girlie?" Zara asked as they stepped inside the darkened interior. "Well, never fear, old Zara will see to it you have a good time." She guided her over to a table and they sat down. The Captain, Maya noted, did not join them, but worked her way over to another table instead.

"Isn't the Captain going to join us?" Maya inquired. She didn't bother to ask about Sarah, who had parted company with them halfway to the bar. She knew that Zara wouldn't tell her anything, and she didn't particularly care either.

"That she will," Zara replied, "but the Captain has some business to do beforehand. So, what'll it be?"

A holomenu sprang up in the air before them, but even though it was written in Standard, the drinks it offered were completely foreign to Maya.

329

She looked at them with a blank expression. "I have no idea what to order," she finally confessed.

"Then let your crewmate pick out something for you," Zara offered, squinting at the menu. "We'll want something that's not too strong. Can't have you training with a hangover." Then after a moment, "Yes, that's just the thing!" She closed her eyes, and two drinks popped up through the tabletop.

"The bar here works off your psiever," she explained, taking one of the glasses for herself. "Mind you, it's convenient, but after you get a few in you, it can turn out to be a pretty expensive set up."

Maya nodded and brought her glass to her nose, examining its contents. The bluish liquid smelled sweet and inviting.

"It's a Blue Firefly," Zara said, sipping at her own drink. "Mines a Red Aalfen. Go ahead, give it a try."

Maya took a small taste. The drink proved to be positively delicious and she drank some more, enjoying the warmth that suddenly filled her.

"Well, do you like it?" Zara asked.

"Yes, I--," the girl started to reply. But just then, a tiny blue point of light flew past her face, and she swatted at it, inexplicably missing the thing. Then another mote joined the first and circled her head. She batted at the newcomer, and missed it as well.

"What *are* these things?" she asked. The *Nulltrekker* had the standard airdoors and repeller fields to keep out insectoids, so she was surprised to see them buzzing around their table so freely.

"What are what?" Zara replied.

"These bugs! Are they supposed to be here? Is this part of the bar?" In Ashkele, just about anything was possible, and for all Maya knew, the tiny blue lights were actually the owners of the establishment.

"Ah!" Zara exclaimed, suddenly comprehending her, "I should have warned you. They're not there, girl. You can give up trying to nail them with your hand."

"I'm sorry," Maya said. "What are you talking about?"

"They're designed illusions," her crewmate responded, gently grabbing her wrist as she brought her hand up for another attack. "Your drink has a drug in it that makes you see them. That's why it's called a

'Blue Firefly.' Each drink here is named for what it makes the drinker see. It's sort of a trademark of the *Nulltrekker*, something they came up with in the last few years, and most of the bars in the Free City have copied it. In fact, I don't think there's a bar anywhere in this City where you can just get straight alcohol any more."

"If you say so," Maya retorted. The little fireflies certainly *looked* real enough to her. But at least the drink was soothing, she decided, although its side effects would take some getting used to. She drank some more, pointedly ignoring the illusions as they continued to orbit around her.

Zara interrupted her with an elbow in the ribs, and inclined her head towards Bel Lissa's table. "Well, it looks like the Captain's guest is here," the Engineer observed. "You might as well order another drink. Inish will be awhile with this one."

***

Valeri t'Tina sat down without asking for an invitation. Since she was the OAE Sector Chief for the Xee Protectorate, she didn't need one.

"So, Captain," she began, "I see that Sarah isn't with you. That's a disappointment. I'd hoped to speak with both of you together, but, I'm sure she'll contact us soon enough. I take it that our business with the Hriss went well?"

"Yes, it did," Bel Lissa replied. "We even managed to turn a nice profit. Can I order you a drink?"

T'Tina thought about it for a moment, and then nodded. "Why not? I'm on duty, but who's watching? I'll take something light."

Bel Lissa placed her order, and after a moment, it popped up through the table.

"G'nar'varkka went for the torpedo just like we thought he would," she said. "I imagine the thing will be duplicated before the end of a week and sent out to every Hriss ship in his clan." Although it was really Sarah's place to deliver this news, she knew that the Sisterhood spy didn't mind hearing it from her.

"Probably," T'Tina agreed. "Which will make fighting him a lot easier than it has been. In the meantime, I'll let you know in advance that we may

331

need you for another mission in a few days. I'll get in touch with Sarah to discuss the particulars if it gets the go-ahead."

"Sounds like the usual fun and games," Bel Lissa commented, toasting her. "Until next time."

The agent drained her glass, and departed.

When she walked over to join her crewmates, Maya couldn't help but notice that the Captain had a mischievous grin painted on her face.

"While we were talking, I ordered her a Green Devil," Bel Lissa said. "It hits a lot slower than most of the drinks here, but it should give her a night to remember, courtesy of the *JUDI*. It's our way of saying thank you for that little run through the gas-giant."

Everyone laughed at the prank and wished T'Tina an eventful night in her absence. Then Bel Lissa reached into her flight jacket, and withdrew a tiny box. She passed it across the table to Maya.

"What's this? "Maya asked.

"It's another thank you, from us to you, Maya."

Maya opened it and saw a tiny earring, sporting a golden skull.

"It's a badge of honor," Zara told her. "You've made your first run in space as a smuggler, and that shows that you are now a member of a very special group of women."

"A very *junior* member," Bel Lissa cautioned, "but still a member."

"Does this group have a name?" Maya asked. "Or do they just call themselves the 'specials'?"

Zara laughed. "They like to call themselves by their old Gaian name, Standardized and modernized of course. They're the 'Sisters of the Coast. It's sort of a loose association of fellow *entrepreneurs;* we help each other out now and again. Another sister sees that in your ear and they'll know you're one of them. It can come in handy."

That was when Maya realized that she'd seen Bel Lissa and Zara sporting the little golden skulls in their own ears now and again. They were wearing them just then, in fact. Looking at them closely, she observed that their skulls had little stylized bones under their jaws. Zara's had one, and Bel Lissa's, two.

"One bone for a first mate, and two for the captain, right?" Maya guessed.

"That's it," Bel Lissa nodded.

"So, is this an Agency thing?" the girl inquired.

"No, girl," Zara answered, "think of it as a business association that the *JUDI* belongs to. It's nothing the Agency is involved in, although they know all about it. Almost all of the ships in our line of work are part of the Sisters, the *Belle Star* for one. It makes it a lot easier for everyone to get the goods and services they need."

"Well, thank you," Maya said. "I get a ride through a gas giant, get shot at, earn some credits, and now I get to be part of a secret club too! What a *wonderful* day!" Her companions laughed with her.

"One other little thing," Zara added, tapping her earring with her finger, "Always wear it in your left ear. If you wear it in your right, it warns other sisters that someone is not to be trusted, and to be on their gaurd."

"I'll keep that in mind--sisters," Maya answered, making certain to put hers on properly. Then she raised her glass, and they returned her salute heartily.

***

Maya rose early, and was waiting for Skylaar when she arrived.

"May morning's light find and bless you, Cho-sena," Skylaar said as she came out onto the lawn. Sarah was following behind her.

"Today, we will practice our normal drills," the Nemesian stated, "but before this, I would like you to sit and observe something."

Maya bowed and took her place on the grass. "Yes, Sena-tai. I would be honored if you would teach me."

"To this point," Skylaar began, "we have practiced under conditions that are normal to any woman, and this is especially true for Sarah. The reason for this has been simple; in order to properly learn the Art, one must first master its basics by working slowly and precisely. Only then can speed and power be added, for without precision they are nothing.'

"As you know, Sarah's reflexes have been augmented bio-electronically, as have mine. We will now engage in a match using our full abilities, so that you can appreciate the difference in performance."

Sarah had mentioned augmentation to her, but without going into any details, and Maya had never followed up on it. Now, not quite certain how these enhancements would influence the sparring session, she waited and watched, her curiosity thoroughly piqued.

The pair bowed to one another, and stepped back. At a nod from Skylaar, Sarah attacked, and Maya was instantly impressed. The woman had been standing roughly four meters from her teacher, and she had simply vanished. Then, in less than a blink of an eye, she reappeared, suddenly less than a meter away. Before Maya's jaw could even begin to drop in astonishment, Sarah immediately followed through with a punch aimed directly at Skylaar's face.

Skylaar was not overawed in the least, and reacted just as swiftly. In a blur of movement that was almost too fast for Maya to even detect, her teacher blocked the strike and whipped around with her prehensile tail to sweep Sarah off her feet.

Sarah responded with a backwards roll that was more or less at normal speed, and as she came back up on her feet, vanished again only to re-materialize behind Skylaar. Right away, she moved in and caught Skylaar's neck in an arm-bar, throwing a punch into her kidneys at the same time. The blow was audible, and although Maya expected to see a display of pain, nothing registered on her teacher's face.

Instead, the Nemesian replied with a rear head butt. At the same time, she grasped Sarah's arm and threw her in a motion that was so rapid that Maya only registered it after Sarah had landed, and returned to her feet. The girl was fairly certain that a forward roll had been involved at some point, but except for a shadowy blur, low to the ground, she had not caught any of it.

Then Sarah did something that made no apparent sense. Once again, she was about three meters from Skylaar, and shouted as she punched into the empty air with her fist.

But as useless as the gesture seemed, it had an immediate and inexplicable effect. The air in front of the Nemesian seemed to ripple and flatten itself into a tangible wave, and when the disturbance hit her, Skylaar was tossed backwards. She recovered from the impact by throwing herself into a rearwards roll.

The moment that she was standing again, she bowed to Sarah, ending the match, and turned to address Maya.

334

"That, Cho-sena, is how one who studies our Art benefits from augmentation. Now that you have had the opportunity to witness it, I am sure that you can fully appreciate why a normal woman, with standard reflexes and abilities, could not prevail against anyone so enhanced. I must admit that even I cannot withstand the pure blast of *Ki-Ah* that Sarah, as an augmented psi, can project.'

"I would also like to point out that she did not send it at me full-force, or I would have been greatly injured. She also did not employ any of her abilities to cloud or confuse my mind, or our match might have ended much sooner than it did.'

"Perhaps, being a psi yourself, and a student of the Art, you might consider augmentation for yourself in the future. You would definitely benefit from it."

"I--I will," Maya stammered, still getting over her astonishment at the match.

Skylaar nodded her thanks to Sarah, who smiled, and reciprocated the gesture.

"Now, at normal training speed, let us practice our drills from the last class. We will begin with forward punches and blocks."

***

Several days elapsed before Sarah announced their next assignment. She made it during a meal cooked by Zara. The engineer's specialty was Kalian cuisine, and she had prepared a Chandikan curry for the occasion.

"We're going on another Agency run," Sarah told them as she delicately spooned some of the curry onto her plate. "It will be in the Sagana Territory and its objective is to deliver a shipment of hand-weapons to a Sisterhood world.'

"The colonists on a little planet called Storm, in the Agleope system, are taking it upon themselves to stockpile arms in the event of an attack by the Hriss, and the Agency wants to keep track of their activities. Naturally, the weapons will have tracers inside of them, so we will get a very good idea of where they go once they have been delivered, and whom they are stored with."

"Are there any special risks that we need to worry about?" Bel Lissa asked as she dished out a serving for herself.

"None really," Sarah answered. "We might be inspected by the Territorial Marshals, but they will probably look the other way. It is the Navy that we might have any concern about, but according to the Agency, their presence is fairly thin in the area. So, all in all, it should be a simple run."

"When do we leave?" Maya asked. She had been hoping to spend a few more days training with Skylaar.

"Tomorrow morning," Sarah replied. "I think we can anticipate a voyage of one to two days at the most, and we should be back before the end of the week. Skylaar has also asked that we use any spare time we might have during the mission to practice our lessons."

Maya acknowledged this with a nod. Now that she had had some opportunities to work out with Sarah, she had come to appreciate the woman's skills. While she didn't exactly relish her company, she understood the value of their sessions together.

"So," Bel Lissa interjected. "Eat up and get plenty of rest. Let's look for take off at 02:28 hours."

CSS *C-JUDI-GO*, Agleope System, Sagana Territory, United Sisterhood of Suns, 1043.02|15|06:33:58

Because of the increased naval presence in the area, the *JUDI* had joined up with a legitimate merchanter convoy. The idea had been to blend in with the other ships and escape official notice.

And when the convoy came out of Null, and disbanded, it seemed as if the tactic was going to work. But when they were a little more than halfway to their destination, an In-System Patrol ship sent out a hail.

"Merchant ship *C-JUDI-GO*, this is the Territorial Marshals Service. Heave to and prepare to be boarded for inspection. Have your manifests and records ready for download."

"Well, Maya," Bel Lissa observed as she started ramping the engines down, "It looks like another first for you. Welcome to another feature of a moonrunner's life; being boarded by the authorities."

"Should I celebrate this landmark event?" Maya asked dryly.

"Only after the stop's over and we're on our way," Zara said. "Don't worry though, our cargo's well hidden, and I've yet to meet a kaaper that even came close to ever finding anything on the *JUDI*."

The engineer rapped on her console affectionately. "She's a clever girl, our *JUDI* and she knows how to hide her little secrets well."

"Just be polite when they come aboard and do what they say," Sarah advised. "I have often found that this is the best way to behave with law enforcement when fighting is not an option."

The patrol ship docked with them several minutes later and a group of Territorial Marshals came aboard. They were accompanied by two Navy women, who stood out because of their black uniforms, and unfriendly expressions.

Bel Lissa met the group at the docking tube. "Officers? I am Captain bel Lissa. How can I assist you?"

"We're conducting a routine cargo and safety inspection, Captain," a Marshal explained. "We'll need to see your manifests and inspect the ship. If everything is in order, you'll be on your way in no time."

"Here you go," Bel Lissa replied, handing her an elzlate pad. "You'll find everything you need here, and my engineer and her mate will assist you with anything you require."

One of the Navy women stepped forwards and took the data pad away from the Marshal. "We're also looking for smugglers," she said brusquely. "What's your cargo and where are you headed?"

"We're hauling a shipment of replacement parts for the mining operations on Storm," Bel Lissa answered, ignoring her rudeness. "You'll find it all right here in our cargo bay."

"We'll just see what we'll find and where we find it," the woman retorted. "And we won't need any 'help' from your crew. You can all stay right here with the Marshals." The sailor waved to a pair of Marshals carrying a large case to follow her. They pushed past Bel Lissa into the main egress way and began to unpack what Maya guessed was equipment to scan for contraband.

It all looked very sophisticated, and as they started their search, she was tempted to worry, but Zara's words to her, and the confidence that Bel

Lissa placed in her Engineer, helped to reassure her. And for their parts, none of her crewmates appeared to be concerned in the slightest. Sarah in particular, seemed the most unperturbed, and leaned casually against a bulkhead, her eyes half-shut as if she were starting to doze off.

Maya knew her too well to believe this for a nano, however, Sarah was *never* truly relaxed, which meant that she was up to something. What that was exactly, she had no idea.

When the search party returned, it was clear that the Navy woman was unhappy with the results of their hunt. "They're clean," she announced with a frown.

Then she stomped into the docking tube, rubbing at her temples. "Lets try to catch up with the rest of those ships from the convoy," she said to one of the Marshals, "and get me something for this goddess-cursed headache. I don't want to have it with me all afternoon."

"Thank you for your cooperation, Captain," the first Marshal said. "Sorry for the delay we caused, but *she* insisted."

"I fully understand, Officer," Bel Lissa returned. "You have a job to do, and it's not always pleasant."

"No," the Marshal agreed, looking meaningfully in the direction of the docking tube and the retreating sailor. "It's not. Thank you for bringing us your cargo. I know that Colony Manager n'Marni will be very glad to get it. Storm is short on those kinds of parts and we may need them very soon."

"Our pleasure," Bel Lissa replied. "Have a safe patrol." The Marshal flashed her a conspiratorial smile and then went up the docking tube herself.

Once it was sealed and retracted, the *JUDI's* crew returned to the control cabin to get the ship under-weigh again.

"You see?" Zara said as she took her station, "No worries. The kaapers found nothing."

"Yeah," Maya observed. "And I imagine that you weren't doing anything to make sure they didn't, and that headache the Navy bitch got was just a coincidence." She had directed this to Sarah.

"Headaches happen, Maya," the woman replied off-handidly, "and even if instruments say one thing, the mind can always be convinced to perceive something else. Not that I'm belittling Zara's fine ship, or its clever little hiding places."

"Why thank you, Sarah! It's always nice to get my share of the credit now and again," Zara said. "Every little bit helps, eh, Captain?"

"That it does," Bel Lissa agreed as she watched the In-System patrol ship moving away on their scanners. "Let's be on our way to Storm, ladies."

***

Darna n'Marni walked among the crates of military long arms with a suspicious expression. From the moment they had met, it was clear that the Colony Manager did not trust, or like smugglers.

"How do I know these energy rifles even work?" she asked, peering skeptically into an open crate. "We've had shipments before that turned out to be nothing but junk."

"If you like, we can test-fire a few of them," Bel Lissa replied. "Pick any crate."

"Fine," N'Marni returned. "I'll take a rifle from this crate, and two more from those containers on the bottom." She signaled for her assistants to come forwards. Each of the women selected a Mark-7, and N'Marni took one as well.

She inspected the weapon carefully, and then looked at Bel Lissa. "Where are the battery packs?"

"Those are in another container," Bel Lissa responded, bending over a smaller cargo box. She unlocked it, and stood up, holding three of them in her hands.

To Maya's astonishment, she casually handed them over to N'Marni and her companions. If the deal was going to go bad, she thought, this was where it would happen, and she couldn't believe that Bel Lissa was being so careless. *If* she was being careless, the girl corrected herself.

She glanced over at Sarah to see what her reaction was. The woman had reassumed her aura of nonchalance, and seemed utterly disinterested in the exchange. After seeing the same performance just a half an hour earlier, Maya relaxed a bit. Sarah was on the job.

339

"If these are good like you say they are, "N'Marni said as she slapped her battery into place, "Then what's to keep me from just taking them?" Her expression became sly and calculating.

"Well," Bel Lissa replied calmly, "Two things. The first would be your desire to maintain our business relationship. You said yourself that you had had problems in the past getting quality merchandise."

N'Marni had switched on the power, and was starting to level the barrel of her weapon in Bel Lissa's general direction. "And what's the second thing?" the Colony Manager asked.

Maya felt a breeze as something passed by, and her eyes registered the brief flicker of a shadow moving across the room.

Sarah was now standing behind N'Marni with a knife pressed against her throat.

"The second thing," she whispered silkily as she dimpled the woman's flesh with its point, "is that you might have some difficulties carrying these crates all by yourself and with your throat slashed open."

N'Marni lowered her rifle, and cautiously looked over her shoulder past Sarah. Her two assistants were lying on the ground, unconscious. Her eyes widened in fear, and Sarah smiled and planted a little kiss on the woman's ear.

"So," Bel Lissa asked, "May we conclude our deal? We'd like to get back to our ship and be on our way."

Everyone knew the answer to this. Given her situation, Darna n'Marni was really not in any position to renegotiate their contract.

***

After the *JUDI* was outbound from Storm, and headed to their transit point, Maya took the opportunity to speak with Sarah. Rather than distract Bel Lissa or Zara from their duties, she used her psiever and opened a private channel.

Back there, that was your augmentation again, wasn't it? Maya asked.

As you already know, it was, Sarah replied.

How do I get augmented? What's involved? Maya hated the fact that this amounted to nothing less than capitulating to Sarah's desires, but the abilities that augmentation offered were simply too impressive to be overlooked any longer.

Sarah responded with a knowing mental smile that grated on the girl. *You will have to go to Nyx for that,* she thought in reply. *They have doctors there that specialize in this. The procedure itself is fairly simple.*

Maya could also sense that there was something else about the process that Sarah was not revealing to her. *And?*

And just being augmented is not enough, Sarah informed her. *You have to learn how to safely use your new abilities. For that, you need to train under a qualified teacher. I know just such a woman.*

Just like you've wanted me to do all along, right? Maya was angry that Sarah had somehow managed to maneuver her to this point, and she didn't bother to mask the emotion.

As you say, Sarah replied coolly. Irritated beyond belief, Maya cut their connection and brooded for a while. Just as they were about to cut the gate into Null, she called Sarah again.

Yes, Maya?

I'll do it, Maya thought. *I'll go to Nyx and do everything you say. I want the augmentation.*

That is good, Sarah answered. *I'll speak with the Captain when I have the opportunity, and see about getting us some time off.*

If she felt any smugness, the woman didn't allow it to color her thoughts. But Maya wasn't fooled for a moment; she knew that Sarah had to be savoring her victory.

But I'm not doing this for you, Maya vowed privately. *It's for me. It's my decision, and when this is over, I'll go my own way and use my abilities for what I want!*

***

Back in the Free City, the crew of the *JUDI* observed their customary ritual of visiting the *Nulltrekker* for drinks. They were on their second round and Maya had started to order herself another Blue Firefly, which she had become rather fond of, when Zara stopped her and ordered something else.

"You'll love this," Zara assured her, thrusting a tall glass that was filled to the top with a dark red liquid which resembled human blood. "A Red Specter! It's a real nulltrekker's drink!"

Maya eyed the offering doubtfully, but Zara insisted that she sample it. "It's a bit stronger than those Blue Firefly's," she warned, "but trust your crewmate, it's worth the risk. Eh, Captain?"

"That it is," Bel Lissa agreed hoisting her own crimson filled glass, "and after a voyage like this last one, it's the only drink that's fitting to toast with!"

Maya took the glass and tried it. Deep, pleasurable warmth filled her immediately, and she felt the stress drain from her muscles.

"That *is* nice," she agreed. The fact that a red-robed wraith with gaunt features and emaciated limbs had appeared, and was floating menacingly around her companions didn't faze her in the least.

Go ahead and float there, you ugly bitch, she thought, taking another, deeper pull on the beverage, *float to your heart's content.* She was at peace, and that was all that mattered.

"A toast!" Zara suddenly cried, spilling fully half her drink onto the table, "Here's to the nulltrekkers! May they find rest in the clouds of forever!"

"Here, here!" Bel Lissa replied, knocking her glass against Zara's, "And here's to the *Indies*! May the winds blow them to tatters and shreds!"

"And here's to the *Shovelheads*," Zara responded, "may they stay as stupid as ever! Goddess keep their pointed heads filled with bone and nothing else!"

"*Aye-yah!*" Bel Lissa answered, draining her glass. Maya enthusiastically joined her crewmates in this toast.

"And here's to the *JUDI*," she shouted, "Long may she outwit her enemies!"

"*Aye-yah* and that, too," Zara laughed. "May she be as slippery as an *alishk* and as hard to track as a *faalax!*"

Maya had no idea what either of these creatures where, nor what planet they hailed from, but she was suddenly too drunk to care, and added her own "Here, here!" to that of her companions.

"So, Captain, my captain," Zara finally said, "What are we to do next? Has Sarah been given another voyage for the *JUDI*? Some far off place that might hide business under its blouse?"

"We have one at that," Bel Lissa answered. "But this time the mission came looking for me, and *I'll* be the one briefing Sarah. It looks like we're going to be taking a trip aboard the *Star of Aphrodite* and doing some work for an old friend of mine."

"The *Aphrodite*?" Zara asked incredulously, "Isn't that--?"

"The very same, Zara," Bel Lissa replied before looking over at Maya. "She's one of the finest liners the Luxar Lines runs. We're to be given luxury accommodations aboard her, courtesy of my friend, and with the Agency's blessings.'

"In exchange for that, we'll provide a few services for her during the voyage. It's easy work, and we'll be traveling Platinum Class. I wasn't sure if the job was going to come our way or not, but when I checked the omni at the spaceport tonight, my friend had sent word that she needed us after all."

"That's some friend you have, Captain," Maya remarked. In all her life, she'd never imagined that she would travel aboard one of the great luxury star-liners, much less in such a high style. As impressed as she was however, she knew that there had to be a catch. "What *services* does this friend of yours expect exactly?"

Bel Lissa looked around the room for a moment before she answered the girl. "I'll fill you all in on the details the day after tomorrow after a few more things get confirmed. If it all comes together, we'll board the *Aphrodite* the day after that."

"Sounds exciting," Maya grinned. So far, Zara had been right. Her job with the *JUDI* had not been boring, or routine. She was equally certain that whatever it was that the Captain's "friend" had in mind, it would be just as interesting, and as lucrative.

***

Maya waited on the lawn, eager for Skylaar's arrival. Thanks to a hangover cure that Zara had slipped her the night before, she felt well rested, and ready to train.

As always, the Nemesian arrived right on time, with Sarah accompanying her. She had them begin with their usual drills, and then, as had become her custom, she announced the topic of the day's lesson.

"Cho-sena," she said. "Up to this point we have concentrated on the basic fundamentals of hand-to-hand techniques, but Sarah has advised me that you will be going on a mission where other skills might become necessary. So, today we are going to focus on learning to use a common weapon." With that, she reached into the pleather case that she always brought with her, and produced a needlegun.

"It is important as a fighter not only to know the fundamentals of body movements, but also how to apply them when a weapon is in their hand. This is one of the most universal weapons in use today."

Maya had seen plenty of needleguns, but she had never learned to use one. They were expensive, and thieves like her didn't need them. Stealth and trickery had always been the tools of her trade.

"I have asked Sarah to begin our lesson by tutoring you in the basic use and operation of this gun, and then we will work on techniques for disarming an opponent."

At a signal from Skylaar, Sarah went back inside for a moment, and returned with a hovertarget floating behind her. It was shaped roughly like a woman, but without arms or legs, and a series of concentric rings were painted on what corresponded to its chest. When she stopped, the hovertarget drifted off to take up a position at the opposite side of the lawn. Then she took the needlegun from Skylaar and addressed Maya.

"First, you should understand the operating principles behind this weapon. The needlegun uses a system of powerful magnets that propel the needles down the barrel and out towards the target. It is really a small version of the rail-guns that are used on Navy ships and fighters."

She pressed a stud on the side of the weapon and released the clip, making sure to show Maya how this mechanism worked.

"The needle itself can be a simple solid projectile, or it can be 'smart' and employ tiny fins to home in on a target and then penetrate and destroy vital organs. Of course, the needles can also carry anything from simple tranquilizers to nerve toxins. There are even explosive versions, and rounds that divide into flechettes. The needles are really quite versatile.'

"Today I have loaded the weapon with simple dumb rounds, but we will also try some of the smart ones as well. Personally, I like to carry a clip with several dumb rounds and then several smart ones, or explosive rounds, just in case I need to follow up with my shots."

With that said, Sarah re-inserted the clip and cocked the weapon. "There are also two sighting modes on this particular weapon, which is a feature that you will not see in most needleguns on the street. You can sight in on your target using the sights, or use your psiever to acquire your point of aim.'

"Additionally, you can fire at your target with single shots, or in bursts of three. This is also something special to this particular gun. Most needleguns can only fire a single round with each trigger pull."

She brought the weapon up in both hands and squeezed off a shot. A sharp sizzling noise and a loud *crack* issued from the weapon as the round left the barrel at supersonic speed. Maya flinched involuntarily, and when she looked down-range, she saw a soft red glow in the middle of the target's chest, plainly announcing that Sarah had hit it dead center.

"I am now sending a signal from my psiever telling the needlegun to switch to the burst fire mode," Sarah continued. She squeezed the trigger again, and this time, three rounds left the barrel. Once again, her aim was perfect, and Maya suspected that she was using the psiever-aided targeting feature to accomplish this.

Sarah knew exactly what direction Maya's thoughts had taken and explained her accuracy. "Just in case you are wondering, Maya, I am *not* using the psiever to track my point of aim, and it is better to get into the habit of doing without that feature. If something blocks the signal to the gun, or it malfunctions and you don't know the fundamentals of shooting, you could find yourself in a very precarious situation.'

"Now, let us address those fundamentals." She handed the girl the weapon, and proceeded to tutor her.

By the time that the lesson was over, Maya had managed to do a passable job of hitting the hovertarget (which had turned out to be much harder to accomplish than she had imagined), and then Skylaar took over the class and instructed her in various techniques for disarming an armed opponent. At the end of their session, she made one more announcement.

"Captain bel Lissa informed me that your mission may require your services as a body-guard. Therefore, the needlegun that we practiced with today is yours to keep, and the Captain will expect you to have it with you at all times during your voyage.'

"I strongly suggest that you avail yourself of Sarah's experience in the meantime, and get as much practice as possible with it. She will also provide you with some Psionic Training System feeds to help you build up your skills."

Maya bowed solemnly to her teacher. Up to that stage, she hadn't learned anything more from Bel Lissa or Sarah about their mission. Now, with the presentation of the weapon, she realized that whoever the Captain's friend was, she was someone *very* important, and that there was definitely some kind of risk involved, luxury liner or no. The whole thing was starting to feel like something out of an adventure-realie, set against exotic backdrops, and filled with spies and conspiracies.

But this would not be a simulation, she thought soberly, and she had been with the *JUDI* long enough now to know that things could get very rough. Hoping that she would never have to use it, Maya pocketed the needlegun and made a point of arranging for the PTS feed with Sarah.

Dinner that evening was delivered from a local restaurant by an armored delivery vehicle. It was a large Tipandian dish that Maya had never encountered before. Zara had said that it was called a "pizza", and aside from the fact that the vegetables and the meat on it came from several Sisterhood worlds, it was one of the few dishes that had remained virtually unchanged since its creation on Old Gaia.

While Maya got used to handling her slice and keeping the thick Zommerlaandar cheese under control, Bel Lissa finally announced the specifics of their upcoming assignment.

"Maya, I know that you've been wondering about our trip, and it's time to give everyone the details. My friend is Senatrix Layna n'Calysher. You might have heard of her."

Maya nearly dropped her pizza. Although she wasn't given to watching newsfeeds, or paging through holomags, she recognized the name right away. Like many prominent Thermadonians, the Calyshers had retained their family surname instead of using the matronymic, and they had always been at the forefront of Sisterhood politics. And of all the women in their illustrious line, Senatrix Layna n'Calysher was without a doubt, the most powerful and successful. She was the leader of the ruling Galaxa party, and an advisor to the Chairwoman herself.

She is the Captain's friend? she thought in amazement.

Suddenly, Maya began to appreciate Bel Lissa in an entirely new light. There was much more to the ex-Navy smuggler than she had previously imagined. "Yes," she said at last. "I've heard of her."

"I thought you might have," Bel Lissa replied, clearly amused by Maya's astonishment. "She's also a very good friend of the OAE, and she's asked us, and the Agency, for a favor. She's going to be traveling on the *Star of Aphrodite* with her daughter on vacation, and she wants us to join her."

"But there's something else that she's really there for?" Maya ventured. The feeling that she was in a realie had returned in full force.

"Yes," Bel Lissa said, taking a drink of her wine. "She's actually waiting to be contacted by members of a group called the Rampart. We met some of them when we went to Sagana; they're a collection of worlds that are banding together to defend themselves against the Hriss."

"By arming themselves with smuggled weapons?" Maya asked.

"Exactly. Most women haven't heard of them or just how heavily they're arming themselves. Some of them are even suggesting secession from the Sisterhood and negotiating their own treaty with the Hriss."

Maya was aghast. "That would mean rebellion!" Despite its flaws, and her own cynicism, she had always unconsciously maintained an image of the Sisterhood as one cohesive body, operating with total solidarity.

"It will not happen," Sarah reassured her. "For one, the Navy is going to be coming into the Territory in a significant way, and quite soon. That event will be public, and billed as an effort to inject more security into the area, which it certainly is.'

"It will also be a bargaining chip for the Senatrix in her negotiations with the Rampart leaders. She is going to be offering them the establishment of a permanent base in the Territory in exchange for them agreeing to disband themselves.'

"In addition, the faction that wants the separate treaty with the Hriss is small and doesn't have much influence yet, but another incident like the raid on Persephone could change that, which is why the Navy is stepping things up.'

"The real danger is their process of self-arming, and the very fact that there are some women who are suggesting secession. That news, if it became known, would be an embarrassment to the current government, and to the Senatrix herself. She is hoping to heal the breach before that can occur."

"So why are we getting involved?" Maya asked.

"The meeting's going to be secret," Bel Lissa replied. "Only the Rampart leadership and the Senatrix are aware of it. With any luck, when it's over, the public will never even know that the Rampart ever existed and life will go on as always. You know, 'Sisters United' and all that. Knowing the Senatrix as I do, I think she'll manage to settle things down, especially if the Rampart sees that the government is serious enough to establish a permanent naval base."

Maya reached for her own glass of wine, and took a deep drink. "But?"

"*But*, the Senatrix and the Chairwoman have powerful enemies within the Supreme Circle itself," Sarah said. "If they knew that this meeting was occurring, and there is a chance that they *will* find out, they would want to prevent it and let the situation get far enough out of hand to force the Chairwoman to resign.'

"Some of these same women would also like to see the Senatrix dead for reasons that have nothing to do with the Rampart. Add to this equation the fanatics within the Rampart who have a vested interest in preventing any form of settlement, and you have a very volatile situation that depends on complete secrecy and vacuum-tight security to guarantee its success."

"And here I thought that being a Senatrix was just a bunch of dull speeches and boring committee meetings," Maya remarked. "So, her going on vacation is some kind of cover?"

"Yes, it is," Sarah said. "Her security people are hoping that no one would suspect her of doing anything clandestine when she is on a holiday cruise with her daughter. That sort of thing just doesn't fit the usual cloak and dagger mold." She smiled in amusement at this, and then went on. "With luck, the ruse will work, and her enemies will be caught completely off guard."

"What about a group of smugglers hanging around with her?" Maya countered, "Isn't *that* just a little bit suspicious?"

"Not in the least," Sarah responded. "Like any powerful woman, the Senatrix is known for her varied associations. Assuming that they even manage to identify us as smugglers, and not merely another component of her security detail, anyone who is aware of the weapons being smuggled into Sagana will think that we are representatives of the Sisters of the Coast, trying to bargain with the government before the Navy increases its presence. They may even come to believe that this is the whole point of her trip."

Maya saluted the plan with an appreciative toast. "Very cute."

"Our basic task," Bel Lissa said, "will be to help her security staff with their protective details while she's aboard the liner. As soon as we find out where the meeting is, we get her off the ship, to the meeting, and back aboard before anyone is the wiser. With luck, and the Goddess' blessings, Senatrix n'Calysher will come home from her vacation with nothing more newsworthy than some gossip about how she was dressed for dinner.'

"*Your* job, Maya, will be to safeguard the Senatrix's daughter, which should be fairly easy work. As for the rest of us, and especially Sarah, we'll be staying close to the Senatrix, and ready at a moment's notice to get her aboard the *JUDI* for the meeting."

"So I'm stuck playing babysitter for a spoiled little rich girl?" Maya frowned. The idea of shepherding some brainless little ninny around while she complained about the temperature of her soup, or the way her flowers had been arranged, didn't sound terribly appealing.

Bel Lissa nodded affirmatively, and Maya sighed raggedly in resignation. "Well, here's hoping that she's not a *total* bitch."

"It could be worse," Zara offered. "It's light duty and I hear the food's good at the Platinum class tables. Just the same, when you're not busy powdering the girl's bottom, keep a sharp eye out and your needlegun handy. Some of the women that hate the Senatrix are pretty nasty and wouldn't flinch at a chance to hurt the Senatrix through her daughter. I've even heard tale that the Bio Action Army has a contract out on both of them. Being on the liner wouldn't stop their kind one *nano*. In fact, they'd welcome the publicity that'd create."

The Bio Action Army was one of the few real terrorist groups in the Sisterhood. They believed that the Sisterhood had abandoned the principles of the old Bio Movement in favor of conventional terraforming, which they labeled 'bioimperialism.'

On several occasions, they had managed to make the headlines by committing sensational acts of violence. The worst had been the notorious Fiveday Evening Attack of 1023.04, when the main magnorail station on Thelta in the Chandi Elant had been attacked with chemical agents. One hundred commuters had lost their lives, and thousands more had been injured.

Although the Sisterhood had managed to destroy most of their cells following this event, the Bio Action Army was still a force to be reckoned with. Their potential presence sobered Maya, but it also mollified her in a way. Even if she was only to play the role of an armed babysitter, the possibility of real danger, however remote, *did* manage to make the job seem just a little bit more important and worthwhile.

"Okay, I'll do it," Maya agreed. "And who knows? Maybe while you're all off playing hovertaxi drivers, I'll be the one to rescue the beautiful girl from imminent peril. So, when do we start this thrilling, action-packed adventure?"

Bel Lissa chuckled. "Be up and ready by 03:75," she answered. "We'll fly out of the port by 04:16, transit and meet with the liner by 05:20. She should be in the Artemi Elant by then and we'll catch up with the *Aphrodite* when she makes port at Chione."

CHAPTER 11

As Ophida had agreed, the wedding ceremony for the two crewwomen took place just before the *Athena* was scheduled to head out on patrol. The event was held in the ship's Temple, and Lilith and Katrinn atttended. Like everyone else in the room, they were in their dress uniforms, and sat together near the cylindrical altar.

Katrinn nudged Lilith as the traditional pairing song began to chime and the two brides entered the Temple. "Here they come," her Second said breathlessly. "Aren't they beautiful?"

Lilith looked back over her shoulder at the couple and had to agree. They were positively radiant.

In keeping with the Selenite faith, they wore matching green gowns, the color of fertility and happiness, which were trimmed with silver in homage to the moon goddess. Their faces were also veiled, but as they passed by, and walked down the aisle together, Lilith could still see the utter joy on their faces.

One of them (she thought it was Ensign t'Marria from Stores) was doing her best not to cry and reached up to blot at her eyes as they stepped up to the altar. Their handmaidens, attired in their finest dress uniforms, stopped behind them and took their places to either side.

Ophida n'Marsi raised her arms in a gesture of benediction. "Sisters," she declared, "we are met here today to witness the union of these two women, Ensign Sharala t'Marria and Lieutenant Karol Gretasdaater to be joined together as loving partners in the eyes of the Lady from this day forwards.'

"Their pairing is like the face of the Lady herself, the moon that once shined upon the planet of our birth. Here and now in this sacred Temple, it is waxing, as the fullness of their love for one another brings them together in a sacred bond. And as they go forth from here, and face life's challenges, their pairing and their love shall increase in its fullness, outshining everything around them.'

"In time, as their days grow short, their light shall seem to wane, but their bond will be eternal and follow them as they pass into darkness, only to be renewed again in an eternal binding of two souls, imperishable and undivided. Witness then, the pairing of Sharala and Karol and know the secret of eternal life; it is love that unites and transcends all things, including death itself."

An Assistant Priestess stepped forwards and brought forth a small pillow. On it rested the couple's silver pairing rings, gleaming in the gentle overhead lighting.

"Sharala," Ophida asked, "is it your wish to be paired with this woman? To be her partner in all things, both good and ill? To have her for all time as your mate?"

"I do," Sharala replied.

Ophida reached for the first ring and handed it to her. "Please place your ring upon her finger as a sign of your promise."

Sharala slid the ring onto her partner's finger and Ophida looked at the other woman.

"And is it your wish, Karol," she asked, "to be paired with this woman? To be her partner in all things, both good and ill? To have her for all time as your mate?"

"I do," Karol replied.

"Please place your ring upon her finger as a sign of your promise." As Karol placed her ring on Sharala's finger, someone in the audience stifled a sob of happiness and Lilith felt a knot starting to grow in her own throat.

"Then in the name of the Lady, and by the powers granted to me by the Great Temple of Selene, the Office of the Chaplain General of the United Sisterhood of Suns Naval Forces, and in the eyes of all here assembled, I declare that you are wedded to one another from this day forwards. Daughters, remove your veils so that you might gaze upon one another as pairmates."

As the two women raised each other's veils, and gazed at one another, the wedding guests stood and applauded the new couple.

Katrinn reached out and squeezed Lilith's arm. "Oh, isn't this just wonderful?" she asked. Her eyes were bright with tears and Lilith nodded in silent agreement.

It *was* wonderful, she thought, watching as the newly married women shared a glass of wine from a special silver cup. Karol was a tall blond who reminded her strongly of Ingrit, and an image came to her, of herself, standing up at the altar in Sharala's place, and looking into her lover's eyes as they faced a new life together.

Could that ever be? she wondered. Would a time ever arise in her life when she would give up her career as an officer to join with Ingrit as her wife?

Up to that point she'd never really considered any other life for herself. But as she watched the happy couple, the sweetness of their shared moment tugged on her heartstrings.

Perhaps, she thought. Not today or tomorrow, but someday.

USSMC Training Facility, 75th Training Battalion, Hella's World, Hecate System, Artemi Elant, United Sisterhood of Suns, 1043.02|17|03:36:63

Kaly ran at the wall and jumped. She was just able to get her fingers over the top lip before she lost her grip and slipped off.

Sa'Tela was standing on the sidelines, watching her lack of progress with obvious disapproval. "Get back to the jump-off site and try it *again*, N'Deena!"

Kaly swore under her breath and tried a second time to mount the wooden barrier, but she was unable to master it.

"All right, N'Deena," Sa'Tela hollered. "You're holding up the line. Go around the *fekking* wall!!"

Humiliated, Kaly ran around to the next obstacle, a maze of low wires that she was forced to crawl under on her belly. This at least was something that she was good at. Most of the other girls were larger than her, and she was able to get through this part of the course without getting hung up.

Troop Leader n'Teri, who was waiting for her on the other side, didn't shower her with praises, however. The DI gave her a shove and yelled at her to move on to the next phase.

This was a length of rope suspended over a deep, dry pit. The objective was simple enough: to swing across the expanse on the rope and reach the other side. When Kaly reached the station, she stopped to catch the rope before attempting to swing over. This cost her the energy that she needed to complete the trip and she came up just short of the opposite side. Remembering her experiences as a child on a swing, she pushed straight out against the bank with her feet and sent herself backwards, creating enough momentum for another try. It did the trick. She was able to crest the lip of the pit, and she let go, landing on the opposite side at last.

Troop Leader N'Vera was anything but congratulatory. "What the *fek* was *that* supposed to be, N'Deena? Do you think you'll have that kind of *time* in real combat? Run back and do that maneuver again in *one* swing!"

Kaly obeyed, but this time, she came up short, and was left hanging in the air above the pit.

"Drop the fek off, N'Deena!" N'Vera howled, "and go back and do it over!"

Kaly tried to cross several more times after this, but with an equal lack of success. Finally N'Vera had had enough of her and waved her on to the next station.

A rope bridge, with two lines attatched to it that served as primitive hand rails, awaited her. It was suspended over a pool of muddy water.

As the recruit in front of her negotiated the bridge, it swayed wildly. Halfway across, the hatchie lost her footing and fell into the evil looking pool. Watching her, Kaly's guts churned at the prospect of trying to cross over it herself. N'Vera didn't give her any options though; the DI was right behind her, screaming at her to move along.

With no other choice, Kaly stepped out onto the rope and grabbed hold of the hand lines, feeling like a tightrope walker from some old realie. It took her a few steps before she got the knack of walking with one foot in front of the other, and even then, her progress was slow. Reaching the middle of the span, she saw a place where the rope had been worn smooth by the feet of countless hatchies and she stepped over it carefully, and reached the other side.

Even so, N'Vera was not pleased. "You were too slow N'Deena!" she shouted. "Just for that, I want you to turn around and go back and *this* time you'd better get across faster!"

Kaly obeyed and started across the bridge. When she reached the center again, she attempted to step over the smooth spot on the rope, but this time she misplaced her foot and slipped.

For an instant, she hung there, grasping the hand lines and trying desperately to get back up on the footrope. It was hopeless though, and finally, she surrendered to the inevitable and let herself drop into the water. She surfaced a moment later, covered with mud and filth.

N'Vera was livid. "N'Deena, you *fekking screw-up!* I told you to go *across*, not to go *swimming!* Get to the end of the line and go across that bridge again, and *keep* going until I tell you to stop!"

By the end of the day, she had made dozens of crossings, falling into the water a third of the time. At last, cold and wet, she was hustled back to the barracks double-quick by N'Vera and her mood was dark by the time they arrived.

"There's a trick to making it through the obstacle course, you know," Bel Anny said as Kaly dejectedly changed out of her sodden clothing.

"Oh?" Kaly asked doubtfully.

"Yep," Bel Anny replied. "It's all in your momentum. You have to come at the wall at a run and then jump up just before you hit it. If you slow down, or stop, you'll never make it over the top.'

"The same goes with the rope. If you take it running, you'll have plenty of energy to make it over the first time. As for the bridge—well, all I can say is to watch your feet, but I guess you know that by now."

Kaly sighed raggedly. "Jana, I'm not sure I can get through this course."

"That's half the reason you fail," Bel Anny suggested. "You have to *believe* that you can succeed, and then you will. Give it a try."

***

Kaly faced her opponent with grim determination. The wooden wall stood there, a huge and implacable barrier, seemingly defying her to conquer it. She was on her free time, and she'd come to the confidence course with her fellow recruits to get in some practice before the next official training session.

"I'm going to master you," she vowed, visualizing herself topping the wall just like Bel Anny had instructed. Taking a deep breath, she started off, running at it for all she was worth. When she came to within a stride, she pushed off and leapt upwards. To her amazement, her fingers touched

355

the top, and she hauled herself over with all the strength that her arms had to give.

"Yes!" N'Gari cried as she watched her from the sidelines.

"That's it, Kaly!" Bel Anny yelled, raising a triumphant fist in the air.

Kaly dropped to the ground, and grinned. Then she trotted back to the starting line for another try, pleased and just a little amazed at her success.

Her next session on the confidence course proved to be an entirely different experience. She powered over the wall with ease and swung across the rope like a super-heroine. Even Troop Leader n'Vera had to give her a grudging nod of approval as she completed the course.

"I wouldn't have thought you'd make it, N'Deena," N'Vera said. This was as close to a compliment as N'Vera was capable of, and Kaly was glad to hear it, knowing how hard it had been for the DI to admit it.

Another round of self-defense training took up the rest of the morning, centering on basic throws. The platoon managed to collect a fair assortment of bruises from the practice, including Kaly.

Despite this, she was in high spirits as she filed into the PTS auditorium for their afternoon class, and her elation was shared by many of her classmates. Their collective mood was about to change radically, however.

"For today's class we have a guest speaker," Sa'Tela announced. Kaly half-expected that their guest was going to be another Hriss, or something equally distasteful.

It wasn't.

An officer, about the Troop Leader's age, came into the PTS room, dressed in a class "A" Marine uniform that was covered in medals. One of them was the Supreme Circle's Medal of Honor, the highest decoration awarded for bravery and service to the Sisterhood.

Kaly realized that this was no average Marine.

The woman walked up to the small stage with a pronounced limp and there was a drawn, haunted expression on her face that bothered Kaly on a visceral level.

She looks like a ghost, the girl thought. It turned out that she wasn't far from the truth.

356

"I have the honor of introducing Major Rana n'Hila," Sa'Tela said, "Currently assigned to the 501st Intelligence Battalion. Major, perhaps you would like to tell everyone the topic of today's lesson?"

The Major nodded and took her place behind the podium. She looked at the recruits for some time, with a gaze that seemed to see past them, to something distant and unknown that only she could perceive. Finally, she spoke. "The subject for today's class is becoming a prisoner of war."

She let her words hang in the air for a long moment before continuing. "You may already know from your PTS feeds, that the Code of Military Justice specifies that all women who are taken as prisoners of war are only expected to furnish their name, rank and service number, and that treaties agreed to through the agency of the Galactic Collective, stipulate that all prisoners are to be treated according to strict humanitarian guidelines. Can anyone tell me what some of those guidelines are?"

Bel Anny stood up and answered for the platoon. "Ma'am, some of those guidelines would be that prisoners are not to be subjected to torture and that they must have adequate food, water and shelter, ma'am."

"Yes, they do say that don't they?" the Major replied, smiling as if she had just been told a bad joke. "One would therefore expect that becoming a prisoner wouldn't be that bad, wouldn't they?" No one tried to contradict her.

"They would be incorrect," the Major continued. "Even though the Sisterhood's Armed Forces subscribes to the humane treatment of its prisoners, and even though the member races of the Galactic Collective say that they do so as well, the truth is quite different.'

"I am currently assigned to an Intel Unit. However, I wasn't always part of the 501st. My original assignment was with a Mobile Infantry Company, stationed aboard the USSNS *Gloriana*."

She paused to see if anyone in the room understood what this implied before pressing on. "My Company saw action in the Battle for Adralaun in the War of the Prophet, and my sisters and I had the misfortune of being captured by the Hriss. We expected that, like ourselves, they would abide by a similar code of prisoner treatment. We were dead wrong."

357

Kaly was just beginning to understand the point of the lecture. Without realizing it, she gripped the arms of her seat tightly, knowing instinctively what the Major would tell them next, and dreading to hear it.

"You see, ladies," the officer said, her voice oddly flat and emotionless, "The Hriss have no concept of 'humane' treatment. Their language has no words for 'mercy' or 'compassion.' And they view anyone who is taken prisoner as a lesser being, worthy only of contempt."

"Those of us who were not killed outright were taken off-planet to a special facility where they studied us. Being an entirely patriarchal society, the Hriss are fascinated by a race of females that can fight, and they were determined to learn what our weaknesses were."

"The women that survived their initial capture were subjected to horrible experiments and tortures of every kind, without any regard for the conventions of war, or decency."

"I am one of the three members of the two hundred women in my Company to survive that experience. I was lucky enough to be rescued by a Marine Special Forces team when they raided the installation.'

"However, it still took many years of rehabilitation, both mental and physical, before I was ready for active service again, or to be able to speak about what I had experienced. I could stand here and tell you what happened to me and to my fellow prisoners, but words are not always enough to get the point across. Let me show you some images of what I experienced instead."

A series of holograms appeared in the air. From the data tags, Kaly could tell that they were shots taken from the helmet-cams of the Marines who had attacked the facility.

The place was dark, and the images were grainy, which proved to be a blessing. What Kaly did manage to see brought back memories of her own experiences in the Gathering Square on the night of the raid on Persephone.

In one shot, a room was shown strewn with body parts and corpses, left to lie there on the floor like discarded scraps of meat from a predator's meal. Others showed women attached to strange devices in various stages of death, and yet another depicted a primitive operating room of sorts, with dissected bodies sprawled on the tables. From the restraints on the wrists and legs, it was all too obvious that the dissections had been performed while the victims had still been alive.

While the holo-show progressed, several of the recruits became ill and fled the room. Kaly was not one of them though. She remained, frozen in her seat, and unable to look away. Lena, who was in tears, tried to grab onto her for comfort, but Kaly barely noticed her, caught up in an inner maelstrom of fascination, horror, and anger.

Finally, mercifully, the images ceased.

"Where the Hriss are concerned," the Major said, "there are no rules of war. The lesson for today is simple; do not allow yourself to be taken alive. Resist with everything you have in you, or suffer the same fate that my sisters and I did. Thank you for your attention."

She regarded them with a strange smile, and hobbled off the stage.

The recruits marched out of the auditorium in silence. To the last, they were deeply shaken. There was very little conversation as they went about the daily chores of cleaning their barracks and inspecting their weapons, and Kaly immersed herself in field stripping her Mark 7, trying to ignore the profound depression that sat atop her like a living being.

She suddenly felt old, and she realized that up to that day, a part of her had still been a little girl filled with hopeful illusions. That she had been holding onto the belief that what had happened on Persephone had only been an aberration, a freak event. That the galaxy wasn't the awful, savage place that the Major had described.

She knew better now, and her existence seemed all the more dark and forbidding for it. Perhaps this was an integral part of growing up, she reflected, the point where childish hopes were set aside and the savagery of life was acknowledged at last.

The notion of someday going out and facing that in battle and possibly even experiencing the horrors that she'd seen during the lecture, filled her with dread, but also with resolution.

Her path was decided. She was going to be one of the few who would stand up to such monstrosities. She would be a part of the "thin grey line" that N'Teri had described to them so often, and she would save others from the atrocities that the universe was capable of inflicting.

Filled with a renewed sense of purpose and strength, she started to reassemble *Athena*, and Lena came over and sat down on the cot next to her. For a long time, the girl said nothing to her, but then, in a quiet voice, too low for the others to hear, her battle sister spoke at last.

"Kaly," she said. "I want you to promise me, if it ever comes down to it—" But she couldn't finish what she had started to say. She didn't need to.

Kaly carefully put down the cleaning rag that she'd been polishing her blaster with and gently caressed Lena's cheek. "It won't," she vowed. "I won't let it."

USSNS *Pallas Athena*, In Space-Dock, Rixa Naval Base, Rixa, Belletrix System, Pantari Elant, United Sisterhood of Suns, 1043.02|18|06:32:92

With only two days left before their scheduled departure for Sagana, Lilith was working in her office reviewing the mission folio when the Com sounded.

"Commander?" It was Marga bel Lyra, her Chief Engineer. To make room for all of the special equipment the Marine Engineer detachment needed to bring with them, Bel Lyra had been overseeing modifications to deck 12.

"Yes, Marga?"

"We just finished removing bulkhead 1250A."

"Did your crews trip over any more ghosts?" Lilith asked with a dry smirk.

"Not...exactly," Bel Lyra responded hesitantly.

"Marga? Don't tell me that you believe in such nonsense?" Lilith was shocked. Bel Lyra was one of the most pragmatic women she had ever known. Her universe consisted of the hard reality of engine systems, duct controls and the laws of applied physics. Not the occult.

"Well, no, ma'am, I don't. Not usually. But in this case..." Bel Lyra replied, "Well, I can just say that I've been down on 12 with the crews, and I've seen what they've been reporting. I've also heard the knocking sounds, and now...this."

Lilith suddenly found herself wondering if Bel Lyra hadn't been working too many hours. *Maybe a shore leave is in order*, she thought, upcoming patrol or no.

"Now this, *what?*" she asked her.

"Well, perhaps you'd better just come down and see, ma'am. Make up your own mind," Bel Lyra suggested. "I've already called Reverend n'Marsi."

"Fine," Lilith agreed. "I'm on my way."

On deck 12, she found most of the expansion crew and a group of Marine engineers huddled around the end of an auxiliary passageway, talking to each other in low, fearful voices. Ophida n' Marsi was also there, along with the Chief Engineer.

"Blessings of the Lady, Commander," Ophida said. "It seems that some of what the crew has been reporting has some merit after all."

"How so?" Lilith inquired. Now she was wondering if N' Marsi needed shore leave as well.

"Perhaps we should just show her," Bel Lyra proposed.

"Yes," Ophida agreed. "Commander?"

The priestess walked down the corridor, beckoning for Lilith and Bel Lyra to follow. They worked their way past stacks of new wall sections and pipes, and stepped over temporary hose lines until they reached the section where the bulkhead had been removed. There, the work had revealed a hollow cavity that had existed between it and the next bulkhead.

Inside, Lilith saw what she thought were old clothes, but as Bel Lyra illuminated the area with a hand light, she realized what had really been concealed there, and gasped.

The body inside the moldering spacesuit had long since mummified and partially collapsed in on itself, but it was clearly human. The suit was old-fashioned, but still easily recognizable as a construction-worker's spacesuit with a heavier than usual helmet and armored plates suited for hard work in a vacuum.

"That suit's at least 300 years standard," Bel Lyra stated. "From the insignia, I'd say that she was one of the original builders of the *Athena*."

Lilith was incredulous. "But how..?"

"Back then, we were in a big hurry to get a navy built," Bel Lyra said. "There was a lot of high-speed automation; robots did a lot of the plate-laying. I figure that whoever she was, she got sealed in by a 'bot and died in there. The plating in this area is so heavy that her distress signal probably didn't get out, if she was even conscious at the time. It's happened before with big ships, even before space travel existed."

"May the All Merciful Lady grant her peace after all these long years," Ophida interjected, making the Lady's sign over the corpse. Bel Lyra and Lilith solemnly copied her.

"Perhaps this is a positive thing," the priestess ventured, "A sign of good luck for the ship. Putting her to rest now, before shipping out, may herald a more fortunate outcome for our mission."

"Perhaps," Lilith replied, carefully masking her skepticism. Even though it was obvious that the entire affair had been nothing more than a series of odd coincidences which could be explained rationally, the crew would still need some closure. That was what really mattered. Ship morale couldn't be allowed to flag.

Presently, the Medstaff arrived, and removed the body. After a brief autopsy in the MedBay, the High Priestess performed a formal funeral ceremony and the corpse of the hapless construction worker was sent into space with full military honors.

After that, there were no more reports of ghosts on deck 12.

***

The body on deck 12 wasn't the only surprise waiting for the *Athena*, or her Commander. The next came the following day.

Like any starship dedicated to keeping the peace, the *Athena* used an automated system for loading the tons of ordinance required to supply its weapons batteries. In the *Athena's* case, this consisted of a massive array of conveyor belts that fed bomb clusters and rockets up from Ord Stores into the waiting guns and launching tubes. For the most part, the system worked quickly and efficiently, but on occasion, things did go wrong, and then workers like Jon were required to lend their flesh and blood assistance.

The neoman was in charge of a cluster of space-to-space anti-ship missiles that needed to be switched out with another set that didn't match the battery that they were intended to feed. The pod, consisting of twenty missiles, was securely held by his lifter's grasping arms, and according to the HUD display on the driver's compartment, he was right on target. When the laser guides told him that he was in line, he edged forwards until the sensors agreed that the pod had made contact with the cradle, and then he released his load.

As soon as the on-board computer verified that the load was secure, and that it matched with the requisition orders for the slot, Jon backed his vehicle out and headed back to the main stores area for another consignment. On his way through the inner blast doors that protected the rest of Ordinance Stores from the conveyor system, he passed a group of women from Engineering moving in the opposite direction.

Part of the system had been shut down, and they were fixing one of the belts that had been suffering from malfunctions. It was an important repair, given the vital nature of the belt's job, but it hadn't mandated shutting down the entire delivery system.

Jon waved at the crew, but just as he had expected, they didn't return his greeting. The neoman sighed in resignation and drove on.

He was in the process of picking up a crate of rail-gun ammunition when he overheard that the repair crew had arrived at their destination in row 130 and was starting their work on the conveyor belt. It shouldn't have concerned him, but something about the transmission made his hair stand on end. It was a premonition of disaster.

Something terrible was about to happen, he realized. Suddenly, he was at war with himself, just as Jesu had struggled when Shaitan had tempted him. His talent was never incorrect about such things. Someone was about to be killed. He was certain of it, and he started to turn the 'lifter around when he stopped.

Don't be a fool, he told himself. *If you go back there before the accident, they will know about your talent and then all will be lost.*

But the feeling of immanent disaster was simply too much for him to bear. He could almost feel the agonizing pain that was about to visit itself upon the crewwomen, and he could not resist the call of his vision. Even though they were unbelievers, they were still human and he knew that he could never live with himself if he didn't at least *try* to intervene.

A Marine would do that, he reasoned. A Believer would do that too and the *Revalation* stated it plainly; '*Show ye charity and aid to all those in distress. Know that to aid them is a holy thing, and to stay thy hand when one could have acted is a sin.*' There was really no choice.

Jon hit the brakes and turned the vehicle around. Immediately, a psiever message flashed in his vision. It was from his supervisor: "Fa'Teela!" it read, "Turn around now and stow that ord-load!"

Heedless of the prohibition against using it, Jon keyed his voice com. "The belt!" he started to say, seeing it in his mind, "Get the crew out now! Hurry! The brace is about to--"

But he was already too late. There was a cry of alarm over the general Com and then an agonized scream. Jon gunned the engine of his lifter and raced back to the conveyor belts. The lifter's plastic and rubber tires squealed and smoked as he hurtled down towards row 130.

He had no trouble finding it; a frantic Engineer came running out, waving her arms at him. Jon pulled up and jumped out of the cab.

Up the row, he saw the metal conveyor belt. The techs had been working on its internal wheels and their guide tracks, and had used a special metal brace to hold back the belt's sections and create a workspace inside of it.

The brace had failed and it had come back down the track with the full weight of the belt behind it. One woman was pinned at the waist, and as he came nearer, he saw another woman, lying inside, neatly decapitated.

"We need help!" Jon yelled into his com-mike. "I have one deceased and one in critical condition!"

"What happened?" someone, probably an Officer, demanded.

The one woman who had not been injured spoke up. "The brace--it--it collapsed. We were running a diagnostic when it came back down. Oh, Goddess, I can't believe it--" the rest of what she had been trying to say was cut off as she collapsed to her knees and sobbed.

Jon ignored her. It was the crewmember pinned in by the brace that commanded his full attention instead. She was about his age, he realized, and with her dark hair and eyes, she could have been his sister. Her skin was chalk-white and her lips were turning blue as she gazed back up at him with eyes that were bright with shock.

"My legs," she said quietly.

They weren't attached to her anymore, he realized in horror. The brace had cut her in half at the waist and he knew that the only thing keeping her alive at the moment was the pressure of the metal against her abdomen. But shock was quickly reversing any benefit that this might have lent.

"C-cold," the woman rasped through dry lips. "S--so cold."

Jon took off his light duty jacket and placed it over her. In a more profound sense than at any other time in his life, he felt completely helpless, knowing that there was nothing else he could do for her. Tears welled up in his eyes as he reached out and gently stroked her sweat-streaked forehead, silently reciting a prayer for her.

"Myra!" the woman behind him urged, "the medics are coming. Hold on a little longer. Please, goddess, hold on. They'll save you!"

But Myra knew better and so did Jon. He looked down into her eyes and saw that death was staring back out at him.

"I tried," he said, his voice choking. "I'm sorry, so very sorry."

"I know," Myra replied, smiling back at him like one of the angels at Jesu's side. "T-thank you."

Then she slipped away.

***

Dr. elle'Kaari showed Jon out of her Office with a 'script for some anti-depressants and then went over to her desk. *Open case file,* she thought. *Fa'Teela, Jon.*

Jon's classified file came up and she considered her words carefully. When she felt ready, she spoke.

"According to the report I received from the Ordnancemistress, the subject had a premonition of the events that transpired there. In the statement given by the Ord Stores officer, the subject not only named the specifics of the event, but also responded to the location of the accident without any external direction. He knew where it was, and what had happened.'

"This event supports the data that we already have concerning his talents and should be added to the index of his precognitive ability set. If Fa'Teela is an average sample as we suspect, then it must be concluded that neomen score highly in this particular area, which would agree with his other psi test results.'

"Also, due to the overt nature of the event, it is unavoidable that this matter must be discussed with the Commander of this vessel, and we should anticipate an inquiry by the Navy. It is also highly probable that he will come under scrutiny by naval psi's as part of their investigation.'

"My recommendation is that any psionic mental manipulation of him by our operatives should be delayed until we are certain that they will not be detected. Please furnish instructions regarding the parameters of any discussion with non-Agency personnel."

She saved her entry, and then sent a copy of it for immediate review by Ophida.

***

Lilith replayed the log of the accident in Ordnance Stores and then addressed her officers.

"So," she said, taking a long speculative pull off her *czigavar*, "It would seem that 'our' neoman reacted to the emergency in Ord Stores in a very surprising manner. His response was apparently the result of a precognitive insight, if the record is accurate."

"It was nothing but wild chance," Col. Lislsdaater said dismissively. "In my book it was also blatant insubordination. He disobeyed a direct order to continue with his duties, and I think that this rises to a level that needs to be addressed."

"The ships psi's might argue with you about it being mere luck, Colonel," Lilith countered, "and from the log, I would have to agree with them.'

"I'm not sure what the Admiralty will think of all this, but I'd venture a guess from what Dr. elle'Kaari has told me, that his premonition was either a one-time event as she believes it was, or that it might actually represent latent talents that he has concealed from us for some reason; most likely in order not to stand out."

366

"Commander, talents or not, he should be brought up on charges, pure and simple," Col. Lislsdaater insisted. "He could have endangered his fellow Marines with that mad dash through Ord Stores, and added himself to the casualties."

Lilith shook her head. "No. Not only would that be a disastrous blow to the public relations effort surrounding him, but I do not personally agree."

"Commander, with all *due* respect," the Colonel said rising, "the neoman is *my* Marine and this is a *Marine* matter."

"True," Lilith replied with a calm smile. "But as part of the Marine detachment assigned to this ship, he is also part of *my* crew and the Navy has a vested interest in the *honest* outcome of its experiment with him. If he fails, it has to be something that is clearly and unquestionably a failure. If it came to it, the public at large might view this event as an act of heroism on his part, not disobedience. Do you want *that* on your record?"

"No, ma'am," Lislsdaater agreed, reseating herself.

"Now," Lilith said, extinguishing her *czigavar*, "I think that the specific issue of his talents should be kept quiet. I'd also like Dr. elle'Kaari to study him further and determine if they exist to any meaningful degree. In addition, I'd like to see Fa'Teela taken out of Ord Stores and included in any special details that might fit his *actual* MOS. Be inventive."

"You want him transferred *out* of Ord Stores?" the Colonel asked. As competent an officer as she was, Lilith sometimes thought that she could be especially dense when it came to subtleties.

"Yes, Colonel, if you would," she replied. "If he fails, then it should be in a decisive and dramatic manner. If not, then he will have the chance to distinguish himself and bring credit to the armed services. Either outcome would be satisfactory as far as I am concerned. As for his talents, I'll leave it to the Navy to decide what to do with him. That's a matter well outside of my purview. Dismissed."

***

The funeral for the two engineers was held that evening in the Ships Temple, with Ophida and her assistants presiding.

367

One of the deceased had been an Amerite, a worshiper of the ancient sun goddess, Ameratsu, and everyone who had attended the funeral honored her memory by dressing themselves in white, the traditional death color. The other woman had been a Selenite, like Lilith, and out of respect for her beliefs, the woman's mate and close friends had added black sashes to signify their mourning.

The tiny group sat together at the front of the room, comforting one another as the High Priestess intoned the funeral rite over the two bodies, which were in the center of the Temple, in closed coffins.

Lilith followed along with everyone, reading from the script for the service, rising, sitting and singing as it directed. Grief, it seemed was universal, no matter the framework in which it was experienced, she thought, seeking out the neoman in the assembly.

Jon fa'Teela had very nearly missed the service; his Troop Leader had assigned him to work a double shift that day, clearly intending to prevent him from attending. Only the express wishes of one of the widows, and Lilith's personal intervention, had overridden this.

The neoman was seated at the back of the Temple by himself, and Lilith watched him carefully for his reactions to the service. She was by no means the only one in the room observing him with a critical eye as the rite went on.

From what she saw, the Marionite seemed just as moved as everyone else. Lilith caught him a few times, superstitiously crossing himself at key points in the proceedings, but he made a show of participating in the rite and demonstrated proper respect for the deceased, and their beliefs, where it was expected.

Perhaps he isn't as uncivilized as Col. Lislsdaater makes him out to be, she reflected. His attempt to rescue the engineers had been at a level equal to what any woman in his position would have done. That in and of itself, tended to belie the common notion that all males were selfish and insensitive. At the very least, it would make for an interesting discussion with Mearinn d'Rann and Dana bel Hanna, Lilith decided.

By this point, the service had reached the point where the congregation was expected to bid the deceased farewell and to show their respects to their survivors. Lilith got up with Katrinn and filed up with her to the mate of the Selenite engineer. Now, it was her turn to perform a ritual, and one that was just as somber as the funeral rite. She drew in a deep breath before she took a Sisterhood flag from her second. It had been folded up into the traditional presentation triangle.

"On behalf of the Star Service and the entire crew of this ship," she said, offering the flag out to the tearful woman, "please accept this humble symbol of our respect. We cannot ever replace what you have lost, but the Sisterhood is grateful for your mate's service, and for the sacrifice that she made in the line of duty."

She saluted her. The woman clutched the flag to her breast and managed a strangled acknowledgement before she burst into another round of tears. Lilith stepped back and moved respectfully away.

When Jon's turn came, he whispered something to the grief stricken woman and took her hands in his for a moment. The widow listened, and then reached up and touched his cheek.

"Thank you," she said. "I know you did everything for her that you could."

A tear coursed down Fa'Teela's features as he gave her his own salute. Even Troop Leader da'Saana, who was behind him in line, was forced to nod in grudging approval at the exchange.

CSS *C-JUDI-GO*, Chione, Oreithyia System, Artemi Elant, United Sisterhood of Suns 1043.02|19|04:58:99

Chione in the Oreithyia system was a small world, known mainly for its exotic caves, breathtaking mountains and excellent skiing resorts. For that reason, it was a regular stop for luxury liners on their tours of the Artemi Elant. Once again, the *JUDI* had joined up with a conventional convoy to make their transit, and as soon as they were back in normal space, they took an in-system route to the planet. At that time of the standard year, the bulk of the ships parked *upside* were either liners, or vessels that supplied the resorts below.

And like a queen holding court over all of them, was the *Star of Aphrodite* herself.

Maya gasped when she saw the ship. The *Aphrodite* was more than two kilometers long; bigger in fact than a Navy supercruiser, and all of its length was a study in smooth lines and soft curves. Its graceful, gleaming white hull was accented here and there with gold striping and its tail was emblazoned with the golden sun logo of the Luxar Lines.

It was, without any doubt, one of the most beautiful starships she had ever seen, and more than complimented the goddess that was its namesake. It reminded Maya of a graceful bird that had once lived on Gaia. A swan, she recalled, a pure white swan.

"It's so beautiful," she said drinking in the sight of the liner's elegant form.

"That she is," Bel Lissa agreed. "Did you know that the *Aphrodite* is actually considered a national treasure? There's nothing else like her in the entire Sisterhood. Other shipbuilders have tried to surpass her, but so far no one has managed it." There was a wistful look in her eyes that Maya thought she understood. For any Captain who truly loved space and the ships that flew there, commanding the *Aphrodite* would be the pinnacle of any civilian career, and something to envy.

Maya let her have her moment of reverie, and then spoke. "Captain, the *Aphrodite* seems a bit delicate to be traveling through Null." In fact, she looked to be an all too tempting target for the *Indies*.

"I've traveled aboard the *Aphrodite* before," Bel Lissa told her, "and she's not all the soft gentlelady that she appears to be. The *Aphrodite's* got more blast armor than some military ships and enough guns hidden under that pretty skin to hold her own. Not that she needs to; you see those Navy cruisers parked off her port side?" Bel Lissa pointed to the grim, dark shapes of a pair of medium *Macha*-Class warships.

"Yes," Maya answered.

"Luxar Lines leases the services of ships like that from the Sisterhood Navy as added insurance. Nothing short of a battle-fleet could get through them to the liner. We can rest assured that our trip will be without interference from the *Indies,* or the Hriss."

Bel Lissa gave the liner one more longing glance and then hailed her. Instead of the usual voice transmissions and data displays back and forth, a full-size holo of a handsome woman in a conservative blue and gold comerci appeared in the middle of the control cabin.

"Greetings Captain bel Lissa, and the crew of the *C-JUDI-GO*," the image said, "On behalf of the Luxar Lines, welcome to the *Star of Aphrodite*. We at Luxar trust that you will find every aspect of your stay aboard her pleasant and relaxing. We value the business of premium customers like yourselves, and hope that you will grace our voyages with your presence for years to come. Is there anything that I can do for you before you begin the docking procedures?"

"No, thank you," Bel Lissa replied.

"Very well, then, gentleladies," the holo replied. "Your ship will now be auto-guided to the hangar. Enjoy your stay with us."

The holo vanished and the classical strains of Karena n'Ishande's *Spring Symphony for Esyllt* filled the cabin. At a signal from the liner, the autopilot engaged to bring the *JUDI* around into a slow, banking turn that displayed the luxury vessel to her best advantage. The music ended precisely as the *JUDI* entered the cavernous hangar-bay and docking arms swung down to engage her hull.

The little merchanter was not the only ship inside the bay by any means. Dozens of vessels were there, and nearly all of them were as sleek and as graceful as the *Aphrodite* herself. These were the private yachts of the rich and powerful, brought along for short jaunts when the liner made port. Alongside them, the *JUDI* seemed every bit the ugly duckling of the ancient Gaian fairy tale.

Feeling intimidated by this display of wealth, Maya got up with her crewmates and followed them as they made their way to the *JUDI's* egress hatch in the cargo bay. When the egress doors opened, she was greeted by a gentle fragrance that she could not place. There was the usual scan of their inoculars, and once they had passed inspection, the doors at the opposite end opened.

A group of live hostesses were waiting for them there. One of the women flashed them a perfect smile and as they came up to her, handed each of them an elegant gold pendant, fashioned in the image of the Luxar Lines corporate logo.

371

"Gentleladies," she explained, "These are your room passes, and complimentary pathminders for the entire ship. Please keep them with you at all times while you are on board." As she told them this, another smiling hostess handed them small bouquets of flowers. Maya accepted the gift and put the pendant around her neck right away.

"Just state where you wish to go and the pathminder will point the way," the lead hostess explained. "On behalf of the Captain, Elayna bel Mandi and her crew, we would like to welcome you aboard the *Star of Aphrodite*, the crown jewel of the Luxar fleet. If you will follow my assistants, they will see you to your suites. We have arranged for accommodations in our most exclusive lodgings on the Platinum Deck. I do hope that they will meet with your expectations."

Maya just gaped, completely overwhelmed and totally devoid of *any* expectations. Her crewmates on the other hand, seemed completely blasé as the hostesses led them through a series of plush corridors, and up a private elevator to their cabins.

"Your pendants will also allow you the use of these private lifts," their guide told them. "This will provide you with complete privacy when you desire it. Only Platinum Class guests and their servants have access to these lifts."

Servants? Maya wondered. *Just how 'exclusive' are these accommodations?* When the lift arrived at their deck, she found out. A long hallway stretched away to either side, lined with expensive carpeting from Sita, and appointed with tasteful works of art that all looked expensive enough to pay for the *JUDI* herself, several times over.

"I'm afraid that we were forced to book a portion of the deck over to Senatrix n'Calysher and her party," their hostess said, somewhat nervously, "but I'm sure that you will still find your own quarters in this wing private enough to suit your needs."

"That's perfectly acceptable," Bel Lissa responded smoothly, "the Senatrix and I are old friends. I'm sure that she won't mind having us as neighbors. Please, send her my regards."

"Very well, gentlelady," the woman replied with visible relief. "Also, Captain bel Mandi sends her greetings and her personal invitation for you to join her at her table tonight. If you wish, we can send our dressmaker up to your rooms before dinner."

"Thank the Captain for me. I will look forward to dining with her again," Bel Lissa returned. "When should we expect the dressmaker? I hope that it will be Madame n'Fawnele. I do so adore her creations."

"Yes, gentlelady," the hostess said, clearly impressed by Bel Lissa's good taste, "I will, and it *is* she who will visit you. Will 07:08 hours be convenient?"

Bel Lissa nodded with a regal acceptance that in any other setting would have seemed ludicrous, but here, her manner was expected and their hostess seemed to approve.

"Then I will take my leave of you, gentleladies," the hostess said, "enjoy your stay." She bowed and quickly retreated down the corridor, leaving them alone at the door to their suite.

"Shall we see what the good women of Luxar have provided for us in the way of lodgings?" Bel Lissa asked, gesturing for Maya and her companions to enter.

To have called the suite "spectacular" would have failed to do it full justice. Like the ship itself, everything within it was gentle curves and smooth transitions. The walls of the foyer were covered in a fine Eidarian alabaster accented with dark Nemesian Tigarri-wood ribbing. A thick, rich off-white carpet covered the floor.

In the center of the room, a finely detailed bronze statue of the famous Nemesian Huntress overlooked a sunken circle of richly appointed couches that had to be made from real leather, also from the wilds of Nemesis.

The light seemed to come from everywhere and nowhere at once. It took a moment for Maya to realize that the source came from behind the alabaster walls and vaulted ceiling, suffusing the space with an even soft glow that banished the shadows and seemed to make everything somehow richer in tone and color.

"Greetings, Captain bel Lissa and crew," a voice said. The image of a beautiful auburn haired woman, clad like their holo greeter had been, appeared to one side of the entry. "I am your private maidservant. If there is anything you desire, I will provide it. If you do not find my present form pleasing, I have 14,436 alternate personas for you to choose from."

373

"Your present form is more than satisfactory," Bel Lissa said. "Perhaps you could fix us some light refreshment while we inspect our quarters? Some sparkling kelberry wine would do nicely."

"Of course, gentlelady," the maid replied, "we have a fine Tipandian vintage from the south side of the Berandin Hills that I recommend."

"That will be acceptable," Bel Lissa returned, dismissing the apparition and taking Maya's hand. "Maya, I think I am safe in saying that you're going to find the bathrooms here to be a truly celestial experience."

Maya let Bel Lissa lead her through their rooms, each fit for a queen. Once she was alone in her own palatial space, she set down her kit bag, and went outside into the main corridor to spend some time alone. Her head was spinning, and the glass of Tipandian wine that Zara had pressed into her hand wasn't helping things one nanobit.

All of this was more than she had ever, in her wildest dreams, expected to encounter when she'd shipped out for a new life in Thermadon. The huge city and its dirty side-streets now seemed as far away as a half-remembered dream, and yet her present reality felt just as ethereal and strange. She stared down at the hall carpet; a masterpiece of woven gold intermingled with more shades of blue than she had ever known existed, and took a breath to steady herself.

It's all so incredible, she thought.

Just then, the doors to the private lift opened, interrupting her thoughts, and a trio of young women who were roughly her own age stepped out of it, but that was where any similarity between them ended. They were all stylishly attired in soft glowgowns and glittering jewelry, and Maya felt shabby and out of place in her flight suit and jacket.

The elegant group paused and regarded her for a long moment, before one of them, a beautiful blond with long luxurious curls, gave her a look of undisguised contempt. "I didn't know that they allowed *servants* from below-decks to wander about up here."

Her companion, an equally statuesque redhead sneered at Maya, "You, girl, aren't you a bit lost? How did *your* kind manage to get up on *this* deck?"

Maya started to explain that she was as much a guest as they were, when the redhead turned to the blond. "I think this is outrageous, Mellissy!

374

To allow someone from *below-decks* to be here on the Senatrix's private floor! We should call security and have her shown out!"

Mellissy started to produce her pendant, when the third girl, an achingly beautiful brunette, stayed her hand. "No," she said, "Can't you see she has a pass just like us? Clearly she has just arrived from some exotic location and simply hasn't had the time to freshen up."

"Yes," Maya managed to interject, "I just arrived with my crewma— my companions. We're staying down the hall from you."

"To *think* that the Captain would allow that!" Mellissy snarled. "I thought that this floor was exclusive! We should complain!"

"You can complain if you want, Mellissy n'Dwavaa" the brunette warned, "but I'd best know *who* I was complaining about before I went and embarrassed myself. As for me, let me introduce myself, I am Lady Felecia n'Calysher." The girl extended her hand in a greeting and Maya took it, her breath taken away by the girl's loveliness.

"I-I'm Maya n'Kaaryn," she managed to stammer back. "I'm with Captain Inish bel Lissa and her party."

"I knew it!" Mellissy hissed, "She's some kind of *common sailor!*"

"No," Felecia corrected, "not a common sailor at all. My mother knows Captain bel Lissa, and our family owes them many debts."

She rewarded Maya with a dazzlingly perfect smile. "Welcome, Maya. Perhaps we'll have a chance to meet again during the voyage."

Maya nodded dumbly, unable to cognate a sophisticated reply.

"Well!" Mellissy sputtered indignantly, "*I* for one have seen enough! To imagine that Felecia n'Calysher, of all the girls I know, would treat with a—a *common dock hand*. Come, Chandel," she said to the redhead. "Let us take our leave."

"Please, forgive their boorishness," Felecia said as her companions flounced away. "Their families have been wealthy for far too long and they forgot their manners somewhere along the way. *Bian sarà,* Maya n'Kaaryn."

Maya watched Felecia go, enthralled by the girl's graceful form as she seemed to float down the hallway to her quarters. This was the Senatrix's daughter, she suddenly realized. The one that she was supposed to guard.

And she was far from the "spoiled little ninny" that Maya had expected. Instead, Lady Felecia n'Calysher was most desirable, and the most attractive girl that she had ever encountered. Just like a princess in an old story.

But would a princess like her ever want someone like me? She wondered. A 'common dock-hand'?

Haunted by the question, and still stinging from Mellissy's insult, Maya turned around and returned to their quarters. Sarah was there, lounging on the couches in the central foyer like a cat waiting for some prey to wander by before pouncing on it.

"I take it from your thoughts that you encountered someone... interesting," the woman remarked with a knowing smile.

"Yes," Maya admitted. More than interesting, she thought. Captivating. Mezmerizing.

"I see," Sarah said. "And obviously, she is someone that I will refrain from *reading* you about any further. We all have our private desires, and they are best left that way. True talent is knowing not only *when* to read, but also *when not to*. Wouldn't you tend to agree?"

"Yes." Maya noded. She didn't add her thanks, but she was grateful to the psi nonetheless for this small consideration.

***

Madame n' Fawnele arrived at their staterooms at 07:08:33 hours, attended by two other women carrying heavy cases. She entered the suite like a force of nature.

"I see that I have arrived just in time!" the woman proclaimed as she eyed Maya. "Such loveliness, and hidden under so many layers of common roughness! This *simply* will not do!" She gestured to her companions and the women opened their cases. One of them handed her a scanner.

"Young lady," Madame n' Fawnele commanded, "gather up your hair so that I can get a good scan of you, and take off that terrible jacket and those wretched flight clothes. Go ahead—*strip!*"

Bel Lissa, who had overheard the commotion, came out and stood nearby, clearly entertained by the whole affair. "Good day, Madame n'Fawnele" she said. "I see that you have discovered our little diamond in the rough."

"I should say!" N'Fawnele replied. "But she is not too rough to resist my artistic touch. *I* will remake her into a vision of elegance!"

In the meantime, Maya had stripped down to her undergarments and piled her hair up into a loose bun, flushing with embarrassment at the dressmaker's words.

But the woman paid her discomfiture no attention. To her, Maya was simply clay to be re-molded into a more pleasing shape. "Young lady!" N'Fawnele suddenly snapped, "Stand straight, arms at your sides. I simply can't get a decent body scan until you stop standing there like a deformed hunch-back."

Maya bit back a rude response and obeyed. The dressmaker drew the scanner over her, taking a reading from head to toe, and then repeated the operation over her backside.

"Good!" N'Fawnele proclaimed. "You can breathe now. I have all I need to create the new you." Her assistants had set up a holojector and a small terminal, and Madame n' Fawnele shooed them away and went right to work.

A perfect hologram of Maya appeared in the center of the room. "Yes," the woman said, more to herself than anyone else, "Definitely a diamond in the rough. So, some adjustments."

She zoomed in on Maya's face and with a few pecks at the holographic keyboard, applied layers of virtual make-up.

"Given her skin tones and her eye color, this is what I would suggest." The girl looking back at them was similar to Maya, but the dressmaker had managed to find, and accentuate her features, bringing out their most attractive attributes. Bel Lissa regarded the final product carefully, and after she had nodded her approval, Madame n'Fawnele snapped her fingers at one of her attendants.

The attendant produced a small case and guided Maya to a portable stool. The instant that the girl was seated, the woman went to work applying the makeup to her face exactly as her mistress had decreed.

"Now, for the hair," the dressmaker announced, "she really does have lovely hair. It's unfortunate that she has just let it grow all loose and wild, but this is easily corrected."

A few taps of the keys, and several elegant hairstyles appeared on Maya's image. Madame n' Fawnele considered a few of them, and then settled on one that piled her hair up into a simple bun, with a few thin wisps to either side of her face. The effect that this produced was to accent her face even further.

"This should do for tonight's affair," N'Fawnele remarked, "and I strongly suggest that in the future she consider styles like it that reveal her features, instead of hiding them away under such a frightful tangle." She glanced over her shoulder at her attendant, who was just completing her work on Maya's make-up.

"While my assistant finishes, let us consider the gown. I have several glowgowns that I wanted you to see, Captain bel Lissa; two of the latest designs from Thermadon in the Consular style, and one from a very promising designer from Sita."

The dressmaker adjusted the hologram and pulled back out until they were all looking at a full figure again. "This first one" she said, tapping out instructions, "will bring out her green eyes and her skin tone very nicely."

The gown appeared, a classic affair composed of loose flowing layers and a long train, complimented by a long sleeved over blouse. The theme woven into its holographic fabric was a dark wooded forest, with only hints of light showing through the animated trees.

"This next one, I personally like," the dressmaker said. "It is also from Thermadon, in the Consular style." This time the dress was a sleeveless affair, and the image of deep ocean waters, dark and inviting, coursed through it. It seemed to bring Maya's features completely into focus, and even her untrained eye could appreciate the end result.

"That's it," Bel Lissa said. "It is, as you and I both know, perfect."

"Yes," Madame n' Fawnele agreed. "I was going to try out one more style, but you have a dressmaker's eye. Now, for the jewels."

A few more taps, and a set of light gold earrings appeared, made of delicate chains and reaching down to just caress the image's shoulders. A matching necklace with a large Kalian emerald completed the ensemble.

What stared back at Maya and everyone else in the room was every bit the princess that Felecia n'Calysher had been. The transformation was breathtaking.

"Excellent!" Madame n' Fawnele exclaimed. She clapped her hands and the second attendant began to work on Maya's hair. "We will order the jewels and have them brought up with the dress within the hour. That should give you plenty of time to dress her and get to the Captain's table for dinner."

"As always, Madame n' Fawnele," Bel Lissa replied, "it's been a pleasure and an honor to witness your work."

***

Maya's dress arrived six standard minutes after Madame n' Fawnele had concluded her visit. Bel Lissa and Sarah quickly helped her into it, and then left her alone to go and get changed themselves.

While she waited for them, Maya looked in the mirror in her stateroom, still not quite believing the transformation that the dressmaker had wrought. Living on the streets, and in and out of spaceports, she had always eschewed frilly things in favor of the practical, but now, looking at herself, she had to admit that she *liked* what she saw. Maybe not for everyday wear, but there were touches that she wanted to carry over into more casual settings.

She finished admiring herself, and walked back into the central foyer. Bel Lissa and Sarah soon joined her there, accompanied by Zara, and each of them was as transformed in their appearance as she was.

Bel Lissa had chosen to wear a fine silver-grey comerci with a dark wine, colored cravess offset with simple gold earrings. Maya recognized them immediately as finer copies of her single Sisters of the Coast earring. Zara had followed her Captain's lead and had gone with a dark brown comerci and a crème colored cravess, but true to her nature, had retained her single earring.

It was Sarah who had altered her appearance the most, opting for a dark hologown that portrayed the farthest reaches of the Outer Arm, complete with slowly spinning images of neighboring galaxies. Dark,

379

filmy gauze covered her arms and shoulders, which Maya found to be a bit odd, but not being familiar with the latest fashions, she assumed that it was in style nonetheless. If anything, the dress made what skin she had left exposed appear even more ethereal and exotic than ever.

Like Maya, her dark hair had also been piled high. In her case, in a neat French twist. Her Daughter's earring had been suspended on a thin gold chain, and she was sporting a pair of platinum earrings with dark purple gems in her ears. She looked like a mysterious queen from some unknown and forgotten world.

"You all look so wonderful," Maya said.

"So do you, Maya," Sarah replied. "Now, shall we go to the Captain's table and dine?"

The women made their way out of the suite and over to the private lift. After consulting Bel Lissa's pathminder, they boarded it and started down towards the ship's dining room. On the way, Maya's crewmates did their best to prepare her for the experience of formal dining. For someone used to using only a knife and spork, the list of do's and don'ts proved to be extremely daunting.

"Now, remember, Maya," Bel Lissa advised, "Keep your feet flat, with the hand you are not using in your lap, and your elbows close to your body. You can be a bit more casual when the meal is over."

"Yes, definitely," Zara agreed, "Also, make sure to use your silverware from the outside in. Oh, and cut only one piece of food at a time. And when you're done, leave the knife above the fork, blade facing you. The knife blade should *always* face you on the table and on the plate."

"Oh yes, and Maya," Bel Lissa interjected, "Make sure you take your spoon away from you when you eat with it. Don't blow on the soup, and eat off the *side* of the spoon."

Until just then, Maya had believed that she already *knew* how to eat. What her crewmates seemed to be describing was more like some strange alien ritual than an evening repast. Her head spun as she tried to take in everything her companions were telling her.

"Stop it, you two!" Sarah finally said. "Can't you see that you're overwhelming her with details? Maya, just watch me and follow what I do.

Don't worry much about it. This is, after all, your first time and you're bound to make mistakes."

"Yes," Maya replied doubtfully, trying to work up her confidence with a deep breath.

The lift reached its destination and the doors opened onto the Versailles, the *Aphrodite's* main dining room. The Versailles was a gigantic vaulted chamber, with tall slim windows that opened out onto a dramatic view of space. Literally hundreds of tables dotted the expanse, and, raised above them all, was the Captain's Table itself. A huge golden image of the goddess Aphrodite stared down from a pedestal behind this, as if overseeing the entire affair herself.

A hostess greeted them as they stepped out of the lift. "Good' eve, gentleladies," the woman smiled. "If you will come with me, I will escort you to the Captain's Table."

Maya followed her friends closely, suddenly realizing that the thousands of diners in the room were watching them as they made their way across it. If a hole had opened up in the deck right then, she would have gladly thrown herself into it and hidden from their stares.

As it was, no escape offered itself and she was forced to keep walking, desperately hoping that she did nothing to embarrass herself in front of so many onlookers. A real princess, like the Lady Felecia, would have handled it all with more aplomb, but gown or no, she felt like a pretender.

"Our main courses tonight," the hostess was saying as they reached the Captain's Table, "are fresh quadsa with wild jasa rice, and chisan salad on the side with a fine lemonaisé dressing, or lamb saafora complimented with fletch'a and krechi-leaf pasta. Our featured wine is a Zommerlaandar veizenwien. Dessert is a choice of house pastries, or yemyem l'Aphrodite."

Maya only recognized one or two of the dishes, but she wasn't worried about how edible the meal would be. Her stomach was so tied up in knots that even a simple bowl of Chikka-broth would have been a challenge to get down.

Most of the diners at the Captain's Table had already been seated, among them Lady Felecia n'Calysher and her companions, along with an older, stately woman that Maya decided had to be the Senatrix herself.

381

Following their hostess up to the huge table, Maya and Felecia made eye contact. There was no mistaking the welcome in the young patrician's eyes, or the spitefulness of her companions.

"Do you see that, Chandel?" Mellissy n'Dwavaa remarked, just loud enough for Maya to overhear, "They're letting *her* eat up here with us! I'd think that a girl like *that* should be fed in the kitchen with the rest of the help."

Chandel responded with a malicious laugh and Maya would have gladly smacked the haughty looks off their delicate faces, but she remembered herself and walked on with her crewmates.

Their seats turned out to be just to the other side of the Senatrix and her daughter, at the Captain's right hand. This alone, caused some chatter among the other diners, and a look of pure outrage on Mellissy and Chandel's faces; only guests of the highest status were afforded such seats. Maya rewarded the two girls with a smile of pure triumph as the Captain stood to personally greet Bel Lissa.

"Inish!" Captain bel Mandi exclaimed, embracing her, "I had heard you were aboard! Good to see you again, old friend."

"Captain bel Mandi," Bel Lissa said, indicating her companions, "you already know Zara and Sarah. Meet our newest crewmember, Maya n'Kaaryn."

"It's always a pleasure to meet a crewmate of Inish's," the Captain replied warmly. Then Maya noticed the single earring of the Sisters of the Coast in Bel Mandi's left ear.

A smuggler, she thought, or a former one at the very least. A thousand questions suddenly begged to be asked, but Maya simply returned her smile.

"I take it that Hari didn't work out?" Captain bel Mandi observed with a noticeable twinkle in her eye.

"Uh, no," Bel Lissa said. "You might recall that she was always a bit too emotional for our kind of work."

"Just as well then," Bel Mandi agreed. "But I am forgetting myself. Let's be seated before our fellow diners perish from hunger!"

They took their seats, which was a signal to the waitresses to begin serving the dinner. "So, tell me, Inish," the Captain was saying, "How fares the *JUDI*? Is she still just as fast as I remember?"

"Even faster," Bel Lissa responded. "Zara's made a few modifications to her since you were last aboard."

Last aboard? Maya wondered. Captain bel Mandi hardly seemed the type to take a ride on a smuggler ship, but there was no denying the Sister's earring that she was wearing. *Mystery upon mystery,* she thought.

The conversation quickly drifted away from the *JUDI* to less interesting subjects, and a waitress came up and offered her a holomenu.

"Gentlelady? What may I serve you for dinner?"

Maya looked at it, completely baffled. The menu might as well have been written in some alien language.

"She will have the quadsa with wild jasa rice, and the chisan salad," Sarah interposed, "and I will have the same."

She reached over and gave Maya's hand a gentle, reassuring squeeze. "Don't worry," she said quietly, "this will go fine. Just follow my lead. Now, take your napkin and put it in your lap."

Maya did as instructed and then took stock of her utensils for the first time. She was horrified at how many forks and how many spoons were arrayed in front of her.

Three wine glasses? What in all space were *they* for?

"Remember, Maya," Sarah whispered, "Just use the first utensil on the outside and work your way in with each course."

Maya picked up her fork and looked at it as if she were seeing one for the first time. Down the table, she overheard a hateful laugh and saw that Mellissy was watching her, clearly enjoying her perplexity.

"*Bitch!*" she silently mouthed back. To her immense satisfaction, the girl's jaw dropped open in shock. Felecia, who had noticed the exchange, rewarded Maya with a smile that she hid from the others as she pretended to blot her mouth with her napkin. How such a girl could stand companions like Mellissy and Chandel was as much a conundrum to Maya as Captain bel Mandi and her connection with the *JUDI*.

Go ahead and sneer, she thought, glaring at Mellissy with undisguised malice, *and maybe this "common dockworker" will teach you a thing or two.* The image of ripping out Mellissy's fine golden curls by their roots brought her spirits back up sharply, and she smiled at something someone said with genuine pleasure.

Their meal, although exotic, turned out to be surprisingly delicious. Quadsa with wild jasa rice was an instant favorite the moment that Maya tried it. The flying insectoid, a native of Nemesis, proved to be a rich meaty creature that tasted like heaven with drawn butter and garleeq, and the chisan salad was a light, but extremely rewarding experience. Maya resolved from that point on, not to be as hesitant in trying out new foods. In one sitting, she learned that an entire universe of gastronomical delights was waiting to be discovered. Even better, with Sarah's patient guidance, she also managed to complete the meal without humiliating herself.

After dessert, the Captain rose, which was a signal to her guests that the meal was officially over. While she and Bel Lissa moved off to the side to discuss something in private, Sarah gently guided Maya down to the dance floor.

"Now, Maya," she said, "I think its time that you reacquainted yourself with your young friend. I believe that the Lady Felecia was watching you through the entire meal, and if I *read* her right, she is secretly hoping for a dance with you."

"With *me?*" Maya gaped.

"Yes, it was unmistakable," Sarah replied. "Even without my talents, I could tell that she finds you incredibly exciting. You would be best advised to honor that." Before Maya could object, Sarah took her over to where Felecia and her companions were standing.

Mellissy and Chandel, realizing that they were approaching, tried to draw Felecia away, but the girl remained where she was. Then Mellissy's expression became pained, and she rubbed at her temples.

"Oh, I have the most dreadful headache," she complained.

"I'm not feeling very well either, "Chandel added. "It must have been something that we ate."

"Perhaps you should both go and lie down for a bit in your staterooms," Felecia suggested. Niether girl protested and they quickly took their leave of her and left the dining room in haste.

Watching them depart, Sarah winked at Maya. "Consider that a small favor to be repaid at another time," she said in a low voice. "Now, shall we go and claim your prize?"

Maya suppressed her delight at her enemies' retreat and walked up to Felecia with her crewmate.

"Lady n'Calysher?" Sarah said, "I understand that you and your entourage are staying on the Platinum Deck with us?"

"Why, yes," Felecia responded, "but I am afraid that we have not been formally introduced, gentlelady. You have me at somewhat of a disadvantage."

"I am Sarah n'Jan and of course, you already know my crewmate, Maya n'Kaaryn. We are serving with Captain bel Lissa. No doubt you saw Captain bel Mandi and her conversing together before dinner?"

"Yes, I did, gentlelady," the girl replied, "and by the way, I must say Maya, that your gown is very striking. You look quite lovely in it."

Just then, Sarah pretended to recognize someone in the room, and excused herself. "I hope that you two ladies enjoy the remainder of your evening," she said. "It was a pleasure to meet you, Lady n'Calysher."

With Sarah gone, Maya suddenly felt awkward and shy again. Sensing this, Felecia quickly made small talk. "Did you enjoy the meal?"

"Yes," Maya replied, "It was quite good. I've never had food like that before." She instantly regretted the remark, knowing that this made her look rough and unsophisticated, but Felecia was unfazed.

"Yes, I gathered that some of this was rather new to you," she replied, "and I imagine that it might even seem a bit silly."

"Some of it," Maya admitted, "but other things are wonderful."

"Yes," Felecia agreed, looking into her eyes. "Some things are at that." Maya flushed, and suddenly her knees felt weak.

Glancing around her to see if anyone was near enough to overhear, Felecia leaned in a little closer, "I understand from my mother that Captain bel Lissa is some kind of pirate, or a spy. Is that *true*?"

"Well," Maya stammered, at a complete loss for words, "not exactly. I mean--"

Martin Schiller

"I fully understand," Felecia replied conspiratorially, "You couldn't tell me if she was—or if *you* were. Just the same, I'd imagine that your lives are full of daring adventures and not nearly as boring as mine."

Maya said nothing.

"I knew it!" Felecia said delightedly, "Just by your silence alone, I can tell that it's the truth! You really *are* pirates. Oh, how incredibly exciting! And here I thought this voyage would be another dull round of dinners and tedious conversations!'

"Rest assured though, I'll keep your secret to myself. I believe that Mellissy and Chandel are scandalized enough thinking you a common sailor. The shock of finding this out would *simply* kill them! And even though they do deserve to die for the terrible way they have treated you, their mothers *are* friends of my mother and their deaths would prove somewhat… awkward."

Maya laughed, and relaxed a bit.

"Would you like to dance?" Felecia asked. Before Maya could refuse, she added. "I know, you probably don't have much experience with dancing as an interstellar secret agent, but I'll help you just like your friend did through dinner. Really, it's a lot of fun once you get the steps right, and besides, no one will dare laugh at Senatrix n'Calysher's daughter, or her friend."

She extended her hand, and led Maya out onto the floor to join a Corrissan waltz that was just beginning.

Felecia proved to be correct; once Maya had learned the basics, dancing was actually quite pleasant. Especially with Felecia in her arms.

***

The crew of the *JUDI* decided to use the next day to tour the ship. Bel Lissa was determined to go shopping, but Zara and Sarah had an eye towards doing some gambling in the liner's casino. Intially, Maya had wanted to join Bel Lissa, but by the end of their breakfast together, they had convinced her to join them instead.

"I'm not sure that I approve of you two scoundrels showing her your evil ways," Bel Lissa commented as they waited together at the lifts. "It's

386

bad enough that you two are going to cheat the Luxar Lines out of its hard-earned money."

"*Pah!*" Zara exclaimed. "Hard-earned, indeed! That casino of won its credits the same as us, through straight-up cheating or my name's Molla n'Dayr. Everyone *knows* that the house stacks the cards in their favor. This is just leveling the odds up a bit."

"And if she is to be a proper sailor," Sarah added, "Maya needs to learn a few social skills, even if she hasn't a taste for gambling."

Bel Lissa shook her head in mock disgust. "'Skills,' indeed! You too are just looking for another accomplice to help you with your wicked plans. Ah wells, at least we know Luxar will earn it all back from the other passengers."

"Exactly," Sarah agreed. "So no harm really done."

Bel Lissa dismissed her crewmates with a wave of her hand. "I'll meet you three bandits back here for supper."

"Of course, Captain," Sarah answered with a mischievous half-smile.

***

The *Aphrodite's* casino took up half of a deck just aft and above the formal dining room. It was filled with every kind of game imaginable; from venerable slot machines (which Zara had called "one armed bandits" for some reason Maya could not fathom), to more contemporary games from every corner of the Sisterhood and beyond. Maya found herself quickly overwhelmed by the lights and the noise of the place, but her companions seemed perfectly at home in the carnival-like confusion.

"Well," Zara announced over the sound of a jackpot being won, "I'm off for a good old fashioned game of Hriss *Thre'vash* or maybe some Stars. I know that Sarah here has a taste for wagering on *Bat-Bat*. You'd probably like that, Maya."

"Yes," Maya agreed, having only the faintest idea what *Thre'vash* or Stars were. Not that she was interested in anything that the Hriss might have to offer, even if it were merely for entertainment.

"Best of luck," Sarah replied with a wink, "though I doubt you'll need it, Zara."

387

She took Maya's hand and guided her through the crowds to the center of the casino. When Zara had mentioned wagering on Bat-Bat, Maya had assumed it would take the form of placing bets by holoviewer. The very last thing she expected to encounter was a full size Bat-Bat field, enclosed by a plastiglass viewing area and real live teams.

Bat-Bat was *the* game for the citizens of the Sisterhood, and even Maya had played a rough version of it in the streets of Ashkele. Eight players composed a team, with one player acting as a guard for each side. All of the players were equipped with body armor, a plastic shield and a flat bat roughly the length of a woman's arm, with the goal-guard possessing a slightly larger shield and bat.

The *batlyball*, which was the object of both team's attentions, was a small thing; roughly a quarter of the size of an average woman's head, and made of pleather. Once it was in play, players could only strike it with their bats or their shields. If a player struck the batlyball with a body part, a penalty was awarded to her team, and it would be re-served in favor of the opposition.

The object of Bat-Bat was simple; to drive the batlyball into the friendly goal area, with a point being gained for each goal until ten rounds had been played. The winner was the team with the highest amount of points.

What made the game challenging was that while the rules forbade contact with the batlyball with anything but shield and bat, anything else was fair game, even other players. Bat-Bat tournaments were famous, or infamous, depending on whom a woman asked, for the number of players knocked into unconsciousness, or badly injured, by a shield strike, or a hit from an opponents bat. And full-scale melees between rival teams were not uncommon.

For this reason, the Supreme Circle had debated outlawing Bat-Bat on and off for years, but with little popular support. Just as the Roman Empire had discovered with its famed circuses, the Senatrixs had learned that the women of the Sisterhood craved the aggressive outlet that Bat-Bat provided.

Maya read the holodisplays. The teams playing that day were the Zommerlaandar *Aegliles* and the Thermadonian *Tigarri*, and the odds strongly favored the *Aegiles*. Looking down at the rectangular playing field, she could see why. Dressed in menacing black and red armor, the Zommerlaanders were gigantic. They looked as if they would simply roll over their smaller opposition without even breaking a sweat.

Sarah had another opinion however. "Do not let appearances deceive you," she cautioned. "The *Tigarri* may not by favored, but their speed and dexterity may yet win over the larger *Aegliles* team. That and certain, let us say, *tricks*, played on them by fortune."

She addressed the holodisplay; "I'll take 1,000 credits on the *Tigarri* to win, please."

"Do you also wish to bet on a winning score?" the AI asked her. "The odds are much higher, but so is the pay out."

"Yes, please," Sarah replied, "I will bet that the final score will be 8 *Tigarri*, 2 *Aegliles*."

"Your wager has been recorded, jantildam. Enjoy the game."

Maya understood enough about Sarah's talents to realize that the outcome would be exactly as she had wagered, however implausible it might have seemed. Sarah smiled, clearly aware of the girl's thoughts, and then nodded to a group across the field.

"It seems that the Lady Felecia n'Calysher and her companions are also attending the game today. Perhaps after the match we can pay our respects to the gentlelady."

Maya blushed, but couldn't resist seeking the young woman out with her eyes. Once she caught sight of her, Maya's pulse started to race out of control and her breath caught in her throat. Heady memories of holding Felecia in her arms came back to her so strongly that she almost missed the beginning of the match.

"Welcome to this special All Worlds Bat-Bat League game, hosted by Luxar Lines aboard their five-star flagship, the *Aphrodite*, where elegance and travel meet," an announcer said. "The Zommerlaandar *Aegiles* are facing off against the Thermadonian *Tigrarri* to determine who will become this year's League Champions. This promises to be an exciting match between a veteran team with an unbroken winning streak and an ambitious challenger hoping to take the title for themselves."

Then, "The referee has given the signal, and the ball is now in play."

Immediately, the *Aegliles* charged across the field, swinging savagely with their bats and shields as they captured the batlyball and drove the *Tigarri* back. But just when it seemed that their path to the goal was clear, a *Tigarri* dashed in and attempted to steal the ball away by diving to the ground and swatting at it with her shield.

The nearest *Aegliles* player did her best to block the interloper with her own shield, but she was just a hair too slow. This enabled the Tigarri to complete her maneuver and serve the ball to a fellow team member, who rushed it down the field.

Already committed to their headlong charge, the *Aegliles* took a moment to compensate, and although they attempted to intercept the supporting *Tigarri* players with some vicious shield blows, nothing could stop the ball from making it to the goal. The *Tigarris* had scored their first point.

Undaunted, the *Aegliles* were determined to regain the upper hand and counterattacked viciously. Time and time again though, their players were outmaneuvered by the faster, cleverer *Tigarris*. Although they finally managed to score two points, these were widely spaced and dearly bought; two of their team members suffered injuries that took them out of the game and reserve players had to come onto the field to replace them.

Not that the *Tigarris* emerged wholly unscathed. In one play, as a *Tigarri* player was attempting to come to the aid of her sisters, she suffered a vicious blow under her chin from an *Aegliles* bat. It sent her flying backwards and knocked her unconscious.

But despite this, and other equally ferocious exchanges, the outcome, in the end, was without question. The *Tigarris*, who had been the underdogs, had won soundly over the *Aegliles*, scoring eight points to two.

"Shall we go and collect our winnings and then console the Lady n'Calysher?" Sarah asked. "I believe that she wagered on the *Aegliles*, as most of the audience did, and I am sure that she could use some cheer."

She took Maya over to the cashier and after collecting a neat 10,000 credits, maneuvered them around the gallery to the Lady n'Calysher's party. Mellissy and Chandel scowled at them as they walked up, but Maya ignored this.

"Lady n'Calysher?" Sarah asked, "Did you enjoy the game?"

"No," she replied sadly, "I am afraid that I bet against the *Tigarris* when my heart had suggested otherwise. I suppose I should have listened. I might have been a few credits richer for it."

"Our condolences, gentlelady," Sarah offered. "Perhaps you might allow us to treat you to lunch as a way of helping to soothe your loss?"

"Your offer is very gracious," Felecia replied, "but I'm not sure if my companions—"

"Yes, indeed!" Mellissy sneered. "Gracious enough, but we already have a pressing engagement elsewhere, an *important* engagement with women of *substance*."

"How disappointing," Sarah replied, disregarding Mellissy's incivility. "We were so hoping for the pleasure of your company, Lady n'Calysher. I know that Maya here certainly was."

Maya wanted to strike Sarah for saying this, but she was also relieved. The woman had just expressed her innermost wishes.

"My apologies," Felecia replied with genuine regret, "but unfortunately my companion is correct. We are scheduled for another meeting. Perhaps we can arrange it for another time. I would like that very much."

Sarah inclined her head in acknowledgement. "Of course, gentlelady. We will await your pleasure." With that, Lady n'Calysher and her friends departed.

The moment that they were gone, she turned to Maya. "You can breathe now," she said. Then, "Tell me, are you interested in another wager perhaps?"

"Maybe" Maya replied carefully, "What are the stakes?"

"I will wager with you that we will be hearing from the good Lady in short order. Say--a credit or two?"

"Done," Maya said. It was wager that she desperately wanted to lose.

***

A gilded invitation, printed on real paper, arrived just as Maya was eating her breakfast. Sarah walked into the dining room with it.

391

"It seems that the Lady Felecia has requested the honor of your presence this afternoon at tea," she announced.

"She has?" Maya replied, pleased and a little startled at the same time.

"Yes, and only you, Maya," Sarah said with a knowing smile. "Offhand, it would appear that I have won our little wager." She handed the card over to Maya to read for herself.

"What should I wear for this?" the girl asked. "I've never been to a formal tea before."

"Unless I am vastly mistaken," Sarah answered, "I think that the best attire would be your flight suit and leather jacket. I believe that of all the items you could wear, that the Lady Felecia would find those garments to be the most appealing ensemble."

"But how should I act?" Maya wondered. "What do I do at a tea?"

"Just be who you are," her crewmate suggested. "As for the tea, I think that it will take care of itself."

***

A servant in a simple, but well-tailored comerci met Maya at the front door of Senatrix n'Calysher's suite.

"Ms. N'Kaaryn?" the woman asked, "The Lady Felecia has been expecting you. If you will follow me."

The servant led her through the suite, which was just as opulent as her own. Felecia was waiting for her in the dining area, accompanied by a dour, older woman who stood off to one side. As Maya entered the room, the woman scrutinized her with a cold, professional stare.

But Felecia smiled at her, dispelling the chill that emanated from her companion. "Maya, I am so glad that you came!" she exclaimed, "I was worried that business matters or something else might have detained you. This is Sharra," she said indicating the hard-faced figure. "She is my bodyguard."

Maya vaguely recalled seeing her at dinner the night before, but hadn't paid her much attention. Now Sharra's frank inspection suddenly made perfect sense and she was tempted to tell Felecia that protecting her was also her assignment, but stopped herself.

Bel Lissa had never mentioned whether or not the girl was aware of what was going on, and she didn't want to jeopardize their mission. Besides which, with Sharra on duty, and neither of them the wiser, she could relax and enjoy her time with Felecia.

"Why would you need a bodyguard?" she asked instead.

Felecia sighed tiredly. "Oh, my mother *insists* on it. Being a Senatrix means that you sometimes make enemies."

Maya raised her eyebrows in feigned surprise. "I had no idea that your lives were like that."

"Yes, it is all a terrible nuisance," Felecia said dismissively. She gestured to a nearby couch and not to the formal place setting at the table. "Shall we sit? We can enjoy our tea here. I think it would be much more comfortable."

The servant who had shown her in, brought an elegant Kaddasian silver tray laden with a small teapot and some delicious looking cakes, which she put down on the small table in front of the couch. But instead of waiting on them as Maya had expected, she hurriedly departed.

"Isn't anyone else joining us?" Maya asked, desperately hoping that Felecia's answer would be negative.

"No," Felecia replied, gracefully pouring out a cup of tea for each of them. "Mellissy and Chandel are out shopping, and my mother is attending some kind of dreary meeting. She was going to hold it here in our staterooms, but I convinced her to take her guests to lunch at *La Floresé* instead. It had something to do with terraforming and mineral rights on some planet or another… and was far, far too tiresome for my tastes."

Maya recalled that the *La Floresé* was one of the many restaurants aboard the *Aphrodite*. It was an expensive place, but also very private and probably more suited to a business luncheon than the staterooms would have been. It also gave her time alone with Felecia, even if her bodyguard still hovered in the background.

"Knowing the way that such affairs go, no one will be back for *hours*," Felecia said. "Which reminds me…" She looked over her shoulder at the bodyguard. "Sharra? I have just realized that I have a few things that need to be picked up from the dressmaker and the jewelers. Could you be a dear and take care of those errands for me before they close?"

393

Martin Schiller

"Lady Felecia," the bodyguard answered reproachfully, "you know that your mother wants me to attend you personally."

"Oh yes," Felecia replied, waving her objection away, "I know. You have your silly little *orders*. Really, I'll be quite safe here with Maya, and I promise that we won't leave these rooms until you return. Please, I'm sure that my mother would understand, just this once."

Sharra's expression became set. "I'm sorry, my Lady but I cannot do that. The Senatrix's instructions were very explicit. I'll send someone from the household staff to take care of the matter."

"Very well," Felecia sighed. "But surely, you can protect me from outside? In the corridor? There is no one in here except us, and it *is* the only entrance."

"My Lady, I already have one of my staff members posted there," Sharra advised, "and someone needs to remain inside the suite."

"Yes, I understand; 'defense in depth'." Felecia acknowledged tiredly. "But can't you defend me from the foyer just as easily? That *is* inside, isn't it?"

Sharra nodded, clearly uncomfortable with the idea, but unable to compose a counter-argument.

"And could you ask whoever that you send on my errands to take some extra time to shop for my mother's birthday gift?" Felecia added, "It is only a few days off, and I would so hate to disappoint her."

"Of course, my Lady," Sharra said, finally grasping her mistress' full intent. "We certainly can't rush things when it comes to the Senatrix's birthday. I'll be in the foyer if you need me. Enjoy your tea together." She left them with a knowing gleam in her eye.

Felecia watched her leave, and as soon as the door had closed, she visibly relaxed. "I thought we'd *never* have a moment alone! Honestly, Maya, you can't imagine how *stifling* it can be sometimes. There's always *someone* with you wherever you are. You're lucky to have as much privacy as you do."

Maya had never given this much thought, but she had to agree. "Yes, I guess there are some drawbacks to being a Senatrix's daughter after all," she said, partly distracted by Felecia's perfume. It had a subtle, haunting fragrance that she could not identify and she felt herself becoming aroused.

394

A clinical part of her wondered if there were pheromones in its ingredients, but then she decided that she didn't really care after all.

"Yes," Felecia replied. "One of the biggest problems is meeting someone special, and finding the time and the place to spend with them. Alone." She moved a bit closer to Maya on the couch and took her hand. "I am glad you came today, Maya."

"I'm glad that I could be here," Maya said, cautiously placing her free hand over Felecia's.

The girl returned her gesture with a gentle, reassuring squeeze and looked up at her through her long dark lashes. "You can kiss me if you like," she said quietly.

Maya didn't need to be asked twice, and leaned in to meet Felecia's eager lips. Their tongues met in a hot electric embrace, and Felecia brought Maya's hand up to her breast with a soft moan.

Maya responded with enthusiasm, grabbing its softness in her hand and squeezing it gently. And as she explored Felecia's neck with her mouth, she discovered that the young woman's elegant coif was only held in place by a trio of large golden pins. She pulled them free, and Felecia's soft scented tresses spilled out over the couch as Maya eased her down.

She had had sex before, but nothing compared to what she was experiencing with Felecia. Everything else seemed transitory and pale in comparison, and she felt a wild sense of abandon come over her, as if she had been starving up until that very point in her life. In return, Felecia gave herself utterly to her, letting Maya have all of her with an unreserved passion. Slowly, Maya worked her way down Felecia's perfect body, building their mutual passions until they reached their peak. When that moment finally came, their simultaneous orgasms were a blinding sweetness beyond words.

Afterwards, they lay together in a warm, naked embrace, hovering in a delicious place that was somewhere between waking and sleep, enjoying the lazy afterglow of their lovemaking.

"I think I could get to like formal tea," Maya whispered.

"I thought that you might feel that way," Felecia smiled, an unmistakable desire in her eyes. "Let me do it this time," she said softly, starting to work over Maya's breast with her tongue.

Abruptly, the universe around them was shattered into a thousand sharp pieces by the piercing wail of an alarm klaxon.

"Exo Alert!" a recorded voice barked from a hidden speaker somewhere above them, "Exo Alert! This cabin has registered the presence of a hostile foreign organism! You have 60 seconds to seek shelter before sterilization commences! Exo Alert! Exo Alert!"

"W-what?" Felecia stammered.

Maya was the first to rise, grabbing the girl by the wrist and pulling her up with her. "Come on!" she shouted over the siren's ear-piercing scream. "If we don't get out of here now, we'll be *kakked* for sure!"

An Exo Alarm aboard a ship meant that the compartment would soon be flooded with deadly gamma radiation and poison gas.

"Where are the survival shelters in here?" she asked Felecia. Although most vessels had shelters for the crew to duck into when an Exo Alarm sounded, she wasn't sure if a liner had the same thing available for its passengers or not. If it did, then the shelter had not popped open and revealed itself like it was supposed to.

"I d-don't know!" Felecia replied, her features wild with terror.

Maya looked around her, and then she spotted a small plate set in one of the bulkheads that she recognized immediately. It was the cover for an emergency manual release handle.

"There!" she cried, dragging Felecia with her. Overhead, hatches in the ceiling had popped open and evil-looking pipes with silver nozzles were beginning to descend.

"Exo Alert!" the pre-recorded message said, "Sterilization devices are now being engaged. You have 30 seconds to reach safe shelter!"

Maya yanked the plate off and found what she had been praying for; a bright yellow handle. She turned it and a section of the bulkhead in front of her started to open. But then, inexplicably, the shelter hatch started to close again. She reacted fast, grabbing a small chair and thrusting it into the opening.

"Malfunction!" the recording replied, "The hatch for shelter 17201-EA1 is jammed. Malfunction!" In the meantime, the hatch was doing its level best to crush the chair and reseal itself.

"Help me!" Maya shouted, as she pulled with all her might against the hatch. Felecia joined her and together they managed to force it open. But almost immediately, it started to close shut again.

"Exo Alert!" the voice insisted. "You now have 20 seconds to seek shelter!"

"Get in!" Maya urged. "I'll jump in behind you!" She shifted position and planted herself in the opening, pushing desperately against the mindless force of the hatch with all of the strength she had.

"But—" Felecia started to argue, but Maya would hear none of it.

"Get in, *now!*"

Felecia leapt into the tiny closet-like space, and Maya knew that she had only a few more seconds before she would be unable to keep the hatch from closing altogether. She took a deep breath and let go, throwing herself in backwards and praying to the Goddess that the hatch wouldn't amputate anything as it sealed itself. The door slammed shut, missing her left ankle by mere centimeters as she landed on top of Felecia.

"Exo Alert! Sterilization procedures commencing!" the voice warned. Maya pulled Felecia to her, holding her tightly and hoping that the airtight seal hadn't been compromised with all of their fighting with the hatch.

The seal held however, and the suite outside was flooded with invisible death. The two girls waited in the semi darkness until finally, the recorded voice announced the all-clear.

"Event termination! No viable organisms detected. Shelters will now open. Be advised that security clean-up crews are enroute to collect any specimins. Do not attempt to touch anything. Vacate this cabin immediately and stand by for further decontamination instructions."

The hatch opened, revealing the room covered in a fine, whitish dust. "Let's get to the entrance," Maya said.

Felecia started to reach for a nearby tapestry to cover them with, but she stopped her. "No. Let's not worry about that right now. There's no telling what's in this dust. The clean-up crews will probably give us a blanket."

They made their way together to the foyer. A solid steel wall, obviously intended to seal off the suite from the rest of the ship, slid up and away as they approached it, allowing them to hear the frantic pounding on the other side of the decorative wooden entrance doors.

"Lady n'Calysher!" a voice shouted. "Are you all right?"

Someone else said something, and then the flimsy doors collapsed as Felecia's bodyguard smashed her way through. Hands reached in and pulled them out into the main corridor. From somewhere, two blankets materialized and were hastily thrown over them.

"My Lady!" Sharra exclaimed, "Thank the Goddess you're alive!"

Behind her a worried looking group of uniformed technicians was approaching rapidly, led by a senior ship's officer.

"Lady n'Calysher, please accept our profoundest apologies!" the officer exclaimed. "There must have been some kind of malfunction!"

Felecia waved the woman off and let Maya pull her towards her own suite, with her bodyguard in tow behind them.

Once they reached Maya's stateroom, Felecia was administered a sedative by the Ship's Doctor and given the chance to rest. Maya meanwhile, went to the living area. Captain bel Lissa and the others were there, waiting with the Senatrix for the Captain of the *Aphrodite*.

When Captain bel Mandi arrived, the Senatrix smiled pleasantly at her, but her expression was belied by the hard gleam in her eyes.

"Captain bel Mandi?"

"Senatrix," Bel Mandi replied stiffly, "on behalf of the *Aphrodite* and her crew, I wish to express my regrets at this unfortunate incident. I've spoken with our Senior Engineer, and after reviewing the event logs, we have only been able to determine that some kind of software error must have occurred, causing the ship's computer to register the false alarm. Nothing like this has ever happened before aboard this ship; the Exo Alert System has always functioned without a single mishap until now. I'm just glad that there was no loss of life."

"As am I," the Senatrix responded coolly.

"Let me assure you that there will be a full investigation into this event and any responsible parties will be punished," the Captain added.

"Thank you for your report, Captain," the Senatrix replied. "You may now take your leave of us. We wish to be alone."

Captain bel Mandi started to say something, but wisely bit it back and marched out of the suite instead, her staff officers trailing behind her.

"I wish to thank you for the life of my daughter, Maya," the Senatrix said formally. "If not for your quick thinking and fast action…"

She paused, and a single tear gathered at the corner of her face and slid down the curve of her cheek. The moisture cut a path through the carefully applied layers of makeup, leaving behind a trail of slightly ashen skin.

"…since my wife died, Felecia is all I have left in this universe. When I think of what might have happened…" The rest of her statement was cut off by a harsh sob and she bowed her head and looked away.

She's in shock, Maya thought, suddenly feeling like an interloper.

Finally, the Senatrix managed to compose herself, and straightened, become the cool, self-assured politician that the Sisterhood had always known.

"It seems that I owe the crew of the *C-JUDI-GO* another debt," she said evenly. "I assure you, this is not an obligation that will be casually forgotten, nor left unpaid. Thank you all."

"Don't mention it. We're just glad that we prevented a disaster," Bel Lissa replied.

"Despite this 'accident,' I did manage to make contact with the courier during my luncheon," N'Calysher informed them. "Our meeting with the Rampart is to be on Nemesis. My Security Chief will discuss the particulars with you, but in the light of what has happened, I must insist that Lady Felecia accompany us. I no longer feel that the *Aphrodite* is a safe place for her. I apologize in advance for any inconvenience this might cause you or your crew."

"I'm sure that with the help of your security team, we can modify our plans accordingly," Bel Lissa replied. At that, the Senatrix rose and left the suite.

"I feel sorry for Captain bel Mandi," Bel Lissa said once they were alone. "It must have been difficult for her to stand there and recite all that nonsense about a software error, but I suppose she had no choice. What did you tell me the odds were on such a malfunction, Zara?"

"Something on the order of a million to 1, Captain," the engineer replied. "Exo Alert Systems have to be foolproof. There's too much of a chance they'd kill a ship's crew otherwise. Sabotage is the only answer."

"Sharra, do you have any thoughts on who might have been behind this little *accident*?" Sarah asked.

The security chief, who had been waiting off to the side, stepped forwards. "Nothing solid yet," Sharra answered, "but I have my people looking into the matter. My guess is that they'll find that the Bio Action Army was behind it, but it's who's behind *them* that interests me more. If I had to come up with a suspect, I'd say Senatrix Danna ebed Haria, but we're not likely to trace a clear path back to her."

"I've heard of her," Sarah said. "I understand that she is one of Senatrix n'Calysher's greatest opponents in the Supreme Circle."

"Yes, she is," Sharra replied. "There have been plenty of rumors connecting her with the Bios, but nothing that could ever be substantiated. I'd say the odds your engineer just quoted would also apply to the possibility that she's *not* involved."

"Please, keep us informed of any developments in your investigation," Sarah requested. "Perhaps, if a credible link can be established it might justify my special attention." There was a speculative, predatory gleam in her eye that Sharra did not miss.

"I will," the security chief agreed. "The Senatrix has been beset by Ebed Haria for some time and if we can prove her connection, your services might be just what is required to *adjust* the situation."

Then she addressed Bel Lissa. "As the Senatrix said, we're bound for Nemesis and our meeting will be taking place at the Shadow Lake Lodge. We should have complete privacy; it's the off-season there, so we will be the only guests. I apologize for having to include the Lady Felecia but the Senatrix absolutely refused my suggestion to have her transported back to Thermadon on a civilian or military transport. Apparently, she only seems to have faith in your ship."

"Which we hope we will be able to justify," Bel Lissa returned. "Lady Felecia is a complication, but nothing that we can't work with. I just hope that she and her mother won't be too uncomfortable on the *JUDI*. She's a small ship and doesn't have very many amenities to offer."

Sharra laughed. "I don't think the Senatrix is too concerned about the amenities at the moment. Provided that we can get her to Nemesis, and then see her and her daughter back to Thermadon safely, I'm sure she'll be more than satisfied with whatever you have to offer."

"Good," Bel Lissa said. "Please try to make sure that the Senatrix and Lady Felecia pack lightly."

"I'll do my best," Sharra grinned.

Bel Lissa smiled back. "We'll take off in one hour."

***

A small contingent of the Senatrix's security women escorted the crew of the *JUDI* and their passengers as far as the lift to the Guest Hangars. After that, they were left on their own.

The servants had been careful to dress Felecia and her mother in plain jumpsuits and spare flight-jackets. All of their finery had been reduced to the barest essentials, stowed away in non-descript flight bags. By all appearances, they looked just like members of the merchanter's crew, and no one paid them any undue attention as they made their way to the vessel.

"There she is," Maya said to Felecia, gesturing expansively. "That's our *JUDI*. Isn't she wonderful?"

"Yes," Felecia agreed politely, clearly taken aback by the merchanter. Maya realized that in her fantasies, Felecia had probably envisioned the *JUDI* possessing a more dramatic appearance.

"I must confess that I had always thought of your ship as being a little... bigger," Felecia admitted, "If only to accommodate enough cargo to make your trips profitable."

"Mark me," Zara said, "She can hold more than enough in her belly to make us a profit on every trip." She gave the *JUDI's* metal hull an affectionate pat and let the scanner read her aural signature at the exterior egress hatch.

"What she's saying is that most of the cargo we haul is small in volume, but special enough to pay for itself," Maya explained. They followed the engineer into the vessel. "The *JUDI* isn't in the business of hauling bulk materials like other merchanters are."

"I suppose not," Felecia agreed. "I must admit that it is quite a thrill to be aboard an *actual* pirate ship."

"That's *moonrunner*, girl!" Zara retorted, "And a proud profession it is! *Pirates* indeed! You'd think we're walking around all the time with parrots on our shoulders and swinging cutlasses in the air! *Pah!*"

"My apologies, Zara," Felecia said diplomatically. "I meant no offense. Please excuse my ignorance."

Zara snorted indignantly and crossed the cargo hold over to the main egressway, muttering something about 'pieces of eight'. Felecia looked at everyone around her with a bewildered expression. "I really didn't mean to affront anyone. It's just that I thought--."

"Don't mind Zara. She's just a bit sensitive on the subject," Bel Lissa interjected. "She always has been. I can imagine that to you the *JUDI would* seem to be a pirate ship. No worries though, it's all a matter of semantics. Welcome aboard the *JUDI,* gentleladies…whatever she is." The captain finished her words with an elaborate bow and a wave that elicited a laugh from everyone.

Bel Lissa went up to the control cockpit, and Maya suddenly found herself playing the tour guide for the Senatrix and her daughter, guiding them down the main egress way. "This is the Crews Quarters," Maya said as she opened the hatch. "You can stow your luggage in here until we can find a place for it in the cargo hold. There's also a bathroom in here in case you need to use the facilities." She stepped aside and let Felecia and her mother peer inside the tiny chamber.

"But there are only two beds!" Felecia exclaimed. "How do you all manage to sleep in here?"

"A good question!" Zara laughed as she squeezed by them. "Welcome to the world of commercial space faring!"

"We don't all sleep at once," Maya told the girl. "It's really only meant for occasional passengers, and a quick nap now and again."

This elicited a confused expression and Maya elaborated. "Most of the trips through Null are short, no more than a few hours, so we don't really need berths like a liner would. If we have to, we take turns, but usually we reach port and get ourselves rooms there. Besides, it saves more space for cargo not having regular quarters. Only Sarah has her own cabin, and she rarely uses it."

Felecia nodded and she and her mother put their bags down on the cabin deck. Then they accompanied Maya back out into the corridor.

"This is where we eat," Maya said, indicating a tiny autochef set in a notch in the opposite side of the bulkhead. There was a small folding table and two swing-out chairs. "You can dial up just about anything on the 'chef, and most of the time it comes out pretty much like it should."

"But again, you normally eat when you get to port?" Felecia guessed.

"Yes," Sarah said, making her way past them, "but for the really long trips we can grab a bite in our escort ship's galley once we're out of Null. The food is usually quite good."

"That, and rent bunk-space and showers as we need them," Maya added. " I prefer port-side lodgings myself."

"As would I," Felecia agreed. Maya ascended the ladder to the command cabin and gestured for them to come up.

"I think I'll stay below," the Senatrix said. "I've seen the *JUDI's* control cabin before, and I could use the opportunity to rest. It's been a rather trying day." She left Felecia alone with Maya.

"Watch your head," Maya warned. They climbed the ladder together and when they reached Maya's station, she pulled out one of the ship's two guest chairs from its recess in the wall next to her. "Here," she said, snapping it open, "you can sit next to me."

Felecia took her seat and let Maya strap her in. She flashed her a suggestive smile as Maya's hands made contact with her body and Maya flushed. She also took a little more time than she actually needed to adjust the straps. *After all*, she told herself, it's *very important to make sure that everyone is properly secured.*

"All right," Bel Lissa announced, "Captain bel Mandi just confirmed that we will leave the *Aphrodite* registered as the *Justine*, one of those toy boats out there, and she'll erase the rest of the departure data to cover our tracks. As far as anyone will know, you and your mother will still be aboard the liner, locked away in your new staterooms, and recovering from the day's events. That should hold us until we've reached Nemesis. Let's be off, shall we?"

Felecia nodded, clearly excited at being in the control cabin. "You know, I have never been up in front like this before. I have always been in the back, or in a stateroom. Where is our escort? Where's the convoy? Shouldn't they be here by now?"

Maya hesitated, and glanced up at Sarah questioningly. When the woman nodded her assent, Maya answered Felecia's question. "Well, you see, Felecia, we don't actually *have* an escort or a convoy. We go it alone."

"What?!" Felecia replied in alarm. "No escort? No other ships? How in the Mother's name can we do that? How can we even *get* into Null?"

"That's the *JUDI's* little secret," Bel Lissa told her. "We have our own Null-wings, and 'special' defenses to deal with the *Indies*. You'll see."

"Yah," Zara added warningly, "and now that you know about it, you'll have to keep your silence, or we'll make you walk the plank."

Felecia looked more confused than ever, and Maya calmed her. "Don't listen to Zara," she said. "There's no 'plank', but it *is* something that you'll have to keep quiet about. And don't worry, we've done this before many times, and we'll get through Null just fine."

"So hold on tight, me hearties!" Zara cackled, "We're weighing anchor and setting sail in search of buried treasure! *Aaaarrrr!*" Even Sarah laughed as she started to focus energy into the Null-wings.

***

Their passage through Null proved both exhilarating and terrifying for Felecia.

"Oh Maya!" she said breathlessly as they flew under an arch made of crimson gases. "It is spectacular! I never imagined that Null was so exquisite! I'd always thought it to be somewhat dull-looking. I can see now why you became a nulltrekker."

"It *is* amazing," Maya agreed. "Don't let its looks fool you though, it's also very dangerous."

"Yes," Felecia replied. "The Indwellers. Do you think... do you think we'll actually see one?" There was a distinct note of fear in her voice.

"As a matter of fact, we will--right now," Bel Lissa answered. "Sarah, we have two, no make that three Indies closing from heading 270.5.14 You should see them at about your 02:91 position."

"Confirmed," Sarah replied. "I also sense a fourth and a fifth somewhere below us, contemplating an ambush while the other three distract us."

Maya glanced at the displays and saw that the Indies were closing the distance rapidly. And the temperature, which had already dropped when they had entered Null, was plummeting rapidly.

"Initiating evasive action," Bel Lisa said, steering the *JUDI* on a course away from the oncoming creatures. Sarah meanwhile, had closed her eyes and was beginning to concentrate.

Seeing this, Felecia clasped Maya's arm. "What is she doing?" the girl asked, mystified.

"Getting ready to fight," Maya told her.

By now, the Indwellers had drawn close enough for them to register visually on the *JUDI's* sitscreens, and Felecia squeaked in fright. Maya took her hand, but she also kept her eyes on the engine power just in case they needed the additional energy for the ship's weapons.

Then Sarah let out a small breath and the two Indies that were below them abruptly broke off and flew away in opposite directions. This did not stop the other three however, and the woman's brow knotted in concentration as she pushed at them with her talents. Although this made the trio of black forms slow down, it didn't stop them. They kept coming.

Sarah pushed again, and this time it had an effect. The largest of the Indwellers halted and its form shuddered. As sweat broke out on Sarah's brow, the thing suddenly folded over, and then shot away into the clouds. This still left the final pair, and suddenly it was Bel Lissa's turn to defend the ship.

"Maximum power to the forward guns, now!" she commanded.

Maya let go of Felecia and quickly entered in the command to the reactors. The instant that their power level peaked, Bel Lissa fired at the nearest Indweller, hitting it squarely in the center of its mass.

An unearthly howl reverberated through the entire ship as the *JUDI's* energy guns ripped a hole in the thing. It tried to continue moving forwards,

405

but as it did, the guns continued to do their work, tearing a long ragged gash, and finally, the creature was forced to ascend.

Only the third and last Indweller remained, and although it took multiple hits from the guns, it continued to come at them.

"Maya," Sarah said. "Come here. I need your help!" Maya unbuckled immediately and hurried over to her.

"Take my hand," Sarah instructed. "Concentrate on the last Indweller. *Push* out at it with your talents. Imagine that your fist is hitting it in the center of its body."

The moment that she made contact with Sarah, Maya could see the Indweller through her eyes. More than ever, she could also sense its absolute malevolence, and she did her best to ignore this as she put all of her will into her visualization.

"That did it!" Bel Lissa declared. "That sent it running."

Maya opened her eyes. The thing was speeding away from them, trying to catch up with its companions.

"It is like that sometimes," Sarah said to her with a weak smile. "They do not always react the way I want them to, and there were many more this time than I normally deal with. Thank you for helping me." She seemed paler than usual, and Maya felt a stab of concern.

"I will be fine," Sarah assured her. "A moment to collect myself is all that I need. Go back to your station." The girl left her and rejoined Felecia, who looked equally wan.

"T-that was *terrifying*," Felecia stammered. "I-I don't know how you can stand to do this all the time. They were so *evil*. They--they *hated* us!"

"It's the price we pay for taking a short-cut through the universe," Bel Lissa explained. "The locals don't welcome visitors."

Felecia nodded, and then leaned in close to Maya. "Maya?" she said in a small voice, "Can you help me....please?"

Maya looked down, and saw what was wrong and then glanced over to Zara. "Lady Felecia needs my help. Are you good here?"

"Yah, girl. Go take care of her."

Maya helped Felecia unbuckle, then assisted her down the ladder. The girl was red-faced with shame, and Maya tried not to look at the dark urine stain between her legs. When they reached the correct stores locker, she helped her find another jumpsuit and showed her to the bathroom with as much dignity and tact as was possible.

The life of a nulltrekker wasn't for everyone.

***

Sarah waited until Maya had descended from the control cabin with Felecia before she allowed herself the luxury of a private smile. Although the Indwellers had attacked the *JUDI* in greater numbers than usual, it hadn't been anything that she couldn't have handled and *had* handled many times before. Enlisting Maya's assistance had forced the girl to act out of loyalty and a sense of teamwork; two qualities that she had never bothered to nuture. Whether she realized it or not, Maya was changing, and being changed, one step at a time.

The Goddess wills the way, she reflected, *but it is our hand that brings that Will to fruition.*

More than ever, she was certain of what the cards had predicted for Maya, and had she been able, she would have thanked the Indies for the part that they had unwittingly played in helping this to become reality.

CHAPTER 12

A golden statue of the goddess Athena stood in a niche behind Lilith's chair in the ship's conference room. One-quarter life-size, the figure was old, having been created over three hundred years earlier, when the *Pallas Athena* had still been a new ship. It had been given to the crew by a master craftswoman as a token of gratitude for saving her planet during the Second Widow's War.

Lilith let her eyes travel over the figure, drinking in its rich detail. Whoever the model had been for the statue, the artist had chosen her well, she decided. Beneath the armored headdress, the goddesses' eyes seemed to exude all of the patience and wisdom in the universe.

Although Lilith worshiped Selene, the goddess of lunar change, it was at times like these that she made a special point to pay homage to her ship's divine patroness. Activating a small votive holocandle at the figure's feet, she whispered a prayer to the guardian of ancient Athens to watch over the ship as she always had. Then she turned and took her seat to await her officers.

Katrinn and Mearinn filed in first, followed by Dr. elle'Kaari, Ellyn n'Dira, Col. Lislsdaater, Bel Sarra and finally, Erin taur Minna. In addition, Lilith had invited Captain Veera t'Gwen, the chief of the *Athena's* Internal Security Detachment to join them.

"Ladies," Lilith said after everyone had taken their seats, "to put it mildly, this has been an eventful week. Between the body that was found on deck 12 and the tragic incident in Ord Stores, I have to say, that I for one, am quite glad that we are shipping out. I don't think I could tolerate any more of the 'peace and quiet' that we've enjoyed here in space dock." There was a smattering of laughter around the room before Lilith continued.

"As you all know, we have been given a unique assignment to undertake. Although we have been on many missions, I doubt that any of them will compare with the demands that this one may put on us, on our crews, or our respective ships.'

"Our first port of call will be Thenti, the Territorial Capitol, and our next leg will be determined from there, based on the local situation. Although, goddess willing, certain portions of our patrol may be uneventful, I want each of you to make sure that your people are at full readiness at all times. We cannot predict when or where we may be called upon to respond in an emergency.'

"In addition, because of the risk of interference by dissident elements, I will be relying on each of you to maintain a high state of vigilance and work closely with Captain t'Gwen and her Security Patrolwomen. Captain, do you have any special remarks that you'd like to make?"

The platinum blond nodded. "Yes, I do" she replied, "One of our major concerns will be access to our ships and the transport shuttles serving them. All passengers will be checked, and entry aboard any vessel will only be granted with the proper identification. We will also be scrutinizing any supplies transported aboard and keeping a watch on any civilian visitors, regardless of rank or position.'

"In addition to our normal shore patrol, my girls will also provide protective detachments for any officers going downside. I realize that all of this might seem quite extreme, but given the uncertain political climate in the Territory, my department feels that these measures are necessary, and we will do all that we can to make sure that our presence is as unobtrusive as possible. Thank you."

"Thank you, Captain," Lilith said. "I know that everyone here understands the need for these steps and will provide you with any assistance you require."

Then she addressed the others. "Captain t'Gwen will be in charge of the Battle Group's overall security forces, and she will meet with the heads of security for the *Artemis* and *Demeter* and work with them to see to it that our combined efforts are in sync. Col. Lislsdaater, I know that I don't need to ask for your military policewomen to assist in this effort."

Lislsdaater smiled. "It will be our pleasure, Commander." Her MP's worked hand in hand with the naval security women as a matter of routine, and Lilith knew that she could count on them, and their commander, to help wherever they were needed to get the job done.

"Well, then, unless anyone else has some special details that we need to go over, I think we can consider this briefing over," Lilith announced.

No one spoke up and Lilith rose from her place. "Let's make preparations to get under weigh. Have your Helmsmistresses set their course for Thenti. I want transit to Null in 1 hour."

Thenti City, Sagana Territorial Capitol, Thenti, Sagana System, Sagana Territory, United Sisterhood of Suns, 1043.02|22|05.20.25

Thenti was an airless rock, one of twelve satellites that orbited around a central gas giant. It was far from barren though. Lilith gazed out of the Territorial Manager's Office onto a bizarre landscape made of solid rock whose shapes suggested strange alien creatures and fluid, abstract forms.

One stone reminded her of a humanoid figure, but with a wildly distorted and mushroom-shaped head. Another looked like a sand beast from the desert world of Razka, complete with its deadly razor–spines, and its neighbor seemed like a woman trying to shield her ears from a scream that only she could hear.

The formations had been created by some geologic process that was utterly unknown to her, and stretched out and away from the view port at until their individuality was lost in the sheer confusion of their numbers and the harsh interplay of light and shadow.

"Thenti's 'Stone People' can be quite enthralling," her host said. Marylyn ebed Terri handed her a glass of Corrissan tea and joined her her at the view port. "As one might expect, after several generations of colonists, there are also many tales told about them. One story is about a woman who went out among them and became so enchanted that she fell under their spell and actually turned to stone herself.'

"Some of the older miners even swear that the stones will come alive when you're out among them long enough. They even say that if you're clever like one woman, I think her name was Fionn n'Cara, and you learn their secret names, they'll lead you to their treasure hoard. Fanciful little tales, wouldn't you say?"

"Yes," Lilith agreed, taking a sip. "Quite." The tea was exquisite, and without parallel except for the teas of her motherworld. "We had similar stories back on Ara. It was very much like Thenti, although we had an atmosphere. Thank you for the tea, by the way."

410

"My pleasure, Commander. We're really quite grateful for the *Athena's* visit," Ebed Terri said. "Aside from the danger that the Hriss pose, especially with our mineral resources, I was hoping that you'd be able to aid us in sorting out a local problem."

Lilith turned to face her. "And that problem is, Governess?"

"Please, Commander, the title is not official yet," Ebed Terri demurred, "Madame Manager, or just Marylyn will do. The ruling to declare us the 12th Elant is still waiting for the Chairwoman's signature, and that's heady enough for this old miner."

As a naval officer who dealt with colonial affairs on a regular basis, Lilith understood the situation perfectly. Becoming an elant, a state, wasn't easy or automatic by any means.

First, viable colonies had to exist and they had to produce a marketable resource of some kind. They also had to have become at least 50 percent self-sustaining within two generations of their founding.

Then, the colonies had to agree to merger with their neighbors under the management of a single member colony, and apply for membership as a territory.

Once this license was granted, the final challenge came when the territory petitioned to become a permanent elant. In order to qualify, the prospective state had to possess Articles of Constitution that were the equal of the Concordance, boast a population of no less than 80,000 souls, have an official capital, and elected representatives who met there on a regular basis. If all this was accomplished, and the Supreme Circle and the Chairwoman ratified the petition, then statehood, with full representation within the Circle, would be awarded.

Even though Thenti and her sister worlds had surmounted all of these hurdles and was on the verge of achieving their goal, a serious local issue could undo everything and bring their space under the interim governance of an appointed committee. And few territories emerged from under the talons of such committees very quickly. Thanks to a trade war between two of its worlds and mutual embargoes, the petition by the Artemi Territories had floundered for decades before it had finally been granted full elant status. This was not a lesson easily forgotten by any group of worlds hoping for greater things.

411

"Very well, Marylyn," Lilith replied, "What can we help you with?"

"Storm and Siren," the Manager said, calling up a holo and zooming in on two worlds in the Agleope system. "The women on these two planets have been at odds with one another for years. It all started over a lost minebot, with one party claiming that the other one stole it. There was a counter-accusation about mining rights being violated, and it went downside from there.'

"Recently, things have gotten worse. Neither planet officially acknowledges the other and both of them are claiming sovereignty over the Agleope system. Each planet sends its own representative to the Territorial House and both of them have claimed the same seat. We've even had to have the women ejected from the floor on several occasions.

"That's in addition to having everything from personal duels, to near-battles between mining parties. Nothing major, mind you, but enough to be a constant headache for the Territorial Marshals.'

"Now, to make things even worse, a group of scientists from Siren have turned up missing during an unauthorized trip to Storm. Siren is charging Storm with kidnapping, and Storm is charging Siren with trespassing and espionage. It's a glorious mess. We've tried to mediate, but neither party will make the slightest concession. I was hoping that a more… official…intervention might knock some sense into their heads."

"A glorious mess, indeed," Lilith agreed. "I don't know how much a warship can do to help heal this breach, but we were sent out here to try and consolidate things against a possible Hriss incursion. I can't promise you a miracle, but we'll certainly see what we can accomplish.'

"By the way, what *was* the scientific team doing on Storm in the first place? That would seem to be a rather perilous venture, given the state of local politics."

"Searching the Drow'Voi ruins," Ebed Teri answered. "They were looking for artifacts, working ones. Their team leader was certain that there were some down there, and she managed to convince everyone that it was worth the risk. Pure folly if you ask me, but there you have it."

It did sound like a foolish venture to Lilith. Scientists had been scouring the Drow'Voi ruins for decades all over the Sisterhood, and had never found a single working device. The ancient culture had not only vanished entirely, it had also made sure to thoroughly clean house before doing so.

"Very well," Lilith said, finishing her tea. "We'll do what we can. And who knows, maybe we'll even discover some Drow'voi artifacts—or even manage to settle this little feud once and for all."

"Stranger things have happened," the Colony Manager said, refilling Lilith's cup.

USSNS *Pallas Athena*, Agleope System, Sagana Territory, United Sisterhood of Suns, 1043.02|22|07:22:29

"Agleope Control, this is the USSNS *Pallas Athena*, Battle Group Golden, requesting approach and orbital coordinates," the Navcom officer said.

For a long moment there was only silence, although the *Athena's* sensors confirmed that there were women on Siren and Storm listening to their signal.

Finally, someone answered. "This is Agleope Control, Station Siren. Please proceed on our coordinates and assume station as delineated. Welcome to our system." A data burst followed this announcement, which was fed into the Navcom computer terminals.

"Well," Lilith said to Katrinn, "that wasn't so bad. Maybe the locals have solved their problems all on their own." Katrinn rewarded her with a doubtful expression and was about to voice her misgivings, when another transmission came over the Com.

"*Pallas Athena*—this is Storm In-System Traffic Control. Disregard that previous message. Proceed to *our* coordinates and assume station over Storm. The *legitimate* government of this system welcomes you."

With that, Navcom received an entirely different set of coordinates. This was immediately followed by a group of targets rising from Storm. According to Fire Control, they were older-style Norn interceptors.

"We are also sending an escort to guide you to us," the Storm controller informed them.

413

Not to be outdone, another set of targets registered coming up from Siren. They were also surplus interceptor-fighters. "Pay no attention to Storm Control, *Athena*. *We* are sending an escort to guide you in!"

"Well," Lilith remarked, arching an eyebrow, "that's something different. What say you, ladies? Shall we let them fight over us?"

"Commander!" Ellyn n'Dira exclaimed, "You can't be serious!"

"Don't worry, Ellyn," Lilith replied. "As entertaining as that would be to watch, we won't allow such an event to occur."

The women of Storm and Siren had much different ideas however. The *Athena's* sensors showed both escort groups powering up their weapons and targeting each other as they closed distance.

Salus n'Hera, the Senior Fire Controller contacted her. "Commander? They look like they're going to get serious. Instructions?"

"Navcom," Lilith said. "Open a joint frequency between the two flights and inform them that if they do not power down, both of them, *right now*, that we *will* fire on them.'

"Assuming that they *do* calm down, notify both In-System Control stations. Tell them that we will send delegate ships to assume orbit over their worlds and that the *Athena* will visit them when we see fit to do so."

"An excellent decision, Commander," N'Dira commented.

"Now, let's just hope they're sane enough to comply," Katrinn said.

"I can see now why the Manager on Thenti was so concerned," Mearinn d'Rann interjected. "This is exactly the kind of thing that would doom any chance at full statehood. Frankly, I'm amazed that this situation has been overlooked for so long."

"According to the OAE file, Thenti has some powerful friends in the Circle," Lilith said, "and strong backers in the industrial sector that are hoping for full statehood. That adds up to a lot of overlooking."

"Commander?" It was Salus n' Hera again. "The two groups have powered down and are turning away from one another."

"Oh, I am just *overjoyed!*" Lilith replied acerbically. "Now, let's get on with this. I feel like a mother settling a dispute between two siblings over a toy. I'd say that a good corrective swat on the rear end is in order for both parties. Fire Control, if we see a repeat of any hostilities, disable the aggressor immediately."

***

Darna n'Marni, the Colony Manager of Storm, and, if one took her claim seriously, the Manager of the entire Agleope system, sat at the conference table aboard the *Athena* tapping her fingers on the table top in irritation. It had been obvious from the moment that Lilith had laid eyes on the woman that she was used to having her way in all things.

"Madame n'Marni," Ellyn n'Dira was saying, "The Navy's position is a simple one. We are not in the business of recognizing the legitimacy of any group's claim of governance. That job is for politicians, not sailors, and I strongly suggest that if you believe that Storm has a legitimate claim that you take up the matter with the Territorial Manager on Thenti."

"We *have*, Advocate!" N'Marni retorted, her jaw clenching in anger. "And that weak-willed woman has done everything she could to avoid giving us an answer. We are tired of waiting, especially now that the Sireens have seen fit to *invade* our planet!"

Her opposition sat across from her, shaking her head and smiling. Sussanhya n'Tanaaya, the Colony Manager of Siren, was radically different in appearance to Darna n'Marni.

Due to the deadly levels of ultraviolet radiation on her motherworld, her skin was jet black, and this was offset by startling golden eyes and honey-colored hair. Thanks to a local insect that gave out a mating call high enough to permanently damage a normal woman's ears she had also been born completely deaf.

And although N'Tanaaya could have easily used her psiever to communicate, she signed out her rebuttal to N'Marni's argument with her hands instead. This proved to be far more eloquent. Her response came across with the same vehemence. She flatly denied N'Marni's charges and angrily leveled a counter-accusation against the Stormites over an earlier incursion into their asteroid mining fields. She ended her statement with a rather rude and ancient gesture that had nothing to do with Standard Sign Language. Her middle finger.

"Did you see what that black skinned bitch just said to me? *That's* what we've had to deal with for years!" N'Marni yelled. "Their arrogance

415

knows no bounds, even here! Commander, I demand that you intercede on our behalf as the only legitimate governing body in this system and aid us to bring order at last."

Not to be outdone, N'Tanaaya made a similar plea and then pointedly turned her back on the Stormite.

Lilith had reached her limits. "Excuse me, but I can see that these negotiations are going nowhere," she said. "So, I will refer to my Advocate here. Ellyn? I believe that in a case where civil disorder exists, that the Navy is empowered to establish a militarized zone of operations and impose martial law. Isn't that so?"

"Why, yes, Commander," N'Dira replied. "That's true, but it hasn't been done in over three hundred—"

Lilith cut her off. "Case law *is* on our side, is it not, Advocate? I believe you'll find a reference to it in the Colony Mandates, volume 12, section 6101, subsection Freda."

"Yes—" the Advocate agreed, calling the text up on holo, "Yes, it would seem that you are right."

"Commander? What in the Lady's name are you proposing? I demand that you—" N'Marni began.

"Madame, *shut up!*" Lilith snapped, "or I will have you and your sister colonist here clapped in irons as my first step in imposing some *real* order! I, for one, have listened to both of you bicker for the better part of a standard hour and I have heard more than enough. You two, with the aid of our learned Advocate, *will* reach a settlement and agree to some form of co-regency."

She got up from the table. "Now, I am going to get a cup of tea for myself and some fresh air. When I return, you will either present me with a sisterly set of compromises, or *I* will dictate *our* terms. Is that clear to both of you?"

Neither of them responded, and Lilith did not press the matter. Instead, she left them together in the conference room and headed straight for the serenity and silence of her quarters for a peaceful cup of tea and a *czigavar*. She needed both.

***

The scene that greeted Lilith when she returned brought a frown to her lips. The Sireeni was standing with her back to the Stormite woman, her arms folded in a pose that clearly expressed her refusal to communicate any further. And Darna n'Marni was staring out into space with her jaw set in defiant silence. Ellyn n'Dira shook her head and rose from her chair.

"I *see*," Lilith said. "Apparently, this must be how you handled the previous attempts by the Teritorial Manager to settle things. Well, I am not going to respond like her. *Security!*" This was directed to the Marine guards at the door. "Take these two to the brig straightaway!"

"Commander!" Darna n'Marni cried, "This is outrageous! How dare you!"

"I think we have already discussed how I dare," Lilith responded, "Volume 12, section 6101, subsection Freda. And if you think *this* is bold, just wait until I send our Marine detachment down to your respective planets and lock everything down. *Then* you might have a legitimate reason to complain. It's a pity that we'll probably wind up having your Colony Charters revoked, but the Sisterhood will not tolerate this ridiculous little civil war that you two seem to be so bent on waging."

She waved to the two Marines, who began to escort the pair out of the room. As she was being led away, Darna n'Marni's shouts could be heard all the way down the corridor, and if Sussanhya n'Tanaaya had had a voice, Lilith was certain she would have joined in the chorus of dissent. Thankfully she didn't, and couldn't.

"I'd say without exaggerating that that went rather poorly," Ellyn n'Dira observed sourly.

"I hadn't expected any better," Lilith replied. "I just hope that a night or two in the brig will force them to see reason. Otherwise, I might have to make good on my threat to send down the Marines."

She called up Security on the com and reached Captain t'Gwen in her squad room. "I've just sent two prisoners down to you, Captain. Please make sure to put them in a cell together and also make certain that they have only one prisoner kit between them. One blanket, and one set of eating utensils. No more."

Her security chief replied affirmatively and Lilith cut the connection. "That might help get the message across."

"The Goddess wills the way" N'Dira said, but her tone belied her doubts.

'A night or two in the brig' actually turned out to be several days. In the end however, Captain t'Gwen notified Lilith that the two women had finally agreed to renew negotiations. This time, when the meeting was reconvened in the conference room, both parties were in a more reasonable frame of mind.

USSNS *Pallas Athena*, Storm, Agleope System, Sagana Territory, United Sisterhood of Suns, 1043.02|25|05:69:27

Jon fa'Teela ignored the looks that he was receiving from the women around him as he rechecked his chair harness one final time. The shuttle had just entered the atmosphere of Storm and they had been warned to prepare themselves for the intense winds that circled the planet.

Troop Leader bel Taralynn, the leader of the Marine Special Search and Rescue team, Red Squad, took advantage of the relatively calm layer that they were traveling through, and braced herself against a support strut as the shuttle rose and dipped.

"All right, ladies," she said, "listen-up! This is a rescue and support mission. This afternoon, the two colonies of Storm and Siren agreed to cooperate in a joint effort with our forces to locate a scientific team that was lost on the Plain of Screams. They checked several Drow'Voi archaeological sites in the area and found the dig at site number 4081. Two of our SAR teams have already been downside for the last 12 hours, and we're going in to augment their efforts.'

"Our mission will be to work with the locals, and search areas that haven't been covered by the other two teams. If we find anyone, we'll conduct a rescue op. I've been told that we're taking along our neoman here because the brass had some *warpy* notion that he might actually be useful out here. I don't know what that means, but at least he can carry all the heavy stuff while we do the real work!"

A few of the Marines laughed and even Jon cracked a small smile. In reality, he had been attached to the S and R team for two very good reasons; the first was because the teams needed all the extra hands they could get to cover the huge search area. The second was because he had had some S and R training as part of his Infantry Specialist Courses, and wasn't anywhere as 'green' as the Troop Leader was making him out to be. Not that he was about to contradict anyone. Just being involved in the special operation was a welcome respite from the monotony of the Ord Stores.

The lighting in the cabin changed from white to red and Bel Taralynn listened to her com headset. "The pilot says that we're leaving the calm air and headed for some *real* turbulence. Buckle up, troopies! It looks like it's going to be one wild ride down!"

The Troop Leader hastily took her seat and strapped in just seconds before the winds hit them. The entire ship reverberated with a loud bang and the vessal was tossed sideways. Then another gust slammed into them from the opposite side with equal violence.

Even though he was intellectually aware that the battle-ready shuttle could withstand the savage forces that were battering against it, Jon found himself praying fervently to Jesu and Mari that they would reach the ground safely.

His fellow Marines adopted a more laissez-faire attitude about the whole adventure, with the Zommerlaandars in particular letting out loud rodeo cheers. One of them even yodeled when the shuttle suddenly encountered a particularly nasty patch of air and dropped before regaining control. Everyone around him seemed to find this extremely funny and laughed and shouted to each other over the screaming winds.

Five long minutes passed before Jon's earnest petitions to the divine were finally granted, and the shuttle touched down on the surface.

"Go-time, troopies!" Bel Taralynn shouted. "The pilot tells me that we've managed to land in a relatively calm area, pretty much right on top of the dig site. Grab your gear and follow my lead. Use your helmet HUD to keep track of the team and our objective." This last remark was directed to Jon, and he nodded his understanding.

Bel Taralynn regarded him uncertainly, and then grabbed up her pack off the storage racks and buckled it on. She dropped her helmet visor and ordered the egress door to open with her psiever. Grey dust and howling winds immediately filled the cabin as she stepped outside, vanishing like a ghost into the swirling maelstrom. Jon was the third person out of the hatch.

He quickly discovered that the 'relatively calm area' that they'd landed in was gusting at no less than 88 kph according to his HUD. The neoman struggled just to stay erect, and followed his teammates as best as he was able. Just walking forward proved to be a major effort and he realized that without the HUD giving him a reference point to travel towards, that he would have gotten himself hopelessly lost just a few meters from the shuttle.

The Drow'Voi ruins, such as they were, proved disappointing. Instead of the imposing towers that were so common elsewhere in the galaxy, all Jon could see when the grit cleared, were piles of wind-blasted rubble. Over the eons, the ferocious climate of Storm had destroyed everything that the Drow'Voi had built on the surface and scoured the area nearly flat. To Jon's untrained eye, the place seemed to be nothing more than a rock-strewn plain and he wondered how the Sireeni science team had even found the location, much less known to dig for anything below the surface.

As Bel Taralynn had promised, the S and R team didn't have far to travel. The dig site was only a hundred or so meters from their landing zone, designated by a single battered marker light on a pole. The entrance to the site turned out to be a rough hole in the ground that the group was forced to enter one at a time.

When Jon's turn came, he dropped down into it without hesitation and landed in a small, dust-filled chamber. Even though they had only descended a few meters, the wind's noise was halved and he was able to see around him without the aid of the HUD. The chamber that they were in was smooth and white with only the rough edges of the entrance to mar its otherwise ageless perfection. At the far end, an oval shaped tunnel led off into the darkness. Bel Taralynn turned on her helmet light and walked straight into it without looking back to see if anyone was following.

The team traveled down the tunnel for the next ten minutes, with only their lights to give the passage any shape or form in the otherwise seamless blackness. Then, up ahead, Jon thought he saw a faint glow. Drawing nearer, he realized that it wasn't just an illusion created by his mind. The tunnel suddenly opened out onto a much larger chamber, lit from the corners by portable work lamps. A group of women, some in Marine greys, others in navy black or the olive drab of the Territorial Marshals were waiting for them, examining a map on a folding table along with a rotating holo of the tunnel complex. The senior-most Marshal and a Marine officer looked up from their work and came over together to greet the team.

"Lieutenant Barbara t'Charli, 10th Territorial Marshals" the Stormite said, saluting them. "Welcome to the wild *gaanz*-hunt."

"Glad to have you ladies aboard," the Marine officer added. "Captain Vera n'Lissa. I'm coordinating the operations of the other two search teams."

Troop Leader bel Taralynn returned their salutes and gestured for everyone in her team to drop their packs and join the group at the table.

Looking over their shoulders, Jon saw that the tunnel system had only been partially mapped. Some levels were clearly delineated, while other portions were vague. And in other spots, even these tentative markings faded out into large empty voids populated only by question marks.

"These are the maps the science team was using," the Lieutenant explained. "From what we can tell from their logs, they used 'bots to perform their initial explorations, and then went in on foot to explore the sections themselves. Their main base camp is down this tunnel in a chamber they called the 'Inner Ear.' They were doing some kind of experiments with ultrasonics there." She indicated the route with her finger.

"Everything down there's just like they left it, right down to the lunch they were eating. We don't know what happened to the group, but something must have occurred that made them all leave together in a hurry.'

"We think they went out of the Inner Ear and deeper into the tunnels through this structure, which they labeled the 'Cathedral.' At the end of it, there are three separate tunnels, each leading off into its own set of sub-tunnels and chambers. The other two S and R teams are already covering the left and middle sectors. Your search area will be down the right hand tunnel, with the Cathedral as your starting point."

421

"Any recent aural tracings or bio-spore?" Bel Taralynn asked.

"Only for a short ways away from the camp, then nothing. Not even good old fashioned foot prints," the Lieutenant responded. "The sci-team just plain vanished. Once you get past this spot," she said, pointing to the furthest mapped tunnel, "there's nothing except dust and the microbes that have been there since the Drow'Voi left. So, we know that they managed to vanish somewhere within the mapped portions, but we don't know how, or why. We're missing maybe ten or fifteen women." She nodded back towards the curved wall behind her where a holo showing the pictures of each member of the party floated as a reference for the rescuers.

"So, you neomen afraid of ghosts?" a Marine to Jon's left asked him.

Jon didn't reply, but another trooper did. "Nah, zat's probably why zhey zent him. *Denn gaasten* will get vun look at his ugly face and zhey'll go runnin t'otter vey, yah?"

"Yah" the first replied, "maybe. I would if I saw him coming up on me in the dark."

"Seal it!" Bel Taralynn said sharply. "We don't have time for jokes. We need to get focused, ladies. There are a lot of things that could explain what happened here and ghosts aren't at the top of my list. The Sci-team might have been caught up in some kind of trap, a cave-in, or maybe just gotten lost. These passages go on for kilometers and we're going to have to walk careful or find ourselves in the same situation.'

"Corporal Astridsdaater and Corporal n'Wendi, you're going to work with me and we're going to devise our search plan. The rest of you double check your gear and suit up for S and R."

With a reconbot scouting ahead, and accompanied by two marshals, the team worked its way from the base camp and down a gently spiraling tunnel that emptied into the second level. The descent proved easy enough; the ancient tunnels were smooth and reasonably free of debris. The wind's roar was a thing of the past now, and except for the crunch of their boots on the gritty floors, the passage was completely still.

Eventually, the tunnel opened out again into a large ellipse shaped chamber, and Jon could appreciate the name the researchers had given it. The room was gently curved with odd folds that flowed seamlessly into the clean white walls. It was overlooked by a large balcony or platform that stretched away into the silent darkness. Just as the Marshal had told them, everything in the chamber was exactly as the scientists had left it. Folding bunks and tables were neatly arranged around a group of work tables and to one side, a makeshift kitchen still held the desiccated remains of the researcher's lunch.

The Marines didn't tarry, and quickly ascended to the balcony level, which in turn led into another chamber filled with delicate pillar-like structures that fused with a high, arched ceiling. The space had been aptly named, resembling in every respect an ancient Gaian cathedral. The awesome structure was at once familiar and utterly alien to Jon's eyes.

Marching among the pillars, he wondered at the nature of the beings that had built the place. Nothing had ever been found at any site anywhere in the Galaxy depicting the ancient architects, and none of the structures that they'd left behind had ever yielded any clues either. The neoman found himself imagining the master builders as everything from humanoid life forms to strange insectoids, all the while feeling in his gut that the truth was probably far, far stranger.

At the end of the Cathedral, the search team took the tunnel to the farthest right. The minutes stretched into hours with no results.

Finally, the Troop Leader called a halt, and after setting markers and a 'bot to act as a sentry, had them turn around and go back the way they had come. Once they were back at the Inner Ear, she called the base camp on her com. By the time that she'd finished speaking with them, however, she was wearing a deep frown.

"It seems that the nice weather we had on the surface is ending," she announced. "The *Athena* just reported a major storm front moving in on our position from the east, with winds estimated at 321 kilometers per hour and higher. Our shuttles are leaving for the night, which means that everyone is stuck here. The storm should pass in about 12 hours and the shuttles will return then."

A few of the troopers groaned their displeasure and Bel Taralynn waved them to silence. "Let's make camp and break out the rations. We'll plan on returning down the tunnel and go deeper in tomorrow morning."

Aside from setting out sentrybots on the perimeters and laying out their sleeping bags, there was little more to do than eat and socialize. Jon was used to being an outcast and didn't force himself into any of the conversations. Instead, he sat off to one side and worked at his meal. A few sentences still came to him now and again, and he pretended not to hear them. They were mostly about him, and none were flattering.

Finishing his meal, he bedded down for the night. His fellow troopers did the same not long afterwards, and the camp became quiet except for the faint hum of the sentrybots patrolling around them in the darkness.

Then, dreams came. At first they were nothing extraordinary; just visions of endless tunnels being walked in darkness, and howling winds. They soon morphed into images of the Inner Ear chamber, but the walls were glowing, and pulsing with a strange energy that seemed to emanate from somewhere behind them.

There were also women there, not Marines, but civilians, and they were running through the camp. Their bodies were transparent and they seemed as if they were part of another reality, just one step removed from the world that the troopers were sleeping in. Jon saw one woman clearly and the expression on her face was utter terror.

He tried to reach out to her, but she ran through him as if he was not even there. The sensation as she passed felt as if a warm wind had somehow blown through his body and the vividness of this shocked him.

Suddenly, he heard alarms sounding and realized that someone was shaking him awake. When his eyes fluttered open, he saw that the walls around them *were* glowing, though not as brightly as they had in his dream, and fading rapidly in intensity.

That wasn't all. The troopers were standing around something lying on the floor and Bel Taralynn was having a hurried conversation with the Ops officers up at the main base camp on her com.

"That's correct, ma'am," she was saying, "the bots' proximity alarms went off and then we woke up and found the survivor right here in the middle of camp.'

"No, ma'am she is not conscious and there seems to be something very *strange* about her. Yes, I'll send you a feed right away. Wait one." She pushed her way through the small crowd of troopers and bent over the prone figure so that her suit cam could capture the image.

424

Edging closer, Jon recognized the unconscious woman immediately. She was a member of the missing science team, and one of the few non-Sireeni's in the party, although her name escaped him. What definitely qualified as 'strange' was her skin.

Weird lights, each no longer than a centimeter, were traveling underneath it, giving off a soft, bluish-white glow. They were everywhere, moving in and through the layers of flesh as if they were following some unknown purpose.

And when the paramedic opened her eyes to examine her pupils, there was another surprise waiting. Instead of finding an iris surrounded by sclera, the victim's eyes were featureless and smoldered with the same unearthly light as the motes. A few of the Marines made signs against evil and backed away, but Bel Taralynn was having none of it.

"You and you," she said, singling out two of the more squeamish troopers. "Get a stretcher and help the 'medic prep her for transport. The rest of you break camp. We're taking this survivor up to the base and putting her aboard a shuttle as soon as the weather lifts."

***

The survivor was positively identified as Dr. Shandra n'Aida, an assistant to the still missing team leader. Just as soon as the weather had more or less settled down, the Marine shuttle returned and she was transported up to the *Athena*.

Once aboard, N'Aida was put in a portable isolation chamber and everyone in the S and R team was whisked to the medbay for isolation and examination. Even the shuttle and its crew were quarantined until they received passing marks from Dr. elle'Kaari and her staff.

The glowing lights had disappeared by this point, and N'Aida's eyes had returned to normal, leaving no clues about what had caused the phenomena. What was clear though, was that N'Aida was in a deep coma that resisted all efforts to revive her.

Then N'Aida's s lab results came back. Dr. elle'Kaari reviewed them personally, and as soon as she was certain that they were accurate, she contacted Lilith.

"Commander," she said over a private com channel, "I can't find any reason for my patient's present state. Other than a genetic anomaly, she seems to be perfectly healthy and should be alert and awake."

"An anomaly?" Lilith asked, relieved that nothing had been found that might have posed a danger to her ship and crew. "What kind of anomaly?"

"Ma'am, I've never seen anything like it in all my years of practice. It appears as if half of her DNA structure has been altered. I can't explain why this happened or even recognize what the new genetic pattern is. The Ships Computer has been consulted, but so far it has found no match with any race, or species anywhere. For all intensive purposes, our patient is half human and half...something else...with a lot of blanks left in between."

"I see, Doctor," Lilith replied thoughtfully. "Let me know if you arrive at any definite conclusions. She'll be your patient until we make port at Thenti and I'm sure that the doctors there will appreciate any advance work that you can do for them."

***

That afternoon, Jon came to the medbay for his usual testing session with Dr. elle'Kaari, but the physician was busy analyzing more data that had been gathered from Shandra n'Aida.

"I'll be right with you, Jon," she said, hurrying past him into her office and waving impatiently for an assistant to follow.

With nothing else to do, Jon wandered over to N'Aida's bed. The scientist had not been found to be contagious, and had been released from her isolation chamber. Now, she lay on one of the beds in the central medbay, with only a simple sheet covering her motionless body.

He looked down at her features, wondering as everyone else had since their return, what strange processes the woman had experienced that had put her in such a state and, for the thousandth time, what had happened to her companions. He'd heard the rumors of course; that she was now only half-human, and having seen the bizarre lights dancing in her body, and the eerie glow in her eyes, he fully believed them.

Then an inspiration came to him. The sisters back on New Covenant would be fascinated with a genetic sample from such an odd hybrid, he reflected. It was even possible that the woman's altered DNA would provide the vital components that they needed for the completion of the Great Work.

This was the special calling that Sister n'Avenal had mentioned to him, he realized. God wanted him to serve His church by getting a sample to the Sister-Scientists. He was as sure of this as he was of Mother Mari's love.

Glancing around to make sure that no one was watching, he plucked a few hairs from her head and put them in his pocket. How he would get them back to New Covenant completely eluded him, but he was certain that Jesu and Mari would open the way.

Seconds later, Elle'Kaari came out of her office. "I'm sorry for the delay, Jon, but our patient here has taken up just a bit of my time. Please, come in. We can still spend a few minutes together."

Jon smiled and walked through the light barrier into the doctor's office as casually as he was able. Inwardly, however, he was terrified. The Sisterhood had been born from a plague, and the Regs on the importation of any biological material were stringent. The only thing that separated him from a military courts martial and lengthy imprisonment, was the thin fabric of his uniform pocket.

***

Jon wasn't aware of it, but he was not alone in his interest in obtaining a sample of Dr. Shandra n'Aida's altered gene structure by any means. Shortly after he had left the medbay, Ophida n'Marsi paid her own visit to Dr. elle'Kaari.

"I saw Fa'Teela go by in the passageway," she remarked. "What did he want?"

"Nothing special," the physician replied. "He was reporting for his usual testing session."

"Is he still pretending not to have any talents?" N' Marsi asked.

"We only touched on the incident briefly, and he seemed to be taking the same line that we've been. That it was a fluke and nothing more."

Elle'Kaari handed the priestess a sealed vial of n'Aida's blood, and the woman quickly put it into the folds of her robe.

"Thank you," Ophida replied, "I'll see to it that this makes its way to Thermadon right away. As for fa'Teela, I'd suggest that we play along with his little charade for now. In the meantime, we'll continue to maintain our surveillance and see what more we can learn. The Agency will need all the information that it can get about these psychic neomen before any recommendations can be made to shut the Marionite project down."

Elle'Kaari nodded. "I understand, and I'll keep you updated on any new information we gather. If he stays consistent, I think that we're looking at percentages that would easily qualify him to work as a military grade psi- -if he were a woman of course."

"Of course," Ophida agreed.

With that, they parted company and the priestess hurried back to the temple with her sample, and started making her arrangements to get the vial to Thermadon immediately. What Elle'Kaari didn't know, what she didn't have the security clearance *to know* was that the vial wouldn't be traveling alone. Instead, the notes from the science team's lead researcher would accompany it. One of her other agents among the Marines, had seen to it that they were handed over to her, and that all other copies had been destroyed.

Although Ophida was no theoretical physicist, she had understood enough of the seized material to realize how revolutionary the find on Storm had actually been. If what the scientists had concluded was true, then the entire balance of power in the Far Arm stood on the brink of radical transformation, with the Agency, and by extension herself, basking in the glow.

USSMC Training Facility, 75th Training Battalion, Hella's World, Hecate System, Artemi Elant, United Sisterhood of Suns, 1043.02|27|02:93:65

"Atten-*shun!*"

In perfect unison, Platoon Carli snapped to attention, the crack of their boots sounding across the open parade ground. Sa'Tela walked down the line, looking for even the slightest deviation from the prescribed positions. She did not find any of the recruits lacking however.

"Parade, left!" she ordered.

"Parade, right!"

She marched the group across the parade ground. "Forward!! Your left, your left, your left."

The recruits performed flawlessly, keeping in perfect step with her. All of their daily drills had paid off. Like the rest of them, Kaly was able to change smartly from position to position, and march with the group with movements that had become second nature.

After a few minutes of this, Sa'Tela halted them. "Well, I see we can finally stand like Marines and even march like Marines," she remarked dryly. "Now, we'll see if we can run and maybe even manage to *sound* like Marines. Shall we give it a try, ladies?"

"Ma'am, yes, ma'am!" the platoon replied.

"Parade, right. Step off and reply." Sa'Tela instructed. The DI started off at a slow run, with the platoon keeping formation with her.

"1, 2, 3, 4, Sister-hood Ma-rine Corps!" she chanted, glancing over her shoulder to make sure they were keeping together. "Let me hear you reply, ladies!"

"1, 2, 3, 4, Sister-hood Mar-ine Corps!" the recruits answered.

"Yes! Good and loud!" Sa'Tela said. She started calling the cadence, "I've got a blaster on my back, a helmet on my head and a 30-kee pack! Sound off! 1, 2, 3, 4, Sisterhood Mar-ine Corps!"

"1, 2, 3, 4, Sisterhood Marine Corps!"

"My mommas said that I was crazy. Said I should go and join the Navy! Sound off!"

"1, 2, 3, 4, Sisterhood Marine Corps!"

"I didn't listen to what they said. I went and joined the Marines instead! Sound off!"

"1, 2, 3, 4, Sisterhood Marine Corps!"

"Signed my name the same day and they just watched me march away! Sound off!"

"1, 2, 3, 4, Sisterhood Marine Corps!"

429

"They say the Navy's pretty grand. But when trouble comes, they need our hand! Sound off!"

"1, 2, 3, 4, Sisterhood Marine Corps!"

"We'll fight on land, we'll fight in air. Where we're needed, we'll be there! Sound off!"

"1, 2, 3, 4, Sisterhood Marine Corps!"

"We'll fight in space, we'll fight on the sea. We'll fight wherever there's an enemy! Sound off!"

"1, 2, 3, 4, Sisterhood Marine Corps!"

"I don't know, but I've been told. Walkin' in space is mighty cold. Sound off!"

"1, 2, 3, 4, Sisterhood Marine Corps!"

"But I don't care, just send me there. All I need is a bottle of air! Sound off!"

"1, 2, 3, 4, Sisterhood Marine Corps!"

Only a few weeks earlier, Kaly might have laughed at the cadence Sa'Tela was calling, or at the very least, considered it childish and primitive. Now, as she ran in time with the other recruits and shouted out her replies, it seemed completely appropriate and even energizing. She barely noticed how long and how far the platoon ran that day.

Afterwards they attended a class on infantry weapons, and it centered on Hriss armament in particular. The speaker was a Lieutenant from the base armory, who had been introduced to the platoon as an expert on foreign weapons.

"An unknown general," she began, "from Old Gaia, once remarked, *'Before you ride off to war, know your enemy.'* With this in mind, we will study our primary opponent, the Hriss Warrior, and his weapons."

At the officer's command, a holo appeared on the small stage in the PTS auditorium. It was a fully armed Hriss.

"When the Sisterhood first encountered Hriss ground forces, there was no standard equipment or load out, per se. Instead, what the Warrior carried, or how he was armored, depended on the clan he belonged to, and personal preference," the Lieutenant explained.

"However, as successive wars with the Hriss Empire occurred, their Warriors adopted a more or less uniform layout. This was thought to be in

430

response to the effectiveness of our own standardization. Although there are still some minor equipment and armor variations from clan-sept to clan-sept, the Warrior pictured here is more or less what you can expect to encounter on the modern battlefield."

"Goddess, what a horrible brute," Bel Anny commented under her breath. Kaly silently inclined her head in agreement, hoping that Bel Anny would get the hint and shut up. She didn't want to get in trouble for talking, and she really *wanted* to hear what the officer was telling them. *Know your enemy,* she thought. *Know them and defeat them.* That was definitely the way.

"Physically, the average Hriss male is considerably taller and larger than a woman. The norm is around 200 centimeters. His upper arm strength is also significantly greater than ours. Some Warriors have been reported to have been strong enough to literally rip a woman's arm from its socket."

The Lieutenant let them ponder this mental image for a moment.

"While you may have already mastered some of the basics of hand-to-hand combat," she continued, "unless you are on par with Troop Leader n'Teri, in my opinion, this is one opponent you would be better advised not to grapple with if you can help it.'

"In addition to his overall size and powerful frame, the Hriss comes with a set of retractable fighting claws. These claws are just as sharp as your RB-22's and just as deadly in close quarters."

The holo zoomed in on the creature's right hand and showed the claws in their extended position. The image of Hvaarka out on the training floor, exposing his own claws at N'Teri came to Kaly's mind, and her level of admiration for the DI's prowess rose even higher.

"That's what nature gave to the Hriss. Now, let's look at what technology has brought to the table. Some of you might be aware that the Hriss are not mechanically oriented. Most, if not all of their weaponry, and their technology for that matter, comes from the hands of their slaves, a race we know of as the *Anx'Ma.*'

"The Anx'Ma have worked under the Hriss boot for eons, and what you see here is the result of their research and development efforts. While you might think that this would produce inferior products, you would be wrong; the Anx'Ma work for the Hriss with great enthusiasm. Even after

431

centuries of enslavement, they regard their masters with something akin to love and devotion."

"That's absolutely the *sickest* thing I think I've ever heard," Lena n'Gari remarked with disgust.

"Well, we *are* talking about *Shovelheads*," Bel Anny added.

Kaly gave them both a reproachful glance. "*Shh!* Quiet *down* you two!"

Their exchange alerted Sa'Tela, who had stationed herself in the back corner of the room. The DI started to look in their general direction and Bel Anny and N'Gari wisely kept any further commentary to themselves.

"The Warrior we see here," the Lieutenant was saying, "comes dressed in an energy-pulse resistant armor which is similar to our own fighting suits, although it is not as durable and not as strong as what we wear. Like our armor, the suit has the ability to change colors to match the surrounding terrain and it masks their heat signature with almost 99.99 percent effectiveness. Of course, as you have already learned on the grenade course, it does not mask their bio-signature at all."

The Lieutenant moved over to a display table off to one side of the small stage and pulled back the cover. "Now this" the woman said, picking up a weapon that Kaly instantly recognized from the first night of the Persephone raid, "Is the Hriss equivalent of our Mark-7 Blaster."

The weapon she was holding was larger than the Mark-7 and made of curved polished shapes that glinted evilly in the auditorium spotlights.

"The Hriss call it the *Xkaxa'k't*. However, for convenience's sake, the Corps has designated it the XK-74. The XK-74 is on par with the Mark 7, but has a smaller and less powerful battery, with a shorter life span.'

"It also lacks any form of psiever targeting augmentation which brings up an interesting point. The Hriss do not possess psiever technology in *any* form. Instead, they rely on more primitive computer-aided aiming systems, or simply on their own individual hand-eye skills. There have been some reports that the Anx'Ma have shown an interest now and again in psiever technology, but Hriss cultural and religious values have prevented them from adopting anything involving the use of bioplasmic energy. The only exception is Nullspace travel, which the Hriss leave to the Anx'Ma to handle.'

432

"Apparently, the Hriss regard it both as dishonorable and a sacrilege to augment the body with bioelectronic and bioplasmic devices. Personally, I thank the Goddess that the Hriss are so devout. It makes them poorer shots, and much easier targets to hit."

This elicited some laughter from the recruits.

"Now, to compensate for its deficiencies, the XK-74 not only fires an energy burst, but also comes equipped with a chemical slug thrower or a grenade launcher." The Lieutenant indicated the paired barrels in the blaster's snout.

"The grenades it fires are similar to our GSG-20's in that they are also hunter-seekers, but they home in on heat and scent signatures from sources like sweat and human blood. Like the GSG-20's, they can sense and travel up to a kilometer to their target. The slugs on the other hand, are shorter ranged ordnance, and are really intended for close quarters. Don't let that lull you into any false sense of confidence though. They're made of depleted atomic materials and are designed to pierce fighting suit armor, which they do with ease."

Then the Lieutenant put down the blaster and produced another weapon. This time it was a curved sword. "This is another Hriss favorite. They call it the *Akskakt't*, which roughly translated, means the 'Sword of Honor'."

"A Warrior's stature in their society can be gauged by the size of their sword. *Akskakt't* range from what we would consider to be daggers to the full sized version we have here. They regard the swords as such important symbols of their personal honor that Hriss have been known to commit suicide with grenades rather than allow them to be captured by an enemy. Like our bayonets, the *Akskakt't* is generally employed as a weapon of last resort.'

"But it is also used in ritual duels between Hriss clan-members, or for executing prisoners who they consider to be of high rank, and therefore worthy of death by it. And that, ladies, concludes my lecture."

Sa'Tela walked down to the stage and faced everyone. "All right, you have half an hour of free time which you'd better use for PT or something like it. *Dis*-missed!"

433

CSS *C-JUDI-GO*, Nemesis, Rahdwa System, Thalestris Elant, United Sisterhood of Suns 1043.02|27|07:96:29

The first thing that struck Maya when she gazed down upon Nemesis was how *green* it was. The planet hung in space like a giant emerald, swathed in thick bands of clouds. The only exception to the seemingly endless rainforests were several oceans bisecting one giant continent, a few deserts, and a jagged mountain range that ran its length almost from pole to pole like the protruding spine of some extinct animal. From upside, there were very few signs that the world was even inhabited.

Here and there, she thought she caught a glimpse or two of a monorail track, or a building, but the cloud cover and the forest canopy conspired to make these sightings doubtful at best. A classic Bio World, the inhabitants of Nemesis had done their utmost to minimize the impact of humanity on it. It was only when the *JUDI* had entered the atmosphere, and begun its descent, that she was able to pick out the landing area, and the resort that they were headed for.

"Isn't it just awesome?" Felecia asked, squeezing her hand. "What an untamed place it seems."

"Indeed," Sarah remarked from her station, "The Nemesians pride themselves on the preservation of their environment. As well they should; Nemesis is home to many of the drugs and medicines that the rest of us depend upon. Without their forests intact, many of the cures that we now take for granted would be completely unknown."

"Yes, I have heard that most of their industrial facilities are underground," Felecia replied.

"That they are," Bel Lissa said. "Except for the Shadow Lake Lodge and a few other locations, it's illegal to build permanent structures above ground or to disturb the rain-forest. Even their logging operations are designed for minimal impact. They only pick certain trees and fly them straight out by hoverlifters rather than risk damaging the undergrowth in any way."

"That is amazing! Being a big-city girl, it is hard to imagine a world without tall buildings," Felecia admitted. "Even Zommerlaand has a few

434

large cities. Nemesis is certainly singular in its wildness. You know, I have never met a Nemesian before."

Maya's knowledge of them came from Skylaar, and her teacher had shared only a little about her birth planet and its unique culture. She found herself wondering what the native Nemesian women were like in comparison.

"It's quite an experience," Bel Lissa told Felecia. "They're a tough, independent breed, built for survival in the forest, which is no mean feat. Most of the successful life forms on Nemesis evolved as carnivores. In fact, they're considered to be some of the most dangerous creatures on any planet in the Sisterhood."

"My, it does sound like a terribly fierce place," Felecia said. "Nothing at all like Thermadon."

"With respect, I would tend to disagree, Lady Felecia," Sarah interjected. "Thermadon has its own *special* dangers that are just as dire. It simply conceals them within another kind of jungle."

"Yes," Felecia conceded. "I suppose it does at that."

The *JUDI* had entered the atmosphere by this stage and was making its descent. The jungle rose up around them and rushed by, and Felecia pointed excitedly at their destination. It was displayed on the ship's sitscreens.

"Look at those trees!" she exclaimed. "They're so huge, they must be centuries upon centuries old! And that lake! Have you ever seen anything so beautiful?" She gasped with childlike wonder and squeezed Maya's hand.

It *was* beautiful, Maya thought as she looked at the scene.

Shadow Lake Lodge was nestled at the edge of an ancient forest, overlooking a long dark lake. The lodge itself was a gigantic structure, constructed mainly of native wood, but the trees nearby made it seem like a doll house in comparison. They soared up into the sky to fantastic heights and the forest that they created was a thing shrouded in darkness, a primeval wall of ancient mystery, and silence.

The lake, for which the lodge had been named, was no less enigmatic than the trees that bordered it. Its surface was as flat and as featureless as a mirror made from smoked glass, and Maya could only imagine what

435

strange creatures the forest and the lake conspired to hide within their respective depths.

The *JUDI* touched down a minute later. When everyone filed out of the vessel, the rich earth scents of the forest around them, combined with real wood-smoke coming from a dozen fireplaces within the lodge, met their nostrils.

To Maya, the air seemed richer than what she was used to breathing, almost as if it were something that she could consume and gain nourishment from. Like anyone, she had heard that women sometimes came to Nemesis when they were very ill, and now she could appreciate why. The purity of the place was undeniable.

Maybe the Nemesians have it a' right, she thought as she stepped out across the concrete landing pad. Maybe a Bio World like Nemesis wasn't 'taking things too far,' as some women tended to believe. Maybe it was simply heading in the right direction. It was suddenly very easy for her to understand why the Biosync Movement had been such a powerful political force, and why groups like the Bio Action Army were so fanatical.

"An astute observation," Sarah said under her voice. "Although the Bio Action Army might be our enemy, it is always wise to see the world through an opponent's perspective to know their hearts. If you know an enemies heart, you know them, and that is the first stage in overcoming them."

"Yes," Maya replied. "I see what you mean."

"But also bear in mind, that despite all of this," Sarah added, gesturing at the forest around them, "what it is they would destroy just as casually and as ruthlessly as the terraformers that they hate so much. The fact that they are so willing to take human life is where their ideas fall short and they betray their own ideals. Hypocrisy is always the pitfall of the fanatic, however noble their cause."

Members of the Lodge staff had come out to meet them by this point, and their leader walked up to the Senatrix.

"Sa'la jantildamé," she said, bowing "Welcome to the Shadow Lake Lodge. We are honored to have you here as our guests. The other party that you were expecting has already arrived."

The Senatrix returned the bow. "The honor is all ours. Thank you for accommodating us on such short notice."

"Thank you, Senatrix," the woman gushed. "Rest assured that you and your guests will have all the privacy that you require. We pride ourselves here on our discretion. I also trust you will be pleased with our conference facilities. Our lodge may look rustic, but I assure you that our amenities are state of the art. Now, if we can show you and your associates to your quarters?"

"Please, lead the way," the Senatrix replied.

**

The interior of the lodge was a tribute to a style that was uniquely Nemesian. Its walls were created from huge timbers cleverly laid together and sealed off from the elements. Large colorful carpets made from local plant fibers covered the polished wood floors, and light was admitted into the enormous building from simple windows made of plain glass and polished wood.

True to their hostesses' claim, the rustic setting cleverly concealed all of the services of modern technology under its wooden skin. When Maya dropped her flight bag in her room and thought about the lights, they came on, illuminating the space from a quaint-looking lamp that shone with a very realistic holographic flame.

The chamber itself was dominated by a large four posted bed, which, like everything else, was made of wood, but in this case, it was intricately carved with floral patterns and decorative images of strange, fierce-looking creatures that were undoubtedly native to the planet's rainforests. Even though they were merely images, none of them looked like anything she would have wanted to encounter face to face, but in their own way, they had a certain wild beauty to them that she had to admire.

She sat down on the edge of the soft mattress and looked out of the room's single window to the forest beyond. It was open and the gentle draft coming in to her room brought with it not only the scents of the woodland, but its sounds as well.

The planet's sun was just beginning to set in the west and the darkening wall of trees was coming alive with strange noises. Odd clicks and howls and occasionally something that sounded very close to a child crying, came to her ears over the breeze as the night-animals of the jungle began their nocturnal prowling just beyond the Lodge's impeller field fencing. She listened to them for a while, trying to imagine their sources and then feeling a chill, got up and closed the window.

As she returned to her luggage to begin unpacking, a holo of Sharra appeared in the center of the room, projected from a cleverly concealed holojector set in what she had initially dismissed as a decorative polished sphere of translucent stone.

"Hello, Maya," the Security Chief said, "I hope I wasn't interrupting anything, but I wanted to let you and your crewmates know what our schedule for tomorrow is. The Senatrix will be meeting with the Rampart leaders at 03:75 hours at the Modrel Cultural Center, which is adjacent to the lodge in the east wing.'

"She has specifically asked that you escort Lady Felecia while she conducts this meeting. I suggest that you think of taking her to the museum, which is next door to the Cultural Center. She might find that of interest. In the meantime, dinner will be held tonight in the lodge's main dining room at 07:50 sharp. Attire is informal."

Maya nodded.

"There is one other thing," the image added, "If you have one, keep your needlegun on you and stay alert. Things seem quiet for the moment, but there's no telling if there will be another attempt on Lady Felecia or the Senatrix."

"Yes," Maya replied, "I will."

Shara smiled wryly. "Good. I thought as much."

***

That night, after dinner, everyone headed back to their staterooms for bed and an early start in the morning. Maya was trying without success to fall asleep, when there was a soft knock at the door. She grabbed up her needlegun and walked over to it.

"Who is it?" she asked.

"It's me," she heard Felecia whisper, "Let me in." Maya admitted her and closed the door.

"I was waiting for a chance to get away from everyone," Felecia said. "The security people have been watching me like *aerhawks*, and I never thought I would get a single moment alone." Then she saw the needlegun in Maya's hand. "What's that for?" Felecia asked with an innocent concern.

"Nothing," Maya lied, "just a habit I picked up." The deception worked, and Felecia's expression changed from unease to affection as Maya laid the weapon down on the night table.

"Is that a *smuggler's* habit?" Felecia asked. "I suppose that a pirate *would* have to be just a little more cautious about a knock at the door than most other women."

She undid her hair and came into Maya's arms. "I seem to recall a promise I made to you back on the ship that I never got the chance to fulfill," she said with a sensuous smile. "And I have felt absolutely *terrible* about it ever since."

"Well," Maya replied with mock concern. "We can't have *that* hanging over your head, now can we?" Then she kissed Felecia deeply and pulled her down onto the bed.

CHAPTER 13

The *Athena* returned to Thenti and when the ship had put into orbit, the entire crew, with the exception of those required for the ship's basic operations, was granted a brief shore leave. It was limited to the territorial capital, and only for one standard day; basically time enough to see Dr. Shandra n'Aida safely ensconced in the local hospital.

Jesu and Mari had heard Jon's prayers.

Praising their names, he wasted no time in getting to his rack and retrieving the hair samples from their hiding place. He had sealed them in a simple plastic bag, and he tucked this into an inside pocket of his fatigues and then joined the rest of his platoon at the shuttle bay.

As fate had ordained, his shuttle was also the same one assigned to carry Dr. n'Aida downside. While this translated into a longer delay at the port as she and her escort of Navy medics was processed through, it also meant that he received less individual scrutiny from the customs officers himself.

With the exception of their Inoculars, the usual scans for biological hazards and contraband were drastically truncated, and any anomalies that *were* detected were simply attributed to their strange passenger. This and the fact that the baggie he carried was partially masked by his own body readings got it and him through the port without registering any alarms. Despite a second glance from the customs officers because of his gender, he walked into the main terminal of the spaceport unmolested.

He quickly made his way to an omni, hoping that his incredible luck would hold. And when he searched the city listings, he found what he had been praying for. It was an entry for one Mari n'Deo.

N'Deo didn't really exist, not as a person at least. It was a name from the *Revelation of Mari*; Mother Mari's formal name in Standard, 'Mari, daughter of God'.

To Jon and any other missionary, this was a clear sign that one of the Faithful was working undercover in Thenti to convert the pagan masses. Depending on the elant, the penalty for such noble work ranged from simple fines, to deportation back to New Covenant, or imprisonment. There were even tales of beatings, and missionaries who had simply disappeared in police custody, never to be heard from again.

In the Sisterhood, spreading God's word could be a very risky calling. Despite these hazards though, a Sister had taken up residence in the city and had left this sign for someone like him to follow. Hands trembling with excitement, Jon crossed himself and called the number.

A woman answered with a somewhat shocked expression when she saw him on her screen. "Blessings," he said, reciting the simple code he had been taught. "I am new to this world. Can you guide me?"

"W-Why, yes. I will point the way," the woman said, giving him the counter-reply. "Come to my shop on Epsilon Street." She supplied him with the directions and cut their connection.

Jon left the terminal and walked out into the large complex of domes that made up Thenti City. His movement through the town was accomplished by negotiating a network of moviwalks, tubeways, elevators and mini-trains, but he managed to stay on course through the maze until at last, he arrived at the block where the shop was located.

That was when a police hovercar landed next to the moviwalk he was traveling on. At a signal from the car, the moving sidewalk immediately came to a gentle stop and two Thentian policewomen got out. Jon felt as if his heart was going to stop beating as they walked up.

It wasn't the first time he'd been stopped by the local police. In fact, this was a fairly regular occurrence, given his strange appearance and the relative rarity of neomen throughout the Sisterhood. But the presence of the hair sample in his pocket made this particular event a new and terrifying experience. For the first time, he genuinely had something to hide, and he found himself saying a silent, desperate prayer to Jesu and Mari, and all of the saints and martyrs, that the officers would only ask him a few questions, and not subject him to a physical search.

"You there," the first officer said as her partner took up a guarding position off to his left and behind him. "Neo! Come here."

Jon obeyed without protest, hoping that the kaaper wouldn't detect his nervousness and become any more suspicious than she already was.

"What are you doing here?" the woman demanded. "What's your business? Do you understand me, Neo?"

"Yes, ma'am, I do," Jon replied. "I'm on a one-day shore leave from the *Pallas Athena*. She just put into orbit upside. I'm on my way to a local shop to buy myself a guidebook."

"*You're* on shore leave?" the officer retorted disbelievingly. "*You're* with the Navy?"

"The Marines, ma'am," he answered. "If you scan me, you'll confirm my service number and assignment."

"Yeah, sure," the woman behind him said doubtfully. "More like someone dressed you up in that costume as some kind of sick joke."

"Now, Maarva," the first officer said wagging a finger at her, "he might actually be some kind of pet, a mascot. We had a pet *scavvas* on the ship I served on. But we'll see one way or the other."

The blue light of the officer's data monocle played over him for a second. "I'll be damned by the Goddess and my soul set to wander," she declared. "Sh--*he's* a Marine all right."

"Wait," her partner interjected "Now, I know what's going on here. He's that Neo freak that was on the news a few weeks back. He's the one they're trying out as a test to see if Neos can make the grade."

The first woman spat on the ground. "What's the service coming to? Goddess blast it!" Then she addressed Jon. "All right *Neo*, your story checks out--for now. Just the same, we'll send word to your CO that we stopped and questioned you for suspicious activity."

"Yes, of course, ma'am," Jon replied.

"And you keep your nose clean here on Thenti, you hear me? I'd love to hook you up just out of loyalty to the Corps. Do *we understand* each other?"

Jon nodded meekly as the two policewomen got back into their 'car and flew off. Then he suppressed a shudder. If they had taken things any further...

Jon didn't finish the thought, and quickly moved on. He wanted to gain as much distance as he could before they decided to come back and question him some more.

But he reached his destination without further incident. The shop was small, and specialized in offbeat realies, holovids, and even a few genuine books. The holosign over the entrance read: "The Guiding Stars" and three four-pointed stars accompanied the fanciful lettering. To the uninitiated, they were only decorations. To the Faithful though, these stars represented the Father, His Son and Mother Mari. He had reached a place of safety.

The woman he had spoken with was waiting for him inside the deserted store, behind the counter. Jon knew better than to take any chances though, even at this stage. He made a fist with his right hand, and placed his thumb over the top of it, so that only the tip extended into space, and held this a little ways out from his right side.

It was the traditional sign that one made before making the Cross of Blessing, and the woman noticed it. Cautiously, she placed her right hand on the counter, and duplicated the gesture. Had she placed her thumb inside her fist, and let it protrude between her fore and index fingers instead, it would have made the sign against evil, and warned him that they were being listened to, or watched. For a little while at least, they were alone and free to speak with one another openly.

"Greetings, Sister," he said. "I have something that must be sent back to New Covenant as quickly as possible." He took out the plastic bag and passed it over to her.

She took it from him without asking any questions and gave him a copy of *The Stone People* in return. The hologuide was a compendium of the myths and legends surrounding the odd geology of Thenti, and a general guidebook.

"You'll need this to make the reason for your visit a convincing one," she informed him. "The local authorities might be watching the store. We've had word that one of our flock may have lapsed back into her pagan ways and I can't ignore the possibility of danger."

"I understand, Sister," Jon replied. "May Jesu and Mari watch over you as they have watched over me."

He wasn't alone when he left the store and made his way back to the port, but he also wasn't surprised. His talent had revealed that someone, probably with Ships' Security, was following him all the way back to the port. He only hoped that the shop owner, whatever her real name was, would move quickly and succeed in the mission he had given her. As he re-boarded the shuttle, he made a small, discreet sign of blessing, and prayed for her.

443

***

The *Athena* and her sister vessels headed out from Thenti late that evening and made an immediate transit into Null, coming out above Persephone. There, they took up station for another day, giving a company of Marine engineers the chance to go downside with their equipment to set up an improved anti-space defense system. Once the engineers were downside, and had started to settle in, the battle group resumed its journey and made for the furthest star system in the Sagana Territory, Phantasma.

Lilith was particularly excited by their destination. Although Phantasma 9-A was uninhabited, the planet was the site of Dr. t'Sharalese's alleged find of Old Gaian artifacts, and she was eager to visit the dig herself and see it first-hand.

Before she would be able to avail herself of this pleasure though, duty had its demands. Phantasma was also at the edge of an unclaimed zone of space between the Sisterhood and the Hriss Empire, and the area was the perfect location to drop off replacement surveillance probes.

In the raid on Persephone, many of the original probes had been damaged or destroyed, and the *Athena's* mission was to substitute them with stealthier, improved devices, and also to monitor any transmissions coming from inside of Hriss space. Eavesdropping missions weren't the most glamorous affairs, but they were vital to the defense effort. Even the most trivial sounding communication could have tremendous strategic value. Not that that made this duty any less tedious.

While the ship headed towards open space and its first jump into Null, she promised herself that once they were done with their spying, they would return to Phantasma, if only for a few hours. In the meantime, she resigned herself to a long and lackluster shift, and settled herself into her command chair.

The hours passed slowly, with the battle group making short transits through Null, dropping listening devices, returning to Null, and repeating the process at another spot. Even the Indwellers seemed bored by it all, and only once did one even deign to make a brief appearance before apparently losing interest in them, and turning away.

Finally, when the probes had been positioned, the *Athena* took up station at the first of its listening posts. This was a point in space that was distinguished only by its coordinates and the presence of a small, non-descript star system nearby. While the ships opened up their electronic ears to listen in on the conversations of their enemies, Lilith decided it was finally time for lunch and retired to her office.

She had just ordered it up, when Caleda bel Tridis from Navcom called her. "Commander?" she said. "We've located some very interesting space debris that you might want to take a look at."

"Oh?" Lilith asked. With so many spacefaring races inhabiting the Far Arm, space junk was an unwanted, but ever-present byproduct. Out in interstellar space however, stellar rubbish was comparatively rare. And Lilith also knew that her Senior Helmswoman wouldn't have bothered her about it unless she had found this particular piece of debris worth examining.

"Yes, ma'am," Bel Tridis answered. "It looks like it's part of one of our ships."

Lilith put down her spork.

"I ran a metallurgical analysis of the object, and it came back with a 97% confidence that it was manufactured in the Sisterhood. The alloys all match what we use."

Lilith nodded. "Send it over."

A holo came up over her desk. It displayed a curved piece of metal, half a meter in length and a quarter wide, with jagged edges, tumbling end over end. The object was travelling on a trajectory that was taking it away from a star system which the *Athena's* charts labeled as HSL-48 2124A. According to the data, it had been in space for the last 20 standard years.

"I see," Lilith said. "Do we know what kind of ship this came from?"

"Yes, ma'am," Caleda returned. "I had the Ships Computer run a comparison, and there's an 80% confidence that it's part of the cowling for an in-system drive unit from a Model 3 SVER ship. It also looks like it was hit by some kind of explosive."

Lilith nodded soberly. The *Servis a Vaste Éteine Reshersche,* the Long Range Exploratory Service, specialized in hunting for habitable worlds, and making first contact with other races. It was a dangerous venture, calling for a special kind of woman, and many SVER ships had gone into uncharted space never to be heard from again. The SVER even had its own monument in Thermadon dedicated to all of the missing crews. New stars were added to it every year.

"Do we have any idea which particular ship this was?" she asked.

"Yes, ma'am," Caleda said. "I checked the SVER records and there were several vessels that came through this quadrant during that time period. Only one of them went missing though. It was the USS *Atalanta*."

Another image popped up, showing the vessel itself, along with its particulars. Fifteen women, three officers, and the rest cross-trained sailor/scientists.

Lunch was over. "I'll be right out," Lilith said.

When she exited her office and retook her command chair, she saw that Caleda had already anticipated her next set of questions. The main sitscreen was lit up with a diagram, showing HSL-48 2124A and all of its satellites.

It proved to be a G2V type star, a yellow star like Sol in the Old Gaian system. But unlike Sol, it had only three small worlds in attendance. The only other remarkable feature was that the second world was a T-type planet, making it very similar to Old Gaia herself. It was exactly the kind of thing that would have attracted a SVER ship to come in for a closer look.

And they probably ran into a Hriss anti-ship missile for all their troubles, she thought grimly. Being as close as they were to the Imperium, that much was almost a certainty.

Survivors however, were not. Not after 20 years, and not if the Hriss had been involved. Crash landing on a Hriss-controlled world was the modern equivalent of ancient mariners washing ashore on an island filled with headhunters.

Lilith also knew what the Navy would expect of her. The battle group would have to make an attempt to locate the crew, and if the Hriss were occupying the little star system as she suspected they were, their presence would have to be noted in the *Athena's* surveillance log. Even though HSL-48 2124A wasn't within the Sisterhood's boundaries, it was still close enough to the Sagana Territory to merit some concern.

She called Katrinn up to her chair.

"A habitable world, then? *And* a missing crew?" Katrinn asked, just as intrigued as she was.

"Yes, it would appear so," Lilith replied pensively. "And probably crawling with Hriss. Nav? Are we picking up any energy signatures in that system?"

Again, Caleda was ready with the answers. It was one of the qualities that Lilith appreciated the most in her senior officers.

"Ma'am," the senior tech informed her. "We have warp trails going in and out of the system. The newest one is 6 months old. We also have energy readings coming from several of the moons, and from the second planet. Nothing large, but they're there."

Lilith's eyebrows rose. "*Warp* trails?" Like the Sisterhood, the Hriss used gravitronic drives for in-system travel, and Nullspace transits for long distances. So did the T'lakskalans and everyone else. Warp-based drive hadn't been used for centuries by anyone, anywhere in the Far Arm.

"How about that?" Katrinn said, clucking her tongue. "Well, Lily, at least we can't say that we're bored anymore."

"No, we can't" Lilith agreed. Whoever or whatever was inhabiting HSL-48 2124A were not Hriss. Instead, they were an unknown. The only certain thing was, that at one time at least, the natives had been hostile. It was the only explanation for the object that they had found.

A first contact gone wrong, she wondered? It was certainly possible, and this added another layer of responsibility to her shoulders. Now, the battle group would need to gather enough information for the SVER to conduct a follow up, or to provide them with the justification to avoid the area all together.

"Helm." Lilith said, "Take us in for a closer look. Full stealth mode, and launch probes as we finish the transit."

The *battle group* went into Null, and when they came out again, they were at the very limits of the little star system. A group of probes were launched immediately.

Once they arrived at their destinations, the spy devices went to work and began sending their data back to their mother ships. What they reported was surprising. There was a group of anti-ship missile batteries in orbit around the second world, but they were not Hriss devices.

"Well," Katrinn remarked. "I haven't seen anything like those things since the Academy history classes. They look like pre-plague GSF equipment."

"Indeed," Lilith agreed. The batteries were at least two hundred years out of date. And while they posed a formidable threat to a careless exploratory ship, they were no match for the battle group.

Meanwhile, more data was coming in. The probes had spotted multiple buildings on the surface of the planet, surrounded by cultivated fields. There was, in fact, a small town, and near it was a com array. Like the anti-ship batteries, this too was an antique.

Seeing all this, Lilith ordered the probes to make a cautious descent into the atmosphere. When they were at 39,000 meters, the machines discharged a cluster of microbots.

The tiny machines descended and over-flew the settlement. The pictures that they sent back depicted a well-ordered community, complete with rows of trees and open green areas that had to be for common gatherings. But the most surprising images of all were of the inhabitants themselves. They were clearly human, and they were moving about their business as if they were completely unaware of the surveillance taking place.

Lilith sat forwards in her chair and steepled her fingers, considering this development. Then she turned to face the Ship's Advocate, who had come up from her office with Mearinn d'Rann to watch the proceedings.

"Now I am *definitely* interested, Advocate. It seems that we have some kind of human colony down there. If I'm not mistaken, they appear to be a mixture of... what are those? Neomen *and* women? There are even children running about! At a guess, I'd say that this is some kind of renegade Marionite colony."

"If that's so," Katrinn offerred, "then they are still technically part of the Sisterhood, and should have applied for permits to colonize. We'd know about them."

"Which a few minutes ago, we did not," Lilith observed. "We also have the matter of the *Atalanta* to consider. Those batteries might only be for self-defense, but I'd wager that they were responsible for its destruction.

If the explosives in their warheads match what we read off that debris, they'll have to answer for that.'

No one disagreed.

"I also believe that we have an obligation to inspect the colony," Lilith continued, "and make certain that they are in compliance with at least *some* of the Colonial Laws." She looked over at the Advocate, who nodded her agreement.

"There's only one thing about all this that bothers me," Katrinn said. "It's the level of their technology. You'd think that even a renegade colony would still want to enjoy *some* of the benefits of the modern universe."

"That's where history might provide us with an explanation," Mearinn d'Rann interjected. "I would urge you all to recall the example of the Returnals, and the clan-based society that they established on Nemesis. By rejecting most of modern technology, they had hoped to return humankind to a more 'perfect' state of existence by adopting an aboriginal lifestyle. You might also recall that on Old Gaia, there were religious communities in the North American continent who forswore anything that post-dated the 19th century."

"The Amish," Katrinn responded.

"Precisely," Mearinn replied. "And these groups maintained their antiquated lifestyle right up to the MARS epidemic. Perhaps this is a similar situation."

"I've never heard of the Marionites taking things quite this far," Lilith countered. "Unless this is some break-away sect that we don't know about. And it still doesn't explain the warp signatures that we detected. Even if these people are not accepting supplies from an outside source, *someone* has been visiting them who is just as old fashioned, and I'd like to know who they are."

"I can't disagree with you, Commander," Mearinn conceded. "There are some anomalies here that tend to weaken my theory considerably."

Lilith smiled at this admission. Mearinn was an excellent teacher, and it had always been difficult to contradict her arguments.

"We'll know one way or the other soon enough," she said. "Helmsmistress, take us in, and stand ready to jam those batteries. They might be out of date, but I don't fancy any trouble from them."

449

The battle group began to move and the probes continued to send back information. What they reported next changed the entire situation dramatically. A more detailed scan of the settlement picked up psiever signals. These matched the identities of the crewmembers of the lost *Atalanta* exactly. Despite the odds, the women were still alive.

Lilith ordered up a holomap of the settlement and summoned Col. Lislsdaater to the bridge.

"Colonel," she said when the woman arrived, "when we get within range I want you to send a Marauder team down to the surface. Their primary mission will be to conduct a rescue operation of the *Atalanta's* crew. Once those women have been safely secured, we'll send down a security detachment, and sort all of this out with the colony leaders."

"Yes, ma'am," the officer replied. "It will be my pleasure."

"Yes. I'm sure that it will be," Lilith agreed dryly. "I have one other stipulation, Colonel. Because this is a Marionite colony, I want you to include the neoman in your team. He might prove to be a valuable asset."

Lislsdaater started to object, but stopped herself. As much as she disliked the idea, her superior's logic was unarguable. "Yes, ma'am."

"Thank you, Colonel," Lilith said. She faced her senior officers. "Now, ladies, let's get on with this."

USSMC Training Facility, 75th Training Battalion, Hella's World, Hecate System, Artemi Elant, United Sisterhood of Suns, 1043.02|29|05:41:88

"Good afternoon, ladies," Troop Leader n'Teri said as she walked across the training mat. "Today we will work on some more of our hand-to-hand combat skills."

The diminutive blond snapped her fingers and Hvaarka entered the gym, accompanied by his usual armed escort. N'Teri spoke with him briefly in Hriss'ka and then turned back to address the class.

"As you can see, Hvaarka has returned to assist us in our lessons. Hopefully, you've had the chance to practice some of the moves we've been working on, because today I want to see some successful matches between you and him."

450

"Oh, goddess," Bel Anny whispered, "and here it looked like things were going so well."

"We'll see," Kaly replied, her eyes narrowing as she met the creature's pitiless gaze. "He can't always win."

"Yeah" Bel Anny agreed facetiously. "We'll compare notes in medbay."

N'Teri called up the first recruit, Bel Haariet. The woman took her place on the mat, but Kaly could almost smell her uncertainty and her fear. Unsurprisingly, the Hriss made short work of her.

"Confidence," n'Teri said as Bel Haariet was helped over to a bench to recover. "Be confident in what you know and work with that. Your opponent will always try to undermine what you know about yourself and use this to your disadvantage. Recruit n'Deena, you seem to be eager to engage our guest. Have at it."

Kaly walked out onto the mat and faced Hvaarka, who greeted her with a low growl.

You won't psych me out, you fek! she thought, meeting his stare squarely. She was determined not to let the creature unsettle her.

Abruptly, Hvaarka charged at her with a hideous roar. It should have frightened her, but instead, she called on the phrase she'd heard in bayonet drill; *"Remember what we are fighting for!"* With a snarl of her own, Kaly stood her ground, and waited for Hvaarka to close the distance between them.

The Hriss struck at her and Kaly attempted to block him, but he surprised her with a backhanded blow to her face. The girl fell backwards with the impact, but as she hit the mat, she went with her momentum and managed to roll out and regain her footing.

Hvaarka attacked again, attempting to sweep her legs out from under her, but Kaly had the advantage of speed, and danced back and away from his feet. The Hriss responded by lunging forwards, his arms spread wide to engulf her.

Kaly saw her chance and struck the creature in the face with her palm, putting all of her body weight into the blow. The Hriss stumbled backwards, stunned and clearly surprised by this turn of events.

She immediately pressed her advantage with a solid kick to his midsection and Hvaarka doubled over. When he rose, he bared his fighting claws. There was a collective gasp in the gym, and the military policewomen started to draw their side arms, but n'Teri stayed them.

The enraged Hriss charged at Kaly, intent on eviscerating her, but slashed at thin air as she stepped sideways and away from him. He kept at her, trying to reach her with his claws, but she moved away from them, and when an opening occurred, she dove into another roll.

This time she came up behind him. With all the power she had in her, she spun into a hammer blow to the back of Hvaarka's skull, the only place where she knew that the bone turned into soft cartilage. The effect was instantaneous and dramatic; the creature flopped forwards, completely unconscious.

"Stop exercise!" N'Teri shouted. Kaly stepped back to let the MP's and the DI examine the creature, and then a Medic joined them. The woman scanned the Hriss, and administered something to him in a hypo that brought him back to awareness.

As the military policewomen got him to his feet, it was obvious that he was in no shape for any further matches that day.

"Well," N'Teri commented as she watched them lead Hvaarka away. "We seem to have concluded our lesson rather abruptly. Well done, N'Deena. *Very* well done."

***

Platoon Carli got a break from PT that afternoon and attended another class instead. This time the lecture was on the Marine uniform. Kaly thought it was rather silly that an entire class was devoted to the subject, but she did her best to appear interested, and awake.

Their instructor turned out to be none other than Troop Leader n'Teri. The DI had changed out of her sweats and entered the classroom dressed in her Class 'A' uniform; a bright red tunic encrusted with service ribbons, and black pants with a single white stripe running down each leg. Kaly was so accustomed to seeing her in dull grey fatigues, that it took her a moment to recognize the DI.

N'Teri took up a position in front of the seated recruits and smiled at them. "Back on Old Gaia," she began, "one of the proudest moments that a Marine had was when they were issued their Class 'A' uniform. Even though the uniform has changed over the centuries, the pride remains. It is, for everyone who sees it, the very embodiment of the mission of the Corps, and its history, and those who are privileged to wear it are the guardians of that sacred obligation."

"If you pass basic, you will have the honor of wearing this uniform, and the honor of representing the Corps. It will be your responsibility to see to it that dishonor is never brought to it by your actions, or inactions. Now, let's discuss its symbolism. Can anyone tell me what my red tunic stands for?"

Hana n'Keera raised her hand. At the beginning of Basic, she had been one of the troublemakers, but lately, she had distanced herself from Bel Jeera and the others, and started to come around. "Ma'am, the red in your tunic represents the blood shed in defense of the Sisterhood, ma'am."

"And?"

"Ma'am, this recruit does not know, ma'am," N'Keera admitted.

"Well, it looks like someone will need to spend some more time with their Grey Book." N'Teri remarked dryly. "You are partly correct: red does stand for the sacrifices that we've made, but it also stands for the sacrifice that we are *prepared* to make. Our mission *never* ends. Anyone care to venture an idea about the black in my collar and pants?"

Lena n'Gari volunteered. "Ma'am, the black symbolizes both space and the soil of all the planets in the Sisterhood, ma'am."

"Very good!" N'Teri said. "And the white in my piping and in the stripe on my pant legs?"

"Ma'am, the white stands for our honor and the purity of our mission, ma'am," N'Gari supplied.

"Well done, hatchie," N'Teri said. "Now, does anyone here remember the meaning behind the insignia on my collar?"

Kaly responded. "Ma'am, the sun, the sword and the starship represent the suns of the Sisterhood worlds, the sword of our unwavering defense, and the starship, our mobility."

"Perfect. Just as if Senior Troop Leader sa'Tela had recited it," N'Teri said with an approving smile. "But what do all these symbols mean together? How can we sum it all up?"

The class remained silent, so she supplied the answer. "We can bring it all together in the Marine Motto: '*Sorele, Sacrif, Oneur,*' Sisterhood, Sacrifice, Honor. If we understand these basic principles, we are a long ways towards becoming Marines."

"What about 'Sisterhood'? What does that mean?" N'Teri asked them. "Anyone? N'Gari, care to give it a try?"

"Sisterhood means...our fellow women and the nation," N'Gari replied.

"Partly correct, hatchie. What *else* does it mean? N'Keera?"

N'Keera thought about this for a moment, and then answered with some hesitation. "The Corps?"

"Yes!" N'Teri exclaimed. "It also means our sister Marines. Not bad, N'Keera, even if you were guessing. Ladies, for us sisterhood is *not* just a word. It's a commitment.'

"All right, who would like to tell me what we mean by 'Sacrifice'? And don't let me hear you repeating what I said earlier. I want your own thoughts." N'Teri looked around the room, and then pointed at Enggredsdaater. "You, what does it mean?"

"Ma'am, zat means zat ve are villing to give up anything for za Sisterhood," the Zommerlaandar replied.

"Yes it does, including our lives," N'Teri nodded. "And now, what about 'Honor'? What is Honor? N'Deena, any ideas?"

"Honor is..." Kaly began. Then she realized that she'd never really thought about what honor was exactly. "Ma'am, this recruit is not certain," she finally said, "but I think that Honor is doing what's right and sticking to it no matter what."

N'Teri grinned. "Well put, hatchie. Honor is following a code of right conduct, even when everyone else around you doesn't. Honor is not just something you follow when someone is watching you.'

"'And Honor' is also something that you defend. The Corps represents 'Honor' and as a Marine, you *are* the Corps, therefore if you fail to uphold your 'Honor', you have failed the Corps, and your sister Marines.'

"Now as we move forwards in our training, I want you to think about what we've discussed here today. I want each of you, from here onwards, whenever you do anything, to think about the Marine motto and how you can apply it to the situation.'

"It's *not* just a pretty phrase for a branch of the armed services any more than a Marine is *just* a soldier. It is a way of life, and as Marines, it will be *your* way of life. It will stay with you for the rest of your days, and because of that, you will *always* be Marines, even after you leave the service. Thank you for your attention, ladies. You are dismissed."

USSMC Training Facility, 75th Training Battalion, Hella's World, Hecate System, Artemi Elant, United Sisterhood of Suns, 1043.02|30|03:65:65

The fifth week of Basic began and Platoon Carli received something rare for Hella's World; a pleasant surprise. After they'd completed their usual morning PT and parade drills, Senior Troop Leader sa'Tela informed them that they would be able to visit the base PX and shop. There were restrictions, of course. Nothing considered contraband was allowed to return with them, especially when it came to foodstuffs, but otherwise the Senior DI let them know that they were free to spend the credits that they'd earned up to that point.

The very nanosecond that they were dismissed, Kaly, Lena, Enggredsdaater and Bel Anny made right for it. Compared to the famous PX on Rixa, the one on Hella's World was small and stocked mostly essentials, but after the spartan austerity of Basic, everything inside the building seemed like an exotic luxury to the recruits.

Although the Corps issued personal hygiene kits, the very first items the women selected were their civilian counterparts. Like her companions, Kaly had taken for granted the easy availability of such items until she'd reached Basic, and she grabbed them up eagerly, not worrying herself overmuch at their prices. The simple prospect of feeling and smelling *human* again was a pleasure that she was not about to deny herself.

After that, it was on to the racks of holomags. There was a brief debate among the group over whether these would be considered contraband, but Bel Anny quickly settled the matter.

"So long as we only view them on our off time and not after lights out, they'll have to let us keep them," she explained. That was all the encouragement that any of them needed, and they snatched up whatever caught their eye.

Kaly herself had never been much of a fan of the popular holomags, and had always considered their content to be rather inane, and a waste of time. But that was before she had entered the world of the hatchie and experienced the complete media blackout that had accompanied it. In a complete turn-around, she wound up choosing *Glitterati* a 'mag that featured gossipy stories of Thermadon's rich and famous and even worse, *Secret Desires*, which offered up a series of short romance stories set in improbable, but strangely engaging settings. She might have felt a little stupid for selecting them, had her companions not gone right ahead and grabbed up material that was even more mawkish than this.

Halfway back to the barracks, Bel Anny pulled everyone aside between two prefab buildings. "I wanted to make sure we had this before we returned and had it taken away," she said, looking around to see if anyone else was watching. Then she produced a small foil-wrapped *chocalat* bar from her fatigue pants.

"Oh, goddess, I didn't know you'd bought that!" N'Gari gasped, "We're not supposed to have that!"

"Well, that's really a matter of interpretation," Bel Anny countered. "We're not supposed to bring it *back*. That's what they told us."

Standing there looking at the candy in her friend's hand, Kaly found Bel Anny's logic beyond contention. Besides, it *was chocalat* and it seemed like it had been centuries since she'd had such a treat. Her mouth watered as Bel Anny broke the bar into four parts.

"To graduation," Bel Anny said, popping her piece into her mouth. Kaly and the others followed suit. The taste was pure, sweet heaven.

Back at the barracks, they were met by Troop Leader n'Vera who inspected their purchases. Kaly could tell that the DI *knew* that they had been up to something, but there was no evidence left to confirm this. Predictably, the woman frowned when she saw the 'mags, but Bel Anny had been correct about the rules. All N'Vera could do was issue a stern warning against reading them at the wrong times, and nothing more. It was a small victory, but it *was* still a victory.

Ten minutes remained before the next scheduled drill, and with some free time on her hands, Kaly climbed into her rack. Instead of catching up on her sleep, she wound up paging through her romance 'mag. She didn't bother to try to follow any of the stories though. Instead, she just browsed through the plasti pages and enjoyed the animated images embedded in them.

One of these proved utterly enthralling. It was a scene of a beautiful Tethyian beach. The image was incredibly lifelike, and the publishers had even managed to embed the fresh scent of the ocean in the plasti page. Kaly brought it to her nose and took a deep breath, savoring the fresh clean smell. She decided right then and there that when she graduated, she would spend the short leave that followed Basic on the water-world. *No more deserts for me,* she thought. She'd eaten enough sand for a lifetime.

Kaly put the 'mag down and leaned over to share the idea with her battle sister, but before she could say anything, the DI's entered the barracks with another surprise. N'Vera and N'Teri were carrying a pair of sacks.

"Mail call, ladies! You have ten minutes to read and reply!" The stunned recruits clambered out of their racks and gathered around the DI's as they called out their names and passed out plastipaper flimsies.

What shocked Kaly even more was that *her* name was called.

Utterly confused, she went up and took the letter from the DI. *Who would write me?* she wondered as she returned to her rack. Reading the letter's contents, the mystery soon became clear.

The message was from one of the only adult survivors of the colony, and a former primary teacher of hers, Bella n'Mari.

"Dearest Kaly," it began. *"I had heard that you had joined the Marines from the Red Star people, and I knew from my own time in the service how much it means to hear from those at home. I wish that it was one of your friends, or even your mothers writing this, but the Goddess decided otherwise when She took them from us. So, please accept my words instead.'*

457

"The colony is getting back on its feet and getting a lot of help from the government. I heard last week that new colonists are coming here to join us and to help us rebuild.'

"I know that with a lot of hard work, we will accomplish this, and I hope that when you graduate from your training you will come and visit us. I know that it's not easy to think of that right now, but Persephone is your home, and everyone here would welcome you with open arms. In the meantime, know that our hearts are with you."

"May the Lady watch over you, Bella n'Mari."

Tears came to her eyes and Kaly blotted them with her sleeve, hoping that no one around her had noticed. But everyone else was too busy with their own letters and her moment of weakness passed without discovery.

There was simply nothing she had to say in reply, she realized. Not now at least. N'Mari had been absolutely right; the mere thought of returning to Persephone was too painful to even consider just then.

She needed time. Time to heal and time to come to terms with all that she had lost there. Quietly, she folded the letter up and stuffed it into her pocket.

Shortly after this, Troop Leader n'Vera reentered the barracks and collected everyone's replies. When she reached Kaly, the girl demurred, and the DI moved on without comment.

After that, the platoon made ready for their next drill, which was out on the firing range. As they were issued their weapons, and marched off to the range, there was a visible improvement in everyone's morale.

Everyone's, except Kaly's.

Shadow Lake Lodge, Nemesis, Rahdwa System, Thalestris Elant, United Sisterhood of Suns, 1043.02|30|05:41:67

Maya didn't envy the task that the Senatrix had ahead of her. The meeting with the Rampart leadership would be a long and difficult one. Silently wishing the politician well, she escorted Felecia out of the Lodge and over to the museum.

Despite the dangers, known and unknown, Felecia was in a cheerful mood and took Maya's hand when they were finally alone. The path to the museum was lined with beautiful trees and plants, and with a soft warm breeze caressing them, it was easy to imagine that they were somewhere else, far away from the galaxy's problems.

While they exchanged small talk, Maya took in the subtle scent of Felecia's perfume, mixed with the exotic aromas of the wild blooms around them and sighed. *If only life stayed like this*, she mused, *a pleasant afternoon that lasted forever.* But she knew life better than that, and did her best to drink in the moment while it lasted.

They reached the Nemesian Cultural Museum and began their tour of the place. True to its name, it was a testament to the hardy explorers that had discovered the planet and eventually settled in its dangerous jungles. They learned that Major Matthew Modrel, the leader of the first expedition was both a local hero and something of a spiritual icon to the women of Nemesis who saw *him* as a sort of father figure to their genetically altered race.

They also discovered that like many of the early pioneers, he had died violently in an encounter with one of the many predators native to the world. Despite such harsh conditions however, the early settlers had found enough reasons to remain and had adapted their offspring to live in the unforgiving environment. One entire wing of the place was devoted to the genetic alterations that each generation had undergone until they had found forms that were equal to the jungles challenges.

Nothing had been equal to the Great Plague however. Like the rest of what would later be called the Sisterhood, Nemesis lost all of its men, and the women of the forest had been compelled to live on without them.

Felecia paused at a holographic representation of the local Widow's Stone. "You know, Maya," she said thoughtfully, "There's one of these in Thermadon City. In my first year of primary, we went out and visited it at the Memorial Park, but I suppose I was too young to really understand what it meant. Now, I think I can start to appreciate what those women went through. It must have been terrible to lose someone that you loved to something you couldn't stop."

"Yes," Maya agreed somberly, "it is."

"Oh, goddess! I'm sorry. I didn't realize," Felecia stammered, "Did something happen to your world? Do you want to tell me about it?"

459

Part of her wanted to simply refuse Felecia, but another part of her wanted to share her history with her. She didn't trust most women, but even though their relationship had been a short one, something about Felecia made her feel that it was safe to open up, even if only a little bit.

"All right," Maya said tentatively. "You want to know my story, here it is." And then she told her; about the colony, the plague that had wiped it out, the Xee orphanage and her life on the streets. And at the end of her narrative, she looked away and bowed her head. Even after al the intervening years, the pain was still sharp.

Felecia gave Maya her moment, and then broke the silence between them. "What were your mothers like?" she asked gently.

Maya looked up at her, her eyes red rimmed with pain. "Yes, my *mothers*," she replied bitterly. "I guess that's what you'd call them. They were hydraulics engineers, which made them pretty important to the colony since it was an agro operation.'

"They never should have gotten their birthing license, but what they did for the colony made the Colony Mothers turn a blind eye when it came to their parenting scores.'

"Not that they had much time to be parents. There was always plenty of work for them to do, a new field being laid out, or some water project or another to go out on. They were never there, and when they were, Jora and Kaaryn fought. Goddess, how they fought! You can't imagine how many nights I lay awake listening to them scream at each other.'

"I think they got paired because it was the 'right thing to do', and maybe that's why they had me too. Whatever the reasons were, by the time I was eight, they'd separated and Kaaryn, the one who was around the most, raised me. Well, not raised; she basically handed me over to the childcare center and left me to go do her business.'

"Did you make some friends there, at least?" Felecia asked.

"No. I played by myself, or I watched adventure holos."

"Adventure holos? Like what?"

"It was silly, really," Maya answered, brightening a little, "but I used to watch episodes of *Laana, the Far Star Ranger* when we could get them from the supply ships. I really loved that show. She'd fly around the universe, run into strange beings and save their worlds. I even used to have fantasies about growing up and being just like her."

"It looks like you did in a way," Felecia offered. "I mean, maybe you're not a Long Range Recon Explorer like her, but you must see a lot of exciting things on the *JUDI*."

"Yeah," Maya agreed. "But Lana was never lonely, she was always strong. I wasn't, and I guess I envied her for that."

"What about your teachers, and the other girls? Couldn't you have reached out to them?" Felecia asked.

"Yes," Maya admitted, "I suppose I could have, but once you get into the habit of being alone, it's hard to break it and suddenly be 'little-miss-social.' At least if you're alone, no one can hurt you."

"You're not alone now, Maya," Felecia offerred, taking her hand.

"No," Maya replied. She almost added, "Not for now," but she left that thought unspoken.

"You know," Felecia said, changing the subject, "there's supposed to be a wonderful garden with some native carvings next door. That sounds like it would be lovely to visit, don't you think?"

Maya took her hand and let Felecia lead her out of the museum. After her confession, she felt raw inside, but also strangely relieved. Her memories certainly weren't gone; the ghosts were still there. But something, some small part of the burden that she had been carrying in silence up to that point, felt like it had ben lifted from her.

The Ki'ask'a Garden was behind the cultural center in a clearing all its own. Felecia proved correct about the place. Once Maya was outside the museum, she felt her well-being returning, and gladly let herself become distracted by the garden's displays.

The exhibits there made this easy to do. Massive logs had been planted in the ground and intricately carved and painted to depict creatures from Nemesian myth and legend. A holosign informed them that one of the first settlers, an engineer, a male, and a descendant of an aboriginal Gaian tribe called the Salish, had introduced the tradition of carving totem poles, or *ki'ask'as* to their new world. The creatures and the symbols on the poles were entirely Nemesian however, derived from what the first settlers and their descendants had encountered as they explored the jungles.

461

Maya walked up to the largest and most imposing of these monuments and examined it closely. At the bottom of the pole was the unmistakable shape of a stylized spaceship. Perched atop this was a helmeted woman.

No, Maya realized, it was a *man;* the facial hair on his upper lip made that a certainty. Above *him* was a fierce looking creature with multiple legs and sharp fangs, and then a representation of a Nemesian woman complete with her prehensile tail and claws.

A pale white flower with a distinct grouping of five petals surmounted the figures, and finally, capping off the entire pole, was an intimidating creature with a large membrane between its forward-most set of arms that seemed to give it the ability to glide, if not fly. Although the representations were crude, they exuded a raw sense of power and meaning.

"That is Modrel's *Ki'ask'a,*" a voice said from behind. Maya whirled around to face a pair of Nemesian women standing there, regarding them. Neither Maya nor Felecia had heard them approach, and they took a step back.

Both native women were tall and wiry, with light emerald-colored skin and dark braided green hair. A crisscrossing of scars marred their complexions, and their muscles looked as hard as steel. They also sported intricate tattoos on the left sides of their faces that Maya knew, represented their clan affiliation.

Their clothing, she saw, was made from leather. Not vat grown, but genuine leather that had been fashioned from the hides of real animals and sewn together. The garments consisted of a simple strap to act as a brassiere of sorts, and long knee length shorts that were equipped with large pockets. Heavy leather belts rode at their hips, with pouches of varying sizes hanging off of them, and everything had been dyed in various shades of green or brown.

They were also armed. Well-worn chemical rifles were slung casually over their shoulders, and knives at least a half-meter long that Maya knew were their Tej knives, sat in elaborately beaded sheaths on their belts.

Overall, they were a tough-looking duo and, looking at them, Maya had no doubt in her mind that they had fought more than their fair share of lethal predators, and personal duels, to the death.

The Nemesian nearest her folded her arms and looked at them with bright golden-orange eyes that were slitted like a kaatze. "You must be two of the *hwa'ni'tem* that came here to meet with each other," the woman said, her prehensile tail flicking with either curiosity, or as a warning to be careful of their answer.

Maya didn't know what *hwa'ni'tem* meant, but from the woman's tone and her supercilious posture, she guessed that it wasn't entirely complimentary. "Maybe," she answered cautiously, "Maybe we're not. Who are you?"

The Nemesian woman's eyes narrowed and she regarded Maya for a long moment with an appraising expression.

"You are cautious for an outsider," the woman finally said, relaxing slightly, "that is rare among your kind. Most *hwa'ni'tem* charge straight into the jungle without looking to see where their feet are taking them. And they die."

Maya didn't reply, and waited.

Finally, the woman spoke again. "Very well," she said, "I will tell you *one* name that I am called. I am Keela taur Minna. My Hunting Sister here is Laa'ret taur Minna, but we have other names that only our Clan Sisters will ever know."

"And my name is Maya n' Kaaryn," Maya replied. She wasn't certain if it was safe or not to tell them who her companion was, so she added, "This is my friend, Tarylynn n'Betsi."

Keela's slitted eyes narrowed again, and she sniffed the air as if she were trying to smell the lie. At last, she shrugged in acceptance, and panted lightly, as if she knew that Maya hadn't been forthright, and actually respected her for it. Then she folded her arms across her chest and haughtily inclined her head towards the nearest totem pole.

"Tell me, *Maya of Kaaryn*, do you and your *friend* find these carvings quaint? Perhaps even---*savage?*"

Keela had a smile on her face now. It was just enough to expose the very tips of her fangs. This, Maya understood completly. Nemesians never smiled. It was a warning, and another test to see how she would respond.

"No," Maya replied evenly. "Not savage, just very different from what I know." She meant this. Skylaar had taught her to respect the ways of the

463

jungle women, even if much of it would remain forever beyond her comprehension.

"Another good and thoughtful answer," Keela conceded. "Many women come to this place and dismiss what they see here as so much primitive nonsense. Then they take a trip into the 'Tamed Wood' and think they have truly seen our world." This was accompanied by a sneer, and her partner Laa'ret panted in what had to be derisive laughter.

"In doing so, they miss the *real* song of the Great Mother Forest. Tell me, outlander, do you think that you know what story that *ki'ask'a* in front of you is singing about?"

"I'm not sure. I don't know all of the symbols," Maya admitted, "but I think it's singing about the colonization of this planet."

"You have it a'right," Keela said. "Most *Hwa'ni* don't see that until someone points it out for them. But then, most *Hwa'ni* can't see the trees until they blunder straight into one. Shall I tell you the words to the song, oh, *Outlander-who-can-see-the-trees*?"

"Yes, please," Maya answered. "Tell me the words. I want to hear them."

Keela looked up at the carving. An expression of reverence came over her features. "So be it, and blessings be upon the ancestors who hear my words," she said formally.

"This ki'ask'a sings of the ship that brought humanity from the Land-Above-the-Sky to the great World of Life that *Hwa'ni* foolishly call Nemesis. It sings of Major Modrel and his brave followers, who set foot upon the ancient soil of this place, and of those who met their end at the hands of the Forest People, the creatures that roam our jungles.'

"It sings again of Modrel and his own glorious death at the hands of the *Sallash'kvechka*, the Neversaw Beast, and of the birth of the first forest women. It also sings of Modrel's flower, the Ghost Flower, and of the wonderous cures and the hidden treasures that we, his daughters, have found hidden beneath the forest canopy.'

"And it ends its song with the glorius battle cry of the *Minna'que'tsa*, the fighting bird from which my clan derives its name and its power. That is *our* crest atop it all, Maya of Kaaryn, for our song is sung throughout the Great Mother Forest from the foot of Blood River Falls to the Glen of

Bones as the very first of the Forest Clans. Is that not a mighty song, *Outlander-who-can-see-the-trees*?"

"Yes," Maya replied. "It is. Thank you for singing it for me."

Keela's posture relaxed. "You are wiser than most *Hwa'ni* I meet," she remarked. "We shall see one another again, I think."

Without further ado, the native women turned as one and sprinted towards the trees lining the garden, leaping upwards without any apparent effort onto the nearest branches. Keela gave them one backwards glance before she and her companion jumped across to another pair of limbs and vanished into the confusion of green leaves and concealing branches.

"Great Goddess! They were... magnificent!" Felecia said breathlessly. She laughed and held out her hand. "Look at me, my hands are shaking!"

Maya clasped them in her own trembling hands and looked off in the direction the Nemesians had gone, filled with admiration, and a deeper insight into her martial arts teacher's roots. They were magnificent indeed.

***

On the second day of the Senatrix's conference with the Rampart, Felecia announced that she was officially bored. The girl approached her mother, and after some pleading, convinced the woman to arrange for an imaging safari. This was something that the Shadow Lake Lodge was famous for, and Felecia was overjoyed at the entertainment this would provide, and at the opportunity it offered to go shopping in the Lodge's clothing shop. She was, as she quickly pointed out to Maya, completely unequipped for such an arduous journey into the "wilderness"—even if that so-called wilderness was safely enclosed by impeller fencing and totally devoid of any harmful predators.

Maya let Felecia lead her on her shopping spree, and after a little protest, even allowed her to buy her a souvenir sun hat for the trip. When the girl's shopping was finally done, they returned briefly to their quarters so that she could change into her new outfit; a khaki colored jumpsuit that mimicked more practical garments. Afterwards, they ate a light lunch together in the Lodge's main dining room.

465

Felecia was excited by the prospect of getting away from the resort, and when the staff women came for them, she eagerly led the way to a pair of hoverlifters that were waiting for them outside. The utilitarian craft consisted of flat decks with seats, open pilot's stations at the prow and skirts of clear plastiglass surrounding the entire platform. Suspended beneath this were pairs of tubular anti-grav units.

Overall it was a simple, yet practical design that was perfect for negotiating the Nemesian forests, and Maya learned from the staff that these machines came in a variety of configurations, ranging from fully covered models, to heavy-duty units equipped with lifting cranes for logging operations.

Uniformed crew members, and a small contingent of the Senatrix's security women, were waiting for them at the boarding ladders. So were the two Nemesian women that they had encountered in the Ki'ask'a Garden. Sharra had briefed Maya about them while Felecia had been changing into her new outfit, so she wasn't surprised by their presence, but her companion was.

"Look! It's those two native women that we met," Felecia whispered to her, "What are they doing here?"

"Working for your mother," Maya explained, and Felecia mouthed a silent "oh" of comprehension, suddenly understanding perfectly. Even though they were only going on an imaging safari in a pacified nature preserve, the Senatrix's Security Chief wasn't taking any chances with her safety.

Although they had been employed to accompany them, and lend their wilderness experience and skill as fighters, the Nemesians kept to themselves, and stood off to one side as the staffers ushered Maya and Felecia up the short ladders onto the nearest 'lifter. It was only when everyone had boarded both craft, and had been buckled in, that they finally deigned to join them. From the stiff manner of the Lodge employees, who were all from off planet, and the canine-exposing grins that the Nemesians gave them, it was obvious that the two groups were not used to being in such close proximity to one another.

Maya did not share their unease, and boldly looked over at Keela and her partner as they took their place in the 'lifter. The Nemesian seemed to approve of her audacity, and rewarded her with a slight nod of acknowledgement as the 'lifter rose smoothly into the air.

"Sa'la jantildamé," a staff member said from the front of the 'lifter, "On behalf of the Shadow Lake Lodge, welcome to the Shadow Lake Nature Preserve Imaging Safari, famous throughout the Sisterhood as one of the premier attractions on Nemesis.'

"We will be leaving the Residence Zone which houses the Lodge and its outbuildings, and proceed directly to the Nature Preserve where we will be able to view some of the wonders of the wild and dangerous Nemesian forest."

As she said this, Keela, or her companion (Maya was unsure which) let out a disdainful snort. If the staffer had noticed their scorn, she pretended ignorance, and carried on with her pre-packaged speech with a pleasant, albeit artificial smile.

"I will be your guide on our adventure today. My name is Shirleese. Please feel free to ask me any questions you have." Shirleese was a pretty blond with perfect hair, and she was dressed in an outfit that mimicked Felecia's. Like the rest of her fellow employees, the woman was too clean, too *"civilized"* compared to the Nemesians for her garb to be anything more than a costume worn by an actress in a realie, or in their case, a tour guide.

"The Residence Zone and the nature preserve are protected from the forest's predators by an impeller fence and an array of sonic devices that stretch in an unbroken ring around both zones," Shirleese told them.

"You may already be aware that the Nemesian forests are the source of some of the most fantastic medicinal plants in the Sisterhood, but also home to some of its most fearsome predators. This protective ring, which is in continuous operation, serves to make these zones habitable and completely safe for our guests."

By this time, the two 'lifters had floated past the lodge and were in the process of following the lake shore towards a gap in the tree line. Maya noted that a pair of double gates and impeller fencing separated what had to be the Nature Preserve from the Residence Zone.

Their guide cheerfully continued as the craft turned away from the lake and moved towards the gates. "This pair of gates is an added safety precaution, separating the two zones. If, in the unlikely event that the

467

impeller field surrounding the preserve ever fails, the Lodge would still be afforded the protection of these gates, which rely on a completely separate power grid. The Shadow Lake Lodge has made every effort to ensure that our guests enjoy both the highest level of security and enjoyment of what our unique world has to offer."

The gates, like the impeller field fencing, were enormous. In fact, they were larger than any barrier that Maya had ever seen before, which made her wonder just exactly *what* they were intended to keep out. Their tour of the museum had introduced them to a few of the smaller predators, but even those exhibits had made the frank admission that not *all* of the native species were accounted for. Given the extreme hazards of exploration, most of what scientists knew of the flora and fauna of the Nemesian forests was more legend than fact.

Maya also noticed that the demeanor of the two Nemesians changed subtly as the 'lifter made its passage through the barrier.

They know what the fences keep back, the girl thought, watching as Keela reflexively clutched the handle of the Tej knife on her hip. And for once, Maya was satisfied with her ignorance. She suppressed a shudder as they passed through the gates, trying not to let her imagination run away with her as the forest pressed in close and dark on both sides of the 'lifter.

Once or twice she thought she saw movement just inside the tree line. Whatever they were, they were large, but thankfully nothing rushed out to the impeller fencing to reveal itself. Despite her disquiet, though, Maya had to admit that the forests of Nemesis were quite beautiful, in their own strange and disturbing way.

The hoverlifters came out into a large clearing. Huge trees loomed all around its edges, their trunks almost completely concealed by massive vines, some of which were as thick as the *JUDI's* engine pods. And here and there, hidden in the shadows created by the dense forest, Maya spotted strange, luminescent flowers that lit up the foliage around them with a soft, ghostly light, creating an almost cheerful counterpoint to the otherwise omnipresent gloom.

"Gentleladies," Shirleese said, "Welcome to the nature preserve. This is the Modrel Valley, named after Major Matthew Modrel, the leader of the first team to explore Nemesis."

While the woman was saying this, Maya noticed that both of the Nemesians were making a quick, surreptitious gesture with their hands. She took this as some form of genuflection and looked away, not wanting to intrude on their private ritual. Neither Shirleese, nor her fellow employees seemed to notice it however, and the guide continued with her monologue like some kind of 'bot.

"You may have already spotted some of the exotic flowers native to the forest floor," she said, "and noted their bio-luminescent qualities. For those who haven't seen this yet, an excellent example is coming up on our right; a particularly large patch of what we call the Widow's Bed flower which gives off a distinctive blue glow when the shadows are just right.'

"You may have also noted the large vines that cover nearly every centimeter of the forest's trees, which are known of as blackwood trees. These vines are called strangler vines, but that's a misnomer; the vines don't harm the trees in the least. Instead, they actually provide a protective covering that shields them against wood-boring insects and helps to support their great weight, allowing them to grow as large as they do."

Then Shirleese looked over her shoulder and her perfect smile broadened. "Gentleladies, we are indeed fortunate today. If you look to our right and through the trees, you'll see some examples of traveler plants making their way along the ground. These rare and unique plants use the hydraulic action of the water inside of them to move across the forest floor from one place to another in order to find the best places for sun and nutrients."

Maya seriously doubted that there was really anything rare or unexpected going on here. The imaging safaris were one of the Lodge's major attractions, and their guide certainly knew where everything was located within the preserve. Even so, she kept her cynicism to herself out of deference to Felecia, who was buying the whole thing.

"Look," the girl said to her, pointing. "There they are!" Maya peered down and spotted one of the plants a moment later.

It proved to be a small bush with thin, whip-like branches at its base which it was using to propel itself towards a bright patch of sunlight. When it reached the spot, a thick root dropped down from its midsection and bored into the soft dark earth. Then the plant settled down, and as it spread its appendages outwards, large white flowers with thick petals sprouted open and caught the light.

"Isn't this exciting?" Felecia asked, squeezing her hand. "Such strange plant-life they have here! No wonder the first scientists were so eager to explore this world."

Despite the fact that the whole thing had been staged, Maya had to admit that the sight *was* impressive. She had never encountered plants that could move around on their own. She also found herself wondering if the plants got any kind of kick-back from the Lodge for showing up on cue like this. *Water? Fertilizer? A shiny new pot?*

As she suppressed the urge to laugh at her own sarcasm, a second plant came out of the shadows and Felecia immediately brought up her realicam to film the spectacle. Shirleese nodded to their pilot, who went into a hover, and when Felecia had finished, they flew on.

At a point where the clearing split in two directions, the machine made a right-hand turn that brought it around the edge of the jungle and into an even wider meadow. A small lake dominated it, fed by a waterfall that spilled out from under the jungle canopy from a source somewhere in the shadows high above them. Beyond this, huge jagged mountains rose up in the distance, looking like the teeth of a gigantic predator, and Maya gazed up at their hazy summits, marvelling at their size and grandeur.

Shirleese gestured expansively at the sight. "The mountains you see in the distance are the Chasadaans, which are the location for the famous Sarayanne Hot Springs, known all around the Sisterhood for its unique healing powers. If you are so inclined, arrangements for a trip to the hot-springs can be made when we get back to the lodge."

"Oh, Maya!" Felecia exclaimed, pressing herself in as close as her seat harness would allow, "wouldn't it just be wonderful to go there? I've heard of those springs and it would be simply marvelous to spend a day just soaking in a nice hot tub, don't you think?"

"Yes, it would," Maya replied. The springs did sound inviting, especially if the trip involved spending some time alone with Felecia *in* that tub. "We'll have to see if your mother will let us get away for another day and go up there."

Up ahead of them, an open tent had been erected next to the lake shore. The pleasant aroma of fresh food carried over the gentle breeze as the 'lifter drew near.

"Mmm," Felecia purred. "Doesn't that smell fantastic? I had heard that we would have a little picnic out here, but I didn't think it would be so nice." Maya's stomach rumbled involuntarily in agreement, and Felecia laughed. "I guess I won't be eating alone, then, will I?"

Maya blushed, but Felecia was right. After their light breakfast, the scent of the food was irresistible.

The 'lifter landed and they were shown over to the tent. Predictably, the Nemesians did not join them. Instead, they settled themselves under a nearby tree and broke out packets of rations from their packs, clearly content with the simpler fare, and their own company. Maya gave them a quick respectful nod, and then let Felecia pull her into the shelter.

The food that was waiting for them proved to be just as delicious as its aroma had advertised, and after they had finished their lunch, a waitress came up and offered them cups of kaafra flavored with local Nemesian *chocalat*.

Felecia took hers, and after a delicate sip, sighed in contentment. "Isn't that just divine?" she sighed. "I can see now why Nemesian *chocalat* fetches such a high price off planet. I'll simply *have* to convince Mother's cook to stock some of this for our kitchen. I don't think I could ever drink any other kind now."

Maya tried her own beverage, and when the rich, velvety taste hit her tongue, she found that she couldn't disagree. The local version made everything else that she'd ever tried seem downright tasteless. She drained her cup with relish and nodded back.

"I do hope you're free tonight," Felecia said, putting her cup down. "I wanted to share something with you that is very special to me, and I hope that it won't offend you."

"Nothing you do could offend me," Maya assured her. "Do you want to tell me what it is, or should I wait?"

"Well," Felecia began, making certain that no one was within earshot. "It's something I picked up on my last trip with my mother. Oh, I don't

471

know if I should tell you…please promise me that you'll not breathe a word of it to anyone!"

"Yes," Maya agreed. "I'll keep it a secret, but only if you tell me what 'it' is."

"It's a *converger*," Felecia said almost in a whisper.

"A *what?*"

"It's *very* expensive," the girl explained, "and *very* hard to get. The merchant who sold it to me said that it interfaces with your psiever and the psiever of someone else, and that it switches their signals."

"I don't follow," Maya said. "What's so special about that?"

"It puts you *inside* of the other person. You actually feel like you *are* them, and they *are* you. I thought that it might be something that we would like to try… together."

Maya smiled provocatively at the notion. "I'll give anything a try."

***

After lunch they spent some time taking more images with Felecia's realicam, and then the 'lifters headed back towards the lodge. The sun was just starting to set and the craft followed a different, shorter route up through a narrow side valley in order to return before full dark was upon them.

The jungle was especially thick there, and the 'lifters were forced to rise up almost to the treetops to make their passage. Despite the dense cover, there was still plenty to see below them, as Shirleese cheerfully pointed out.

"If you will look down and to the left," she said, "you should catch a glimpse of one of the most famous flowers on Nemesis, the Modrel Flower, which, as you know, was named for the famous explorer. In the wilds, one of the most curious characteristics of this flower is that it is almost always associated with a predator referred to as the "neversaw," which reportedly guards it wherever it is found. Of course, here in the nature preserve, we don't have to worry about this, and can appreciate the flower for its strange beauty without having any safety concerns."

Maya peered down into the canopy and spotted the flower, a huge milky white growth with five distinct petals, each as large as a woman's head. She recognized it right away from the ki'ask'a carving, and something about the blossom made her skin crawl.

She wasn't alone in her reaction. The two Nemesians next to her were clearly disturbed by the growth and looked around them warily.

"We should not be here," Keela said gravely. "It is never good to be near the ghost flower, even here." Her companion nodded in agreement and began to un-sling her rifle.

Up in the front of the 'lifter, their tour guide was speaking through her ear-bud to someone at the lodge. "*What* happened?" Shirleese asked, her professional polish cracking as her voice took on a note of alarm. "What are you saying?"

A look of concern came over her pretty features and she turned towards her passengers. "Gentleladies," she started to say, "there seems to have been some kind of problem--"

There was a rush of air, as something too fast for the eye to register swooped into the open craft and out again. It took Maya a few seconds to come to the horrible realization that Shirleese's body no longer possessed its head. The woman's corpse stayed erect for a moment, before collapsing onto the deck with a sodden thump. The blood spattered pilot near her screamed in terror and banked the lifter hard and to the left as she accelerated.

It was the wrong manuever. Instead of getting the 'lifter clear of the trees, the edge of the craft caught on a huge limb and flipped over. To Maya's surprise and horror, her harness unbuckled and she was thrown violently from her seat and out into space.

Everything around her became a green blur for a few seconds before she hit a branch. The impact knocked the air out of her and she very nearly tumbled off to the forest floor below, but an instinct from somewhere deep and primeval made her reach out and catch herself.

Using all the strength she had, she pulled herself up and looked around for Felecia and the others. Someone was screaming nearby and she tried to spot the source, but the canopy was too dense for her to see where the woman was, or identify her.

She decided to try to climb down, and gingerly lowered herself to another branch just beneath her. As she stepped onto it, she heard a mew of fear. Human fear.

She looked down and spotted Felecia, clinging with her fingers to another tree-limb, but just barely. The girls' body hung in space with only her tenuous grip preventing her from falling to her death. "Help me!" she whimpered, her eyes bright with terror.

"Hold on!" Maya urged, "For the goddess's sake, hold on! I'll come to you." She tried to lower herself and reached out, but she missed Felecia's hands by a good meter.

"Please!" Felecia cried, "I can't hold on much longer!"

Maya's mind raced, trying to figure out how to save her lover. Then she remembered her flight jacket's special features. Thanking the Goddess and Apee Corporation, she unzipped the compartment in her right arm and withdrew the length of monofilament rescue line. Making a crude loop, she lowered it down to the girl. "Grab the line," she instructed. "I'll pull you up!"

Felecia made a grab for it, but only succeeded in missing the line. Suddenly, she was hanging by only one hand and flailing wildly to grab a hold with the other. "I'm slipping!" she screamed in alarm.

Suddenly, Maya was no longer alone on the branch. It was Keela. Without saying a word, the woman wrapped her prehensile tail around the limb for support and lowered herself downwards, reaching for Felecia. But just as she was about to make contact, Felecia gave out a cry, and lost her grip.

The Nemesian reacted with superhuman speed and just managed to get hold of the girl's arm before it dropped away. Grimacing with the effort, Keela hauled Felecia upwards until she was able to raise herself up onto the branch.

"Oh, goddess!" Felecia sobbed, coming into Maya's arms, "I thought…" The rest was lost in her tears. Holding her close, Maya turned to Keela. "What happened?" she asked.

"We were attacked by the neversaw," Keela answered. "The impeller fencing must have been sabotaged, and I think the same evil hands made certain that our harnesses failed.'

"Now we must get away from here. This is no longer the Tamed Wood, but the True Forest. The neversaw will be close by, and other creatures just as dangerous will soon arrive."

Right then, a scream of agony sounded from somewhere below and off to the right, gruesomely punctuating the Nemesian's statement.

Keela addressed Felecia. "Quickly, climb onto my back and lock your arms around my neck. I will carry you down, then I will return for your mate and we will make our way on the ground. It is not as safe as the Green Road, but neither of you is skilled enough to travel that."

Felecia looked fearfully at the distant forest floor, and then at Maya. "Please, isn't there another way?"

"She's right," Maya said, not sure what Keela had meant by the 'Green Road.' "There's no way my escape line will reach the bottom of this tree. You'll have to do as she says. She knows what she's doing."

"But--"

"There is no time for arguments, girl!" Keela snapped. "The neversaw will find us up here. Now climb on!"

Felecia glanced doubtfully at the ground again, but with a nod of reassurance from her lover, did as the forest woman had ordered.

"You," the Nemesian said to Maya, "secure yourself to this limb with your line. If you are armed, be ready with your weapon until I return for you."

Maya immediately tied one end of her escape line to the branch. It took her a moment to figure out what to do with the other end, but then she recalled the large metal ring she had found inside a flap alongside her jacket's zipper. She pulled this out from its hiding place and fashioning a loop, clipped the monofilament line into it. Then she zipped the jacket up and tested the connection, letting out an audible sigh of relief as she realized that it was securely fastened to the limb. After this, she took out her needlegun, checked its ammunition level, and cocked its action.

Keela nodded approvingly, and then scrambled down the branch with Felecia on her back.

"I will return momentarily," she said back up to Maya. "Keep a sharp eye out for any movement in the canopy and do not hesitate to fire at it. The neversaw will not give you any time to verify your target."

Without waiting to see if Maya understood, she continued her descent to the forest floor with Felecia holding on for dear life. At the main trunk, she sank her claws and foot talons into the softer vines that were covering it and started down. Her passenger squealed with momentary alarm, but Keela's grip was firm.

They were about halfway down the great tree when Maya thought she heard a rustle in the treetops nearby. She brought her pistol up, seeking a target, but failed to locate anything lurking amidst the dense mass of leaves and branches around her.

Something *was* out there though. She couldn't see it or smell it, but her talents could feel it. It was out among the branches, watching her with malevolent eyes and considering its next move. Her palms started to sweat as she ranged the barrel of the needlegun in front of her, trying to spot the creature.

In the next instant, it came at her, a shadowy form half-hidden by the foliage. Maya fired and another scream issued out through the canopy, but this time it came from nothing even remotely human.

The enraged creature burst into view on a nearby branch; a blur of teeth and claws, and it was Maya's turn to cry out as it lunged at her again. Overcome with terror, she forgot where she was and took a step backwards, but there was nothing for her feet to find purchase on. Instead, she slipped and fell backwards off the limb, smashing through several smaller branches before she reached the end of her line and came to a bone-jarring halt.

Up above her, on the limb that she had been perched on was the neversaw. The creature looked vaguely like a tiger from Old Gaia, but with too many limbs and eyes to even pretend a shared lineage. It looked down at her with a giant wedge-shaped head filled with thin razor sharp teeth. Howling with frustration, the predator flicked its prehensile tail and began to work its way down to her.

Maya brought her needlegun to bear for another shot when something dripped down into her face, instantly burning her skin and eyes, and robbing her of the chance to see her target clearly. It took her a moment to realize that the stuff in her eyes was what the predator used for blood. She wiped as much of the loathsome substance off with her arm as she was able and fired a burst upwards. The neversaw leapt away, leaving her unsure if she had even hit the thing.

Maya also didn't intend to stay and find out. The ground was still a long ways off, but the prospect of hanging in mid-air by a thin line with a wounded predator lurking nearby, was less attractive than risking the drop. She let out the line until it reached its end, took in a deep breath and detached.

She fell like a stone. The soft ground turned out to be much closer than she had expected, and she landed hard. Stars filled her vision for a moment, and as they cleared, Felecia and Keela ran over.

"Oh, Maya!" Felecia cried. "Are you okay? Are you all right?" Maya let Keela assist her to her feet and waved Felecia back.

"I'm fine," she replied with a weak smile, "just a little meteor pitting and some scraped paint. No worries." In fact, everything hurt, but nothing seemed to be broken.

"Can you walk?" Keela asked.

Maya nodded.

"Good. We need to be away from here." There was a rustle overhead and Keela brought up her chemical rifle, letting off a burst of automatic fire. Another unearthly shriek issued from the canopy above them, followed by a shadowy form moving rapidly away from them across the treetops.

Keela nodded to herself in satisfaction. "Follow me and do not let yourselves stray too far behind," she said. With that, she started off.

Because the giant trees blocked off most of the life-giving sunlight, the forest floor was relatively clear of undergrowth and Maya and Felecia were just able to keep pace with the Nemesian. The woman set a brutal pace, but after her own encounter with the neversaw, Maya had no objections and urged Felecia along. Once or twice, the city-born girl stumbled on a root, or an uneven patch of earth, but Maya was there to help her and kept her moving.

Reaching a small clearing, Keela gave them a moment to sit and catch their breath. While she waited for them, the woman sniffed the air and listened carefully to the noises around them with her long pointed ears, ranging around her with the barrel of her weapon. When her stance relaxed slightly, Maya could tell that nothing dangerous was lurking nearby. For the moment.

"The nearest large clearing is still far from here," the Nemesian announced, "and we cannot know if our personal rescue beacons have been received; the trees can sometimes block out a signal. We will have to move much faster. The Mother Forest is no place to be after full dark." Maya pulled Felecia up to her feet and followed Keela as she led the way.

Darkness swallowed up the forest around them like a living thing, and on its wings came the same weird cries that Maya had heard from her room on their first night. But they were closer and more frightening without an impeller fence to keep whatever had made them at bay. She gathered Felecia in and kept her needlegun at the ready, staying alert for any sign of danger.

Abruptly, Keela stopped and raised a hand in warning.

Suddenly, a huge multi-eyed creature with a muscular back and short, powerful looking legs sprang at them, its jaws opened wide. Felecia screamed in terror and Maya fired wildly at the monster, her needlegun flashes creating a bizarre strobe effect against the things pale hide as it charged fowards.

Keela fired at the same time and there was a wet *splat* as she scored a direct hit in one of the things primary eyes. The nightmarish creature shuddered and gave out a shriek that threatened to rupture Maya's eardrums as it skittered back and scuttled off into the shadows.

"The *wasauk* will not return," Keela stated, calmly changing her rifle magazine for a fresh one. Then she slung her weapon, took out her Tej knife and slashed her upper arm, twice. Watching her perform this ritual, Maya finally understood the meaning behind the scars there. Each one represented a battle that the Nemesian had won. And both of Keela's arms were covered with them.

Keela re-sheathed her blade. "I injured the beast and it should keep its distance now. Even so, there may be others of its kind nearby. Get your companion to her feet."

Maya looked down and saw that Felecia had collapsed during the attack. She tried to coax her into standing, but her lover was at the very limits of her resources and clung to Maya's legs like a child, sobbing uncontrollably and whimpering for her mother. Finally, she bent down and caressed the girl's head, whispering soft nonsense into her ears until at last, Felecia allowed herself to be pulled upright. Finally, they started off again, and Maya kept a protective arm around her, gently urging her along.

Although the native woman made no comment, the contempt in her eyes was plain, and she didn't bother to slacken her pace one nano. It was obvious that she regarded Felecia as the quitessential *hwa'ni'tem.* Only the fact that she was being paid to protect her, and the ire that her people might face from Felecia's powerful mother, were what prevented her from simply abandoning them both to their fates.

Not that Maya cared. What really mattered was that Keela *was* there and giving them the edge that they needed to get out of the forest alive.

The minutes passed, and finally they reached the edge of the large clearing that the Nemesian had mentioned. Seeing the saw-toothed mountains rising in the distance, Maya realized that she was looking at the Chasadaans, which meant that they were somewhere on the border of the Modrel Valley.

Reassured by something even remotely familiar, she started to walk out into the clearing, but Keela signaled for her to wait. Once again, the woman listened, and smelled the air. At last, she relaxed and waved them forwards.

"My hunting sister is nearby and others of your kind are with her," Keela declared. "We will join them and wait for rescue."

She gestured towards a small fire that had been lit in the center of the meadow. A group of women were huddled around it, and even from that distance, Maya could make out Laa'ret's wiry form, standing watch over them.

Keela waved them past her, keeping her rifle trained on the treeline, and after they had gone a little ways, she retook the lead.

"Our rescue beacons should be readable from here," Keela said as they reached the group of survivors. "If there is not too much trouble back at the Lodge, we should expect rescue by dawn."

"The Lodge!" Felecia's eyes became bright with alarm. "My mother, and all those people!"

479

"We cannot help them," Laa'ret stated flatly. "We can only remain here and hope that they will be able to win their way to us. Until then, we stay. This is the only safe place for offworlders. Get some rest while you can."

"I'm sure that your mother is all right," Maya offered. "She had a full contingent of security staff with her and my crewmates. I'm sure they got her to safety."

"Do you really think so?" Felecia asked in a small voice. Her eyes were bright with hope and fear.

"Yes," Maya replied. "I do. Come, let's sit by the fire."

CHAPTER 14

Unnamed Settlement, Second Planet, HSL-48 2124A System, Unclaimed Territory, 1043.03|02|02:38:33

Jon fa'Teela rose up onto his elbows and peered into the display screen of his manoculars, scanning the town ahead of him. In many respects, the buildings were familiar enough, but he still couldn't see anything that resembled a church. If the town were a Marionite settlement like they thought, there would have been one. But the Marine Marauder team had made a full circle around the community, and there simply didn't appear to be a House of the Faithful anywhere within its boundaries.

His psiever flashed with a message from the Troop Leader. *Well? What's bothering you, Neo?*

Jon shook his head. *Nothing. I just don't think this is a Marionite colony.*

We'll see, the woman replied doubtfully. *I think your friends here just aren't as obvious about it. We're going to move in closer. We need more intel.*

The team moved forwards, keeping low to the brushy ground and making their way towards a road that led out of town into the surrounding fields. Tall bushes lined the side they were on, and this feature, along with the uncertain pre-dawn twilight, made it relatively easy going, even for Jon, who hadn't been on night maneuvers since Basic.

They stopped at the edge of the road and halted when they heard something. Jon thought it had been a woman's voice, singing a simple song, and he turned his head in the direction of the sound. A young girl, possibly 13 standard, was on a bicycle, riding right towards their position. The single headlamp on her vehicle bobbed wildly as the girl interrupted her tune and stepped into the pedals to get her bike over a small rise in the roadway.

She crested it, and as she slowed for a moment, the nearest SpecOps member jumped up and seized her while another Marine took control of the bicycle. It was the perfect kidnapping. In an instant, they had the struggling girl and her bike off the road and out of view. In another second, they had tied her hands, taped over her mouth and covered her eyes with a kerchief.

You! Neo! the Troop Leader thought to Jon. *You can finally do something useful. Carry the prisoner on your back. We'll cover your exit. We're going to waypoint Dana-Eleen. We'll question her there.*

Jon hoisted the girl on his back without comment, bringing her manacled hands over his neck and using them to keep her weight steady. While they moved away from the ambush site, he tried to monitor her breathing, just in case the girl had swallowed her tongue. With the load he was carrying, the trip back to their gathering point proved tougher than it had been coming in, but he managed to get their prisoner there without incident, and he set her down as gently as possible.

At a nod from the Troop Leader, Jon removed the bandana from her eyes, and then carefully peeled the tape off of her mouth.

"Who are you?" the Troop Leader demanded.

The girl looked up at her in confusion, and the trooper repeated her question with the same result.

"Who... are... you?" the trooper asked, pointing towards the girl and then herself. "I... am... Troop Leader... Annasdaater."

Their captive did not reply.

"Maybe she's impaired somehow," another Marine suggested.

The squad's medic came forwards and scanned their prisoner from head to foot and the girl watched the proceedings with a certain frightened fascination. It was as if she had never seen a medical body scanner before.

"No," the medic said at last. "She's fine. She should be able to speak to us without any difficulty."

"Maybe she just doesn't understand Standard," Jon volunteered.

"That's ridiculous!" the Troop Leader snorted. "This is a human colony! Of *course* she knows Standard. She's just playing stupid with us." The Marine bent over and cupped the girls jaw roughly. "Now you listen, girlie!" she snarled, "I want an answer to my question. *Who are you?*"

The terrified girl shook her head and uttered a string of words that were completely foreign to everyone in the squad. Everyone except Jon.

He blinked in disbelief as she repeated herself. *"Miya namey es Reesy!"* she blurted. *It couldn't be*, he thought.

The Troop Leader had noticed his reaction. "Does that gibberish make any sense to you?" she asked. "What did she just say?"

"If she's speaking the language that I think she is," he replied, "then she just answered your question. She said her name is Reesy."

482

"Did she now?" the Troop Leader challenged, planting her hands on her hips. "In what language? What dialect? I speak Standard, Nemesian, Kalian, Zommerlaandartal, Hriss'ka, and even a little Xee. I've never heard anything like that mess of words."

"If you were a Marionite, it wouldn't sound so foreign to you," he retorted.

"*That* would be unlikely" the woman replied with a sneer. "So, what do you *people* know that we don't?"

"A dialect of Old Gaia for one.It's called *Espangla*," Jon answered, more and more confident of his conclusion. "We of the *Faithful,*" he made sure to put an emphasis on that word, "keep it alive because it is one of the few remaining tongues of the planet that gave birth to Jesu, our First Savior. I studied it as a child in our primary school, along with another sacred language called *Latin*. It was part of our religious training."

"So, she speaks a Marionite language, then," the Troop Leader concluded. "That just confirms what Command thought about this place."

"No," Jon countered. "It doesn't. There is no church here and there would be if this was a colony of the Faithful. And no one actually *speaks* Espangla, or Latin. We speak Standard just like everyone else does. The Sisters only use Espangla for rituals. It's too sacred for daily use."

"Well, maybe these people just don't think it's so holy," the Troop Leader retorted. "Maybe they're some kind of offshoot that just uses it for everyday speech."

Jon shook his head. "No, I disagree. Let me try something and we'll see if I'm right."

"Go ahead."

Jon walked up to the girl and tried to smile at her as reassuringly as possible. He knew that the Marine team was terrifying and he wanted to be seen as a friend, despite the circumstances. He got down on his knees so that he was on a level with her eyes, and carefully composed his words.

"*Miya namey es Jon,*" he said, pointing to himself. "*Que es esteya sitia llamar?*"

The girl looked at him in bewilderment, but answered immediately. "*Se llama a la Escaul.*"

"And all that meant?" the Troop Leader demanded impatiently.

Martin Schiller

Jon waved her off and asked the girl another question. *"Has oidia hablaar de el Padrey? Que sabey de el Salvadar de todas nosotra?"*

The girl rewarded him with another perplexed look, and Jon reached forwards slowly and withdrew her necklace from her blouse, reassuring her in Espangla that he meant her no harm. The pendant at the end of the tiny chain confirmed all of his suspicions and he held it up for the squad to see.

"This should be a Star of the Faithful," he explained. "A Marionite star, but it's not. It's a secular piece of jewelry."

"So what?" one of the troopers replied in a bored tone.

"No young Marionite girl would ever be allowed to travel without wearing the sign of Our Lady Mari for protection. It's unthinkable. I also just asked her if she knew the Son of God as her savior and she didn't know what I was talking about."

"Neither do I," the Troop Leader responded with a derisive laugh. Her sisters joined her. "Go on."

Jon ignored their scorn. "She's definitely not a Marionite. If she were, she'd know about Our Savior. Everyone here would, and none of them would deny Him. She also told me that this settlement is called the School. Apparently the town is dedicated to some kind of worldly study. It's *not* a Marionite colony."

"Well what is it, then?" the Troop Leader asked incredulously. "I have to report *something* up to Command."

"It's a settlement that speaks a language that no one has spoken conversationally for over 1,000 years standard," Jon answered. "Who these people are, I don't know, but they're not from any Sisterhood world."

"Of all the *klaxxy shess!*" the Troop Leader sputtered. "She's human! The Doc here would have said if she wasn't. You ask her about the Sisterhood and I'll lay a wager she knows about it just fine."

"I will, Troop Leader," Jon agreed, "but I already think I know the answer." He asked the girl the question and was quickly rewarded with another long string of words.

"So?"

"So, you were right," he said, *"in part.* She knows about the Sisterhood, but she told me that she learned about it from the women who came to live here years ago. She's never been there, and neither has anyone

484

that she knows except for those women." There was a tone to his voice that indicated he was holding something back, and the Troop Leader caught it.

"And? What else?"

"It scares her. She's frightened of the Sisterhood."

"Fine!" the Troop Leader scowled. "I'll just report that we have another *fekking mystery* on our hands. We have a colony of people, humans, that aren't from the Sisterhood and speak an antique tongue that only our pet neoman knows. They'll just *love* that!"

***

After receiving the team's report, Lilith ordered the Battle Group into standby mode. She needed to contact Rixa immediately. This was something that they would definitely want to hear about. Inviting her senior officers into her office, she made the call.

When she answered, Admiral ebed Cya had included two other women in their conversation. They were introduced to Lilith as the Director of the OAE, Susa ben Paula, and Senatrix Barbra d'Salla, Assistant Majority Leader of the Supreme Circle.

"Commander, you seem to have stumbled across something that we've been investigating for some time now," Ben Paula began. "What I'm about to tell you cannot go beyond this group."

"Ma'am?" Lilith asked. She was beginning to wonder if this affair could get any stranger, or more complicated. As it turned out, it did.

"We've known for a while about the existence of a human civilization that survived the Plague just like we did," the Agency Director said. "We learned about them through our partners, the Daughters of the Coast. Nothing solid however—not at first."

So, it's not first contact after all, Lilith thought. *And the 'Lost Colonies' aren't really 'lost'.*

Senatrix d'Salla spoke next. "Once we were certain that they existed, we tried to make contact with them. We wanted to negotiate an alliance and secure trade agreements. You see, they have some things that we want, not the least of which are rich sources of titanium and other important metals."

485

"So you sent the *Atalanta* here to accomplish that mission?" Lilith asked.

"Yes, we did," the Senatrix admitted. "Along with several other SVER ships. They all disappeared and we never received an answer to our proposals. Now we know what happened to one those ships at least, and it's a fair bet that the same thing occured to the others."

Lilith turned to Admiral ebed Cya. "What are your orders, ma'am?"

"Lilith, this situation touches on our foreign policy, and also on our long term goals for the quadrant," Ebed Cya replied carefully. "We need the resources that this star nation has, and we also need to make certain that they don't fall into Hriss hands.'

"In addition, there is the fact that our efforts to forge a partnership have gone unanswered, and that our sailors have not been allowed to contact us, or to return to the Sisterhood."

Lilith nodded. *Given their level of technology, they're probably terrified of us*, she thought. She didn't say this out loud however.

"Commander, we want you to rescue the crew, but we also wish to make a statement here. This star nation must be made to understand that we will not tolerate the destruction of our ships, or the imprisonment of our citizens."

"Yes, ma'am."

"We also want to make it clear," the Senatrix added, "that it would be in their best interests to adopt a friendlier attitude towards us. They need to realize that we must have open communications and that an alliance is in their best interests."

"I'm sorry, Madame Senatrix," Lilith said, "but isn't that the job of the OAE?"

D'Salla gave her a smile that didn't reach her eyes. "It is—but in this case, we feel that our diplomatic efforts have failed to produce the results that we have been looking for. So, the task is being given over to the Navy."

Lilith was immediately reminded of a quote that she had once heard in the Academy as a young cadet. It was from the great military thinker, Karla von Clausewitz. It went; *"War is the continuation of politics by other means."* She kept this to herself as well.

Ebed Cya addressed her again. "Commander, your orders are to neutralize their planetary defenses, and deploy your forces downside. There, you are to secure the settlement and detain the entire population."

Lilith didn't quite believe what she was hearing, and raised a quizzical eyebrow.

"You are to utilize your assets to the *fullest* extent," Ebed Cya continued. "We want the population to have no doubts about our displeasure, or to be given any opportunity to offer up resistance to our presence. This mission will serve as an example to their government, and hopefully, motivate them to initiate an open and constructive dialogue with us."

Or serve as a prelude to open war, Lilith reflected sourly. Suddenly she understood the situation all too clearly. This had very little to do with the rescue of some marooned sailors.

Instead, it was 1852 BSE all over again. These people, and their nation were Imperial Japan, and she had been involuntarily cast in the role of Commodore Perry. Only this was not Tokyo Bay, and her ships were not equipped with iron cannons but planet-buster missiles.

But as horrified as she felt, she was also an officer, and she reminded herself that she had a job to do, however distasteful it was.

"Yes, ma'am," she answered stiffly.

"Very well," Ebed Cya concluded, obviously just as uncomfortable as she was. "You are dismissed, Commander. Carry out your orders."

The call ended, and Lilith let out a deep, ragged sigh.

"What kind of orders were those," Katrinn demanded. "Are they completely klaxxy? They just told us to terrorize those people!"

"They are not klaxxy Kat," Lilith replied grimly. "Far from it. It's called 'gunboat diplomacy'. Ask Mearinn to explain what that means."

With that, she showed everyone out, and took a few minutes to compose herself and come to terms with what she had just been ordered to do.

***

The early morning air was still and quiet. Only the occasional call of a bird, or something very like it, disturbed the silence that enveloped the sleeping settlement. Without any sign to warn of its arrival, a Valkyrie aerospace fighter roared overhead, just meters above the tallest roof. Its engine noise shook the glass of every building as it flew straight down the middle of the town's main street. It banked left and headed out and away over the surrounding fields.

Jon watched as a few lights winked on in some of the houses, and down the street he saw the figure of a man come out and search the sky for the source of the disturbance.

Another Valkyrie thundered past, and the man ran back inside his home. The raid had begun.

Jon looked to Troop Leader Annasdaater and she flashed him a hand sign that told him to wait. Then she withdrew a smoke canister from her web gear, popped the fuse and threw it into the center of the street. A block away, another member of their team did the same thing.

The area began to fill up with grey-white smoke and another sound came to his ears. It was a low rumbling thrum that Jon knew were the fans of hovertanks. A second later they came into view over the roof tops and took up guarding positions, kicking up clouds of dust and sending someone's laundry flying into the air.

The ground troops came in next, rushing by Jon and his squad with their weapons charged and ready. Passing the first few houses, small groups broke off, and covering the entrances with their weapons, kicked the doors open and rushed inside. When they reemerged, they had the stunned residents marching out at gunpoint in front of them, hands atop their heads. This scene was repeated at every home and every building until the entire population was out in the street shivering with fear and the chill in the air. And through it all, a pair of troopers were recording the event with a holocorder.

Jon felt a chill of his own, but it was not from the cold. What he was witnessing here was too similar to the fears that he and other members of the Faithful harbored. Someday, if the right-wing extremists in the Sisterhood ever had their way, this could happen on the Marionite motherworlds, to his people, he thought. He whispered up a tiny prayer against evil.

"Well," Troop Leader Annasdaater said, "I suppose we should go help with the prisoners. It's a damn sight more interesting than standing around here doing nothing."

She hefted her Mark 7 and joined a pair of Marines who were herding their captives down the street towards the open common area at the center of town. Having no alternative, Jon followed her, trying to appear as non-threatening as possible to the frightened townspeople.

In contrast, his fellow Marines all seemed to be enjoying the affair, and once or twice he saw one of them shove a male, or bark out an expletive as they marched their captors along. He looked away from the spectacle.

"Is this job a little too tough for you, Neo?" Annasdaater challenged. "You look like you have a problem."

"No, ma'am," Jon lied. He tried to adopt the same hard expression as the other troopers, but it was difficult. This was even worse than the lies he had been forced to tell Dr. elle' Kaari, or stealing the sample from N'Aida. It went against everything that he believed in.

But he also knew that the Marines around him were watching to see if he would break and he was not about to let that happen. He was a Marine, too, he forcefully reminded himself, and he had a mission to perform. And more than that, he owed the Sisters on his motherworld, and his fellow neomen, his strength. If he succumbed now, if he gave into his revusion and rebelled like he wanted to, then all of their struggles to see his kind succeed would be for naught. Motherthought would be proven right and Shaitan would win.

"You!" he shouted to one male who was lagging a bit, "Get moving! Pick up the pace."

Annasdaater glanced back over her shoulder and gave him a look of grudging approval. He had passed her test. And more importantly, he had resisted temptation. The Evil One would have to wait for another chance to thwart the truth.

At the central gathering area, the officers in charge of the landing force gave the order for the males and females to be segregated. There was some light resistance to this from a few of the captives, but in the end, the town was neatly divided between the two sexes.

This too was documented by the holocamera. When the camera's crew moved on, Jon and several other Marines were assigned to watch over the males, while the females were led into the Main Gathering Hall. Not knowing what else to do, he signaled the men to sit on the grass.

A few of them tried to make eye contact with him, but he avoided it. He couldn't bring himself to meet their eyes. For the first time since becoming a Sisterhood Marine, he felt ashamed of the uniform he wore.

Unnamed Settlement, Second Planet, HSL-48 2124A System, Unclaimed Territory, 1043.03|02|02:73:30

Lilith and Katrinn walked together down the shuttle ramp and stepped into the bright sunlight. The shuttle had landed at the end of the settlement's main street, just behind a Marine hovertank that sat on guard, covering the group of buildings.

Lilith glanced up at the trooper on duty. She was perched atop the turret manning a heavy blaster on a swivel post, and Lilith read the expression on her face. It was boredom mixed with mild confusion, as if the woman wasn't entirely sure why she was there, or what they were doing with so much firepower in the absence of any threat. She envied her for her ignorance.

"This is appalling," she said under her breath. "Absolutely appalling."

Katrinn nodded unhappily. The Zommerlaandars' mouth was set in a tight, unhappy line. "I know. Just keep it together, Lily. We'll do our job, and then we'll get out of here."

Col. Lislsdaater was standing with a group of officers a little further down the street, and when she saw Lilith and Katrinn, she broke away and marched up to them with a decided spring in her step.

"Commander," she said, saluting crisply, "the town is secure and we have the residents detained. The crew of the *Atalanta* has been located and they are in the Main Gathering Hall. We also have the town leaders isolated. They are awaiting your pleasure."

"I see," Lilith responded tightly, returning her salute and frowning at the inference that any of this 'pleased her' at all. "Did you encounter any resistance, Colonel?"

"Almost none, ma'am," the Marine replied. "I'm happy to report that the operation went quite smoothly. I also took the liberty of segregating the males from the female residents. I thought that this measure would make the interviewing process easier."

"I imagine so," Lilith replied, trying not to sound reproachful. "Tell me, have you learned anything from the settlers?"

"We haven't bothered to speak with the males yet. Not that they would have had anything intelligent to say. And the women have proven surprisingly uncooperative, despite being given the opportunity to get away from them. Really, Commander, this place--"

Lislsdaater groped for the right words, "--this place is a complete reversal of what's *right*. The women seem to actually *care* about the males like you or I would care for a *wife*. It's completely bizarre, ma'am. There's no other way to put it."

"Yes. Naturally," Lilith responded tautly. "Now, if you would be kind enough to escort me to the crew of the *Atalanta*?"

"This way, ma'am." Lislsdaater gestured for them to follow. She took one step, and then stopped and turned around to face her superiors once again. "I must warn you before you see them, ma'am. They've... they've changed from what you might expect."

Lilith paused midstride. "Oh? How so?"

"They've, well, to borrow from an ancient expression, they've 'gone native,'" Lislsdaater explained.

"Native?"

"Yes, ma'am. They're like the rest of the women now. Some of them have actually *paired* with the males here and borne *offspring* by them!"

Lislsdaater was clearly disgusted by the concept. "They've refused to speak to us, although we are fairly certain that they still speak Standard. The rest of the population speaks something only the neoman understands, and we've had to use him for most of the interviews, so it's been rather slow going."

"Yes, I can imagine," Lilith grimaced. "Let's get on with this, then."

***

The crew of the *Atalanta* sat around a table inside the Main Gathering Hall, accompanied by several uncomfortable-looking Marine guards. Jon fa'Teela had also been brought in. Lilith signaled for him to stay, but waved the other guards outside as she took her seat.

"According to her psiever signature, that's the Captain there," he said indicating the oldest of the group. "But she hasn't talked to me yet."

Lilith addressed the woman directly. "Captain? My name is Commander Lilith ben Jeni of the United Sisterhood of Suns Naval ship *Pallas Athena*. I want to find out what happened to your vessel, and how you came to be here."

The woman simply glared at her, folding her arms and shaking her head in negation. Jon repeated the question in Espangla, and got the same result.

At that point, one of the younger women, who had been staring at them with an expression of pure contempt, leaned forwards and slammed her fist on the tabletop. "We want our children back! *Now*," she snarled in Standard, "or we're telling you *nothing!*"

The Marine guards started to come back into the room, but Lilith stopped them and addressed Col. Lislsdaater. "Colonel? Is this true? Do we have their *children* in custody as well?"

"Only the males, ma'am. It was—" the officer began to say.

Lilith cut her off, barely able to contain her anger now. Orders or no, she had had enough. "Colonel, find their children and bring them here *immediately.*"

"*All* of them?" Lislsdaater asked incredulously. "Even the *males*?"

"*Yes*," Lilith said coldly. "Straightaway. And while you're at it, release the rest of the people we have in custody. I don't believe that they will prove to be *any* danger to our forces."

"But, Commander--"

"That is a direct order, Colonel!" Lilith snapped. "This farce has gone on long enough."

Before long, a rather harried-looking trooper returned with a crowd of children of varying ages. One of them, a male, maybe 10 years standard, broke away as they entered the hall, and ran to the woman who had hit the table.

Watching them embrace, it was clear to Lilith that she was seeing mother and child, reunited. A moment later, the woman looked up at her, and nodded sullenly in gratitude.

"Now," Lilith said, taking in a breath to master herself, "perhaps we can hear your story now?" This time the captain spoke, and at length. Her Standard, while somewhat out of date, and interspersed with Espangla words, was still quite clear.

***

Dr. Adalpha Martana looked nervous.

And well he should be, Lilith thought as he was brought into the room. As despicable as their own actions had been, what this man had done was just as intolerable. Although he was not entirely the criminal that Colonel Lislsdaater had described, he was also not the angel that the crew of the *Atalanta*, or the native born residents, believed him to be.

Lilith nursed her *czigavar*, glad for the strength that it was lending her, and wishing at the same time that it produced smoke so that she could blow it directly in the man's face.

"Doctor," she said through Jon, "I have had the opportunity to speak with the crew of our long range exploratory ship and they have related to me a most *involved* tale. One that is part aggression, part rescue, and part kidnapping from the sound of it. Frankly, I do not care for its overall tone.'

"For this reason, I have invited our Ship's Advocate to sit in on our interview, as I value her legal opinion." She indicated N'Dira, who had come downside as soon as Lilith had relayed the story to her.

"What we have here, if I understand the circumstances correctly," Lilith said carefully, "is what started as an accident. The *Atalanta* was entering this system and attempting to contact you, when your defensive batteries attacked it. It was forced to make an emergency landing on your planet, sustaining casualties in the process.'

493

"Apparently, the crew did send off a distress beacon, but for some reason that we have yet to determine, it was lost in Null. According to Captain n'Talla, once they had landed, your people found them and cared for their injured. *However,* before they could affect repairs to their ship, you placed them in confinement."

"Commander," the man interrupted in Espangla, "surely you can understand why. We had no idea whether they were friend or foe. We'd never seen anything like their ship before, and we had to take precautions."

"That sir, is a *lie*," Lilith retorted icily. "You nation has been aware of us for a very long time. You confined them because you received orders from your government to do so, and you kept them isolated in this little 'school' of yours for over a year before you released them into your general population. You studied them, and more importantly, you prevented them from leaving by having their ship destroyed."

She paused for a moment. "Why is that, may I ask?"

"We saw no other choice," Dr. Martana explained. "We had to learn what we could about your civilization, and we had to protect ourselves, and our society. It is nowhere near as advanced as yours and we would have had no chance of surviving a conflict."

"Understandable," N'Dira interjected, "but what you did could also be considered an act of war. Those women are our citizens. You held them here, and although they eventually acclimatized to your way of life, their adjustment could easily be interpreted as a form of Stockholm syndrome. The fact is, they were not free to leave, and had no alternatives."

"We saw no other way!" the doctor protested. "Our civilization must be protected! The culture shock alone—"He didn't finish.

"Which brings us to an interesting subject, Doctor," Lilith said steepling her fingers. "This 'civilization' that you are talking about. How often does it send supply ships here? Are they military vessels? And if so, what kind?"

"I won't tell you anything," he answered defiantly.

"No, I didn't imagine that you would," Lilith said, "but I am required to at least ask the questions. I'll leave these, and other equally important matters to be revisited by women more capable than I. Personally, I tend to agree that any sustained interaction between our two cultures would be catastrophic, but again, this is a matter for others to decide."

"However, one issue that I will resolve immediately is the fate of the *Atalanta's* crew. I plan to offer those crewmembers that wish it, passage off this world and the opportunity to return to the Sisterhood. I will also extend the same offer to any native female who wishes it."

"I'm in no position to protest, am I?" the Doctor asked her.

"No, Doctor Martana," Lilith answered. "You most certainly are not."

***

Upon their return to the *Athena*, Lilith and her officers were bio-scanned, and when their inoculars confirmed that they were disease free, they were allowed to pursue their duties. Lilith made for her office immediately and had Navcom contact Naval Command on a secure channel.

This time, when Ebed Cya came on, she was alone, and Lilith was grateful for that. She didn't want to speak with anyone from the OAE, or Thermadon just then.

"It is done, ma'am," she said, keeping her tone carefully formal.

"Good," Ebed Cya replied. "How many members of the *Atalanta's* crew decided to accept your offer of repatriation?"

"Only two," Lilith answered. "The rest have assimilated too much. They have families now. Return for them is not even a possibility. They think of themselves as natives, and frankly, seeing them with their children and their... *husbands*, I can appreciate their sentiments."

Ebed Cya nodded gravely. "Have we had any takers from the native women?"

"No, ma'am."

Her superior paused, then, "Lily, I know how hard that order was to carry out, and for what it's worth, I'm sorry."

"May I speak freely, ma'am?" Lilith asked, and when Ebed Cya assented, she dropped her controlled façade. "What we did down there was wrong!" she said. "We terrorized those people."

"We did," Ebed Cya agreed, "and it was wrong, but the holo that we took is being passed along by the Dauhgters of the Coast to their

495

leadership. It will demonstrate our resolve and I seriously doubt that they will hold any more of our sailors captive, or continue to ignore our requests for a dialogue."

Lilith had very strong misgivings on this score, but she bit her tongue. She had already said enough. Instead, she sat up straighter, and once again, became the professional soldier.

"What will happen to them now?" she asked. "To their world?"

"I'm afraid that you won't like it," Ebed Cya answered gravely. "We're going to stay at HSL-48 2124A. The *Pelé* and her battle group are on their way to relieve you.'

"They will be bringing an extra detachment of Marines with them, along with a group of intelligence specialists, and the battle group will quarantine the system. From here on, Thermadon considers HSL-48 2124A to be a Sisterhood military reservation. That will send a clear message that we can, and will, take what we need—unless our neighbors choose a friendlier alternative."

The Admiral had been completely correct in her surmise. Lilith didn't care for this news one nano, or the part she had been forced to play in it. It was not the place in history that she would have chosen for herself. Nor was this the government that she had upheld and defended for so many years. It had become something else, she had decided. Something that she didn't particulary care for at the moment.

"I see," she said, her features taut with suppressed emotion.

Ebed Cya went on. "Commander, you will immediately classify all data concerning HSL-48 2124A, Class Radiant. You are also to mark that area of space off limits to anything but military vessels and personnel with Radiant-level clearance.'

"While you are awaiting the *Pelé*, remain on station and intercept any non-Sisterhood craft that attempt to come into the area. You are also to notify this command of any such event immediately."

"Yes, ma'am," Lilith said.

"In addition, you will also make certain that all of the personnel involved in the ground action are debriefed fully. To the fullest possible extent. Staff officers such as yourself, are excluded from this requirement however."

Lilith did not understand. "Ma'am?"

"To be a bit plainer, once you are relieved, I want everyone's memories of the place scrubbed during the PTS-debriefing, except for your command staff. We cannot have the news of this civilization leaking out to the general populace. Not now. Not when we are poised for another conflict with the Hriss. We will need total solidarity if it comes to war, goddess forbid."

"I understand, ma'am."

The call ended, and Lilith relayed the information to her subordinates. After that, she gave command over to Katrinn and returned to her quarters. There, she put on her realie headset and re-started the Celina realie. She needed to lose herself in something, and wash the bad taste out of her mouth. The fate of nations would have to wait.

USSMC Training Facility, 75th Training Battalion, Hella's World, Hecate System, Artemi Elant, United Sisterhood of Suns, 1043.03|03|02:50:67

Every week, the recruits were called into Sa'Tela's office for mandatory personal counseling. Normally this involved a review of training scores and a discussion of areas that each recruit needed to improve in, but Kaly found herself dreading the affair as the day approached. She knew that the letter she had received would come up in the conversation.

Sa'Tela confirmed this when she stepped into the DI's office, and stood at attention. "N'Deena," she said, "I understand that you received some mail from home the other day."

"Ma'am, yes, ma'am."

"I also understand that you did not write back. Why not? You know that the Corps encourages recruits to stay in touch with their loved ones."

"Ma'am, this recruit decided not to," Kaly replied.

"And why is that, N'Deena?" sa'Tela inquired.

"Ma'am, this recruit considers that a private matter," Kaly answered.

"Well, its *not*," Sa'Tela informed her. "You've been coming along quite nicely in your scores and the last thing I want is for something from the outside to interfere with your becoming a Marine. *Everything* in your life is my concern. *Nothing* is private as far as the Corps is concerned. So, out with it, hatchie."

Kaly had no choice but to obey. "Ma'am, the letter was from my home. From Persephone. They want me to come back for a visit."

"And?"

"Ma'am," she said. "This recruit—this recruit is not ready. I can't face them. I can't go back there. Not yet."

Sa' Tela nodded slowly. "Believe it or not," she finally said. "I know what you're going through and I also know how hard it might be for you to believe that right now."

Kaly blinked, nonplussed.

"You think I'm some kind of martinet without a human bone in my body, don't you?" Sa'Tela asked her. "You should, it's only natural at your stage of training. You've probably even sworn to show me a thing or two and make me eat my words."

Kaly was astounded at how much the DI knew about her, and felt embarrassed.

"Don't be ashamed," the DI said as if reading her mind. "I was a young recruit once, just like you. And just like you, I stood on that same carpet and told my DI that *my* letter from home was none of *her* business.

You see, I came from a small fringe world just like Persephone that was settled by Kalian immigrants. We were raided by the Hriss, just like you were. I lost half my family in that raid. I watched them die."

"That was back in the last war, and I joined up for exactly the same reason that you did. I wanted to kill the Hriss for what they had done to me and mine. The Corps made sure that I got my chance and then some."

Kaly didn't know how to respond. She'd never given much thought to the personal histories of her instructors. Like everyone else, she had often joked that drill instructors were speed-grown in a vat somewhere and came bursting out as full-fledged Marines, with bayonets clenched in their teeth. It was very hard to picture Sa'Tela as a young woman with loved ones. Or as a clumsy hatchie like herself.

"Trust me in this," Sa'Tela said. "The best thing you can do for yourself is to write her back, and when you're ready, go back for a visit. It's the only way to heal-up. I know. I went through the same thing with my people. That's not an order by the way, just a suggestion from someone who's been there."

"Ma'am, yes, ma'am."

"All right N'Deena, dismissed."

Pensive, Kaly returned to her rack and joined the platoon in a timed drill led by Troop Leader n'Vera, assembling and disassembling her Mark 7. They were all just about perfect by this point, but of course, not perfect enough to suit N'Vera. That, they had learned was an impossibility that rivaled a spaceship surviving a trip through a black hole. By now, everyone just accepted this, even "the rebels."

The assistant DI made them repeat the exercise over and over, and for once Kaly was glad for this. The drill helped take her mind off Sa'Tela's advice. She didn't want to think about Persephone any more.

The recruits had just managed to barely satisfy the assistant DI, when Aliz bel Jeera's turn came up for an interview. After her humiliating defeat at the hands of the Hriss prisoner, Bel Jeera had been strangely withdrawn, and had eschewed even the company of her fellow agitators. She said nothing to anyone as she went into the office, and her expression was dark and troubled.

Shortly after this, a Corporal from Operations appeared in the barracks and went in. When she exited, Bel Jeera was with her. She said nothing to anyone as they left the barracks together, and kept her eyes straight ahead. She was opting out.

As they walked away across the parade ground, Sa'Tela appeared at her doorway and watched them go. Kaly saw an expression of sad resignation cross the DI's face before she closed the door again. Had she not just had her own session alone with the woman, and glimpsed her human side, she would never have believed it.

She had been wrong about the DI's, she realized. Completely wrong. Sa'Tela and her fellow instructors really *did* want everyone to succeed, and pass their training, even N'Vera. After weeks of hating them, and especially Sa'Tela, it was a stunning revelation.

Shadow Lake Lodge Nature Preserve, Nemesis, Rahdwa System, Thalestris Elant, United Sisterhood of Suns, 1043.03|03|02:52:33

Even from a distance, Maya could tell that something was wrong at the Lodge. Although the side facing the nature preserve was intact, white smoke issued from the opposite wing and there were several armored hover vehicles in orbit over the resort. They were emblazoned with the insignia of the Nemesian Planetary Militia. When the rescue 'lifters came out over the shore of the lake, one of the militia vehicles peeled away from the scene and joined up as an escort, its belly guns ranging wide.

The 'lifters and their armored guardian cleared the lake shore and came in for their final approach to the Lodge's main landing pads. Drawing closer, a makeshift morgue came into view. It had been set up at the edge of the landing field and another militia hover vehicle, an ambulance with a bright red pentagram on its side, was parked next to the rows of bodies. Its crew was busy, loading plastic body bags into its main bay while an armed militiawoman stood guard.

Maya tried not to look too closely at the bags, but like everyone else aboard her 'lifter, she wondered if any of them contained someone that she knew and cared for. Felecia reached for her, and Maya put her arm around her as the 'lifter moved over the gruesome scene and settled down onto a clear landing pad.

"I'm sure your mother made it out," she said, countering Felecia's unspoken fears. "I know that Bel Lissa and Sarah would have made sure of it." Felecia responded with a nod, but her eyes were filled with worry and she made no move to get up from her seat.

"Come on," Maya urged, "We have to get off. We have to get on with this." Felecia obeyed woodenly, unbuckling her seatbelt.

"Don't worry. I'll be with you no matter what happens," she promised her. Her lover's features brightened slightly and they disembarked together.

A militiawoman met them at the foot of the ladder. "Are you Lady Felecia n'Calysher?" she asked.

Felecia held onto Maya for support and answered the woman in a tremulous voice. "Y-yes. I am." This was the awful moment of truth, and Maya dreaded what the woman might say next.

"Your mother left instructions for me to escort you personally. Your Security Chief is waiting for you up at the Lodge. If you will follow me."

Felecia let out a ragged sob and embraced Maya. "Oh, goddess! She's alive! Oh, thank the Lady!"

"Can you tell me if everyone else in her group made it?" Maya asked, "Is Captain Inish bel Lissa and the rest of her crew all right?"

"I'm not sure, ma'am. You'll have to check with my commanding officer," the militiawoman replied, somewhat impatiently. "I only know that the Senatrix herself gave me explicit orders to see that her daughter received an escort as soon as she returned from the nature preserve. Now, if you'll follow me."

The soldier led them up into the main lobby. This time, instead of warm, welcoming lights, and smiling clerks waiting to check them in, the Lodge was illuminated by harsh emergency lights and filled with busy looking militiawomen who ignored them completely. An acrid smell hung in the air, a mixture of wood, plastic and something that Maya's mind instinctively recognized as burnt flesh--human and non-human. It was a nightmarish reversal of their first day at the resort.

"Your Security Chief is waiting for you in the main dining room," their guide said, oblivious to the transformation. Maya and Felecia followed her, stepping around a large, dark stain in the lobby's ornate carpet that looked suspiciously like someone's, or *something's,* blood.

Like the lobby, emergency lights lit up the main dining room. The nearest tables had been cleared of their finery, and boxes of supplies sat on their finely polished surfaces. Where a large picture window had once been, there was now a gaping hole that had been crudely covered over with plastic sheeting. It rippled and snapped as the breezes from the forest pushed against it.

Sharra was there, talking on a portable communications phone and as she gestured for them to wait, a militiawoman came up and offered them both cups of hot kaafra, sandwiches and blankets. Maya took the food, and after settling Felecia's blanket around the girl's shoulders, made certain that she ate.

At last, Sharra concluded her call. "Yes, that's right, Major. I want you to send teams out and find who's responsible for this. I'm not too picky about what shape they're in when they come back either. Let me know when you've found something."

501

She hung up, stood, and looked at Maya and Felecia for a long moment. Her features, at first businesslike and professional, softened.

"Lady n'Calysher--," she started to say.

Before she could finish, Felecia cast off her blanket and ran over to her, hugging the security officer fiercely. "I'm so glad you're alive, Sharra!"

Sharra fought back a tear and stepped back, quickly readopting her professional façade. "Your mother is well, and she wanted us to get you back to her as soon as possible. There's a shuttle going *upside* to Treetop Station right now."

"What about my crewmates?" Maya asked. "Are they all right?"

Sharra nodded. "Yes, they are. The minute that the impeller fencing failed and the alarms went off, they took charge of the Senatrix and left with her in the *JUDI* for Treetop. They're up there, and safe."

***

Treetop Station sat in a geostationary orbit directly above the north pole of Nemesis. It was a series of flattened spheres linked by a central spindle that reminded Maya of a child's spinning top, but on a gargantuan scale.

Because of the strict bio laws governing industry on the planet, Treetop Station was more than a mere port for starships. It was also the largest community the planet had, and its main industrial hub. The biggest sphere, taking up over a third of its gigantic mass, was completely dedicated to factories that processed the riches of the world below it into usable commodities. Vital medicines, lumber, cloth and a host of other valuable goods, came out directly from the industrial level to the space docks, and into the ships.

And as soon as one ship left, there were a dozen or more waiting for admittance. The traffic around Treetop was the fourth busiest in the Sisterhood. Hundreds of merchanters, their escort ships, and a host of service craft maneuvered around the station, or sat in space waiting for their turn to approach.

The militia shuttle was subject to no such delay. Once within range of the station's auto-control zone, it was guided past the other ships and straight to the nearest open dock.

The militia shuttle was subject to no such delay. Once within range of the station's auto-control zone, it was guided past the other ships and straight to the nearest open dock.

A trio of militiawomen met them there, armed with energy weapons and wearing fighting armor. The senior-most of them stepped forwards to meet them. "Ladies? The Senatrix has been expecting you," she said, "If you'll come along with us."

The two girls were only too glad to follow as they led them through a confusing series of side corridors and emergency passages that brought them straight to militia headquarters. The place was filled with uniformed women, and Maya saw that many of them were just as heavily armed as their escort was. The attack on the Shadow Lake Lodge had been an embarrassment for the local law enforcement agencies and it was obvious that they were not going to allow another event like it to occur.

Bel Lissa was siting on a bench near the main desk and when Maya saw her, she broke away from the militiawomen.

"Goddess!" she exclaimed, embracing her, "I'm so glad you made it out! Is everyone else okay?" Although she already knew the answer, she had to hear it again, just to confirm its reality.

"Yes," Bel Lissa replied. "We're all fine. Zara got a little banged up and I got a tiny knock to my knee. Of course, Sarah came out of it all without a scratch." Maya looked down and saw that her captain was wearing a smart splint on her right leg.

"Now, come along, both of you. The militia commander loaned out her office and the Senatrix is there, Felecia, waiting for you. I don't think she'll be able to contain herself much longer."

Waving off their escort, Bel Lissa took over and led them into a maze of cubicles until they reached the largest one, and went inside.

The moment that they entered, Felecia ran to her mother. The scene became one of tearful hugs and reassurances. Leaving them to their moment, Bel Lissa drew Maya out of the room. Sarah and Zara joined them as they came out into the hall.

"I'm glad you made it, Maya," Zara said. "We were worried about you."

"I'm glad too," Maya grinned. "It was a close thing."

"Closer than you know," Sarah said. "When the fencing went down, the forest creatures attacked the lodge in force. We barely managed to escape to the *JUDI.*'

"Despite that, the Senatrix achieved her objective; the Rampart has agreed to disarm in exchange for certain promises. Now our task will be to transport her safely back to Thermadon for a special session of the Circle. The agreement with the Rampart is not complete until she can announce it and get the specifics ratified."

A few minutes later, the Senatrix and Felecia were ready to leave, and Sharra and her security staff hustled them aboard the *JUDI,* which took off immediately. On the way towards their transit point, Sharra was contacted by the Militia Chief with fresh news and Zara piped the communication into the control room so that everyone could hear it.

The holo showed the officer, somewhere near the edge of the forest. Keela and Laa'ret hovered in the background.

"We have a good idea now about what happened," the woman informed them. The holocam panned over to a pair of bodies lying at the feet of the Nemesians.

"It looks like the Bio Action Army had a team in place here for some time, working as Lodge maintenance employees. Someone in the Rampart must have tipped them off about the conferance. The Bios set explosive charges to destroy all the power stations for the entire impeller grid at the same time, hoping to catch the Senatrix and the Rampart delegates at the meeting."

"I see," Sharra replied. "And the safari's 'lifter?"

"More sabotage. The Bio's compromised the restraint systems and planted some ghost flower cuttings aboard, wrapped in plastic. This made it too faint for the native women to pick up on, but not the neversaw. Those things can smell the tiniest part from klicks away, and they always go after anything that they think is threatening the plant. We don't know why they do this, but they do."

"So the Lady Felecia was also a target," Sharra concluded.

"Yes, ma'am," the Chief replied. "It seems that they wanted to make good on their threat to harm the Senatrix's family and friends. But there are still a few details that we're following up on."

"Such as?" Sharra asked. There was a slight delay as the answer was transmitted from the surface of the forest world to a Com satellite, and out into space.

"To get their jobs here, the terrorists had to have references. Impeccable ones. From the Lodge records, those seem to have come from some highly placed businesswomen."

"Really?" Sharra asked. At her request, the Chief sent the data, and after she thanked her, and had ended the call, she scrutinized it carefully and cross-checked through the omniplex. Shortly, she beckoned to Sarah and the others to come over and join her.

"I think that we may have a conection with Thermadon here," she said. "One of the references is a staffer who works for Feli n'Debara. N'Debara is a close personal friend of Senatrix Danna ebed Haria. Even though it's possible that the employment references may have been falsified, it does create an interesting trail."

"It does at that," Sarah agreed. "Clearly, this N'Debara will merit further investigation. Do we have any other suspects?"

"Not yet," Sharra replied. "The Chief's people are interviewing anyone who knew the workers and following up on the leads. In the meantime, the most important thing is that the Senatrix gets to Thermadon as soon as possible."

"Don't worry. The *JUDI* will get her there," Bel Lissa promised.

Bel Sharra Memorial Spaceport, Cyrene District, Thermadon City, Thermadon, Myrene System, Thalestris Elant, United Sisterhood of Suns, 1043.03|04|03:13:33

A trio of Valkyrie fighters met the *JUDI* when she reentered normal space in the Myrene System, and all inter-system traffic was routed around their approach to Thermadon. With the exception of providing landing vectors to an airstrip at the edges of Bel Sharra, there was none of the usual chatter with the Needle. The *JUDI* was expected, and as they were making their final approach, Maya saw that in addition to a pair of armored hoverlimos, a cluster of Thermadonian police cruisers and plain unmarked hovercars were also standing by. As for their fighter escort, the three

Valkyries stayed with the merchanter until they reached the tarmac, and then they ascended to assume a patrol over the assembly.

The *JUDI* came to a halt and Bel Lissa opened the cargo bay doors. The moment the ramp was down, a group of plain-clothed women toting compact military energy weapons came aboard. The sight of them drove home the fact that they were saying goodbye to one another, and Maya and Felecia ignored everyone around them, and rushed into each others arms.

"Oh, Maya!" Felecia cried. "I'm going to miss you!" Her eyes were filled with tears. Mayas were equally wet, and she gathered her in.

"We'll see each other again, Felecia. I know it!" Inwardly she wondered if this was really true, and then in a burst of emotion, she kissed Felecia deeply. "Stay safe, please," she said.

One of the security women tried to gently pull Felecia away. "Lady Felecia," she said, "we must be going. The Senatrix needs to get to the Golden Pyramid right away."

Felecia pushed the woman's hand away and embraced Maya again. "No!" she exclaimed, "I won't leave you! I can't!"

Maya silenced her protests. "No," she said, stroking her cheek tenderly. "She's right. Your mother has an important job to do and your place is here, with her. I love you, Felecia, but you must go."

Then she stepped back. Those few short steps turned out to be the hardest thing she had ever done, and she felt Bel Lissa's hand come to rest supportively on her shoulder.

Felecia sobbed in abject misery, but she cooperated with the security women as they strapped on a blast resistant vest and put a blanket over her head to conceal her identity. Then they led her down the ramp to join a group of figures waiting at the bottom. They were also covered with blankets, and by intent, it was impossible to tell who was who among them.

They were quickly shown into the two hoverlimos. And as soon as the gull-wing doors had closed, the convoy sped off towards the city, with their police escorts clearing the way while the fighters flew overwatch.

Felecia was gone.

"Come on, Maya," Bel Lissa urged. "I know a place here in the city that serves the best drinks you can find outside of Ashkele. It's no *Nulltrekker*, but I think it will do for us right about now."

Maya nodded despondently, and turned to go back inside the ship to retrieve her flight jacket.

***

The hoverlimo ascended away from the spaceport, and Felecia pressed her hands against the glass, watching as the *JUDI* was left behind. The little ship was all by itself on the huge runway now, and it was a lonely sight, made even worse by the fact that Maya was down there with it. A fresh wave of tears gushed out of her, and when she felt someone try to reassure her with their touch, she angrily shoved their hand away. Finally, when the *JUDI* disappeared from view, she sat back in her seat, her eyes raw and red.

"Maya is a remarkable young woman," the Senatrix remarked. "She is brave, resourceful, and loyal."

"I love her, mother," Felecia said. "I love her."

The Senatrix smiled patiently. "Yes, I know that you care for her. And as my daughter, and as the Senatrix that you will one day become, it is good for you to have friends like her."

"She's more than a friend!" Felecia retorted angrily. "Didn't you hear me? I *love* her!"

"I heard you, Feli," the woman replied, using her private, pet name. "Now, I will teach you one of the great lessons of statecraft. For those who hold the reins of power there can only be one true desire, and that is for power itself. Everything else must take second place. Even love."

Felecia shook her head in denial, but the Senatrix reached over and gave her hand a gentle pat. "Care for her as you will, Feli. In fact, I encourage your friendship. The day may come when Maya will be the captain of that valuable little ship, and you will need all the assistance that she can offer you. Her affection will guarantee her aid.'

"But *never* let her be anything more than a friend. When you do marry, it will be to someone who will help you consolidate your power base, not to a common smuggler. She is, and must always be, a useful tool, and nothing more."

"No!" Felecia retorted. "You're *wrong* mother! You didn't do that when *you* married!"

507

The Senatrix smiled again, but now there was a hint of saddness in her eyes as she remembered her pairmate, and the pain of losing her. Even after so many years it was still sharp.

"Yes, daughter, I did," she said at last. "You see, your mother and I married for political expediency, not for love. But in time, we grew to care for one another.'

"As for Inish bel Lissa, she and I had our affair, just like you and Maya did, and then we grew apart. But even now, she is still loyal to me. You must do the same thing with Maya. That, my daughter, is what it is to be a Senatrix."

CHAPTER 15

USSNS *Lilya Litvak*, Hella's World, Hecate System, Artemi Elant, United Sisterhood of Suns, 1043.03|04|03:75:00

Kaly stood in line with the rest of her platoon, her spacesuit helmet cradled in one arm. As Sa'Tela walked past, she was careful to keep her face expressionless, but her insides felt as if they were full of icewater. The platoon was about to go on their first space-walk, and her mind was filled with nightmarish images of all the things that might go wrong once they were outside. Although everyone else seemed calm enough, she knew that she wasn't the only one who was frightened. Most of her fellow recruits had never been outside a ship in space either, and the night before their trip upside, there had been plenty of horror stories shared in whispers between the racks.

She was especially worried about how Lena would react. Her battle sister had expressed the most trepidation of all, but Enggredsdaater had quietly assured Kaly that she would help her to keep an eye on their friend.

"All right, recruits," Sa'Tela began, "Today will be our first walk in space. This will be the first phase in your training for EVA, or Extra Vehicular Activity. EVA Training will include basic ship repair, rescue techniques, and zero-g combat. Before we go outside, I want to call your attention to the sign above the airlock. Read it and commit its words to memory."

The sign bore a simple, but forbidding message: "Forget and Die!" Kaly swallowed nervously.

"That, ladies," the DI said, pointing up to the words, "is the operative phrase for any operation in space. If you skip a step putting on your suit, or you forget to clip onto a safety line, or make the mistake of doing any number of other important things, space *will* kill you! And you are *not* allowed to die on my watch. Any questions?"

Naturally, no one spoke.

"Good. I will now inspect your suits. I'd better find that the PTS class on Zero-G suits was taken to heart by each and every one of you. *Stand-to!* Prepare for inspection!"

The platoon came as close as they could to full attention in their grey armored suits. Sa'Tela and the other DI's walked up and down the row, reading everyone's gauges and checking hose lines. Kaly passed muster like most of the class, but another woman down the line was called out.

"Recruit t'Harria!" N'Vera suddenly barked, "Your oxy-tank gauges are reading in the yellow! Is that the way they're supposed to be?"

"Ma'am, no, ma'am!" the woman replied. T'Harria, while no troublemaker like Bel Jeera had been, had had problems adapting to the Marine way of doing things since day one. Even the comparatively simple exercise of making up her rack was still frustrating her.

"Then *why* the *fek* are *you* standing in my line? Get your ass over to the filling station and top this suit off, *now!*" While the woman hustled off to attend to this oversight, Sa' Tela addressed the rest of the platoon.

"*That* woman is a moron," she declared. "She failed to perform a full check of her suit. Watch her carefully! If she failed to take care of such a simple detail, she'll probably fail to catch something else later on. Something that will get *you* killed right along with her.'

"I will now share a gem of wisdom with you; *always* pay attention to what you are doing! Most disasters happen because someone didn't. Think about *that* while we wait for your fellow hatchie to return."

T'Harria came back to the line a few minutes later and the instructors checked her suit again. But this time, they found no fault with it.

"Hatchies, you will now put on your suit helmets on and seal up."

Kaly brought her helmet up and over her head in time with the others, and locked it into place. Fresh air from the suits tanks began circulating right away, as internal HUD displays came to life before her eyes. She quickly read them over and confirmed that all systems were online and functioning.

Then the DI's went over to the airlock door. "Training Platoon Carli preparing for EVA exercise," Sa'Tela said to the *Litvak's* Command Center. "Un-securing the inner hatch."

The door behind her slid open, revealing an immaculate chamber that looked just large enough to fit everyone. At the far end was a small window that framed a view of the universe outside; a flat black expanse of pure nothingness dotted with a few stars.

"All right, hatchies! Step inside the airlock. There, you will snap into the main safety line with the carabiner attached to your suit. Make sure to test your attachments. As soon as you are secured, raise your hand and we will inspect you."

Kaly walked inside and located the line. Clamping herself in, she gave the connection two good tugs, just like her training realie had taught her, and then she raised her hand.

Troop Leader n'Vera came over and checked her connection. Satisfied that she was secure, the woman moved on, inspecting everyone until she was certain that they were all ready.

"I will now close the inner door and evacuate this chamber," Sa'Tela announced. "Once this chamber has been evacuated, I will open the outer hatch. You will remain in place during this process. Once the outer hatch has opened, I will step out. Then you will follow me one at a time until the entire platoon is outside the ship. Zat klaar?"

"Ma'am, yes, ma'am!" the platoon responded. Compensators in their suit speakers kept this from deafening everyone on the shared frequency.

Sa'Tela clipped herself in, and when she was secure, purged the airlock. Then she opened the outer door and exited the chamber. "Make sure to engage your mag-shoes as you step out onto the hull," she advised.

As Kaly waited her turn, she ran through a manual of arms drill in her head to distract her from her fears, and then it was time for her to step outside.

The *Litvak* was in orbit over Hella's World, a mere 32,186 km above the surface, and the sight of the huge mustard-yellow planet took Kaly's breath away. Despite the fact that she knew what a hellish place it really was, the desert world suddenly seemed more like a rare gem to her, nestled in the black velvet of the void.

And instead of being terrifying, she found that space was incredibly beautiful. She was so overcome by the scene around her that she almost forgot to engage her mag-shoes. At the last moment, she turned them on and the shoes locked onto the hull plating with a dull 'clank' that sounded up through her suit and into her helmet.

"All right, hatchies," Sa'Tela said, "We will now walk over to the main com array to simulate a repair. At all times, make sure you are clamped into your safety line, and that your safety line is clamped onto the hull. Keep your eyes on your goal and do not let your attention wander. Move forwards, now."

Obediently, the platoon shuffled across the *Litvak*. Their mag-shoes made it slow going, but they soon reached the massive antennae of the Com array, and halted.

"Now, each of you will clamp onto a restraining loop and walk along the hull until I tell you to stop," Sa'Tela instructed. "This will be by the numbers; the first in line will walk to the port side and the second to starboard, and so on. Take it slowly and carefully. I do *not* want to have to rescue anyone today."

Kaly withdrew a second carabiner from her hip belt and drew out the line. When it was clamped in to a loop on the hull, she released the first one, and with it, her connection to the main safety line.

One step at a time, she told herself. *Don't look up. Just go straight ahead.* Slowly and with infinite care, she moved down along the hull, listening on the platoon's frequency for the Troop Leader's orders.

Instead, she heard the sound of rapid breathing, accompanied by inarticulate cries of fear. One of the other recruits was starting to panic.

"I've got to get back inside!" the woman suddenly wailed. "I've got to get back in before I fall off!"

"T'Harria!" Sa'Tela shouted. "Stop right where you are! Do *not* release that safety line! Do you hear me? *Shess*! Someone get her!"

"Kaly!" Lena yelled."Your right!

She looked over her shoulder just in time to see T'Harria floating by, her limbs flailing helplessly. Without thinking, she grabbed for the woman's leg.

The instant that she made contact, T'Harria's inertia slammed them both onto the hull. The impact momentarily dazed Kaly, but she held on to T'Harria, who continued to struggle against her like a drowning victim. Lena joined them, lending her strength, and then Sa'Tela and the other DI's arrived, clamping T'Harria onto the nearest loop. When she was finally secure, Sa'Tela touched her helmet to Kaly's.

"Are you all right?" she asked, the vibrations of her voice carrying her words through Kaly's helmet.

512

"Yes, ma'am," Kaly answered, realizing that she could taste blood in her mouth. "My suit still has integrity and I can walk back. I think I bit my tongue though."

Sa'Tela chuckled. "You and your battle sister did good, N'Deena. Now get back up to the main line and hook in." With that, the Troop Leader got back on the main platoon frequency and ordered everyone back inside. That day's lesson was definitely over.

Later in the evening, and back on Hella's World, Sa'Tela came into the barracks and made an announcement.

"Hatchies," she said solemnly. "Recruit t'Harria will not be rejoining this platoon after she gets out of medbay. Instead, she will be mustering out on my recommendation. Any Marine who cannot walk in space is useless to the Corps."

Kaly found herself agreeing. The Troop Leader was right, she thought. T'Harria had no business being a Marine if she couldn't even get through the basics of working in space. It was for the best.

Sa'Tela wasn't finished though. "It is also my duty to announce a change. As part of the normal rotation of leadership, Platoon Leader bel Anny is hereby demoted back to Recruit. For her actions upside today, and for her overall performance to date, Recruit n'Deena is hereby promoted to Platoon Leader. Well done, hatchie." Then she turned and marched back through the door without any further ceremony.

"Congratulations, Kaly," Bel Anny said, clapping her on the shoulder. "You deserve it."

"Yah, *gaad vork*, Kaly," Enggredsdaater agreed.

"You're not angry with me?" Kaly asked Bel Anny.

Bel Anny grinned. "Goddess, no! I've had enough responsibility for one life. I was thinking lately about how much I enjoyed just being a plain hatchie, and it looks like Sa'Tela read my mind. You're welcome to it, and all the wonderful ass-chewing sessions that come with it. Congratulations, Platoon Leader."

She gave Kaly a mock salute.

Special Military Quarantine Zone, Second Planet, HSL-48 2124A System, Unclaimed Territory, 1043.03|04|05:10:39

After the USSNS *Penthesilea* and her sister ships had taken up station, the Marines from the 115th were relieved and shuttled back upside to the *Athena*. Once aboard, they had to stand in a long line to present their inoculars and get bio-scanned before they were allowed to go down to Five-bar. In typical Marine fashion, the troopers were given just enough time to stow their equipment at their racks, before being instructed to report for debriefing.

At a command from Col. Lislsdaater, Jon and everyone in his unit put on their headsets and sat back. Although he was unhappy at the idea of losing the memory of his experiences on HSL-48 2124A, he took a certain comfort in the fact that he had at least managed to send the hair sample to New Covenant beforehand.

What he had seen at the School had only strengthened his resolve to support the Great Work in any way that he could. Without the Redeemer, there was simply no hope for the women of the Sisterhood, or humanity.

This was his last coherent thought before the PTS-feed began.

***

Jon sat up from the PTS-chair and blinked away the after-images. His mind felt like it had been run through an autochef, and he found it hard to even recall the events prior to entering the star system. Something had happened after that point, he was certain of it, but except for a dim sense that it had been important, and that time had passed, he could not apprehend the memories. A glance at the other Marines around him told him that they suffered from the same amnesia.

"It must have been a classified mission," Troop Leader Annasdaater opined. "They always scrub our brains after the really high-level stuff. Ah wells, we'll probably get another medal for doing something we can't remember doing, eh, girls?" The women around her laughed and got up from their chairs.

Jon was the last to leave, and made his way back to his bunk deeply troubled by his memory loss. As he lay in his rack, he tried to recapture everything. Fragments surfaced eventually, disconnected visions that danced like half-dreams in his mind. He concentrated on them, putting his talents to work, and slowly, the visions started to become more, and more coherent. By the time it was lights out, it had all come back to him. He remembered everything.

"Be well, Reesy," he thought. "May Jesu and Mari watch over you and your people." He whispered a silent prayer of protection for the girl and drifted off to sleep.

HFS *Pillager,* Black Star Clan (Captured Enemy Asset), In Permanent Orbit, Hella's World, United Sisterhood of Suns, 1043.03|05|03:88:64

"Watch your corners!" Sa'Tela yelled. "Team 2, make sure to cover Team 1 as they move forwards to take the objective! I don't want to see you leaving them unprotected!"

Kaly leveled her Mark 7 at the junction of the passageway ahead of her and rushed past the covering team. Platoon Carli was simulating a boarding operation in an enemy ship, and their job was to secure the engine-room. They'd all found out very quickly that a Hriss ship was laid out much differently than Sisterhood vessels. Vital routes like the one leading to the engine room were a maze of sharp corners and side passages that were deliberately designed to give its defenders a distinct advantage against any boarding party.

Kaly neared the end of the corridor, and then stopped and withdrew a GSG-20 grenade from her hip pouch. She flicked the arming switch to 'on' and let go of the small sphere. It floated in the air for a moment as its computer came to life, and then the grenade flew away and went around the corner.

A sharp ping sounded in her suit speakers as the weapon simulated detonation. According to the AI monitoring the exercise, three enemies had been killed by the blast when the GSG had committed virtual suicide.

"Good work, Team 1," Sa'Tela said. "But you got lucky with that grenade, N'Deena. All this metal could have easily masked the enemy's biosignatures. Try it on dumbfire and just roll it down there next time. That can be just as effective, if not more so, in an environment like this. Now, clear the rest of the way to the objective."

Kaly thought about this and spoke into her suit-mike. "Team 3, send out the battlebot." Team 3, which was behind her, activated the machine and the spider-like robot trundled by, its metal legs clanking loudly through the hull-plates.

As the exercise's Assault Leader, Kaly automatically received a visual feed from the 'bot's electronic eyes. A black and white image appeared in the upper left of her helmet's HUD, showing what the 'bot saw as it moved into hostile territory. The corridor appeared to be clear of enemies and the 'bot stopped just short of a large pressure door at the end, training its weapons on it.

Studying the image for a moment, Kaly realized that the door would require a breaching charge to get past it. Team 2 would have that job, she decided.

"Clear," she said over the platoon's common frequency, waving them forwards. To her satisfaction, Team 2 didn't waste any time. They moved past her and set the charge. Then everyone retreated back around the corner.

"Fire in the hole!" the team leader cried. A bright, blue-white tongue of flame flashed around the edges of the thick metal door, and then the portal tottered and fell inwards, trailing smoke. It slammed onto the decking with a resounding crash and immediately, low-power energy bolts lit up the passage, simulating enemy forces attempting to defend the breach.

The battlebot engaged them instantly, firing its energy guns and launching a hail of grenades. According to the data Kaly received from it, all the virtual defenders had just been eliminated, and the passage was clear. From what she could see through the 'bots feed, the corridor the enemy had guarded only went on for a short distance before it branched into two directions.

"All right, N'Deena," Sa'Tela said. "The defenders may be guarding both sides of the intersection ahead of you, or only one, or neither. Take it whatever way you think is the fastest and safest. But don't take too long to make up your mind."

Kaly considered her options, and then gave her order. "Team 1, advance to the 'bot's current position. Team 3, advance the 'bot ahead of us to the intersection. We'll follow it."

516

While Kaly and her team ran up to the doorway, the battlebot stepped across the threshold and advanced. They followed behind it, keeping a careful distance and covering the space ahead of them with their weapons.

When the machine entered the intersection, a rapid-fire succession of energy bolts lanced out at it from the left, hitting its sensor array and one of its forward legs. Simulating internal damage, the 'bot obediently collapsed and cut its visual feed before Kaly could see what had 'killed' it.

She shrank back from the gunfire and brought out a second grenade. Mindful of Sa'Tela's earler advice, she set it for dumbfire, and threw it at the far wall, bouncing it around the corner. This time, there was no ping announcing a kill. Instead, something destroyed the grenade as it landed and rolled along the deck.

Such pinpoint accuracy told her that whatever was down there was not organic life, and she reasoned that it was probably an enemy battlebot of some kind. A GSG set for tracking bioplasmic would have been useless.

Making a mental note to remember this important lesson, Kaly opened up another pouch on her belt, withdrawing a microbot launcher. It was a diminutive gun-like object that resembled a child's toy, but it had a serious purpose.

As she pressed the trigger, a tiny pellet, that was almost too small for human eyes to detect, emerged. Simultaneously, a visual feed started up in her HUD as the little spy device came to life. Kaly punched in instructions on the controls on her suit arm and the little 'bot flew down the passage and around the corner. It revealed that a large battlebot was guarding the junction.

Her assessment had been correct. "Team 2, guided grenade, now!" she ordered. "Patch onto the micro's signal." At the same time, she ordered the diminutive 'bot to paint the target with a laser beam.

A larger, faster version of the smart grenade flew past her, homing in on the microbot's signal. Then a ping sounded. The enemy battlebot was dead.

"Allright, advance forwards and secure the engine room" Sa'Tela instructed. Kaly ordered her teams into motion.

That night, after they'd completed the exercise, Sa'Tela praised their work. "You did good," she told them. "Most hatchies get caught by that hidden 'bot. You didn't. Just remember what you learned when it comes time to face the real thing."

To underscore how pleased she was, she rewarded the training platoon with one of the latest realies from Thermadon, and a case of Zommerlaandar beer. They'd all come far in the last few weeks and she wanted them to know it.

Kaly took hers outside and sat with Lena on the steps of their barracks. Taking a long, slow pull from her ice-cold bottle, she looked up at the stars and let herself enjoy the moment. Nothing had ever tasted sweeter.

USSMC Training Facility, 75th Training Battalion, Hella's World, Hecate System, Artemi Elant, United Sisterhood of Suns, 1043.03|10|03:33:33

Platoon Leader Kaly n'Deena stood at ease in her Class 'A' uniform, in front of Platoon Carli, which was only a smaller part of a much larger formation made up of all the training platoons that had reached graduation. Intellectually, she knew that this was the very last day of Basic, but she still had a hard time believing it.

Only six metric weeks had passed since she had first stepped out of a crowded shuttle onto Hella's World, but in that time it was as if every part of her former existence had been erased and replaced with the Marine standing there on the concrete parade ground. She felt as if she had always been in training, with no past before day one, with no mothers other than her drill instructors and no family except her fellow recruits. It seemed impossible to her that this phase of her life was now coming to an end.

A group of officers walked out and solemnly mounted a metal platform that stood before the bronze statue of Molla n'Dayr, the famous heroine of the First Widow's War. Kaly and the rest snapped to attention.

Then an honor guard composed of the drill instructors from all the training platoons came forwards and raised the banners of the United Sisterhood of Suns and the Marine Corps on a pair of flagpoles. In tandem with the other platoon leaders, Kaly barked out a command to her group. "Platoon! Attention. Present... *arms!*"

Everyone on the field saluted the two banners as the national anthem, *"Sisters United,"* played out over a speaker.

"United are we, sisters to-gether, Holding hands--across the stars!
Standing bravely, sisters to-gether, We band--against the foe!
United are we, sisters to-gether, Holding hands--across the stars!'

"Working proudly, sisters to-gether, We build--our worlds strong!
Dreaming boldly, sisters to-gether,
We bring--to our daughters,light!
United are we, sisters to-gether, United Sister-hood of Suns!"

Although Kaly had known this song since primary, it had never had the meaning that it suddenly did for her now. Simple words with a simple message that the Marine Corps had incorporated into its motto: "Sisterhood. Sacrifice. Honor." It had been hammered into her very soul in Basic and now, she was proud to be playing a part in the grand scheme that it represented.

The recruits held their salute until the very last notes of the song had played themselves out. Then Col. Rayna n'Pela, the Commanding Officer of the 75th Training Battalion, stepped forward to address them.

"Ladies," she said, "You have reached the end of your training here on Hella's World. You have accomplished what many women would not have the strength, or the courage to achieve, and have become the stronger for it. From this day forwards, you will no longer be referred to as 'hatchies' or 'recruits'. Instead, you will have the honor of being addressed as Marines. Marines who have passed through some of the toughest training of any facility in the Sisterhood.'

"Some of you will go on from here and become support staff. Others will become front-line troopers, facing our enemies on the battlefield. No matter what your assignment is, no matter where you are stationed, and no matter what dangers you might face, nothing will change the fact that you are all part of an elite sisterhood, now and forever.'

"It has been our great honor to oversee your training, and our privilege to be the first to salute you. Congratulations, Marines. The Sisterhood is proud of what you have become." At that, the Colonel, her fellow officers, and the Drill Instructors snapped to attention and saluted the assembly.

Tears welled up in Kaly's eyes and her throat tightened as she and her fellow Marines returned their salutes.

I've made it, she thought, feeling almost dizzy with elation. *By the goddess, I've made it!*

The same scrawny, *klaxxy* girl that had stood in front of a Marine encampment on a cold dawn a lifetime ago, and had endured so many hardships since then, had survived, and been reborn.

I'm a Marine, she told herself. *A Marine.*

***

Having graduated Basic, the former hatchies of Platoon Carli did what soldiers like them had been doing for centuries. They went to the nearest bar to celebrate, and get themselves insensibly drunk. On Hella's World, the one establishment open to enlisted personnel was the *Sun, Sword and Starship.*

It had none of the frills that might have been expected on more cosmopolitan planets, but no one who came there really cared. Like everything else on the training planet, it was simple, functional and kept itself focused on its primary mission. Which in this case, was serving strong alcohol in large quantities.

None of the new Marines had taken the time to change out of their Class 'A' uniforms, and no one bothered them about it. Graduation was one of the few times when a trooper wasn't held to the usual regulations.

The bar was packed to capacity with new Marines, and Kaly had some trouble making her way inside and finding her teammates among a sea of red tunics. Fortunately, Lena n'Gari spotted her and pulled her in through the crowd.

"Kaly!" she laughed, "Come on! Enggredsdaater is having a contest with Bel Anny to see who can down the most shots! My credits are on Berta."

Someone pressed a drink into Kaly's hand as they reached the bar, and she took a long pull on it. Whatever was in her glass burned like fire as it went down her throat and she coughed, but then, a pleasant warmth spread through her body that more than made up for the pain.

Just as Lena had advertised, Enggredsdaater and Bel Anny were downing shots, and Kaly could tell from the number of overturned glasses, and the glow that each of them had, that their contest had been going on for some time. Seeing her, Bel Anny nodded to Kaly with her shot glass, and then downed the contents in one gulp, spilling some of it down her chin and laughing. Not to be outdone, Enggredsdaater took up another glass and drank it down, wobbling unsteadily as the alcohol hit her.

"Come on, Kaly!" Lena urged, holding up her glass, "I know you only took one sip. You've got to join your sisters! We've all got to have the same hangovers in the morning! It's regulations!" Before Kaly could refuse her, Lena pressed the glass up to her lips. She tried to get away with a polite sip, but Enggredsdaater had seen what was happening and threw a huge arm around her.

"Yah, Kaly, *gaane-an, drenkka!*" she laughed.

Trapped between the two of them, Kaly had no choice, and Lena showed her no mercy, pouring in a large mouthful. It was the same rocket fuel that she'd been served a few moments earlier, but it went down easier this time. Either it tasted better, or it had simply managed to deaden her senses enough to seem that way. Although she knew that a truly murderous hangover was going to be waiting for her in the morning, her friends' abandon, and the strong drink, made that concern seem less and less important with each passing second.

In the meantime, Bel Anny and Enggredsdaater were each trying to get her involved in their shots contest. But then Troop Leader n'Vera walked up and surprised them. It was more than the woman's presence that was unexpected however. It was also her expression: for the first time ever, Kaly saw a smile on her face.

What was even more startling was what she said to Kaly as she raised her glass to her. "Congratulations, N'Deena. I knew you'd make it all along."

Not quite certain how to reply, Kaly tentatively returned her toast. The Troop Leader grinned broadly at this and winked at her. Then she turned and disappeared back into the crowd. Lena, who had been watching the entire exchange, was open mouthed with surprise, and when she and Kaly looked at one another, they both burst into laughter.

521

"That must be some pretty strong stuff she was drinking," Kaly declared, shaking her head in disbelief.

"Well, whatever it is, I *want* some!" Lena replied.

The crowd parted for an instant, and Kaly saw Sa'Tela, sitting by herself at the back of the room in a booth. They made eye contact, and Kaly excused herself from her companions, and walked over to join her.

From the half empty bottle and the shine in the Kalian's eyes, she could tell that the woman was well into her cups. True to her nature though, her hand on her glass was rock-steady.

"Do you mind if I join you, or is this private, ma'am?"

Sa'Tela laughed quietly and waved to her to take a seat. "Actually, I was expecting you, N'Deena. Want some of this? It's *Aqqa*, a little something from Sita that's just a bit stronger than that weak tea you've got there." Kaly downed what was left of her drink and held out her empty glass.

Sa'Tela poured her some of the clear liquid. "We're handing out unit assignments tomorrow, then you'll have some leave time before you have to report in. Have you given any thought to what we talked about?"

Kaly knew that she was referring to Persephone, and after considering her drink for a moment, downed the contents. It was as wicked as Sa'Tela had warned, and just about the perfect strength for the topic of their conversation.

"You'll never finish it if you don't go back," Sa'Tela warned. "Even if it's just for a day, you have to go back there. It won't bring anyone back that you lost, but it *will* honor them. They deserve that."

Kaly didn't reply and held out her glass again.

"I went back to my home," Sa'Tela continued as she poured out another glassful. "I went to where they all were and I said a prayer for them, and I left a flower. Then I turned around and didn't look back. I've been marching on ever since, but I know they're back there, watching me. I'd like to think that I've made them proud."

They looked across the table at each other and shared a long silence, then Kaly got up. "Thank you for the drink, Troop Leader—and for everything else."

522

Sa'Tela put down her glass and saluted her. "My pleasure. You are dismissed, Marine." Kaly returned her salute and walked back to the bar.

By this time, Lena was dancing with Bel Anny, and when she saw her, the girl giggled and pulled Kaly in to join her. "Dance with me, Kaly," N'Gari invited, throwing her arms around Kaly's neck, "I want to feel *good* tonight." Her mood was infectious, and Kaly let it sweep her up. It was a night for celebration, she told herself. Persephone could wait.

***

With a few exceptions, most of Platoon Carli made a point of visiting the medbay as their first order of business the following day. Knowing where they had been the night before, and why, the medics treated them with a remedy for hangovers that medical personnel had known for centuries. This was a combination of painkillers, B-12 injections, and pure oxygen. As a result, they were able to present a reasonably military bearing when Sa'Tela and the other DI's had them gather in the barracks for what was to be their last meeting as a platoon.

"Well ladies," Sa'Tela said. "Today is that special day when we find out where everyone is going to be posted."

Despite consuming a massive quantity of *Aqqa*, and goddess knew what else, the DI looked as fresh and as sober as a Marionite Sister. To add insult to injury, her fatigues were even neatly pressed. It was disgusting and Kaly wished she knew how the woman had managed it.

"I'm going to call out each of your names," she informed them, "and you will come up to receive your orders."

Bel Anny was the first of their circle to be called. "Bel Anny, it looks like you're going to pull guard duty on Rixa. Who the *fek* do you know in Command? I want to get my butt powdered and perfumed, too!"

The girl blushed and went up to take her orders from N'Teri. Enggredsdaater was the next one up.

"Enggredsdaater, you're pulling duty with the 201st aboard the USSNS *Roza Shanina*. They're a tough outfit, and they need tough women like you. I'll expect to hear great things about you. *Faalistaar, Zommerlaandar!*"

The big blond smiled shyly and worked her way through everyone's congratulatory pats on the back, including Kaly's. "Zat vas my mother Enggred's old unit," she told them.

"I know she'll be proud of you, Berta. Both your mothers will be," Kaly replied.

"N'Deena!" It was Sa'Tela.

Kaly's head whipped around. "Yes, ma'am?"

"You're serving with the 115th, aboard the USSNS *Pallas Athena,* so I guess you named your blaster right. They're a front line unit like the 201st, so I'll expect you to do us all proud."

She took the flimsy from N'Teri, and gave Lena a reassuring smile. Her battle sister returned it, but weakly, and her green eyes were filled with apprehension. The night before, she had confessed that the prospect of joining a new unit filled with strangers terrified her. That, and the hope that somehow, they would be posted together somewhere.

Goddess, Kaly thought, *grant her wish, please.*

When her name was called, N'Gari jumped up, startled and fearful. "N'Gari!" Sa'Tela said. "You're going to be with N'Deena in the 115th. Watch out for each other."

Lena's relief was palpable. There were tears in her eyes, and her hand shook as she accepted her orders. Flimsy in hand, she rushed over to Kaly and gave her a big and rather un-military hug. "I'm so glad we'll be together!" she sobbed, "Isn't it wonderful?"

Thank you, Lady, Kaly thought as she returned her embrace.

Newhearth Colony, Persephone, Demeter System, Sagana Territory, United Sisterhood of Suns, 1043.03|12|07:72:98

Kaly had to fight the sensation that she was existing in two realities at once. Her eyes told her that the living center was still there, and with the exception of a few extra windows that she didn't recall, it looked exactly the same as it had before the invasion.

Out in the gathering square, gilded by the late afternoon sunlight, there was the same flagpole, flying the banners of the Sisterhood and the Sagana Territory. Underneath this were plastic and metal play-sets that the little ones always used when they weren't in primary. And somewhere ahead of her, she heard the familiar sounds of someone laughing coupled with the soft sighing of the wind coming in over the fields.

At the same time, another scene overlapped this. In that world, it was nighttime and dark pools of blood stained the grass in the square. The corpses of the colonists lay there, their eyes open wide with the uncomprehending stares of the dead. Blaster fire crackled nearby, and the air reeked with a sickening combination of smoke, ozone, and burned flesh.

She shook her head, willing these grim images away and sensing her distress, Lena offered her her hand. Kaly squeezed it with such fierceness that her companion gasped, and she let go and apologized.

A little further down the road, she recognized the broad flat area where the bodies had been buried, and stopped. The earth-moving machines were gone now and grass had covered over the pits. A flat black widow's stone sat in the middle of this expanse in a small gravel covered circle. It was flanked by low benches and flowers. Even from where she stood, Kaly could see the laser carved inscriptions etched on the stone's surface.

Once again, the other universe intruded, tormenting her with its troubling visions. In her mind's eye, she could see past the peaceful shroud of grass to the truth that lay beneath it. The white plastic body bags were still there, lying together in silent ranks like huge bloated earthworms condemned to an eternity of darkness.

I should'nt have come here, she thought. It was too much to bear.

She started to turn around, but Lena retook her hand, and urged her forwards. "Come on, Kaly," she said gently. "We have to do this. They're waiting for us."

Kaly nearly refused, but then after a long moment, she nodded in agreement. Lena was right, and so was Sa'Tela. She had to finish this journey, and she was grateful that N'Gari was there to help her.

Bella n'Mari was waiting for them at the edge of the Gathering Square. Although only six standard weeks had passed, the woman seemed much older than Kaly remembered her, and her eyes were shadowed with their own painful memories. *It must have been even harder for her,* she realized, *to stay here with all these ghosts.*

525

The old woman came up and took Kaly's hand in hers. "Welcome back, Kaly. We've missed you."

She started to answer, but words failed her and she took the schoolteacher into her arms instead. The woman was as frail as a bird, and as they embraced, Kaly could feel how many years of life the invasion had stolen away from her.

At last, she stepped back, and brushed a tear from her eye. "This is Lena," she managed to say. "She and I went through basic training together."

N'Mari smiled sadly. "Welcome to Persephone," she said, and then she led them across the square and into the living center.

The colonists had prepared a dinner for them in their honor and although Kaly tried her best to enjoy it, there were too many faces that she didn't know, and too few that she did. Lena stayed by her side through the whole affair, and with her help, she managed to make it through to the end, but only barely. It was just past sunset by the time they walked back into the gathering square with N'Mari.

"Are you leaving now?" the woman asked her. It was more of a statement than a real question, and she'd been merciful enough not to ask them to spend the night.

"Yes," Kaly replied. "I have one more thing to do and then we're taking the shuttle back."

N'Mari nodded slowly in understanding. "I'm glad that you came, Kaly" the teacher said. "Your mothers would have wanted that. I know that wherever they are now, they're proud of you."

Kaly gave the woman another hug.

"*Bian gà,* Kaly," N'Mari said. "Think of us from time to time, won't you?" They both knew that this was the last time that they would ever see one another again.

"I will," Kaly promised her. The old woman gave her another sad smile, and then turned away and walked back across the square.

Kaly watched her until she had disappeared inside the living center, and then picked up her kit bag and started back down the road. Lena stayed beside her, saying nothing.

When they reached the memorial park again, Kaly set her bag down and walked out to the widow's stone. She touched its cool surface, feeling the names carved into its face with her fingertips. The failing light made it impossible for her to read them, but she didn't need to.

She already knew their names; they were her mothers, her aunts, and all of her friends. Everyone.

At last, when she was ready, she stepped back and rejoined her companion. They walked together towards the fading glow on the horizon, and the shuttle that would take them away from Persephone, but not its ghosts. Those would stay with Kaly wherever she went.

***

They spent the night together in a private cabin aboard the supply ship, the CSS *Sacajawea*, which had come to the Demeter System as part of its normal delivery route. They'd been able to afford the berth thanks to the generous discounts that private businesses gave to military personnel, especially in the light of the raid on Persephone. In the morning, they were scheduled to catch another connection and meet their platoon-mates on the water-world of Tethys. There, they would finish out their leave at one of its many resorts.

Lying in her bunk, despair robbed Kaly of any joy that she might have felt. She knew that visiting Persephone had been the right thing to do, but as she tried to sleep, she could see the widow's stone in her mind, and then the faces of everyone that had died. They passed by in silent review, and the tears that she had been suppressing for so long finally arrived. She wanted to resist them, to dam up everything inside of herself behind a wall of denial just like she had been since the night of the attack, but she no longer possessed the strength.

Her only option was to surrender, and at last, she let the pain flow out of her in long gasping sobs. As the tears flowed freely down her face, her anguish felt so deep and so powerful that it seemed as if she would never be able to stop weeping. And for one terrified instant, she even wondered if her grief would manage to drive her insane.

527

Sensing the crisis, Lena came over to her. Kaly barely felt her as she lay down on the bed and wrapped her arms around her.

Finally, the pain subsided, and Kaly was able to look up at her, her eyes raw with sorrow. "I'm glad you came with me," she stammered. "Thank you, Lena."

"That's what battle sisters are for," Lena answered tenderly, "We take care of each other."

Kaly gave her a weak smile, and they looked into each other's eyes. Then impulsively, she suddenly raised herself up and kissed Lena on the lips.

Lena blinked. For a long moment, her expression was thoughtful, as if she were carefully evaluating what had just happened. Then her features softened, and she leaned in and returned the kiss, long and deeply.

CHAPTER 16

The Grand Abbess of the Abbey of New Bethlehem awoke with a start. The com light was blinking at the other corner of her bedroom. Rising reluctantly, she gathered her nightgown around her and accessed the time on her psiever. It was 01:68.

"This had better be important," she muttered to herself. Morning prayers were only two hours away, and at her age sleep was hard enough to come by as it was.

"Connect," she said wearily. The com came alive, filling the room with light. The image of Sister-Professor Tara n'Amela, head of the Order's ultra-secret *Project Advent* appeared. From the woman's expression, the Abbess could tell that she was very excited.

"Sister-Professor?" she asked, "What brings you to call on me at such an ungodly hour? Is something wrong?"

"Wrong, Grand Abbess?" the woman replied, "No, by Jesu *nothing* is *wrong*! It's quite the opposite. I don't mean to seem boastful, but I almost can't believe what I have to tell you."

"Well? Out with it! I'm an old woman and it's late," the Abbess demanded.

"It's that material we received from our missionary, Jon," the Sister-Professor explained. "We've been working with it ever since we received it. He told us that the sample contained some interesting anomalies. We tested it against our present matrices and…"

"And *what*, Professor? Keep it simple, please. I am just a humble Sister with little knowledge of the sciences."

"It *did* have some interesting properties," the scientist responded breathlessly. "Some *very* interesting ones. I checked and rechecked our computer growth simulations, and what we have, if we go ahead with implantation and germination, may be the answer to all our prayers and hard work.'

"I don't know how the woman's DNA was altered or why, but we're looking at far more than just an anomaly, or even another series of advances in the next generation of neomen. Far, far more. Please, forgive me, but my head is spinning with the implications."

"What exactly are you trying to tell me, Professor?" the Grand Abbess asked.

"That after all these generations of neomen, that the One, that *He* will be the next generation to be born!" the scientist answered.

"That's a rather grand statement, Sister-Professor!" the Abbess retorted in disbelief. She was beginning to wonder if the woman was getting enough sleep herself. She *had* been working long hours lately.

"Yes, yes Grand Abbess, I realize that," the professor responded, "and before I called you, I had Sister-Professor t'Janyya check the growth simulations with the new strain factored in, and she supports my findings. The figures are correct."

"I see," the Abbess replied carefully. "I will have my 'car brought around. Expect me in an hour. In the meantime, speak to no one else about this." She cut the connection.

Could it be? she wondered. *Could the One be ready to come among His people now?*

It was something that she would have to look into with great care. Over the four hundred odd years that the Marionite Order had been involved in Project Advent, there had been many false alarms, each of which had seriously undermined the confidence of the Faithful. She was not about to overexcite her flock needlessly.

But if it *were* true, were they ready? Was *she*? The Abbess let that thought go and quickly dressed.

An hour later, she was seated in the Office of Sister-Professor n'Amela, enjoying a cup of tea that one of the woman's acolytes had brought for her. After the long trip to the laboratory by hovercar it lent warmth to her aged bones, and she sipped at it gratefully.

"If you would direct your attention to the holojector," the Sister-Professor began. An image of a neoman appeared, with a set of statistics that included intelligence factors, projected longevity, psi ratings and a host of other important-looking data whose meaning completely eluded the Abbess.

The Sister-Professor then launched into a short lecture on normal levels of growth and performance, and went on to explain what had been previously expected in terms of improvements in the next generation of neomen. It was all quite abstract, but the Abbess smiled and made certain to nod at what she thought were the right moments.

She remained unconvinced however. So far, nothing that the woman was telling her justified her excitement in any way.

Then the Sister-Professor switched to another holo. It depicted a member of the Adam 16 generation of neomen. There were only a handful of them in existence, and few outside of Project Advent itself even knew that they existed.

Instead of the hard angular lines and overdeveloped muscles commonly associated with neomen, the A-16's were a radical step forwards. Their bodies had soft, feminine curves, a more delicate bone structure, and ample breasts that would have been the envy of any true woman. Their genitalia however, left no doubt whatsoever about their true sex.

They had been made this way on purpose; the genetic engineers working for the Order had long understood that the only acceptable form that a Savior could take was one that would appeal physically to the Sisterhood at large. The A-16's were their solution.

But this still didn't explain the reason for this late night meeting, and the Abbess's patience was nearly exhausted. She was just about to demand that the Sister-Professor get to the point, when a new holo appeared.

For a moment, the Abbess thought that she was looking at another A-16. To be sure, he was an extremely handsome specimen, far lovelier and more perfectly formed than any other A-16's that she was familiar with, but still nothing worth being woken up for.

Then she saw his designation. He wasn't an A-16. He was a 17—a generation that was still only a concept. His figures were also on display, right alongside the normal parameters for A-16's.

The difference between them was astronomical. Even as untrained as she was, she could see that in every respect, this neoman was vastly superior to anything the Project had ever created.

It was his eyes that captivated her the most. They were a pure, piercing blue that radiated a power that she had only dreamed of experiencing in her most fervent prayers. The Sister-Professor had not been boasting after all, she realized.

531

It is Him! she thought. *He has come unto us at last.*

"You see it too, don't you?" the Sister-Professor asked her. "Your Grace, his projected psi abilities are off the charts, his estimated IQ is over 200 and there is more. So much more. He is beyond anything that we had projected for another ten generations at least. It *has* to be Him. I don't know by what grace this good fortune has occurred, but He *is* the One!"

Still entranced, the Abbess nodded absently and continued to stare at the image hovering in the air before her. For decades, she had worked and prayed that the Marionite Order would someday achieve its goal and resurrect the Savior. She had never been prideful enough to think that she would see it in her lifetime however, and yet, she was certain that this was exactly what she was looking at. The reality of it left her awestruck.

"Shall we go ahead with implantation?" the Sister-Professor asked eagerly. "We have a number of suitable host-candidates who are ready to serve the Church as mothers."

"No," the Grand Abbess replied, coming out of her reverie at last. "Not yet. I want these figures checked again, Sister-Professor, and by an independent work group."

"But, Your Grace--" The woman looked utterly crushed.

"If it is Him," the Abbess told her, "then we are obligated to proceed with due reverence and even greater care. Rest assured, Sister-Professor n'Amela, that if the examination of your projections does not reveal any hidden genetic defects, this neoman will be implanted and born to the world. I promise you that.'

"But," she added, holding up a warning finger, "even then, he will still have to be evaluated by the Church's Auditor General for the Signs. If they are witnessed, and the Council of Bishops and the Pope agree with the findings, *then* and *only* then will an announcement be made to the Faithful."

The Sister-Professor knelt down before her superior. There was a noticeable sag in her shoulders. "Yes, Your Grace. I see your wisdom. I...am simply tired."

The Abbess put her hands on the woman's head. "You have done well, Sister-Professor, and the Church is eternally grateful, but now the real work begins. If you are right, then the wait will be well worth it. Let us give our

532

thanks together to Jesu and Mari in prayer and fortify ourselves for this great labor."

Tethys /In-Transit/USSNS *Pallas Athena*, Calandra, Miralindra System, Sagana Territory, United Sisterhood of Suns 1043.03|19|05:67:29

After Basic and her visit to Persephone, Tethys was exactly the vacation Kaly had needed to help herself heal. They had met up with Enggredsdaater and Bel Anny at Oceana, a resort town known for its beaches, and its beautiful weather. Thanks again to the discounts offered to servicewomen, they'd stayed together at the *Wavebreaker*, one of the finer resort hotels on the Blue Coast. The remainder of their leave had been a wonderful blur of alcohol, good food, sand, sun and sex. But as with all such things, the day finally arrived for them to leave Tethys, and report in to their new units.

The 115th was in Sagana with the *Pallas Athena* at the time, and after a tearful goodbye to their two friends, Kaly and Lena made their way to the distant territory through a combination of civilian and military transports.

Neither of them knew about the events in HSL-48 2124A, and several days of unexplained delay elapsed before the *Athena* finally made port. And in true Marine fashion, Kaly and Lena were given notice at the last nanosecond to report *upside* immediately with their gear, and just managed to hitch a ride aboard a Navy shuttle crammed with supplies.

When the shuttle docked, the pair followed the freight-loaders into one of the docking tubes, kit bags in hand and packs on their backs, not quite certain what to do next. Instead of a single Marine standing post to verify their orders, there was a squad of military policewomen stopping everyone and subjecting all the freight to scans and hands-on inspections.

Although their uniforms and gear made it patently obvious who they were, they were still required to present their IDs, and have them verified before they were allowed to pass through the checkpoint. When they finally made their way past the welcome sign into the ship itself, Lena glanced back at Kaly questioningly. She was just as puzzled though, and could only shrug.

Fortunately, a little further on, they encountered another Marine who was friendlier than the MP's, and she summoned someone for them to report to. This proved to be none other than Corporal n'Valri.

"Well, well," the woman said putting her hands on her hips, "Look who's back, and if she isn't a full-fledged goddess damned ground-pounder! I guess that Grey Book that I loaned you came in handy."

"It's good to see you too, Corporal," Kaly said, grinning. *Goddess,* she thought, *talk about coming full circle.*

She indicated Lena. "This is my battle sister. We're here to report for duty with the 115th."

"Well, you've come to the right place, Marines," N'Valri replied. "It just so happens that the 115th is at home right now. Come on, I'll get you to the CO."

As N'Valri led the way, Kaly smiled to herself. This time the pace that the Corporal set was much more leisurely than the first time that she'd been aboard. Apparently, running a new hatchie through the maze of passages at full thrust was part of the fun. Not so with real Marines.

"So, what's with all the security?" she finally asked her.

"Oh, some kind of trouble with the locals," N'Valri said casually. "It gives the MP's something to do, I guess. By the way, you want another leg up?"

"Sure," Kaly replied. "The last one you gave me went a long ways."

"Okay," N'Valri said, "Two things. One; watch out for Troop Leader da'Saana. She's a hard nose, and if you get on her bad side, you're done. Two; no hazing the neoman. The Corps has sent the word down from on high that he's to be left alone."

"The neoman? What neoman?" Kaly inquired.

"I guess that you two didn't hear about him while you were in Basic," the Corporal replied. "The courts decided to let one of them join the unit. He's bunked by himself, and we've been using him on all sorts of special details.'

"The other troopers gave him a pretty hard time at first, and then Command got involved. Now, he's hands-off, but you probably won't have to deal with him. He keeps pretty much to himself when he's not on a detail. 'Just let him be' is the rule. So, stay professional and leave him alone."

"Sure thing," Kaly agreed. She was just fine with that. She didn't have any feelings about neomen one way or the other, and she didn't think that Lena cared either, but neither of them wanted to get themselves involved in anything that would make them stand out. That was *always* a recipe for trouble.

By this point they had reached Troop Leader da'Saana's small office. She was away on a detail, but her assistant, Corporal n'Darei was at her desk. N'Darei called up their files at her data terminal.

"A Platoon Leader, eh? Not bad, N'Deena. And N'Gari, I see you also got good marks. Welcome to *Hekate's Hounds*, Ladies.'

"You'll be replacing two troopers that transferred out to another unit. We're in the middle of our patrol, so things will be a bit hectic, and you'll both have to hit the ground running, but I imagine you're used to that by now. Did you know that I had the same DI's that you did? Tell me; is N'Vera still the same armor-plated bitch she used to be?"

Kaly noticed the Eye of the Goddess pin on the Corporal's tunic, and nodded. "Well, she was a bit of a challenge," she answered carefully.

"That's a very diplomatic way of putting it, N'Deena," the Corporal smirked. "I think that my ass is still sore from all the butt-chewing that I got from that woman."

She stood up. "Okay, let's get you two situated. One question before we do that though: I know that you two are battle sisters. Is there anything more between you?"

"Corporal?" Kaly asked. Relationships in Basic hadn't been discouraged, but they also hadn't been *encouraged* either, not that anyone had had the energy for them at the time. She wasn't entirely sure how to answer.

"That tells me what I wanted to know right there," N'Darei replied. "It's not like Basic here, troopers. The 115th is a family, and our CO, Col. Lislsdaater, understands how things are. If you two have something going with each other, that's fine. We want you to be happy with your posting. Just make sure it doesn't interfere with your jobs and it won't be an issue."

535

Kaly and Lena both relaxed when they heard this, and the Corporal didn't miss the change. "I'll make sure you get adjoining racks," she reassured them. "Welcome aboard."

N'Darei walked them over into Five-Bar. Although it was a new experience for Lena, Kaly already knew what to expect. The racks had seemed tiny when she had first laid eyes on them, but now they seemed positively palatial after the accommodations on Hella's World.

This time, and because it was going to be their home for a while, she paid special attention to the personal touches that the troopers had made to their spaces. A holopic of a beach on Tethys, taped to a bulkhead caught her eye, as did several small vases of flowers sitting wherever there was space for them. She also took note of the bunks where the plain grey privacy drapes had been replaced with bright fabrics. When she got the opportunity, she was going to do the same things for their racks, and she was certain that Lena would agree.

Passing one row, Kaly heard music and turned towards the source. A trooper was sitting on the edge of her cot and playing a mandolin while some of her neighbors listened to her impromptu concert. The musician smiled at them as they walked by, and N'Darei nodded back.

A little further in, they encountered something that she didn't recall on her first visit. It was a grey tabby-kaatze. He sauntered by as if he owned the entire deck, and gave them a brief inspection. Having managed to meet his minimum standards, he moved on to more important business.

"That brassy little fellow is Skipper," the Corporal advised them. "He's the Commander's kaatze, but we've sort've been adopted by him, and he comes down here to see what kind of hand-outs he can get. We're not really supposed to feed him, but he's a master of the art of blackmail, so we have sort of an *informal* arrangement."

Kaly laughed and Lena smiled shyly.

At last, they reached the final pod. "These are your racks," N'Darei announced, indicating a pair of empty compartments. "One on top of the other like I said, and you'll have some privacy back here. There's storage under your beds and two lockers in the bulkhead that you can also use.'

"The PX here isn't bad either; they've got plenty of personal items, and even a few things that you can pick up to make the place a little more personal. The rest you'll pick up as you go through your tour."

Then she handed them a pair of handheld data terminals. "And these are your pathminders. You'll want to look them over, and use them until you get used to the ship's layout. I'll warn you right now though; the *Athena's* a huge ship, and they'll keep you from getting lost and starving to death in some side corridor. N'Deena knows what I'm talking about."

They took them from her and then Lena noticed the grey plastic tarp that seperated the rack behind them from the rest of the pod. She nudged her battle sister and inclined her chin towards it.

"Who's back there?" Kaly asked. But she already suspected that she knew what the answer was.

"Well…that's where the neoman sleeps," Corporal n'Darei answered hesitantly. "I'm really sorry about that, but we had to put him *somewhere*, and you two being new—"

"We understand," Kaly assured her. "Corporal n'Valri told us all about him. As long as he doesn't give us a problem, we don't care."

Lena nodded in agreement. "Really. It's okay."

"Now, that's the attitude that we are under orders to have," N'Darei declaired. "He hasn't given us a problem *yet*, and he keeps to himself. *But* if you girls have *any* trouble from him, any at all, you come straight to me, or Troop Leader da'Saana, and we'll have him in the brig so fast that your heads'll spin into orbit. That's a promise. And if you want to get new rack assignments, just say the word right now and as soon as they come up, I'll move you."

"We'll just see how things go," Kaly volunteered, "and let you know if anything happens."

"That's all we can do for right now, isn't it?" N'Darei agreed. "Hey, are either of you hungry? The mess hall here is pretty good."

"Yes, Corporal," Kaly said, "We are."

"Then come this way, gentleladies," N'Darei said with exaggerated politeness, "and sample some of our fine cuisine. I think that a few of the girls from the unit are up there right now, and you can get a chance to get to know each other over chow." Kaly and Lena dropped their packs and

537

eagerly followed the Corporal out to the Lifts. Neoman or no, they were ready for a good meal.

***

The supply shuttle had brought up more than just Kaly and Lena. In addition to foodstuffs, medical supplies and spare parts, it had also carried something for Lilith. She was just finishing her shift in the Command Center, when a young Ensign from Navcom came up and saluted her.

"Ma'am?"

"Yes, Sailor?"

"Ma'am, I have a letter for you." The young woman handed her an envelope. It was made of real paper, not a plastic flimsy.

Slightly surprised, Lilith took it from her. "Thank you, Sailor."

Like most women, she had never received a real letter from anyone in her entire life. Most communications were performed electronically, or over long distances by satellites beaming the information through Null and back into normal space, through the aid of trained psi's. 'Hard copy' only existed in the form of plastic flimsies. Real paper was extremely rare, and mainly limited to antique books owned by collectors.

It took her a moment to decipher the handwritten combination of Standard and Zommerlaandar characters before she realized who had sent it. It was from Ingrit. She opened it carefully, not wanting to damage the fragile envelope and unfolded the message within.

"My darling, Lilith," it began, *"I was lying here, in our room listening to the night and looking up at the stars. Something flew by, far overhead, and I thought of you out there, looking at the same stars.'*

"I can still feel you lying next to me in the moonlight, and every once in a while, I think I can hear your voice saying something, or the sound of your laughter. At those times, the distance between us is a painful thing, but I tell myself that like Katrinn, you have an important job to do. One that is much more important than the desires of one poor farm girl.'

"But just the same, I miss you. Knowing that this letter will reach you, and be held by your hands, after being touched by mine, helps a little. In a small way, I think it brings us together again, at least for a while.'

538

"Take care of yourself out there, and come back to me when you can. I know that you know what you are doing, and have done it a thousand times, but this superstitious Zommerlaandar still prays every day to the Wise Ones, asking them to watch over you and keep you safe until I can hold you in my arms again.'

"I love you—Ingrit."

Lilith put down the letter for a moment, considering it. She suddenly appreciated why the ancients had used them as a form of communicating, even long after the advent of electronic media. In a strange way, the handwritten message seemed to convey Ingrit's words in a much more intimate and meaningful manner than any display on a screen, or a printed flimsy, could have ever managed. She could almost feel Ingrit's energy, lingering on the paper, and taking it back up, she realized that she could actually *smell* the subtle traces of Ingrit's scent, mixed in with the aroma of fresh earth and grass that was Zommerlaand itself.

I love you too, Ingrit, she thought.

She got up from her chair, taking the letter with her. Her shift was over, and she had two things that needed attending to.

The first was a visit to the *Athena's* PX. Goddess willing, they actually sold paper and a pen, or could at least order them for her. If not, then she knew that Sa'Vika could be relied upon to find it for her somewhere in the universe. The woman had a knack for accomplishing the seemingly impossible, and she always did it with a smile on her face.

The second thing was to keep a promise that she'd made.

***

"I see that you've come back," Dana bel Hanna observed. "I had hoped that we would continue our conversation together."

Lilith took her seat before the holojector. "I made a promise to you," she said. "Part of that was to return, and the other part was to think over what you said the last time we spoke."

"And did you, Commander?" the matrix asked.

"Yes," Lilith replied, "I have, and I must admit that your description of your life after your translation intrigued me."

539

"I sense a certain level of hesitation in your voice, however," Bel Hanna observed. "It certainly doesn't take a great deal of processor power to understand that a full acceptance on your part wouldn't require any further conversation between us. There would have simply been an addition to your file asking that the translation be performed when you died."

"A very accurate assessment," Lilith admitted. "And completely correct. There is one thing that I have to know before my mind is made up."

"And that is?"

"I know from your file that you had relationships when you were in your body, and that you even married. Do you ever think of her? Do you ever miss her?"

"How do I go on without her?" Bel Hanna interjected. "Isn't that the rest of your question? How did I leave an entire life behind and move on to another existence?"

"Yes," Lilith replied. "I find it hard to understand. You see, I've met someone, and I think that when the time is right, that we may have a life together, even daughters. It's hard for me to imagine having that, and then living another life without her."

"I understand, Commander," Bel Hanna said. "I had the same questions when I was in a physical body, but now that I exist as a personality matrix, I realize that they were more a statement of my own ignorance than anything else. I mean no insult by that. I simply say it as an admission of my own limitations at the time.'

"I loved my wife when I was in a body and we shared a life together that was full and rewarding. And when the Goddess decided that it was time for me to die, that life ended, but not my memories of it, or of the ones that I loved.'

"I still love her, even now, and I know from my experience being translated, that we are not destroyed by death, but transformed, just as I was. My transformation was artificial of course, but in the greater scheme of things, it was merely a variation on what the divine intends for us all. The ancients were right, Commander; reincarnation really *does* exist and the spirit *is* eternal."

Lilith was certainly familiar with the concept. In her own faith, it was accepted that the soul went into darkness, and then renewed itself like the

Moon Goddess Herself, waxing, waning, and waxing again, eternally. As a mortal woman though, death was still a very daunting thing to consider.

"I can tell by your increased heart rate that the subject alarms you," Bel Hanna said. "I apologize for eavesdropping, but it *is* hard to ignore. I also appreciate how you feel. You have what you have, and your faith tells you not to be concerned, but the darkness is still out there."

"Yes," Lilith confessed.

"Understandable," Bel Hanna replied, "but I submit that you already have proof of a sort."

Lilith arched an eyebrow. "Do I now?"

"Yes. Your proof is your own existence in your current body. It is not the same body that it was when you were born, and you are not the same person that you once were.'

"With each passing day, every cell in it has changed and been replaced, and you have also changed as a person; from the girl that you once were, to the woman you are now. You have, in a small way, been born, died and been re-born many times already. Why should it be any different in the larger scheme of things?"

"An interesting observation," Lilith said. "You should have been a Priestess."

"Perhaps in another life I will be," Bel Hanna laughed. "And perhaps in a past life, I was. But to return to your central issue, I would offer you some advice."

"And that is?"

"Live. Love this woman of yours and have your life together, and when your time finally comes, honor her through the eternity of your memories."

"I will," Lilith answered.

"Then I will look forwards to the day when you are translated, and if *you* allow it, to share in your memories of this wonderful woman of yours. In the meantime, Commander, be well."

Lilith rose from her seat and the holographic image of Bel Hanna disappeared. For a moment, she listened to the soft hum of the ship's computer reverberating through the walls, and considered the conversation. Then she left the chamber and headed down to Ellyn n'Dira's office.

As always, the woman was hard at work, but she stopped what she was doing and greeted her. "Commander? What brings you down to the dungeons?"

"I need to have my will amended," Lilith said.

***

That same evening, Kaly and Lena lay together in Kaly's bunk. They were half-asleep when they heard Jon enter the pod. There had been plenty of gossip about the neoman at dinner, but because he had been away on work details and visiting the ship's doctor, they had yet to actually encounter him. When Jon walked past their rack, Lena opened her eyes and sat up.

"I think he's here!" she whispered excitedly.

"Come back to bed!" Kaly urged. "I've heard enough about him for one day."

"I have to see what he looks like!" Lena declared. As shy as she tended to be, she was always the first one to show any interest in a mystery, and Kaly thought that she was sometimes too curious for her own good. Before she could object any further, the young woman had gathered up the blanket around her and worked her way over to the corner of the alcove.

"Lena!" Kaly exclaimed, "Come back here!" But Lena was already peeking around the privacy drape, and finally, Kaly moved up to join her.

Jon had his back to them, and he was lifting the tarp that separated his rack from everyone else's. With all of the commotion that Lena had made, Kaly was certain that he knew that they were watching him, but he didn't acknowledge their presence. Instead, he walked around the tarp and let it drop behind him. A moment later, the light from over his rack came on, glowing through the thin plastic sheet.

"Did you see him?" Lena asked her. "He was *huge*! They told us that he was big, but I don't think I'd even come up to his chest!"

"Yes," Kaly replied, putting a hand to her shoulder. "I did, and he was gigantic. Now, please, Lena, come back to bed."

Lena hesitated, and risked one more glance in the direction of Jon's sleeping area before she allowed Kaly to pull her away. Once she was back in her lover's arms, her expression became thoughtful. "You know something, Kaly?" she finally said. "He didn't look like an ape at all." Several of their companions at dinner had described him that way.

"No," Kaly agreed sleepily, "He didn't."

A short silence passed between them, and then Lena added. "It must be lonely for him back there, all by himself. I think that's rather sad."

Kaly sighed and gathered her closer. "Yes, probably so." Thankfully, Lena let the conversation die there, and the two of them managed to drift off to sleep.

Jon was already gone when their psievers woke them, and the two women dressed in their fatigues and reported to Corporal n'Darei.

"You two have a work detail today" she informed them. "You'll be helping engineering down on deck 24, passage 5, sub-passage 14. They've had some leaks in the water pipes down there and they need us to help with the repairs. Private bel Freda is in charge of the Marine end of things. Get down there and see what she needs."

Kaly and Lena saluted the woman and using their pathminders, found their way down to the work detail. Private bel Freda put them right to work.

"The engineers got the replacement pipe up inside the wall already," the Private advised them, "They're having us check the couplings while they run some water through the line to check the seals. You two can go down to the end of the passage and help out."

She pointed down the corridor to two hatches in the overhead and a pair of Marines who were already up inside on ladders. There were open toolboxes at the foot of each ladder. Kaly took her place at the foot of the furthest ladder and Lena went over to the nearer one.

As she did so, the Marine above her dropped their wrench, and started to come down to retrieve it. It was Jon fa'Teela.

Private bel Freda was walking by right as this happened. She glanced down at the tool, and then stepped over it and walked on without making any move to pick it up. Lena grimaced, and handed it up to him.

"Here," she said.

Jon took it and rewarded her with a small, half-smile. "Thank you." Compared to her, his hand was huge and hairy, and the deepness of his voice startled her, but she still managed to meet his eyes and return his smile.

Bel Freda noticed the exchange, and gave them a disapproving glare. But she said nothing and went over to the end of the passage to speak with one of the engineers instead.

Kaly had also witnessed it, and the Private's reaction. Later, after their work had been completed, she spoke with her battle sister on the lift.

"Lena, you don't want to be friendly with the neoman," she warned. "You remember what Corporal n'Darei told us? We don't want to stand out."

"I remember," Lena replied, folding her arms stubbornly, "and Private bel Freda *and* Corporal n'Darei can both stuff it up their pipes if they don't like it. The Private told us to help with the work and that's just what I did. Besides, there's no call for the way she acted. She could have handed the wrench back just like I did. We're all Marines, even him."

"Just the same," Kaly replied, "we're new here and we don't need to get on anyone's bad side."

"I know that, and he may be as ugly as anything the Goddess has ever created," Lena said, "but it was still wrong."

USSNS *Pallas Athena*, Neutral Space, Unclaimed Zone Adjacent to the Sagana Territory, 1043.03|21|00:97:63

Mearinn was on third watch when the *Athena* monitored a transmission from the Agleope system, and as soon as the situation became clear, she woke Katrinn, Lilith and Ellyn. "We have a problem in Agleope," she informed them, "Hriss raiders are attacking the mining operations in the system's asteroid belt."

All three women dressed hurriedly and ran to the lift, very nearly colliding with each other. "It looks like Command was right about the Hriss, Lily," Katrinn said as the lift ascended.

"Yes," Lilith replied. "Now, let's hope we can catch them before they slip away."

The lift opened onto the command deck and as a group, they went straight over to Mearinn. From the displays on the sitscreens, Lilith could tell that they were looking at least one *Hilla*-Class light cruiser and a small group of fighters. And from the transmissions that they were receiving, the Territorial Marshals were doing their best to defend the main mining station, but they were clearly out-matched.

"We're already prepping for Null," Mearinn said as she surrendered the command chair. "We should be making the transit in two minutes, and helm estimates a ten minute passage."

Which meant that they would be too late to prevent any casualties, but still well within an acceptable time-envelope to catch the raiders in-system *if* they were going after the mineral resources. If the raid were merely punitive however, the whole thing would be over and done with before the battle group would arrive.

"With luck they'll be greedy and this is all for minerals," Lilith said, calling up a cup of tea for herself. "Do we have any kind of track showing where they came into the system?"

"Yes, Commander." A holo showed the area where the raiders had exited Null, along with their line of travel to their target.

"Good," she replied. "As soon as we come out of Null I want the signature of their ship and a scan of the stellar neighborhood for any Null points."

Every time a spaceship created a gate to enter Null, a remnant of that rift remained after the transit, and if the ship wasn't in some form of stealth, an energetic trail was left behind by the ship's in-system engines. The same held true for any exit back into normal space.

Each ship's plasma drives also left a distinct signature that was as unique as fingerprints, or a bioplasmic aura. If the Goddess favored them, the raider's energy signature would be detectable, and match a trail leading back to one of the nearby Null transit points. If they were even luckier, the same trail would lead back to the raider's home system.

The odds were long against this though. By and large, the Hriss weren't idiots, and when they had raided Persephone, the gate they had created to enter Null had been well outside the immediate stellar neighborhood, making it anyone's guess where they had come from.

Hopefully, things will be different this time, Lilith thought, and she said a little prayer to the Lady to tip the scales in their favor.

545

"Ma'am," the helmsmistress informed her. "We're ready to make the transit."

"Good," she answered, "let's get to work."

***

The instant that the battle group exited Null, Lilith ordered general quarters sounded and gave the command for the *Nighthunters* to launch their fighter-interceptors. Their exit back into normal space had been as close to the asteroid belt as they had dared to get, and they still had another ten minutes before they would be inside of that zone and within missile range.

When the *Hilla*-Class light cruiser realized that they were there, it began to leave the area immediately, abandoning its own fighters, and their pilots, to their fate. The sitscreens showed the cruiser moving away from the asteroid belt at full in-system thrust, and Lilith only hoped that the Freya interceptors, and their fighter escorts, would have enough time to cut them off before they reached clear space and made their transit. It was going to be a close thing, but the battle group had the terrain in their favor; the asteroids were thick around the cruiser, and it was not as nimble as the smaller interceptors that were closing in on it.

The flight leader hailed the cruiser in Hriss'ka, "Hriss warship! You have entered Sisterhood space and attacked it. Power down and surrender immediately or be destroyed as pirates."

The Hriss captain replied with an expletive, and the small group of enemy fighters turned about and headed at the interceptors. It was a brave, but utterly futile move. The Freya's banked away to engage the light cruiser, while their escorts, the faster Valkyrie aerospace fighters, attacked their Hriss counterparts and drew them away from the Freyas.

Although the Hriss pilots were determined, their fighters were a generation behind the Valkyries, and much less maneuverable. They were also outnumbered three to one. The Valkyries let loose with a volley of anti-spaceship missiles, and as the Hriss fighters tried to evade them, they closed to within gun distance and fired their rail-guns in short bursts.

One Hriss fighter was immediately damaged by a missile, and lost all thruster control. It spun out of control until it hit an asteroid and became a ball of plasma.

The second Hriss fighter was sheared in half by gunfire and the third met its fate when it tried to evade a Valkyrie's rail-guns and flew too close to a stray missile. In a few seconds, only the cruiser remained, and the Freyas were gaining on it like wolves closing in on their prey.

The vessal had just cleared the asteroid field by this stage, and was powering up its Null-wings as its gunners tried to shoot the Freyas down. It was far too late however, and the interceptors were too agile for the energy bolts to find their marks. The Freyas avoided the defensive fire with ease and rolled down at the ship, letting their missiles fly.

The first one hit the cruiser's Null-wings on the left side, shearing them off and making any transit impossible. Its sister plowed into the cruiser's engines and the third and final missile cut the cruiser completely in half when it struck amidships.

This was all the punishment that the vessel could withstand, and it exploded. Debris flew everywhere, and the lead Freya pilot sent her interceptor into a victory roll, cheering over the com. The battle, as such, was over.

"Well, that was certainly short," Lilith remarked dryly, "Did we get a match on that cruiser's engine signature?"

"Yes, we did," Mearinn announced triumphantly. "The engines match to a track leading into a Null point just inside Hriss space. Even better, the track leads straight back from the transit point to a nearby star system. I'd lay odds that that's their base. It looks like they got careless this time." She sent a holo up to Lilith's chair that pinpointed the location.

Lilith noted that the system's star, blandly labeled as CD48 2259, was a G3-4V type. This made it the perfect location for a T-class planet, and for a Hriss raider base. "I agree, Mearinn," she said. "I think 2259 merits a much closer inspection."

"Commander, if we enter Hriss space with our battle group, we could start a war," N'Dira warned.

"I fully appreciate that possibility, Advocate," Lilith returned. "But we may not have any choice in the matter. If it is there, we cannot leave that base operational. I suggest that we send the *Demeter* to tend to any survivors at the mining station and adjourn to my office to confer with Rixa."

An urgent message was sent through Null and out to Rixa, and by the time that Lilith and her officers had settled themselves in her office, Admiral ebed Cya had appeared on the holo.

"I was afraid that we would find the raider's base inside the Hriss territorial boundaries," the Admiral said. "And I agree with the Advocate that this does present us with a delicate situation.'

"However, we have clear evidence that the raider came from *there*. Our legal affairs specialists with the AG's Office were contacted as soon as you sent us word, and they feel that this amounts to nothing less than a clear act of piracy. Unless the Hriss government acknowledges the raiders as an official part of their armed forces, the AG believes that they will stand aside and let us take action.'

"Personally, I agree with their assessment. The Hriss Imperium knows full well that if they *do* acknowledge the raiders, that it would give us reasonable cause to declare hostilities. And the Admiralty does not believe that they desire open war with us at the moment.'

"Therefore, I am ordering you to proceed to the location of the suspected base, and neutralize it. There is one proviso however: because of the recent raids, and a lack of detailed intelligence on current Hriss military strength and intentions, one of your priorities will be to gather whatever intelligence material you can.'

"I realize that it would be swifter and safer to simply bomb the site from space, but we must gain whatever insight we can before the Hriss make another aggressive move.'

"Towards that end, I am also ordering the *Penthesilea* to break off from her picket duty and join your battle group. The *Penthesilea* will provide you with additional firepower, and as you know, she is currently hosting a company of trained intelligence specialists. They will bring their skills to bear once you have isolated and secured the enemy's command and control center. Do any of you have any questions about this mission?"

Lilith nodded, and the Admiral acknowledged her. "Yes, ma'am. I am concerned about the number of casualties that we might suffer in a ground action. Apart from the C and C installation, are there any other assets that we will need to concern ourselves with?"

"None," the Admiral answered. "Aside from securing that specific complex, you have free reign to bomb the rest of the planet to atoms and the goddess damn them all. That should limit your people's exposure and also prevent you from becoming involved in anything protracted.'

"There is one other thing. Once the Intel people have completed their work, we want the C and C complex to be completely destroyed. We don't want to make it easy for the Hriss to determine exactly how much we were actually able to learn. Make your operation as swift as possible Commander, and leave as few traces as you can."

Ellyn n'Dira raised her hand. "How will the political end of things be handled, ma'am?"

"As for that," Ebed Cya replied, "we will recommend that the OAE Diplomatic Corps contact the Hriss ambassador as soon as possible and ascertain their position. If the dialogue exceeds the time that you need to prosecute your action, we will express our regrets to the Hriss, and explain that we were in hot-pursuit of suspected pirates. As my mothers used to say, 'it's always better to apologize than to ask for permission."

N'Dira nodded and shared her superiors dry chuckle.

Erin taur Minna, also had a question for the Admiral. "Is there any chance that the raiders will receive assistance while we are attacking the base?"

"We cannot be sure of that, Captain taur Minna," Ebed Cya admitted. "Quite frankly, we are gambling that the Hriss government will will not send any additional forces to challenge you. There is the remote possibility that they might, which is all the more reason for your battle group to prosecute your action with due haste. Goddess willing, you will be able to gather your intel and destroy the base before any such naval units could respond---if they respond. Does anyone else have concerns that they wish to address?"

"No, ma'am. I believe we are done," Lilith replied. "Thank you."

"I wish I was going out there with you," Ebed Cya said. "My prayers will be with you though. Good luck and good hunting." The Admiral ended the call.

"I wonder how long Naval Command will take to place that call to the Diplomatic Corps," Katrinn asked with a grin. "Or for the diplomats to get around to contacting the Hriss Ambassador?"

"Long enough for us to get across the border and take care of our mission, I'd wager," Lilith opined. "Let's not take a lack of bureaucratic initiative for granted however. I want us ready to transit as quickly as possible. Also, please wake Col. Lislsdaater and Dr. elle'Kaari and have them come topside to meet with me right away; this is going to be a Marine operation once we have the high ground, and we have to expect casualties."

***

Kaly and Lena had been sound asleep when the *Athena* received the distress call from the Agleope system. They were awakened by Corporal n'Valri.

"N'Deena! N'Gari! You two need to get up to the bridge right away," she declared, shaking them awake. "Get your blasters on the way and make sure you have extra battery packs."

"What's going on?" Kaly asked blearily.

"It looks like we're going in after Hriss raiders," N'Valri answered. "I need you and your battle sister to stand watch over the main lift in the command center. Your job will be to control access to the bridge, and repel any Hriss that might board us and try to capture it."

"Yes, Corporal!" Kaly replied, coming to full alertness. Her pulse raced at the thought of having to deal with Hriss Warriors inside of the ship itself, and she could tell that Lena was just as nervous as she was.

"Don't worry," N'Valri assured them, knowing full well where their thoughts were taking them. "It's simple SOP duty. There's never been a hostile boarding in the history of the Navy. They just want to cover all the possibilities. More the like, we'll vaporize the raiders, and that will be that. So, just look tough and stand guard duty until you are relieved."

The Corporal left them to round up some other Marines, and Kaly and Lena dressed and hurried over to the armory lockers. Even though it was unlikely that there would be any emergency that they would personally have to contend with, they were still expected to expedite their response.

Once they had their weapons, they headed topside and entered the command center.

Neither of them had ever had the occasion to visit the place before and they had to force themselves not to gawk in awe at the huge sitscreens and the beehive of activity going on all around them.

Fortunately, they were met by a Private, who patiently directed them to where they needed to be, which turned out to be standing to either side of the lift doors. "Just stay out of everyone's way," she advised, "and wait until someone tells you that you can leave your post. And look at the bright side, you'll get a front row seat for the only action we're likely to have."

The Private proved to be right about "front row seats." They did have a pretty good view of everything that was going on, and were able to watch and listen as the fighters destroyed the enemy cruiser and its escort. It was a short battle, but thrilling to watch, and when the stand-down from general quarters was sounded, they were sent on their way.

They managed to get as far as the armory before they got the word that the "unlikely action" was not only likely, but immanent. They were instructed to report to the Marine Briefing Center and join their unit.

Col. Lislsdaater stood at the head of the room on a low stage, along with the rest of her officers, and the room, although a large affair, was crowded with troopers and their Troop Leaders, and some women had to stand or lean against the bulkheads.

"Marines," she said as a holo of a star system came up at the head of the room, "I have just been informed by Commander ben Jeni that our battle group is headed into Hriss space to attack and destroy an enemy base.'

"As you veterans know, ordinarily the battle group would simply nuke the location from space while we stood security posts aboard ship. That is not the case today.'

"We have been charged with the task of going downside after the high ground has been secured and capturing and securing the enemy's Command and Control Center. We are to neutralize any enemy resistance that we encounter along the way and hold the facility while the Navy Intel people gather vital information. I would show you the layout of the installation, but at this time, we are not certain where on the planet it is, nor its extent.'

"What I *can* tell you is that despite any bombardment from orbit, we can expect heavy resistance, in the form of enemy troops, gun emplacements and even armor. We will have the assistance of Navy fighters, and fire support from the battle group, which will give us an edge.'

"However, I would be lying to you if I said that I thought that this was going to be easy. It won't, and some of you may not come back when this is over." For an instant, she glanced directly at Jon, and catching herself, pointedly looked away to someone else. Lilith hadn't specifically ordered her to include the neoman in the ground action, but Lislsdaater knew, without having to ask her superior, that Lilith would consider the operation as another chance for him to succeed, or as she fully expected, to fail.

If he did fail, then it would be his last failure and they would finally be shut of him. The ground assault would surely be bloody, and quickly claim anyone who was not truly fit to be a Marine. In her estimation, Fa'Teela wasn't fit to be a Marine. Instead, he was a walking casualty. He just didn't know it yet.

"For some of you," she went on, "this operation will be your first taste of combat, and I will offer you this advice: rely on your training and listen to your Troop Leaders. Do what you are told and don't play the heroine. That is all for now, troopers. As soon as we have more information, your unit leaders will be briefed. May the Goddess watch over you. Dismissed."

Kaly and Lena exchanged worried expressions. *This is it,* Kaly thought anxiously. The real thing, what their training on Hella's World had been all about. What it really was to be a Marine. Once again, she recalled Troop Leader Alika's words to her back on Persephone and reflected on them. *Maybe I am a crazy girl just like she said,* she thought, *but here I am.*

She gave Lena's hand a quick squeeze as they stood. "We'll get through this," she said with a confidence she didn't really feel. "We'll get through it, and we'll be all right." Her battle sister nodded, but it was obvious that she was terrified.

On the way to Five-Bar, they passed the Ship's Temple. A long line of troopers were waiting in the corridor, using the brief down-time to visit it, and receive blessings. Lena halted as they reached the tail end of the queue.

"Can we go in?" she asked. "Please? I'd like to. It would make me feel a little better." Kaly assented and they took their place with the others.

Inside, the High Priestess and her staff were doing triple duty, but both of them managed to get themselves blessed. The change in Lena's mood was marked; the moment that an Assistant Priestess placed her hands on the young woman's head and uttered a benediction, her tension seemed to completely disappear. Seeing the transformation, Kaly realized that she hadn't really known until just then that her lover was so devout. The subject had simply never come up, and now she was glad that they had taken the time to come there. The simple ritual had given the young woman comfort, and as they left, Kaly had to admit that she even felt a little better herself.

Back at their racks, everything narrowed down to a process of checking and rechecking their weapons and gear. After that, there was nothing to do but wait.

When the word finally came, it came suddenly and without any warning. One moment, they were seated on the edge of Lena's cot, saying nothing and holding hands. The next, and they were running with everyone else out of Five-Bar to the nearest lift, and crowding inside. At the Hangar Bay, they dashed out to one of the gigantic assault shuttles and pelted up the ramp. There, they were directed by the shuttle's crewwomen past a group of hovertanks to the rear of the cavernous cargo bay, where a row of Armored Personnel Hover-Carriers sat with their sally doors open.

The inside of their APHC was cramped, and the only concession that it made to comfort were padded benches to either side of the troop compartment. The moment that everyone had boarded and taken their seats, the sally-doors closed and they were sealed off from the rest of the universe.

Corporal n'Darei made her way over to them. "Make sure to buckle in securely," she cautioned. "The ride might get rough when we hit atmosphere. And also make sure to undo the chin straps on your helmets before you exit. If you step on a mine while the straps are still on, the blast will take the helmet and your head right along with it."

Sobered by this, the two women hastily buckled themselves in. Snapping the last strap into place, Kaly noticed that Jon had taken a seat directly across from them.

553

From the way that he was fumbling with his own harness, Kaly could tell that he was as nervous as they were, and more than ever, he seemed like everyone else; just another poor ground pounder who was wondering if he would be sitting there on the return trip, or riding back upside in a body bag.

Kaly decided that she would support Lena after all. If her battle sister wanted to object about the way the neoman was being treated, she would back her up all the way. Lena *was* right. It wasn't fair. Not when he was there in the troop compartment right along with the rest of them, taking the same risks.

Just then, the transport hit an air pocket as it entered the atmosphere, and lurched violently. When the craft stabilized, she made a point of meeting the neoman's eyes, and smiling at him. Glancing around to see if anyone else was watching, he carefully returned the expression. It was a small thing, shared wordlessly between them, but it felt right to Kaly. It felt good.

The minutes passed, and the shuttle continued to descend. Finally it landed, and when the AHPC's ramp opened, it was onto absolute chaos. Energy bolts and spent uranium tracer rounds ripped through the air and Kaly's ears were immediately overloaded with a cacophony of shouts, screams and explosions. A hovertank was settling down right next to them, blowing sand into the troop compartment as its main gun fired at something ahead of them and out of view.

Corporal n'Darei was the first one out of her harness, and waved towards the open sally port, but no one needed any encouragement. Everybody was tripping the release catches on their restraining straps and running down the ramp to take cover behind the shuttle and any handy pile of rocks.

Whatever it was that had attracted the hovertank's interest came to bear on the troopers. Kaly had just enough time to see two Marines get blown apart in a spray of blood and steam before she felt someone push her head down. It had been Jon, she realized, and the three of them hunkered down along the shuttles armored body.

"Yes!" she heard Troop Leader da'Saana shouting, "That's affirmative. The enemy is attacking from emplacements just west of our

LZ. We have at least two confirmed KIA. Requesting close air support on my mark. Advise."

Kaly heard the low rumble of a Valkyrie fighter coming in for an attack, and then she felt the wind from its passage as it flew above them, only a dozen or so meters off the ground. A loud whoosh and a sharp bang followed its passage. Simultaneously, the landscape ahead of her turned into a sea of pure, elemental fire and Kaly's eyes stung from the smoke and the stench of burning chemicals.

The gunfire stopped.

"*Ganz fekking tal!*" Da'Saana hollered. "That got the *Aasnaslaaken*! Okay, fly-girl, we'll call you back when there's some more real work for you to do."

The Valkyrie, which was now more than a kilometer away, replied with a saucy shake of its wings, and then it peeled off to find other things to murder.

"Come on," the Troop Leader urged, "we have a base to secure."

They formed up behind her and ran through a tangle of rocks and twisted debris until they reached a platoon of Marines that had taken up positions facing a large, squat structure. Corporal n'Darei was there, and quickly briefed Da'Saana on the situation.

"That's where we think the C and C is," she stated, "but the *shovelheads* have at least two emplacements covering the approach. They're shielded from IR and bio-detection, so we can't be sure of their numbers. I've asked the Valkyries to come in and carpet-bomb the area."

Right on cue, two fighters thundered by and dropped their ordnance on the strip between the Marines and the building. Everyone ducked down as rock and other debris rained down, and when it subsided, a few troopers rose up and cautiously surveyed the landscape.

"Nothing" one woman reported. "They may have taken them out."

"Maybe," Da'Saana replied doubtfully. "Maybe not. Send out a couple of battlebots to make sure."

Corporal n'Darei relayed the request, and presently, a pair of troopers came up, hauling a large grey case. They opened it, and two battlebots unfolded themselves from the interior and clambered up over the rocks. The images that they sent back indicated that the Valkyries had managed to destroy one emplacement, but that the second position was still manned and active.

While the 'bots engaged the Hriss gun-crew and pinpointed its location, Da'Saana called in another air strike. The Valkyries returned for another pass and this time, let go with their rockets, making short work of the gun and its crew. When the smoke cleared, one of the battlebots scurried up over the lip of the emplacement and confirmed that there was nothing left except a few shredded body-parts.

"*Zum Betz!*" Da'Saana announced with satisfaction. "That's more like it. All right, let's move in. Keep a sharp eye out! There could still be more of them out there."

The squad got up and started towards the distant building. A quarter of the way there, a hovertank joined them, and took the point.

Kaly did what everyone else around her was doing, and kept her Mark 7 at waist level, panning its barrel back and forth to cover the rock field around her. The landscape wasn't completely flat, and what might have been a dry wash created by what little water the planet had, cut across their line of march.

There was also a small dirt hill on the other side of the wash, covered with rock. For a moment, she thought she saw the reflection of something coming from the hill, and as her mind began to process this information, the Hriss who had hidden themselves there fired an anti-armor rocket at the hovertank.

It hit the vehicle in the left hover pod and the tank nosed into the sand, belching smoke. A second rocket found its mark and the machine exploded. Another rocket took out the two battlebots.

With their covering armor destroyed, the Hriss opened up on the troopers with everything they had. Everyone dove for the ground, and as Kaly lay there, she managed to fire off a few blind shots from her weapon.

Off to her right and behind her, Lena and Jon were doing the same thing, and Troop Leader da'Saana was alternating between talking on her com and urging everyone to move forwards into the gully. As one, they began to crawl from rock to rock as the Hriss kept up a steady stream of gunfire. Finally, after an infinity of terror, the troopers reached the lip of the wash and rolled down into it.

At the bottom, Kaly realized that they had not reached safety after all. Tiny wire antennae poked up out of the sand. They were in a minefield.

"Don't move!" Da'Saana yelled. "Stay close to this side!" The Troop Leader got back on her com and requested armor and air support, but the news she received was not good.

"What the *fek* do you mean you don't have any air units available?!" Kaly heard the woman growl. "We're stuck in this *fekking* wash and it's a *kekking* minefield! No, I *don't* want fire support from space. We're too close to the target for that, you stupid can-scrubbie. We'll get fried. Fine! We'll just lie around here and wait until you're not too busy."

The Hriss, however, had other plans in mind. Kaly caught movement at the top of the little hill, and then saw something small rolling down into the wash.

"Grenade!" she cried. With nowhere to go, she rolled herself up into a little ball and hugged the dirt wall behind her.

The grenade went off, detonating a mine at the same time. The combined blast slammed into her like a sledgehammer, knocking the wind out of her lungs, but absent a few cuts from the shrapnel, she realized that she was still alive. So was everyone else.

The Goddess had smiled on them. The Hriss Warrior had failed to roll the grenade far enough, and thanks to their aversion to bioplasmic technology, it had been a conventional munition.

Then the Warrior at the top of the hill realized his mistake and sent another grenade tumbling down at them.

Thankfully, this one also fell short. "*Fek!*" Da'Saana shouted as it went off. "All right, Marines, in case you haven't noticed, we're in a bad situation. The only way out is for someone to get up there and take out those *fekking Shovelheads!* I need volunteers."

At that instant, it was as if all of Kaly's life had compressed down to that one point, and had paused, waiting for her to make a choice. A strange calm descended over her, and she knew what that choice was going to be.

"I'll go," she said.

"No!" Lena pleaded. "You can't! They'll kill you!"

"Someone has to," Kaly said flatly. "Or we all die."

557

"Then I'm going with you too!" Lena replied fiercely. "I won't let you go alone! I'm your battle sister. If you try to leave without me, I'll follow you! I swear I will!"

"No," Kaly insisted. "I want you to stay here."

Another grenade landed near them, and this time, it managed to wound one of the other troopers. The woman screamed in pain, and while her companions crawled over to her and applied a field dressing, Da'Saana ended the debate.

"*Both* of you are going!" she said, "Just get your asses up there! I can see a small draw to your north. If you work your way over to it and climb up, you should come up behind their position."

Kaly glared warningly at Lena, but the young woman was resolute. "You heard her Kaly. We both go. Together!"

"Okay, together."

Jon nudged Kaly. "It sounds dangerous," he said evenly. "Mind if I tag along?"

"Fine," Kaly sighed, shaking her head in resignation. "The *three* of us then."

She looked at Da'Saana, and the Troop Leader nodded. "Go ahead and take the Neo. The three of you have a better chance of making it and who knows? Maybe he'll do something useful. We'll give you what covering fire we can. Now move out!"

Kaly crawled forwards, watching for the deadly little wires in the sand. The Hriss grenades had cleared the mines ahead of them, and she could see that the ground was safe all the way to the opposite wall of the wash, and she made for it. Lena and Jon followed, and the rest of the squad began firing up at the hill and throwing GSG's that had been set for dumbfire. None of them did any damage, but they did manage to pin down the Hriss long enough for the trio to reach safety.

Once they were up against the dirt embankment, it was a matter of staying close to it, and working their way down the wash. The mines were only centimeters away, and the loose sand that had gathered near the embankment made the going slippery. Kaly chose her steps with care, knowing that to slide sideways would spell the end of them all.

At last, she reached the draw that Da'Saana had indicated, and took up a position that covered the top of the channel. Lena and Jon joined her and then they started up the slope, keeping as low as possible. When they neared the summit, Kaly peeked up over the lip.

The Hriss were just a few meters away from her, manning a heavy energy cannon. They were behind a protective barrier of earth and steel plates, and visually camouflaged from the air by netting that mimicked the desert vegetation.

They're up there, she thought to her companions. *When we come up out of this wash, we'll be in the open until we reach their position. It's not good.*

GSG's in bio mode? Jon offered.

We can try them, but with all that steel, we can't be completely sure they'll do the job, Kaly replied. *I say GSG's in dumbfire, and then we charge them. The gun is facing away from us and the entrance is on our side."* She looked at her companions for confirmation.

I can't come up with anything better, Jon admitted.

You're right Kaly, Lena agreed, *it's the only way.*

Kaly suddenly recalled Troop Leader n'Teri's lesson to them back in Basic. *"The bayonet is the weapon of last resort for the Marine,"* she had said. *"When your Mark 7 has run out of battery charge, malfunctions, when you need to make a silent attack, or must engage your enemy at extremely close quarters, then you will employ the bayonet."*

"Fix bayonets," she said, snapping her RB-22 into place. She pulled out a pair of grenades from her pouch next. "We'll throw together, and then come over the top."

Lena attached her own bayonet, and looked into Kaly's eyes. "I love you, Kaly," she said.

Kaly stole a moment to reach over and caress her cheek. "I love you, too, Lena."

She switched on the grenades and let them fly. Then she was charging over the top, with Lena and Jon right behind her.

After that, everything became a confused blur of gunfire, screaming, shouts and explosions. The chaos ended with her pulling her bayonet out of a Hriss Warrior's chest, and realizing that everything except for her and her friends was either dead, or wounded beyond the capacity to offer any resistance. Blinking away the fierce red haze that had filled her vision, she went over to Lena.

The young woman was trying to discharge her Mark 7 into a Hriss who was lying on the ground. The Warrior's face had been blown off, and the blaster's battery pack was completely drained. Kaly gently pulled the useless weapon from Lena's grasp and drew her into her arms.

Then Jon walked up and gathered them both in. Neither resisted his embrace and they stood together in silence.

"The squad's coming up," he finally said, but Kaly didn't care. They were still alive and the Hriss weren't. That was all that mattered.

Da'Saana was the first one to reach their position, followed by the rest of the squad. If she, or anyone else, had any reservations at finding them standing together, they kept it to themselves. Instead, the Troop Leader speculatively probed one of the dead Hriss with the toe of her boot, and then ordered the squad's medic to come up and give the trio a quick once-over.

They received a clean bill of health, and while the wounded Marine was evacuated by an AHPC from the wash below, Da' Saana signaled for the squad to move on. Air units had become available again, and would be able to provide them with close support.

Although they met some light resistance on the way, they swept it aside with the aid of the Valkyries, and finally reached the building that they had fought so hard for. Da'Saana had everyone take up covering positions, and then signaled for two Marines to move up to the entrance.

The troopers had just taken their places, when there was a loud explosion from deep inside the structure, followed by a huge fireball that forced everyone to duck. The thick black smoke that billowed out after this told the whole story of what had just happened.

Da'Saana spat on the ground in disgust. "Well, ain't that just *fekking* grand? The *Shovelheads* just blew the place up. Guess they couldn't stand losing to us, eh girls? I'll contact Command and let them know we're guarding a building full of junk. Might as well stand down."

***

Kaly, Lena and Jon were seated together on a piece of broken concrete, waiting for someone to tell them what to do next. They secretly hoped that no one would, and that they would get a chance to enjoy some time off their feet, but when a Navy officer walked up, their brief respite was over. Kaly rose slowly, her muscles protesting from overwork, and gave the woman the crispest salute that she could.

"Yes, ma'am?"

"I'm with the DNI," the officer explained. "I need to have your PIFSDat Units." The Personal Infantry Fighting Suit Data Processors, processed all of the data that their suit cams and other devices took in, and also acted as digital recording devices.

None of them had the slightest idea why the woman would want them, especially so soon after the fight. The information from the PIFSDat units was usually collected just before debriefing aboard ship, but Kaly and her companions didn't argue with her. Instead, they unsealed the little pouches on their shoulders, and unhooked the units from their cables.

The officer took Kaly's first and plugged it into a portable data terminal. From the green flashing light on the side of the PIFSDat, Kaly knew that she was downloading all of the data inside of it.

Finishing, she handed it back to Kaly and worked on Jon and Lena's next. "I made a copy of the data in your units," she said as she returned them, "and if anyone asks you about it, have them see Captain n'Kyla with the Intel Company."

While everyone plugged their units back into their suits, the officer gestured towards the ruined C and C building. "Has anyone been inside that structure?"

"No, ma'am," Kaly answered. "Not yet. We were waiting for some EOD women to come along and check for traps inside."

"Don't worry about it," the woman grinned. "We'll handle the interior. I want you and your troopers to secure the entrance. Other than DNI personnel, I don't want anyone going in, and nothing disturbed inside. Zat klaar, Marine?"

Kaly gave the woman another salute. "Yes, ma'am. *Klaar*."

The officer left, and they gathered up their gear, and shared a questioning look at one another. But Kaly just shrugged.

Why they were being asked to guard a room filled with blown up rubble was beyond their understanding, but being ground-pounders, they also knew that it was none of their business. So they marched down to the building and took up guard positions around the soot-covered entrance.

After several minutes, a team of Navy Intel women arrived, carrying an assortment of cased equipment with them. Whatever they did inside did not take very long, and when they were finished, Kaly and her companions were told to report to the staging area for the APHC's.

This was one order that they *did* comprehend clearly. It was time to leave and return to the *Athena*.

USSNS *Pallas Athena*, Battle Group Golden, Agleope System, Sagana Territory, United Sisterhood of Suns, 1043.03|21|06:64:24

Lilith hadn't seen a holo-conference as large as this since the War of the Prophet. The battle group had returned to Sisterhood space as soon as the Intel women had finished their work on CD48 2259 and transmitted the data back to Rixa.

Now, she was seated in the *Athena's* conference room with all of her senior officers, and surrounded by images of every Commander in the Topaz Fleet. The meeting itself was being led by none other than Jora t'Kayna, the Admiral of the Navy. The Admiral's holo floated over the baaka wood table, flanked by images of Admiral ebed Cya and all the other members of the Admiralty.

"Ladies", T'Kayna began, "I have grave news. Thanks to the information that we received from Battle Group Golden and other sources, we now believe that the Hriss are massing their forces for a general war against the Sisterhood. We predict that this conflict will come in the next six months."

T'Kayna vanished, and a display showing Hriss space replaced her. Where it abutted the Sagana Territory, Lilith could see star systems that had been marked out as supply depots, as well as forward bases. A few of them were old, but many were new, and as the animation played out, groups of

Hriss warships could be seen taking up stations at the very edges of the Imperium's borders.

Most of these vessels were marked, showing their clan affiliation, and those that weren't had been labeled with the DNI's best guess. Quite a few were Imperium forces, and loyal to the Emperor himself. And there were far too many of them to be explained away as either border security, or in system patrols, Lilith concluded.

"Naval Intelligence has picked up chatter that indicates that the clans are getting restless, and that a number of them of have been considering making a bid for the Throne of Bones," T'Kayna's voice continued, "and you all know what that means."

Lilith nodded grimly to herself. Whenever the clans started eyeing the Throne, the Hriss Emperors countered the threat by stirring their warriors up against the Sisterhood, and the clan leaders were more than happy to go along with this. They had threats of their own to deal with from junior clan leaders. Sending the hotheads out to almost certain death by promising them glory and riches had worked well for centuries, and the Sisterhood had always been forced to play the executioner.

Whether it wanted to or not.

T'Kayna went on. "Topaz Fleet, in conjunction with Silver and Onyx, will be posted to the Sagana Territory. Based on enemy movements, this command believes that the attack will begin there, and additional forces are being moved up to bolster the area's defenses. The general public doesn't know about any of this yet, but senior officials in Sagana and elsewhere have been briefed, and they are ready to work with us at a moment's notice."

The last time that this had happened, and despite the best efforts of the Navy to prevent it, civilian lives had still been lost, Lilith recalled. Space was just too vast to prevent every incursion and she shuddered at the thought of the casualties they would suffer when the Hriss managed to sneak through and conduct quick raids. And not for the first time, she whispered up a curse against the Hriss leadership and the Emperor himself.

The display disappeared and T'Kayna's image returned. "I will now turn the briefing over to Admiral ebed Cya and her staff. Thank you for your attention, and May the Goddess watch over us all in the weeks and months ahead."

The holo-conference went on for another twenty minutes, and when it concluded, Lilith and her staff found themselves alone again.

Well," she said to them. "There you have it. Go and brief your department heads, and start instituting more emergency battle drills. I want us to be as sharp as possible."

Katrinn and the others rose, their expressions somber. Lilith however, remained in her seat.

"I'll be up on the bridge in a few minutes," she told them. "I want to replay the data."

After they had departed, Lilith gave herself a moment, and then ran the holo again, watching the Hriss ships as they shifted from one system to the next, and coming closer to the edge of Sisterhood space with every new phase. Although she wanted to, there was no refuting the data, or the Admiralty's conclusions.

Goddess, she thought, *another war. Will it ever stop?*

Leaning back in her seat, she sighed wearily and rubbed at her temples, suddenly feeling very, very old.

"The Hriss never do seem to get tired of their aggression, do they?" an unknown voice asked. "But then neither do we. Especially when it comes to lost branches of humanity."

Startled, Lilith sat bolt upright in her seat and spun around to face the speaker. She was an unremarkable woman, with forgettable features, and dressed in a Captain's uniform. She was also occupying a chair that just a few seconds earlier, had been empty.

Lilith wasn't misled by her uniform though. She knew every officer aboard her ship, and this woman *wasn't* a member of her crew.

"Who are you?" she demanded, immediately sending a thought to the holojector and switching off the display. "How did you get in here? This briefing was classified."

"I'm a friend of a friend," the intruder responded with a wry smile. "We'll call the woman that I know Lady Spider. Her real name is unimportant. What *is* important is that Lady Spider knows your daughter,

564

and she sent me here to deliver a message. Oh, and if you're about to call Security, don't bother. They won't hear you."

Lilith had been in the process of doing that very thing, and had just discovered this for herself. Her psiever simply wasn't detecting the Ship's network of relays. For all intents, she was shut out of the system. But that only happened when the ship, or a psiever, experienced a major malfunction—or when the OAE was involved. Her credits were riding on the Agency.

The stranger nodded. "Yes, I am with the Agency, but it's a special unit that's not tied in with the departments that you normally deal with. We're somewhat—independent—and we don't have to follow the Agency's policies. We operate under our own special mandate.'

'And what you're thinking right now is also correct. I am a psi. But I'm not here to talk about me, or my unit. I'm here to talk with you about your daughter."

"What about my daughter?" Lilith challenged. "What do you know about her?"

The agent leaned back in her seat, steepling her fingers together the way that Lilith herself tended to. "Commander ben Jeni, your daughter is alive. I was sent by my friend to tell you that."

It took several seconds for Lilith to process this. "W-what do mean?" she finally managed to stammer.

"Exactly what I said," her uninvited guest answered. "The Agency has lied to you. Your daughter didn't die and she was never missing. She is alive and well, and very shortly, she'll make contact with you."

Lilith gaped at the woman. Then anger and suspicion replaced shock. "Is this some kind of Agency trick?"

The woman shook her head and laughed softly. "No, Commander. No trick. Just the simple truth. Lady Spider has been her mentor for many years, and she knows your daughter better than your daughter knows herself.'

"And it's time for your daughter to come home. There is much more at stake here than just another Hriss invasion, and Sarah will need you as much as you will need her to get through it. Lady Spider felt that you

565

deserved to know the truth and to be given the opportunity to prepare yourself."

As astounded as she was, Lilith started to rise, intent on reaching the door and summoning the Marine guards. She never even got as far as leaving her seat. The figure vanished into thin air, and she just managed to catch the flicker of a shadow crossing the room. In less than an eyeblink, the woman reappeared. She was standing right next to her now, resting her hand gently on Lilith's shoulder.

Inexplicably, Lilith couldn't move a muscle. Something that the stranger was doing to her was preventing this.

"I've been watching you for several weeks now," the woman said quietly into her ear, "and waiting for the right time to give you the news. You're a good woman, Commander, and a capable leader. After all that she's been through, Sarah is truly blessed to have you for a mother."

A strange compulsion made Lilith look back to where the intruder had been seated. There was an object on the table that hadn't been there before. It was a rose, she realized, but unlike any that she had ever seen before. The flower was completely black. Not simply a dark purple, but a pure ebon hue.

"The rose will tell you everything that you need to know, Commander," the woman said, "and please, don't be angry with Sarah. She was only doing what her country asked of her."

At that, the feeling of the hand on her shoulder went away and Lilith's strange paralysis dissapeared. When she looked behind her, no one was there. She was alone again.

For a moment, she stood there blinking in astonishment and then she recovered, and sent a signal to security. This time, it got through and the Marines rushed in to the room.

"Commander? Is everything all right?"

"Did anyone just leave this room?" Lilith asked them.

"No, ma'am," one of the troopers answered. "My partner and I have been standing outside the whole time. The last people to come out of this compartment were Lt. Commander Bertasdaater and the other staff officers."

566

"I see," Lilith replied slowly. "Very well, trooper. Return to your post." Her next move was to call up the security footage from the room itself and the corridor outside.

All she saw was an image of herself, talking to an empty chair. The rose winked into view towards the end of the clip, as if it had been delivered by some supernatural force.

And Lilith certainly didn't believe in magic.

The intruder must have been wearing some kind of sophisticated cloaking device, she concluded, *and she did something to the vid feeds and the psiever relays.* But the 'what' and the 'how' completly eluded her.

Her eyes fell on the rose again. It was still sitting where it had been left, waiting for her. *The rose will tell you everything that you need to know,* the woman had said.

She went over to it, and examined it. Despite its odd coloration, it seemed to be completely conventional. Gingerly, she brought it to her nose and inhaled.

The scent registered in her brain, followed immediately by a thought. It came to her as clearly as if someone had just sent it to her by psiever. It was accompanied by a vivid mental image of a holojector with a personnel file on display.

Use the 'jector, it suggested. *Call up your daughter's file. You'll find that Sarah n'Jan's information has been amended.*

Hands trembling, Lilith sent the command to the holojector that had been built into the conference table and ordered up the file. When it came up, she had to read and then re-read the status box several times before she could bring herself to believe what it was telling her. Instead of listing her daughter as *'Missing/Presumed Deceased'* as it always had, it now read *'Active/Pending Reassignment.'*

Unable to remain standing, she collapsed into the nearest seat and let her emotions take over. Suddenly, the Hriss and the possibility of a war didn't matter at all. Nothing did except the fact that after all the years of worrying, and wondering, her deepest wish had been granted.

Sarah was alive. *It's true!* she thought. *My daughter is alive!*

***

567

"You did good down there, troopers," N'Darei said. She was only looking at Kaly and Lena, and it was obvious that her praise did not include Jon. Fa'Teela was a non-entity as far as she was concerned.

"You two need to report to the mess hall straightaway." Then she finally deigned to acknowledge the neoman and her smile vanished. "Fa'Teela, you can go stow your gear and stand down in your rack."

"Yes, Corporal," Kaly replied, speaking for all of them. Whatever it was they were needed for in the mess, she desperately hoped that it wasn't going to take too long. They where exhausted, and none of them wanted to do anything more than throw themselves into their racks, and get some sleep. And with the exception of unsealing their boots, the added step of undressing was optional, and highly unlikely.

"Well, let's get it over with," Lena said wearily. They stopped just long enough to stow their blasters at the armory, drop their field packs in their lockers, and then they trudged off to the lifts, leaving Jon to remain behind at his rack as he had been ordered to.

At the mess, Troop Leader da'Saana greeted Kaly and Lena with a grave expression. "Today was the first time that you greenies saw combat, wasn't it?" she asked them.

"Ma'am, yes, ma'am," Kaly answered raggedly.

"Please, come with me," the Troop Leader said. They followed her to one of the tables. A bottle sat in the middle of it, filled with an amber colored liquid. It was unlabeled, and unsealed, and the rest of their unit was gathered around it with serious looks on their faces.

"Have a drink," Da'Saana instructed. "It's something that every trooper does the first time they see action with the *Hounds.*"

Kaly brought it up to her lips, and without further ceremony, drank a mouthful. Whatever it was was on par with the potency of the drinks that she'd had at graduation, including the *Aqqa*. She coughed and nearly dropped the bottle before someone rescued it from her.

Lena went next, and suffered nearly the same reaction. This earned them a smattering of laughter from their fellow Marines, but Da'Saana didn't join in. She took the bottle from Lena, and solemnly toasted them with it.

"Welcome to the 115th," she said, taking her own pull from the bottle, and shuddering slightly as the stuff hit her. Then she slammed it back down onto the table.

That was the signal for the assembly to relax and start passing the bottle around. Kaly and Lena were quickly invited to join in, and in short order, more alcohol was produced and everyone was talking and joking with them as if they had been with the unit for years. Only Lena seemed uncomfortable with all this.

"This is wrong," she finally whispered to Kaly. "Jon should be here too." Her battle sister nodded in agreement, but said nothing.

It was only after they had finally been allowed to leave, and return to their racks, that Kaly revealed the bottle that she had managed smuggle out. It wasn't the rocket fuel they'd been toasted with, but it was still strong.

They went straight with it to Jon's rack. His privacy curtain was down by then, and Kaly gave it a tug. When it opened and Jon peered out, he regarded them quizzically.

"For you," she explained, holding the bottle out to the neoman. "You did good. You deserve this."

Jon took an appreciative sip. "Thank you" he said.

EPILOGUE

Darna n'Marni sat in her office, seething with anger. A month earlier, the fools in the Rampart had agreed to disband, and now she'd received a message that some of her closest associates were backing out of her plan to leave the Sisterhood and form their own union. It was unbelievable!

The women that she had once thought to be so strong and far thinking had turned cowards and had actually *capitulated* to the Sisterhood. She knew that their agreement to build a fancy naval base in Sagana was nothing but nonsense, and she was amazed that her associates--her ex-associates--she reminded herself, had let themselves be duped by such empty promises.

She was not so gullible though. They could let themselves believe whatever they liked, but she was going to make certain that Storm at least, was prepared for the Hriss, and for the future. An *independent* future, free of the weak-willed Sisterhood. The other worlds in the territory would come running to her when they finally saw the light, and she intended to make them grovel for forgiveness.

She erased the message, and started to look around for something to calm her nerves with when she received a call on her com. "Yes?" she snapped. "What is it?"

It was Tia bel Tanya, her storesmistress. "Ma'am, sorry to bother you, but there's something wrong with the guns that those smugglers sold us."

"Something's wrong?" she growled. "What 'something'?"

"It's the battery packs. They... well, you should just come down here and see," Bel Tanya answered.

"Very well," N' Marni retorted. *Now what?* she wondered. Her day seemed to be getting worse by the nanosecond. She got up from her desk and went straightaway down to the colony stores, already rehearsing the verbal drubbing that she was going to give her storesmistress if this turned out to be something trivial.

At the stores, she was surprised to see that Bel Tanya was not alone. There were also two Territorial Marshals with her and a third woman dressed in a plain comerci. Before she got the chance to demand to know what was going on, the woman in the comerci stepped forwards and flashed a badge, a military one.

"Darna n'Marni?" she asked. "I'm Agent Hana t'Sheryl with the DNI and I'm placing you under arrest."

"On what charges?!" N'Marni spluttered. The two Marshals were already stepping up to either side of her and taking hold of her arms.

"Possession of restricted weapons," T'Sheryl answered with a smile, "participating in intersystem smuggling, and my favorite charge, sedition. I can also add disturbing the peace if you'd like. It would make the charges against you a nice even number."

"This is outrageous!" N'Marni shouted, pushing the Marshal's hands away from her. "The Territorial Governess will not stand for this!"

The DNI agent smiled again, even wider. "Actually, she signed off on the arrest warrant personally. I don't think you'll get much assistance from that quarter. If I were you, I'd consider getting myself a good Advocate instead."

***

At the same time that Darna n'Marni and her cache of illegal weapons were being taken into custody, half a dozen employees of XiGen Genetic Labs also found themselves under arrest.

The charges against them ranged from conspiracy, to trafficking in restricted genetic materials. And with these arrests, a complex network of biomaterials smuggling was completely destroyed.

In the meantime, the Marionites had unwittingly given the Agency another means to spy on them by using the stolen samples they had received from Sarah. The samples had been tagged with special gene-markers that would allow the OAE, and other associated agencies, to identify any new neomen that they created, and track their specific generation. Along with the spybots that she had planted, the markers would provide a clearer picture of the progress and the true scope of their clandestine project, and also fill in some of the gaps in the Agency's ongoing investigation.

There was no fanfare however; the OAE shunned publicity. Instead, it made sure that the Department of Bio Security got the credit for everything. They even threw a sop to the Thermadonian Metropolitan Police by allowing them the glory of performing the actual raids on the XiGen Labs.

Light years away on Ashkele, the real heroine behind it all sat in her private booth in the *Orfeo Café*. It was her favorite restaurant in the Free City and it specialized in Nyxian cuisine. As she considered the menu, a servingwoman brought a black rose to the table.

"What's that?" Maya asked between bites. "A flower from a friend I don't know about?"

"In a sense," Sarah replied with her usual mysteriousness. She smelled the bloom and smiled as she learned the news of the arrests and then received the personal note of thanks from the Agency's Director that had been attached with the message.

"May I?" the girl asked.

"Of course" Sarah replied. "In fact, there's something special in this flower for you. Take a deep breath and you'll see what I mean."

Curious, Maya took the flower and sniffed at it, and then her eyes widened. At Sarah's request, one part of the communication had been keyed specifically to both Maya and herself. It was the news of two final apprehensions that were completely unrelated to Sarah's operations.

A false-memory told Maya that Thermadonian Customs Police Officer bel Marda and her partner had been detained by their department's Internal Affairs Division on charges of corruption and conspiracy. The phantom messenger also informed her that according to the official report, both women had opted to commit suicide in their cells before investigators could question them at any length. While foul play was strongly suspected, no proof existed to support this, and no one was looking very closely into the matter either.

"I called in some favors to make certain that justice was properly carried out," Sarah explained after the message ended. "I thought that you would appreciate the news."

Maya put down the rose and grinned. "I *like* how these smell," she remarked. "I like them *very* much."

"As do I," Sarah returned. "Now, finish your meal and let's be on our way home. We've a long trip tomorrow to Nyx."

USSNS *Pallas Athena*, On Station, Calandra, Calandra System, Sagana Territory, United Sisterhood of Suns, 1043.03|22|03:67:60

Following the assault on the raider base, Kaly and Lena were each summoned to Col. Lislsdaater's office individually. Kaly was the first to report.

She saluted and stood at attention until the Colonel looked up from her work. "Trooper n'Deena? You may stand at ease," the woman said. "I've been going over the report from your Troop Leader about the action you saw downside. She speaks very highly of you, and about the initiative you took with that enemy gun emplacement."

"Thank you, ma'am," Kaly replied, keeping her eyes straight ahead.

"Based upon her report and on your personnel file, I'm recommending two things. The first is your promotion to Corporal, effective immediately. You showed excellent leadership under fire, and your previous experience as a Platoon Leader in Basic supports this decision.'

"Secondly, I am recommending you for the Silver Galaxy Medal, First Class, for duty above and beyond the call. Quite frankly, if you hadn't taken that emplacement out, your squad would have suffered a lot more casualties than they did. Pending the Commandant's approval, N'Gari will also receive the same award, Second Class."

Kaly didn't miss the fact that the woman hadn't mentioned Jon or included him in the awards. She also wasn't sure that she really deserved a medal, much less a promotion.

"Thank you, ma'am," she answered instead, feeling a twinge of guilt for not voicing her true feelings.

Even so, Lislsdaater caught the doubt in her tone. "But?"

"Permission to speak freely, ma'am?"

"Granted."

"Ma'am, this trooper is grateful for the medal, but she did what any Marine would have done in such a circumstance." She almost added, 'any Marine, even Jon', but she knew better and left that part out. "She is also not sure she is ready for the rank of Corporal, ma'am."

"Thank you for your frankness, *Corporal*," Lislsdaater replied, "but I have a different opinion on both counts. The medal is yours whether you want it or not. What you did down on there is *not* what any other Marine would have done; it was extraordinary and you *will* be rewarded for it.'

"As for your new rank, the Corps needs good leaders, so get used to it. Corporal n'Darei will show you the particulars of the job and get you up to speed."

"Yes, ma'am. Thank you, ma'am"

"Now, there is one other item of business that I want to address," Lislsdaater continued. "This is your future in the Corps. Have you given any thought to your military career?"

"Ma'am?" Kaly asked. Up to that point she hadn't really considered being anything but a ground-pounder, and the Colonel's question caught her completely by surprise.

"Although you've only been a Marine for a short time, you have distinguished yourself," Lislsdaater explained. "It's time you thought about your career track. There's a lot more to the Corps than just Mobile Infantry Specialists, N'Deena, and the Sisterhood needs good women to serve in key jobs. You scored high on the CAFAT test when you enlisted, and that, combined with your performance to date, opens up a lot of possibilities. I'd like to suggest one job in particular: Special Operations."

"The Marauders, ma'am?" Kaly was incredulous. The Marine Marauders were the elite forces of the Sisterhood Marines. It had been a Marauder unit that had prevented her from getting herself killed when she had tried to engage the Hriss patrol on Persephone. The very last thing that she'd ever expected was for someone to tell her that she had what it took to measure up to *their* standards. The Marauder units were a thing apart, like the super-heroines of the realies, and not something that a simple *anyone* like her could ever aspire to.

"The same outfit, n'Deena," Lislsdaater said. "I spent some time in SpecOps myself before I went to OCS, and they need women who can show leadership and quick thinking under fire. I think you have what it takes, and I'd suggest that you consider it.'

"Naturally, I want the best to serve with *Hekate's Hounds*, but I also want what's best for the Sisterhood. It would mean more training on Hella's World of course, and Larra's Lament, but I think that once you got through it, you'd realize that I was right about it being a good fit for you."

"Yes, ma'am," Kaly answered, but again her tone betrayed her.

"You're concerned about your Battle Sister. Is that it?" Lislsdaater ventured.

"Ma'am, yes, ma'am," Kaly admitted.

"I understand, Corporal," the woman said, "but sometimes personal relationships have to suffer for the greater good. Sometimes they even come out the stronger after they're tested. That's something you'll have to find out on your own, with your partner.'

"But remember what we're here for. It's not for us, N'Deena. It's for the women that we protect, and you owe *them* something too. Think about this, and think about SpecOps. If you decide you want to go through with it, I'll put your application through myself. In the meantime, you are dismissed."

Kaly left the Colonel's office deep in thought. That night, when she saw Lena, she didn't mention what the Colonel had suggested to her, and only talked about the promotion. Aside from mutual congratulations over their medals, and shared commiseration about Jon's unfair treatment, Lena was just as taciturn about her own meeting with the Colonel.

Kaly didn't pry into the reason for this though. She knew that Lena would tell her what was bothering her, when she was ready.

There was no private meeting with Col. Lislsdaater for Jon and as Kaly had rightly guessed, no promotion, or any medal. Instead, he received a notice over his psiever informing him that a note had been placed in his personnel file.

It read simply; *"Trooper fa'Teela assisted his fellow Marines in neutralizing enemy resistance on the third planet in system CD48 2259. This entry is to formally document this fact, and will be included in Fa'Teela's permanent service record. Col. Marya Lislsdaater, Commander, 115th Marine Combined Combat Force."*

Jon wasn't bitter about this snub, nor was he jealous of Kaly and Lena. They deserved the recognition that they had received, and he was genuinely happy for them. The simple fact that he *had* been acknowledged in *any* way was reward enough. It represented one more step towards the acceptance of neomen by the Sisterhood, and beyond this, of the Redeemer Himself when the time came for His coming. Those things were far more important than any worldly awards.

575

And as if in acknowledgement of this, he received another message later that day. The *Athena* had made port at Thenti again to take on supplies, and the mail.

There was a flimsy for him from New Covenant. Per Naval Regs, a censor had already screened the letter, but the body of the message was completely intact.

To any other eyes, it contained nothing more than long scriptural passages from the *Revelation of Mari*, but it was a quote from *Joahnna 14.2* that caught his attention immediately.

"Suffer not the unbelieving to know all that is encompassed by Thy wisdom," it said, *"For it would be turned by them only to evil ends."*

The citation was meant to alert him that a secret message was concealed within the letter's text. Jon drew the privacy curtain around his rack and opened his bible to the *Book of Holy Numbers*. Using this as his cipher key, he carefully decoded the message.

He was stunned by its contents. It was from Sister n'Avenal.

"The One may soon be among us," it read. *"After careful study by the Church and final approval by the Council of Bishops and the Pope, a worthy Sister was chosen and given the honor of being implanted as the Holy Host Mother. May it be the Creator's Will that His day has come unto us at last! Mari be praised to the Heavens!"*

Jon put the flimsy aside and got down on his knees, ignoring the pain that the hard metal flooring inflicted on them. Tears of joy filled his eyes as he thanked Jesu and Mari for the greatest gift of all. The salvation of all humankind.

***

A copy of Jon's flimsy reached Ophida n' Marsi before even Jon had had the chance to read it, and his activities with the *Revelation* were relayed to her private terminal. Her computer immediately deciphered the message and a translated version was waiting for her.

The *Book of Numbers* cipher had been broken for many years, and the Agency had kept this fact a closely guarded secret for situations just like this. As she sat in her office and reviewed the decoded communication, the priestess realized that something very important had occurred in the Marionite genetic project. What it was, she was not entirely certain, but it was quite clear that the Agency had to be notified immediately.

And although Ophida dearly wanted to have Jon detained for questioning right then and there, she knew that she had to resist the temptation. For the moment at least, she simply did not have enough proof to justify such an action. If it came to a formal review, anyone would be able to argue that it was equally as likely that he had received the message as one of the "Faithful," as he might have as a covert agent.

More evidence would be needed to indict him, and she knew it. Without it, all she could really do was instruct her operatives to maintain their surveillance, and hope that he, or his handlers, made a fatal mistake. Goddess willing, they would.

USSNS *Pallas Athena*, Treani, Brin System, Sagana Territory United Sisterhood of Suns, 1043.03|23|07:74:30

With the help of Saara sa'Vika, and the ship's PX, Lilith had managed to get her hands on some paper and a pen, and sat down at her desk to write a letter.

"My Darling Ingrit," she began, *"I have read your letter many times, and always it is your last words to me, 'I love you,' that captures my heart.'*

"I have just completed a very important mission, and it would seem that the Goddess has given me more tasks to fulfill in the next few months. The times ahead will be difficult for all of us, but I will face them as I always have, and do as She commands until she declares that my labors are complete.'

"My dearest, I pray to Her every day; I pray for you and for everyone at the farm, and I pray that when my work is done, and we are all safe at last, that She will see fit to grant me what I have come to realize is my most earnest wish. This is to leave space behind and join you in a life together, there on Zommerlaand.'

"May the Goddess grant that this day comes soon, a day when we will be in each other's arms again, and this time, share our sunsets together until the very last one paints the sky.'

577

"Until then, know that wherever I am, that I love you--Lilith"

Grunvaald Haarmaaneplaatz, Vaalkenstaad Township, Zommerlaand,
Sunna 3, Solara Elant, United Sisterhood of Suns, 1043.03|23|00.00.12

Grammy awoke with a start. It was still dark outside, and her psiever
told her that it was 00:00 hours. She heard a tapping at her window and
realized what it was that had roused her. It was Old Meg, drumming on the
glass with her beak, and when she saw the bird, she knew that something
was wrong. Very wrong.

The old woman went to the window and admitted the creature, which
hopped up onto her shoulder right away and began talking to her in their
special language. Shortly, Meg's message became clear, and she lifted the
bird off of her and set it down on the sill to get dressed.

Ingrit was already waiting for her when she went downstairs, holding
a lantern and a shawl. Grammy wasn't surprised by this. Ingrit had always
had the Sight and had known that something was amiss.

"I had a dream, *Grötdaar*," Ingrit explained. "Something's wrong,
isn't it?"

"*Yah*," Grammy replied. "We must go to the High Place."

Ingrit put the shawl around Grammy's shoulders, and followed her out
of the house and up the trail to the grove. At the High Place, Grammy took
her seat on the carved tree stump, and Old Meg landed on her shoulder.

The two of them talked at length, and when the conversation was over,
the bird took its customary place on a nearby branch and waited. Then
Grammy relayed the message that Old Meg had given her from the *Oude
Mehnsz*.

"The Gods have sent us a warning," she said, "A great evil is coming.
We must be on our guard, and do all that we can to lend our strength and
wisdom to those whom the Gods have ordained will fight against the
Enemy. I fear for them, Granddaughter; there are terrible times ahead.
Terrible."

She made the *Maarkken* against evil and stood, stretching her hands
upwards to the night sky, feeling outwards with her Sight for Katrinn.
Finding her at last, she breathed a sigh of relief.

Katrinn was safe. For the moment.

Not one to take chances, Grammy called on the names of the *Oude Mehnsz* and then she made the *Maarkken* of the Shield and the Spear, chanting their ancient names as she sent them across the vast gulf of space to the *Athena*. Behind her, Ingrit had also raised her arms, and sang in accompaniment as she lent her own power to the old woman's spell.

Then Grammy performed the same ritual for Lilith. Although she was an unbeliever, and not of their soil, she was also a loved one, especially to Ingrit, and deserved the same protection that she had given to her granddaughter.

At last, when it was done, the old woman dropped her arms and pulled her shawl closer. With Ingrit lighting the way, they walked back down the hill together to the farmhouse in silence.

END OF BOOK ONE

The saga continues in Book 2, "Sisterhood of Suns: Widow's War"...

Glossary of Sisterhood Terminology

Aqqa; a distilled alcoholic drink native to Zommerlaand. Clear, colorless, and ranging from 90 to 120 proof, it is the strongest adult beverage legally available in the Sisterhood.

Baaka Wood; a fine grained Nemesian hardwood. Baaka wood is prized for its jet black color, and is used mainly for crafting fine furniture and quality fighting staffs.

Battlebot; an intelligent robot which can be guided either by a human operator, or function independently in a combat role. Specialized battlebots can perform additional tasks such as medical/rescue response, or infiltration assistance for special operations teams.

Battle Group; a common operational unit of the Sisterhood Navy, battle groups typically consist of three ships; two Macha class cruisers, and an Isis-class supercruiser. Battle groups are tasked with general patrol, enforcement of maritime law, and conducting special missions.

Bioplasmic Energy; a term for the energy which interpenetrates and animates all living beings. It manifests as the aura or life-force. The term was coined during the Cold War on Old Gaia as part of experiments by the Soviet Union in psychic phenomena.

Biosyncronism; an environmentalist movement which arose in response to the terraforming of extrasolar planets. The Bios believed that instead of changing an ecosystem, humanity needed to alter itself genetically to adapt to their new environment.

Bio Action Army; a violent extremist group opposed to 'ecological imperialism', basing its philosophy on radical interpretations of the principles of Biosyncronism.

Blast Resistant Armor; utilized by the military in a variety of applications (including vehicle and personal fighting armor), it is made of a classified ceramic which absorbs incoming energy and channels it away from the wearer. Additional layers of other materials also lend it the ability to defeat projectiles.

Comerci; A one or two piece business suit worn on formal occasions, with a high, stiff collar and a monochromatic color scheme. A cravat-like accessory known as the 'cravess' offsets this somber arrangement with bright colors and is often accompanied by elegant stick-pins.

Commander: A Gaian Star Federation rank adopted by the Sisterhood Navy. Commanders are normally in charge of a battle group, and outrank the Captains of its individual ships.

Concordance, The; the founding document of the Sisterhood. The original is enshrined on Thermadon, in Concordance Hall, and is protected by a 24-hour Marine honor guard.

Drow'voi; an extinct non-human race famous for its many ruins, and unknown technology. The most notable of their sites is the 'Necropolis', which is located in Xee space. Drow'voi ruins can be found almost anywhere in the Milky Way galaxy.

Elant; a territorial division of the United Sisterhood of Suns, comprising a specific region of space and overseen by a Governess. Each Elant is represented by a Senatrix (who is appointed by the Sisterhood's supreme executive officer, the Chairwoman), and they serve their region's interests in a governing body known of as the Supreme Circle.

Elzlate: a personal data pad, powered solely by bioplasmic energy, and responsive to psiever commands. A detachable stylus allows the user to input signatures and sketch images.

Gravitronic Engine, *Moteur Gravitronic*; the gravitronic engine is a propellant-less system which allows a modern starship to travel through normal space at speeds that far exceed older antimatter engines, and with much greater efficiency, economy, and safety.

Powered by a hyper-efficient positronic reactor, the engine produces positive gravitronic particles which surround a vessel with an artificial gravity field. At the same time, the engine emits a stream of negatively charged particles (or anti-gravitrons) that push against the positive field, repelling it and generating the motive force.

In addition, this negatively charged field also acts as a shield, protecting the crew from acceleration forces and resisting impacts from foreign objects (making separate 'shields' outmoded). Defensive functions such as the discharge of energy weapons, firing missiles, or launching decoys, is accomplished through an adjustment by the ships computer, which creates a gap in the twin fields just large enough to accommodate the event, and only for as long as it is required.

A byproduct of operating the gravitronic engine is heat. That problem is solved by special vanes sited along the body of the ship, which vector excess radiation outside of the gravity 'bubble' and into space (using the same process that allows for weapons discharges).

Changes in heading are accomplished by vectoring the anti-gravitronic stream in a new direction. This is augmented by thermal anti-matter thrusters, which can deliver additional power during take off, and function as afterburners. They also support the grav bubble's shielding effect by compensating for the drop in inertia otherwise created by any increase to the negative field, thus allowing for the ship to maintain its speed. Currently in their 5th generation, gravitronic drives are the most common form of in-system propulsion in the Sisterhood.

Hriss; a humanoid race occupying a section of space adjacent to the Sisterhood. The Hriss are a patriarchal society divided into clans and ruled by an Emperor. Aggressive and warlike, the Hriss have engaged in numerous conflicts with the Sisterhood, starting with the First Widow's War.

Hriss'ka; the Hriss language, known for its colorful profanities and the custom of using insults as a polite form of conversation.

Indweller, Indie; amorphous creatures that inhabit Nullspace, they will attack any spaceship that enters their dimension. To combat this problem, ships travel through Nullspace in convoys, accompanied by heavily armed escort vessels.

Kaatze; a genetically altered version of the Old Gaian house cat. Kaatzen (plural) are slightly larger than their ancestors, and bred for intelligence. It is the custom for psievers to be implanted in them when they are kittens, allowing for mind-to-mind communications with their human companions.

Ka'na; a single-edged, two-handed sword native to Nemesis, the Ka'na owes its design to the ancient Japanese katana.

Klaxxy; a Zommerlaandar slang word for 'crazy'. Another less popular term, 'warpy' hearkens back to the 24th century (pre-Plague era) and expresses the same idea.

Malandrium; iron particles compressed through a classified industrial process to assume an ultra-dense state. Malandrium is used as a coating for bladed weapons and projectiles, and is recognizable by the black sheen it lends to the treated object.

Mariner; Naval rank equivalent of a Yeoman (replaced in the 24th century by the Gaian Star Federation Navy).

Marionite; a follower of the Church of the New Revelation of Mari, a survival of Christianity. The Marionites are responsible for the reintroduction of human males into society, out of the belief that by doing so, that their savior figure will arise and rescue humanity from its sins.

Mark-7; the standard issue Marine infantry weapon. The Mark-7 discharges a concentrated 'bolt' of energy at a target. It features a gun-to-psiever targeting interface as well as conventional iron sights, and can accept grenade launchers and other attachments. The Mark-7 is also equipped with a bayonet lug, and training with the bayonet is a feature of Marine basic training.

MARS Plague; a gender specific disease, believed to be a bioweapon. Male Acute Respiratory Syndrome was 100 percent fatal to all human males during the late 24th century BSE. This brought about the collapse of the Gaian Star Federation and engendered the rise of the Sisterhood.

Marauder Team; an elite special operations unit of the Sisterhood Marines, consisting of four women; a team leader, sniper/security, explosives/security and medical/communications. Their equivalent in the RSE is called a Special Reaction Unit (or SRU Team).

Merchanter; The common term for a commercial spaceship, generally involved in the transportation of freight from one star system to the next. Merchanters are recognizable by the 'CSS' tag in their name (as in CSS *C-JUDI-GO*).

Motherthought; a pro-female supremacist philosophy that was developed in response to the devastation left behind by the MARS plague. It espouses the idea that men were genetically inferior and that Woman is the summit of human evolution.

Naming Conventions: Modern Sisterhood names are derived from their specific linguistic groups and consist of the individual's personal name, followed by the local term for 'daughter of' and then the name of the birth mother that carried them to term (as in 'Lilith ben Jeni', or 'Lilith, daughter of Jeni'). The only exceptions are where a woman takes the name of a teacher, family or clan as her surname.

Needlegun; a common side-arm, the needlegun is clip fed, and uses magnetic fields to fire 'smart' or 'dumb' 5.588 mm projectiles (.22 caliber). Needlegun rounds can be solid shot, explosive, or even poisoned. Most needleguns are semi-automatic, but military and intelligence versions have a three-shot burst fire capability.

Nemesis, Nemesian; a planet in the Rhadwa system, Thalestris Elant. This world is covered with dense forests and best known for its fierce predators, and unspoiled wilderness. Nemesis is also considered to be the ultimate expression of Biosyncronism. Here, the local women have been genetically modified for survival in their jungle environment, and strict laws are in place to control deforestation and prevent the destruction of the ecosystem. Nemesian women live in clan-based societies, as part of the Bio Movement's belief that an aboriginal lifestyle was the most harmonious and natural way for humans to exist.

Neoman; the product of a formerly secret Marionite genetics program, known of as Project Advent. There are three versions of neomen, based on their generation; Adam 1-15 (who would be considered conventional males by 21st century standards), Adam-16's (who are sterile hermaphrodites with breasts, female features, but male genitalia) and a single Adam-17 who is the end result of the entire program, the Redeemer himself.

Nullspace, Null; an alternate universe which parallels our own, Nullspace offers a shortcut around otherwise insurmountable stellar distances. Rifts in space and time, created by trained psi's, allow a ship to enter Null and travel to destinations in mere hours instead of the weeks, (or even months) that would be required using alternative methods of travel such as warp drive.

Nyx, Nyxian; a planet in the Morpheus system, Thalestris Elant. One of the most unique features about Nyx is that its dominant native life forms developed along nocturnal rather than diurnal lines due to an excess of ultraviolet radiation. Nyxian women were genetically modified using local DNA as the developmental model, both to address this environmental issue, and in keeping with the principles of Biosyncronism. A side-effect of this is super-albinism and an extreme sensitivity to bioplasmic fields, leading many Nyxians to pursue careers in medicine.

Old Gaia; the Sisterhood term for the planet Earth, which was destroyed by the Hriss in the First Widow's War. The location of Old Gaia in the Solara Elant is currently designated as a national monument.

Omniplex; An interstellar information network which extends throughout Sisterhood space. The omniplex is also nicknamed the 'plex, and local terminals are simply called omni's.

Pairmate; an alternative term for a wife. The Sisterhood marriage ceremony is sometimes called Pairing.

Parthenogenic Birth, Parthing (slang); in response to the crisis created by the MARS plague, formerly forbidden techniques for artificially reproducing human life were hastily reexamined. One technique, pioneered by the great geneticist, Dr. Rachel Landa, proved to be the only one which surmounted the technical problems that were otherwise inherent in such an endeavor, and the Landa Method became the reproductive standard used by the Sisterhood.

The birthing process (sometimes also refered to as 'parthing') begins with an application by the mothers to have a child. The candidate mothers are then required to submit samples for a pre-pregnancy genetic screening process. The samples are analyzed and a holographic simulation, which displays their daughter as she would appear at various ages (along with potential health issues) is then presented to the mothers for approval. If any genetic defects have been found, this is also the point where they will be identified, and scheduled for repair.

The next step requires that both mothers be certified as being psychologically fit and financially capable of supporting their offspring. They must also successfully pass a State-approved class in child care.

The final stage is the implantation process itself. A normal, unmodified egg is harvested from the donor mother, and combined with a specially modified egg from the birth mother. The end result is then implanted in the birth mother, and carried to term, resulting in a genetically diverse individual.

Phonetic Alphabet; commonly used by the Sisterhood military to designate letters. The names for each one are: Anna, Betsi, Carli, Dana, Ellyn, Freda, Geri, Hilla, Ida, Jenny, Karyn, Lynda, Mari, Nora, Paula, Queen, Roberta, Sharra, Tina, Una, Viki, Willa, Xari, and Zena.

Primary, Secondary and Tertiary Education; Primary is what societies on Old Gaia would have recognized as a combination of Kindergarten, Elementary School and Junior High. It ends at the 10th Level. Secondary begins at Level 11, and goes through five more stages, and can be compared to a blend of High School and Technical/Trade School. Tertiary School, which has no formal levels, but a degree system, is the equivalent of the Old Gaian university model and like primary and secondary, is free of charge to any woman.

Psi; someone with psychic talents as determined by testing in primary and during induction into the military. An informal term is 'talenti' (as opposed to 'normali').

Psiever; a device implanted at birth by nanites into the human brain. Utilizing an integrated microcomputer, psievers can differentiate between specific conscious thoughts and other brain impulses, translating those thoughts into commands. Such commands are then broadcast by the device to specialized receivers via a ULF radio signal.

Psievers are also capable of receiving signals and relaying their information to the user's brain centers, making induction learning, psiever-to-psiever communications and realies, possible. In addition, psievers also have a number of low-level functions such as a virtual inbox for text messages, a camera-capture application (using signals from the user's visual center) and a clock/alarm mode.

Qada; Due to their extreme vulnerability to ultraviolet radiation, Nyxians are compelled to wear the Qada. This garment covers their bodies from head to toe, protecting them when they venture anywhere where they might be exposed to harmful light.

Realie; Realies, or Reality Induction Simulation utilizes the ability of psievers to receive information and transmit it to the brain to create an artificial reality.

Red Star Relief Organization; a descendant of the Red Cross, the Red Star is a civilian disaster relief organization which provides assistance to communities and planets who are the victims of disaster or war. The Red Star takes its name from its insignia, which is a red interlaced pentagram that reflects the common religious symbolism of the Sisterhood.

Santaj; the Thermadonian art of blackmail, Santaj consists of two components; *Intima* and *Terminér*, ('*her underwear*', or compromising secrets and '*the hard end*', sheer brute force).

Second, Third; the terms used for the officers who are immediately subordinate to the Captain (or Commander) of a starship, and in descending order of authority. They are a 23rd century replacement for the older titles of 'First' and 'Second Officer'. On a Sisterhood ship, the commander of a vessal is always considered to be the First, followed by the Second and the Third.

Seevaan; an insectoid race, possessing a level of technology that is vastly superior to the Sisterhood. The Seevaans are responsible for gifting Humanity with space travel. They are also close allies with the Sisterhood.

Senatrix; a government representative, appointed by the Chairwoman to serve the interests of her Elant in the Supreme Circle.

Ship Classes; although it utilizes many types of vessels to fulfill its mission, the Sisterhood Navy currently fields three basic classes of starship for its battle groups. In descending order of their size and power, these are the Isis (supercruiser), Macha (medium cruiser) and Chandi (light cruiser). Of the three, the most common is the Macha class, which is considered to be the workhorse of the Star Service.

Standard or *Norma*; the shared common language of the Sisterhood, Standard was created just after the establishment of the United Sisterhood of Suns. It is based largely on French, with Spanish, Italian and Romanian influences.

Star Scouts; an organization dedicated to teaching the values of community, sisterhood and self-reliance to young women.

Star Service; an alternate name for the Sisterhood Navy.

Symbiote; a Drow'voi artifact which can attach itself to a living host, and grant them race-specific abilities. In human subjects, this is the power to slow time. Symbiotes are highly classified, and are only introduced to high-level intelligence operatives.

Time and Date Conventions; in the Sisterhood series, many scenes are given location and time headings. The times and dates are based on Thermadonian time, and utilize a metric-based system. The Sisterhood year is calculated from the beginning of the Sisterhood (year 0.0) and has 13 months, of 30 days a piece. Months are further divided into four seven day weeks (known as a 'Sevenday', with each day labeled simply as Oneday, Twoday, etc.). An example of a typical header would be:

"USSNS *Pallas Athena*, Battle Group Golden, Topaz Fleet, In Orbit, Nuvo Bolivar, Argenta Provensa, Esteral Terrana Rapabla, 1048.01|19|02:59:82".

In this entry, "1048.01|19|02:59:82" translates to the year 1048 ASE (After Sisterhood Era), the first month, the 19th day, at 02:59:82 hours (or 5:52:22 AM).

Thermadon, Thermadonian; the capital of the Sisterhood and its largest city. It is also the Sisterhood's main financial and media hub. The term 'Thermadonian' refers to anything native to, or inspired by this metropolis.

Troop Leader; Marine rank equivalent of a Sergeant (replaced in the 24th century by the Gaian Star Federation Marine Corps).

Tej, Tej Knife; a coming-of age-ritual that originated on Nemesis and was later adopted by the Nyxian women, and to a certain degree by the Kalians, Sitalans and Durendelans. Successful completion results in the awarding of the Tej knife (known as the Moonblade on Nyx), which serves as a functional survival tool, a fighting weapon, and a symbol of full adulthood. On Nemesis, Tej knives are custom made, and their markings identify the user's clan.

T'lakskalan (slang, Tee-Lak); a reptilian race, the T'lakskalan's are notorious for their trafficking in slaves. Although not a major political or military force, the Tee-Laks are a constant thorn in the Sisterhood's side, conducting raids on isolated settlements and taking prisoners.

United Sisterhood of Suns; the official name for the Sisterhood (In Standard: *Unité Sorele da Soléz*).

Zommerlaandar; a native of Sunna 3 (formerly Alpha Centauri A) in the Solari Elant. Zommerlaand was settled by a group of Northern European states early in the diaspora from Old Gaia. Its main exports are agricultural products, making it the 'Bread Basket' of the Sisterhood, but it is also home to some of the Sisterhood's foremost military recruits, and many terms from Zommerlaandartal have found their way into Standard.

Xee; a non-human invertebrate species, famous for their business acumen and political neutrality. The Free City on Ashkele, serves as their primary trade-hub with the Sisterhood and other star nations.